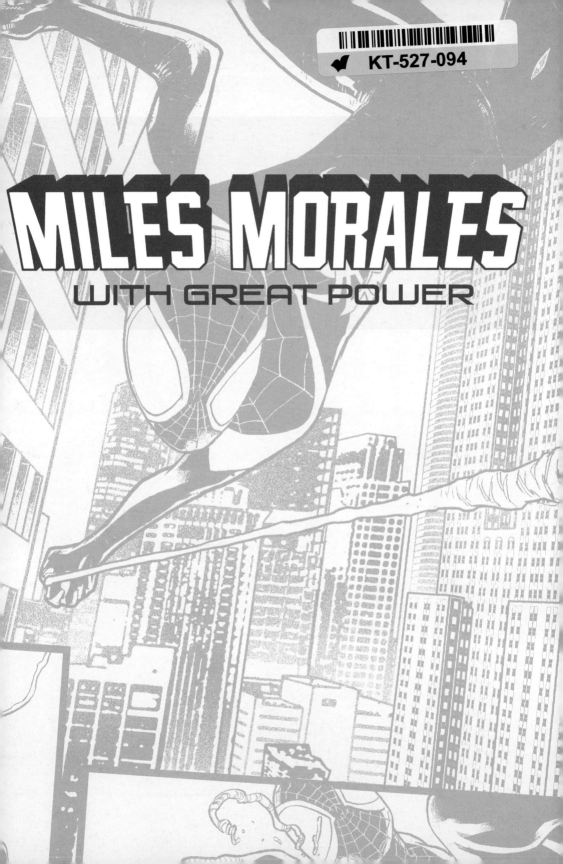

MILES MORALES
WITH GREAT POWER

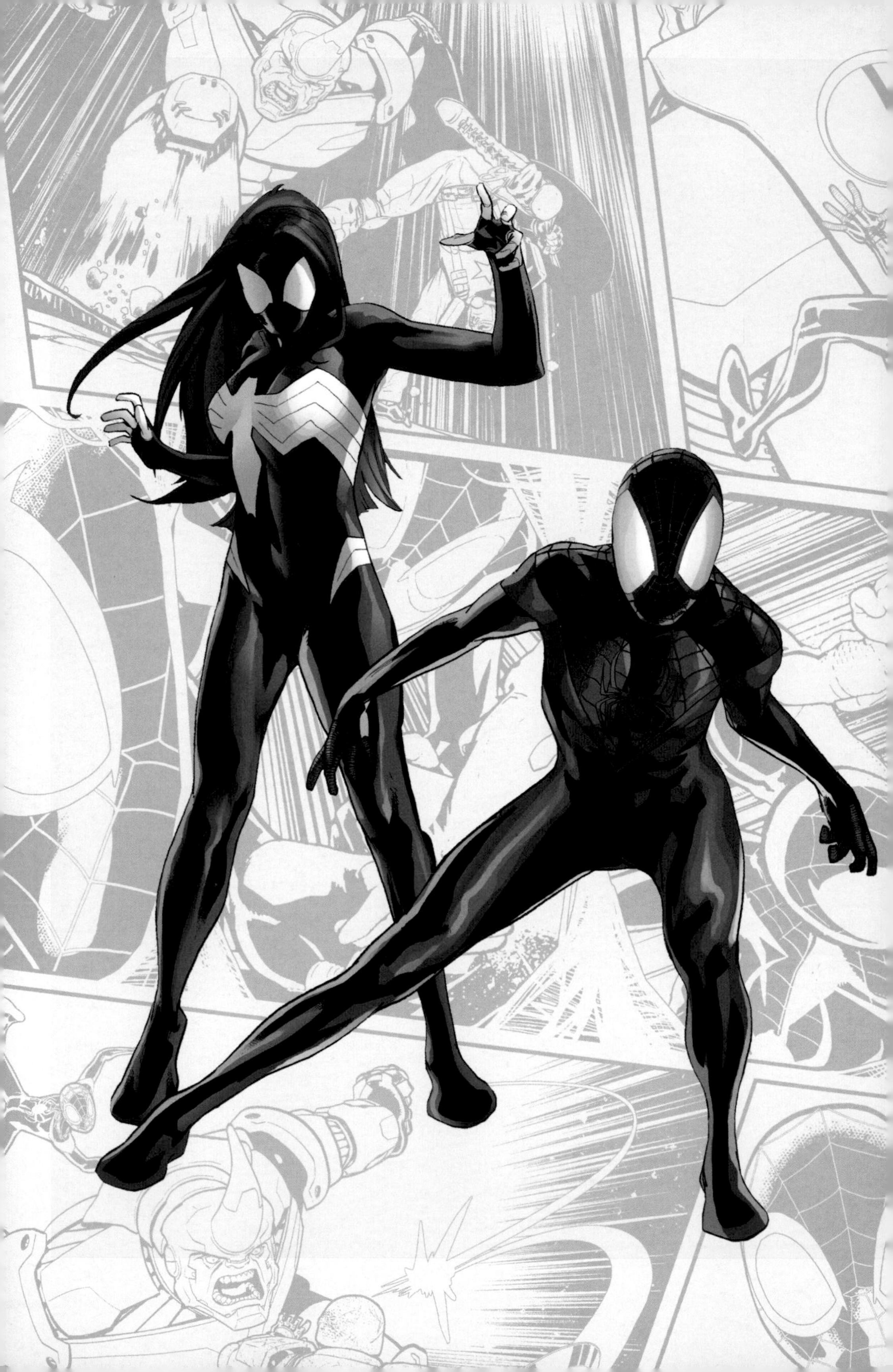

MILES MORALES

WITH GREAT POWER

WRITER
BRIAN MICHAEL BENDIS

ARTISTS
DAVID MARQUEZ (#11-15, #16.1, #18),
PEPE LARRAZ (#16-17)
& SARA PICHELLI (#19-22)

COLOR ARTIST
JUSTIN PONSOR

LETTERER
VC's CORY PETIT

COVER ART
KAARE ANDREWS (#11), JORGE MOLINA (#12-15),
DAVID MARQUEZ & RAIN BEREDO (#16, #18),
DAVID MARQUEZ & JUSTIN PONSOR (#16.1 #17, #19, #21-22)
AND SARA PICHELLI & CHRISTINA STRAIN (#20)

ASSISTANT EDITORS
EMILY SHAW & JON MOISAN

ASSOCIATE EDITOR
SANA AMANAT

SENIOR EDITOR
MARK PANICCIA

Spider-Man created by STAN LEE & STEVE DITKO

collection editor JENNIFER GRÜNWALD
assistant editor CAITLIN O'CONNELL • associate managing editor KATERI WOODY
editor, special projects MARK D. BEAZLEY • vp production & special projects JEFF YOUNGQUIST

director, licensed publishing SVEN LARSEN • svp print, sales & marketing DAVID GABRIEL
editor in chief C.B. CEBULSKI • chief creative officer JOE QUESADA
president DAN BUCKLEY • executive producer ALAN FINE

MILES MORALES: WITH GREAT POWER. Contains material originally published in magazine form as ULTIMATE COMICS SPIDER-MAN #11-22 and #16.1. First printing 2019. ISBN 978-1-302-91977-1. Published by MARVEL WORLDWIDE, INC., a subsidiary of MARVEL ENTERTAINMENT, LLC. OFFICE OF PUBLICATION: 135 West 50th Street, New York, NY 10020. © 2019 MARVEL No similarity between any of the names, characters, persons, and/or institutions in this magazine with those of any living or dead person or institution is intended, and any such similarity which may exist is purely coincidental. **Printed in Canada.** DAN BUCKLEY, President, Marvel Entertainment; JOHN NEE, Publisher; JOE QUESADA, Chief Creative Officer; TOM BREVOORT, SVP of Publishing; DAVID BOGART, Associate Publisher & SVP of Talent Affairs; DAVID GABRIEL, SVP of Sales & Marketing, Publishing; JEFF YOUNGQUIST, VP of Production & Special Projects; DAN CARR, Executive Director of Publishing Technology; ALEX MORALES, Director of Publishing Operations; DAN EDINGTON, Managing Editor; SUSAN CRESPI, Production Manager; STAN LEE, Chairman Emeritus. For information regarding advertising in Marvel Comics or on Marvel.com, please contact Vit DeBellis, Custom Solutions & Integrated Advertising Manager, at vdebellis@marvel.com. For Marvel subscription inquiries, please call 888-511-5480. **Manufactured between 7/19/2019 and 8/20/2019 by SOLISCO PRINTERS, SCOTT, QC, CANADA.**
10 9 8 7 6 5 4 3 2 1

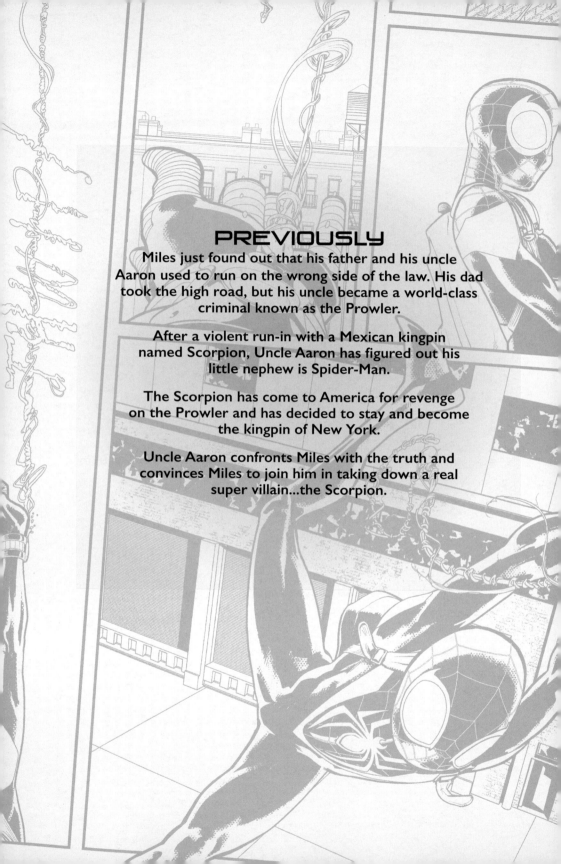

PREVIOUSLY

Miles just found out that his father and his uncle
Aaron used to run on the wrong side of the law. His dad
took the high road, but his uncle became a world-class
criminal known as the Prowler.

After a violent run-in with a Mexican kingpin
named Scorpion, Uncle Aaron has figured out his
little nephew is Spider-Man.

The Scorpion has come to America for revenge
on the Prowler and has decided to stay and become
the kingpin of New York.

Uncle Aaron confronts Miles with the truth and
convinces Miles to join him in taking down a real
super villain...the Scorpion.

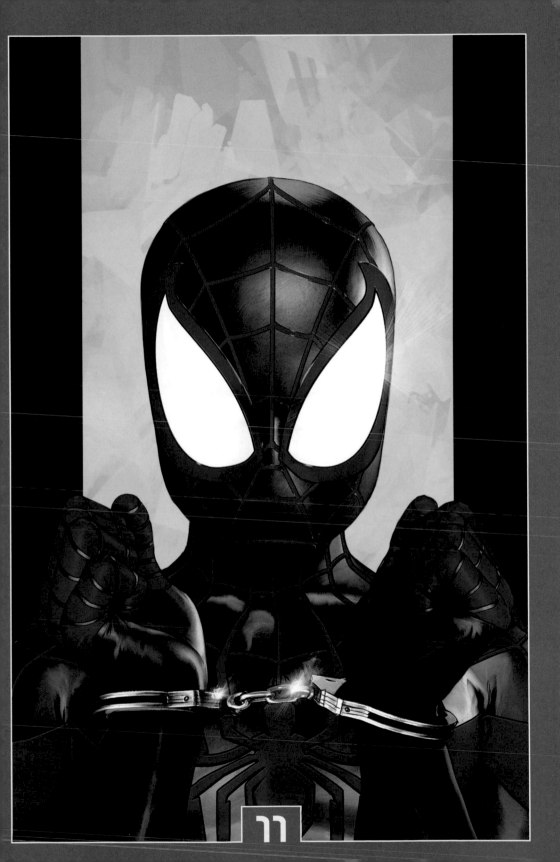

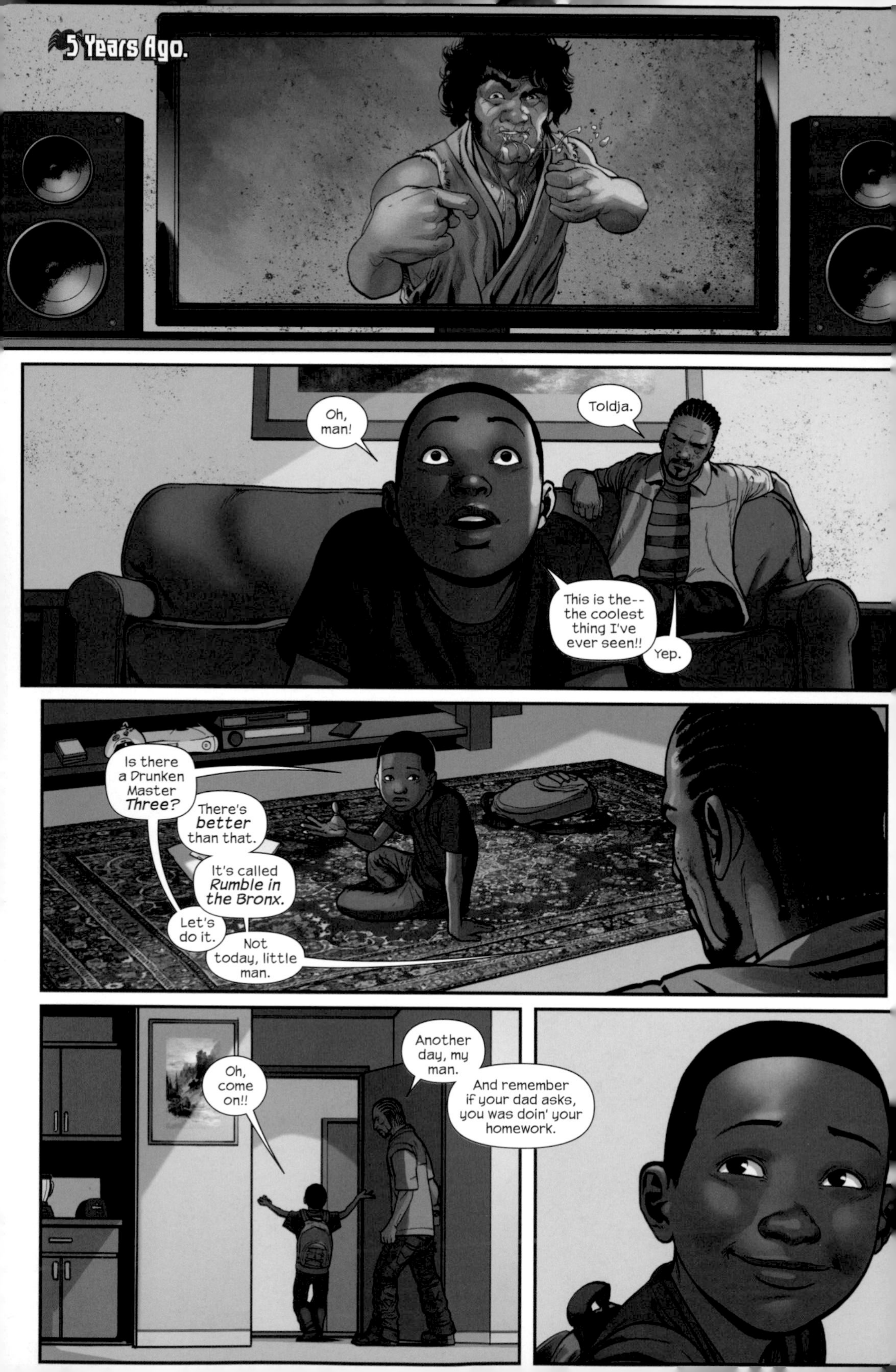
5 Years Ago.
Oh, man!
Toldja.
This is the-- the coolest thing I've ever seen!!
Yep.
Is there a Drunken Master *Three?*
There's *better* than that.
It's called *Rumble in the Bronx.*
Let's do it.
Not today, little man.
Oh, come on!!
Another day, my man.
And remember if your dad asks, you was doin' your homework.

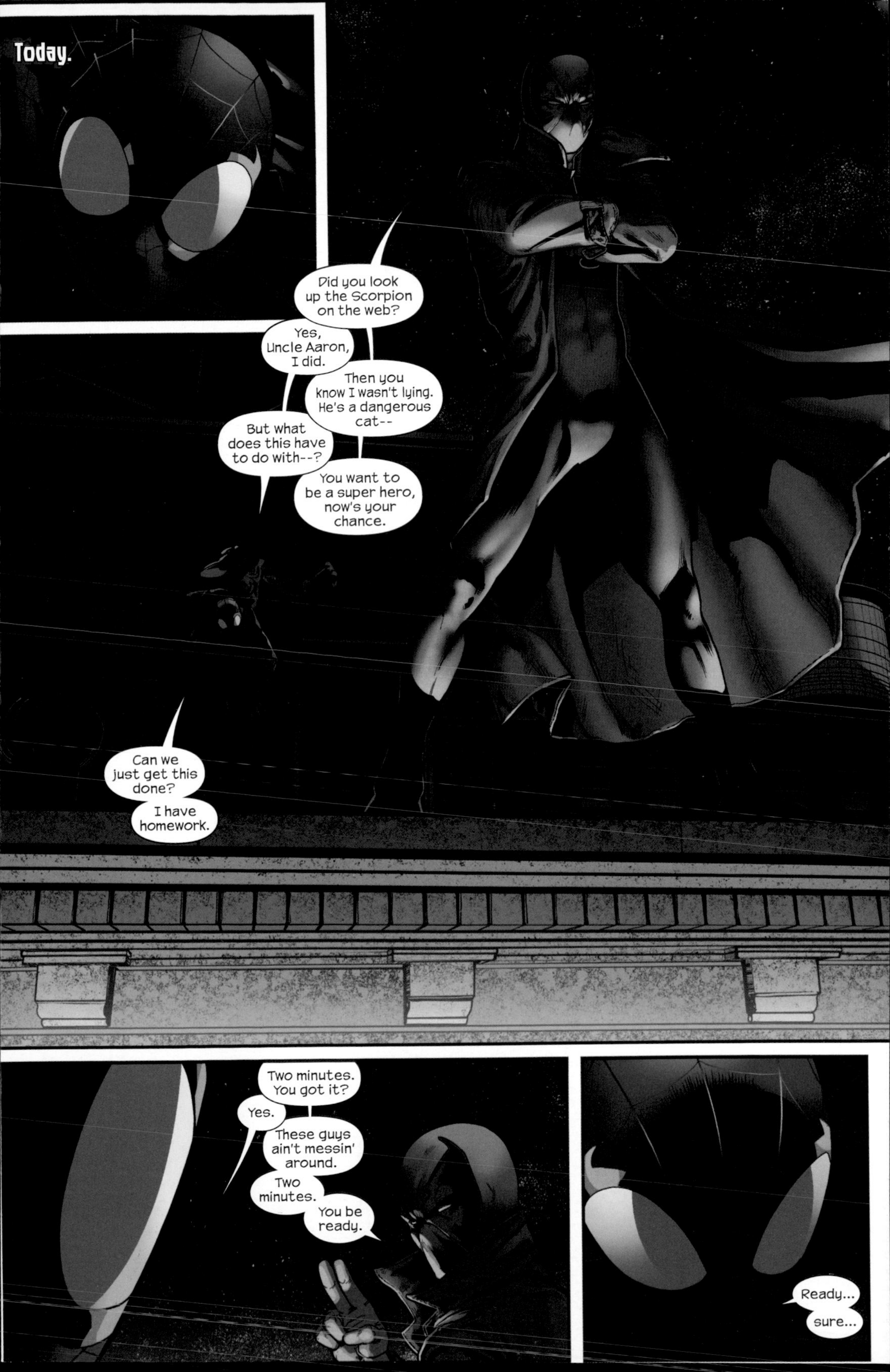
Today.
Did you look up the Scorpion on the web?
Yes, Uncle Aaron, I did.
Then you know I wasn't lying. He's a dangerous cat--
But what does this have to do with--?
You want to be a super hero, now's your chance.
Can we just get this done?
I have homework.
Two minutes. You got it?
Yes.
These guys ain't messin' around.
Two minutes.
You be ready.
Ready...
sure...

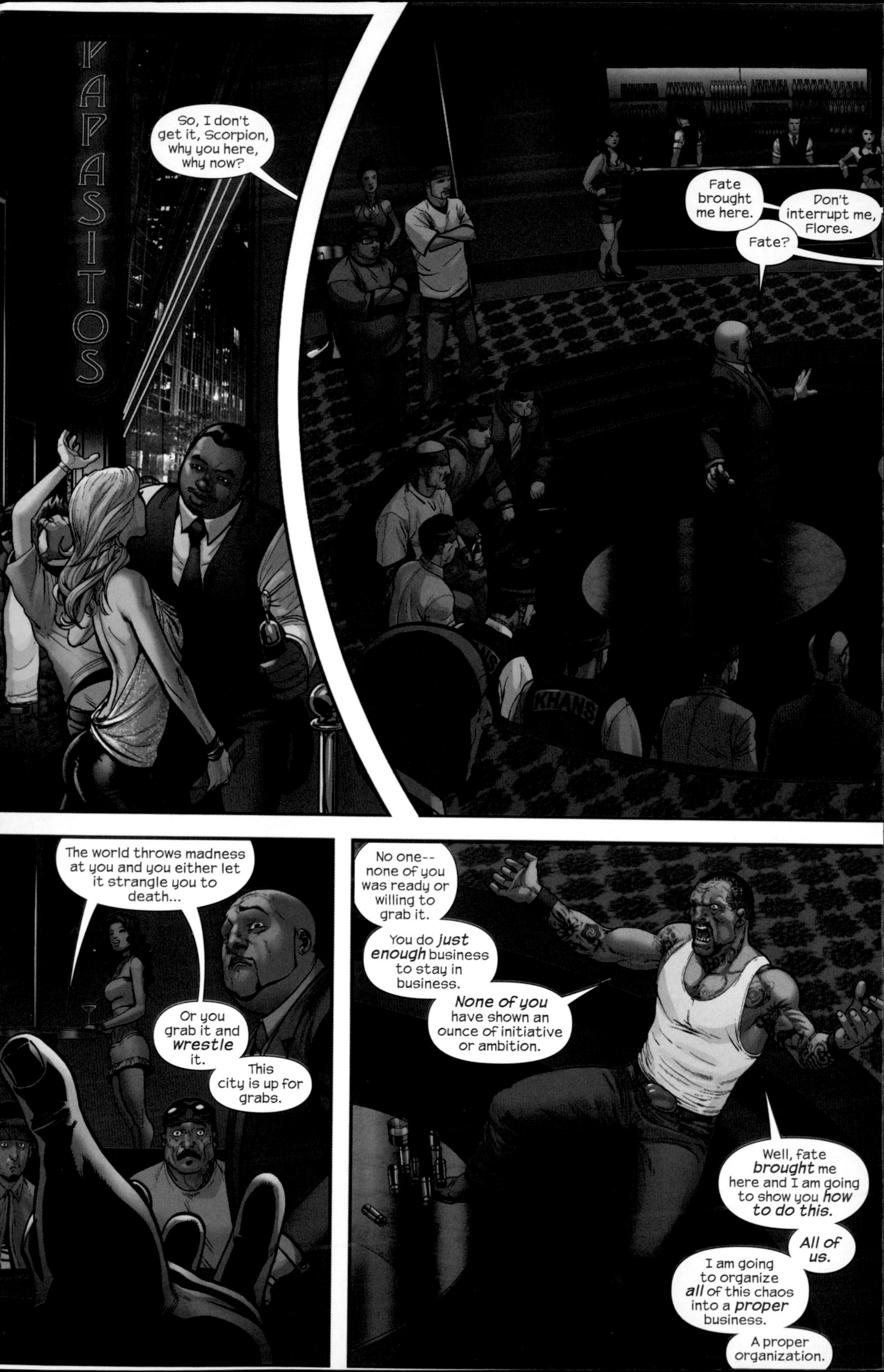

PAPASITOS
So, I don't get it, Scorpion, why you here, why now?
Fate brought me here.
Don't interrupt me, Flores.
Fate?
KHANS
The world throws madness at you and you either let it strangle you to death...
Or you grab it and *wrestle* it.
This city is up for grabs.
No one-- none of you was ready or willing to grab it.
You do *just enough* business to stay in business.
None of you have shown an ounce of initiative or ambition.
Well, fate *brought* me here and I am going to show you *how to do this.*
All of us.
I am going to organize *all* of this chaos into a *proper* business.
A proper organization.

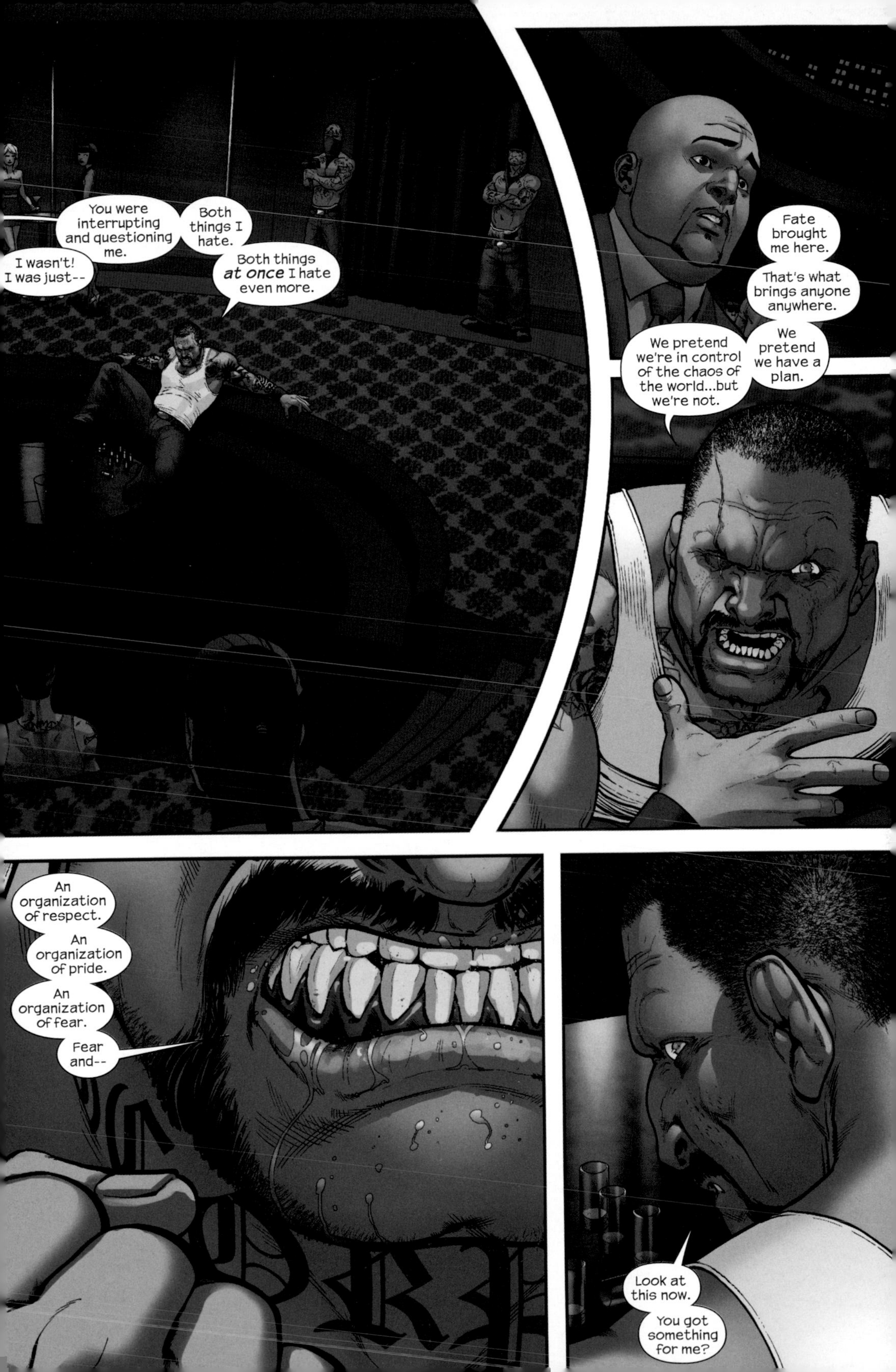
You were interrupting and questioning me.
I wasn't! I was just--
Both things I hate.
Both things at once I hate even more.
Fate brought me here.
That's what brings anyone anywhere.
We pretend we have a plan.
We pretend we're in control of the chaos of the world...but we're not.
An organization of respect.
An organization of pride.
An organization of fear.
Fear and--
Look at this now.
You got something for me?

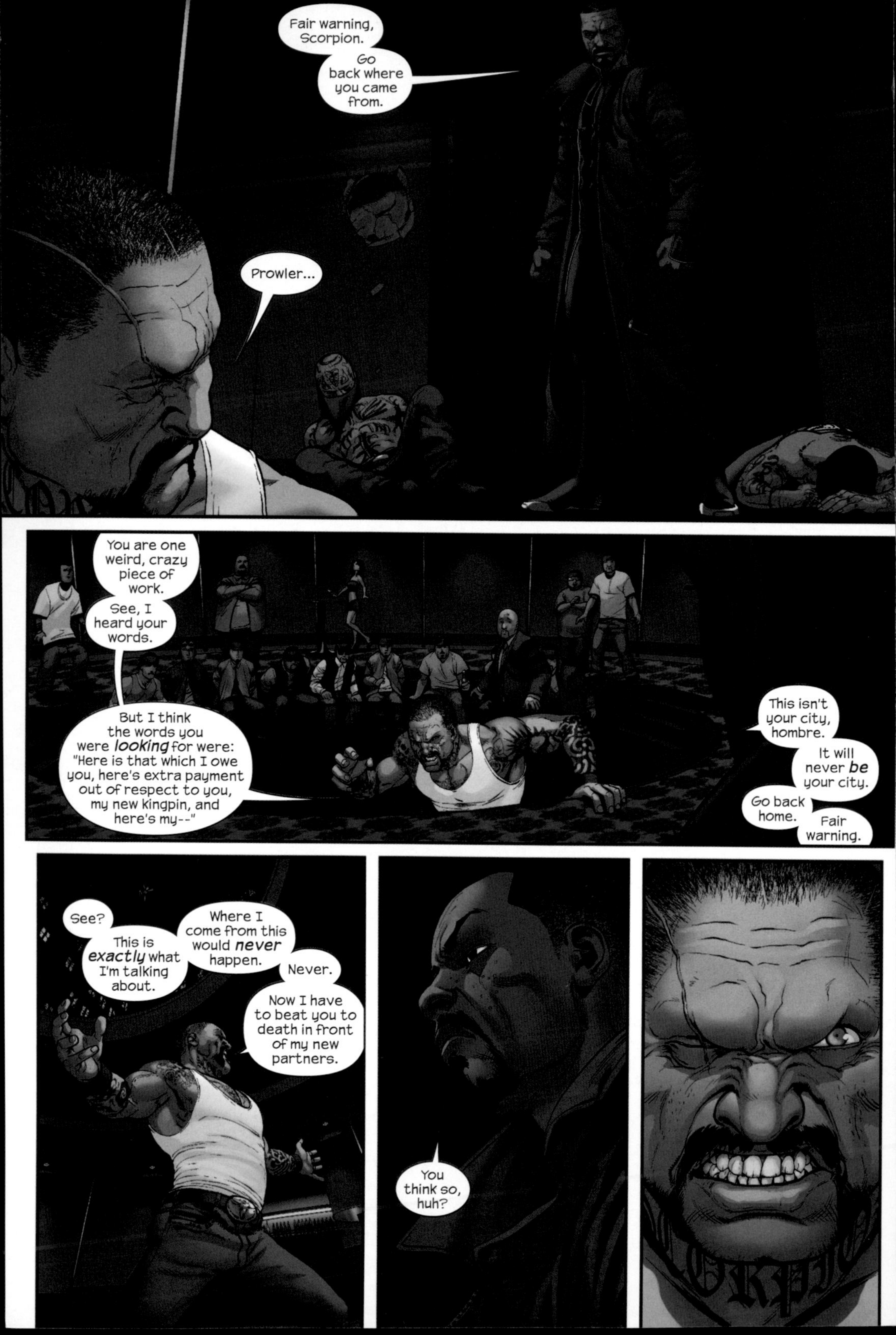

Fair warning, Scorpion.
Go back where you came from.
Prowler...
You are one weird, crazy piece of work.
See, I heard your words.
But I think the words you were *looking* for were: "Here is that which I owe you, here's extra payment out of respect to you, my new kingpin, and here's my--"
This isn't your city, hombre.
It will never *be* your city.
Go back home.
Fair warning.
See?
This is *exactly* what I'm talking about.
Where I come from this would *never* happen.
Never.
Now I have to beat you to death in front of my new partners.
You think so, huh?

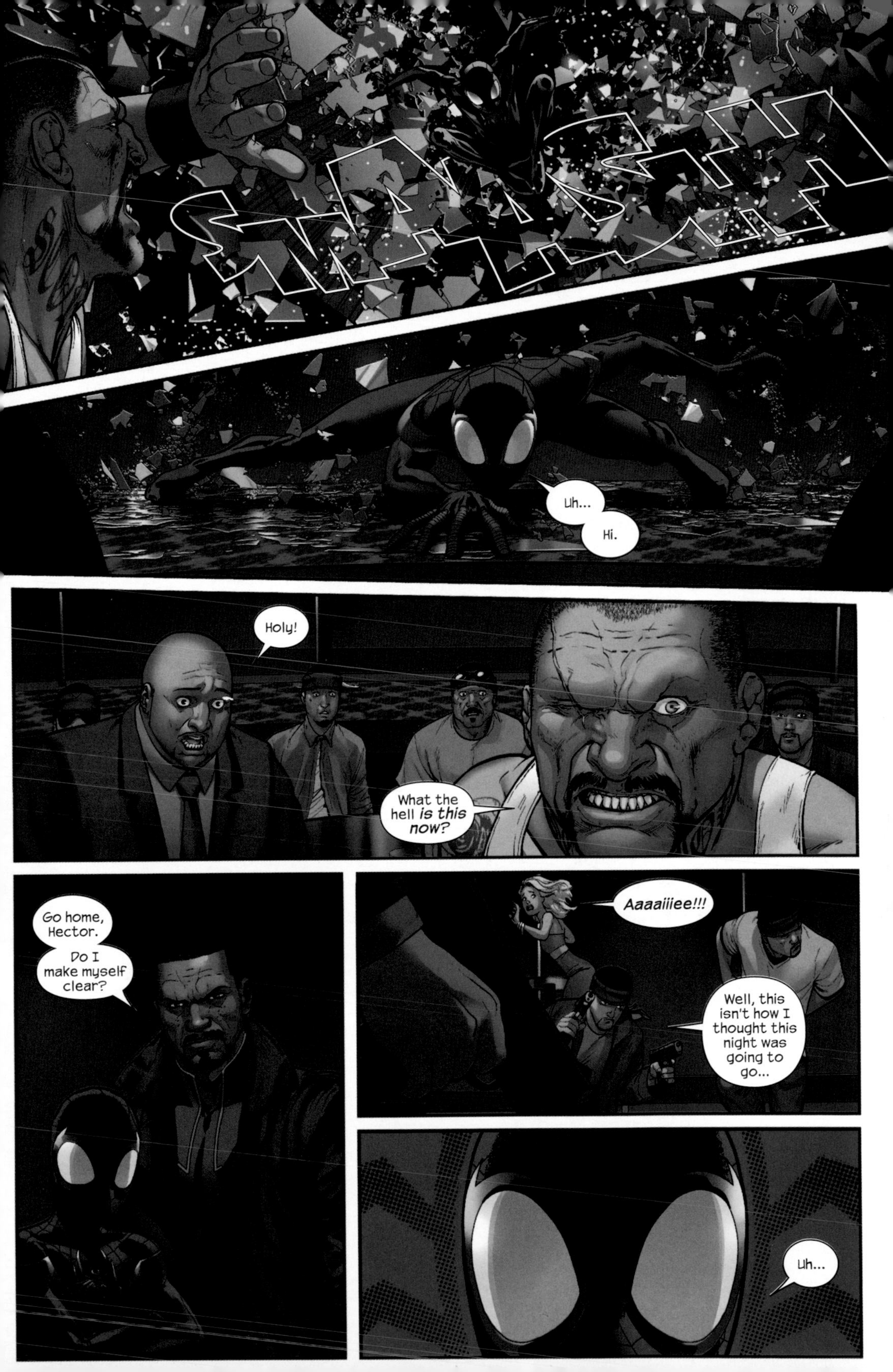
SMASH
Uh...
Hi.
Holy!
What the hell is this now?
Go home, Hector.
Do I make myself clear?
Aaaaiiiee!!!
Well, this isn't how I thought this night was going to go...
Uh...

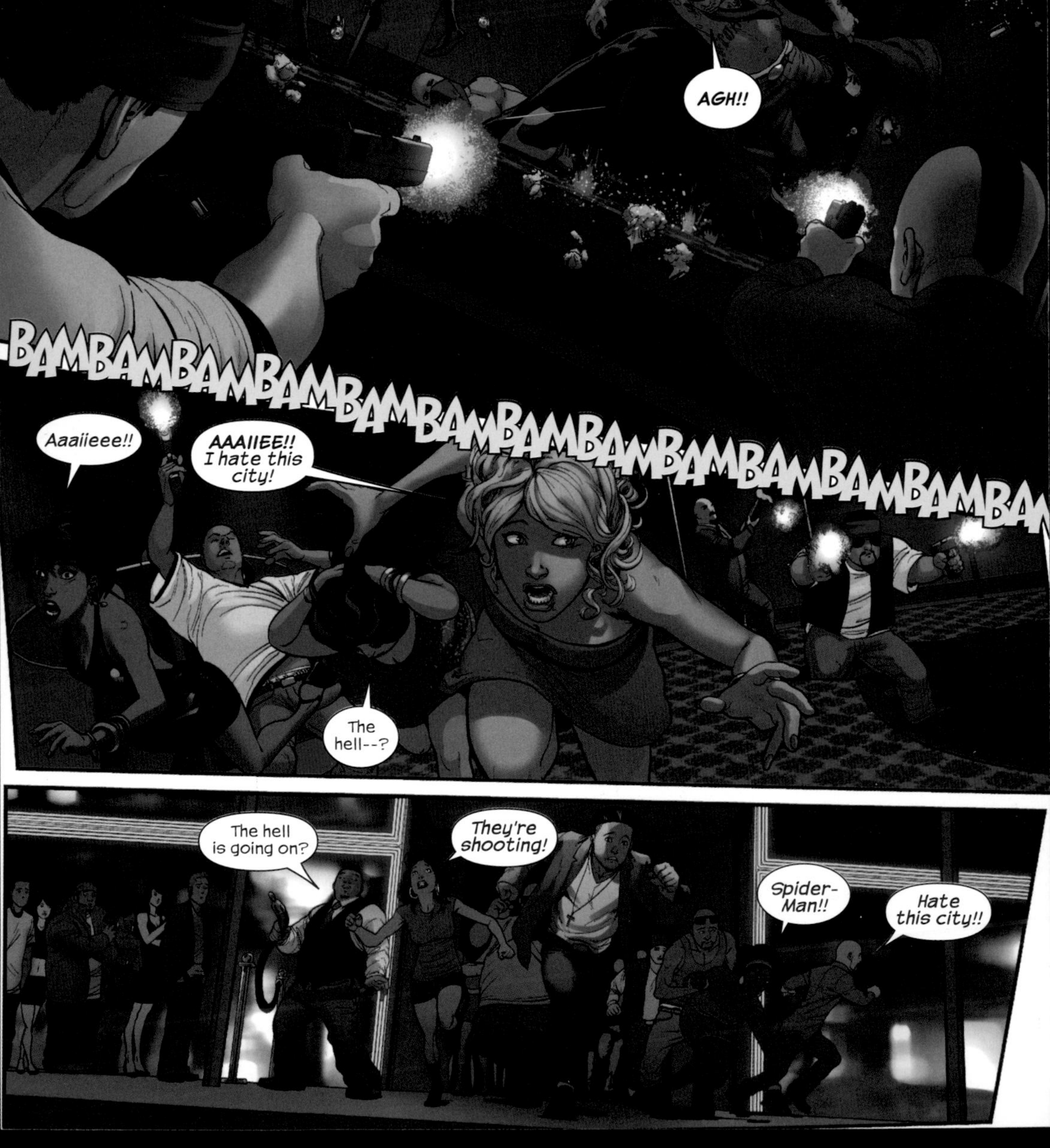
AGH!!
BAMBAMBAMBAMBAMBAMBAMBAMBAMBAMBAMBAMBAMBAM
Aaaiieee!!
AAAIIEE!! I hate this city!
The hell--?
The hell is going on?
They're shooting!
Spider-Man!!
Hate this city!!

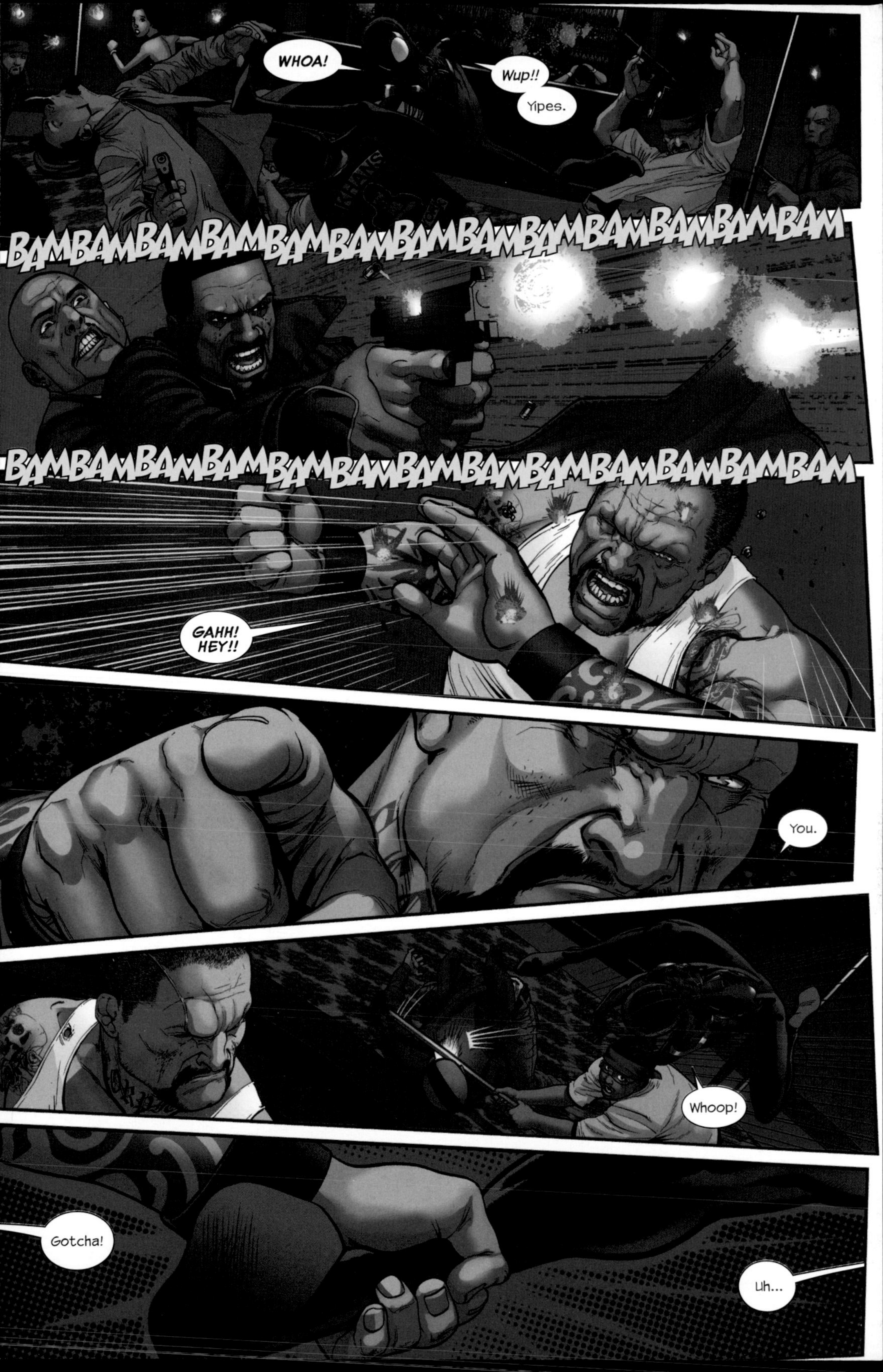
WHOA!
Wup!!
Yipes.
BAMBAMBAMBAMBAMBAMBAMBAMBAMBAMBAMBAMBAM
BAMBAMBAMBAMBAMBAMBAMBAMBAMBAMBAMBAMBAM
GAHH! HEY!!
You.
Whoop!
Gotcha!
Uh...

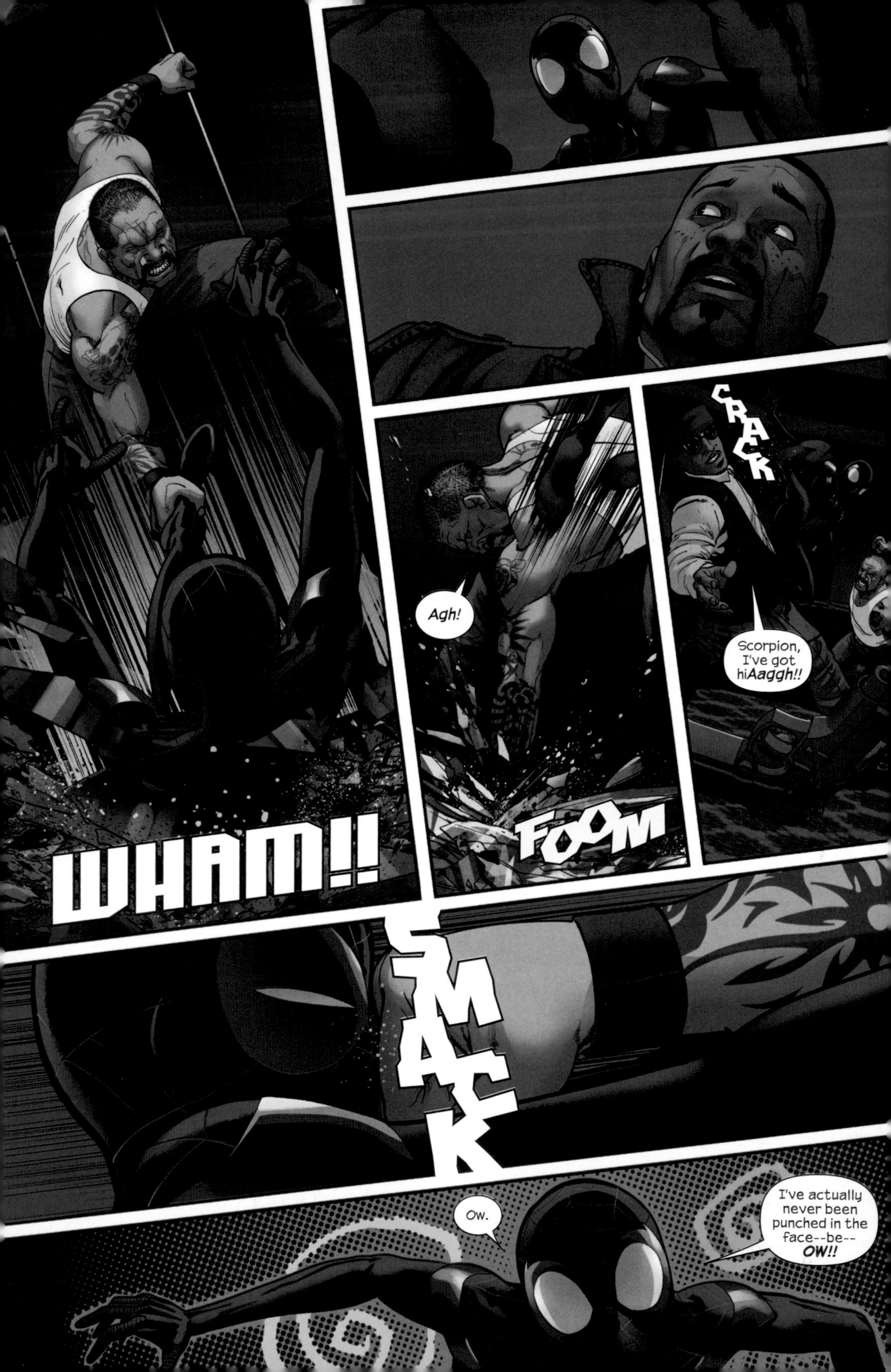
WHAM!!
Agh!
FOOM
CRACK
Scorpion, I've got hiAaggh!!
SMACK
Ow.
I've actually never been punched in the face--be-- OW!!

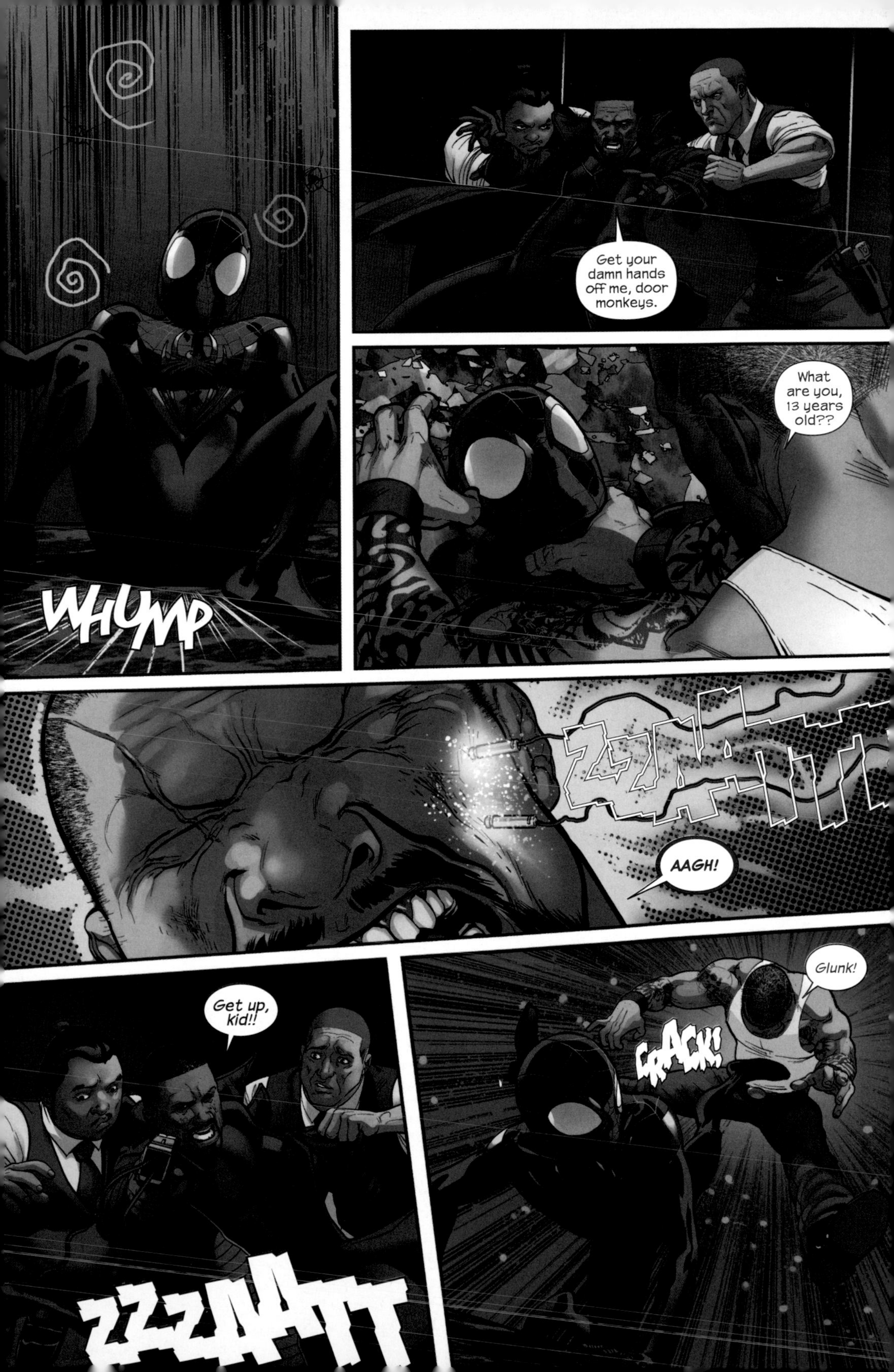
WHUMP
Get your damn hands off me, door monkeys.
What are you, 13 years old??
ZZZAATT
AAGH!
Get up, kid!!
ZZZAATT
Glunk!
CRACK!

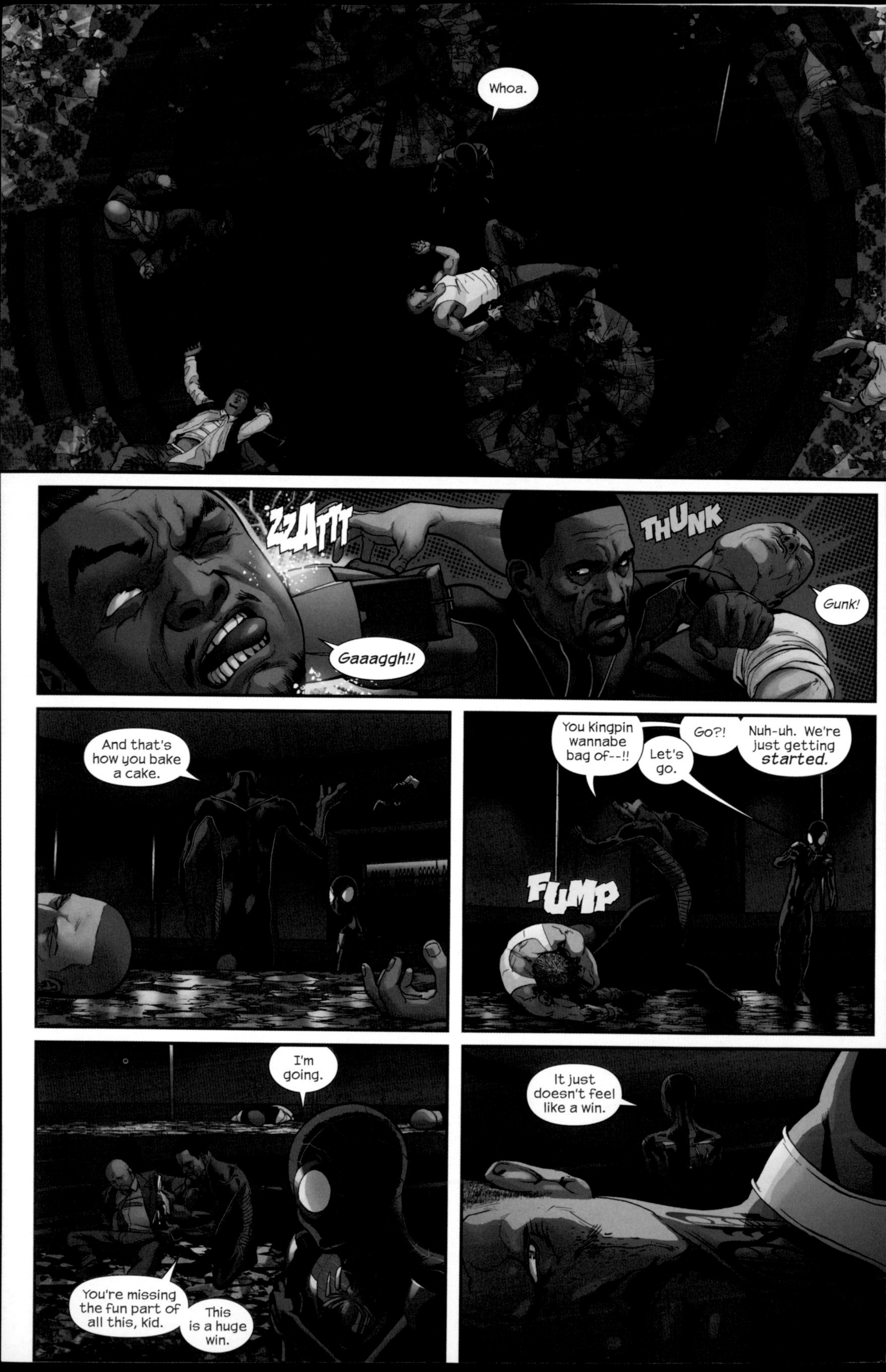
Whoa.
ZZATTT
Gaaagh!!
THUNK
Gunk!
And that's how you bake a cake.
You kingpin wannabe bag of--!!
Let's go.
Go?!
Nuh-uh. We're just getting *started.*
FUMP
I'm going.
You're missing the fun part of all this, kid.
This is a huge win.
It just doesn't feel like a win.

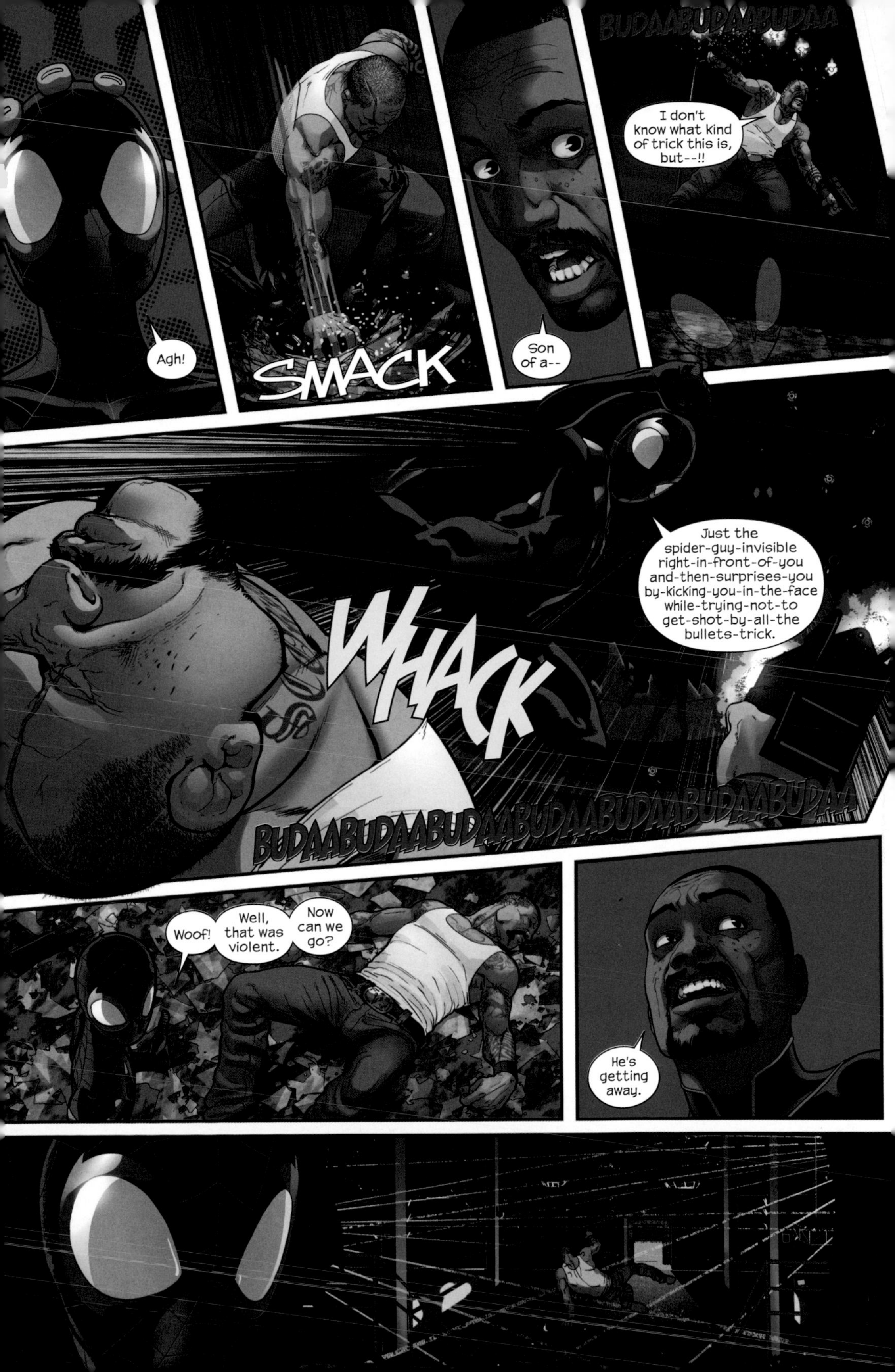
BUDAABUDAABUDAA
I don't know what kind of trick this is, but--!!
Agh!
SMACK
Son of a--
Just the spider-guy-invisible right-in-front-of-you and-then-surprises-you by-kicking-you-in-the-face while-trying-not-to get-shot-by-all-the bullets-trick.
WHACK
BUDAABUDAABUDAABUDAABUDAA
Woof!
Well, that was violent.
Now can we go?
He's getting away.

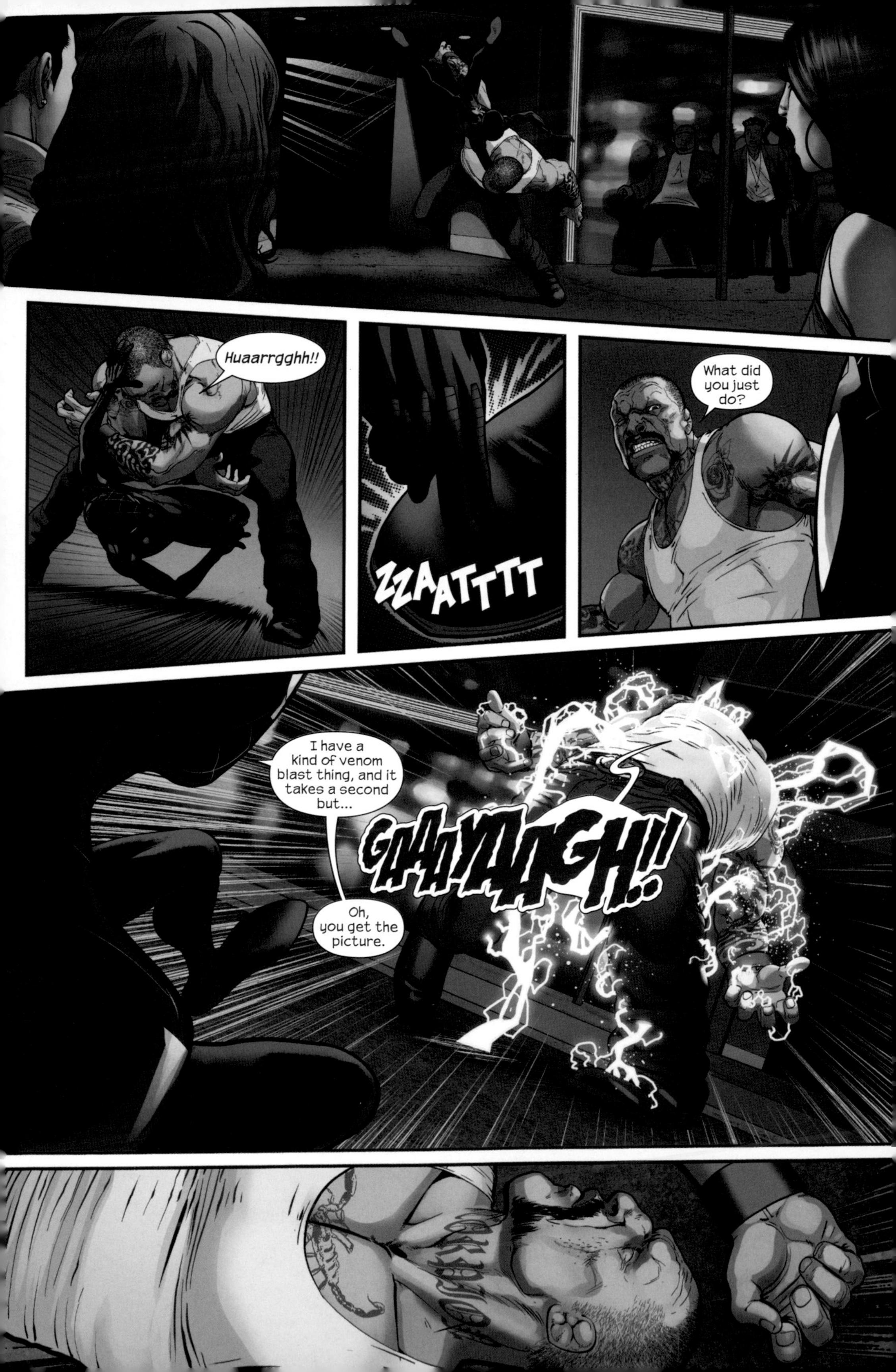
Huaarrgghh!!
ZZAATTTT
What did you just do?
I have a kind of venom blast thing, and it takes a second but...
GZAAAYAAAGH!!
Oh, you get the picture.

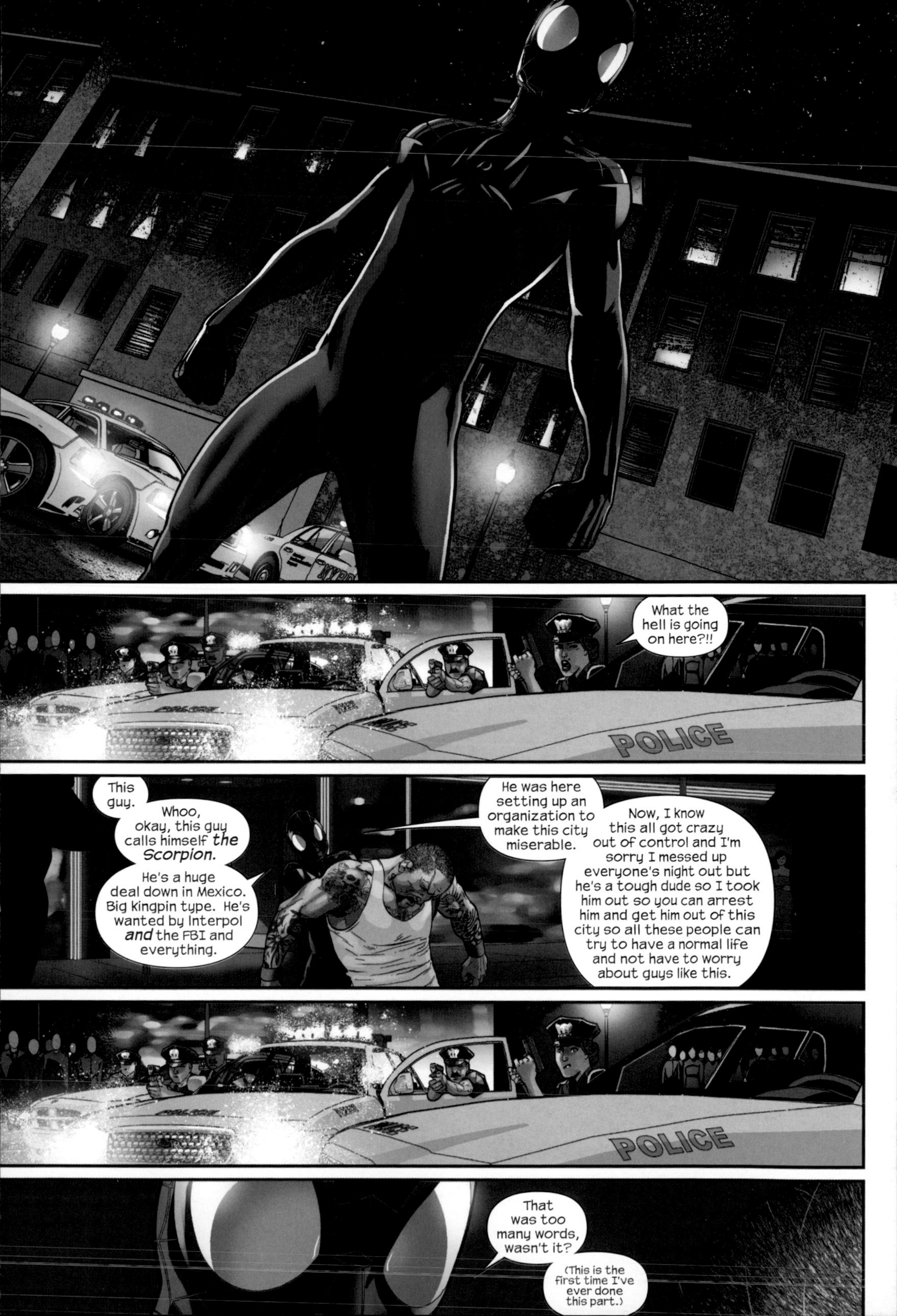
What the hell is going on here?!!
This guy.
Whoo, okay, this guy calls himself *the Scorpion.*
He's a huge deal down in Mexico. Big kingpin type. He's wanted by Interpol *and* the FBI and everything.
He was here setting up an organization to make this city miserable.
Now, I know this all got crazy out of control and I'm sorry I messed up everyone's night out but he's a tough dude so I took him out so you can arrest him and get him out of this city so all these people can try to have a normal life and not have to worry about guys like this.
That was too many words, wasn't it?
(This is the first time I've ever done this part.)

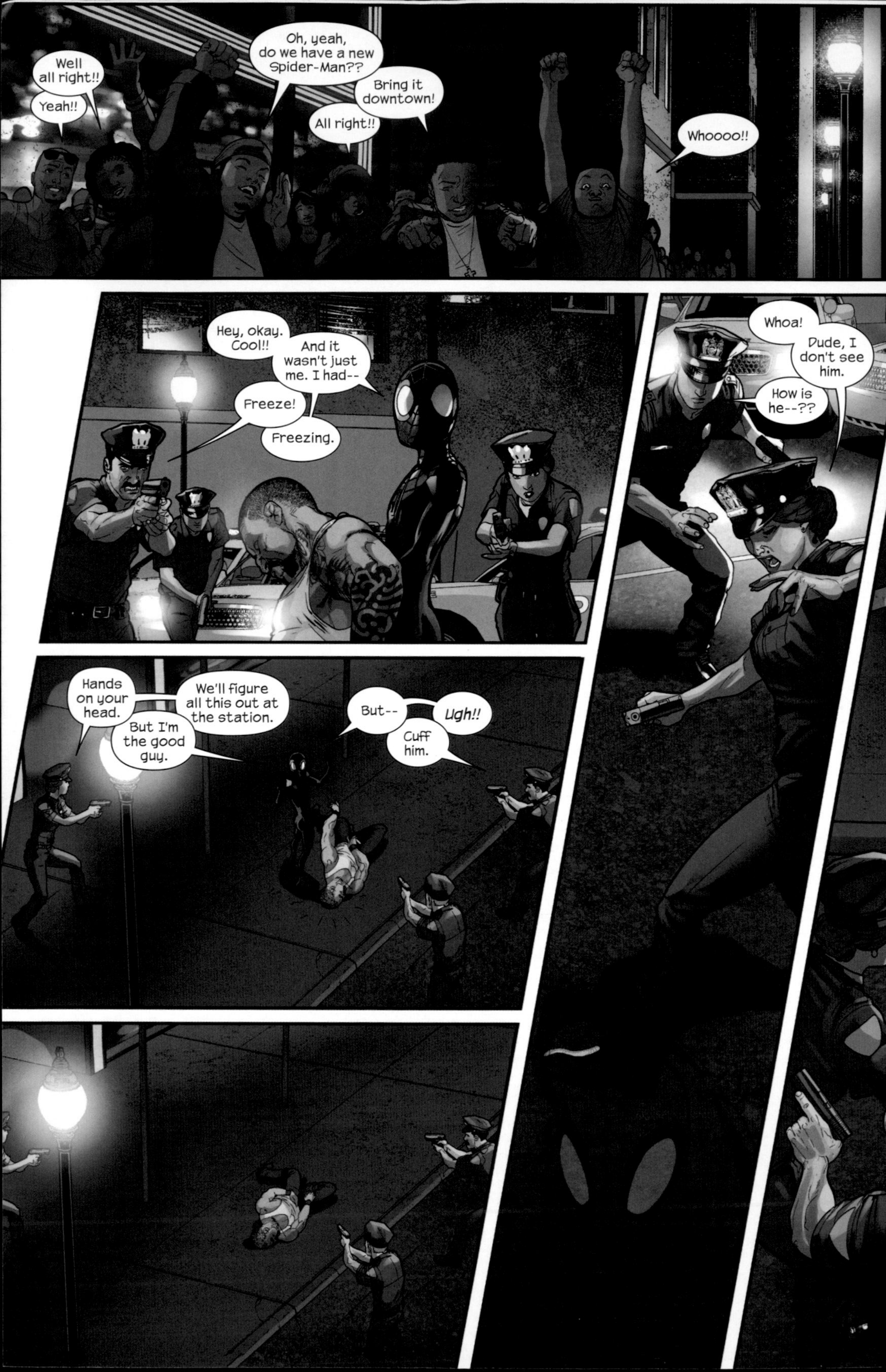
Well all right!!
Yeah!!
Oh, yeah, do we have a new Spider-Man??
All right!!
Bring it downtown!
Whoooo!!
Hey, okay. Cool!!
And it wasn't just me. I had--
Freeze!
Freezing.
Whoa!
Dude, I don't see him.
How is he--??
Hands on your head.
We'll figure all this out at the station.
But I'm the good guy.
But--
Ugh!!
Cuff him.

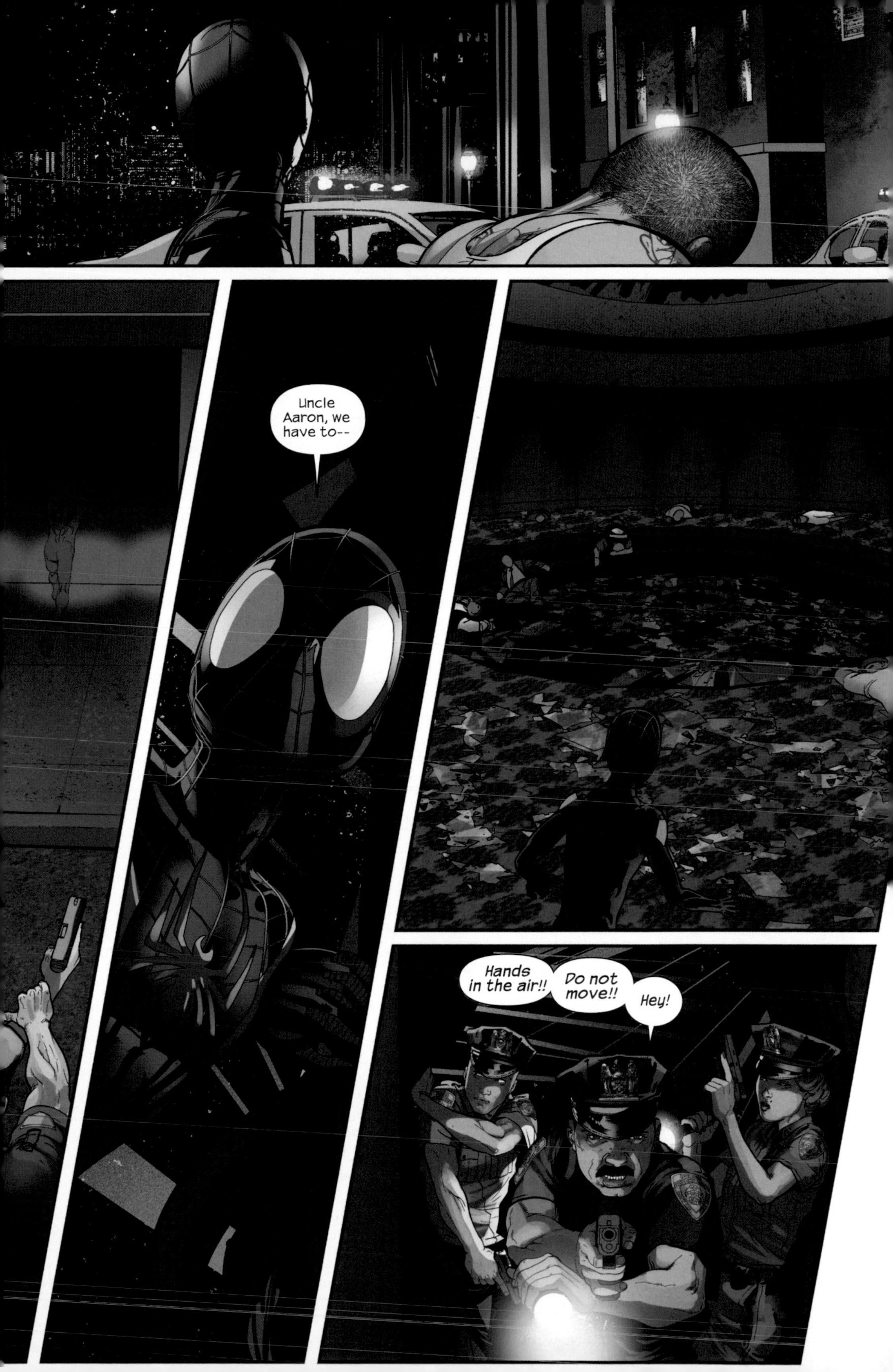
Uncle Aaron, we have to--
Hands in the air!!
Do not move!!
Hey!

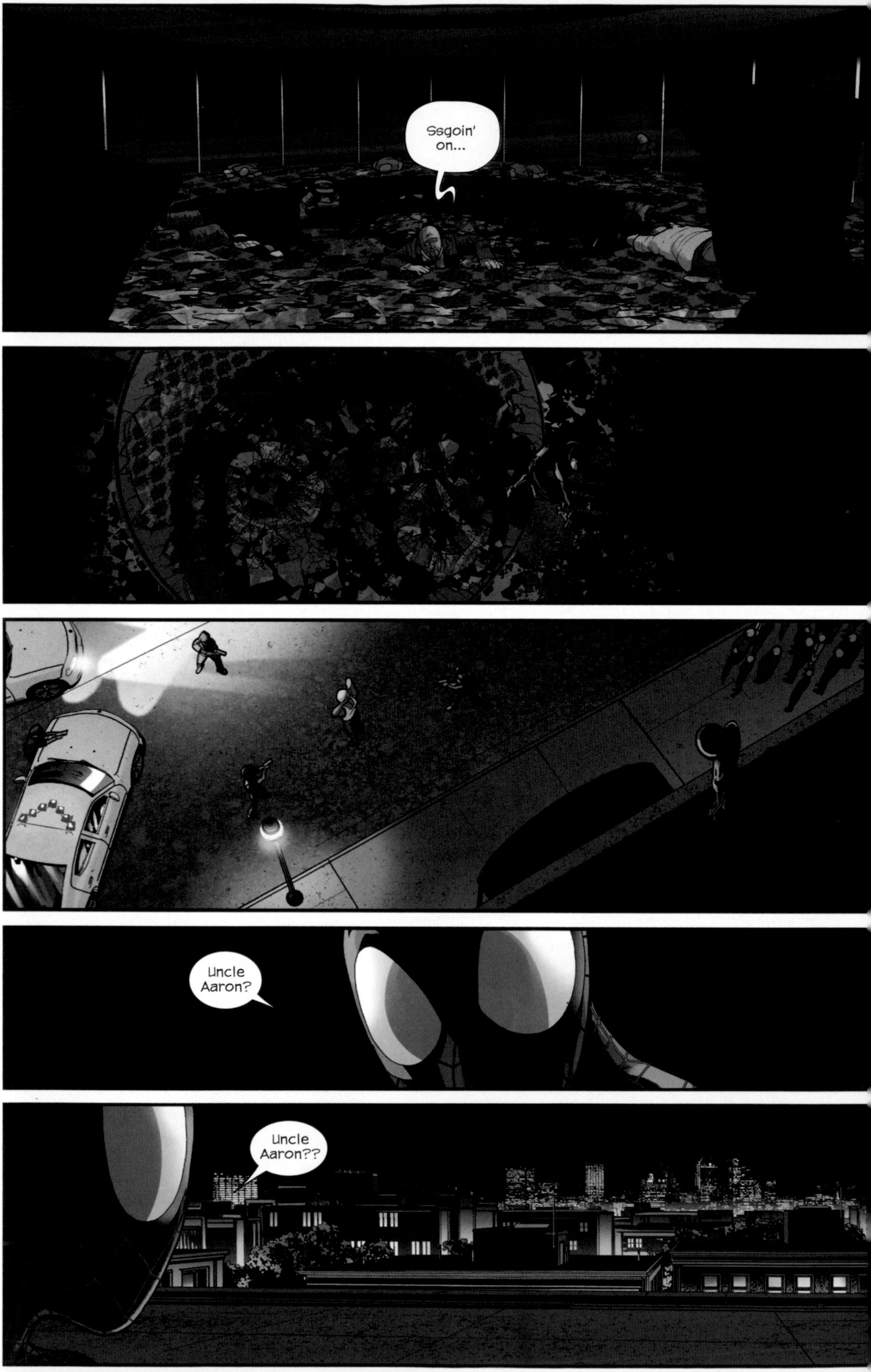
Ssgoin' on...
Uncle Aaron?
Uncle Aaron??

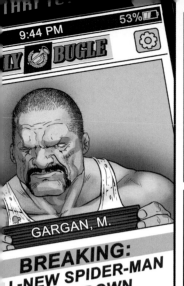

9:44 PM   53%

GARGAN, M.

BREAKING:
L-NEW SPIDER-MAN TAKES DOWN THE SCORPION

REFRESH FOR DETAILS

Holy macaroli...

Jeez!

Hey...

Miles, you okay?

Where's Judge?

Shower.

Good, good...

You do this?

Kinda, yeah.

Dude, who *are* you?

You would not believe the night I'm having.

BBZZZZ

It's been buzzing all night.

Who is it?

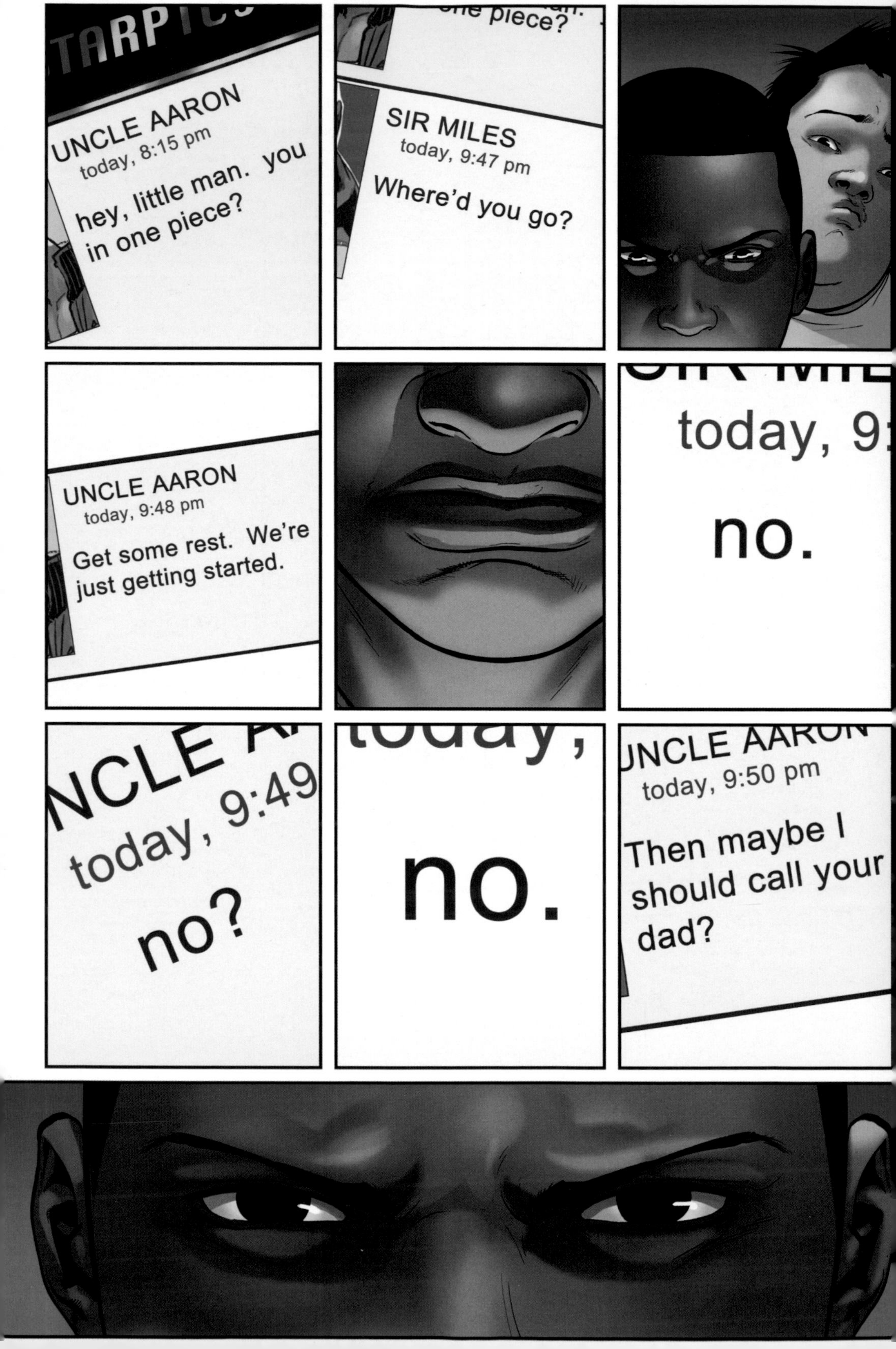

UNCLE AARON
today, 8:15 pm
hey, little man. you in one piece?
SIR MILES
today, 9:47 pm
Where'd you go?
UNCLE AARON
today, 9:48 pm
Get some rest. We're just getting started.
today, 9
no.
today, 9:49
no?
today,
no.
UNCLE AARON
today, 9:50 pm
Then maybe I should call your dad?

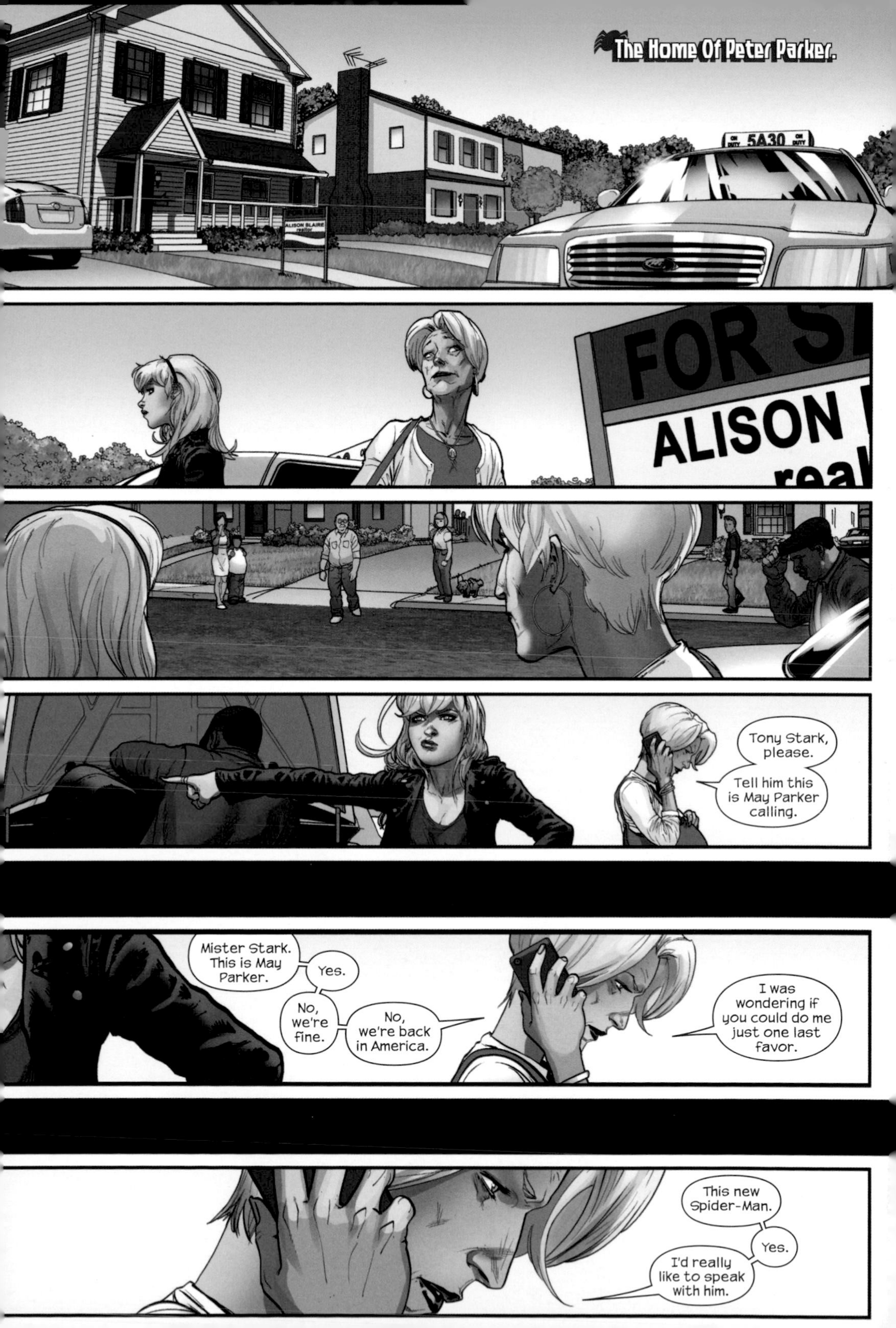
The Home Of Peter Parker.
5A30
FOR SALE
ALISON BLAIRE
realtor
FOR S
ALISON
real
Tony Stark, please.
Tell him this is May Parker calling.
Mister Stark. This is May Parker.
Yes.
No, we're fine.
No, we're back in America.
I was wondering if you could do me just one last favor.
This new Spider-Man.
Yes.
I'd really like to speak with him.

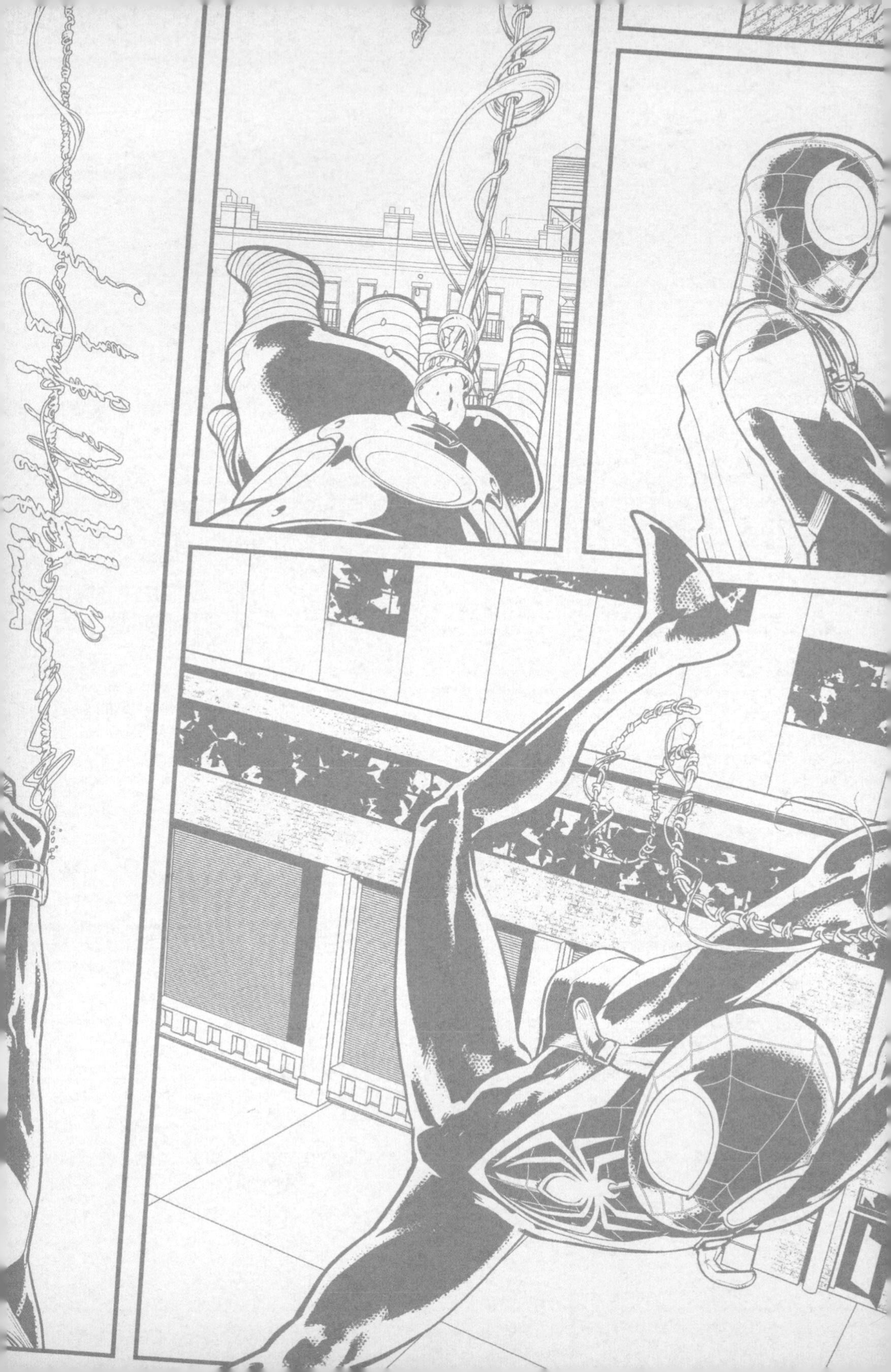

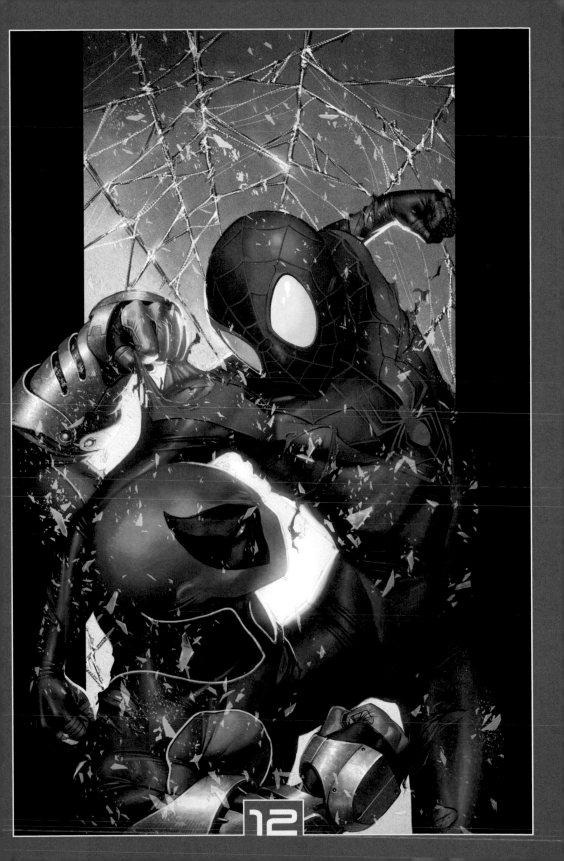

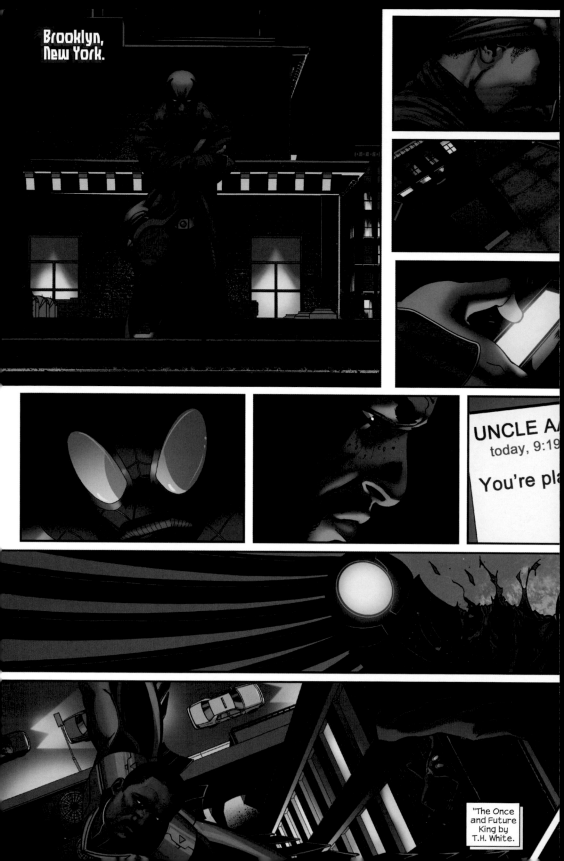

Brooklyn,
New York.

UNCLE A
today, 9:19

You're pla

"The Once
and Future
King by
T.H. White.

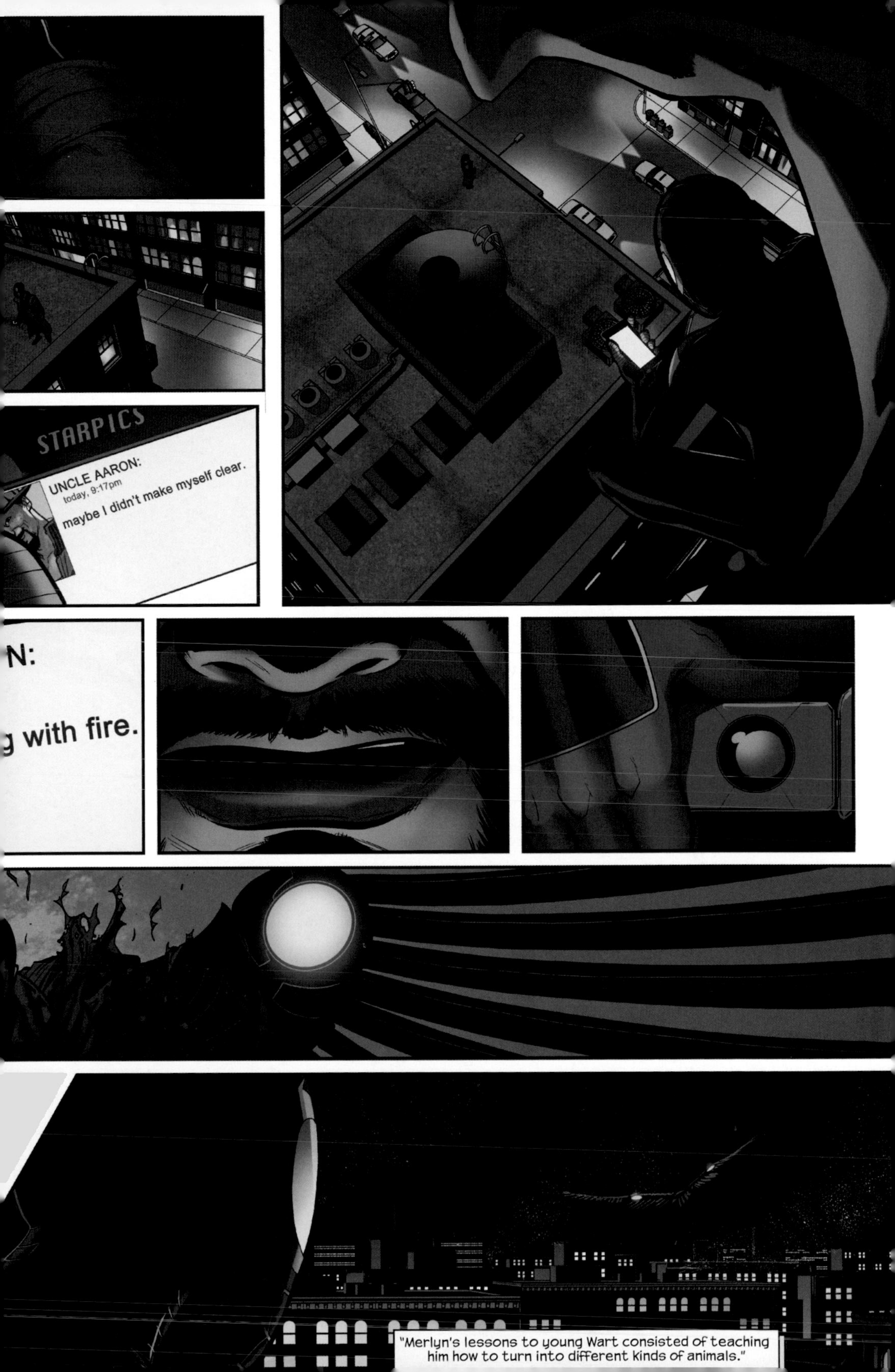
STARPICS
UNCLE AARON:
today, 9:17pm
maybe I didn't make myself clear.
N:
g with fire.
"Merlyn's lessons to young Wart consisted of teaching him how to turn into different kinds of animals."

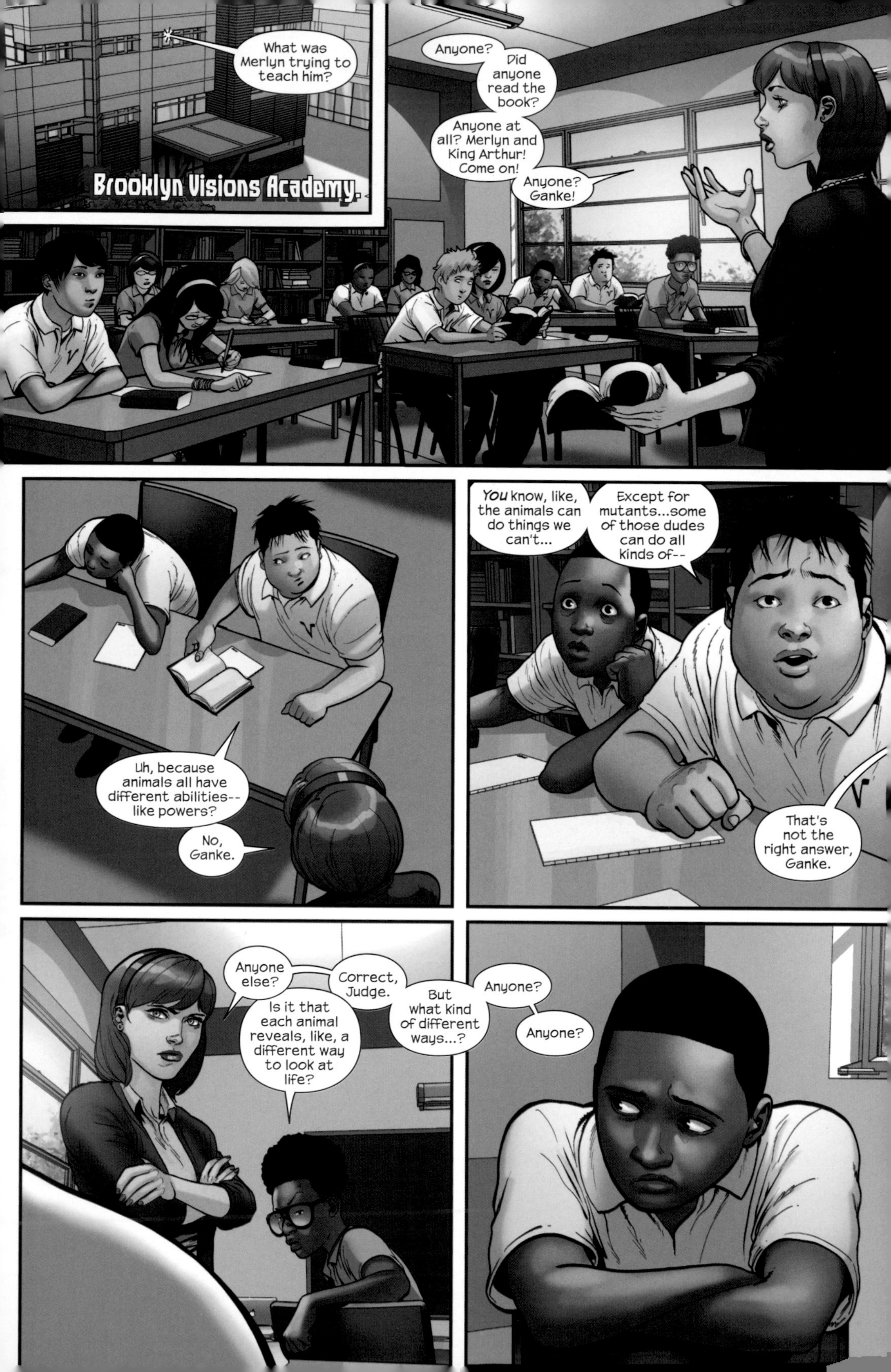
Brooklyn Visions Academy.
What was Merlyn trying to teach him?
Anyone?
Did anyone read the book?
Anyone at all? Merlyn and King Arthur! Come on!
Anyone? Ganke!
Uh, because animals all have different abilities--like powers?
No, Ganke.
YOU know, like, the animals can do things we can't...
Except for mutants...some of those dudes can do all kinds of--
That's not the right answer, Ganke.
Anyone else?
Is it that each animal reveals, like, a different way to look at life?
Correct, Judge.
But what kind of different ways...?
Anyone?
Anyone?

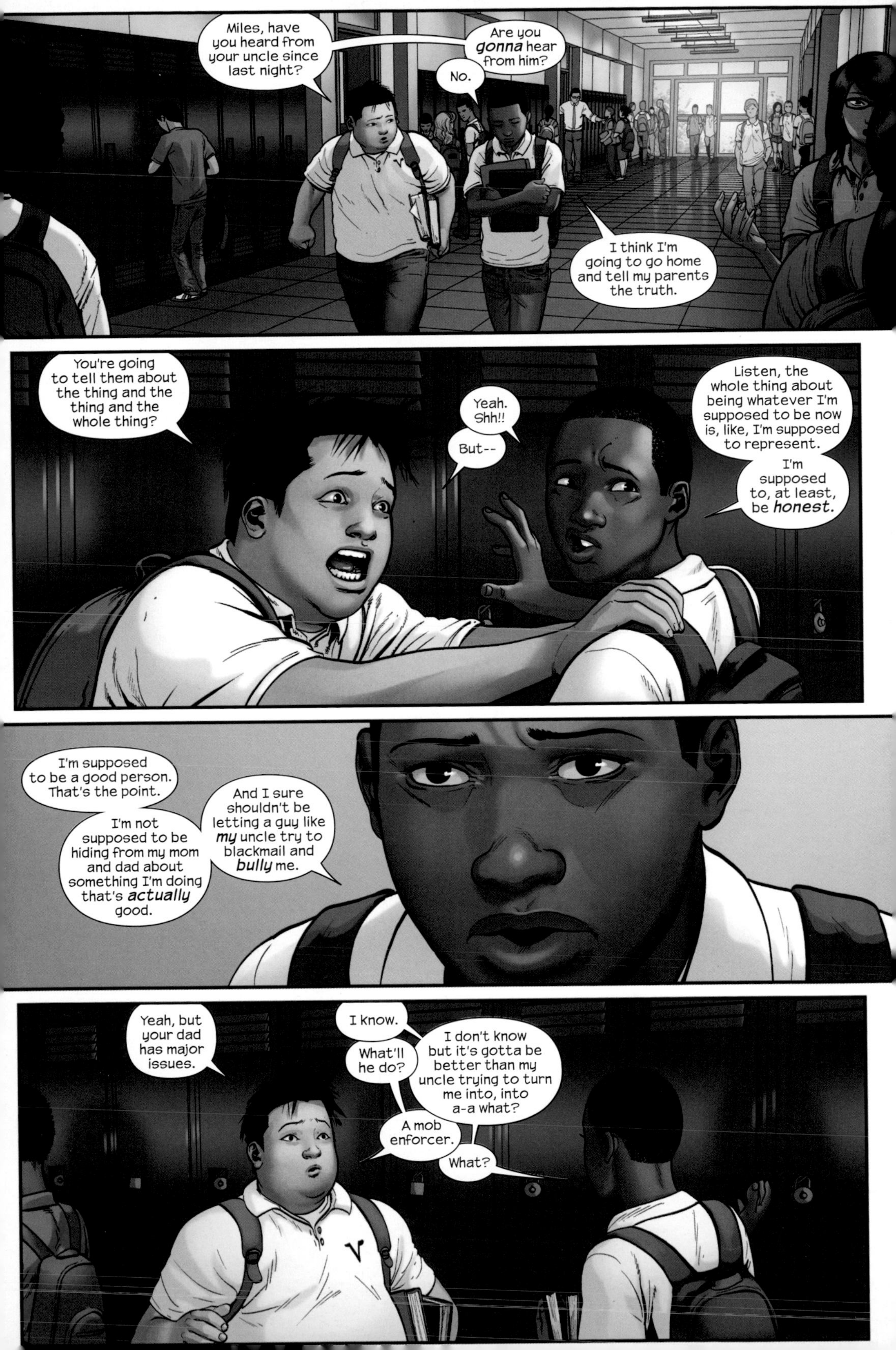
Miles, have you heard from your uncle since last night?
No.
Are you *gonna* hear from him?
I think I'm going to go home and tell my parents the truth.
You're going to tell them about the thing and the thing and the whole thing?
Yeah. Shh!!
But--
Listen, the whole thing about being whatever I'm supposed to be now is, like, I'm supposed to represent.
I'm supposed to, at least, be *honest.*
I'm supposed to be a good person. That's the point.
I'm not supposed to be hiding from my mom and dad about something I'm doing that's *actually* good.
And I sure shouldn't be letting a guy like *my* uncle try to blackmail and *bully* me.
Yeah, but your dad has major issues.
I know.
What'll he do?
I don't know but it's gotta be better than my uncle trying to turn me into, into a-a what?
A mob enforcer.
What?

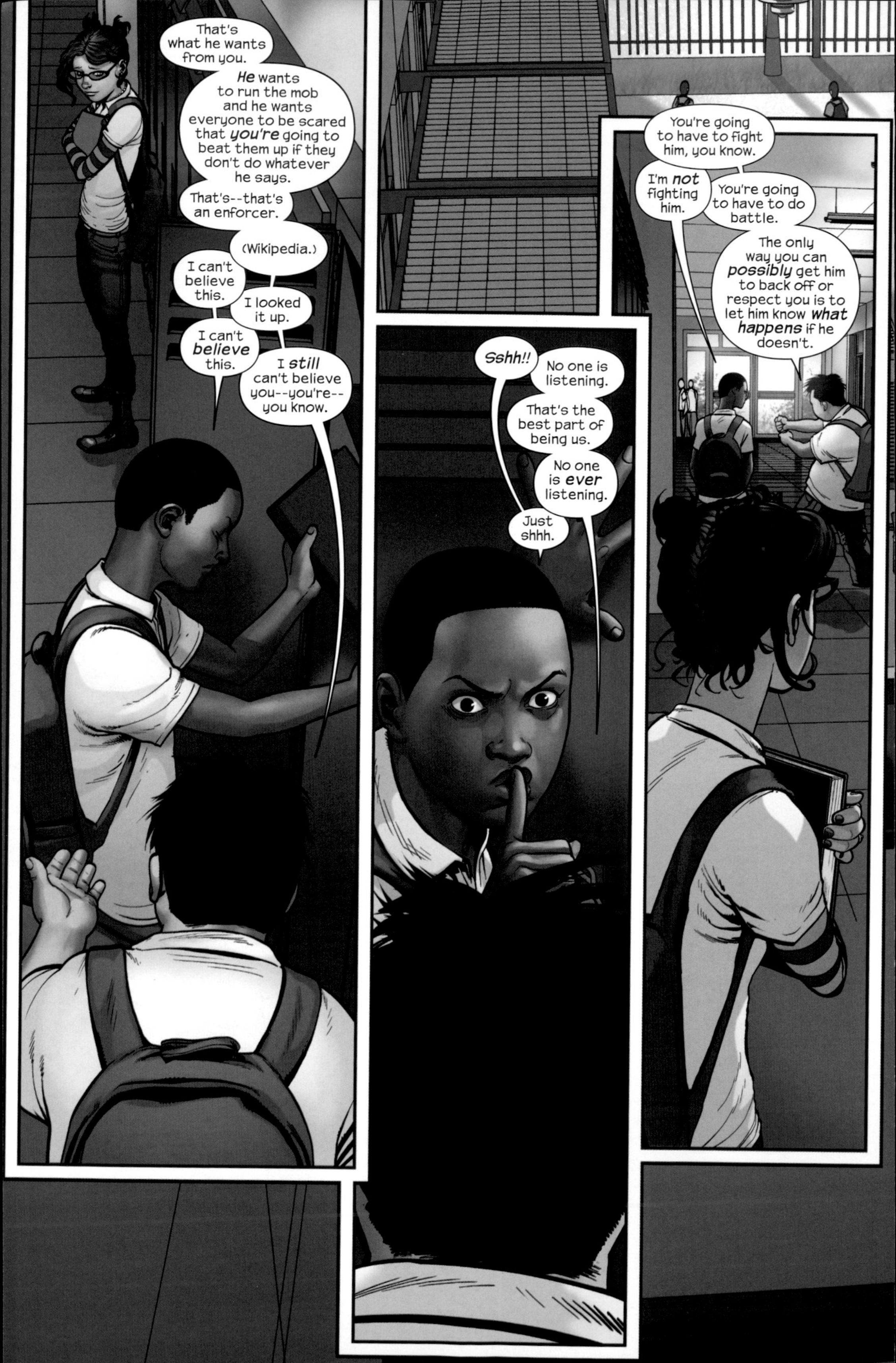
That's what he wants from you.
He wants to run the mob and he wants everyone to be scared that you're going to beat them up if they don't do whatever he says.
That's--that's an enforcer.
(Wikipedia.)
I can't believe this.
I looked it up.
I can't believe this.
I still can't believe you--you're--you know.
Sshh!!
No one is listening.
That's the best part of being us.
No one is ever listening.
Just shhh.
You're going to have to fight him, you know.
I'm not fighting him.
You're going to have to do battle.
The only way you can possibly get him to back off or respect you is to let him know what happens if he doesn't.

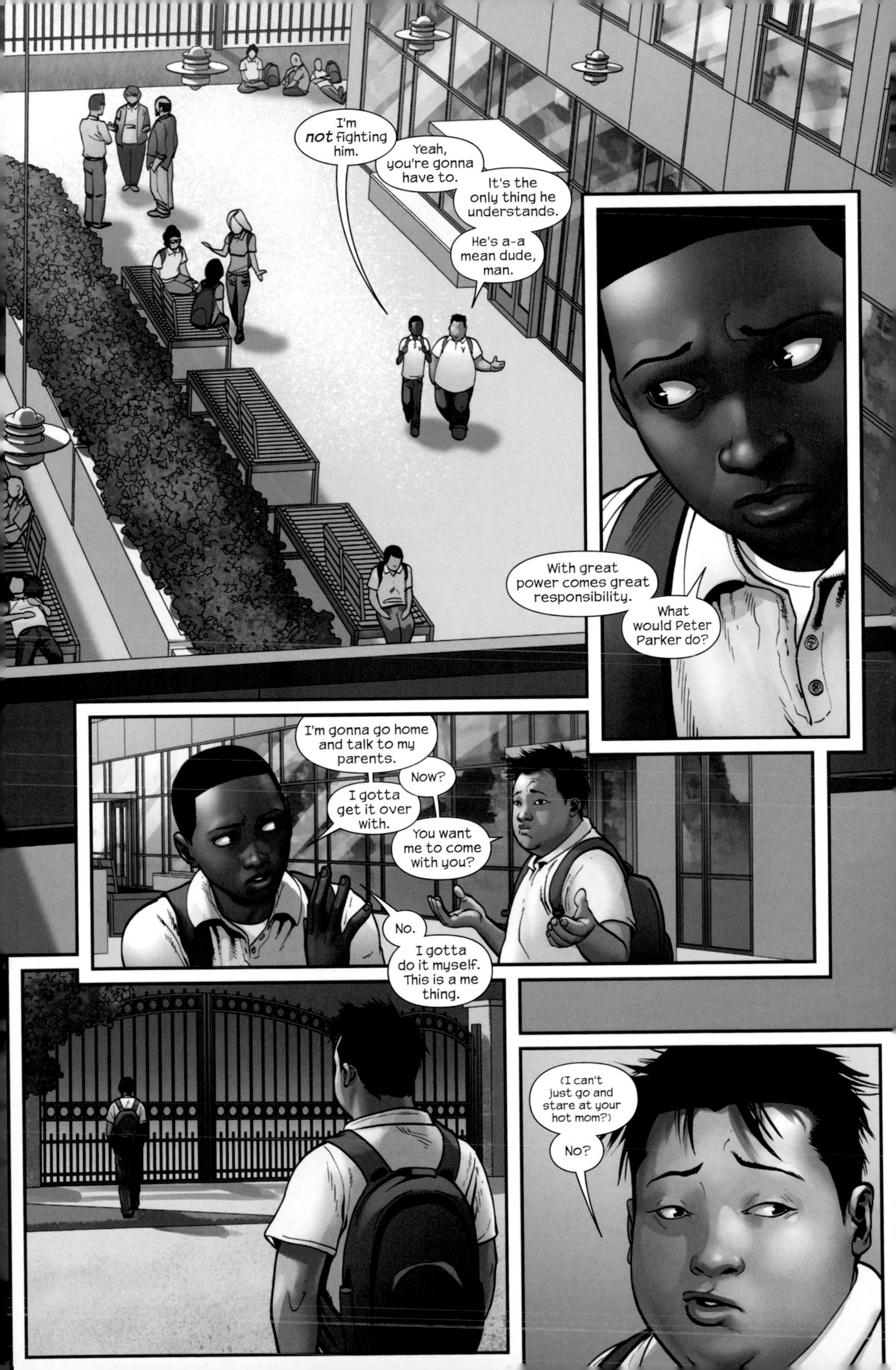

I'm *not* fighting him.
Yeah, you're gonna have to.
It's the only thing he understands.
He's a-a mean dude, man.
With great power comes great responsibility.
What would Peter Parker do?
I'm gonna go home and talk to my parents.
Now?
I gotta get it over with.
You want me to come with you?
No.
I gotta do it myself. This is a me thing.
(I can't just go and stare at your hot mom?)
No?

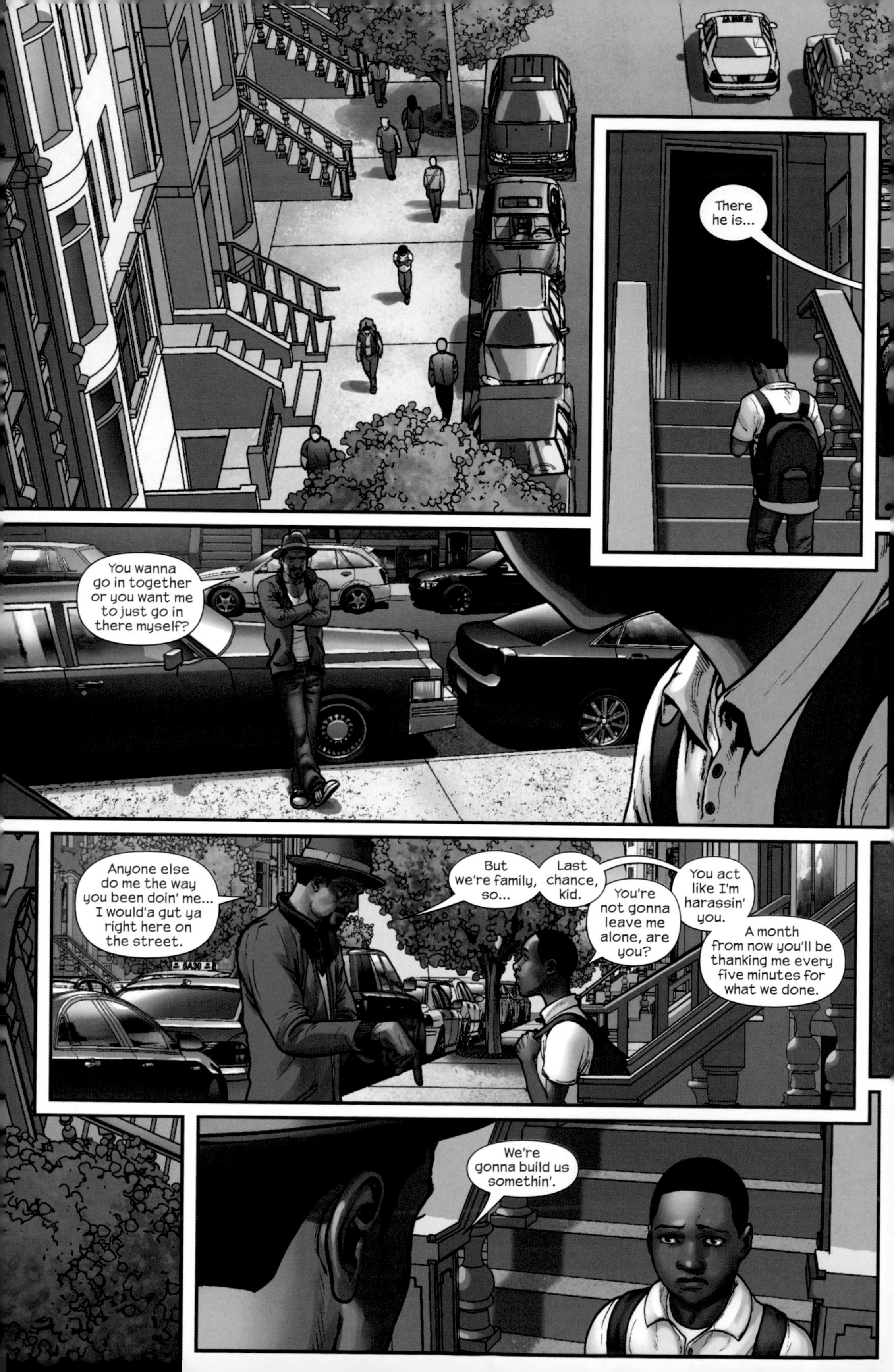
There he is...
You wanna go in together or you want me to just go in there myself?
Anyone else do me the way you been doin' me... I would'a gut ya right here on the street.
But we're family, so...
Last chance, kid.
You're not gonna leave me alone, are you?
You act like I'm harassin' you.
A month from now you'll be thanking me every five minutes for what we done.
We're gonna build us somethin'.

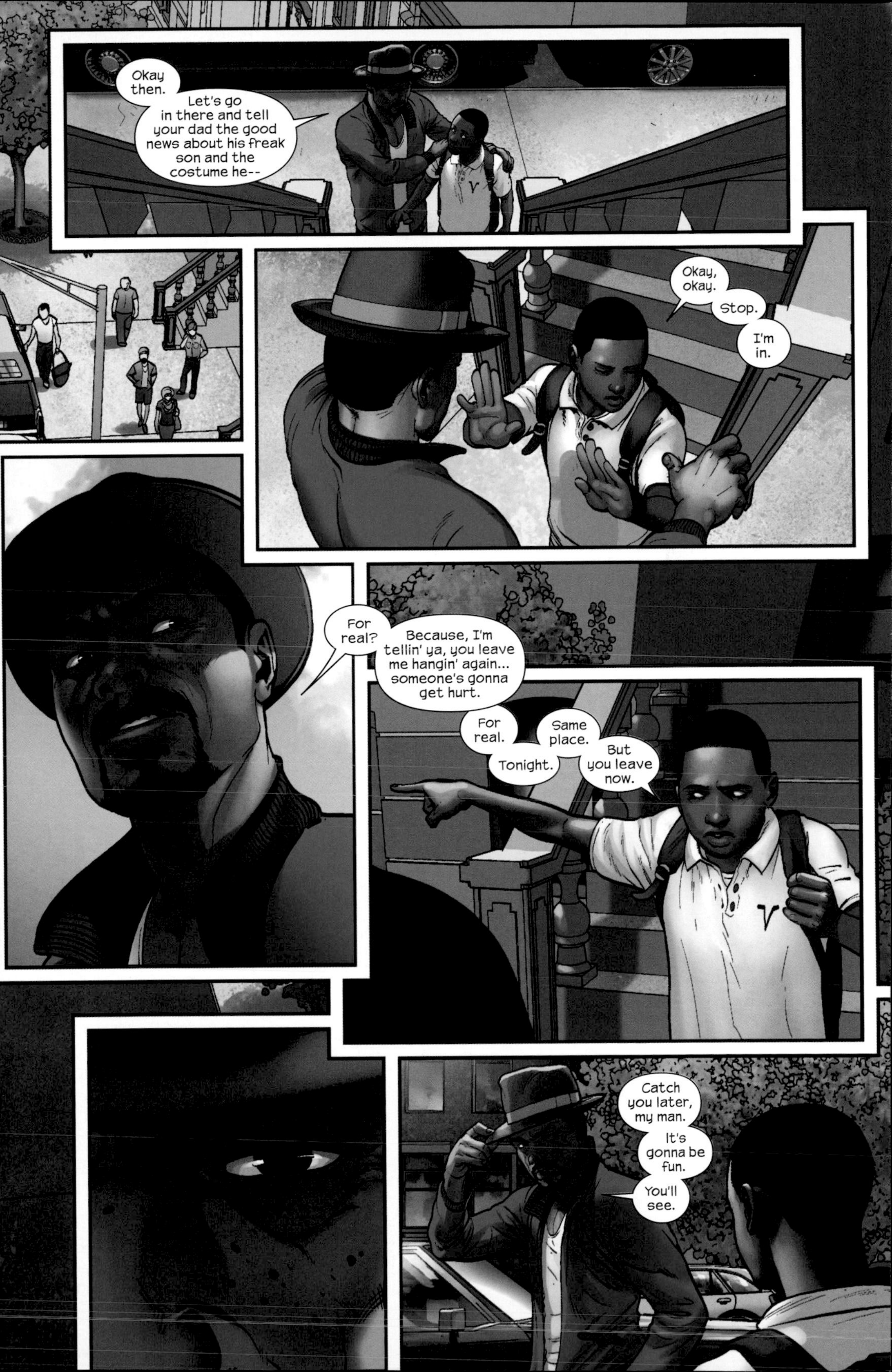
Okay then.
Let's go in there and tell your dad the good news about his freak son and the costume he--
Okay, okay.
Stop.
I'm in.
For real?
Because, I'm tellin' ya, you leave me hangin' again... someone's gonna get hurt.
For real.
Tonight.
Same place.
But you leave now.
Catch you later, my man.
It's gonna be fun.
You'll see.

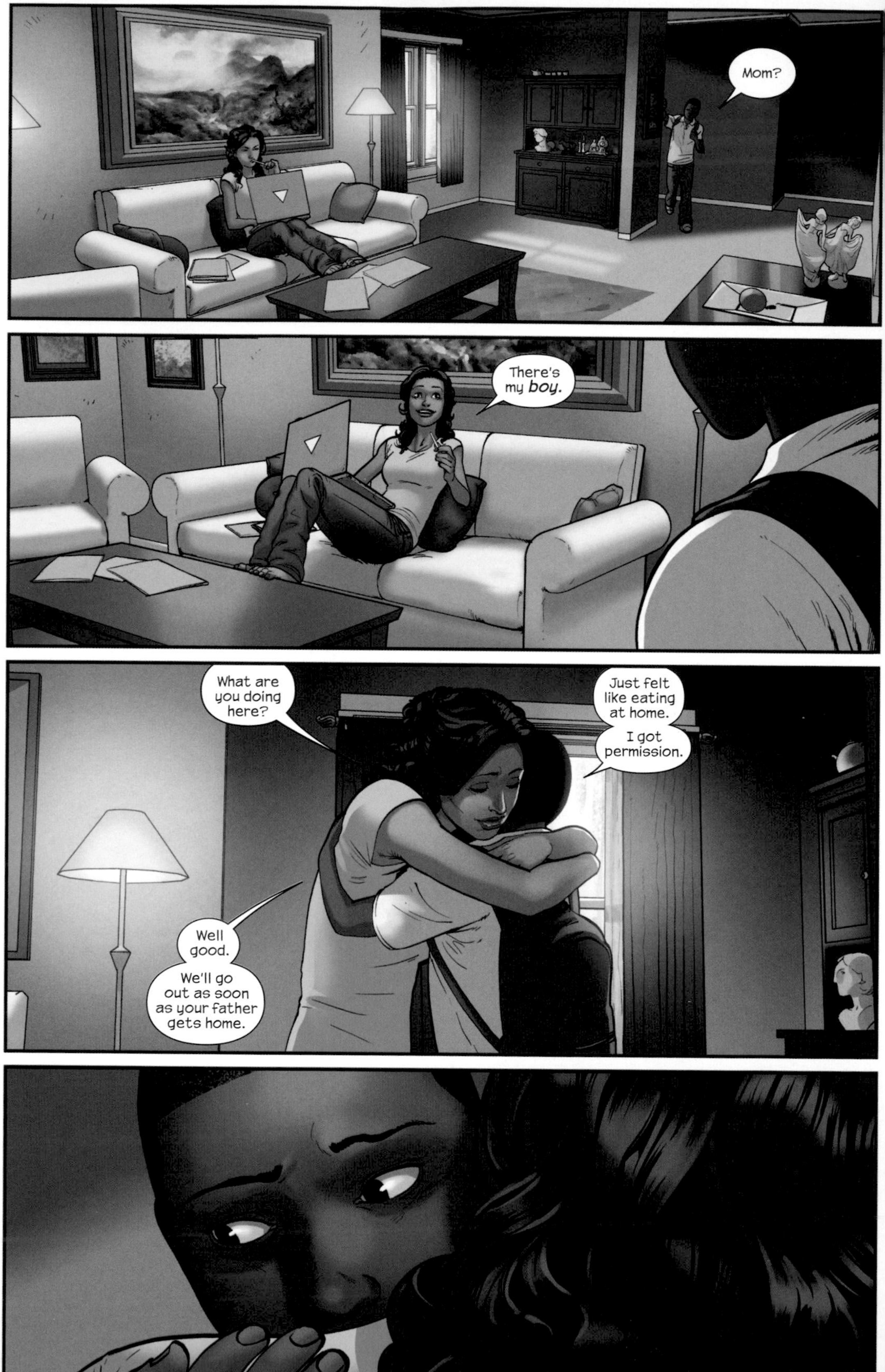
Mom?
There's my *boy.*
What are you doing here?
Just felt like eating at home.
I got permission.
Well good.
We'll go out as soon as your father gets home.

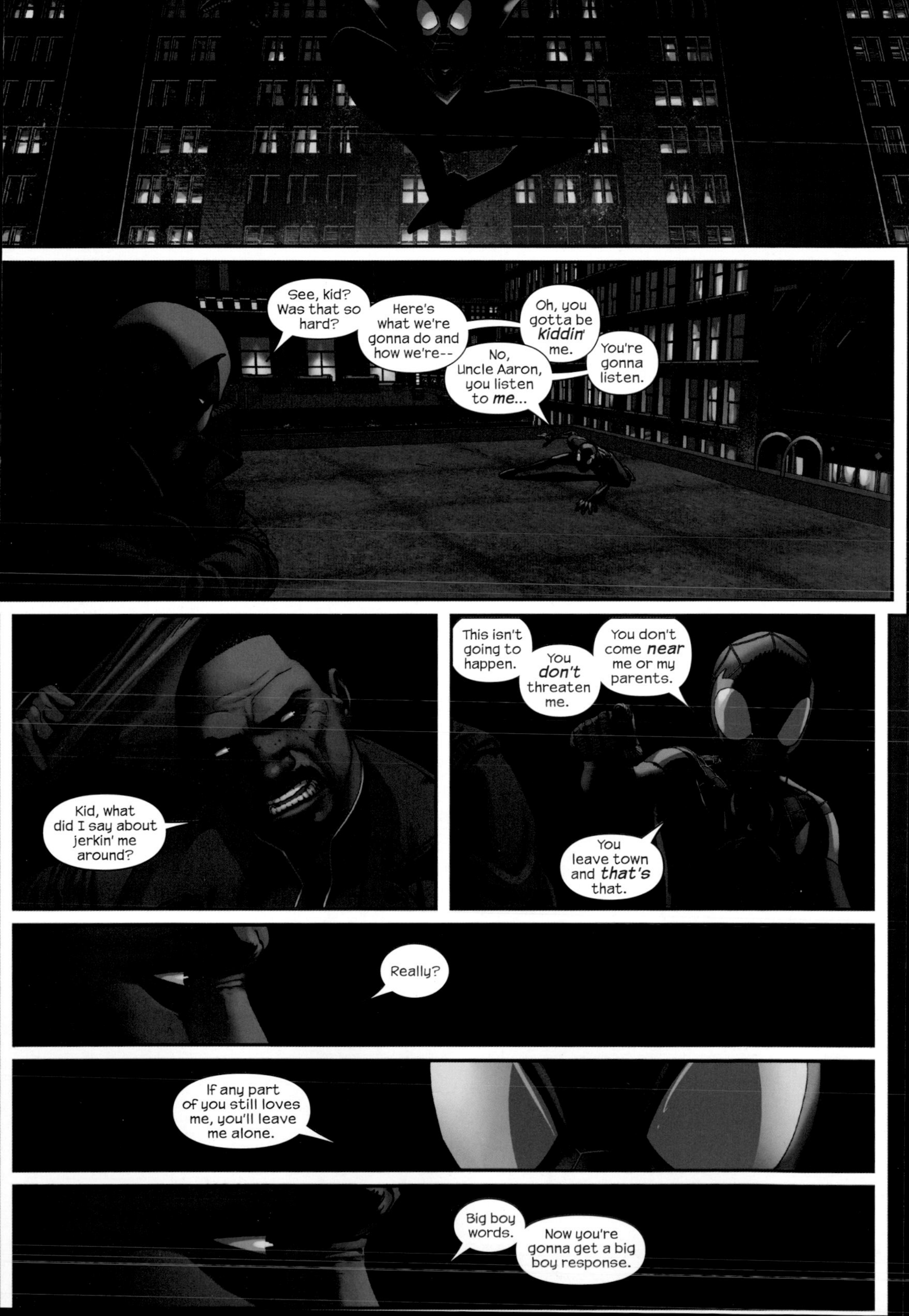
See, kid? Was that so hard?
Here's what we're gonna do and how we're--
Oh, you gotta be *kiddin'* me.
No, Uncle Aaron, you listen to *me*...
You're gonna listen.
Kid, what did I say about jerkin' me around?
This isn't going to happen.
You *don't* threaten me.
You don't come *near* me or my parents.
You leave town and *that's* that.
Really?
If any part of you still loves me, you'll leave me alone.
Big boy words.
Now you're gonna get a big boy response.

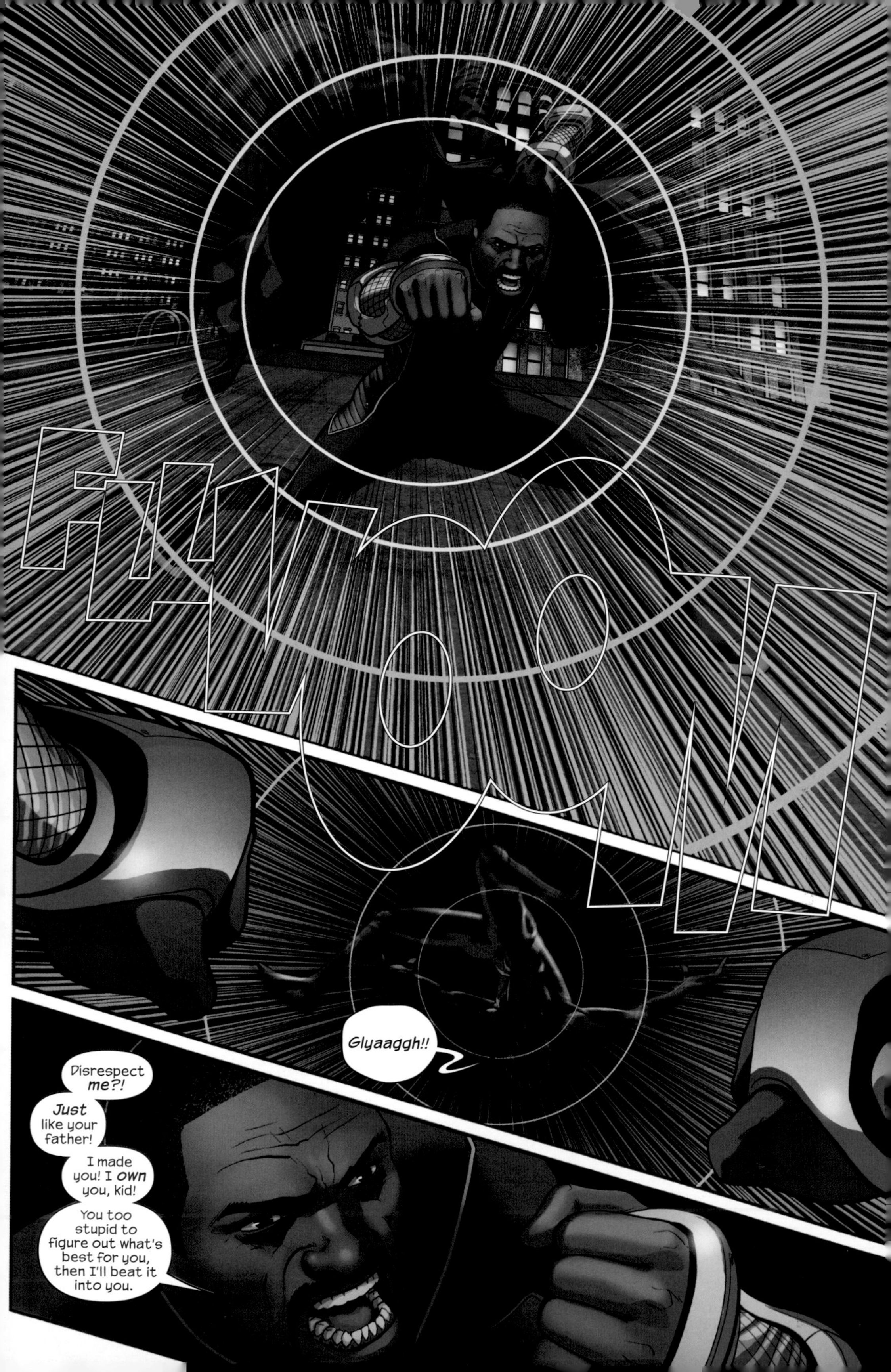
FZZWOOOM
Glyaaggh!!
Disrespect *me?!*
Just like your father!
I made you! I *own* you, kid!
You too stupid to figure out what's best for you, then I'll beat it into you.

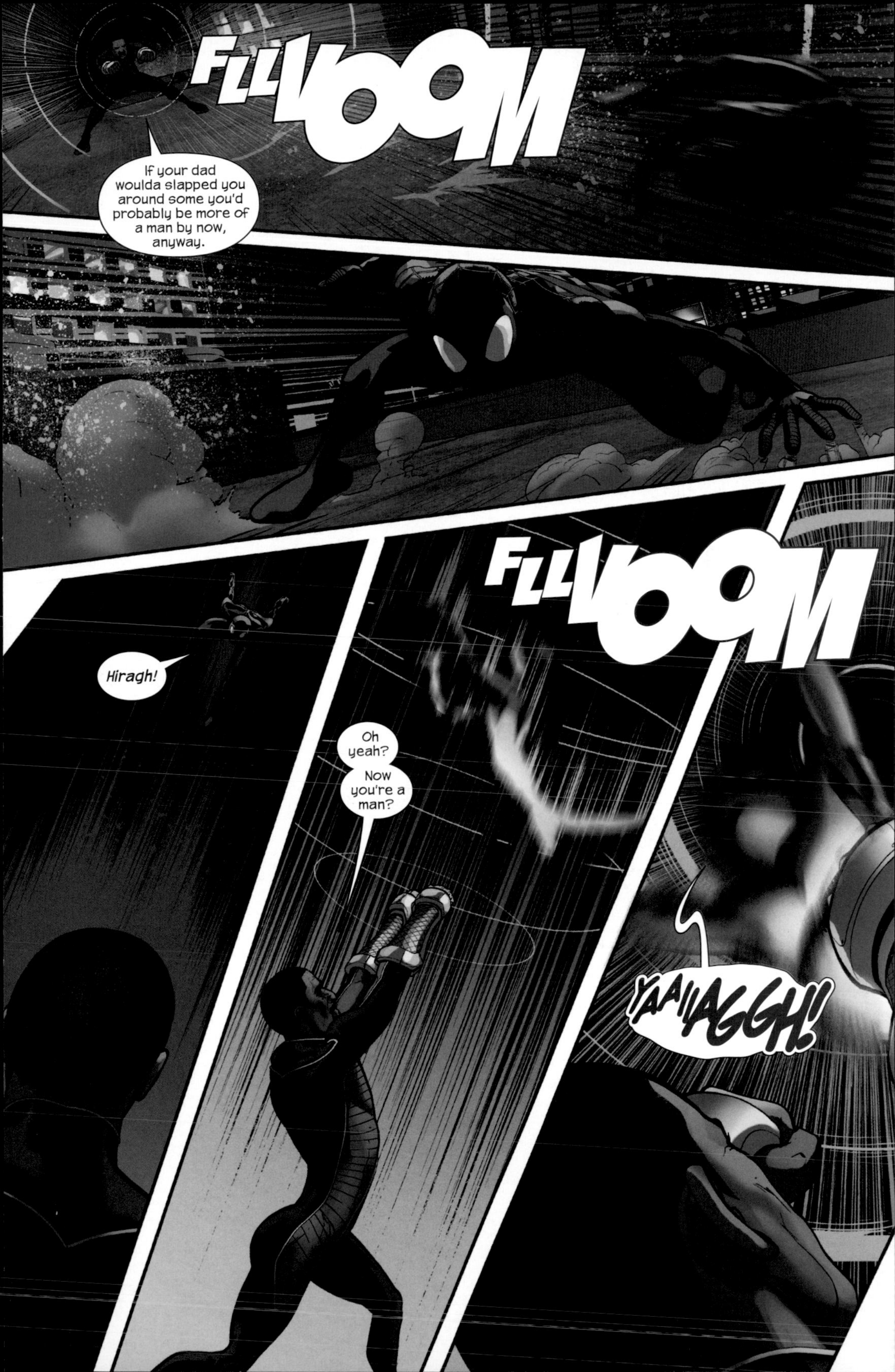
FLLVOOM
If your dad woulda slapped you around some you'd probably be more of a man by now, anyway.
FLLVOOM
Hiragh!
Oh yeah?
Now you're a man?
YAAAAGGH!

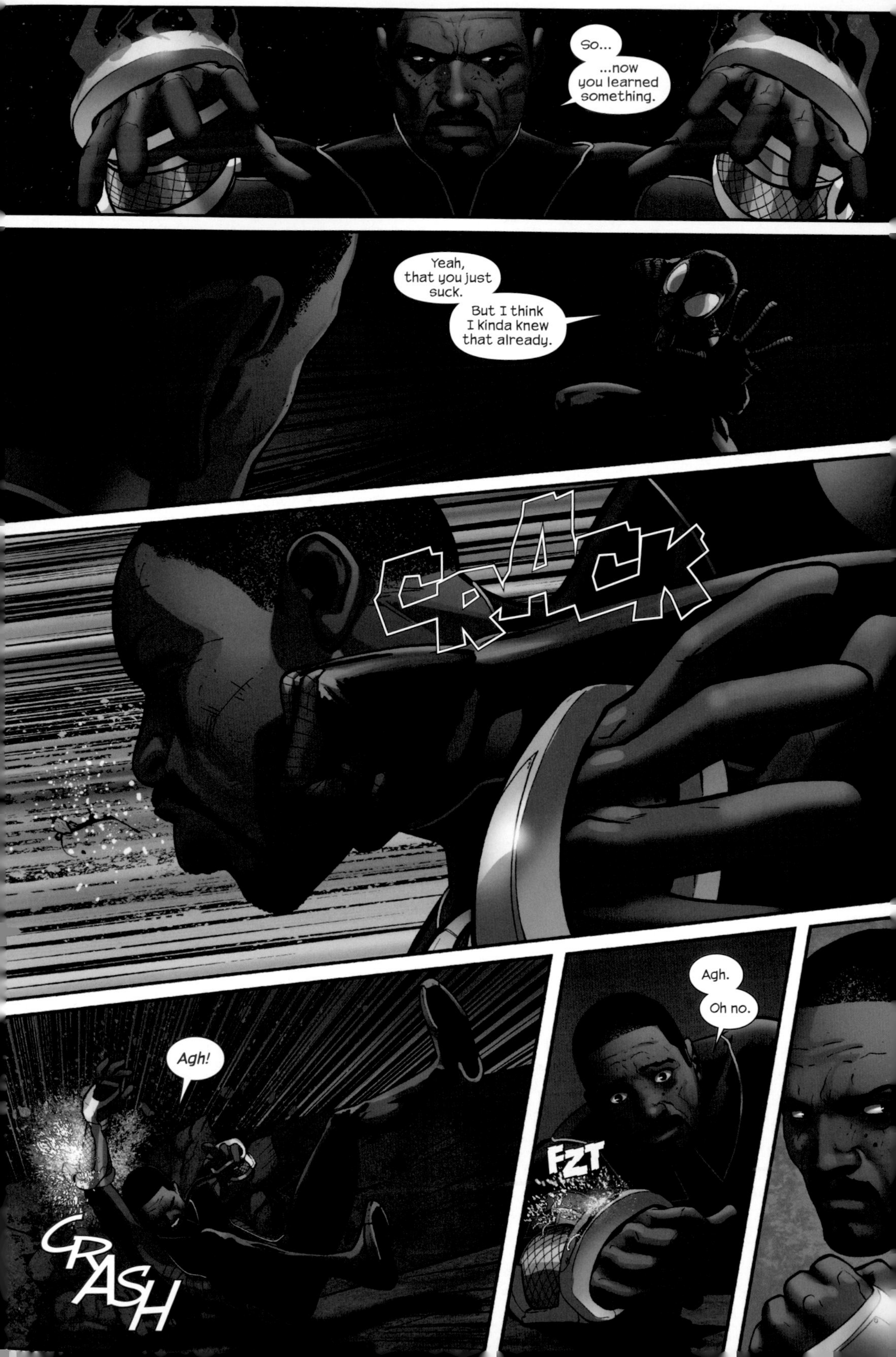
So...
...now you learned something.
Yeah, that you just suck.
But I think I kinda knew that already.
CRACK
Agh!
CRASH
Agh.
Oh no.
FZT

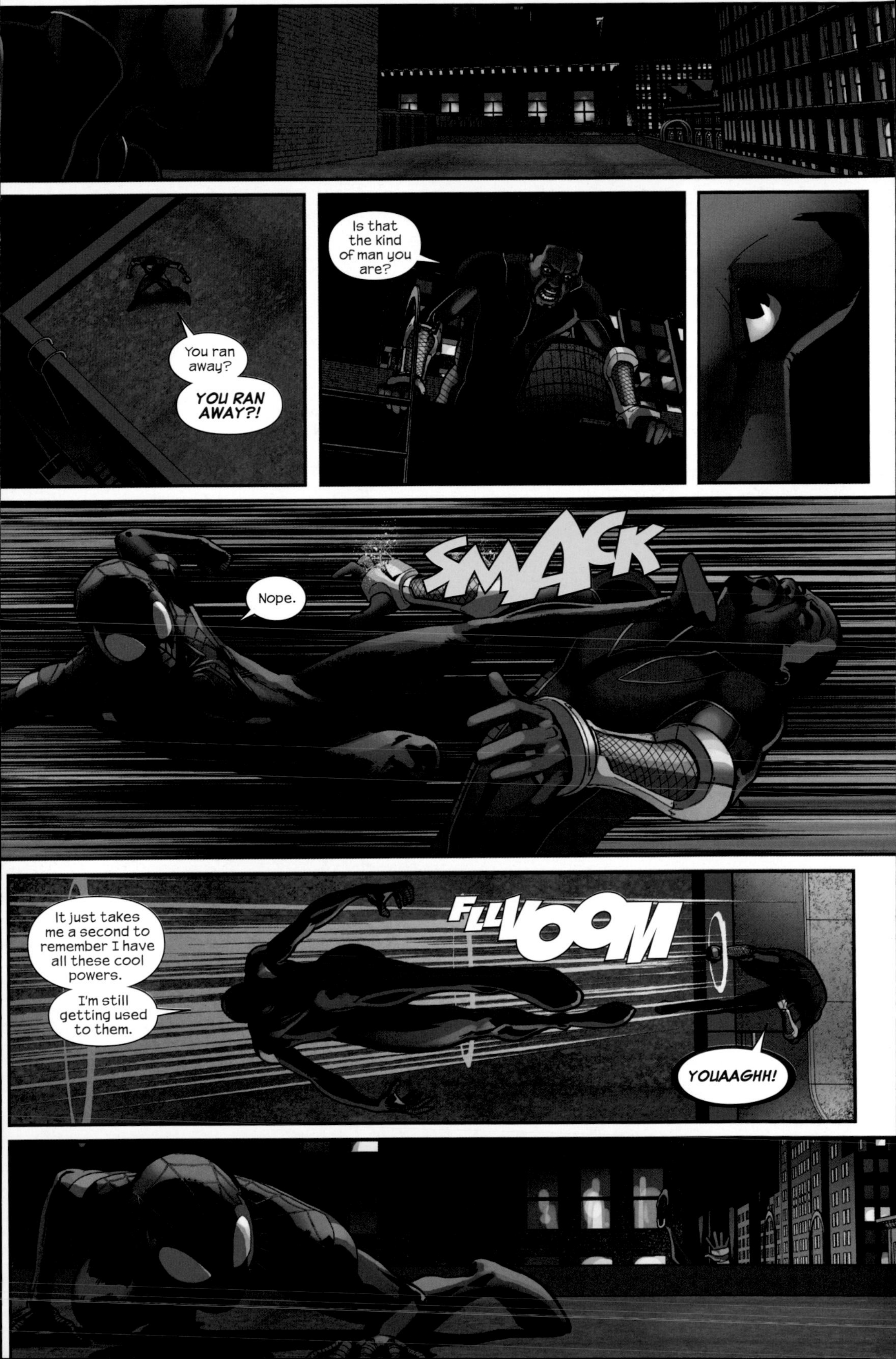
You ran away?
YOU RAN AWAY?!
Is that the kind of man you are?
Nope.
SMACK
It just takes me a second to remember I have all these cool powers.
I'm still getting used to them.
FLLLVOOM
YOUAAGHH!

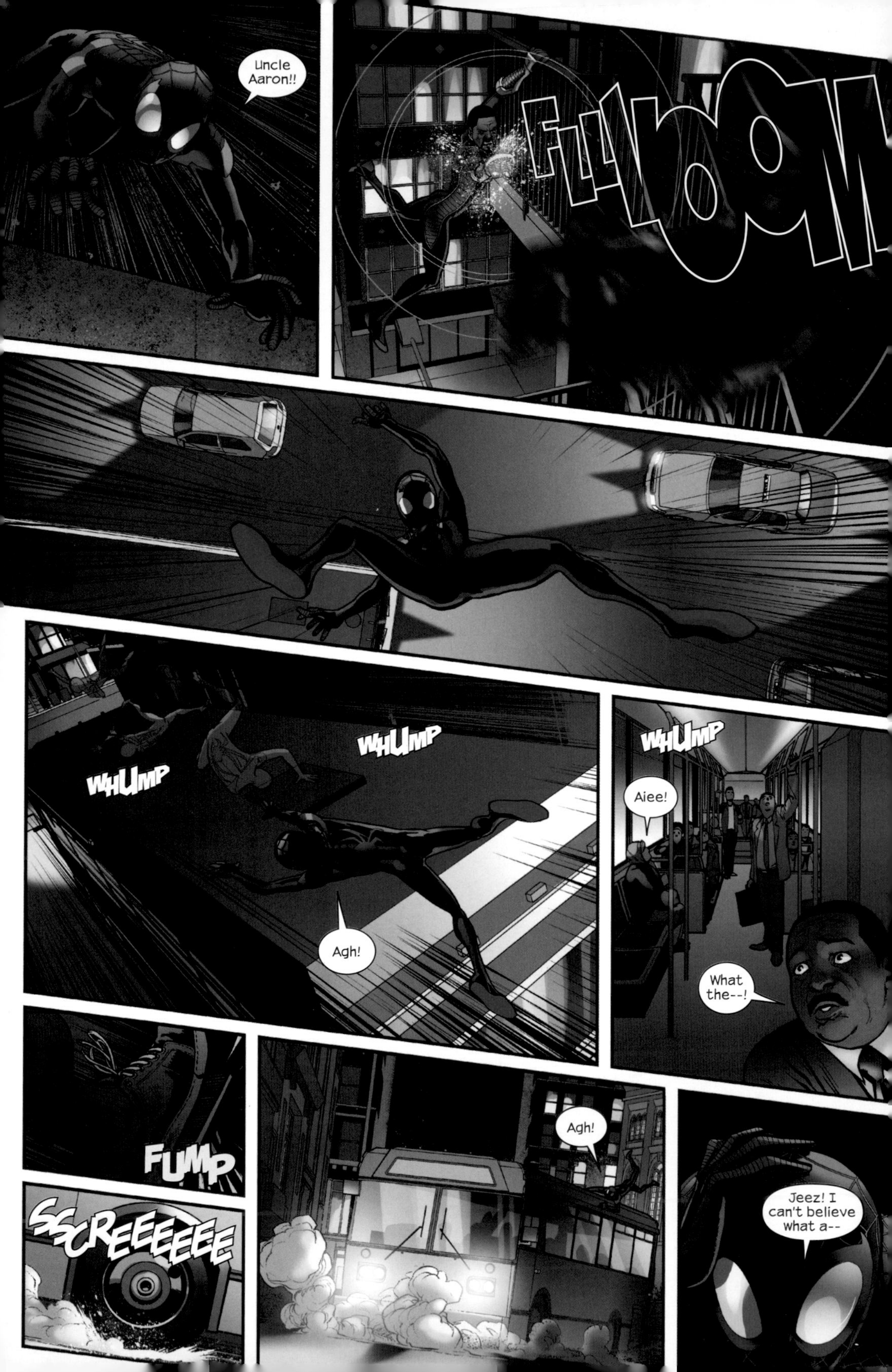
Uncle Aaron!!
FLLLBOOM
WHUMP
WHUMP
Agh!
WHUMP
Aiee!
What the--!
FUMP
SSCREEEEEEEE
Agh!
Jeez! I can't believe what a--

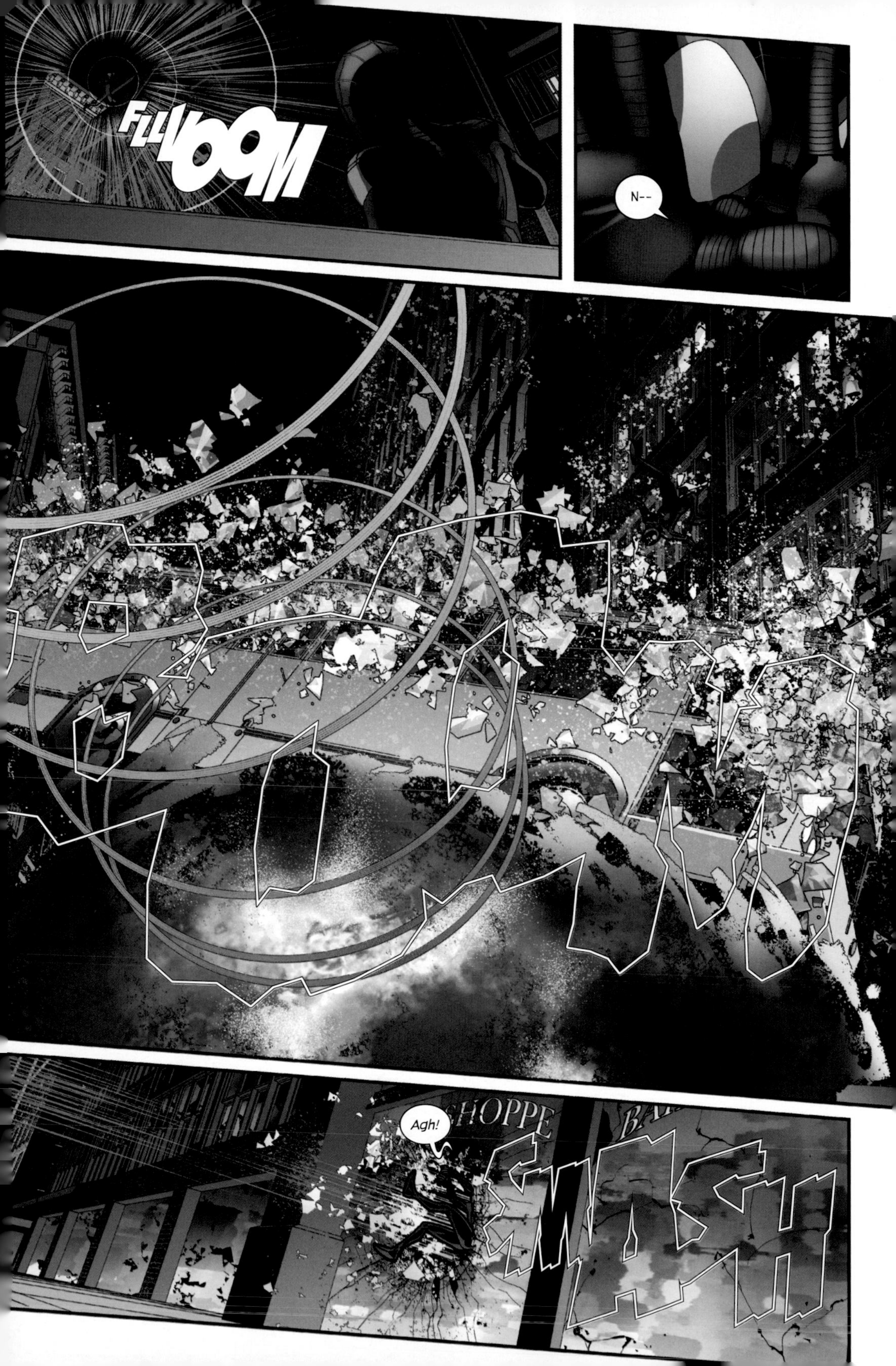
FLLVOOM
N--
Agh!
SHOPPE

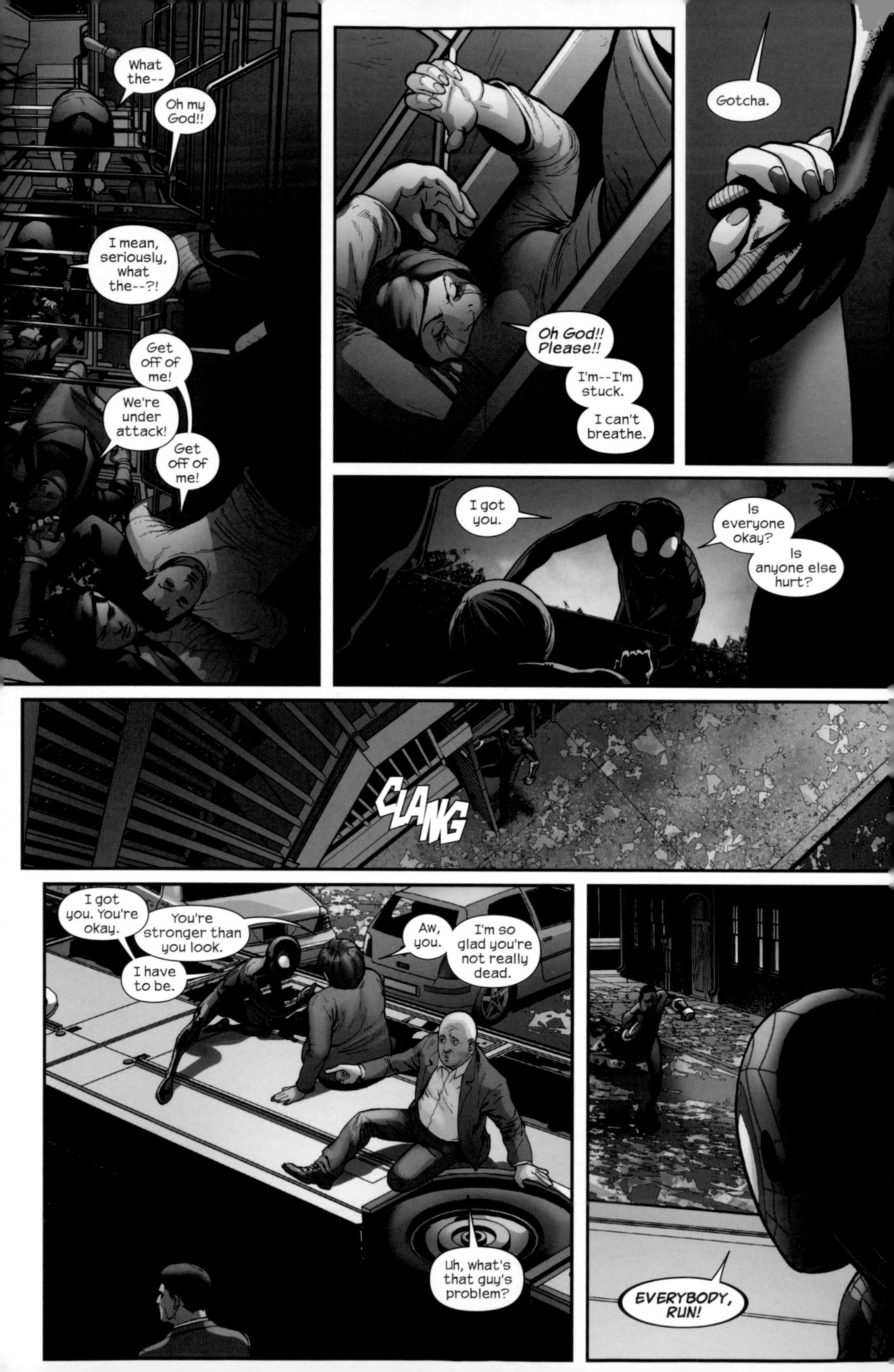
What the--
Oh my God!!
I mean, seriously, what the--?!
Get off of me!
We're under attack!
Get off of me!
Oh God!! Please!!
I'm--I'm stuck.
I can't breathe.
Gotcha.
I got you.
Is everyone okay?
Is anyone else hurt?
CLANG
I got you. You're okay.
You're stronger than you look.
I have to be.
Aw, you.
I'm so glad you're not really dead.
Uh, what's that guy's problem?
EVERYBODY, RUN!

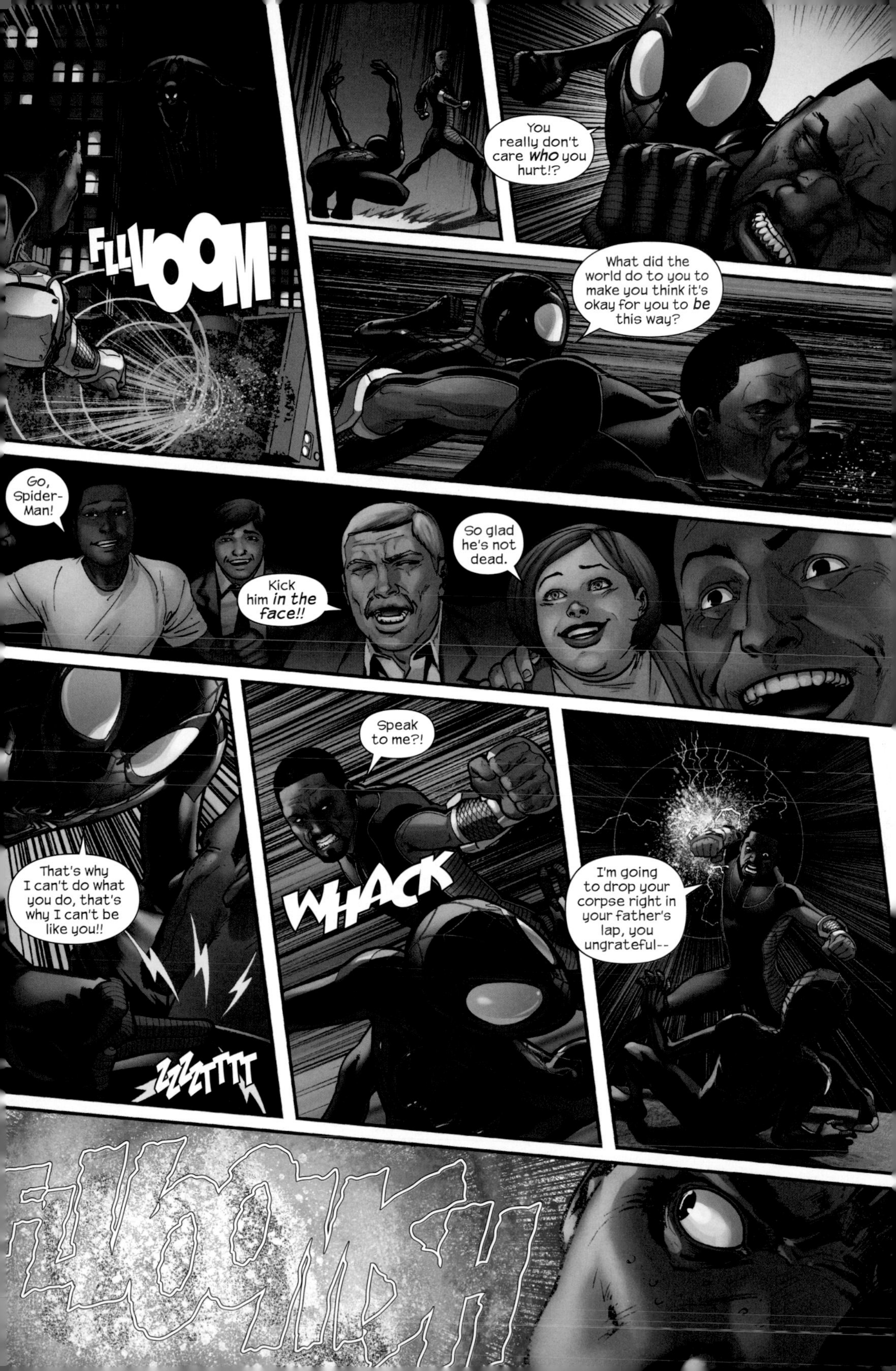
FLLVOOM
You really don't care *who* you hurt!?
What did the world do to you to make you think it's okay for you to *be* this way?
Go, Spider-Man!
Kick him *in the face!!*
So glad he's not dead.
That's why I can't do what you do, that's why I can't be like you!!
Speak to me?!
WHACK
I'm going to drop your corpse right in your father's lap, you ungrateful--

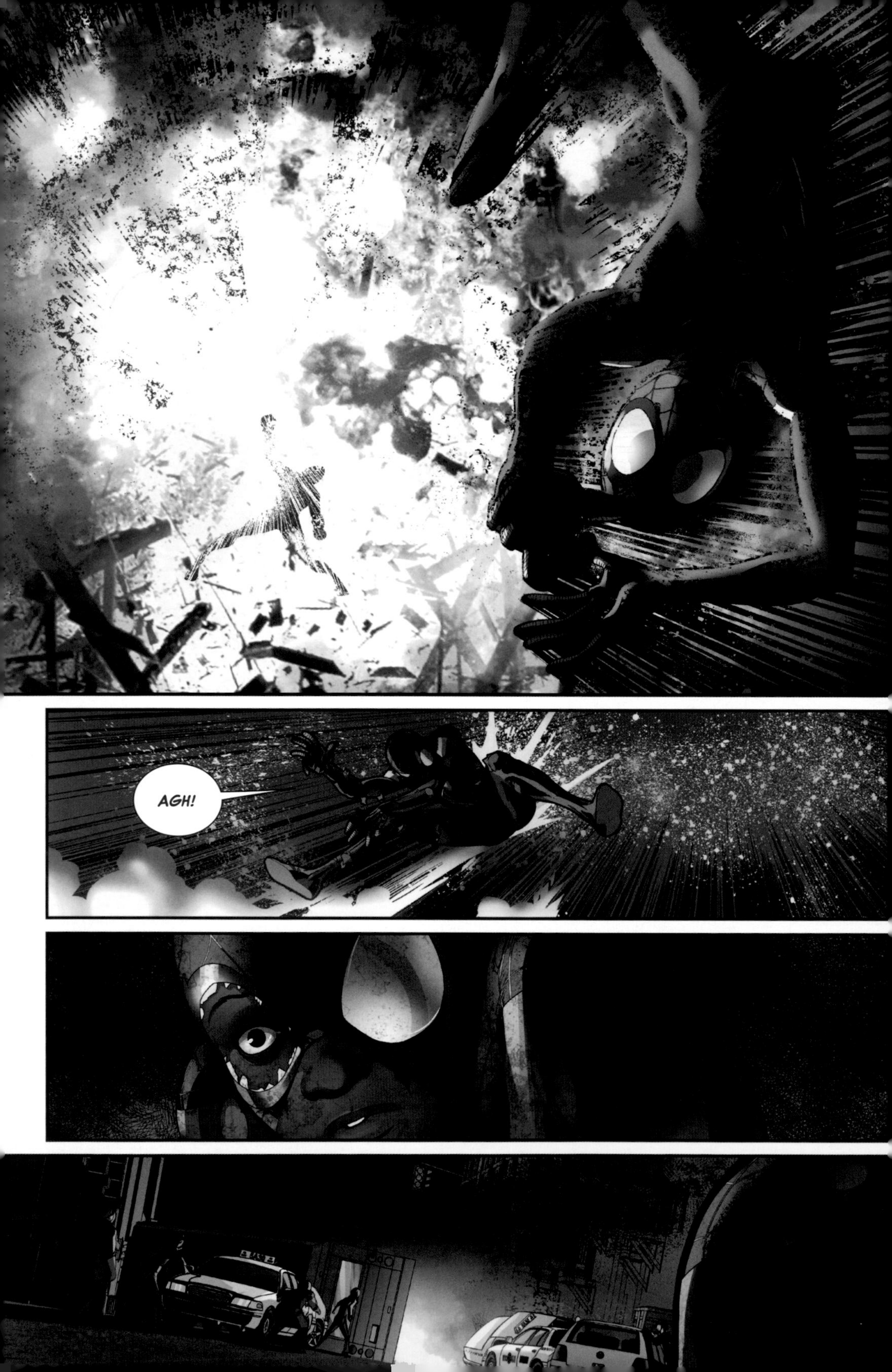
AGH!

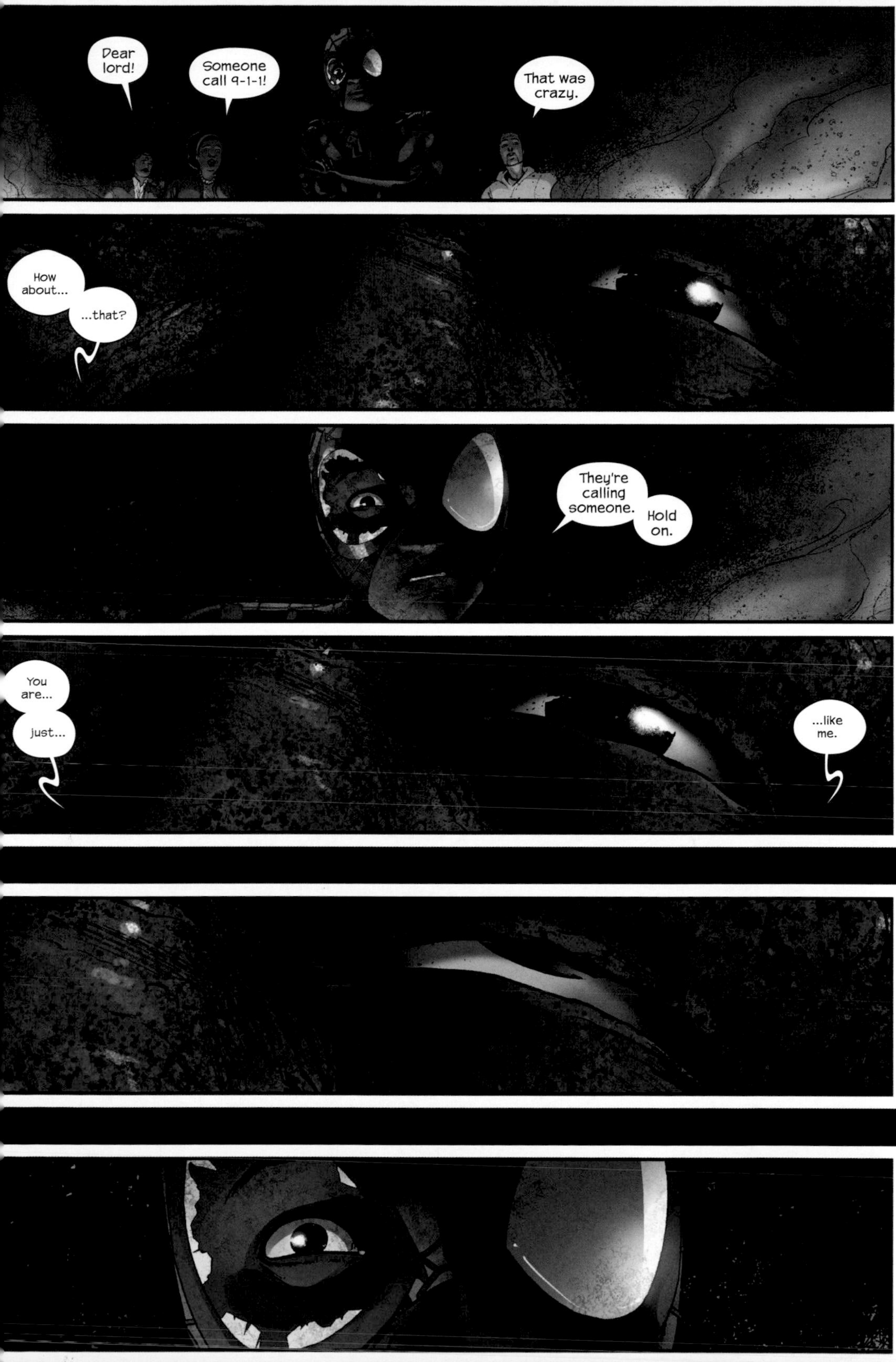

Dear lord!
Someone call 9-1-1!
That was crazy.
How about...
...that?
They're calling someone.
Hold on.
You are...
just...
...like me.

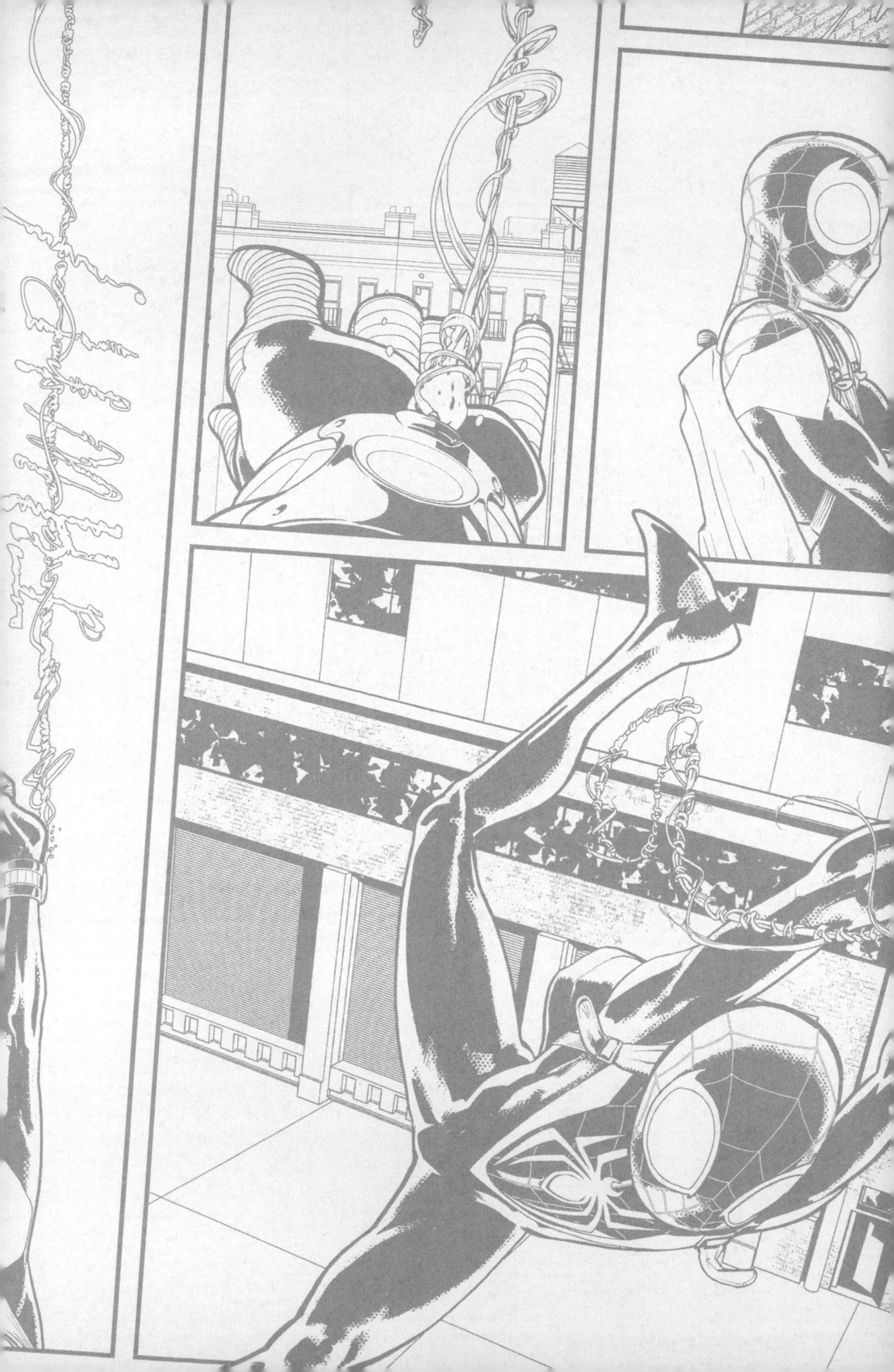

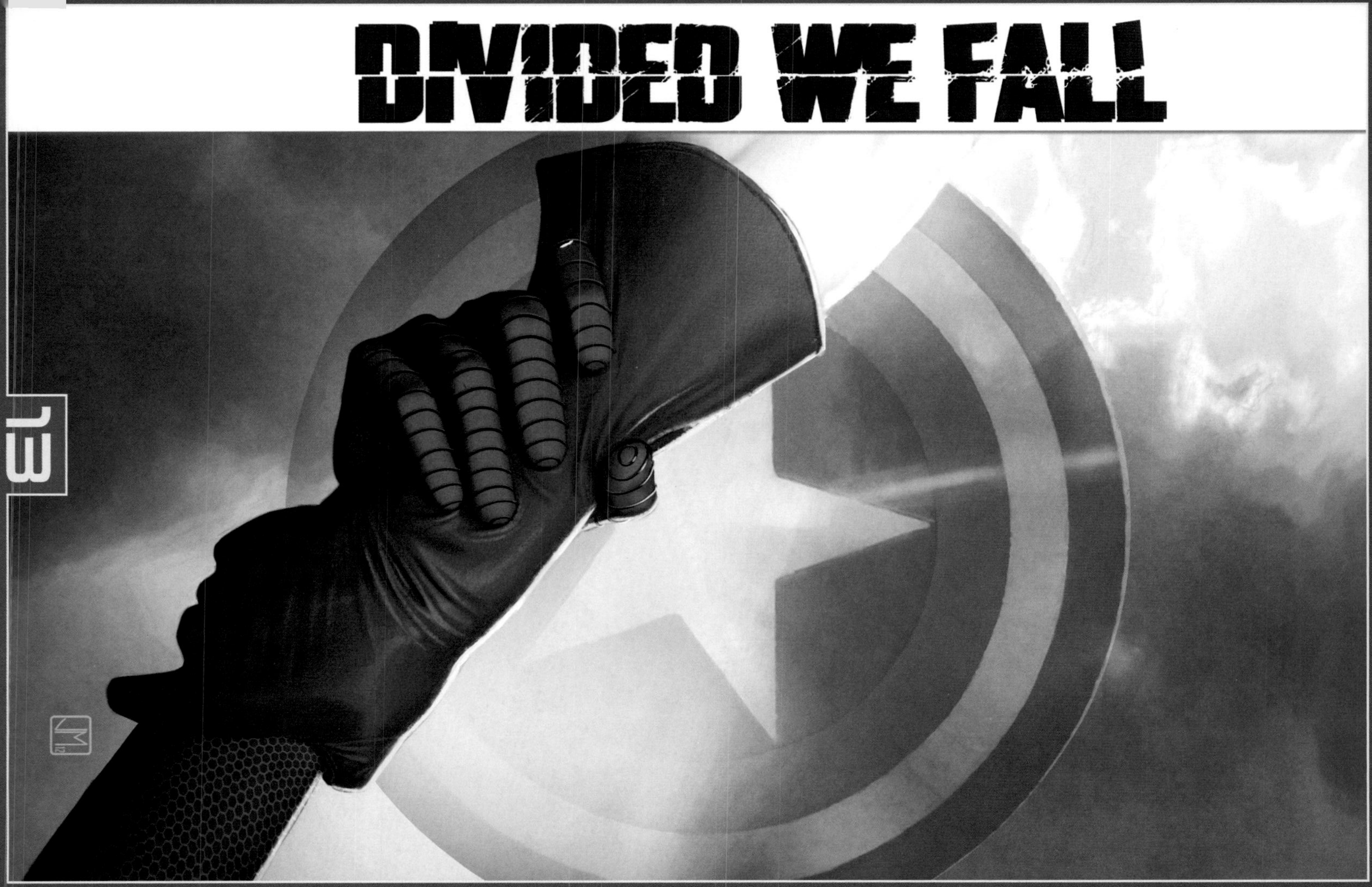
DIVIDED WE FALL
13

MONTHS BEFORE PETER PARKER WAS SHOT AND KILLED, GRADE-SCHOOLER MILES MORALES WAS ABOUT TO START A NEW CHAPTER IN HIS LIFE AT A NEW SCHOOL--WHEN HE WAS SUDDENLY BITTEN BY A STOLEN, GENETICALLY ALTERED SPIDER THAT GAVE HIM INCREDIBLE ARACHNID-LIKE POWERS.

ULTIMATE COMICS ALL-NEW SPIDER-MAN

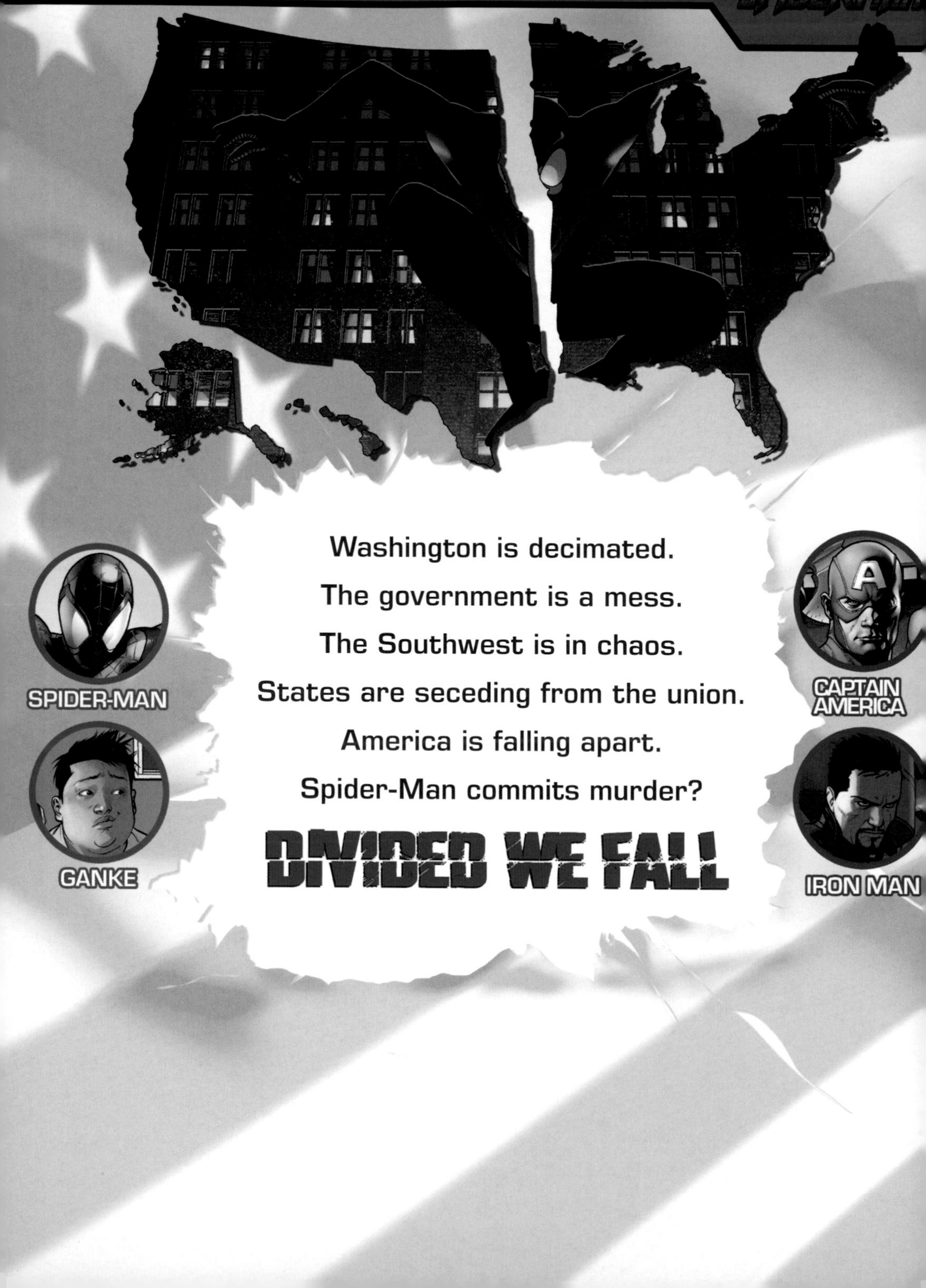

Washington is decimated.
The government is a mess.
The Southwest is in chaos.
States are seceding from the union.
America is falling apart.
Spider-Man commits murder?
DIVIDED WE FALL
SPIDER-MAN
GANKE
CAPTAIN AMERICA
IRON MAN

S.H.I.E.L.D. SITUATION MAP:

[Anti-government militia hot spots]

Montana, N. Dakota
S. Dakota, Wyoming
Arizona, New Mexico
N. Carolina, S. Carolina,
Georgia

[Eastern seaboard control zone]

New England,
New York,
New Jersey,
Delaware,
Washington, D.C.,
Maryland,
Virginia

secured by National Guard under emergency powers committee

[the West Coast]

California, Oregon
Washington

status unknown

[Great Lakes states]

Minnesota,
Wisconsin,
Michigan,
Illinois,
Indiana, Ohio

status unknown

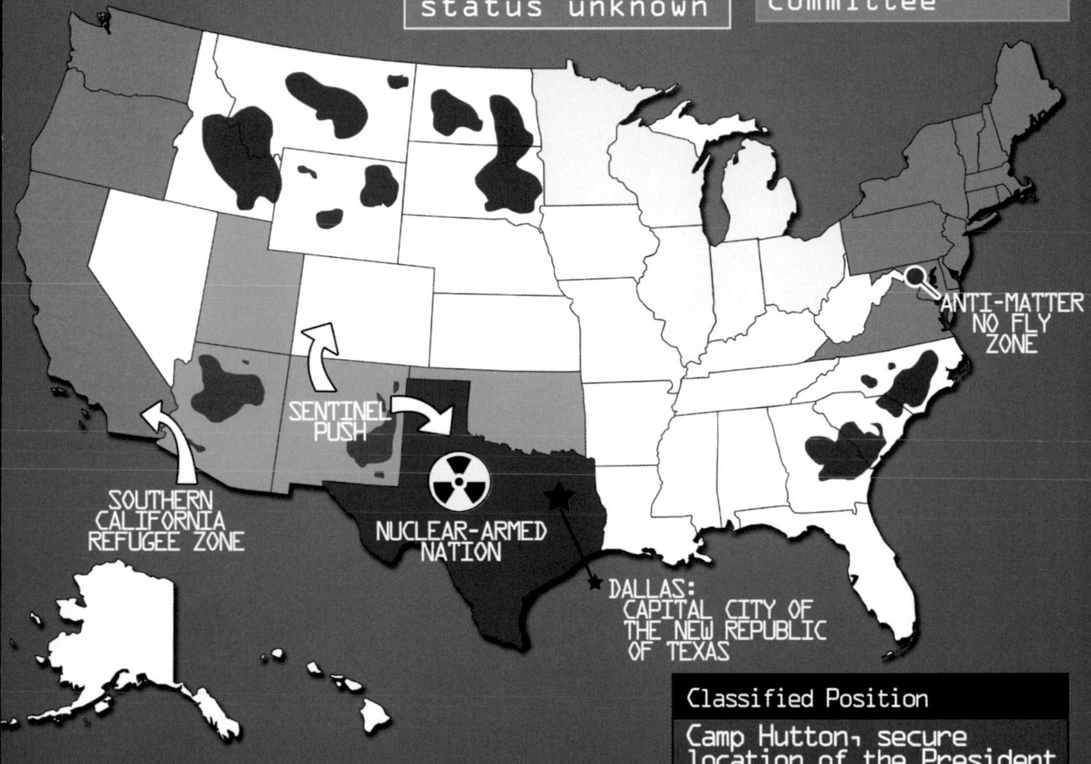

ANTI-MATTER NO FLY ZONE
SENTINEL PUSH
SOUTHERN CALIFORNIA REFUGEE ZONE
NUCLEAR-ARMED NATION
DALLAS: CAPITAL CITY OF THE NEW REPUBLIC OF TEXAS

Classified Position

Camp Hutton, secure location of the President of the United States

[Sentinel-controlled no-man's-land]

New Mexico, Arizona
Utah, Oklahoma

abandoned by the U.S. government

[The New Republic of Texas]

Texas

declared state independence

ALL STATES SHOWN IN WHITE ARE U.S. GOVERNMENT-CONTROLLED ZONES

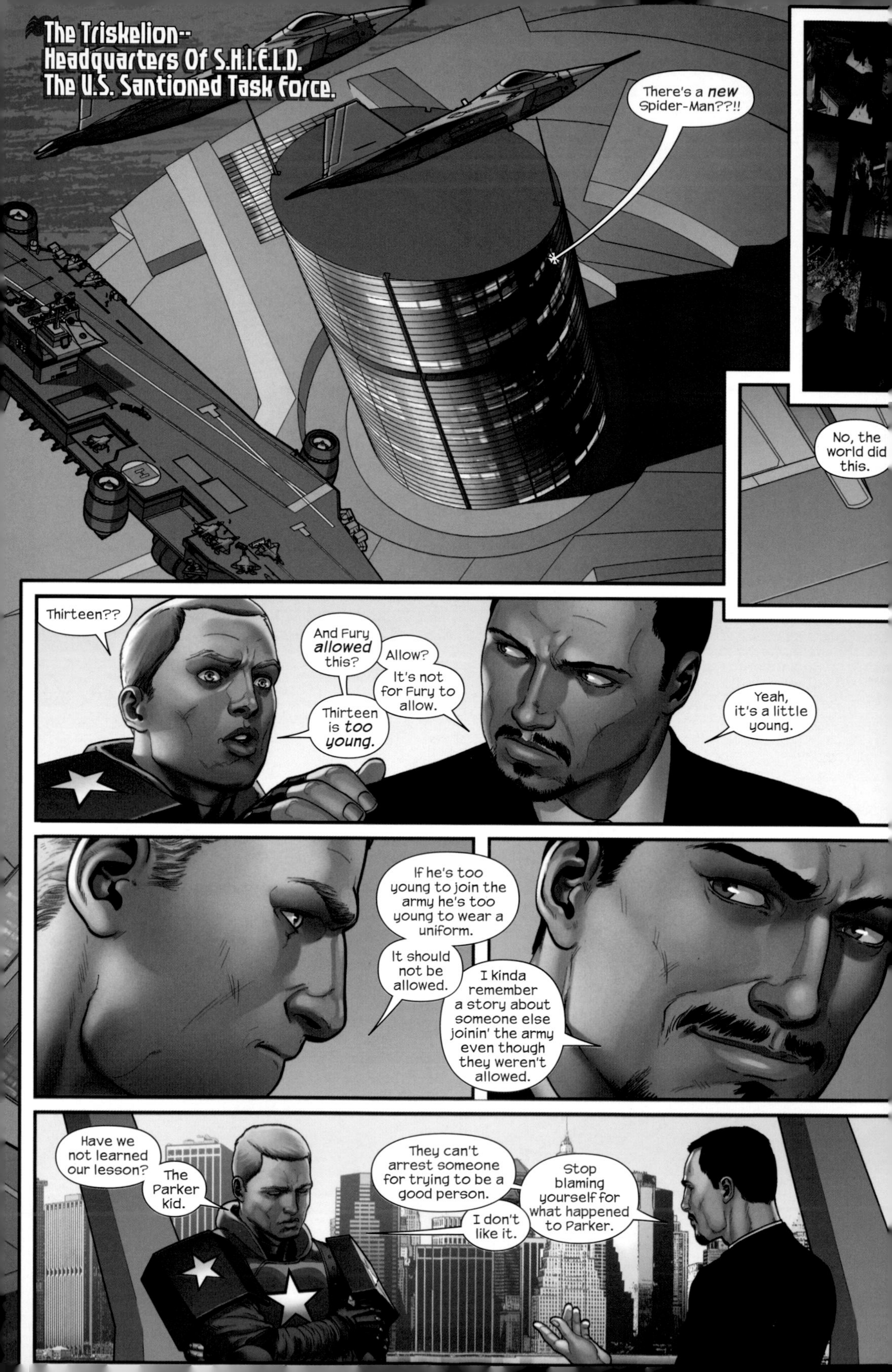

The Triskelion--
Headquarters Of S.H.I.E.L.D.
The U.S. Santioned Task Force.
There's a *new* Spider-Man??!!
No, the world did this.
Thirteen??
And Fury *allowed* this?
Thirteen is *too young.*
Allow?
It's not for Fury to allow.
Yeah, it's a little young.
If he's too young to join the army he's too young to wear a uniform.
It should not be allowed.
I kinda remember a story about someone else joinin' the army even though they weren't allowed.
Have we not learned our lesson?
The Parker kid.
They can't arrest someone for trying to be a good person.
I don't like it.
Stop blaming yourself for what happened to Parker.

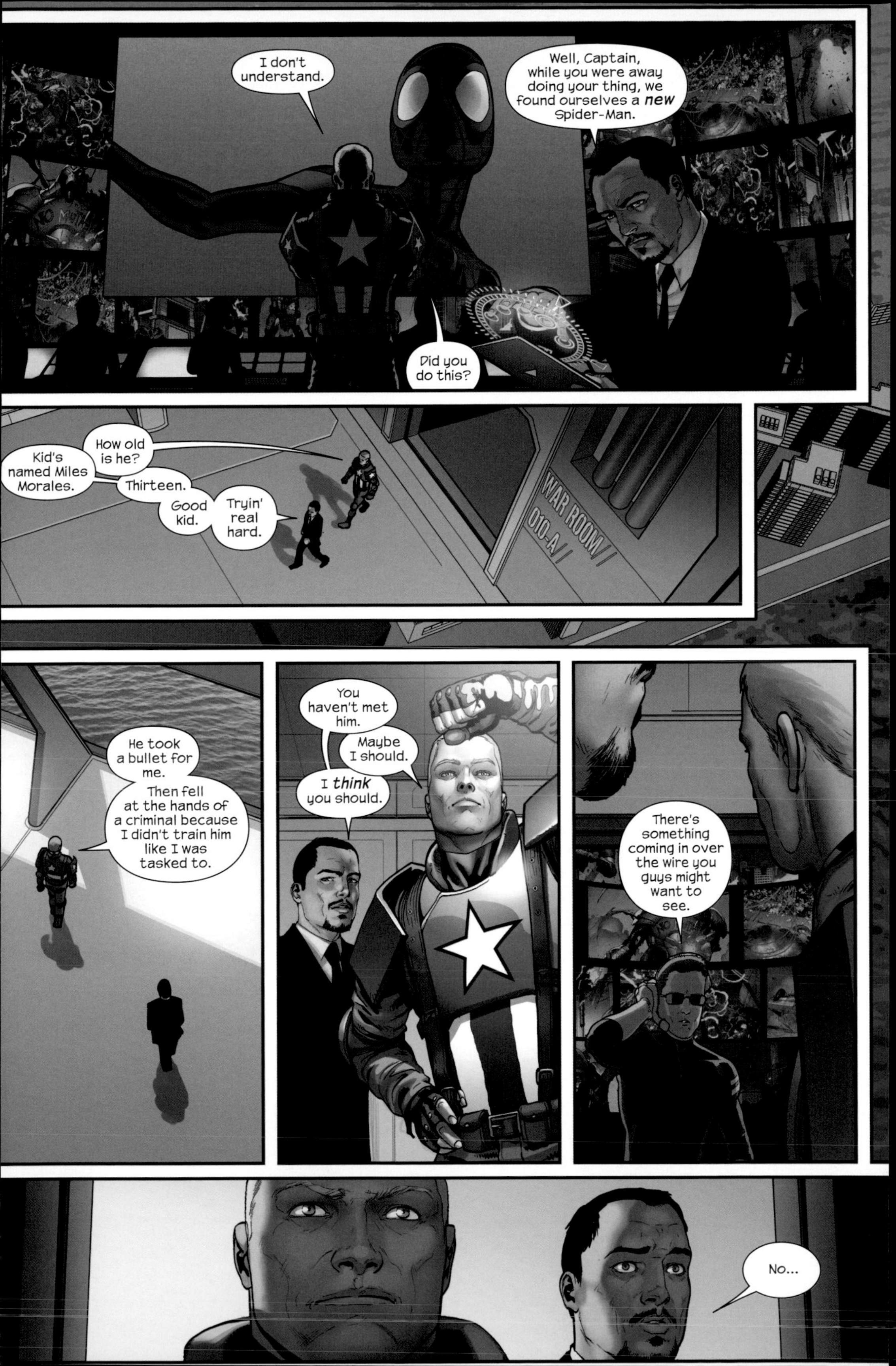
I don't understand.
Well, Captain, while you were away doing your thing, we found ourselves a new Spider-Man.
Did you do this?
How old is he?
Kid's named Miles Morales.
Thirteen.
Good kid.
Tryin' real hard.
WAR ROOM // 010-A//
He took a bullet for me.
Then fell at the hands of a criminal because I didn't train him like I was tasked to.
You haven't met him.
Maybe I should.
I think you should.
There's something coming in over the wire you guys might want to see.
No...

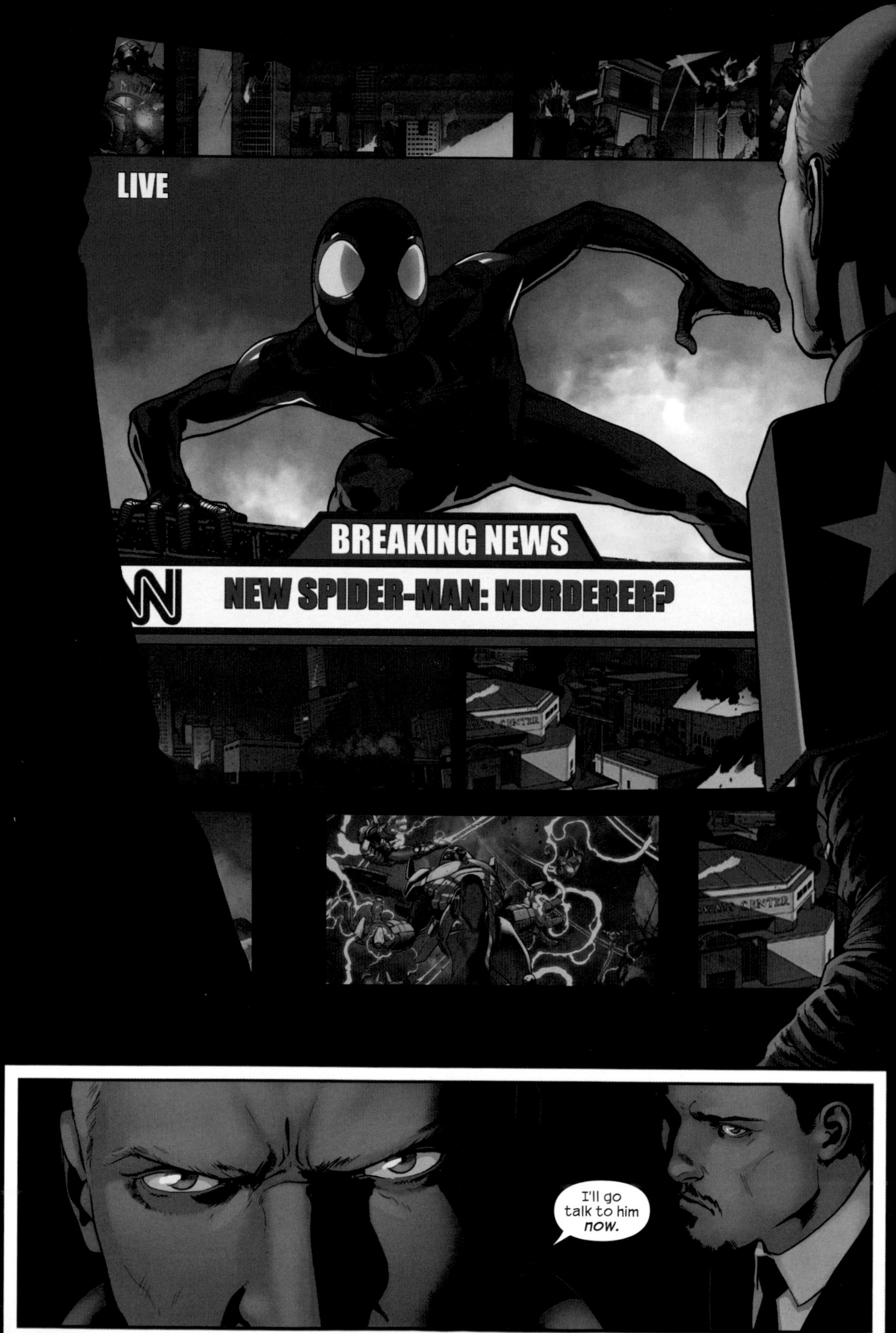
LIVE
BREAKING NEWS
NEW SPIDER-MAN: MURDERER?
I'll go talk to him *now*.

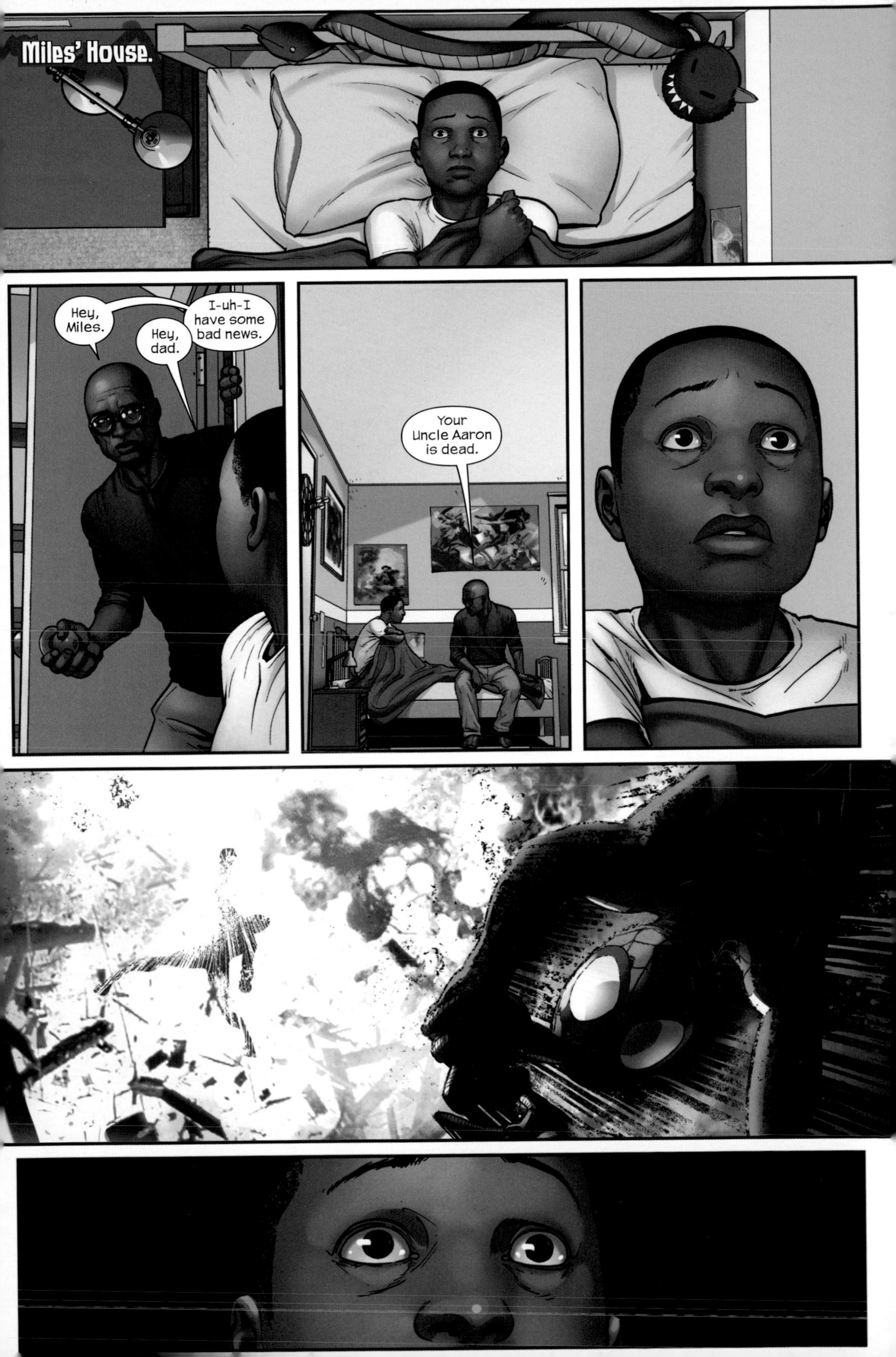

Miles' House.
Hey, Miles.
Hey, dad.
I-uh-I have some bad news.
Your Uncle Aaron is dead.

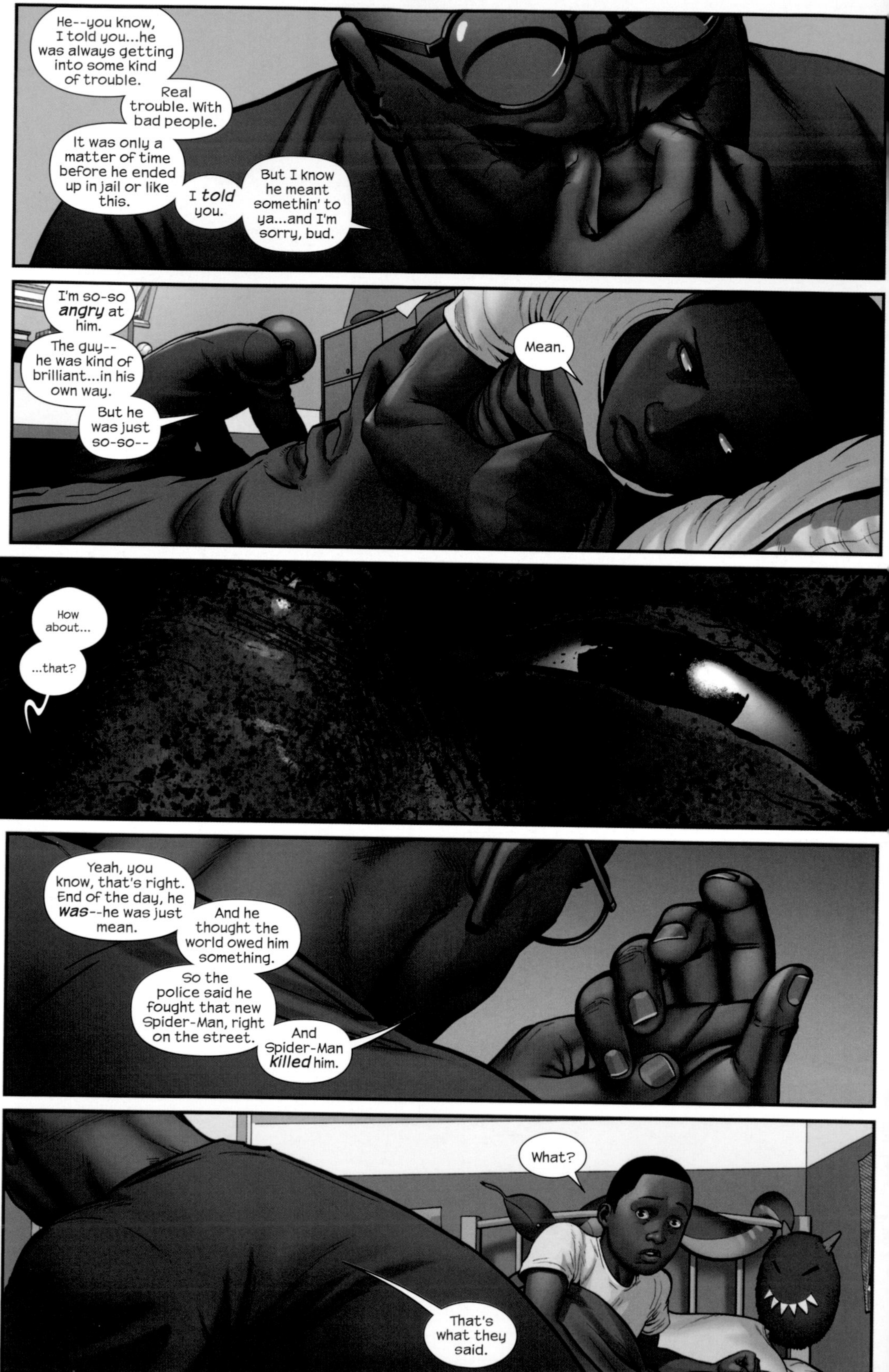
He--you know, I told you...he was always getting into some kind of trouble.
Real trouble. With bad people.
It was only a matter of time before he ended up in jail or like this.
I *told* you.
But I know he meant somethin' to ya...and I'm sorry, bud.
I'm so-so *angry* at him.
The guy--he was kind of brilliant...in his own way.
But he was just so-so--
Mean.
How about...
...that?
Yeah, you know, that's right. End of the day, he *was*--he was just mean.
And he thought the world owed him something.
So the police said he fought that new Spider-Man, right on the street.
And Spider-Man *killed* him.
What?
That's what they said.

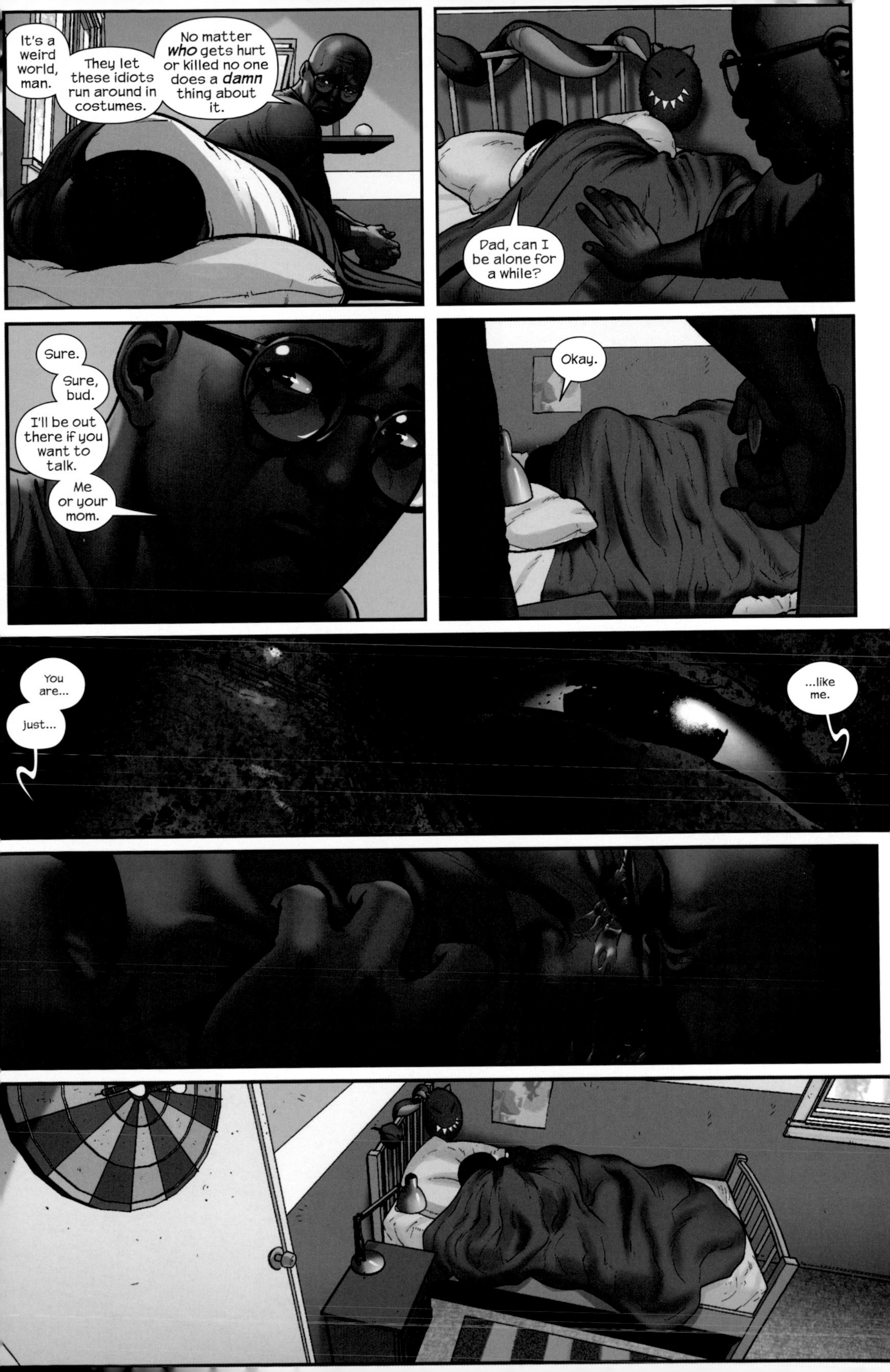
It's a weird world, man.
They let these idiots run around in costumes.
No matter *who* gets hurt or killed no one does a *damn* thing about it.
Dad, can I be alone for a while?
Sure.
Sure, bud.
I'll be out there if you want to talk.
Me or your mom.
Okay.
You are...
just...
...like me.

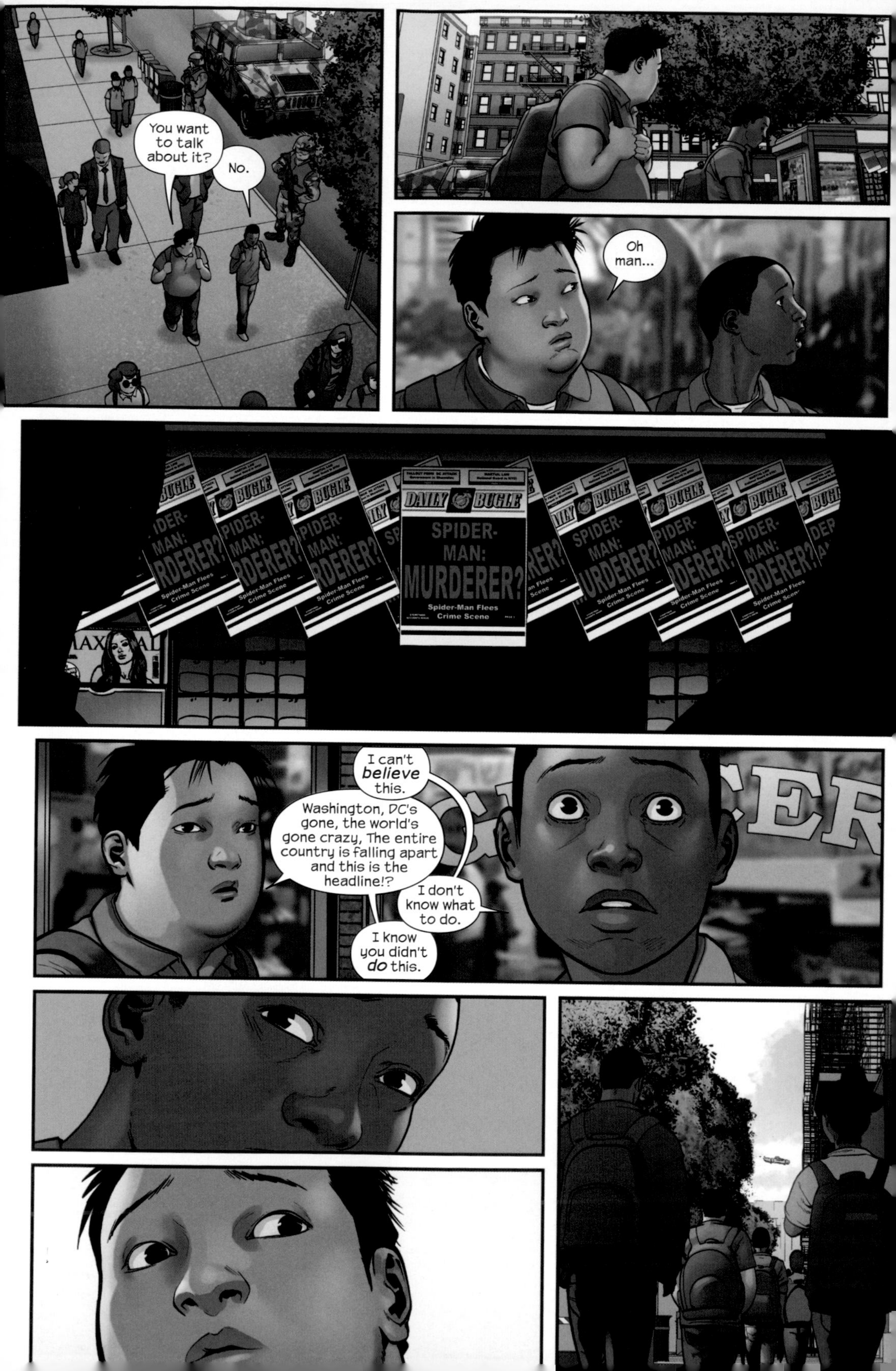

You want to talk about it?
No.
Oh man...
DAILY BUGLE
SPIDER-MAN: MURDERER?
Spider-Man Flees Crime Scene
I can't *believe* this.
Washington, DC's gone, the world's gone crazy, The entire country is falling apart and this is the headline!?
I don't know what to do.
I know you didn't *do* this.

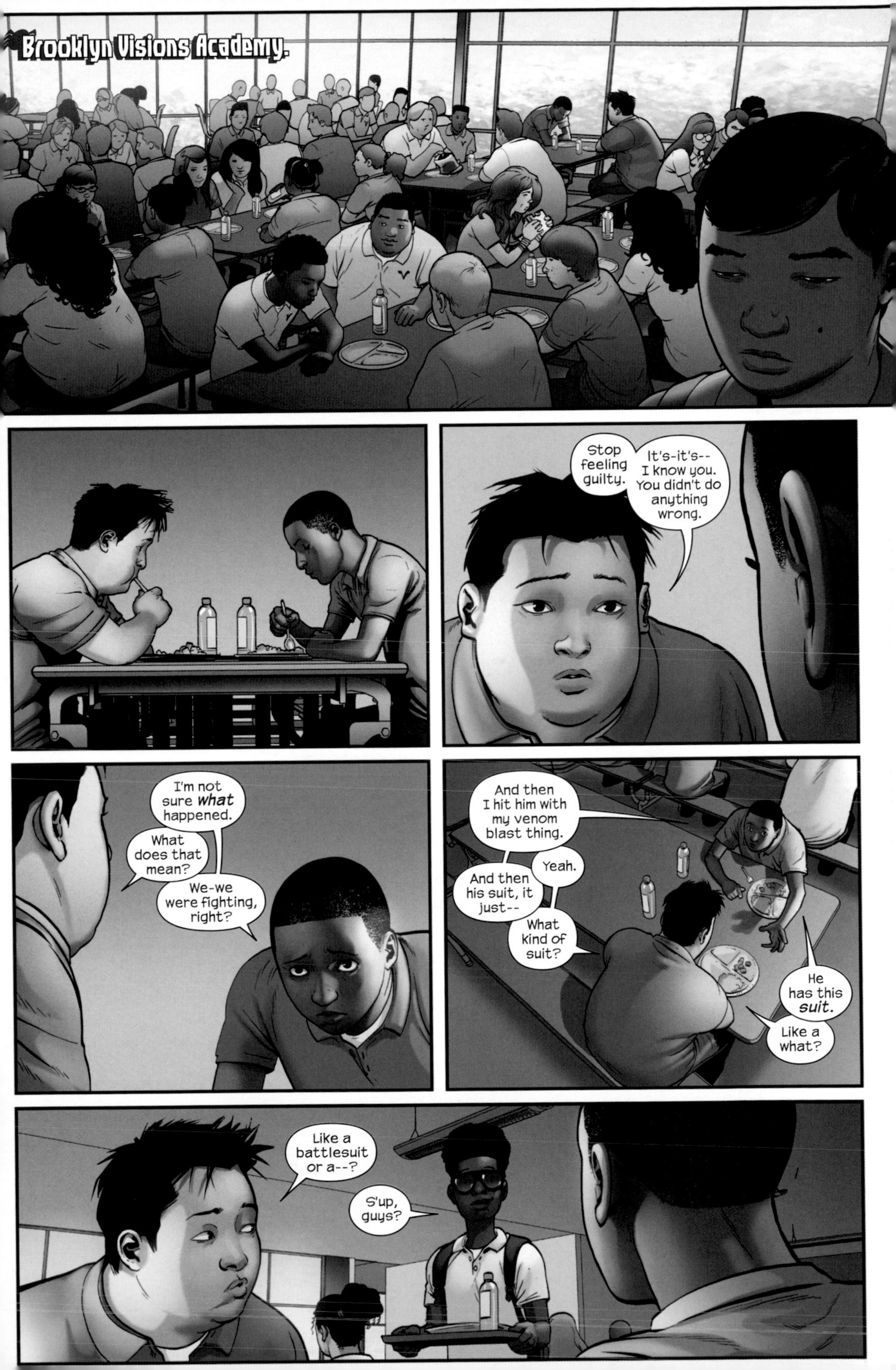
Brooklyn Visions Academy.
Stop feeling guilty.
It's-it's-- I know you. You didn't do anything wrong.
I'm not sure *what* happened.
What does that mean?
We-we were fighting, right?
And then I hit him with my venom blast thing.
Yeah.
And then his suit, it just--
What kind of suit?
He has this *suit.*
Like a what?
Like a battlesuit or a--?
S'up, guys?

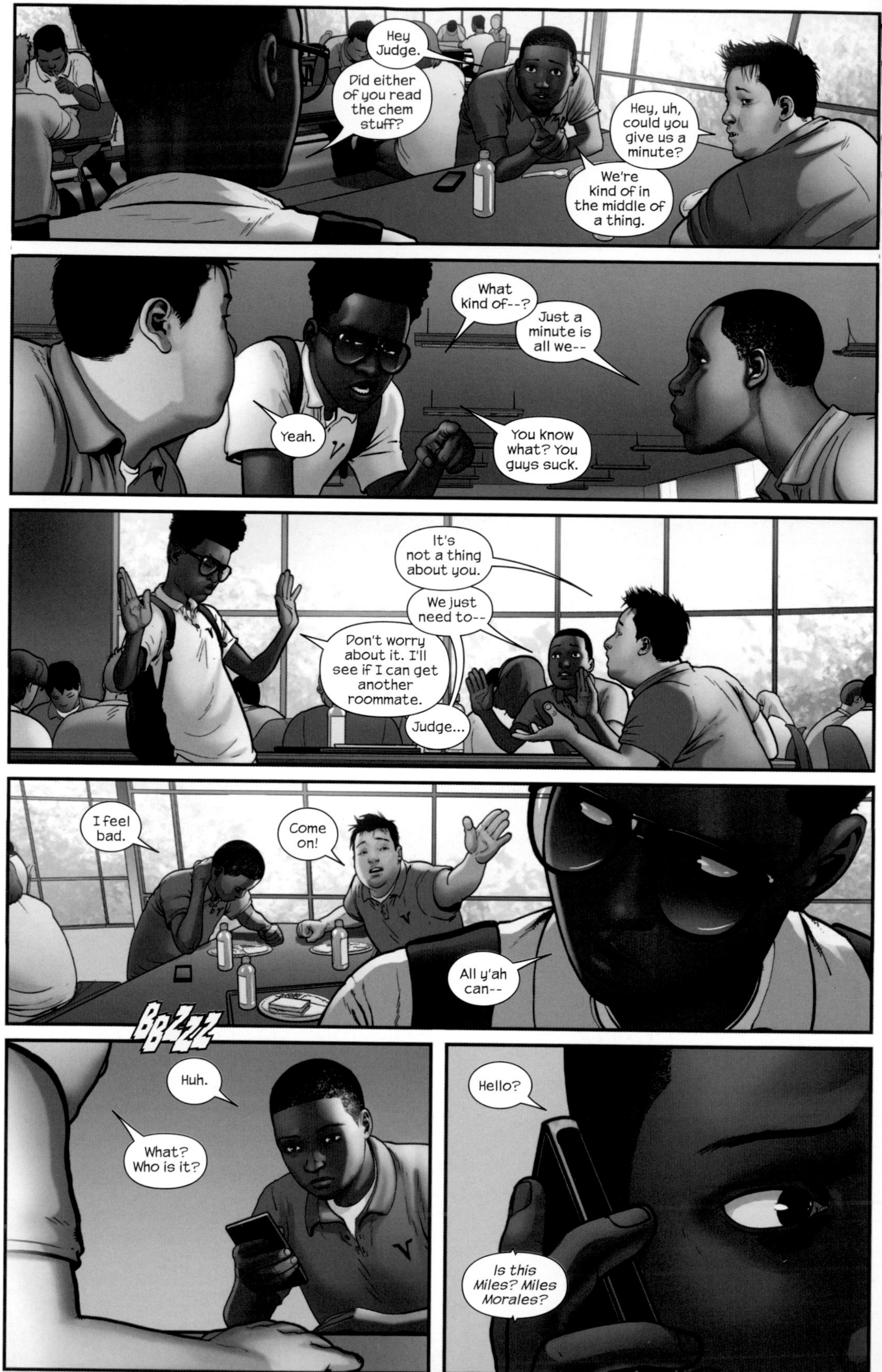
Hey Judge.
Did either of you read the chem stuff?
Hey, uh, could you give us a minute?
We're kind of in the middle of a thing.
What kind of--?
Just a minute is all we--
Yeah.
You know what? You guys suck.
It's not a thing about you.
We just need to--
Don't worry about it. I'll see if I can get another roommate.
Judge...
I feel bad.
Come on!
All y'ah can--
BBZZZ
Huh.
What? Who is it?
Hello?
Is this Miles? Miles Morales?

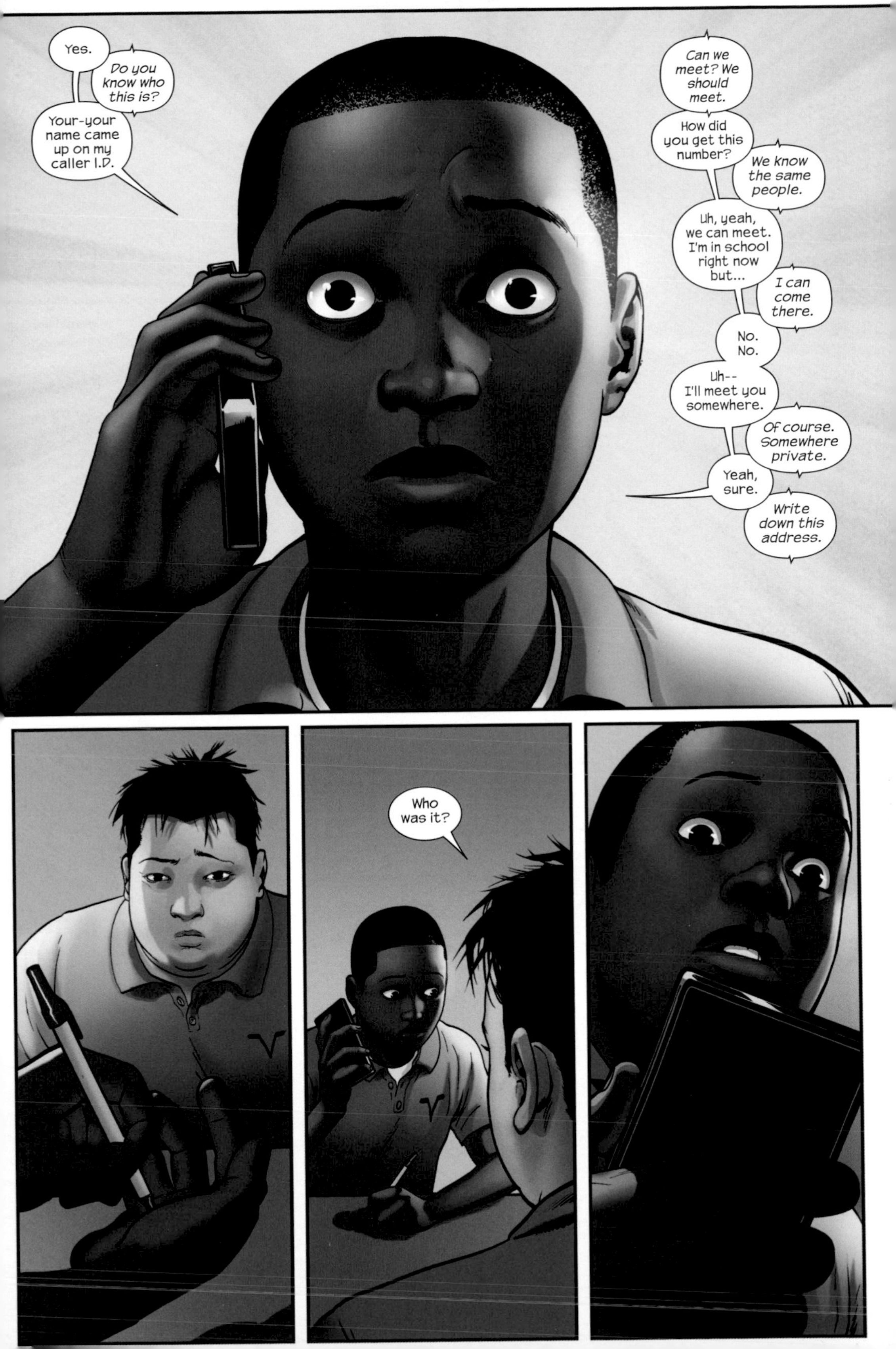
Yes.
Do you know who this is?
Your-your name came up on my caller I.D.
Can we meet? We should meet.
How did you get this number?
We know the same people.
Uh, yeah, we can meet. I'm in school right now but...
I can come there.
No. No.
Uh-- I'll meet you somewhere.
Of course. Somewhere private.
Yeah, sure.
Write down this address.
Who was it?

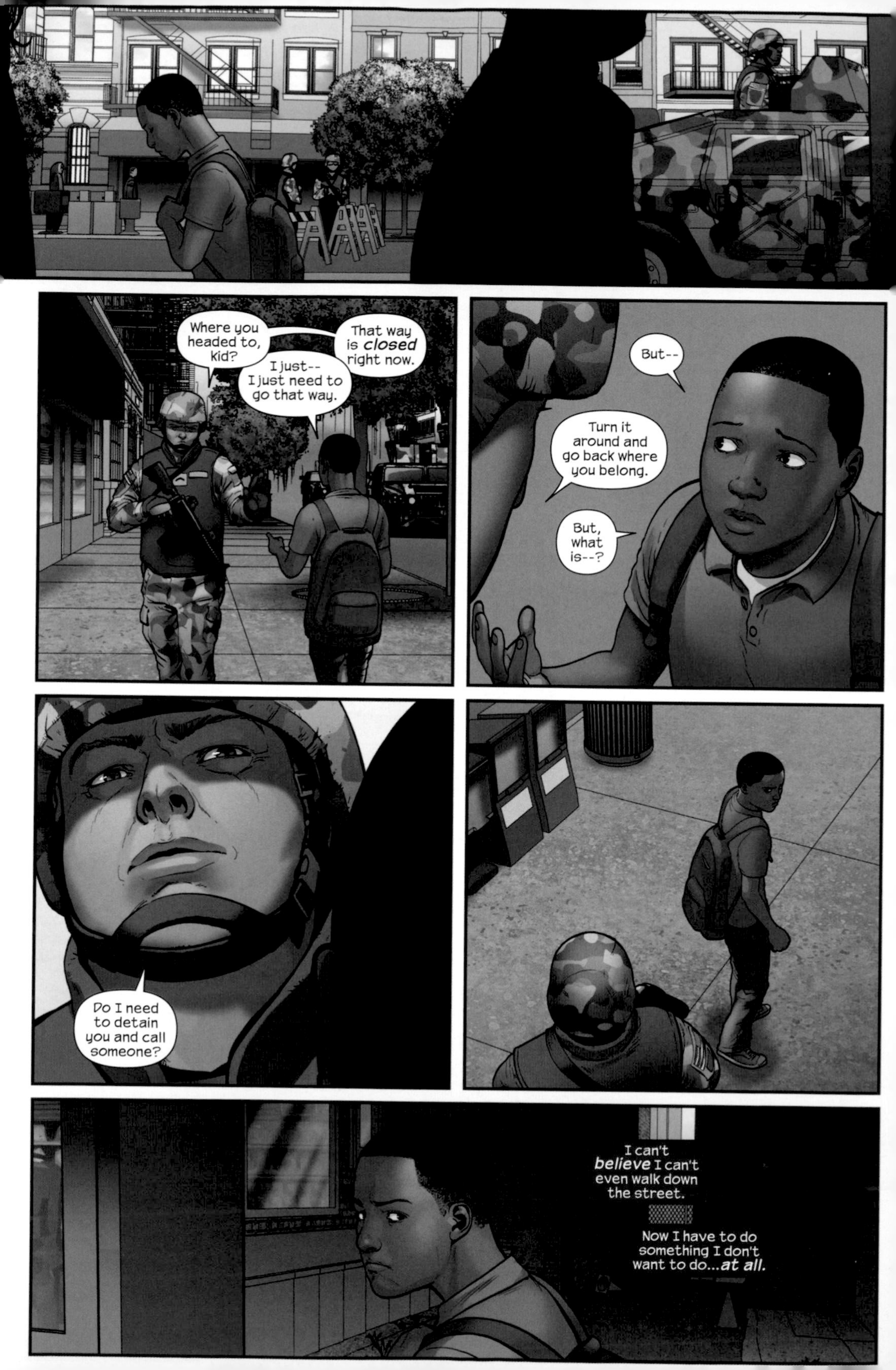

Where you headed to, kid?
That way is *closed* right now.
I just-- I just need to go that way.
But--
Turn it around and go back where you belong.
But, what is--?
Do I need to detain you and call someone?
I can't *believe* I can't even walk down the street.
Now I have to do something I don't want to do...*at all.*

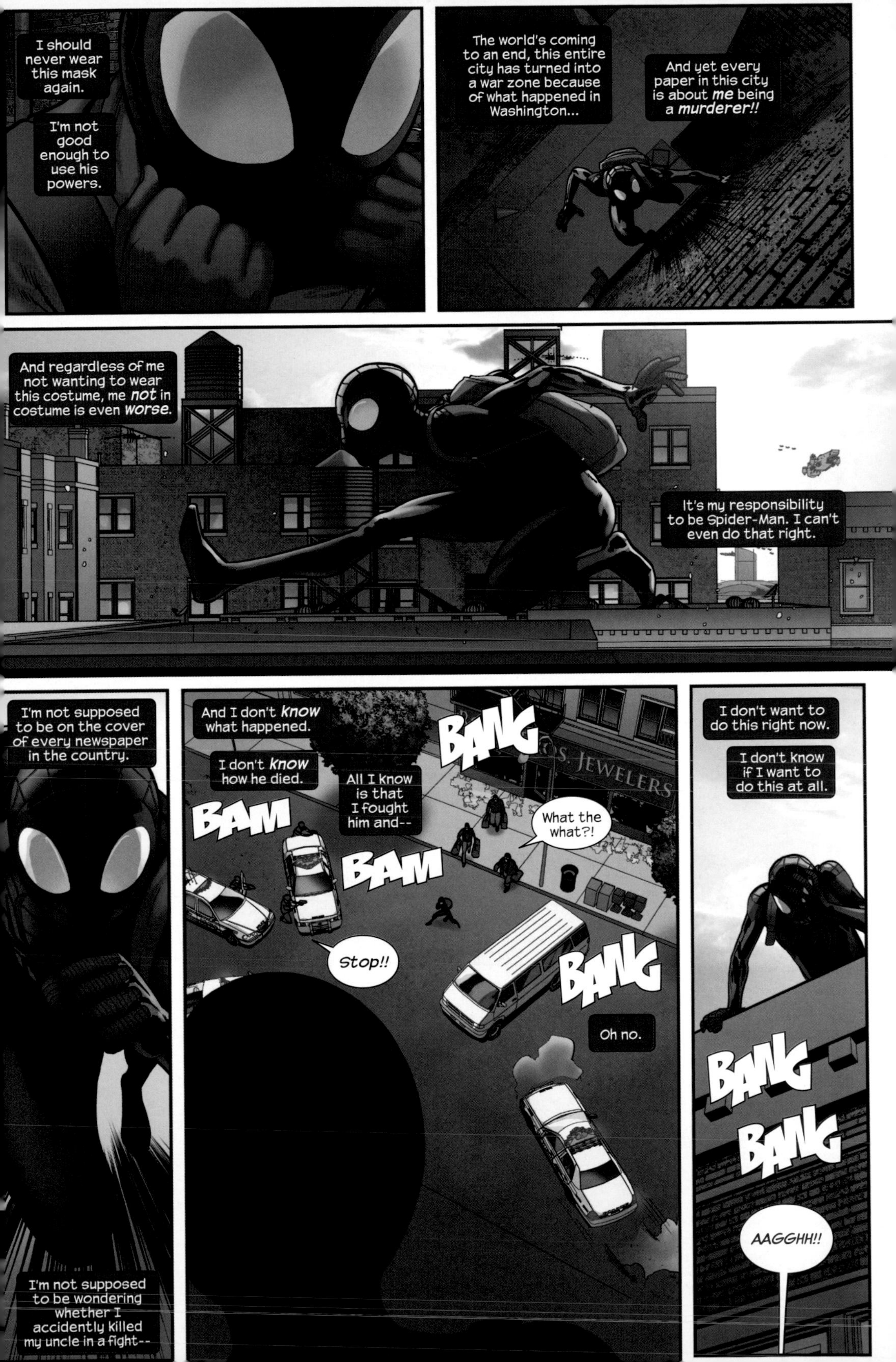

I should never wear this mask again.
I'm not good enough to use his powers.
The world's coming to an end, this entire city has turned into a war zone because of what happened in Washington...
And yet every paper in this city is about *me* being a *murderer!!*
And regardless of me not wanting to wear this costume, me *not* in costume is even *worse*.
It's my responsibility to be Spider-Man. I can't even do that right.
I'm not supposed to be on the cover of every newspaper in the country.
I'm not supposed to be wondering whether I accidently killed my uncle in a fight--
And I don't *know* what happened.
BANG
I don't *know* how he died.
All I know is that I fought him and--
BAM
JEWELERS
What the what?!
BAM
Stop!!
BANG
Oh no.
I don't want to do this right now.
I don't know if I want to do this at all.
BANG
BANG
AAGGHH!!

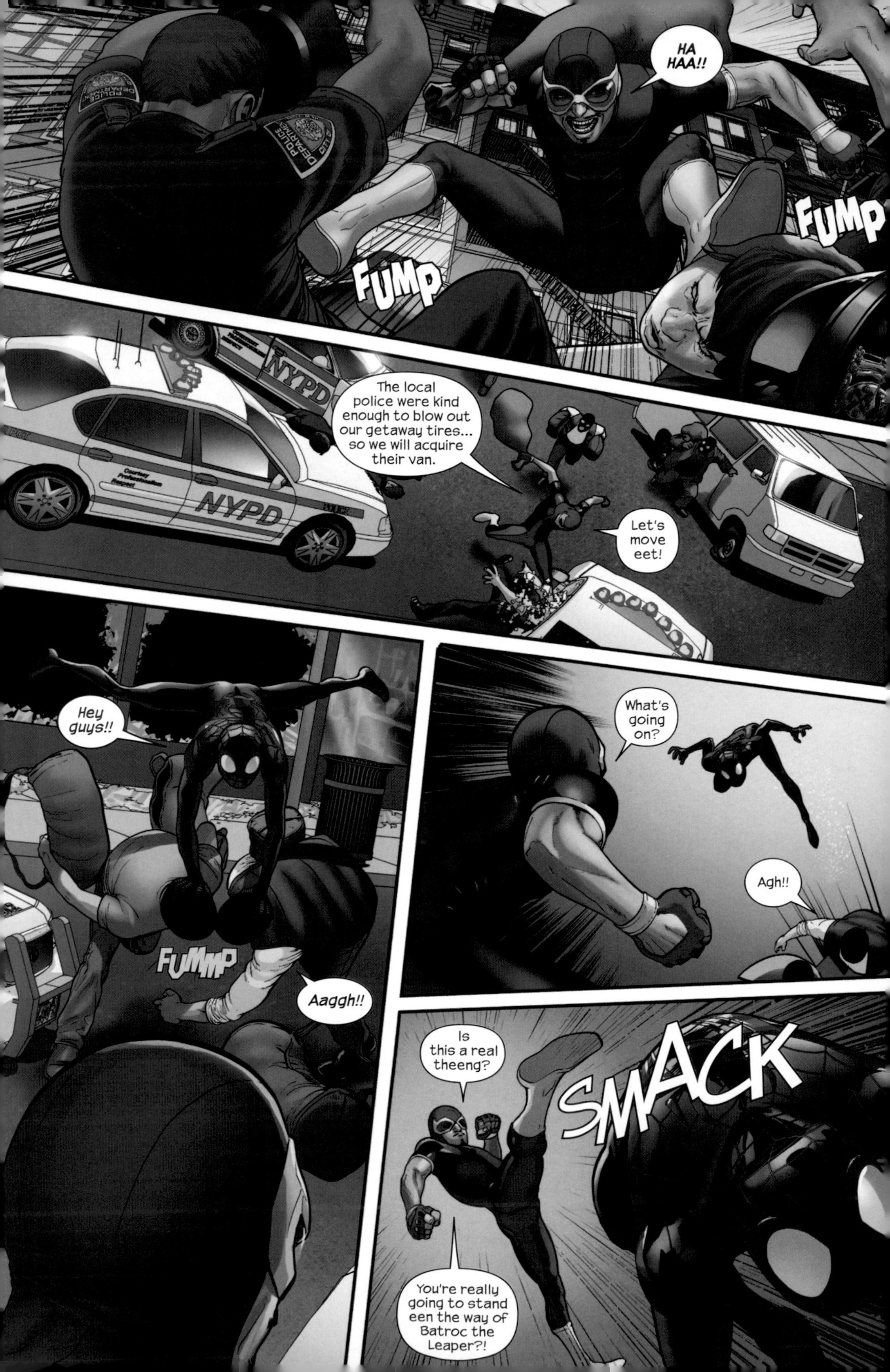
HA HAA!!
FUMP
FUMP
The local police were kind enough to blow out our getaway tires... so we will acquire their van.
Let's move eet!
Hey guys!!
FUMMP
Aagggh!!
What's going on?
Agh!!
Is this a real theeng?
SMACK
You're really going to stand een the way of Batroc the Leaper?!

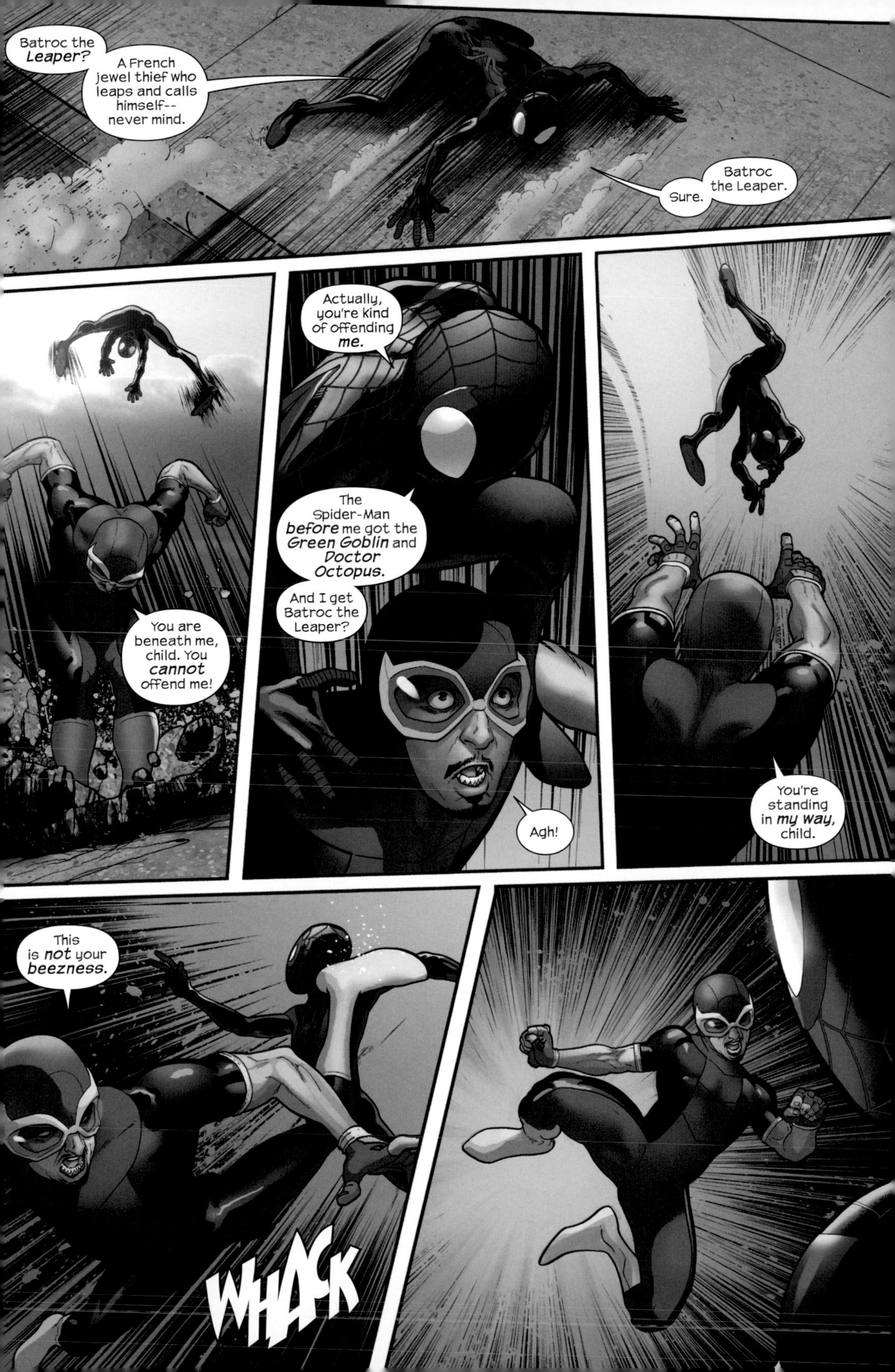

Batroc the *Leaper?*
A French jewel thief who leaps and calls himself-- never mind.
Sure.
Batroc the Leaper.
Actually, you're kind of offending *me.*
You are beneath me, child. You *cannot* offend me!
The Spider-Man *before* me got the *Green Goblin* and *Doctor Octopus.*
And I get Batroc the Leaper?
Agh!
You're standing in *my way,* child.
This is *not* your *beezness.*
WHACK

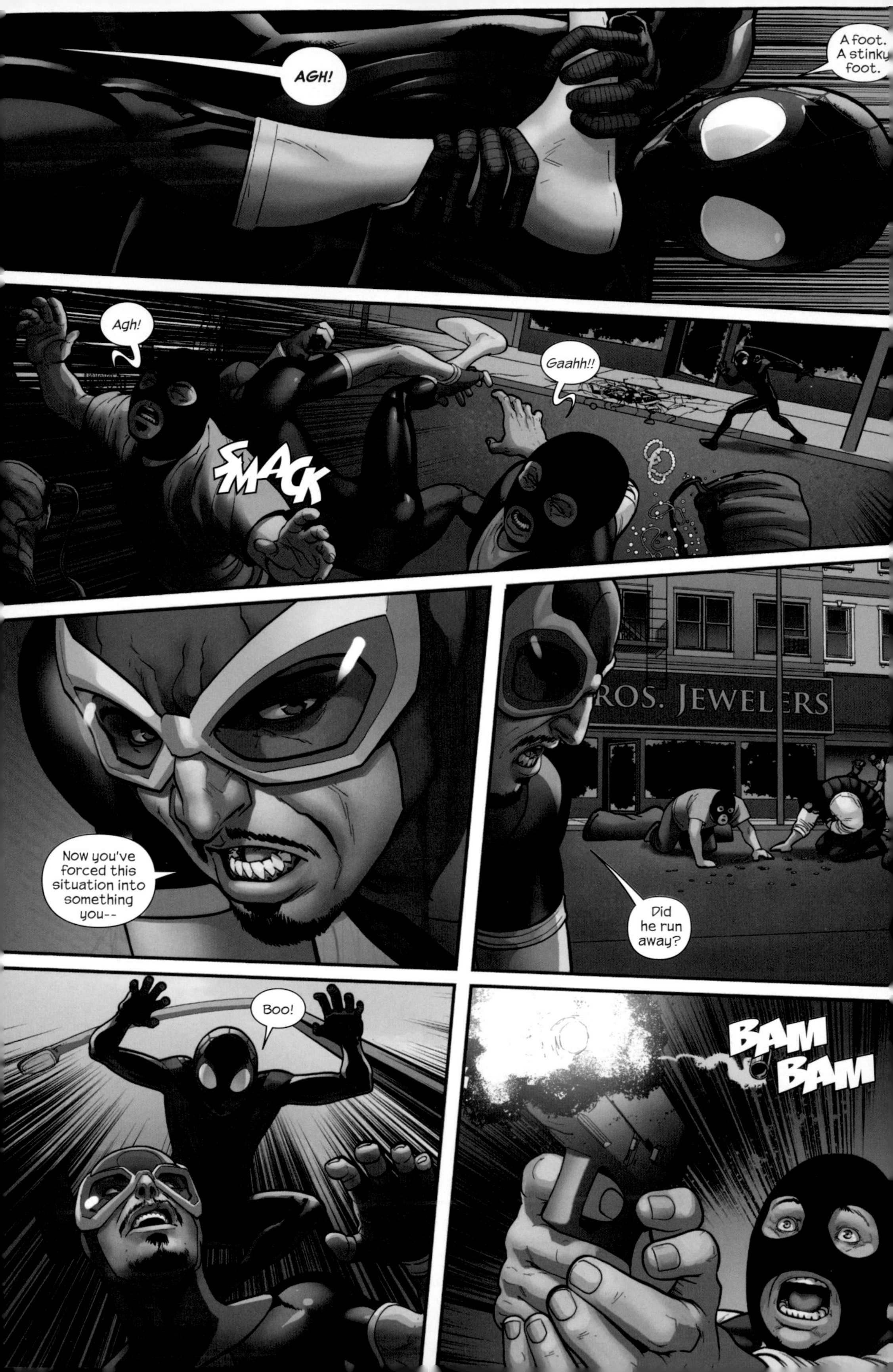
AGH!
A foot. A stinky foot.
Agh!
SMACK
Gaahh!!
ROS. JEWELERS
Now you've forced this situation into something you--
Did he run away?
Boo!
BAM BAM

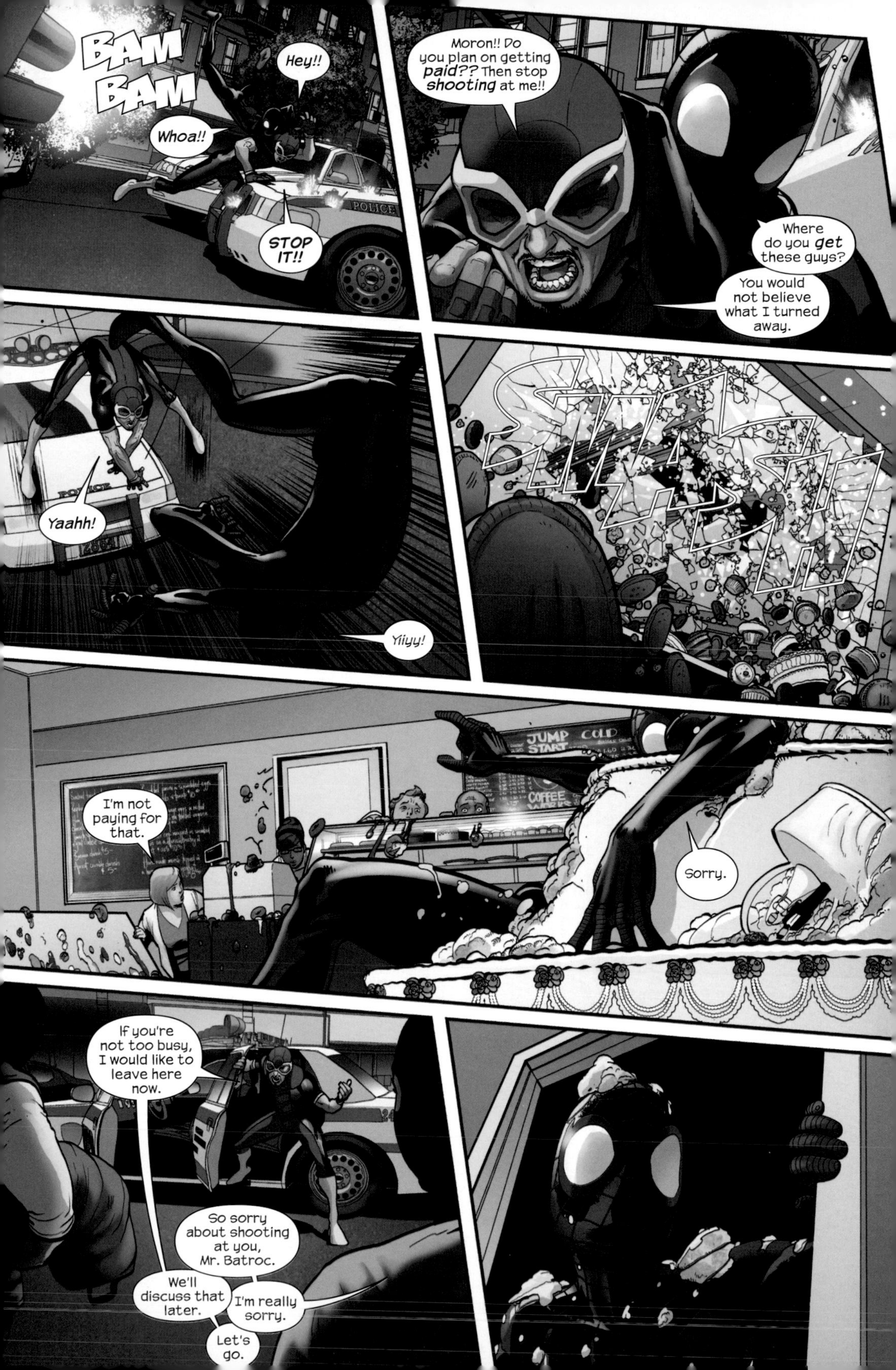
BAM
BAM
Hey!!
Whoa!!
STOP IT!!
Moron!! Do you plan on getting paid?? Then stop shooting at me!!
Where do you get these guys?
You would not believe what I turned away.
Yaahh!
Yiiyy!
JUMP START
COLD
COFFEE
I'm not paying for that.
Sorry.
If you're not too busy, I would like to leave here now.
So sorry about shooting at you, Mr. Batroc.
We'll discuss that later.
I'm really sorry.
Let's go.

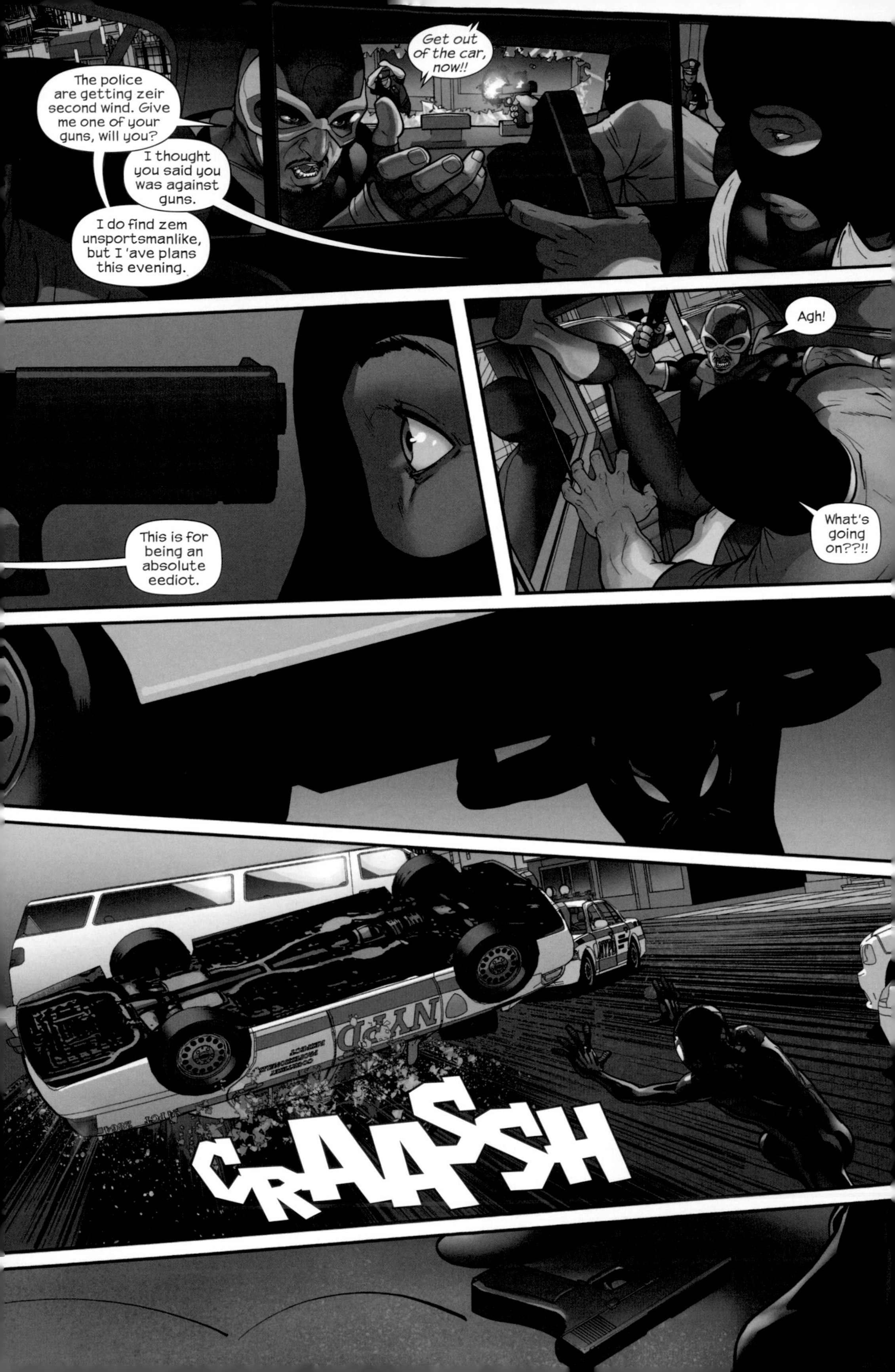

The police are getting zeir second wind. Give me one of your guns, will you?
Get out of the car, now!!
I thought you said you was against guns.
I do find zem unsportsmanlike, but I 'ave plans this evening.
This is for being an absolute eediot.
Agh!
What's going on??!!
CRAASSH

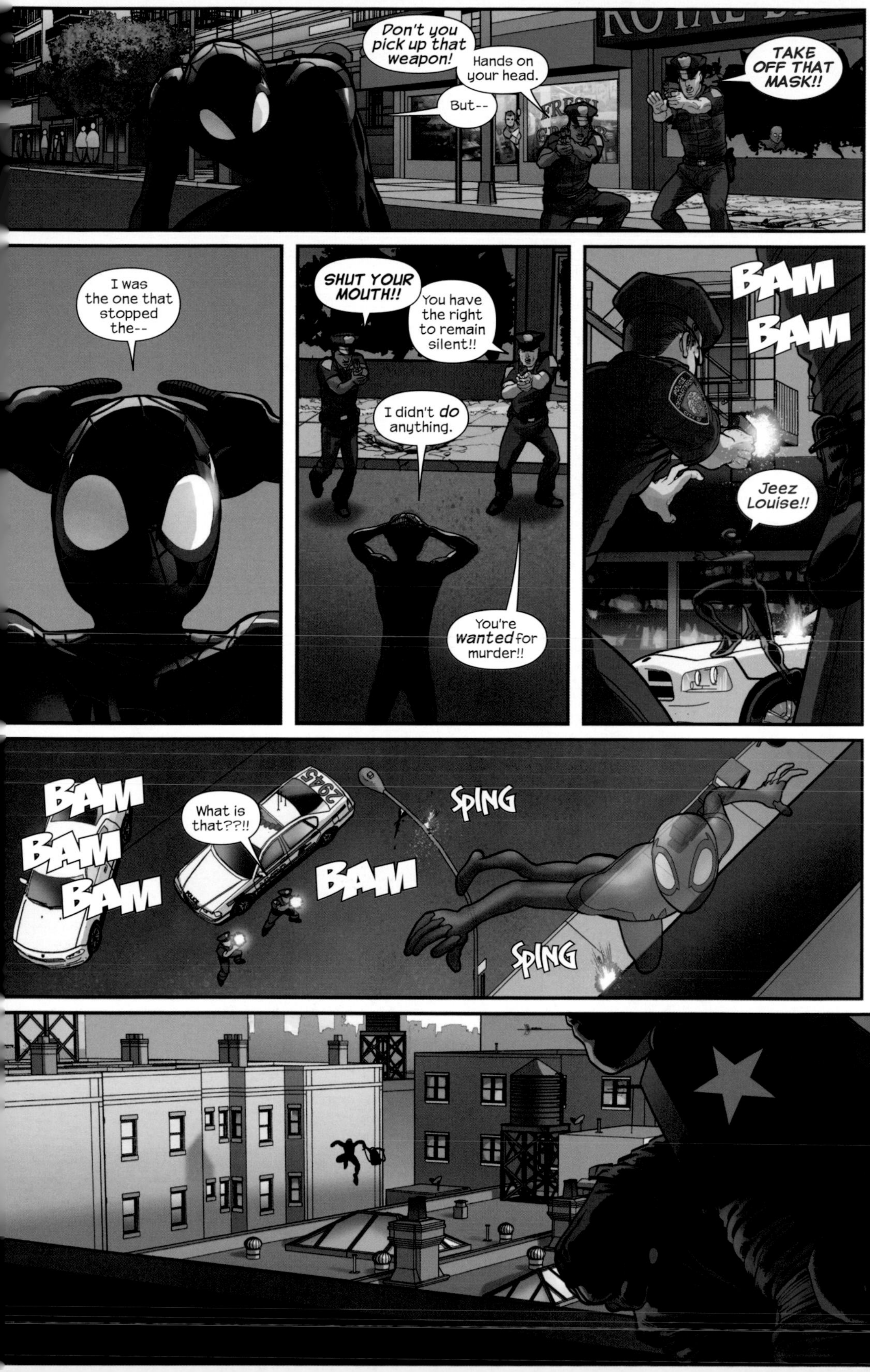
Don't you pick up that weapon!
Hands on your head.
But--
TAKE OFF THAT MASK!!
I was the one that stopped the--
SHUT YOUR MOUTH!!
You have the right to remain silent!!
I didn't do anything.
You're wanted for murder!!
BAM
BAM
Jeez Louise!!
BAM
BAM
BAM
What is that??!!
SPING
BAM
SPING

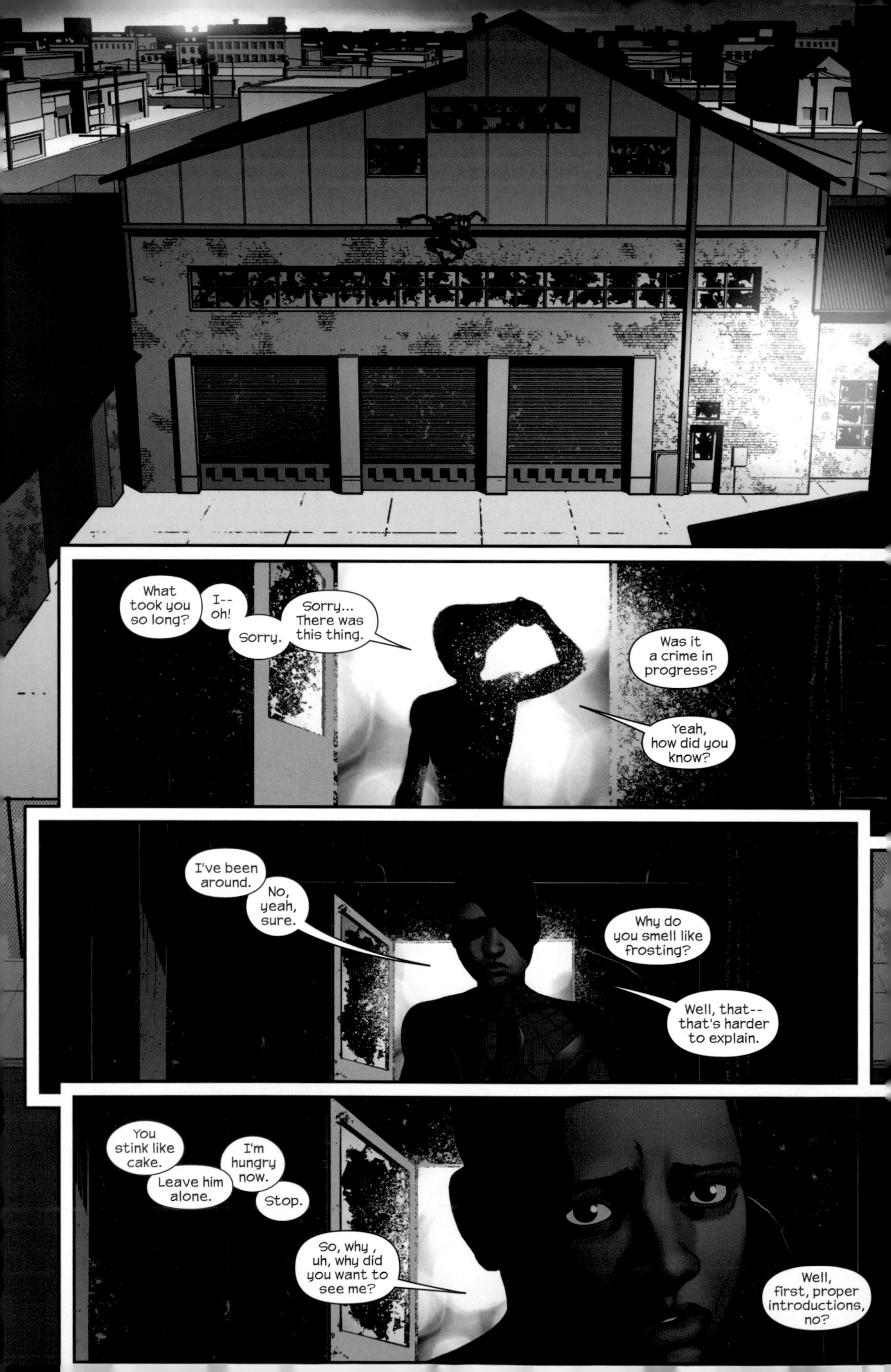
What took you so long?
I-- oh!
Sorry.
Sorry... There was this thing.
Was it a crime in progress?
Yeah, how did you know?
I've been around.
No, yeah, sure.
Why do you smell like frosting?
Well, that-- that's harder to explain.
You stink like cake.
I'm hungry now.
Leave him alone.
Stop.
So, why , uh, why did you want to see me?
Well, first, proper introductions, no?

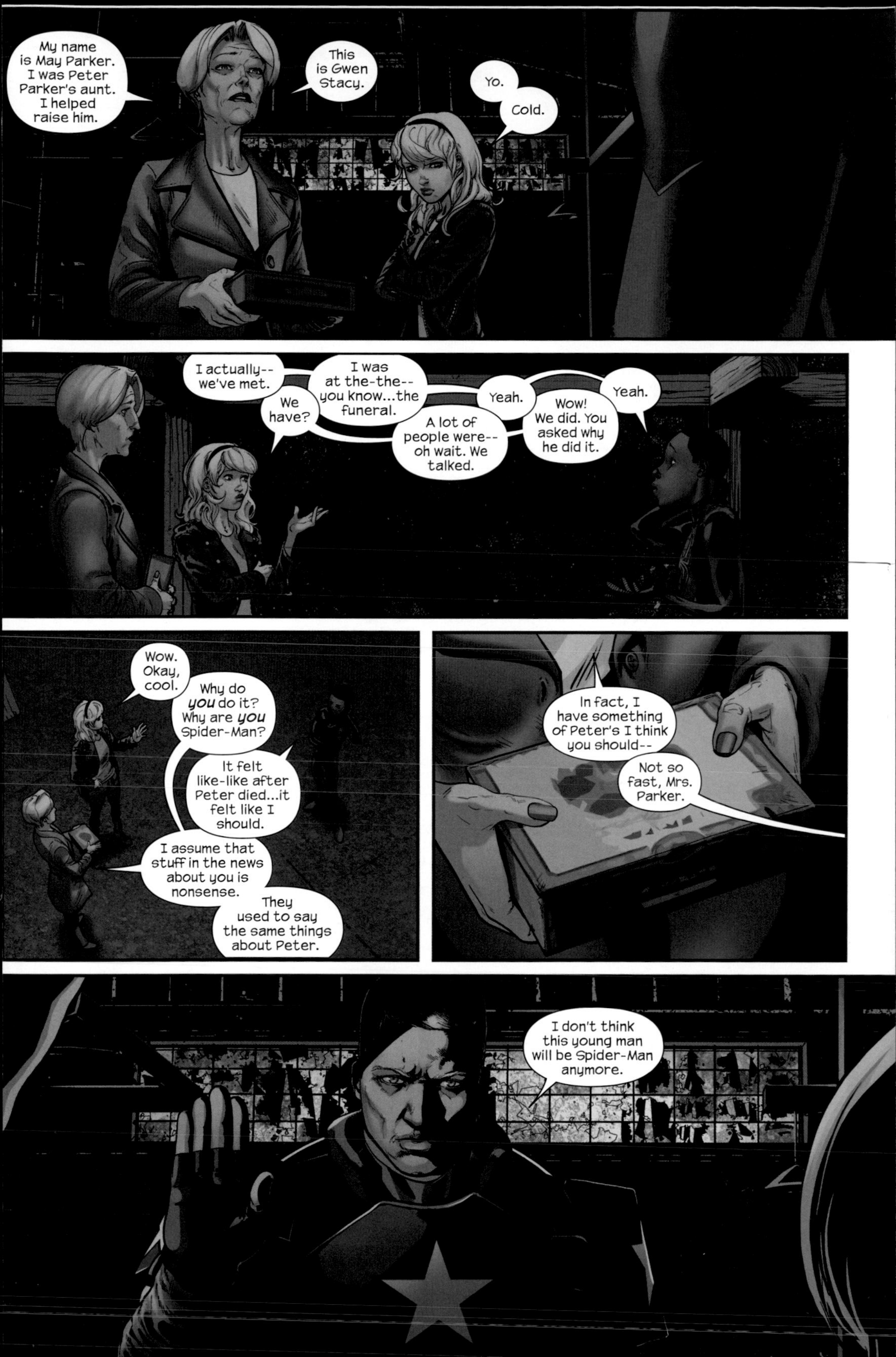

My name is May Parker. I was Peter Parker's aunt. I helped raise him.
This is Gwen Stacy.
Yo.
Cold.
I actually-- we've met.
We have?
I was at the-the-- you know...the funeral.
Yeah.
A lot of people were-- oh wait. We talked.
Wow! We did. You asked why he did it.
Yeah.
Wow. Okay, cool.
Why do *you* do it? Why are *you* Spider-Man?
It felt like-like after Peter died...it felt like I should.
I assume that stuff in the news about you is nonsense.
They used to say the same things about Peter.
In fact, I have something of Peter's I think you should--
Not so fast, Mrs. Parker.
I don't think this young man will be Spider-Man anymore.

CAPTAIN AMERICA, YOU ARE A JERK!!

GWEN STACY!!

Well, he is, Aunt May!!

You can't come in here and just tell Spider-Man he can't be Spider-Man.

I can, actually.

Well then you're Captain Jerk of the-the-the Ultimate Jerk Squad of America.

Wait, hold on!!

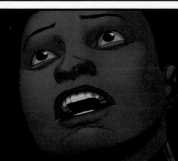

How did you-- we're literally hiding in a run-down broken warehouse in the middle of Queens--

How did you even find us here?

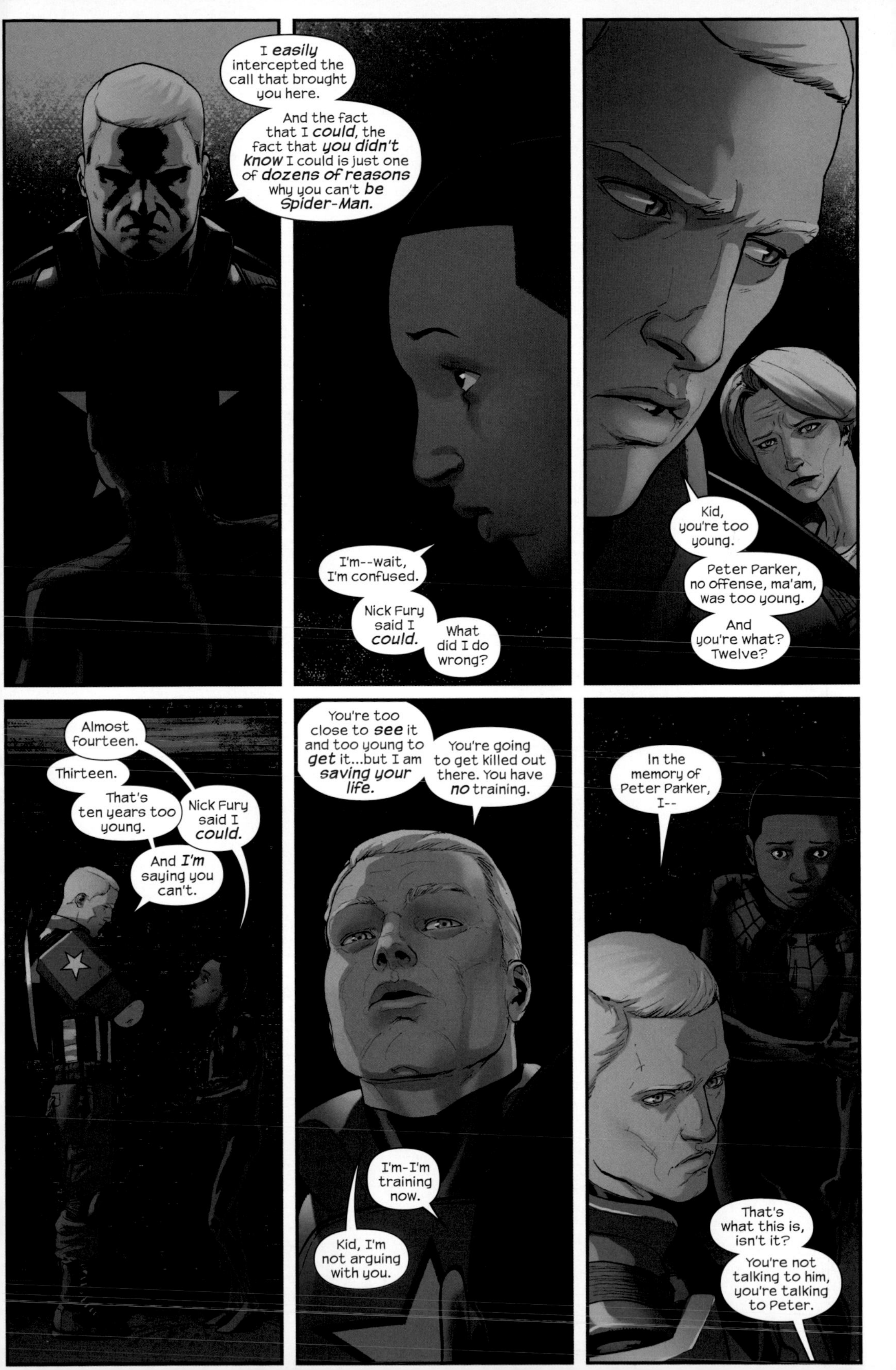
I easily intercepted the call that brought you here.
And the fact that I could, the fact that you didn't know I could is just one of dozens of reasons why you can't be Spider-Man.
I'm--wait, I'm confused.
Nick Fury said I could.
What did I do wrong?
Kid, you're too young.
Peter Parker, no offense, ma'am, was too young.
And you're what? Twelve?
Almost fourteen.
Thirteen.
That's ten years too young.
Nick Fury said I could.
And I'm saying you can't.
You're too close to see it and too young to get it...but I am saving your life.
You're going to get killed out there. You have no training.
I'm-I'm training now.
Kid, I'm not arguing with you.
In the memory of Peter Parker, I--
That's what this is, isn't it?
You're not talking to him, you're talking to Peter.

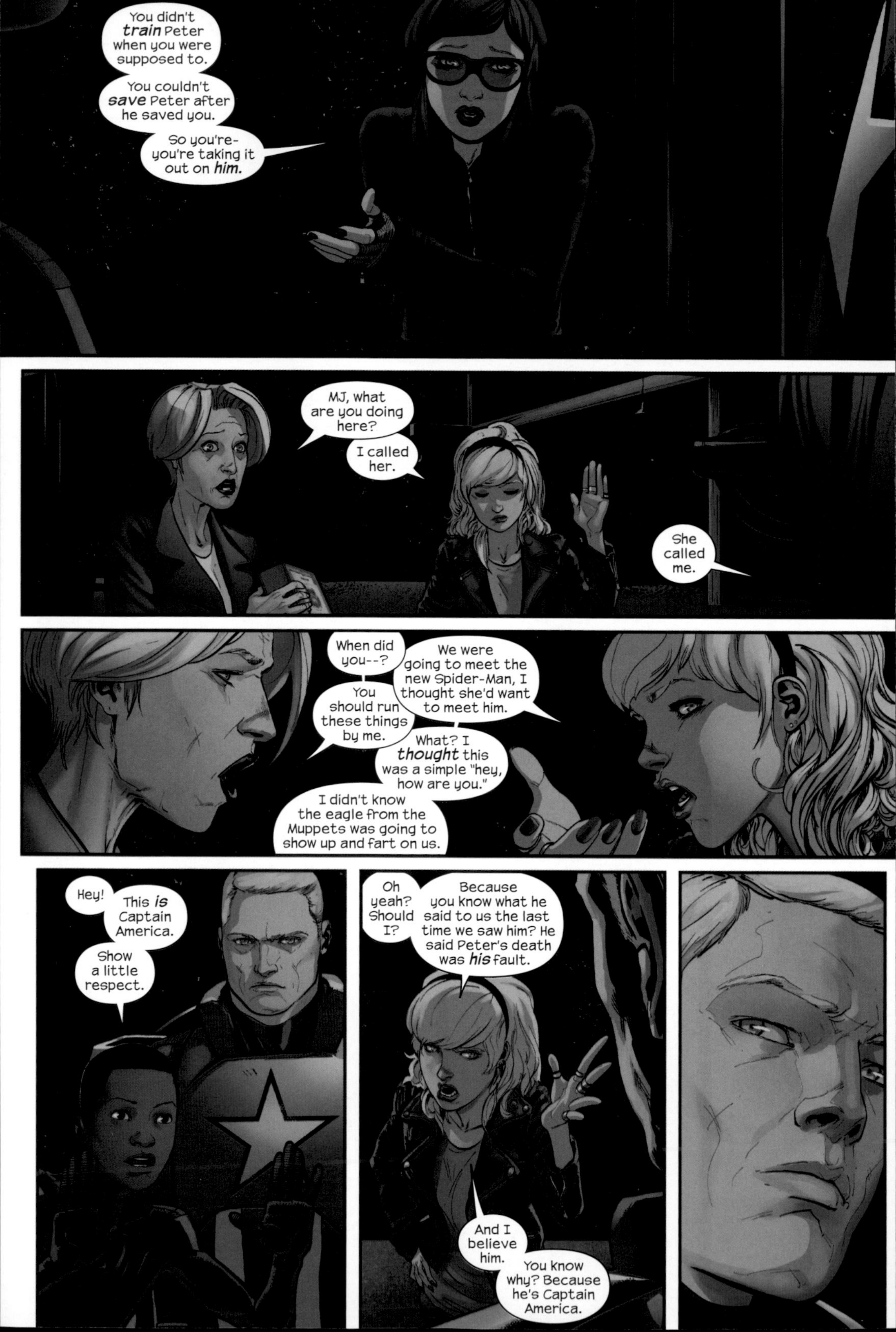

You didn't *train* Peter when you were supposed to.
You couldn't *save* Peter after he saved you.
So you're- you're taking it out on *him.*
MJ, what are you doing here?
I called her.
She called me.
When did you--?
We were going to meet the new Spider-Man, I thought she'd want to meet him.
You should run these things by me.
What? I *thought* this was a simple "hey, how are you."
I didn't know the eagle from the Muppets was going to show up and fart on us.
Hey!
This *is* Captain America.
Show a little respect.
Oh yeah? Should I?
Because you know what he said to us the last time we saw him? He said Peter's death was *his* fault.
And I believe him.
You know why? Because he's Captain America.

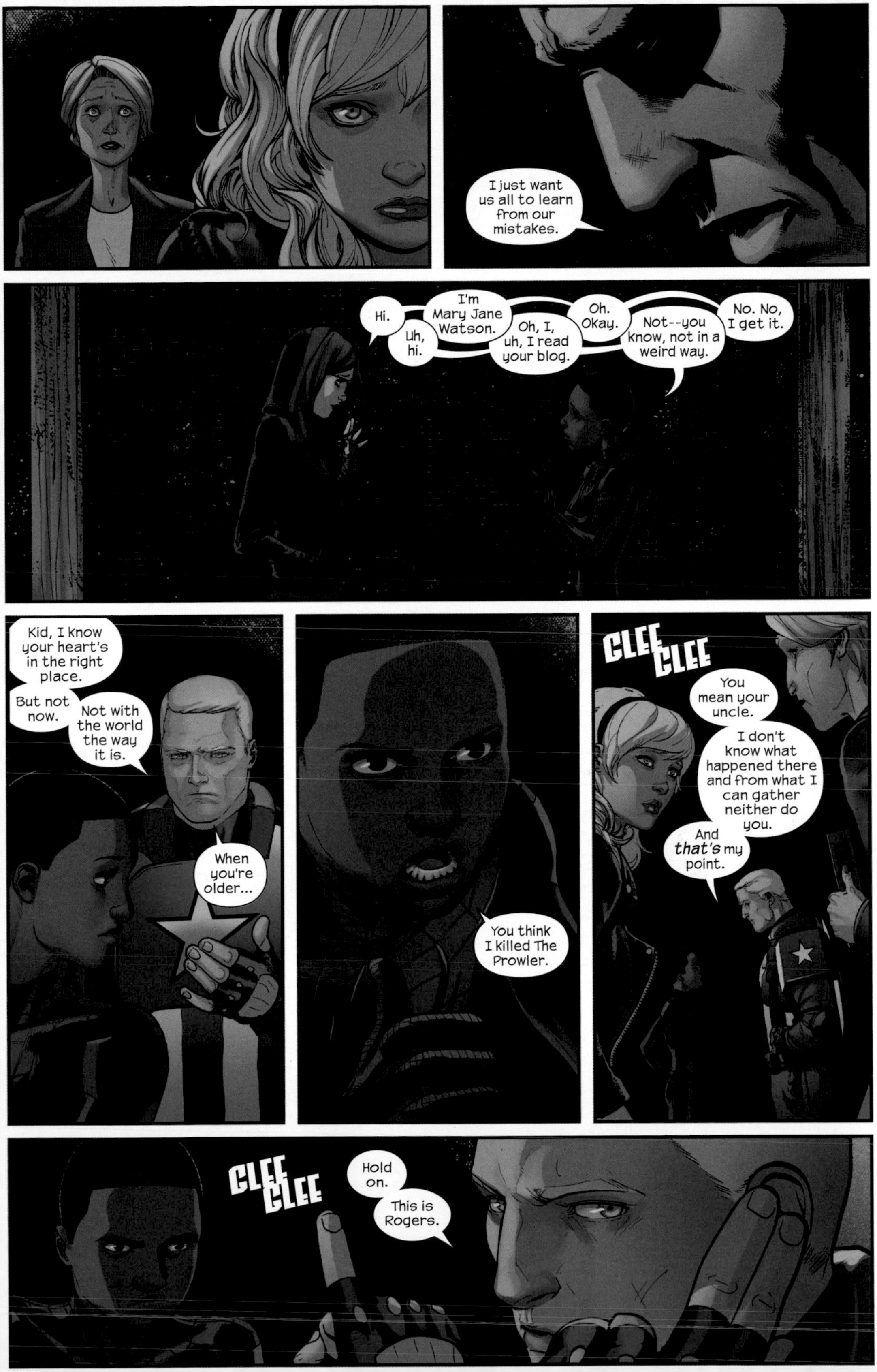
I just want us all to learn from our mistakes.
Hi.
Uh, hi.
I'm Mary Jane Watson.
Oh, I, uh, I read your blog.
Oh. Okay.
Not--you know, not in a weird way.
No. No, I get it.
Kid, I know your heart's in the right place.
But not now.
Not with the world the way it is.
When you're older...
You think I killed The Prowler.
CLEE CLEE
You mean your uncle.
I don't know what happened there and from what I can gather neither do you.
And *that's* my point.
CLEE CLEE
Hold on.
This is Rogers.

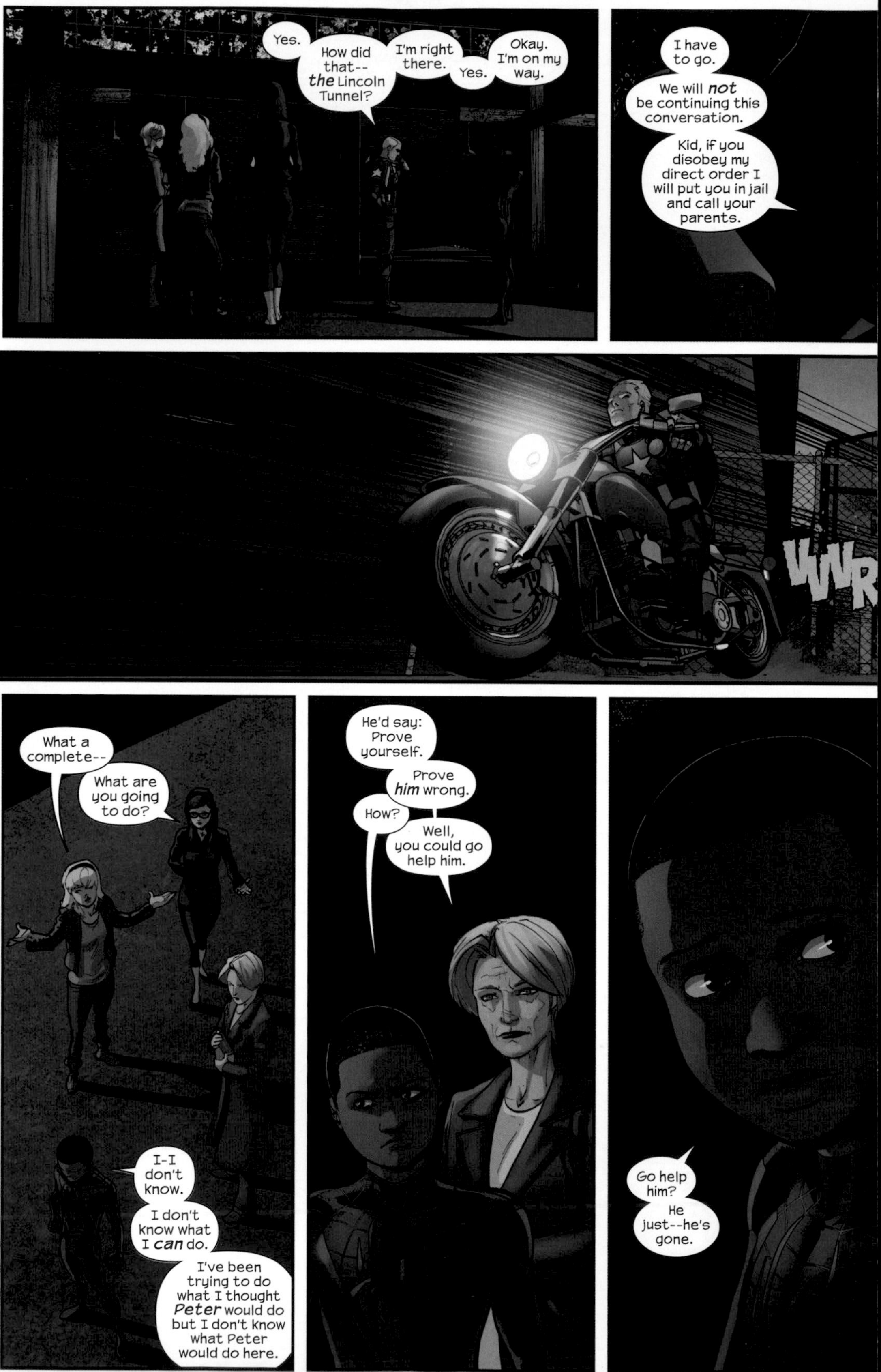
Yes.
How did that-- *the* Lincoln Tunnel?
I'm right there.
Yes.
Okay. I'm on my way.
I have to go.
We will *not* be continuing this conversation.
Kid, if you disobey my direct order I will put you in jail and call your parents.
VVVR
What a complete--
What are you going to do?
I-I don't know.
I don't know what I *can* do.
I've been trying to do what I thought *Peter* would do but I don't know what Peter would do here.
He'd say: Prove yourself.
Prove *him* wrong.
How?
Well, you could go help him.
Go help him?
He just--he's gone.

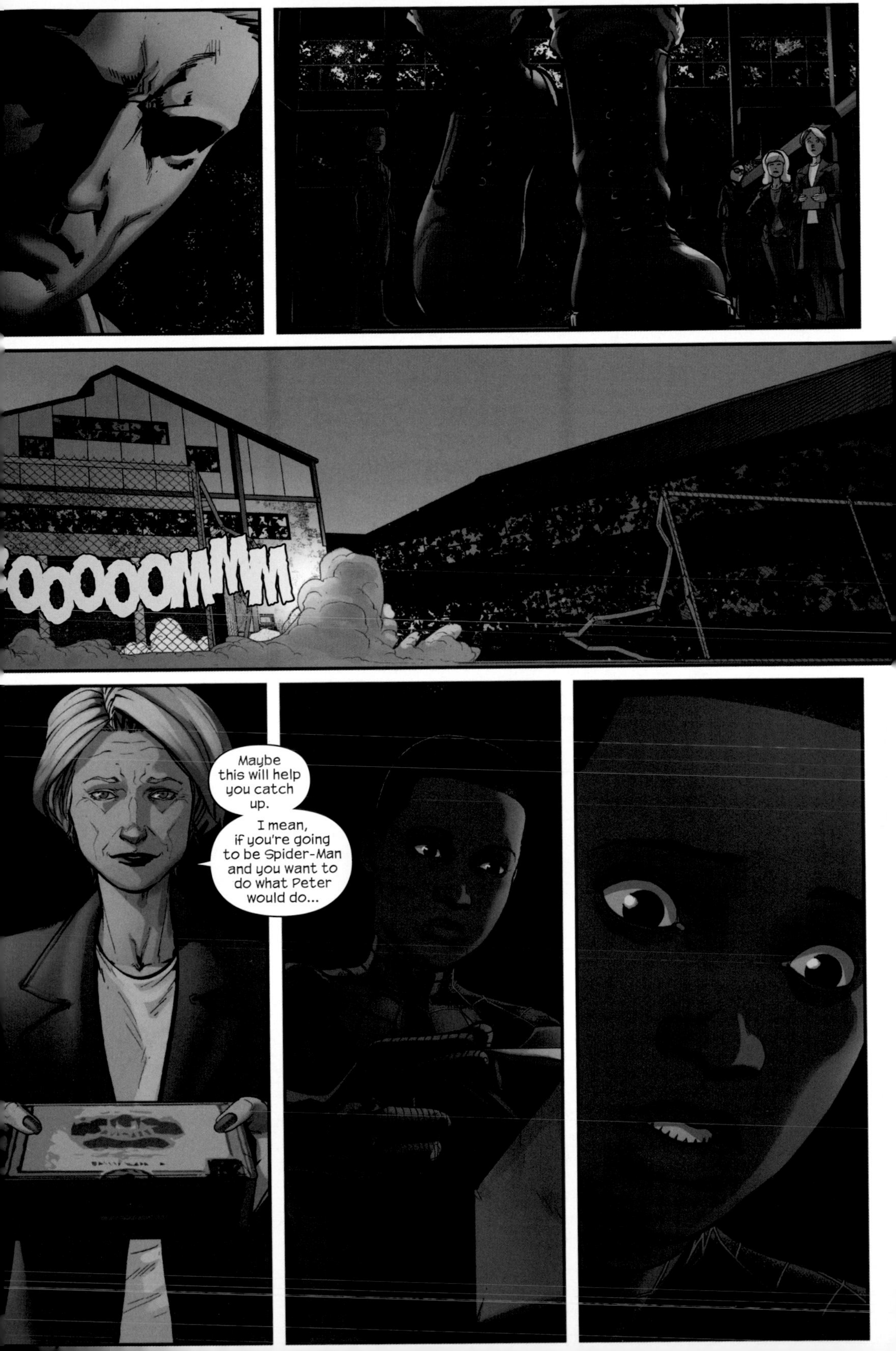
OOOOOOMMMM
Maybe this will help you catch up.
I mean, if you're going to be Spider-Man and you want to do what Peter would do...

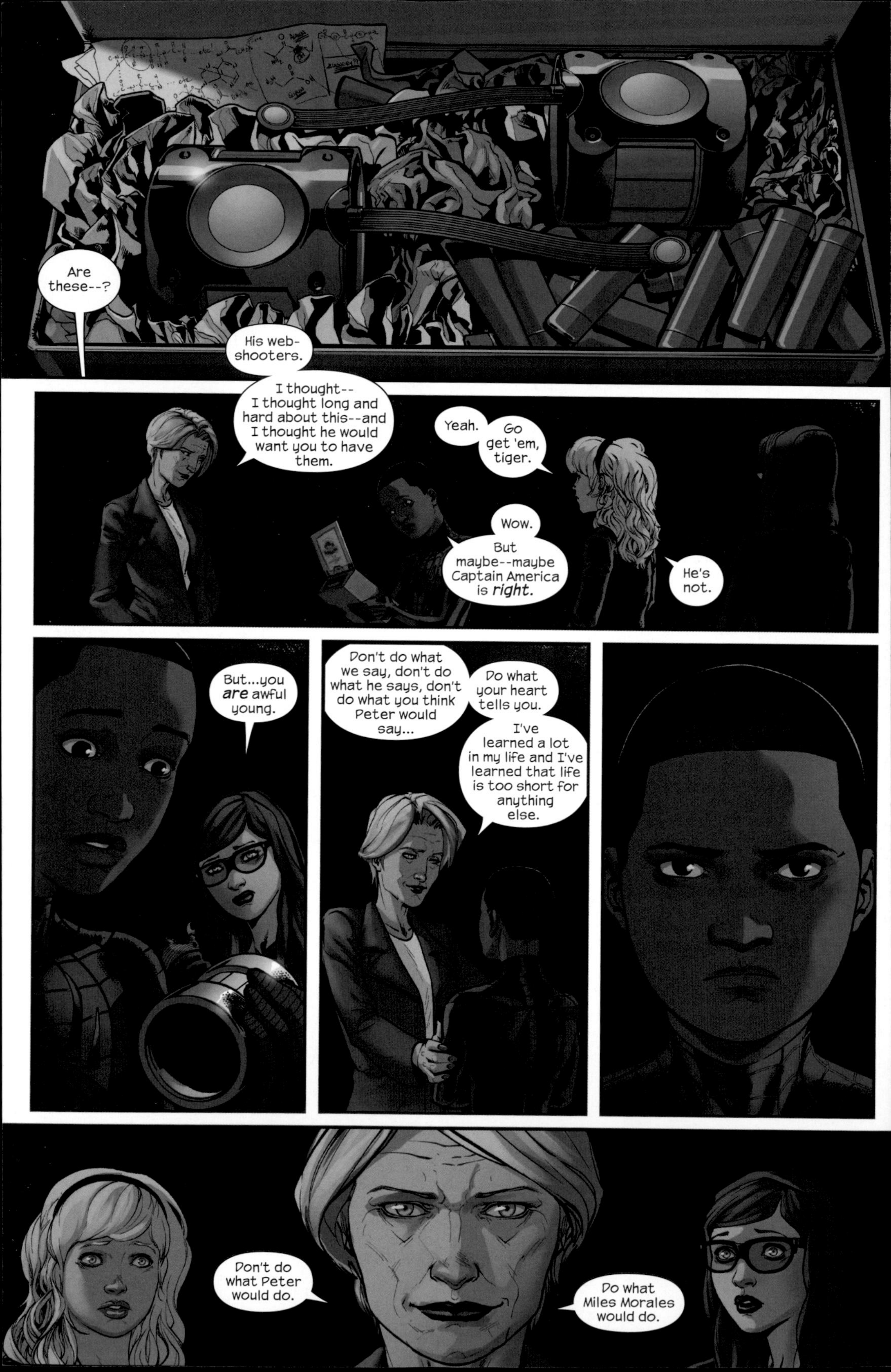

Are these--?
His web-shooters.
I thought-- I thought long and hard about this--and I thought he would want you to have them.
Yeah.
Go get 'em, tiger.
Wow.
But maybe--maybe Captain America is *right.*
He's not.
But...you *are* awful young.
Don't do what we say, don't do what he says, don't do what you think Peter would say...
Do what your heart tells you.
I've learned a lot in my life and I've learned that life is too short for anything else.
Don't do what Peter would do.
Do what Miles Morales would do.

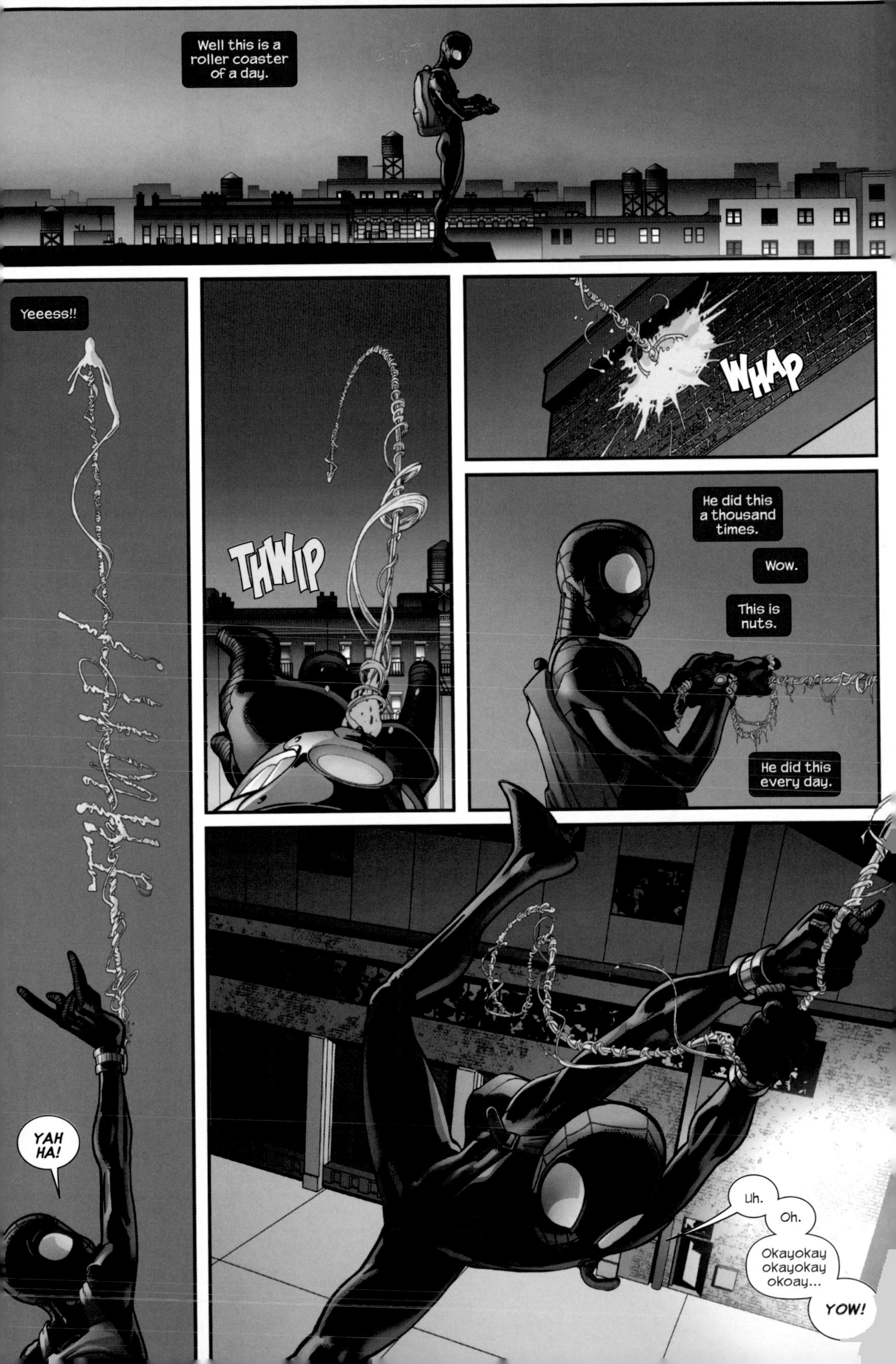
Well this is a roller coaster of a day.
Yeeess!!
YAH HA!
THWIP
WHAP
He did this a thousand times.
Wow.
This is nuts.
He did this every day.
Uh.
Oh.
Okayokay okayokay okoay...
YOW!

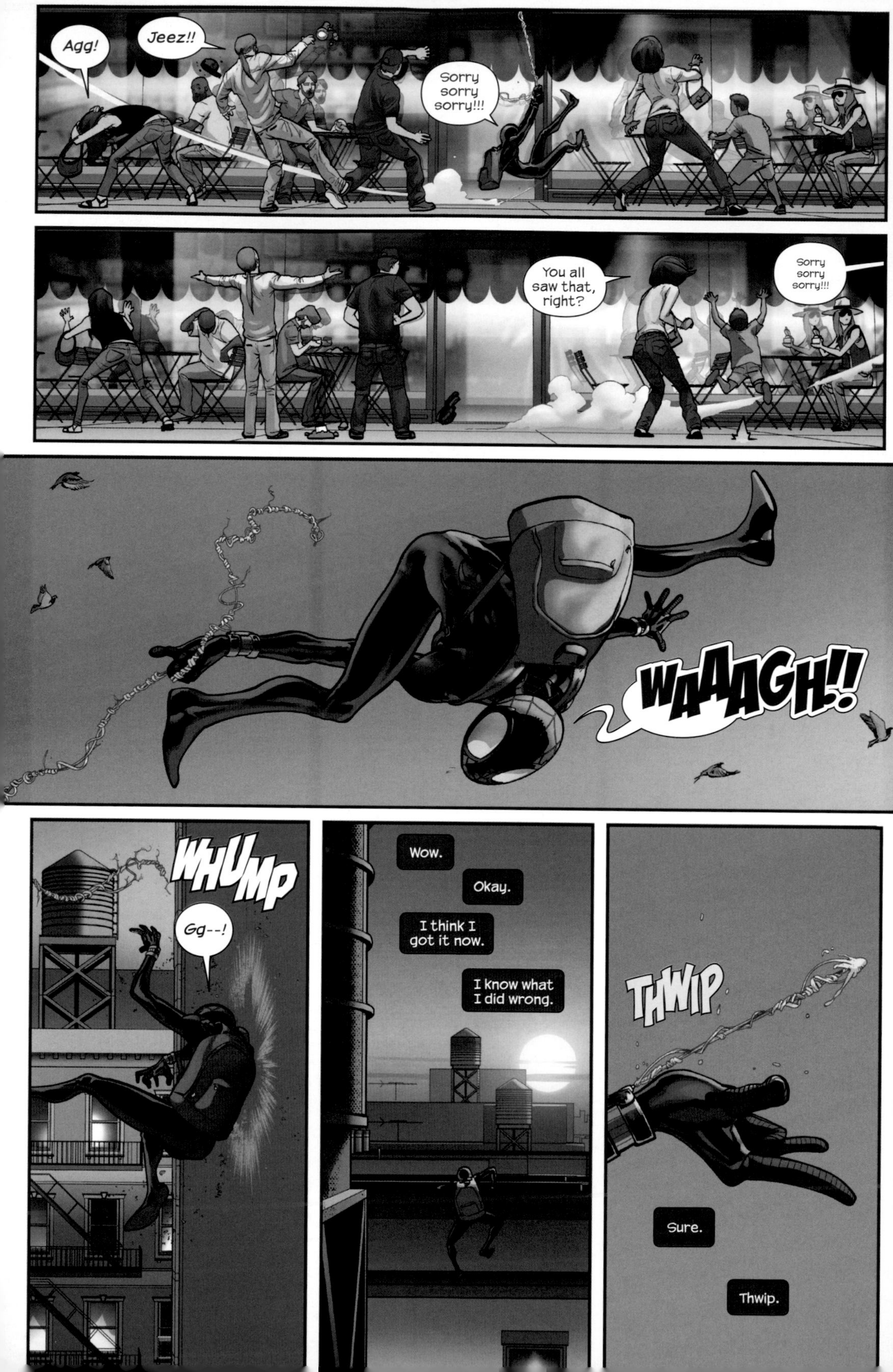
Agg!
Jeez!!
Sorry sorry sorry!!!
You all saw that, right?
Sorry sorry sorry!!!
WAAAGH!!
WHUMP
Gg--!
Wow.
Okay.
I think I got it now.
I know what I did wrong.
THWIP
Sure.
Thwip.

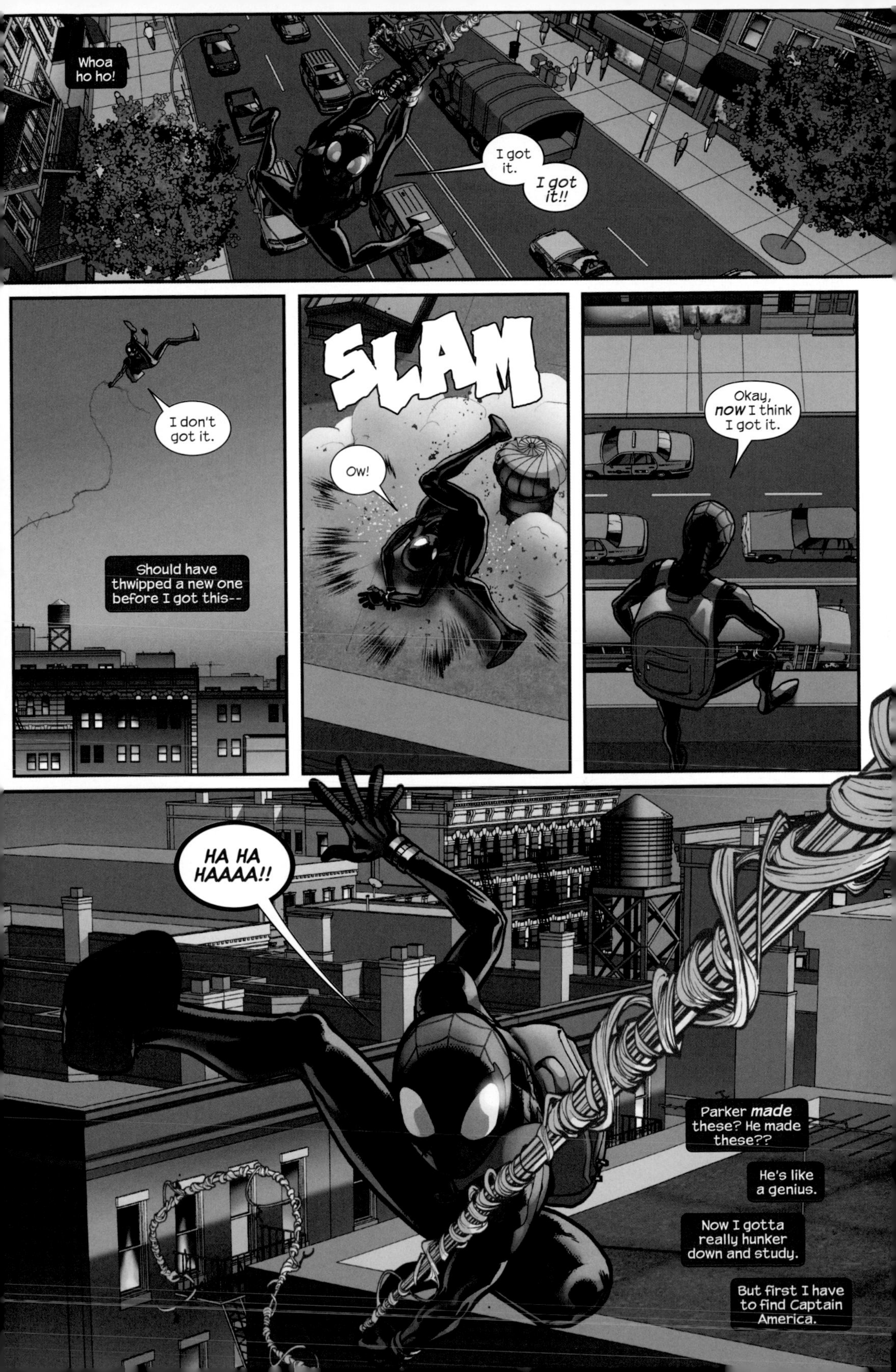
Whoa ho ho!
I got it.
I got it!!
I don't got it.
Should have thwipped a new one before I got this--
SLAM
Ow!
Okay, now I think I got it.
HA HA HAAAA!!
Parker made these? He made these??
He's like a genius.
Now I gotta really hunker down and study.
But first I have to find Captain America.

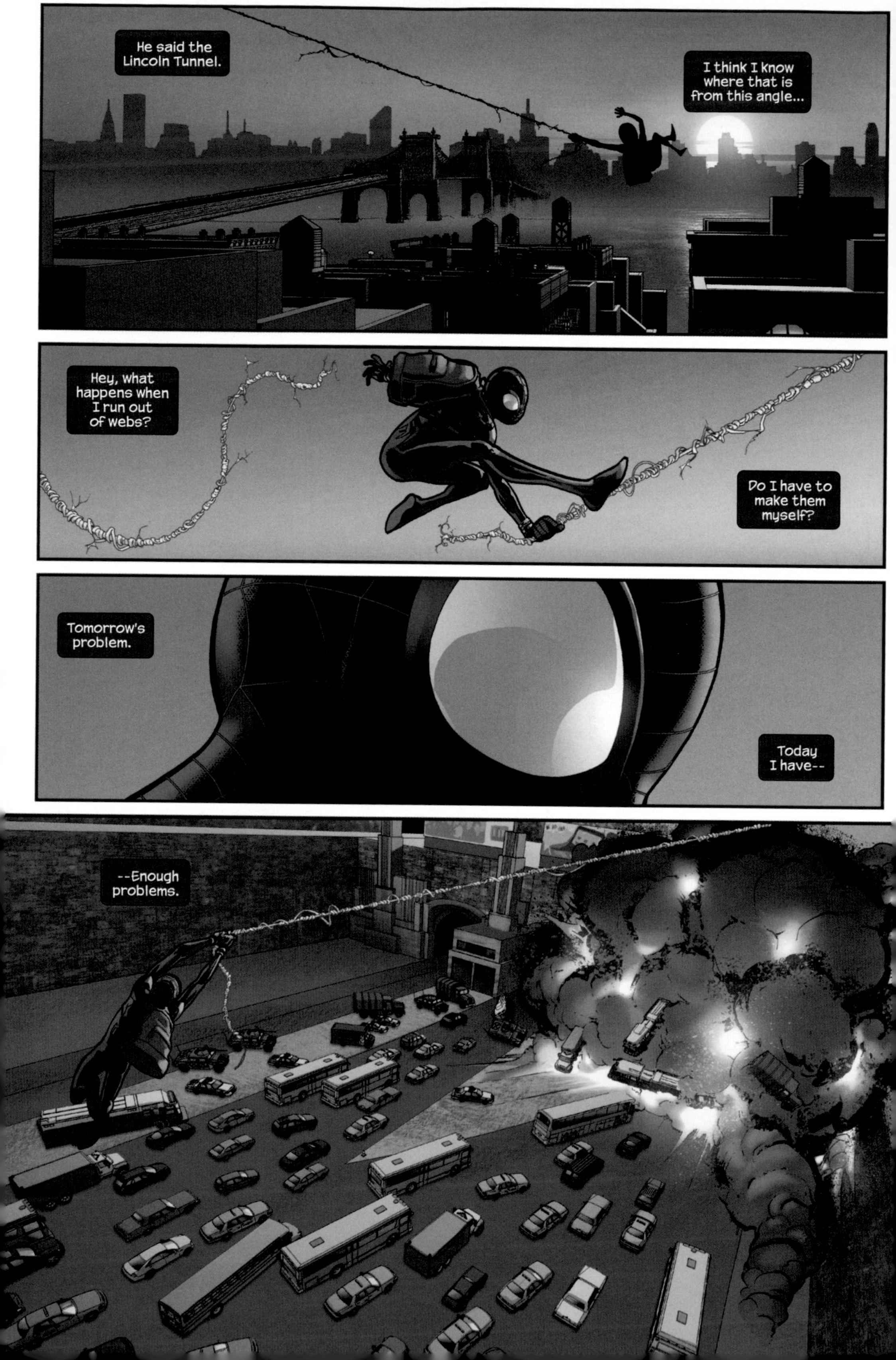
He said the Lincoln Tunnel.
I think I know where that is from this angle...
Hey, what happens when I run out of webs?
Do I have to make them myself?
Tomorrow's problem.
Today I have--
--Enough problems.

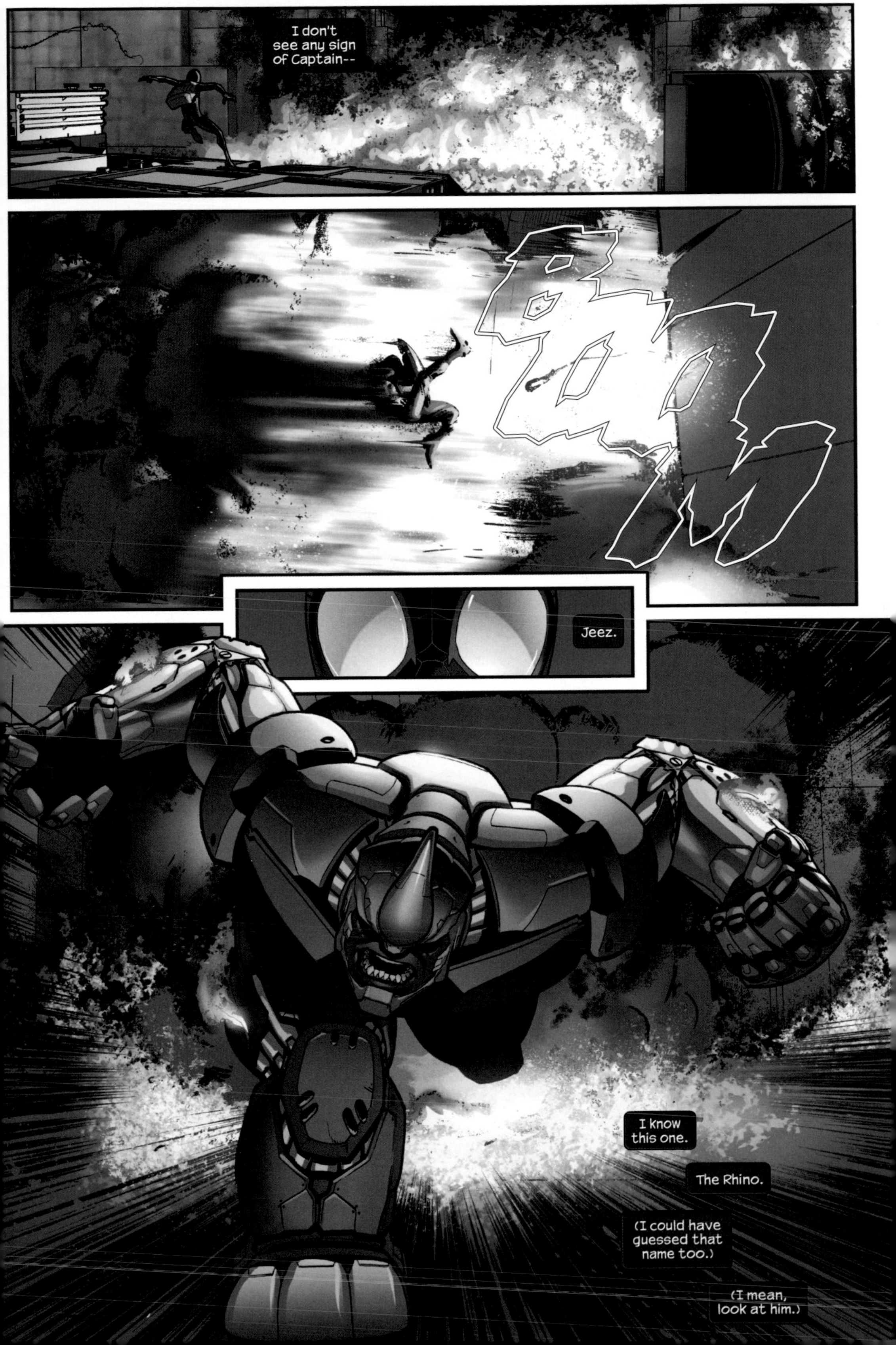
I don't see any sign of Captain--
BOOM
Jeez.
I know this one.
The Rhino.
(I could have guessed that name too.)
(I mean, look at him.)

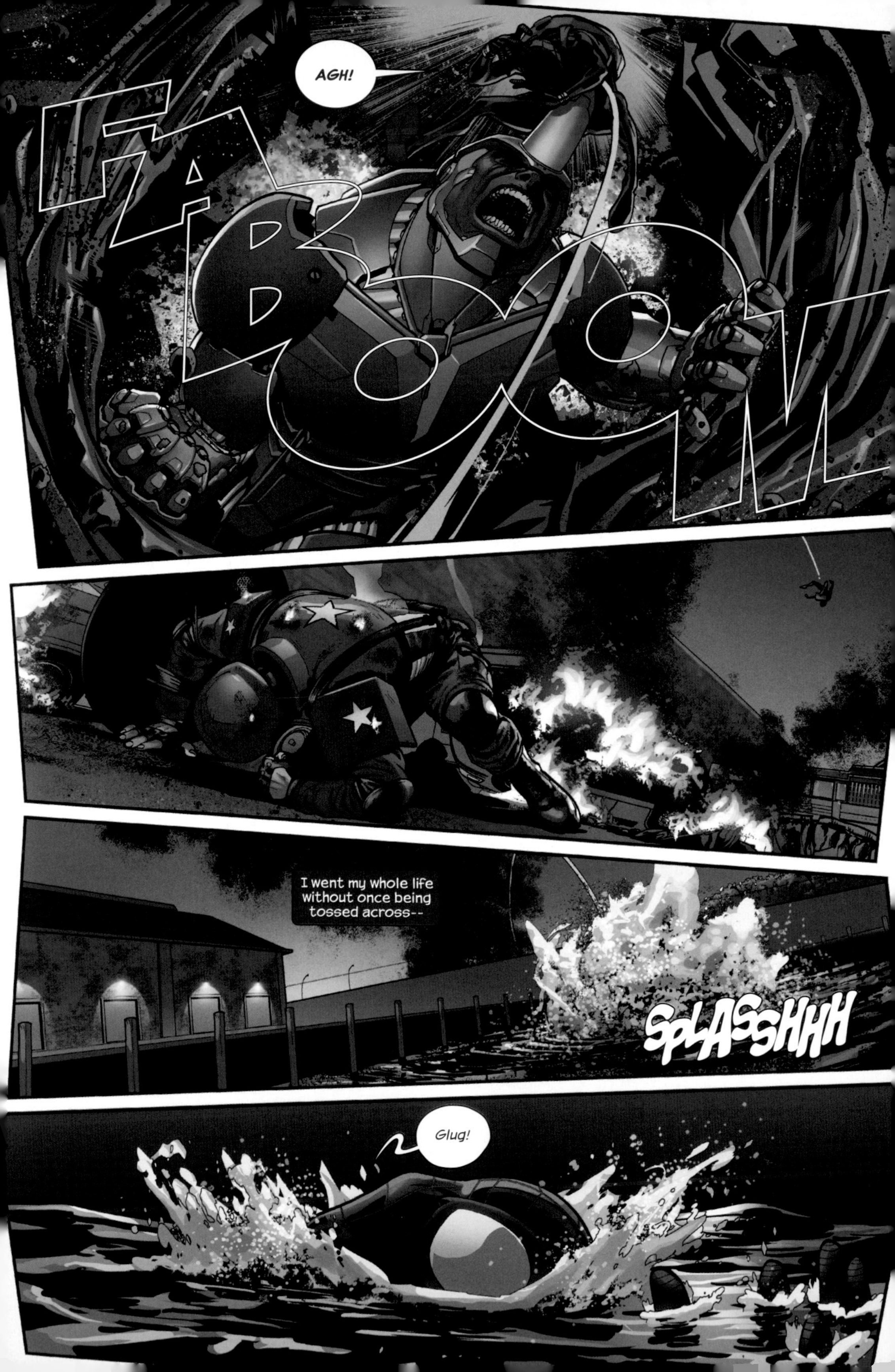
AGH!
FABOOM
I went my whole life without once being tossed across--
SPLASSHHH
Glug!

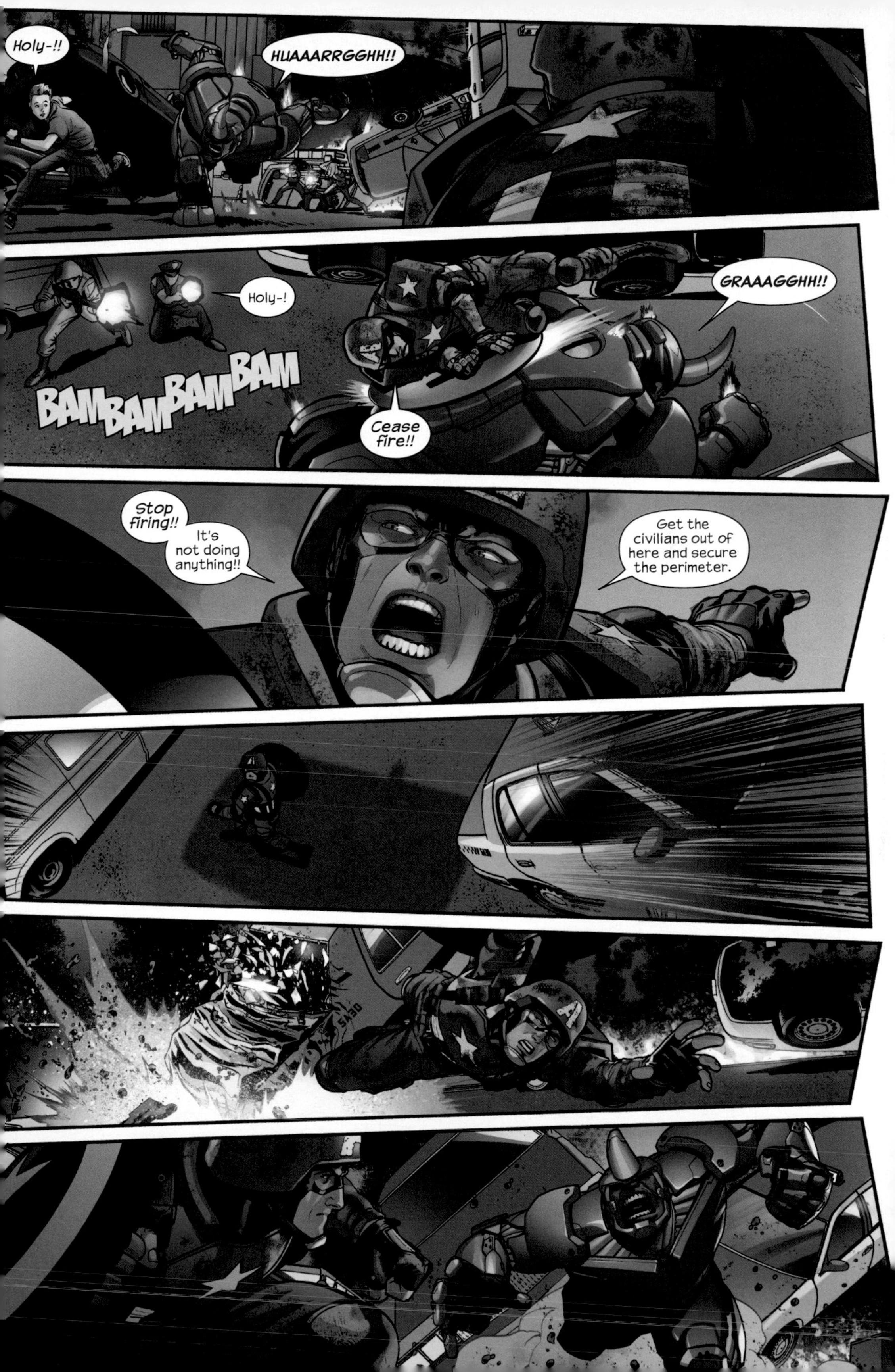
Holy-!!
HUAAARRGGHH!!
Holy-!
GRAAAGGHH!!
BAMBAMBAMBAM
Cease fire!!
Stop firing!!
It's not doing anything!!
Get the civilians out of here and secure the perimeter.

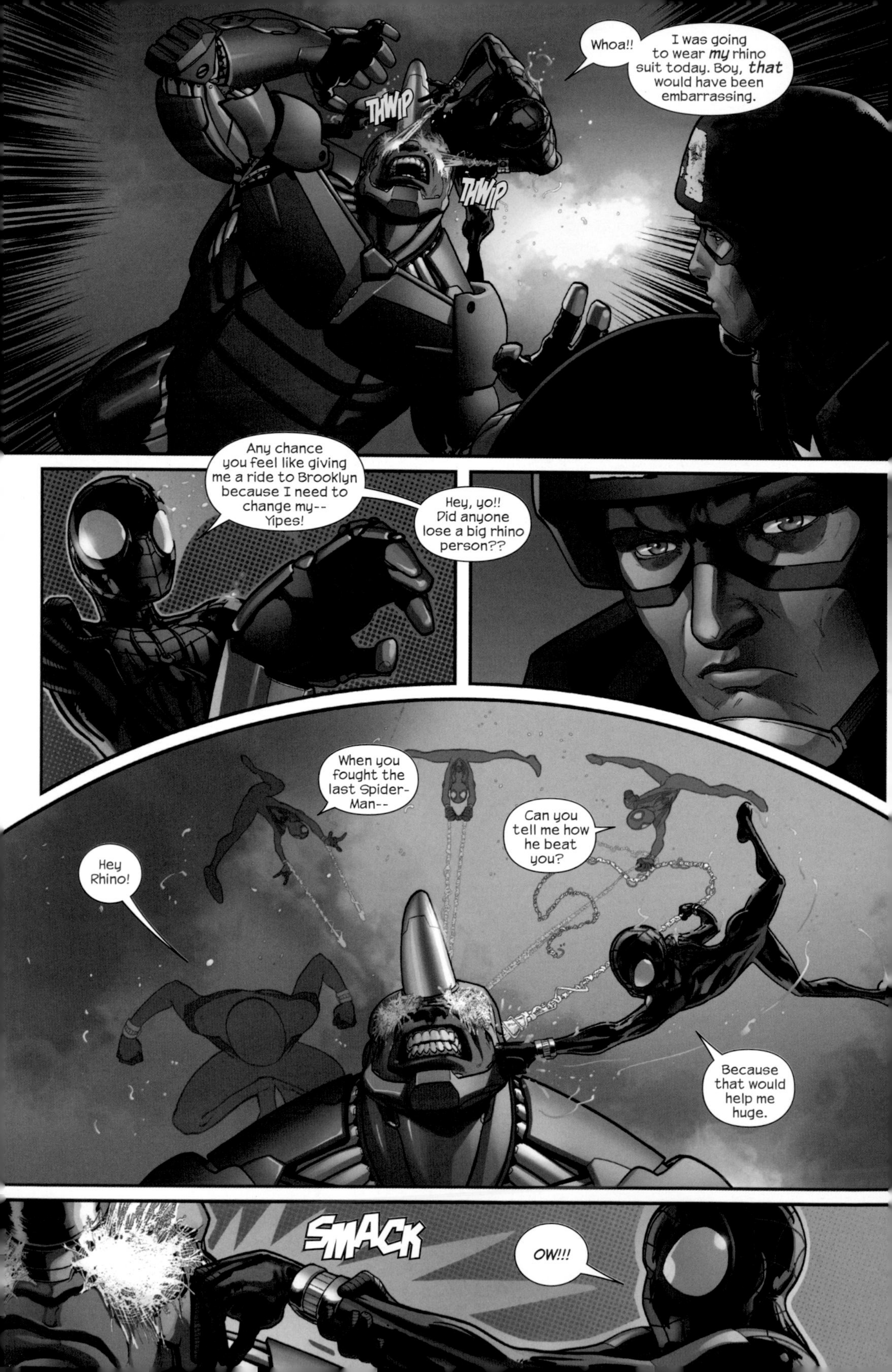
THWIP
THWIP
Whoa!!
I was going to wear *my* rhino suit today. Boy, *that* would have been embarrassing.
Any chance you feel like giving me a ride to Brooklyn because I need to change my-- Yipes!
Hey, yo!! Did anyone lose a big rhino person??
When you fought the last Spider-Man--
Can you tell me how he beat you?
Hey Rhino!
Because that would help me huge.
SMACK
OW!!!

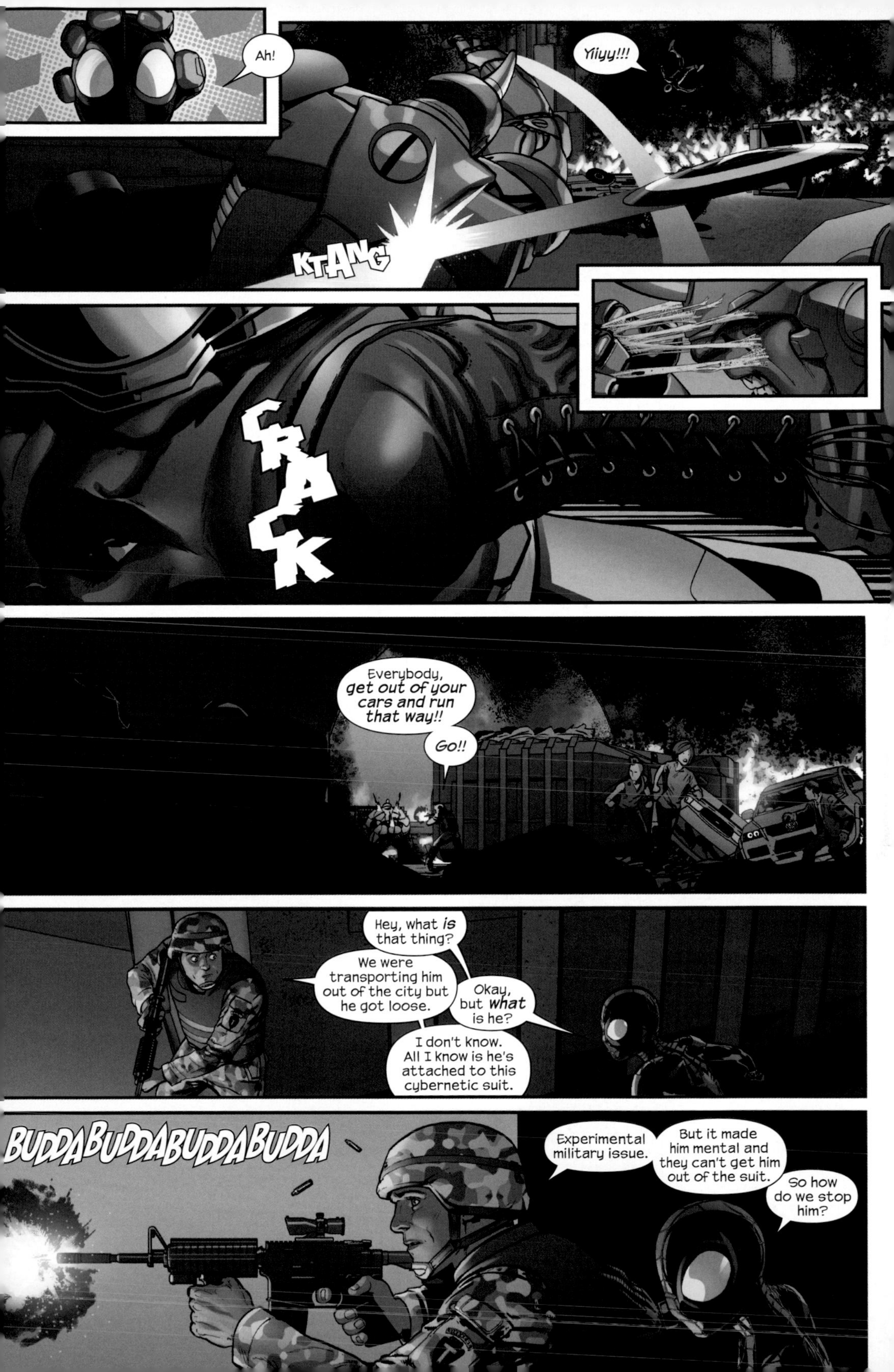
Ah!
Yiiyy!!!
KTANG
CRACK
Everybody, get out of your cars and run that way!!
Go!!
Hey, what is that thing?
We were transporting him out of the city but he got loose.
Okay, but what is he?
I don't know. All I know is he's attached to this cybernetic suit.
BUDDABUDDABUDDABUDDA
Experimental military issue.
But it made him mental and they can't get him out of the suit.
So how do we stop him?

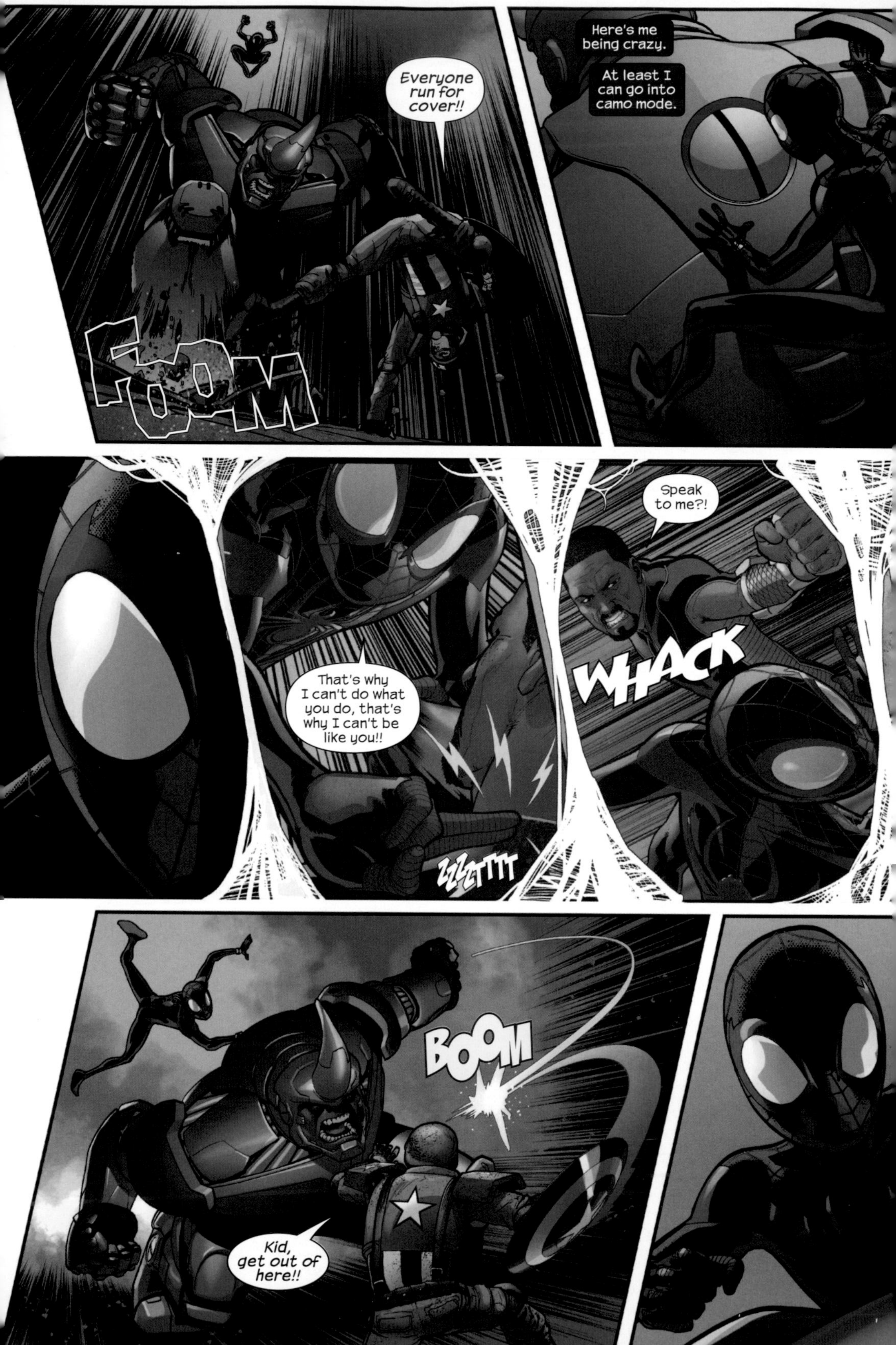
Everyone run for cover!!
FOOM
Here's me being crazy.
At least I can go into camo mode.
That's why I can't do what you do, that's why I can't be like you!!
ZZZZTTTT
Speak to me?!
WHACK
BOOM
Kid, get out of here!!

But the Army guy said he had a control panel and-- yep, there it is.

Maybe some of my venom blast, which is what I'm now going to call it, can do the--

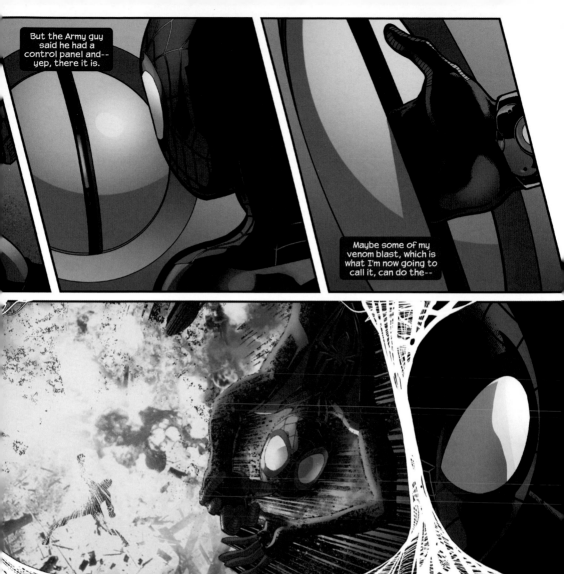

ZZTTTT

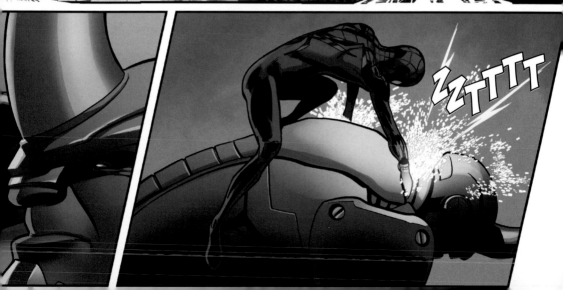

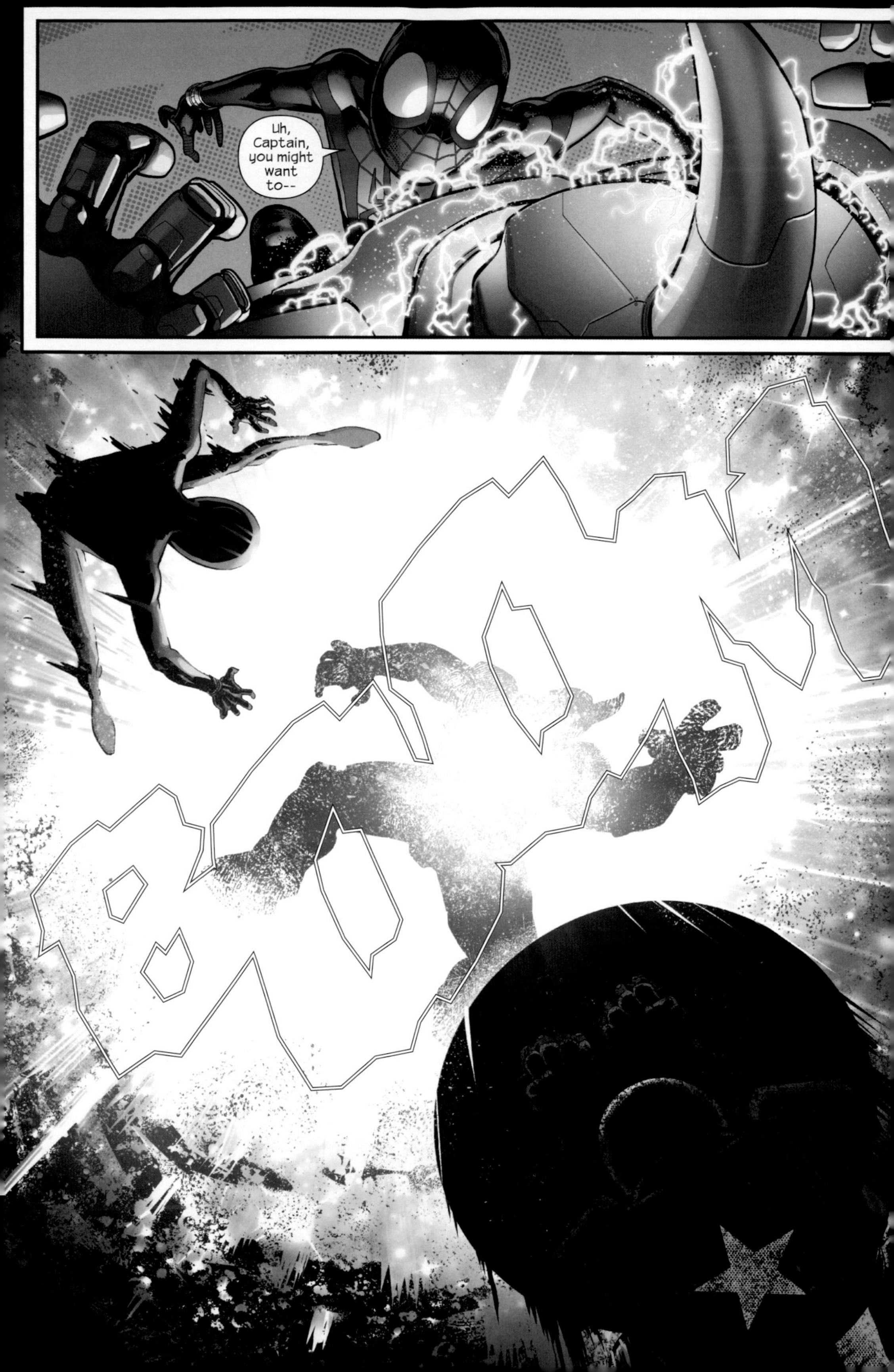
Uh, Captain, you might want to--
BOOM

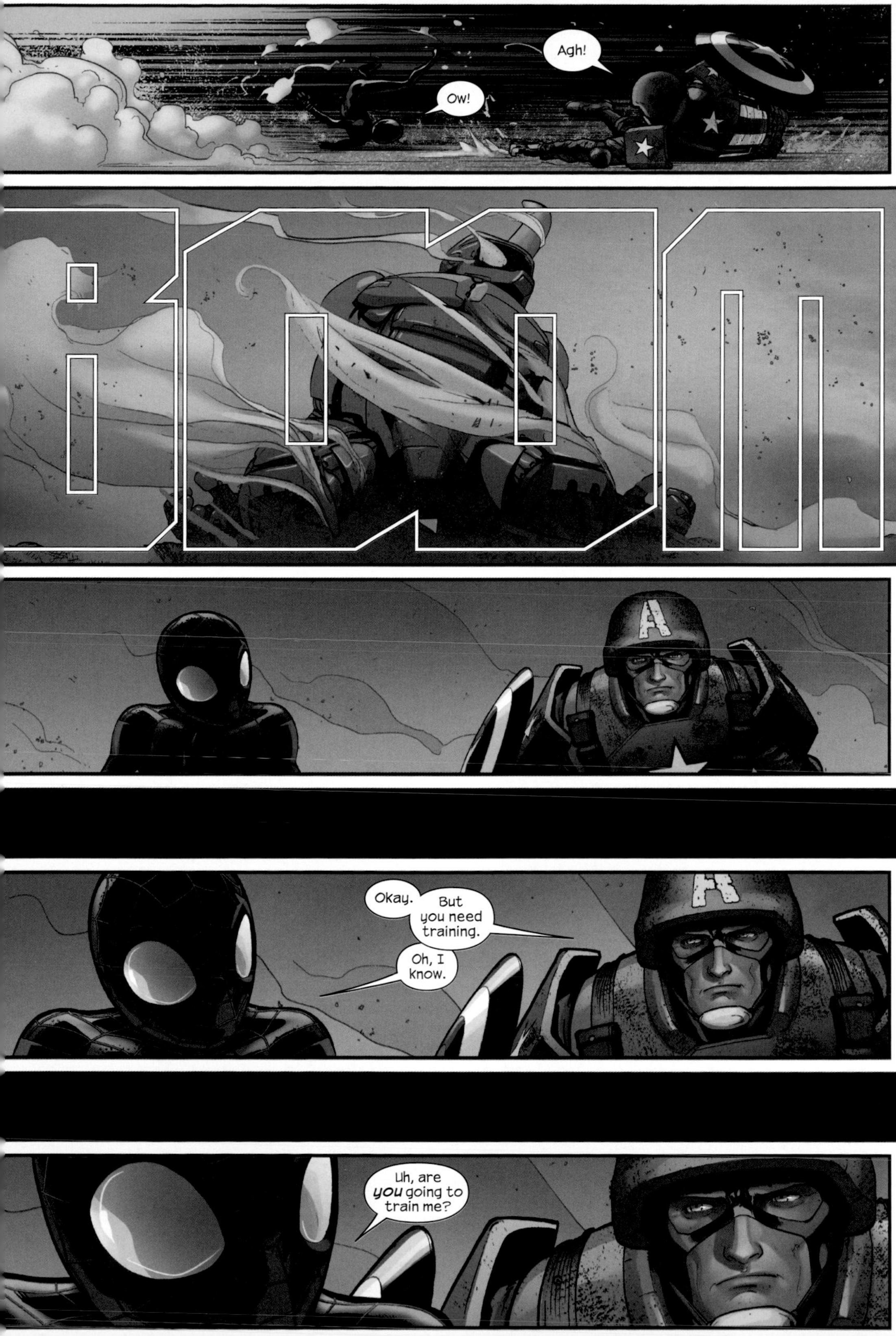
Agh!
Ow!
BOOM
Okay.
But you need training.
Oh, I know.
Uh, are *you* going to train me?

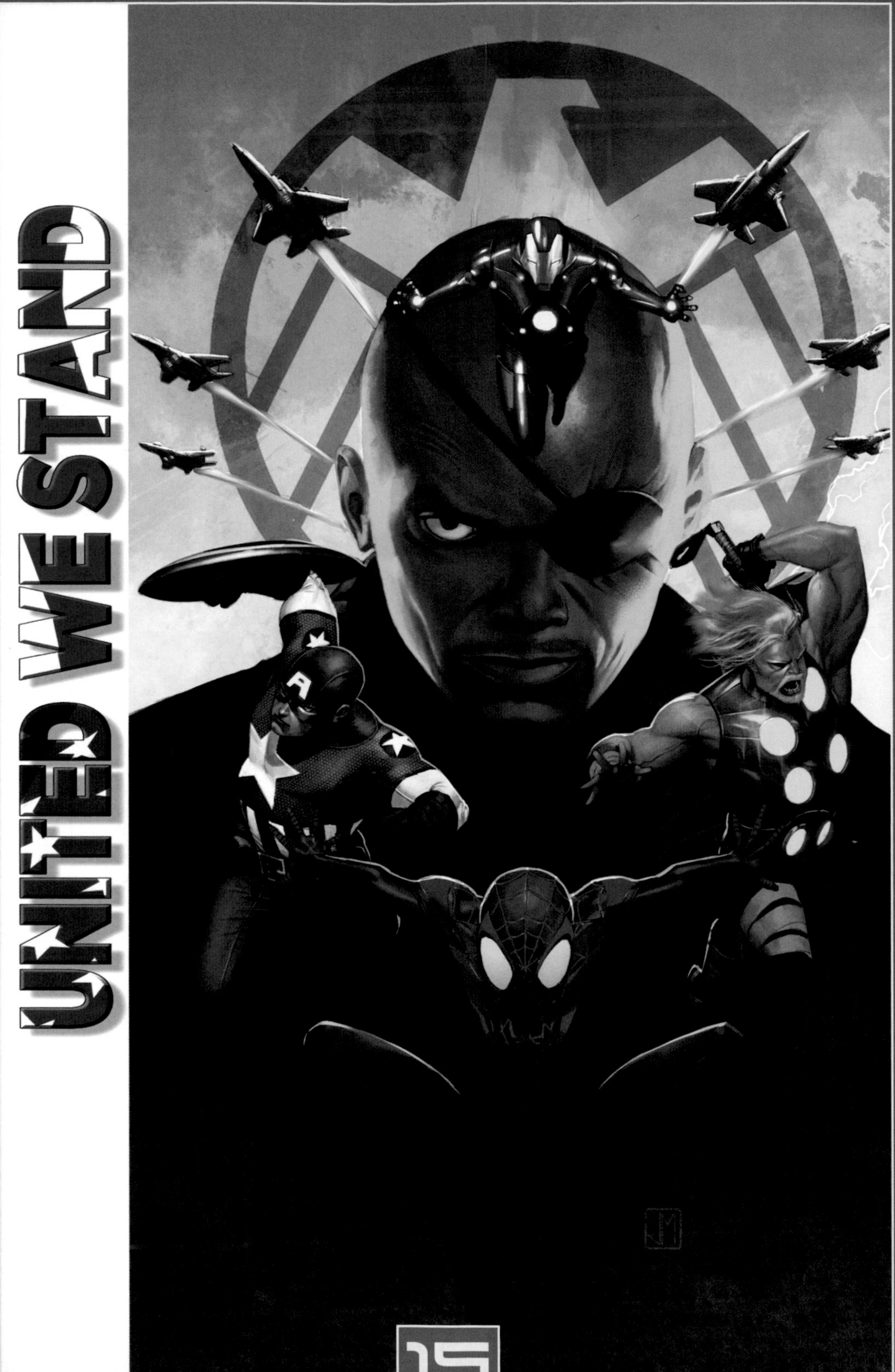
UNITED WE STAND
15

S.H.I.E.L.D. SITUATION MAP:

[Anti-government militia hot spots]

Montana, N. Dakota, S. Dakota, Wyoming, Arizona, New Mexico, N. Carolina, S. Carolina, Georgia, Idaho

[Eastern seaboard control zone]

New England, New York, New Jersey, Delaware, Washington D.C., Maryland, Virginia, Pennsylvania

secured by National Guard under emergency powers committee

[the West Coast]

California, Oregon, Washington

status unknown

[Great Lakes states]

Minnesota, Wisconsin, Michigan, Illinois, Indiana, Ohio

status unknown

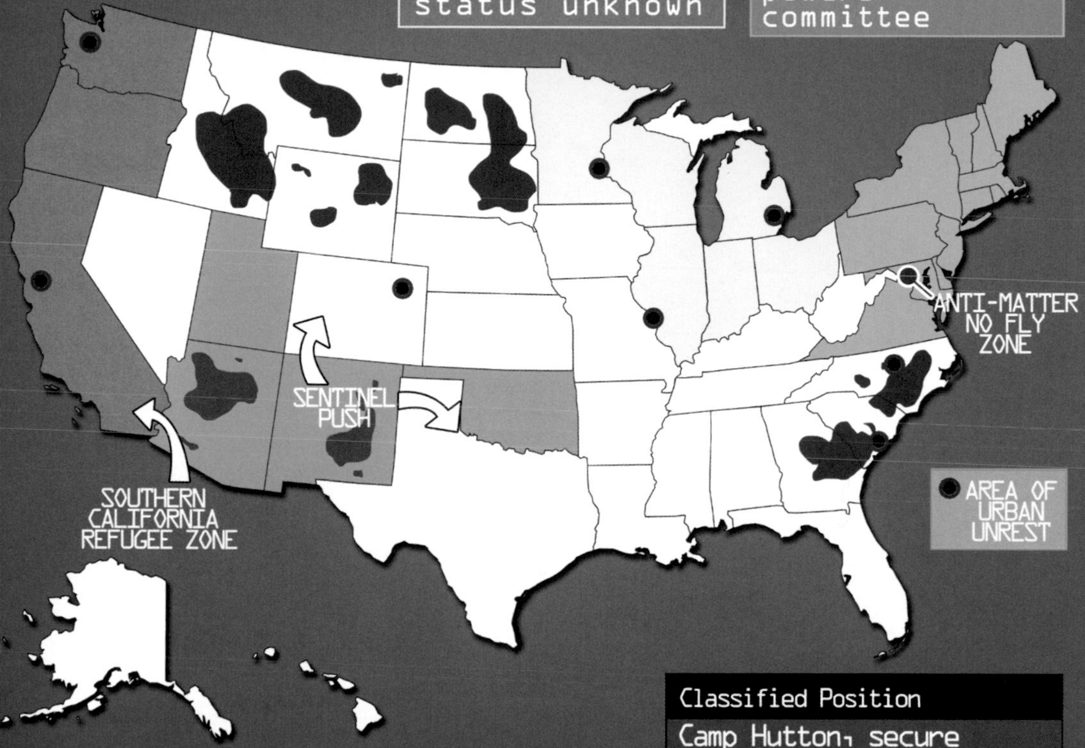
SENTINEL PUSH
SOUTHERN CALIFORNIA REFUGEE ZONE
ANTI-MATTER NO FLY ZONE
AREA OF URBAN UNREST

Classified Position

Camp Hutton, secure location of the President of the United States

[Sentinel-controlled no-man's-land]

New Mexico, Arizona, Utah, Oklahoma

abandoned by the U.S. government

ALL STATES SHOWN IN WHITE ARE U.S. GOVERNMENT-CONTROLLED ZONES

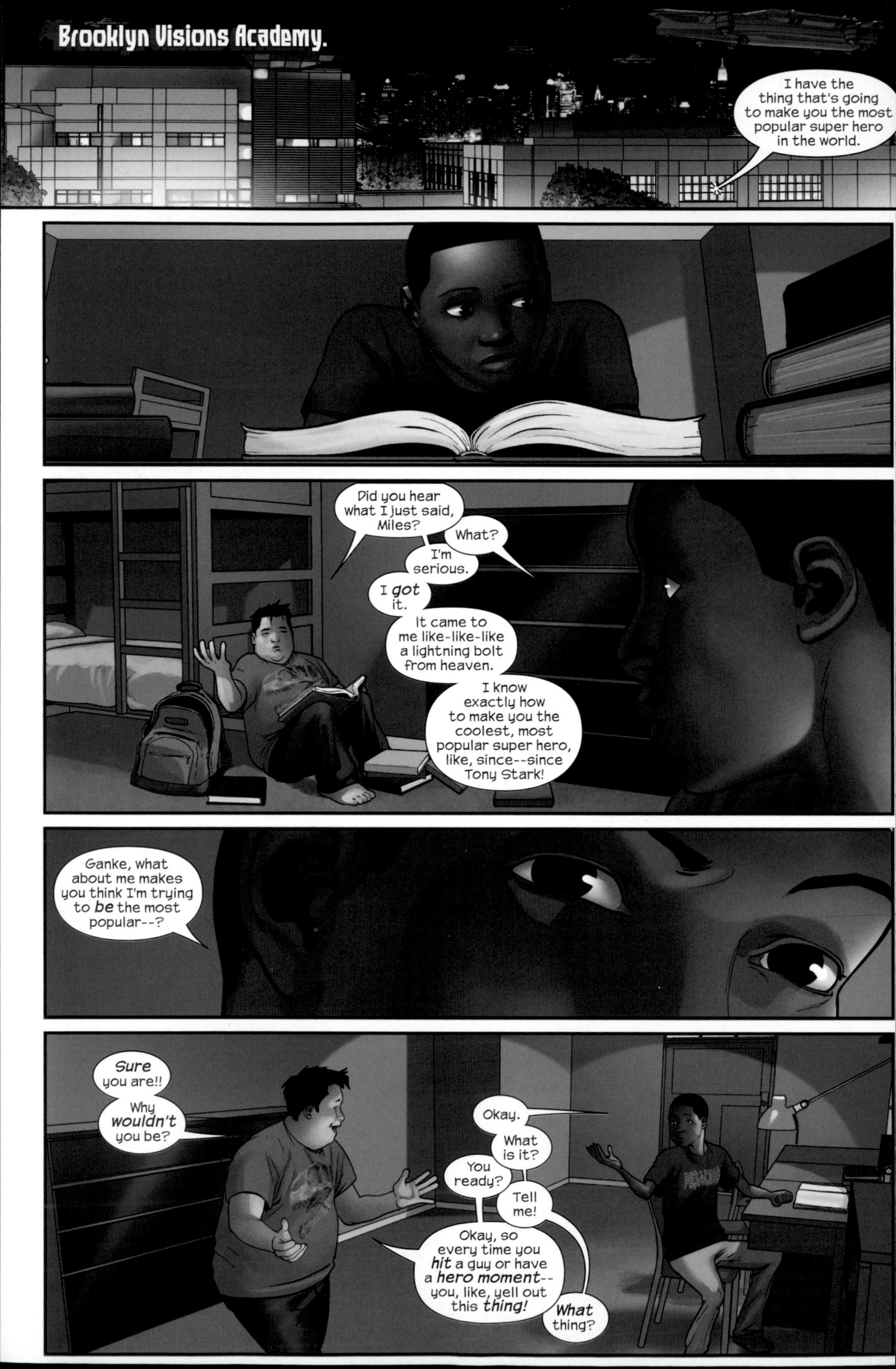
Brooklyn Visions Academy.
I have the thing that's going to make you the most popular super hero in the world.
Did you hear what I just said, Miles?
What?
I'm serious.
I *got* it.
It came to me like-like-like a lightning bolt from heaven.
I know exactly how to make you the coolest, most popular super hero, like, since--since Tony Stark!
Ganke, what about me makes you think I'm trying to *be* the most popular--?
Sure you are!!
Why *wouldn't* you be?
Okay.
What is it?
You ready?
Tell me!
Okay, so every time you *hit* a guy or have a *hero moment*--you, like, yell out this *thing!*
What thing?

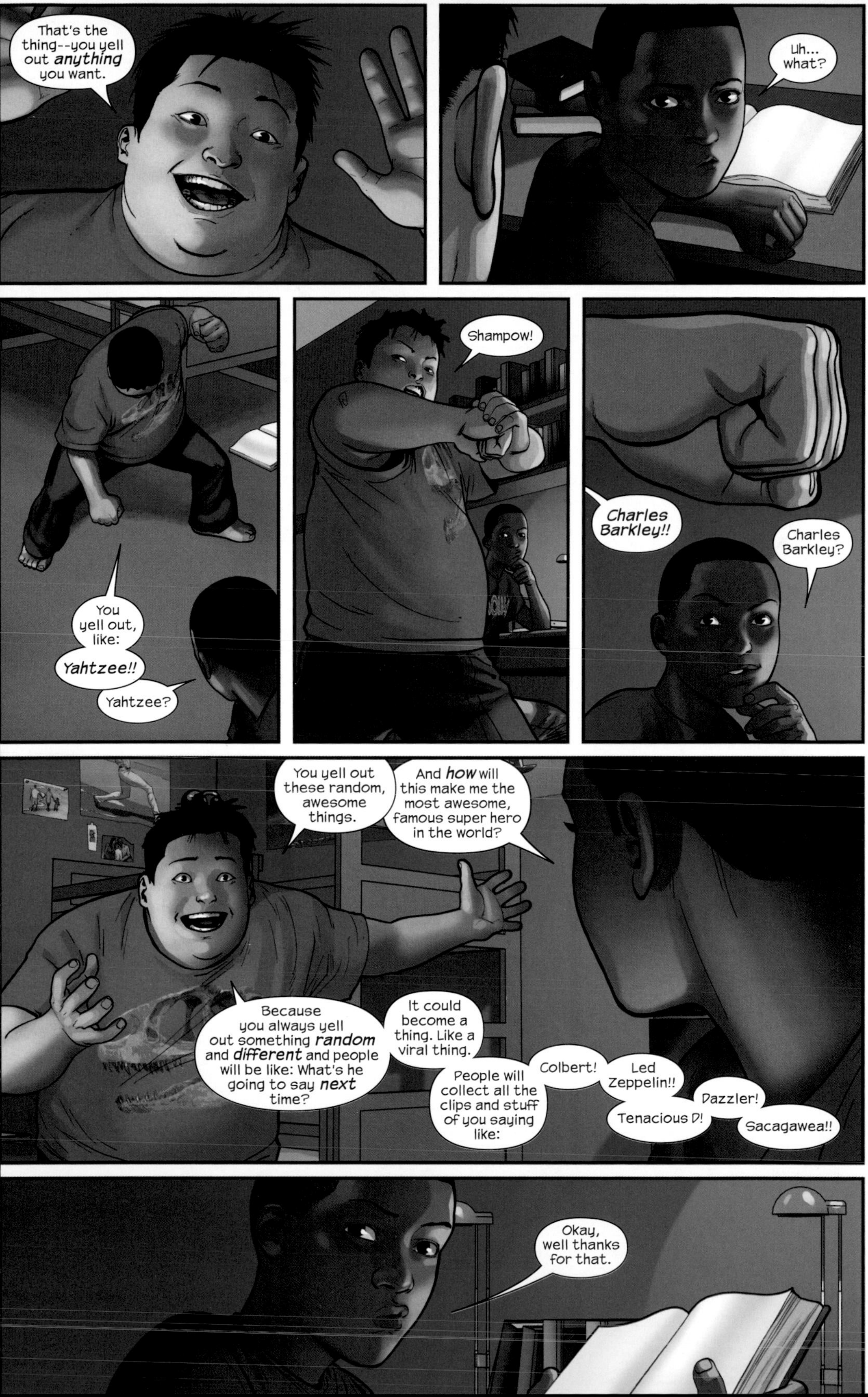
That's the thing--you yell out *anything* you want.
Uh... what?
You yell out, like:
Yahtzee!!
Yahtzee?
Shampow!
Charles Barkley!!
Charles Barkley?
You yell out these random, awesome things.
And *how* will this make me the most awesome, famous super hero in the world?
Because you always yell out something *random* and *different* and people will be like: What's he going to say *next* time?
It could become a thing. Like a viral thing.
People will collect all the clips and stuff of you saying like:
Colbert!
Led Zeppelin!!
Tenacious D!
Dazzler!
Sacagawea!!
Okay, well thanks for that.

James Brown!! Roman-burger!! Philip Seymour Hoffman!

Study!

No, see, that's not a good one. You need to be so random that people couldn't even *guess* what you were going to--

Study!!

I told you we're not going to study until you show them to me.

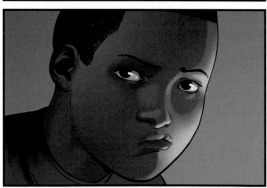

Okay.
Lock the door.

Wow. Right?

The web shooters. And his aunt just *gave* them to you? Yup.

And these were *his*? These were the actual ones *he* wore?

And he *invented* them.

How do you do *that*?

I think he might have been some kind of genius.

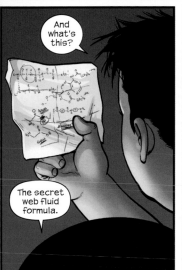

And what's this?

The secret web fluid formula.

So we have to make more?

When this runs out.

Uh-oh.

I was hoping that's where you would come in.

Me?

You're the smart one.

I mean, I--I don't--

I can't!

If you can make a Death Star out of Legos using your own designs...

Yeah.

But-but-but chemistry.

Oops.

Hey!

Hey, why won't this door open?!

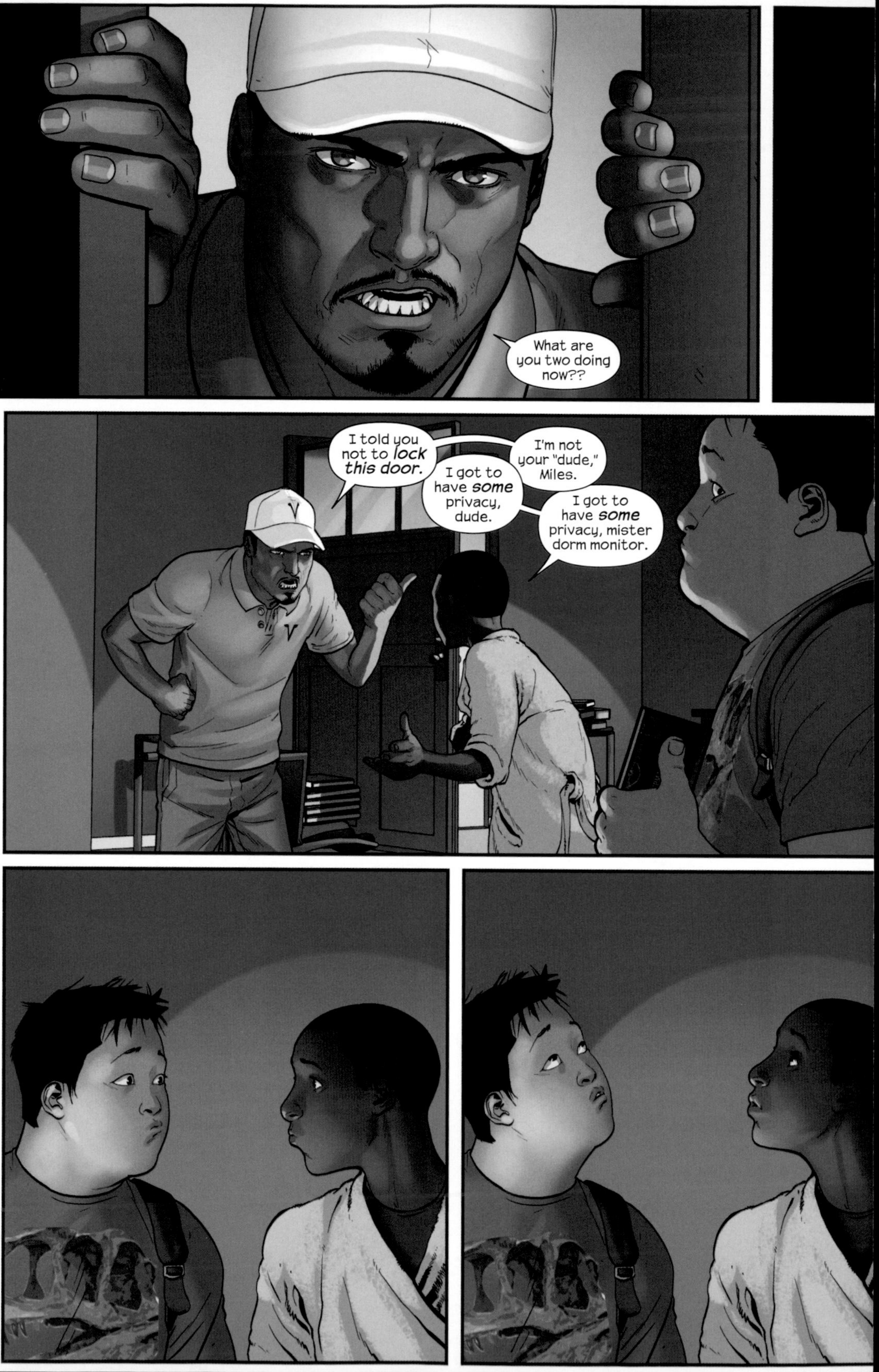

What are you two doing now??
I told you not to *lock this door.*
I got to have *some* privacy, dude.
I'm not your "dude," Miles.
I got to have *some* privacy, mister dorm monitor.

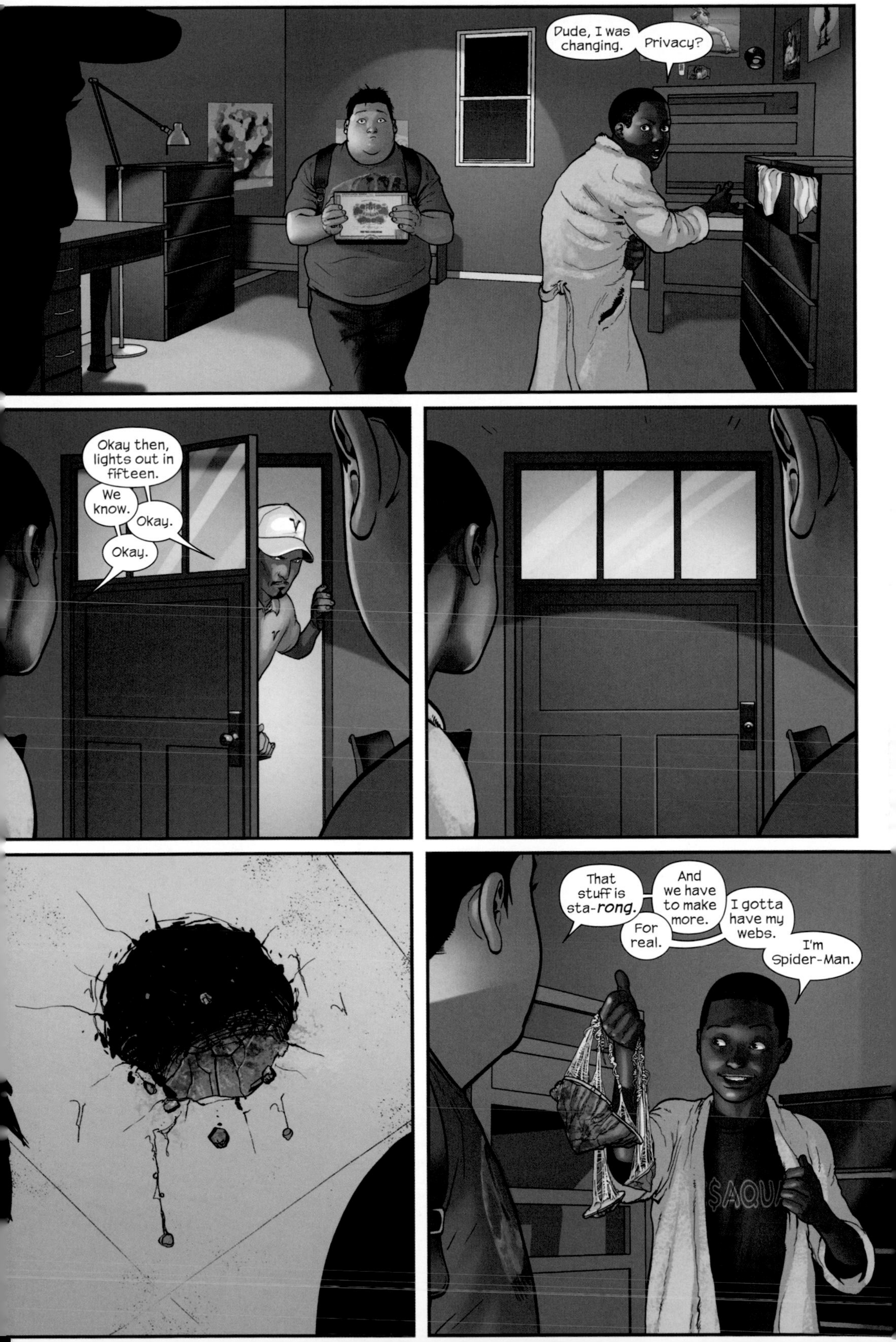
Dude, I was changing.
Privacy?
Okay then, lights out in fifteen.
We know.
Okay.
Okay.
That stuff is sta-***rong.***
And we have to make more.
For real.
I gotta have my webs.
I'm Spider-Man.

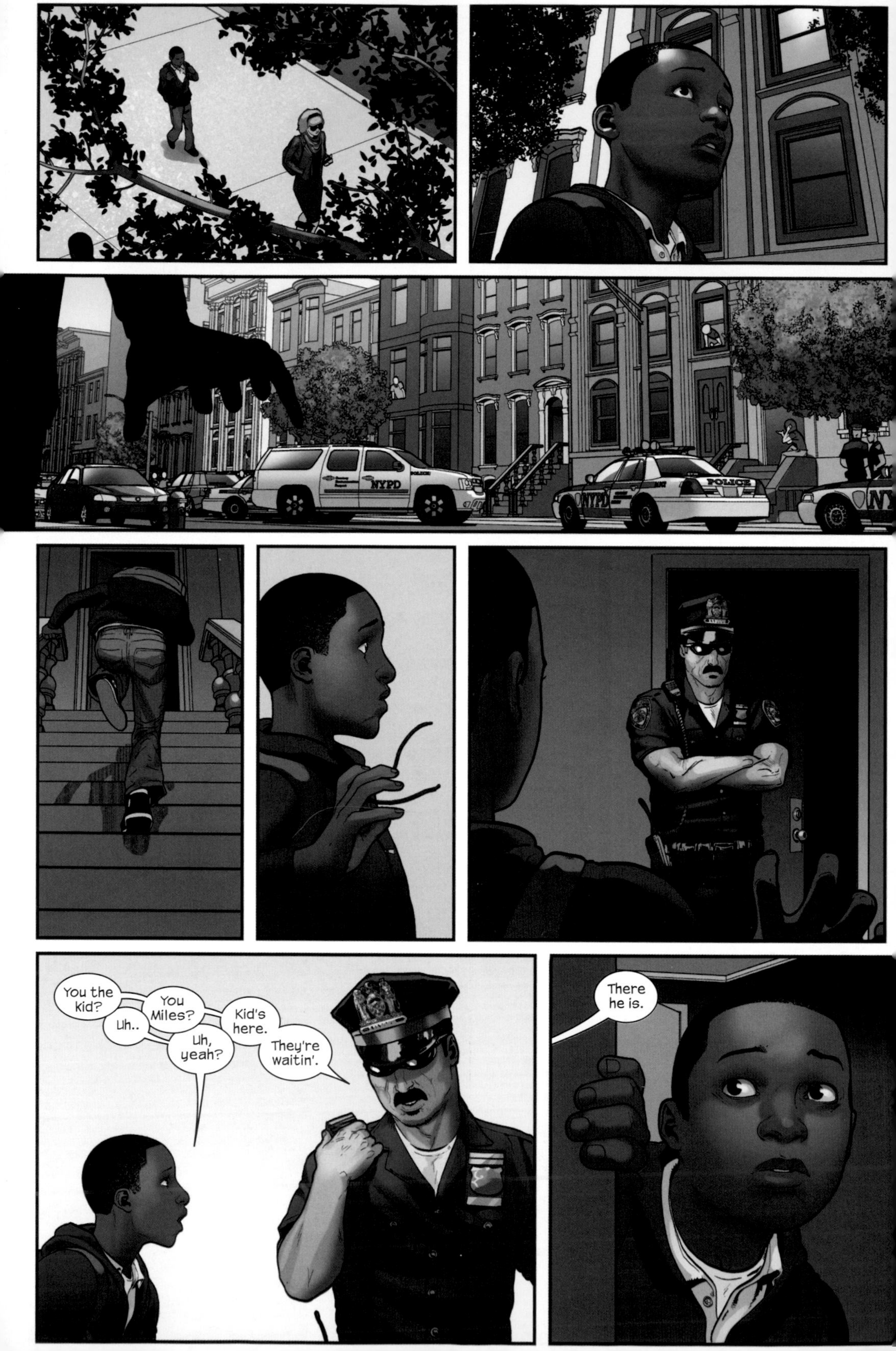
NYPD
POLICE
NYPD
POLICE
You the kid?
Uh..
You Miles?
Uh, yeah?
Kid's here.
They're waitin'.
There he is.

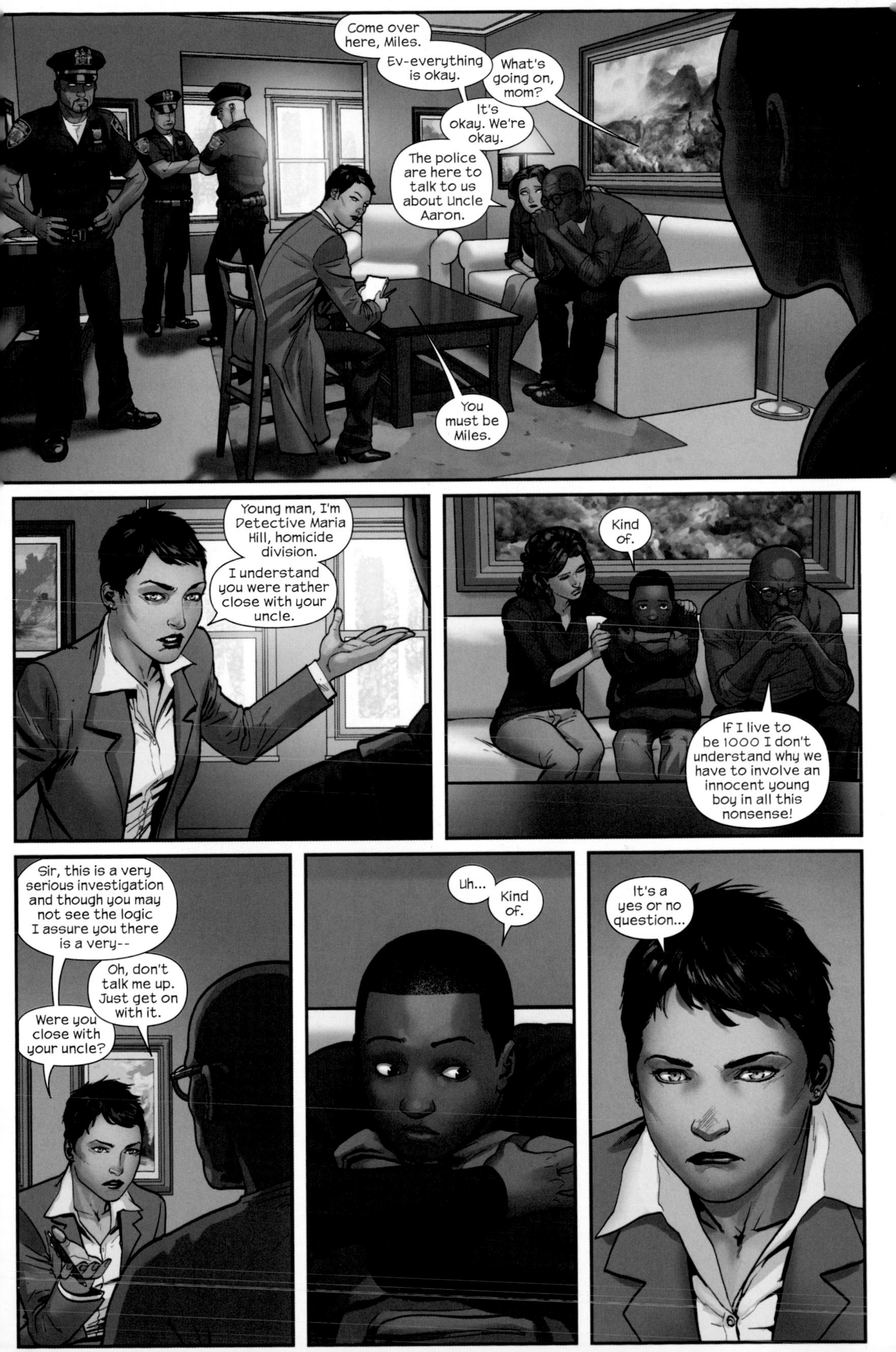
Come over here, Miles.
Ev-everything is okay.
What's going on, mom?
It's okay. We're okay.
The police are here to talk to us about Uncle Aaron.
You must be Miles.
Young man, I'm Detective Maria Hill, homicide division.
I understand you were rather close with your uncle.
Kind of.
If I live to be 1000 I don't understand why we have to involve an innocent young boy in all this nonsense!
Sir, this is a very serious investigation and though you may not see the logic I assure you there is a very--
Oh, don't talk me up. Just get on with it.
Were you close with your uncle?
Uh...
Kind of.
It's a yes or no question...

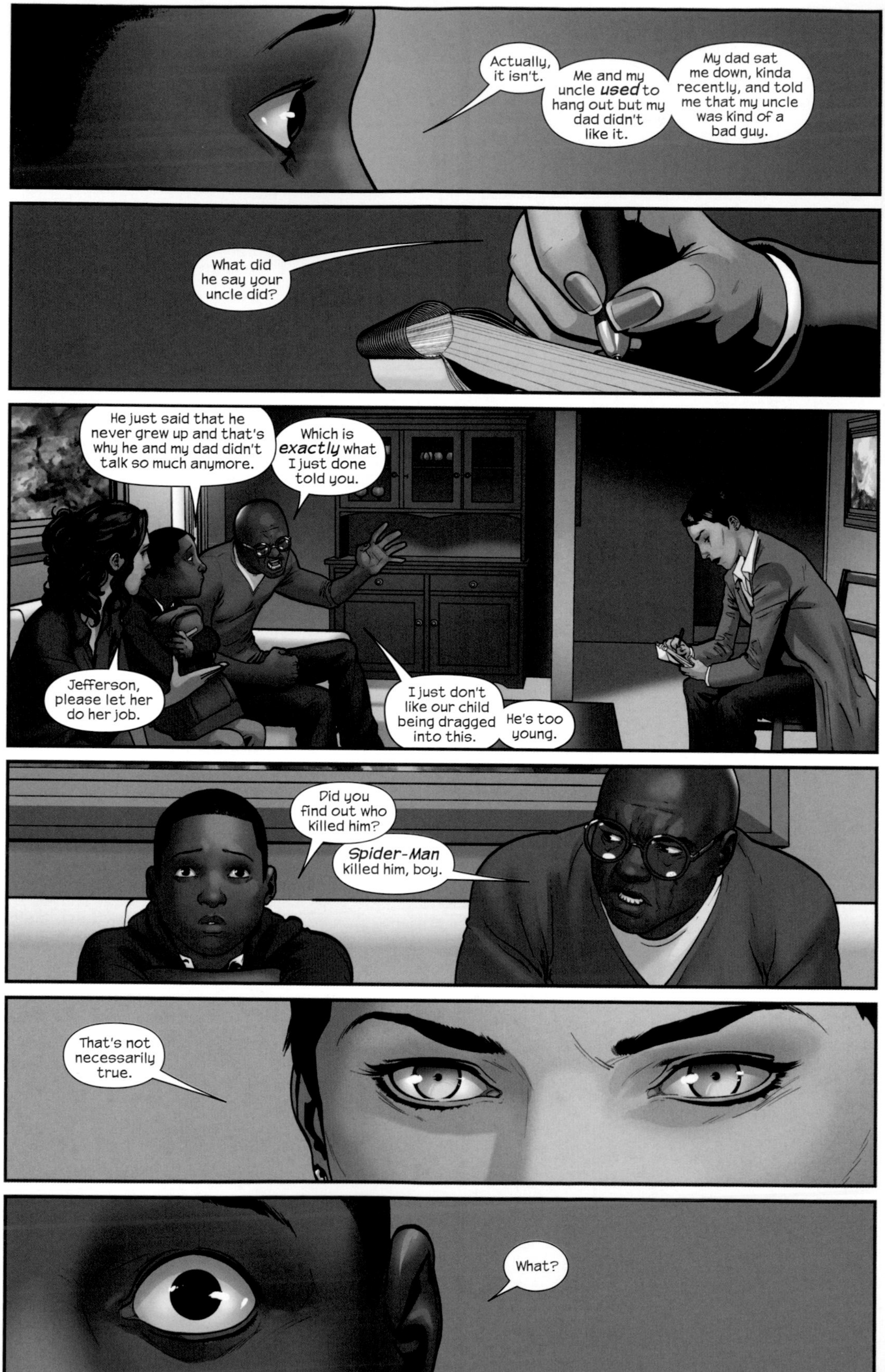
Actually, it isn't.
Me and my uncle *used* to hang out but my dad didn't like it.
My dad sat me down, kinda recently, and told me that my uncle was kind of a bad guy.
What did he say your uncle did?
He just said that he never grew up and that's why he and my dad didn't talk so much anymore.
Which is *exactly* what I just done told you.
Jefferson, please let her do her job.
I just don't like our child being dragged into this.
He's too young.
Did you find out who killed him?
Spider-Man killed him, boy.
That's not necessarily true.
What?

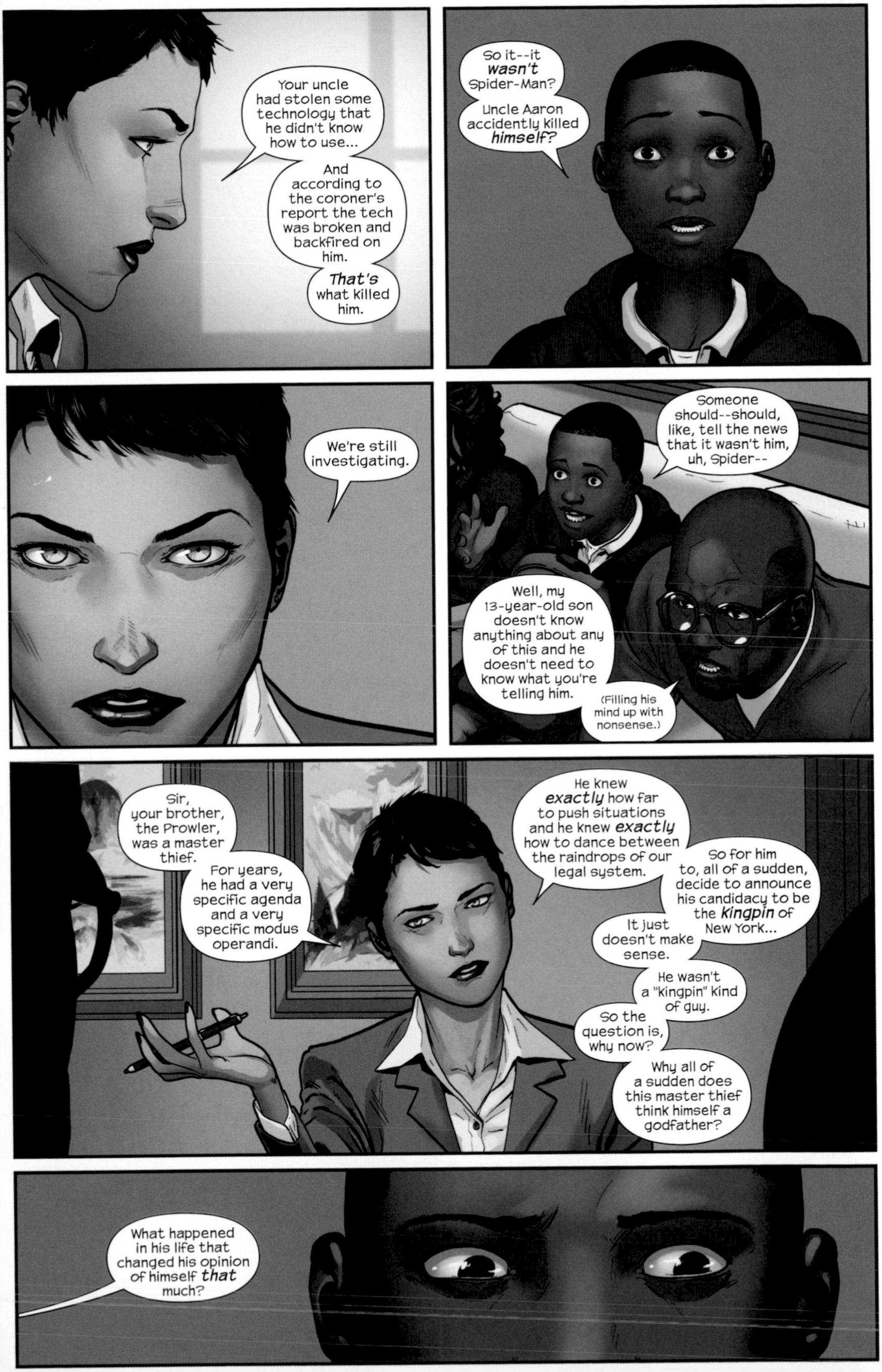
Your uncle had stolen some technology that he didn't know how to use...
And according to the coroner's report the tech was broken and backfired on him.
That's what killed him.
So it--it *wasn't* Spider-Man?
Uncle Aaron accidently killed *himself?*
We're still investigating.
Someone should--should, like, tell the news that it wasn't him, uh, Spider--
Well, my 13-year-old son doesn't know anything about any of this and he doesn't need to know what you're telling him.
(Filling his mind up with nonsense.)
Sir, your brother, the Prowler, was a master thief.
For years, he had a very specific agenda and a very specific modus operandi.
He knew *exactly* how far to push situations and he knew *exactly* how to dance between the raindrops of our legal system.
So for him to, all of a sudden, decide to announce his candidacy to be the *kingpin* of New York...
It just doesn't make sense.
He wasn't a "kingpin" kind of guy.
So the question is, why now?
Why all of a sudden does this master thief think himself a godfather?
What happened in his life that changed his opinion of himself *that* much?

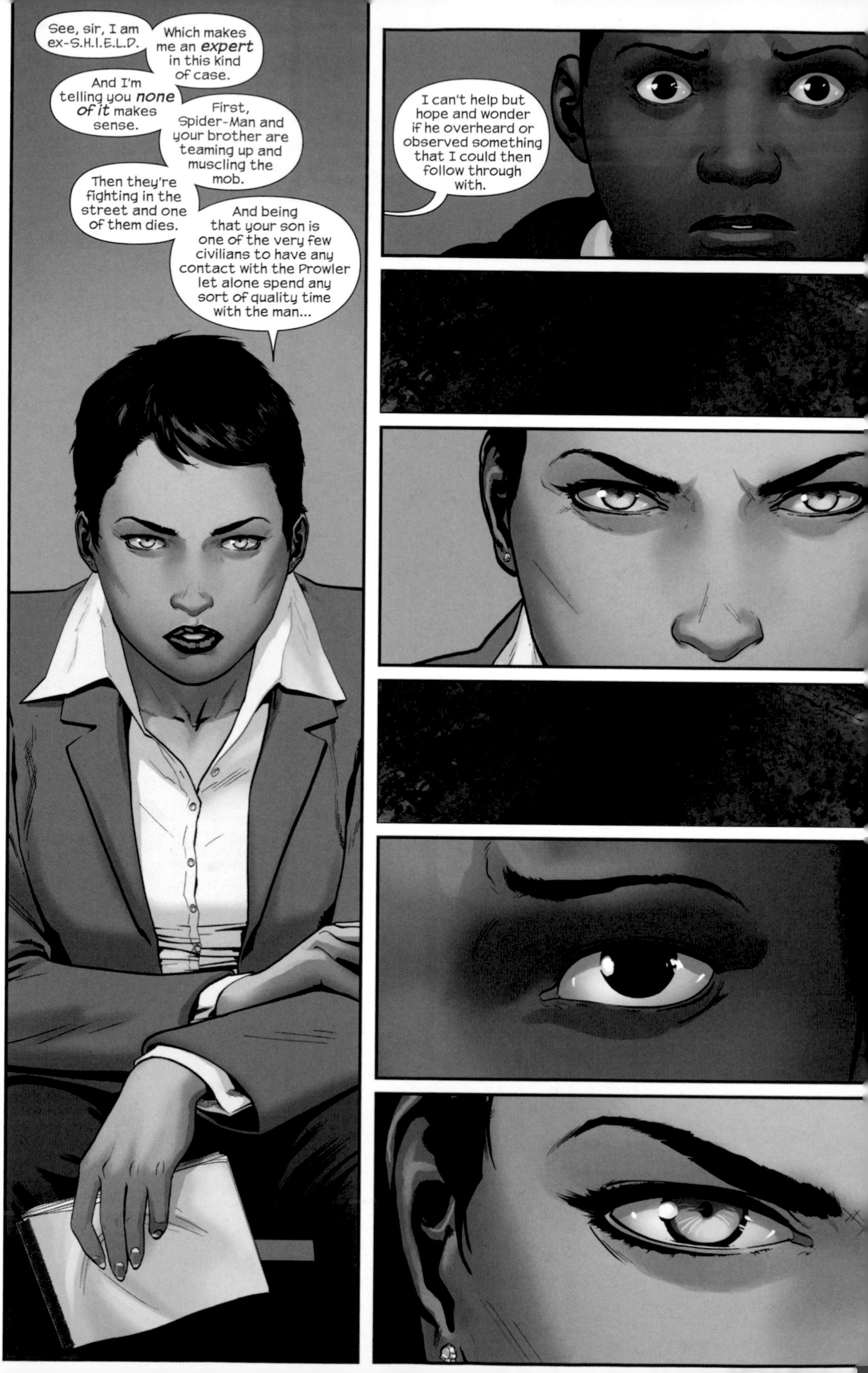
See, sir, I am ex-S.H.I.E.L.D.
Which makes me an *expert* in this kind of case.
And I'm telling you ***none of it*** makes sense.
First, Spider-Man and your brother are teaming up and muscling the mob.
Then they're fighting in the street and one of them dies.
And being that your son is one of the very few civilians to have any contact with the Prowler let alone spend any sort of quality time with the man...
I can't help but hope and wonder if he overheard or observed something that I could then follow through with.

So, Miles, did you see or hear anything?

Did your uncle say anything to you about anything?

You are... just... ...like me.

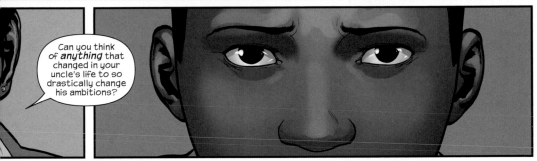

Can you think of *anything* that changed in your uncle's life to so drastically change his ambitions?

just... ...like me.

Uh, no, like I said... My dad told me not to hang around him anymore.

Well, I guess we're done here.

Again, I'm sorry for the intrusion.

It's just-- you get where I'm coming from.

You're the dad, I get it.

What's more important than your boy?

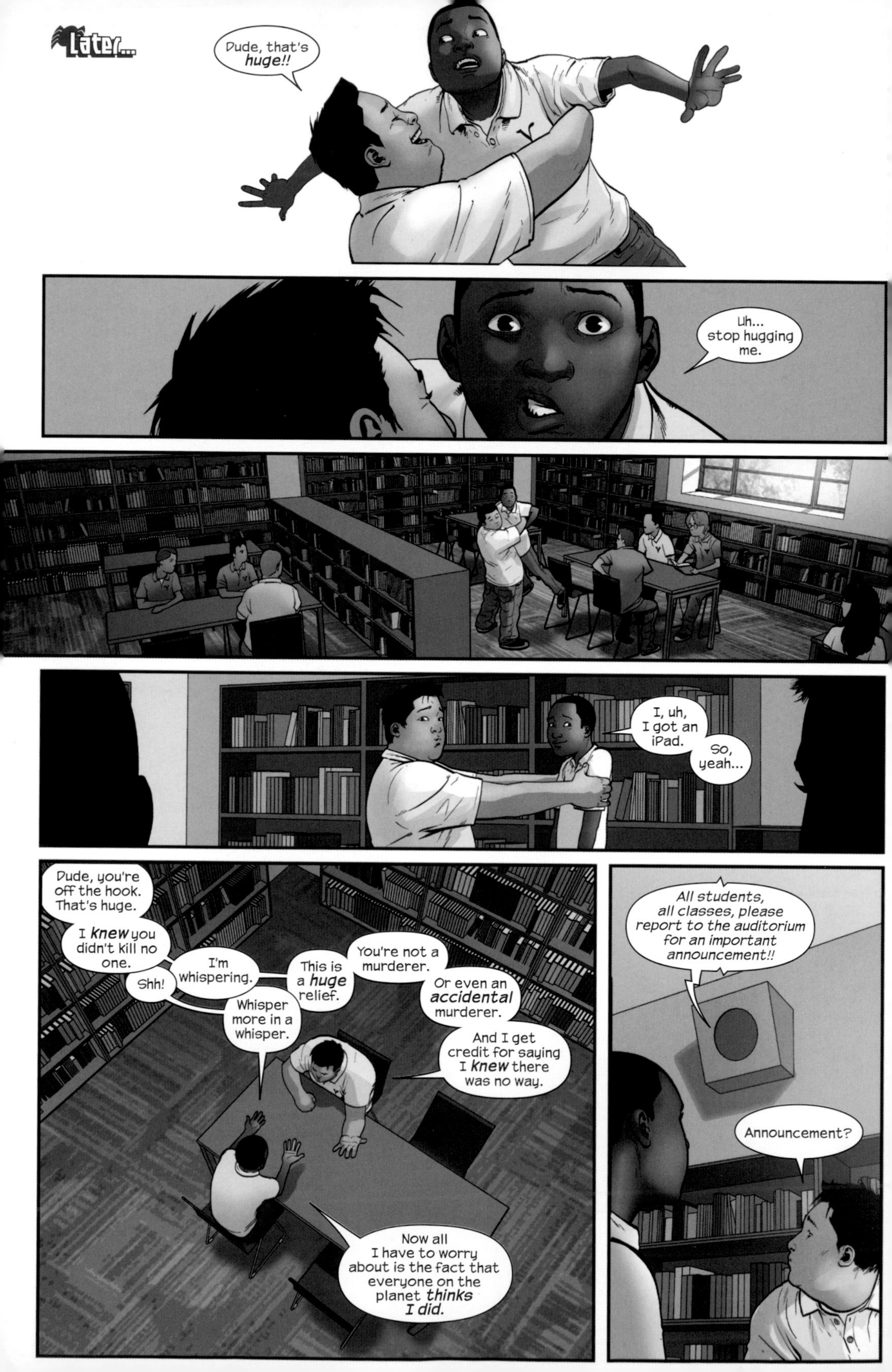
Later...
Dude, that's *huge!!*
Uh... stop hugging me.
I, uh, I got an iPad.
So, yeah...
Dude, you're off the hook. That's huge.
I *knew* you didn't kill no one.
Shh!
I'm whispering.
Whisper more in a whisper.
This is a *huge* relief.
You're not a murderer.
Or even an *accidental* murderer.
And I get credit for saying I *knew* there was no way.
Now all I have to worry about is the fact that everyone on the planet *thinks* *I did.*
All students, all classes, please report to the auditorium for an important announcement!!
Announcement?

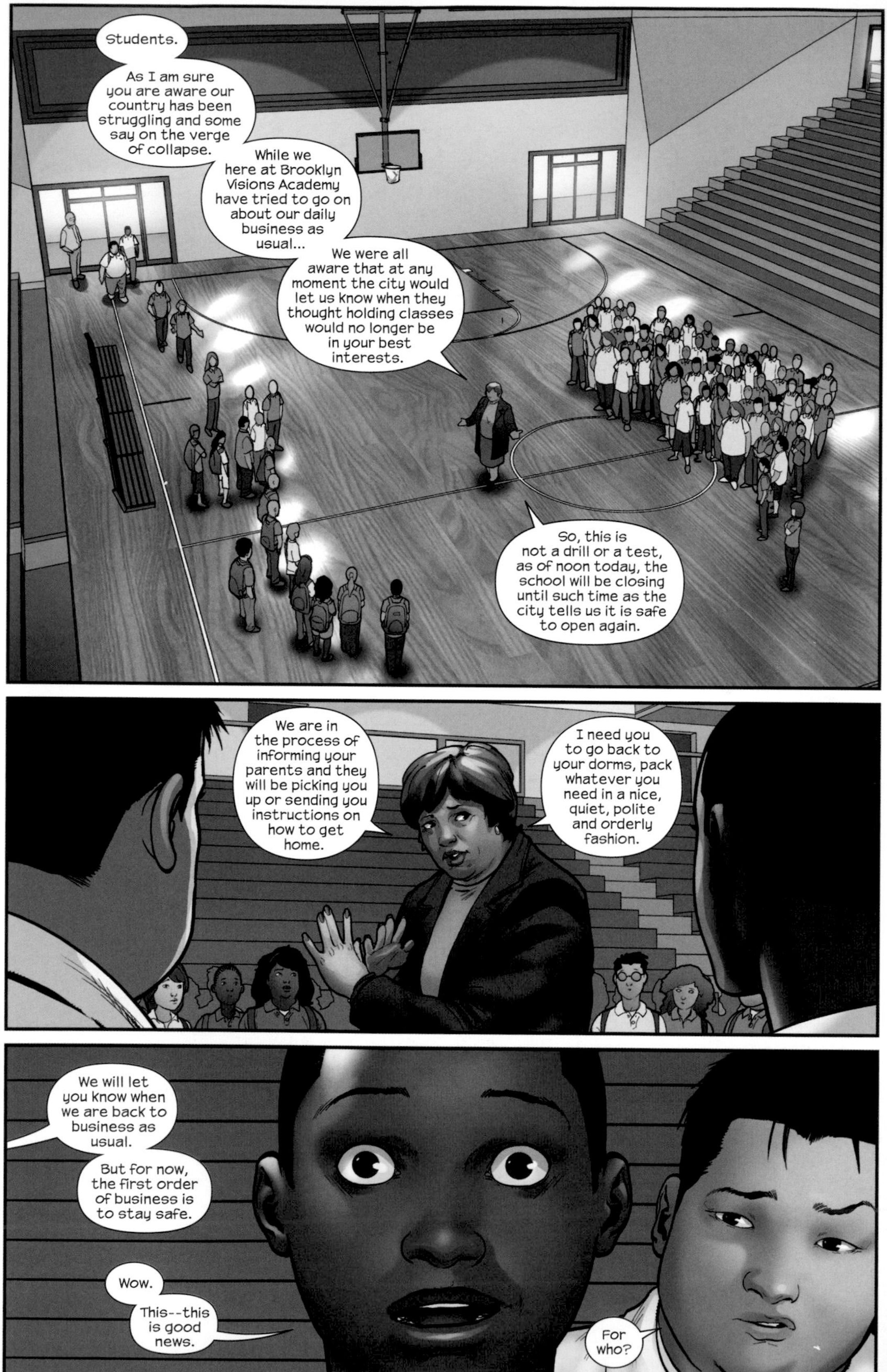
Students.
As I am sure you are aware our country has been struggling and some say on the verge of collapse.
While we here at Brooklyn Visions Academy have tried to go on about our daily business as usual...
We were all aware that at any moment the city would let us know when they thought holding classes would no longer be in your best interests.
So, this is not a drill or a test, as of noon today, the school will be closing until such time as the city tells us it is safe to open again.
We are in the process of informing your parents and they will be picking you up or sending you instructions on how to get home.
I need you to go back to your dorms, pack whatever you need in a nice, quiet, polite and orderly fashion.
We will let you know when we are back to business as usual.
But for now, the first order of business is to stay safe.
Wow.
This--this is good news.
For who?

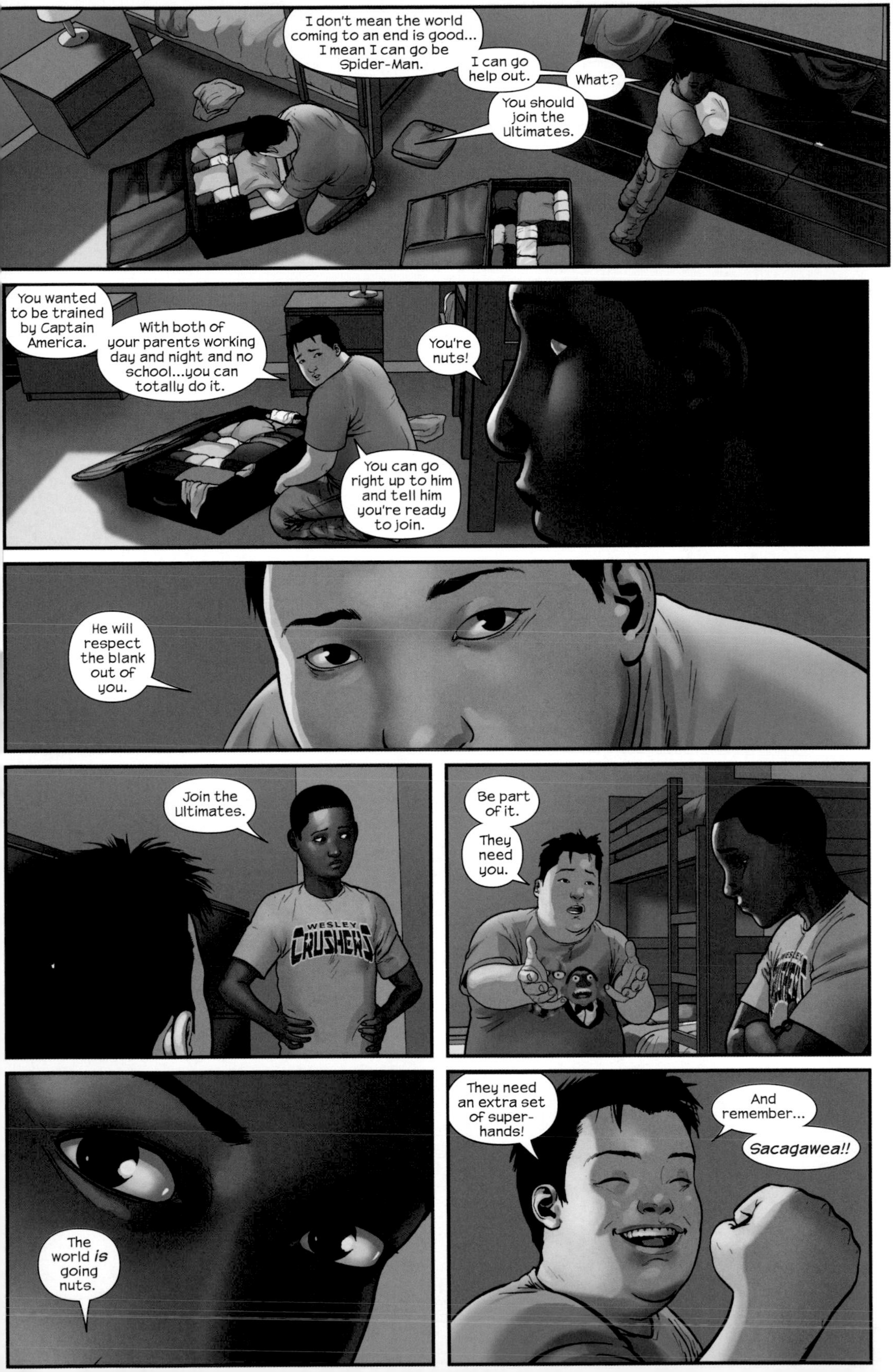
I don't mean the world coming to an end is good... I mean I can go be Spider-Man.
I can go help out.
What?
You should join the Ultimates.
You wanted to be trained by Captain America.
With both of your parents working day and night and no school...you can totally do it.
You're nuts!
You can go right up to him and tell him you're ready to join.
He will respect the blank out of you.
Join the Ultimates.
WESLEY CRUSHERS
Be part of it.
They need you.
They need an extra set of super-hands!
And remember...
Sacagawea!!
The world is going nuts.

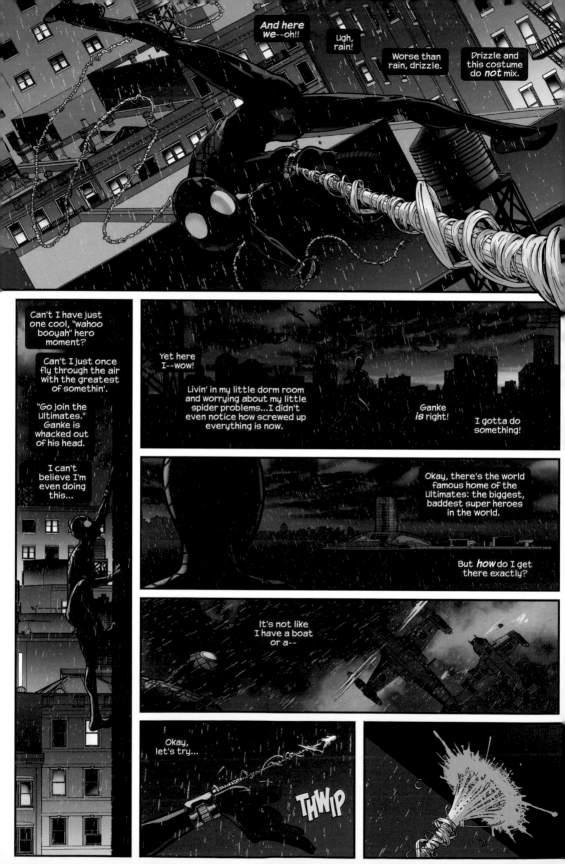

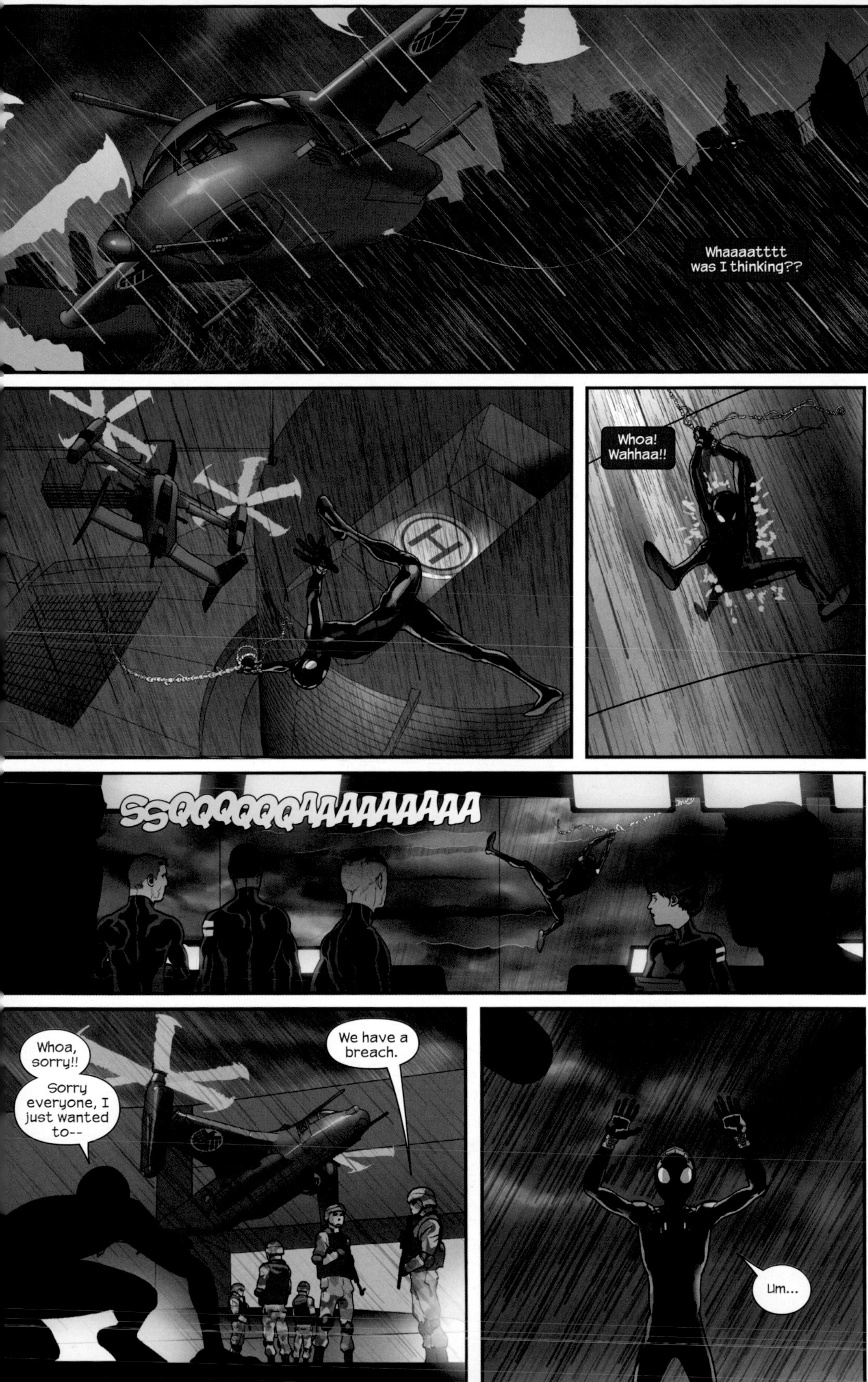
Whaaaatttt
was I thinking??
Whoa!
Wahhaa!!
SSQQQQQQAAAAAAAAA
Whoa,
sorry!!
Sorry
everyone, I
just wanted
to--
We have a
breach.
Um...

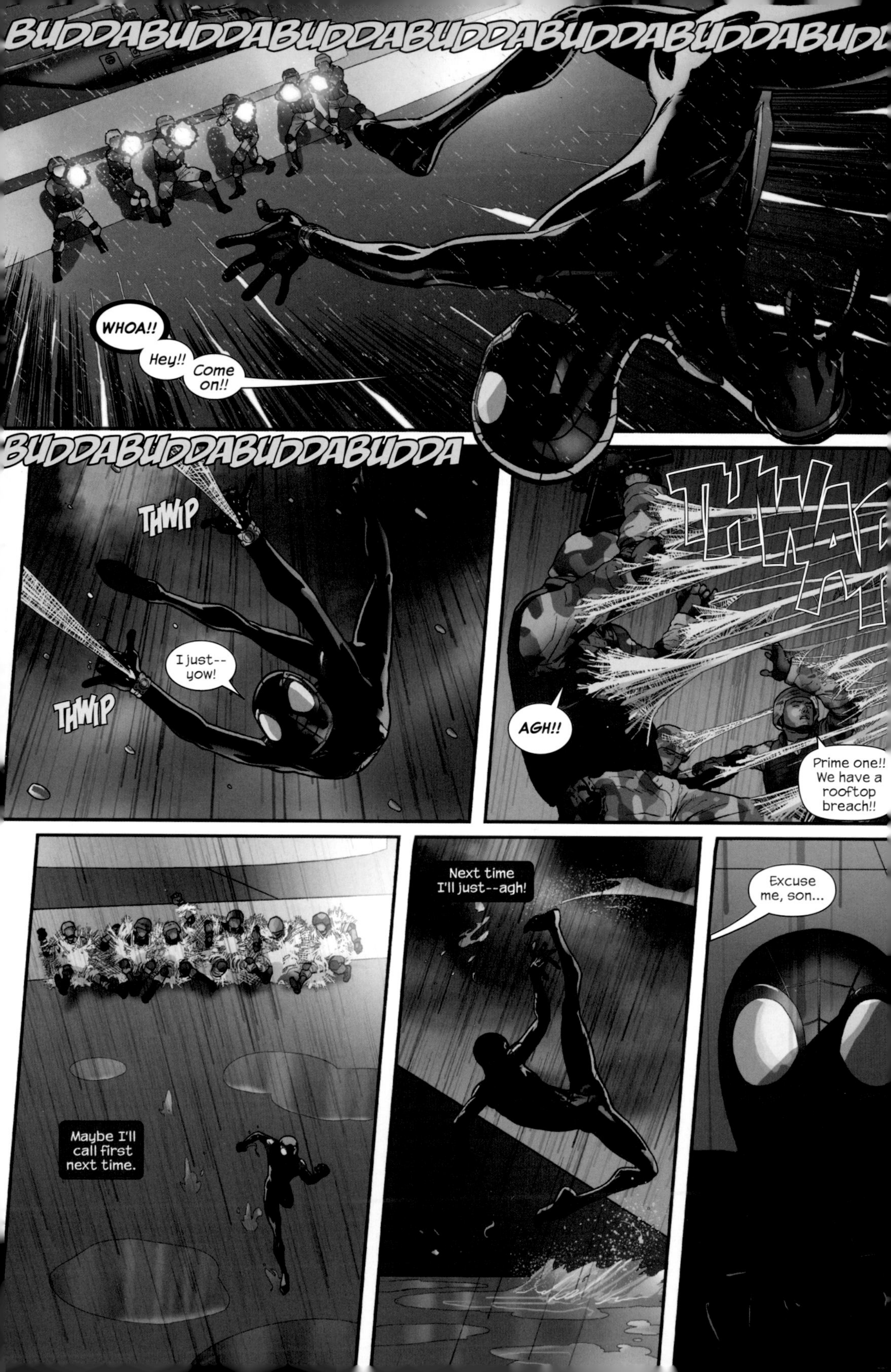
BUDDABUDDABUDDABUDDABUDDABUDDABUDD
WHOA!!
Hey!!
Come on!!
BUDDABUDDABUDDABUDDA
THWIP
I just-- yow!
THWIP
AGH!!
Prime one!! We have a rooftop breach!!
Maybe I'll call first next time.
Next time I'll just--agh!
Excuse me, son...

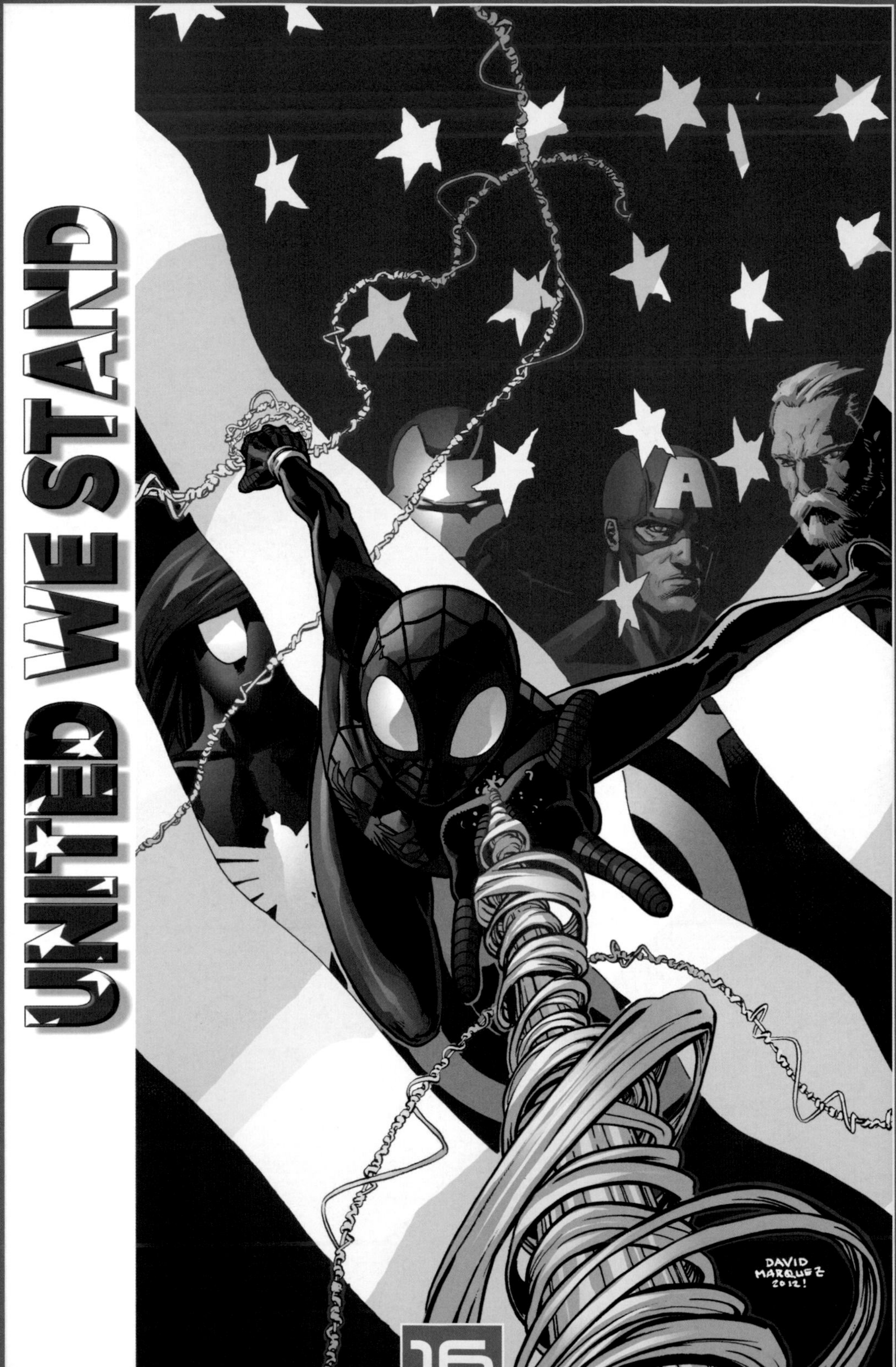
UNITED WE STAND
DAVID MARQUEZ 2012!
16

S.H.I.E.L.D. SITUATION MAP:

[Anti-government militia hot spots]

Idaho,Montana,
N.Dakota,S.Dakota,
Arizona,New Mexico,
N.Carolina,
S.Carolina,Georgia

[Eastern seaboard control zone]

New England,
New York,
New Jersey,
Delaware,
Washington, D.C.,
Maryland,
Pennsylvania,
Virginia

secured by
National Guard
under emergency
powers
committee

[The West Coast Nation]

California,Oregon,
Washington
Independent nation

Wyoming
status unknown

PROJECT
PEGASUS

ANTI-MATTER
NO FLY
ZONE

SENTINEL
PUSH

AREA OF
URBAN
UNREST

SOUTHERN
CALIFORNIA
REFUGEE ZONE

[Great Lakes Alliance]

Minnesota,
Wisconsin,
Michigan,
Illinois,
Indiana,Ohio

Independent
nation

[Sentinel-controlled no-man's-land]

New Mexico,Arizona,
Utah,Oklahoma
abandoned by the
U.S. government

ALL STATES
SHOWN IN WHITE
ARE U.S. GOVERNMENT-
CONTROLLED ZONES

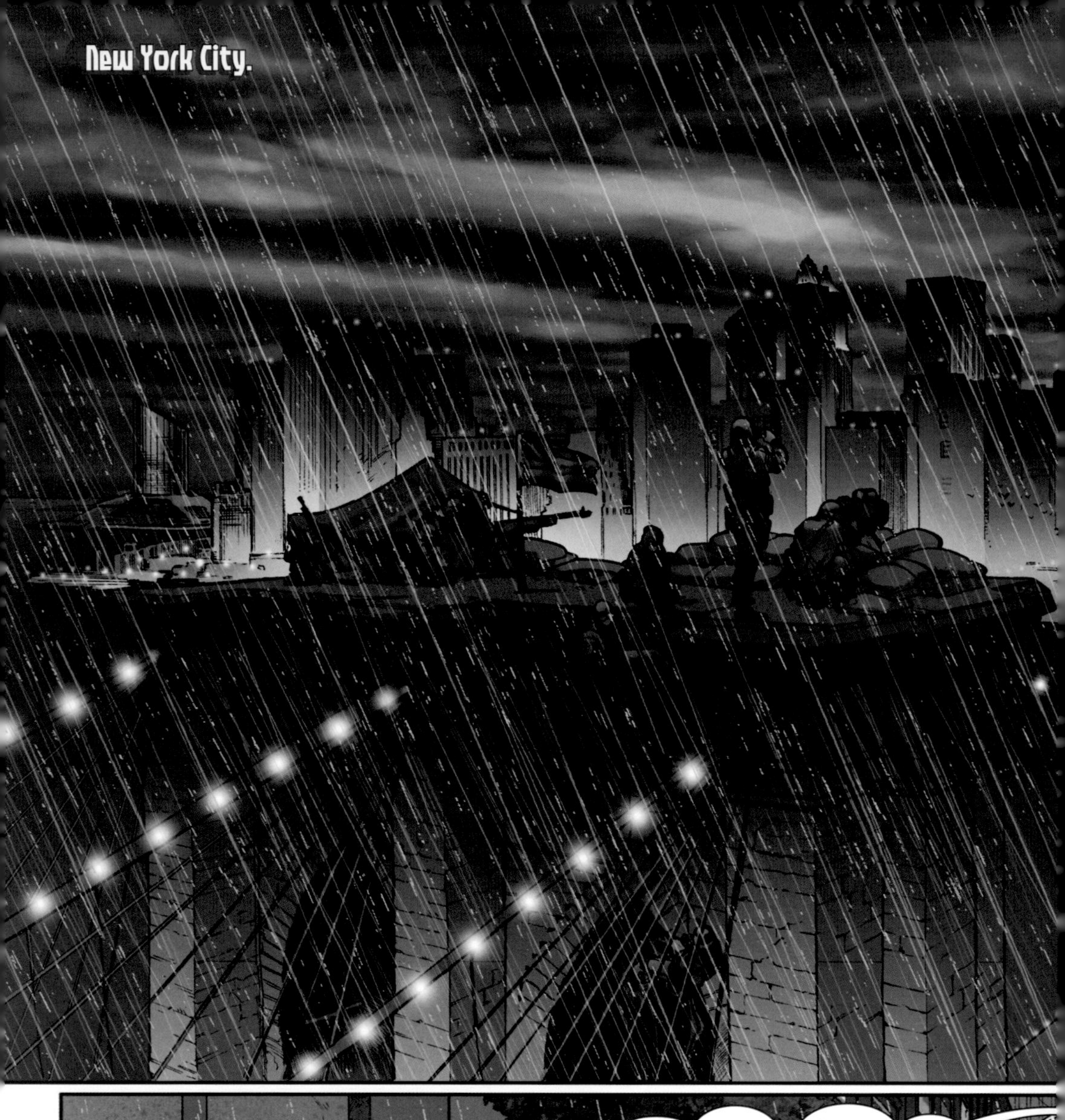
New York City.

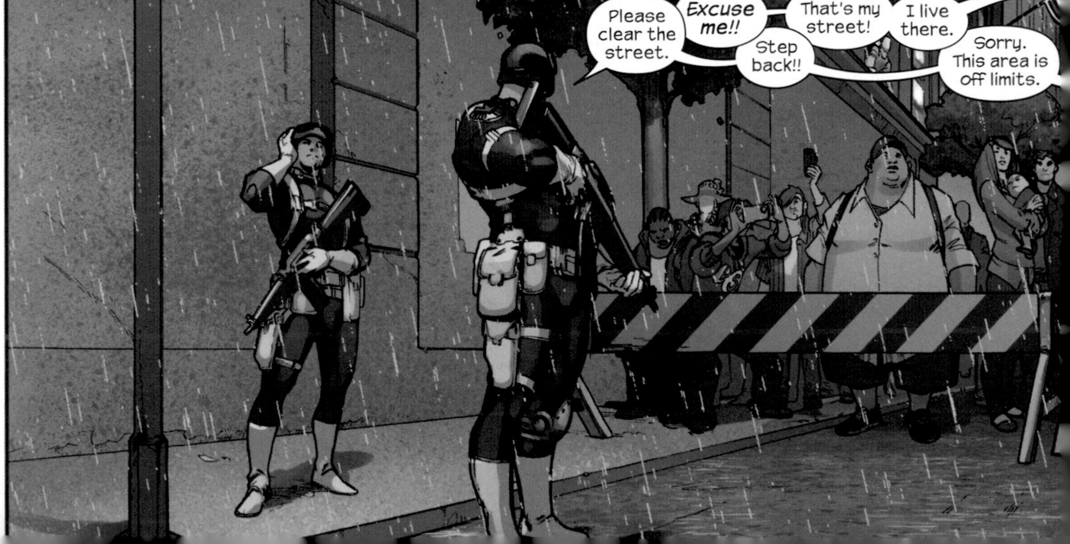
Please clear the street.
Excuse me!!
Step back!!
That's my street!
I live there.
Sorry. This area is off limits.

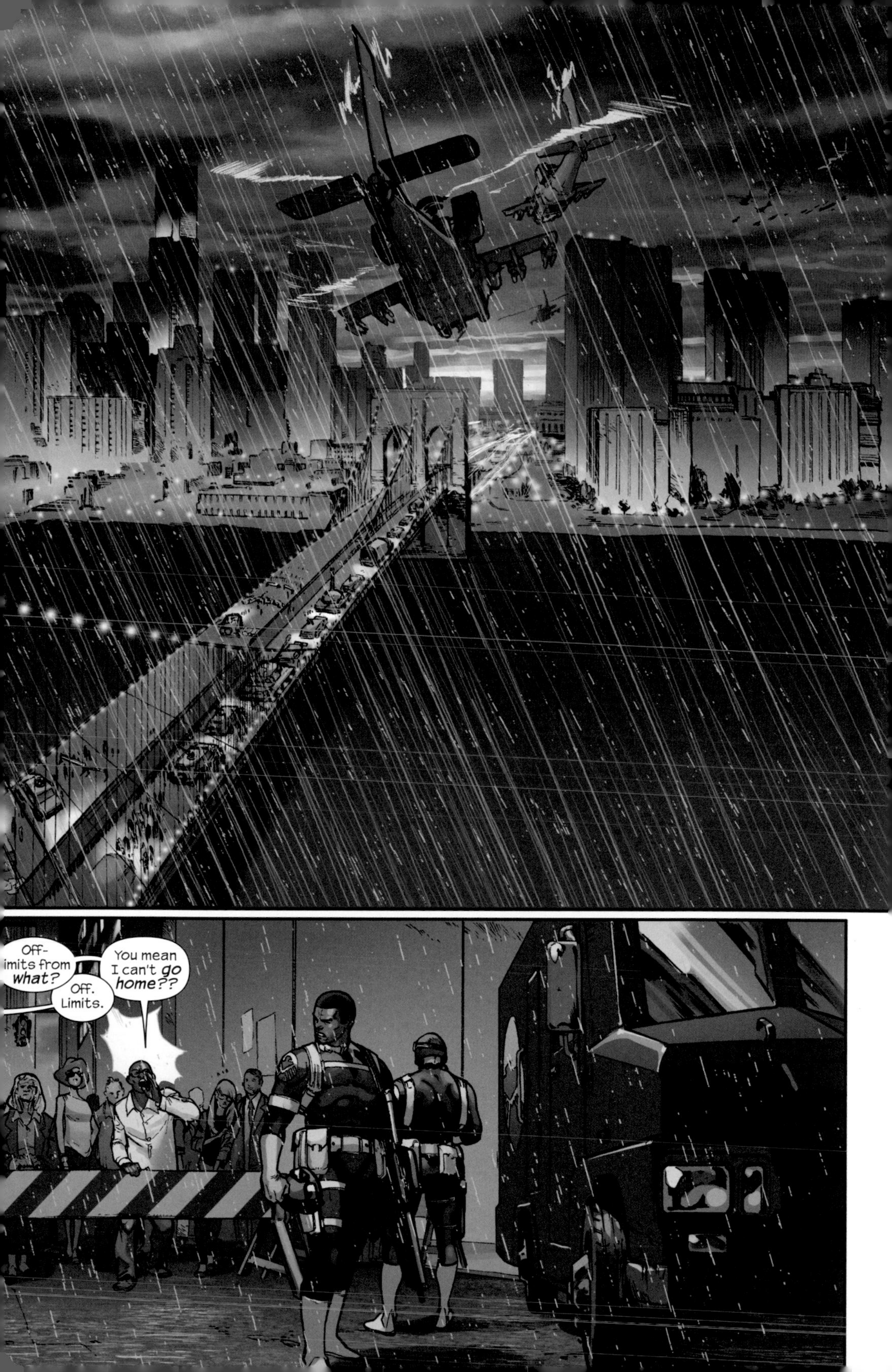
Off-limits from what?
You mean I can't go home??
Off. Limits.

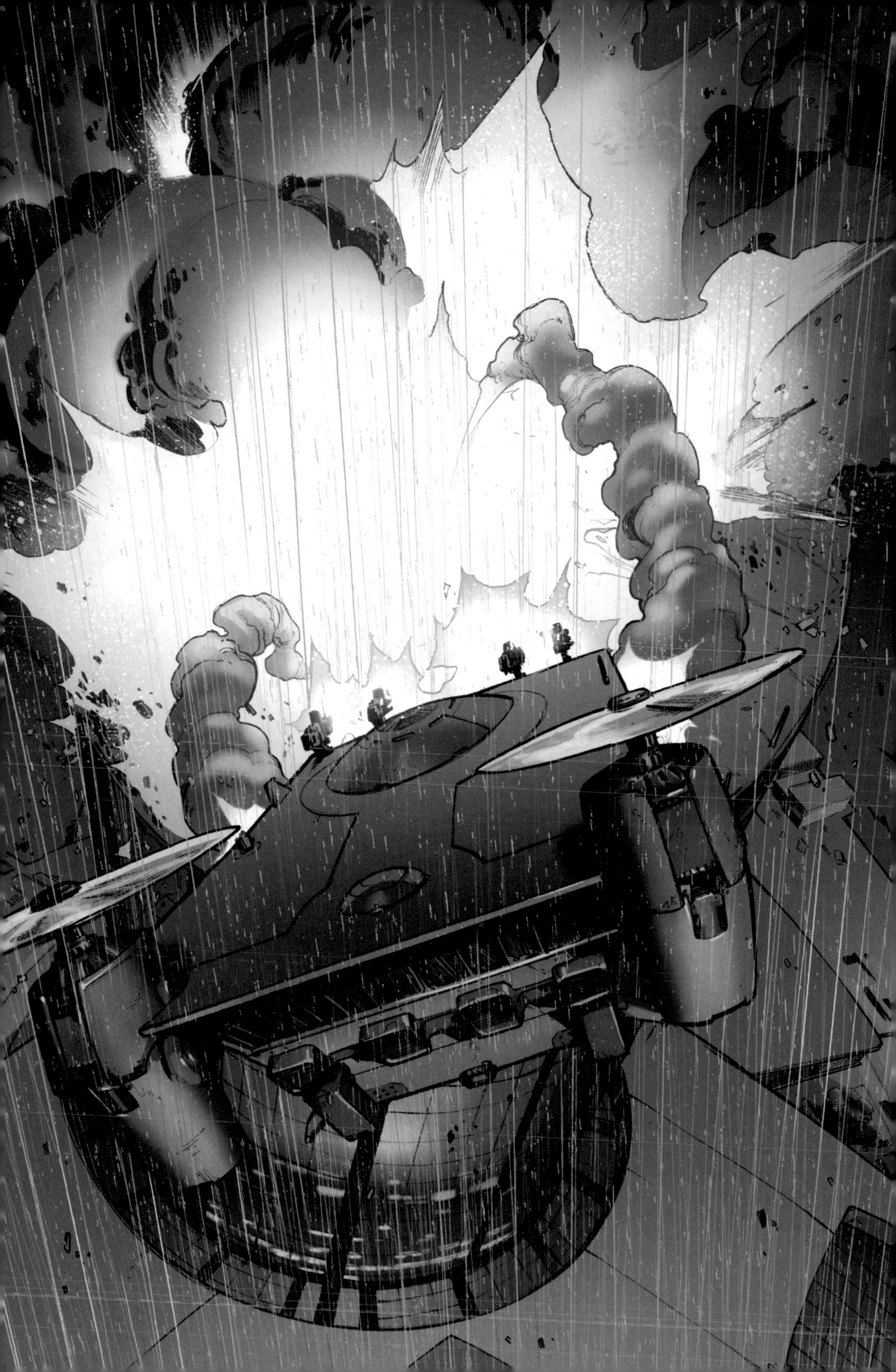

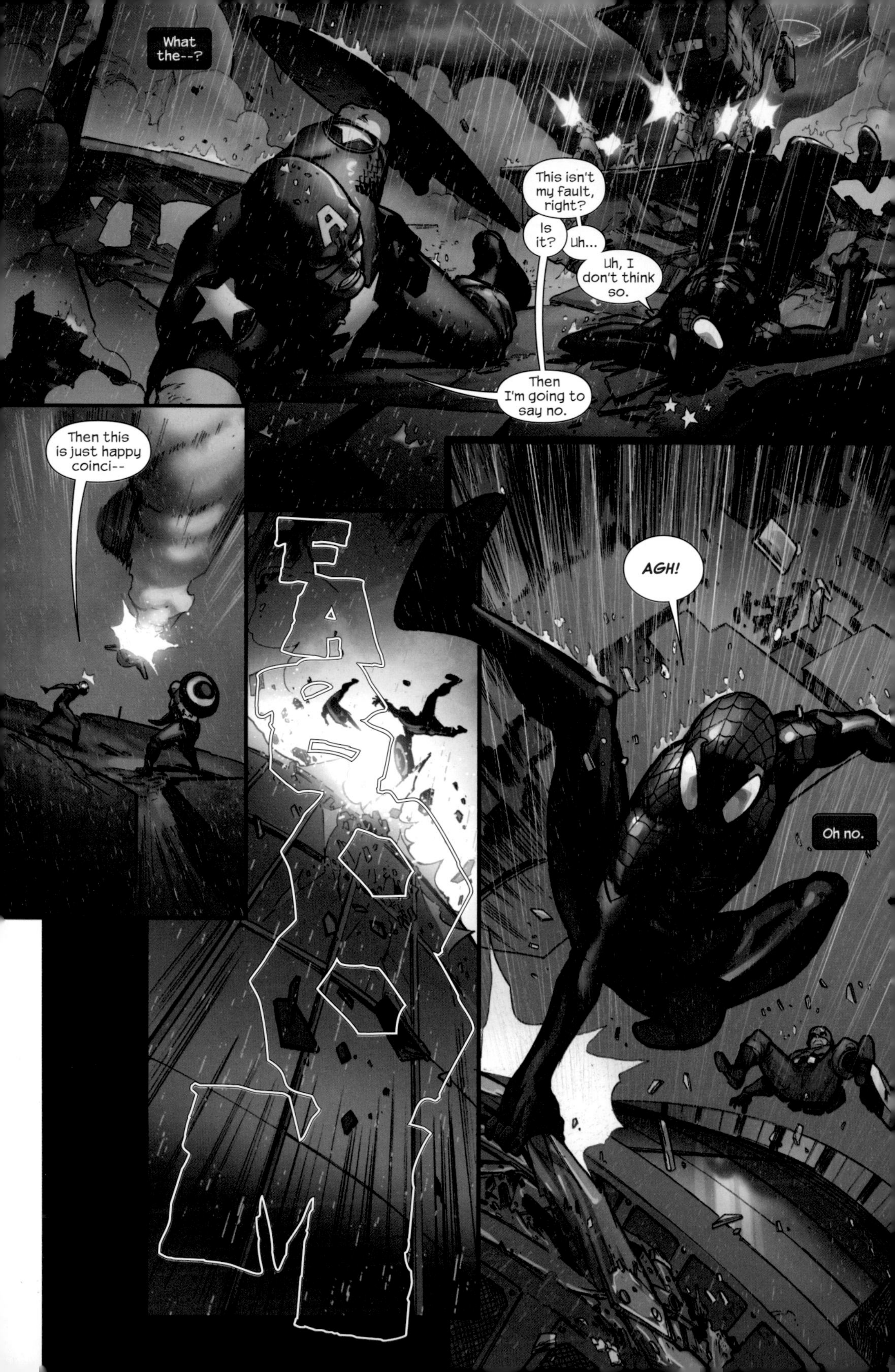
What the--?
This isn't my fault, right?
Is it?
Uh...
Uh, I don't think so.
Then I'm going to say no.
Then this is just happy coinci--
AGH!
Oh no.

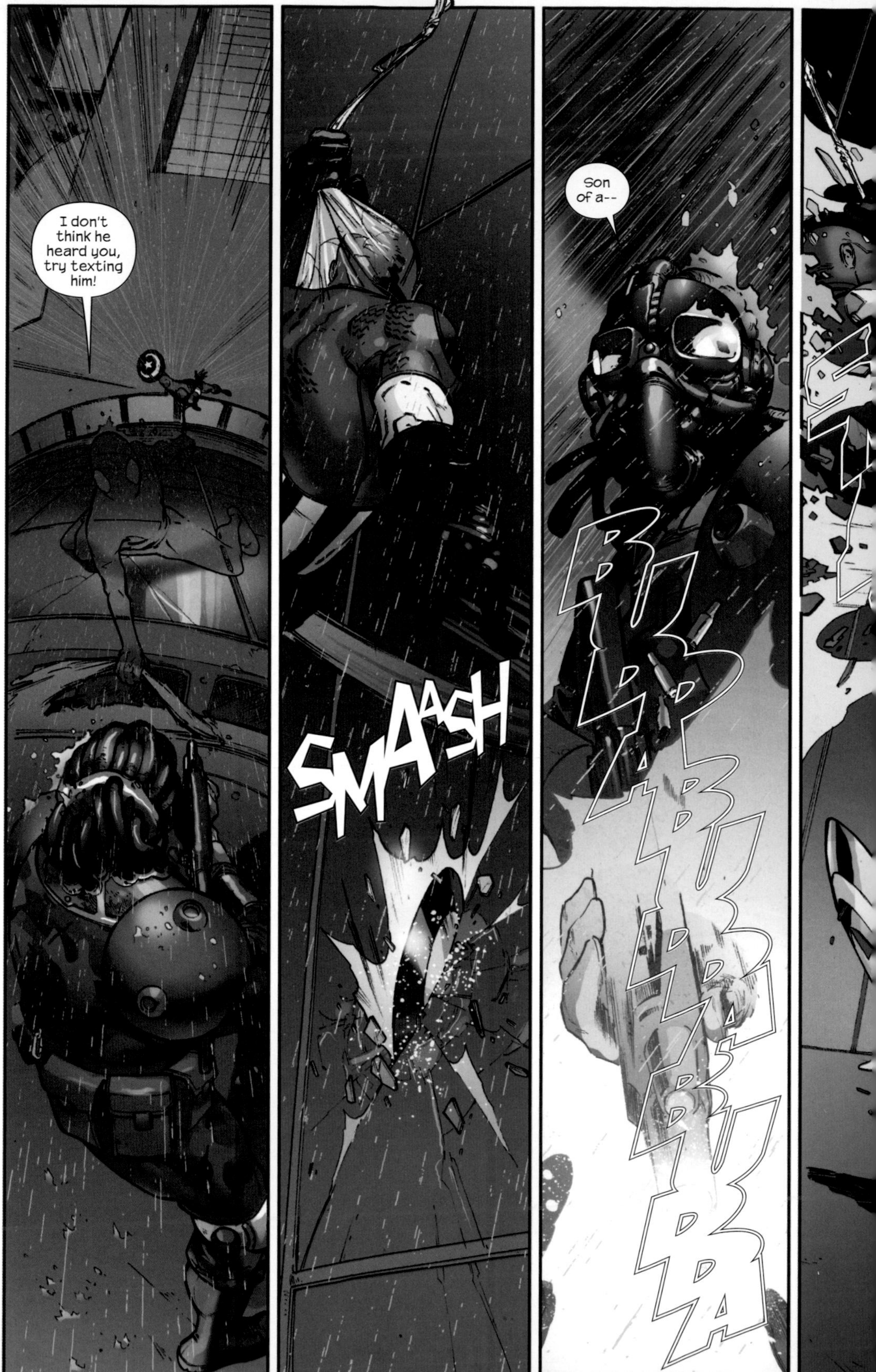
I don't think he heard you, try texting him!
SMAASH
Son of a--

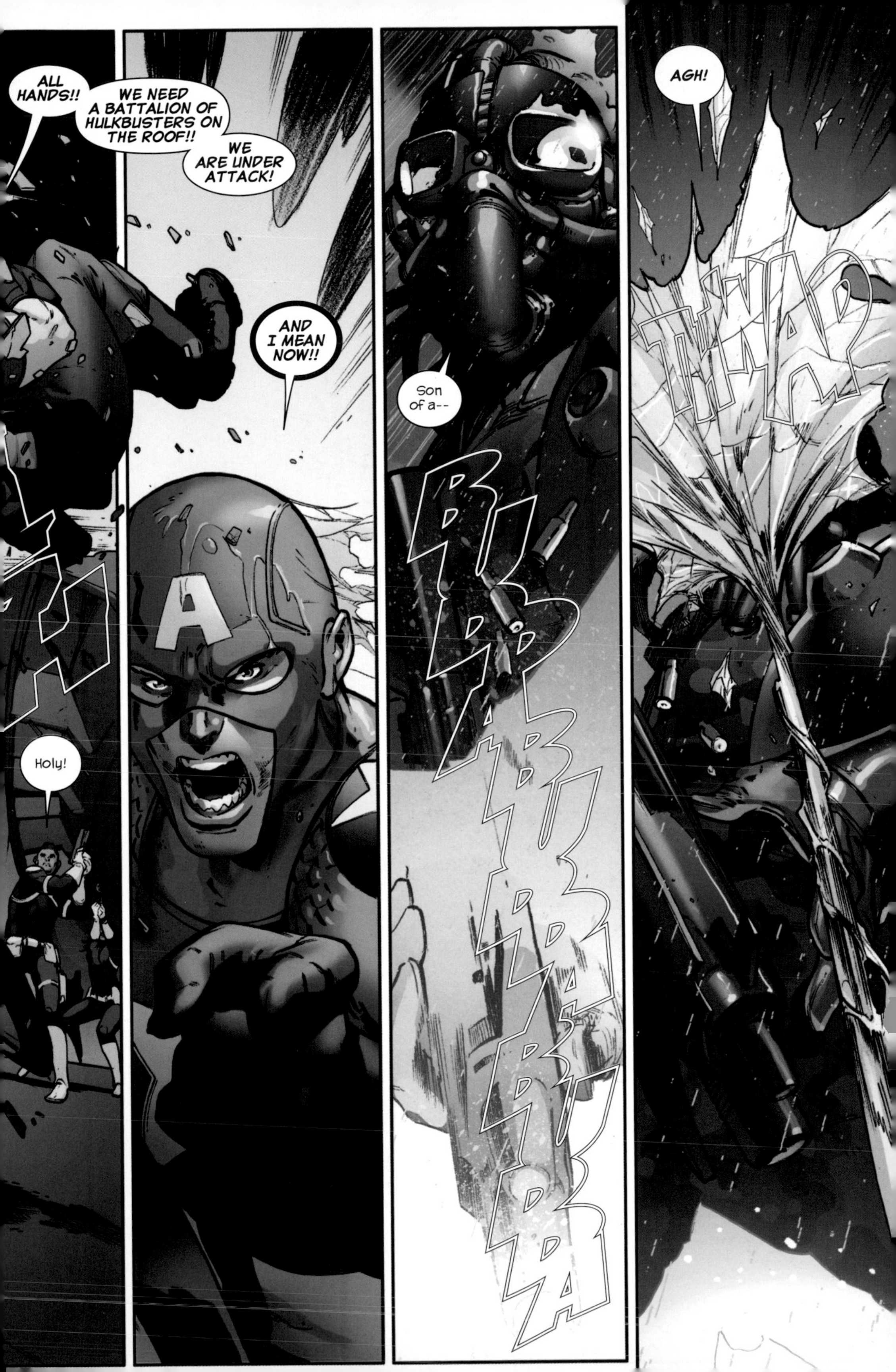
ALL HANDS!!
WE NEED A BATTALION OF HULKBUSTERS ON THE ROOF!!
WE ARE UNDER ATTACK!
AND I MEAN NOW!!
Holy!
Son of a--
RUBBABUBBUBBADDA
AGH!
THWAP

SHA BOOM

FLA BOOM

On it!

Hulkbuster squad in formation.

Roger that!!

Quincarrier.

Whoa.

I want one.

Okay, now I'm part of a Hulkbuster squad.

I really hope there's no Hulk coming that needs busting.

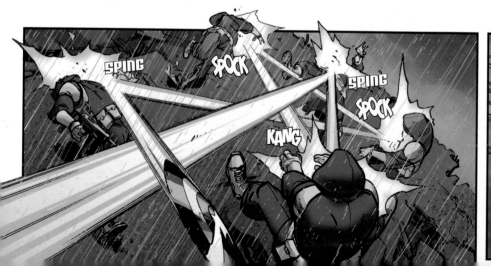

SPING

SPOCK

SPING

SPOCK

KANG

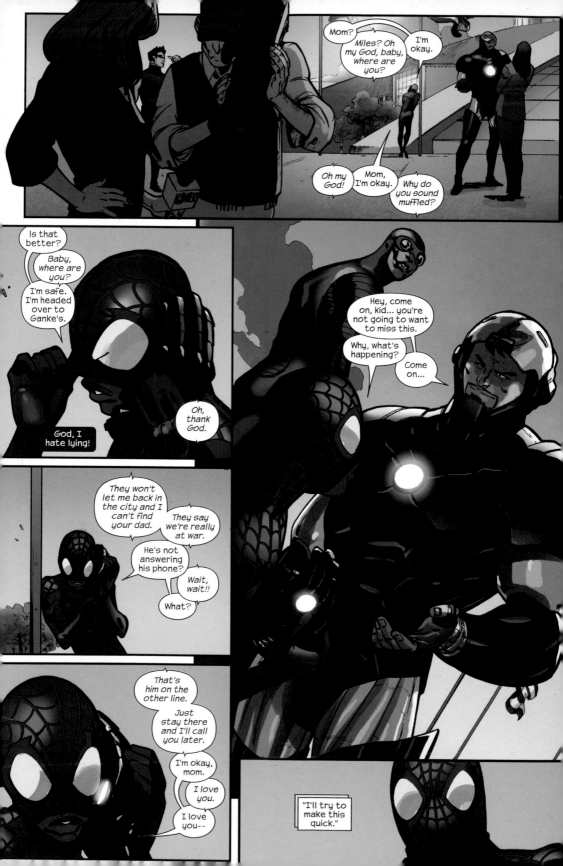

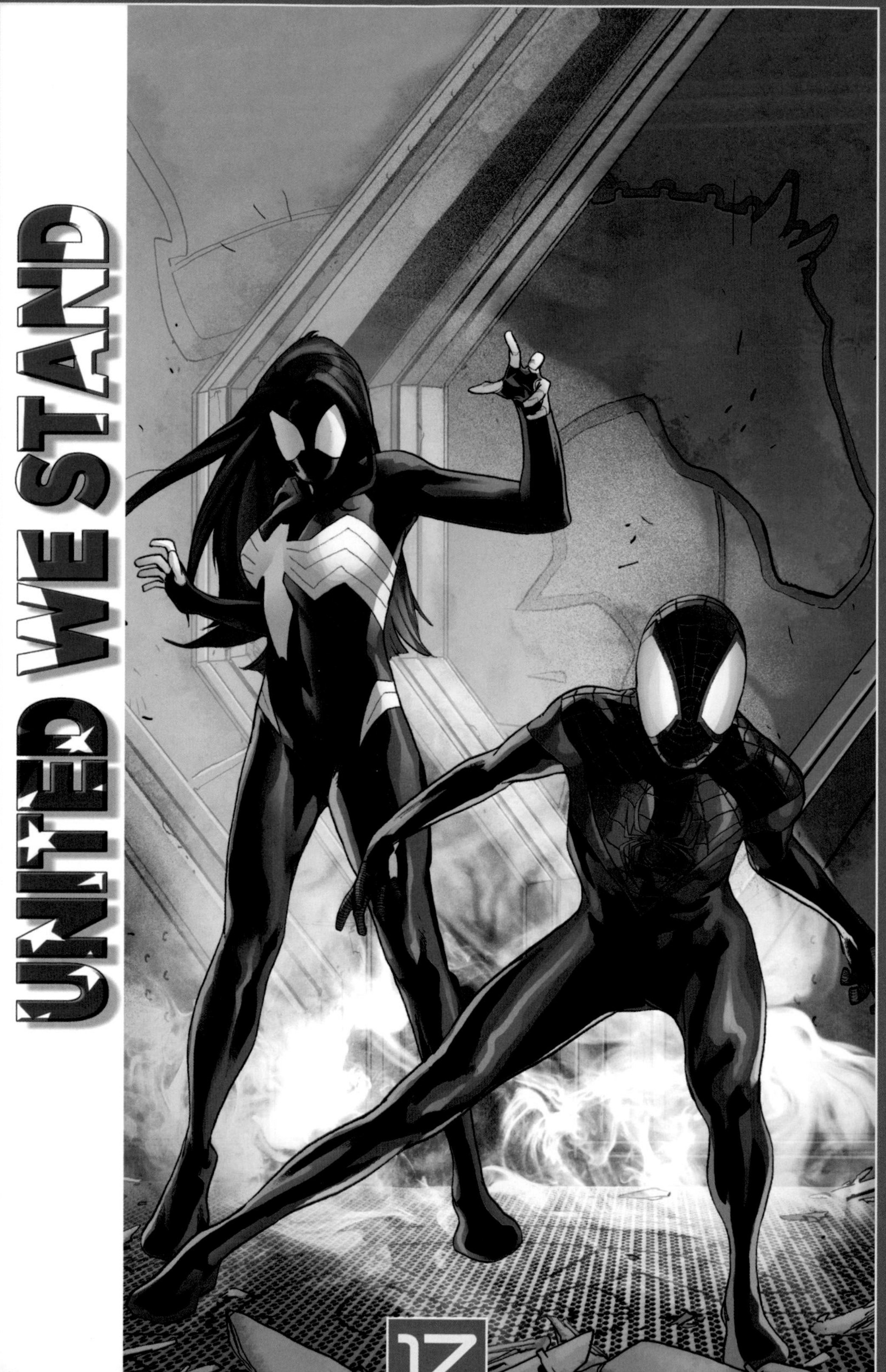
UNITED WE STAND
17

S.H.I.E.L.D. SITUATION MAP:

[Anti-government militia hot spots]

Idaho,Montana,
N.Dakota, S.Dakota,
Arizona, Wyoming

Wyoming
status unknown

[Eastern seaboard control zone]

New England,
New York,
New Jersey,
Delaware,
Washington, D.C.,
Maryland,
Pennsylvania,
Virginia

secured by
National Guard
under emergency
powers
committee

PROJECT
PEGASUS

ANTI-MATTER
NO FLY
ZONE

AREA OF
URBAN
UNREST

[Great Lakes Alliance]

Minnesota,
Wisconsin,
Michigan,
Illinois,
Indiana,Ohio

Independent
nation

ALL STATES
SHOWN IN WHITE
ARE U.S. GOVERNMENT-
CONTROLLED ZONES

Okay, so, listen up...

I know a lot of you have done a lot of admirable things but very few of you have gone to war. *This* is war. Actual war.

Falcon, you take to the sky.

Anything that's up there...you bring down here.

Susan Storm, you take your invisible powers and your crazy force fields and you create chaos.

You *knock* them off their game.

You keep them charging into invisible force fields until they run out of steam.

And Spider-Man and Spider-Woman, you two stick together.

You are a tag team.

Done.

Uh, actually, um, I'm just going to do my own thing out there.

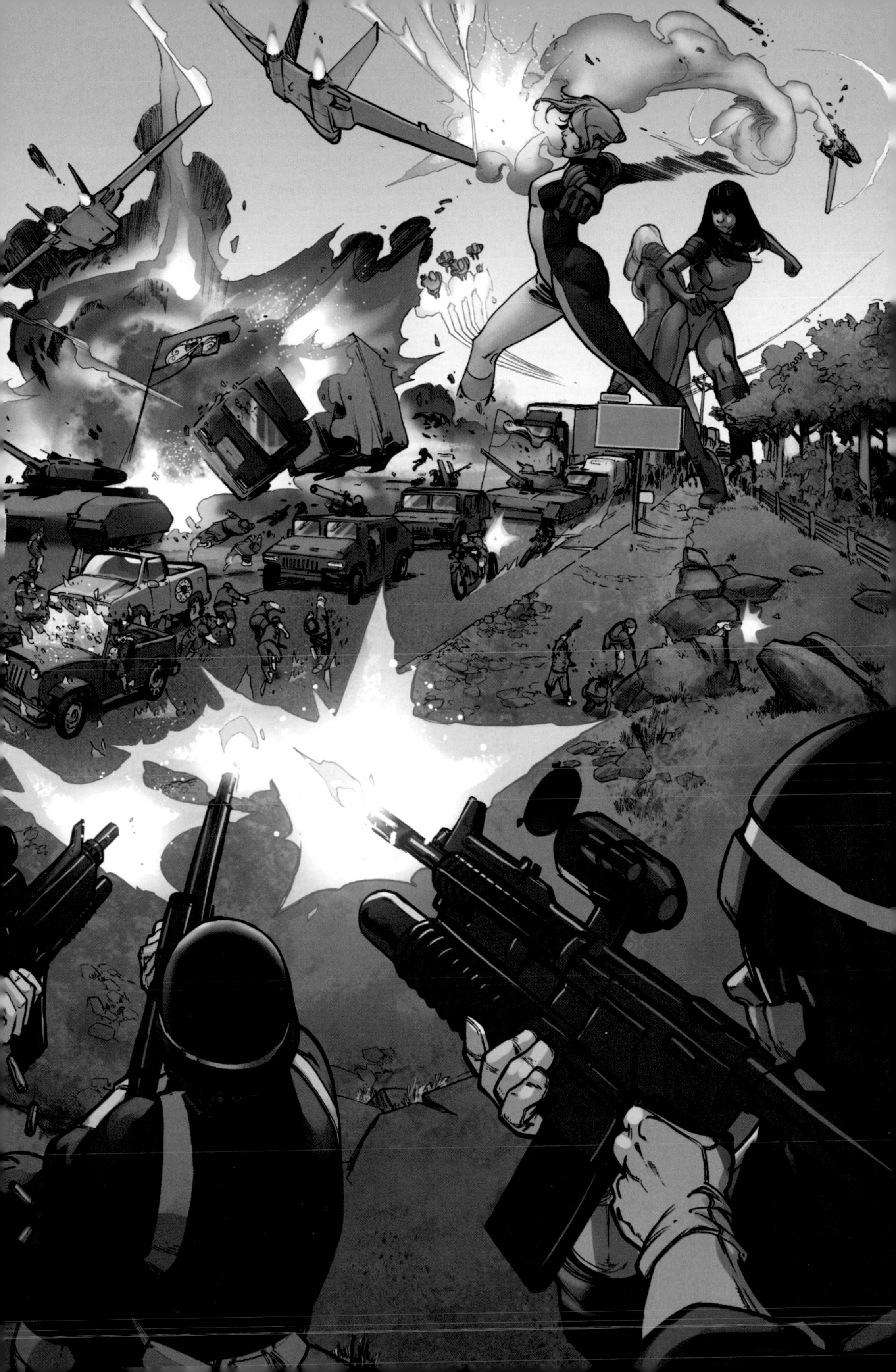

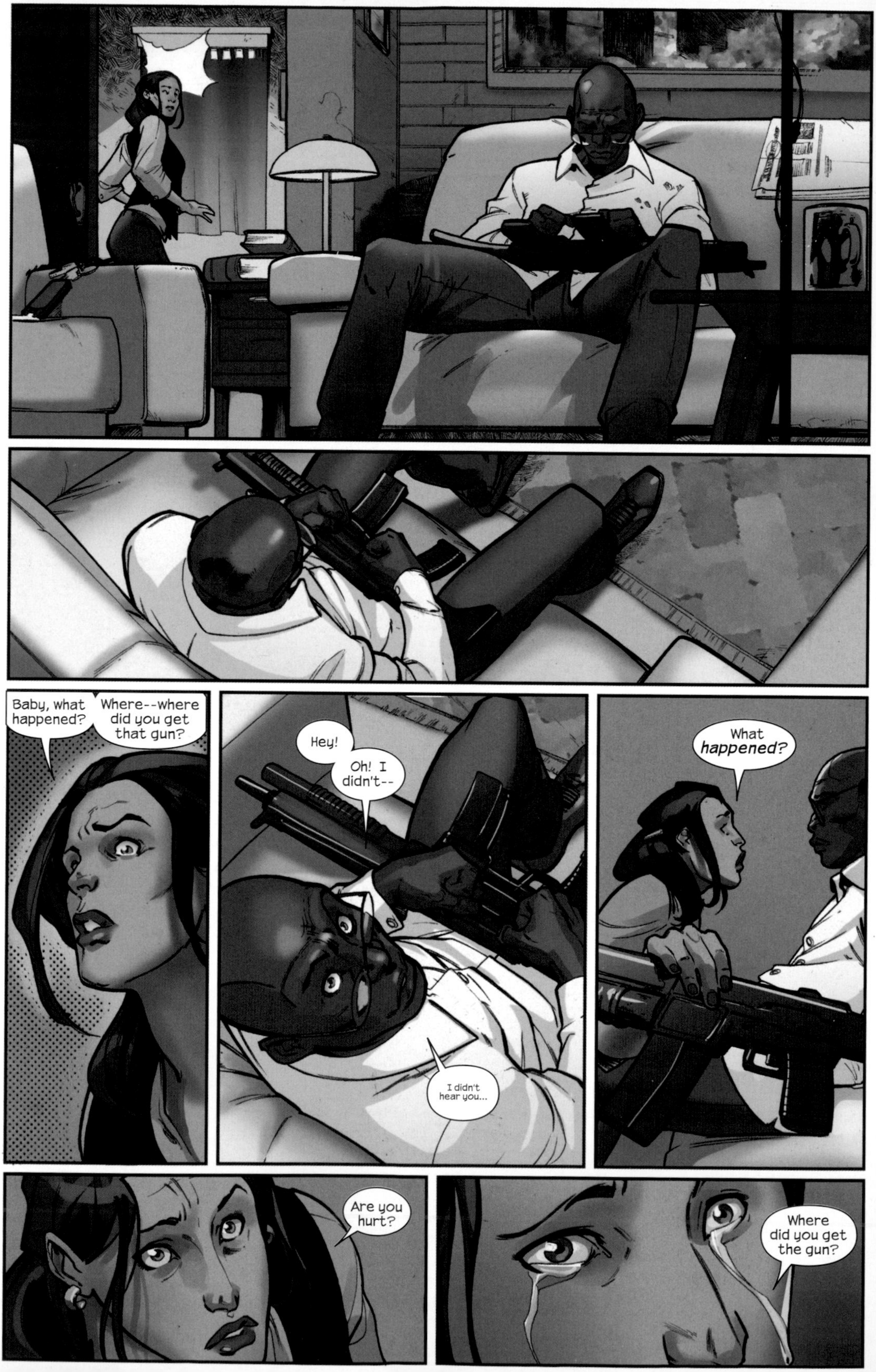

Baby, what happened?
Where--where did you get that gun?
Hey!
Oh! I didn't--
I didn't hear you...
What *happened?*
Are you hurt?
Where did you get the gun?

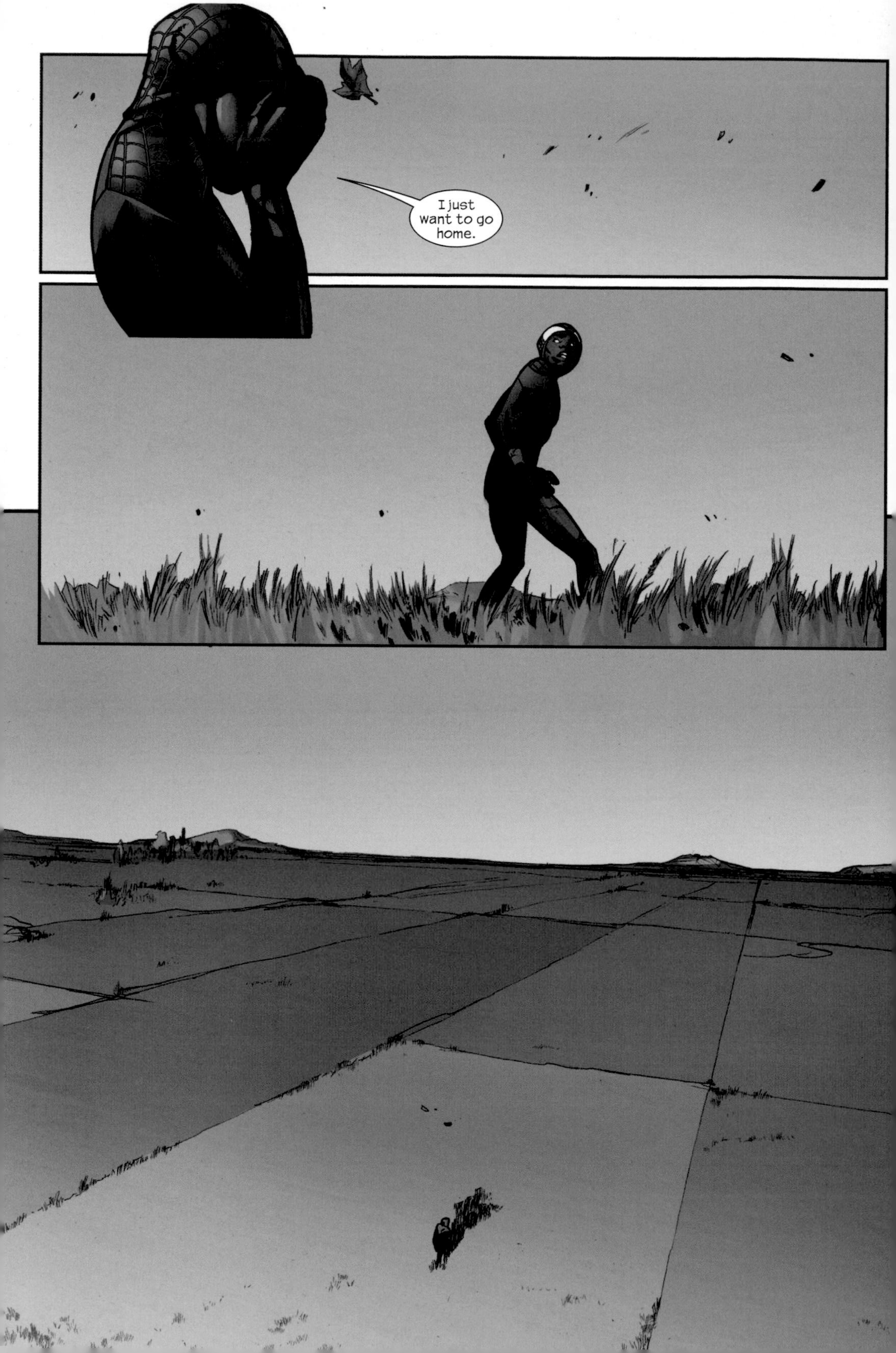
I just want to go home.

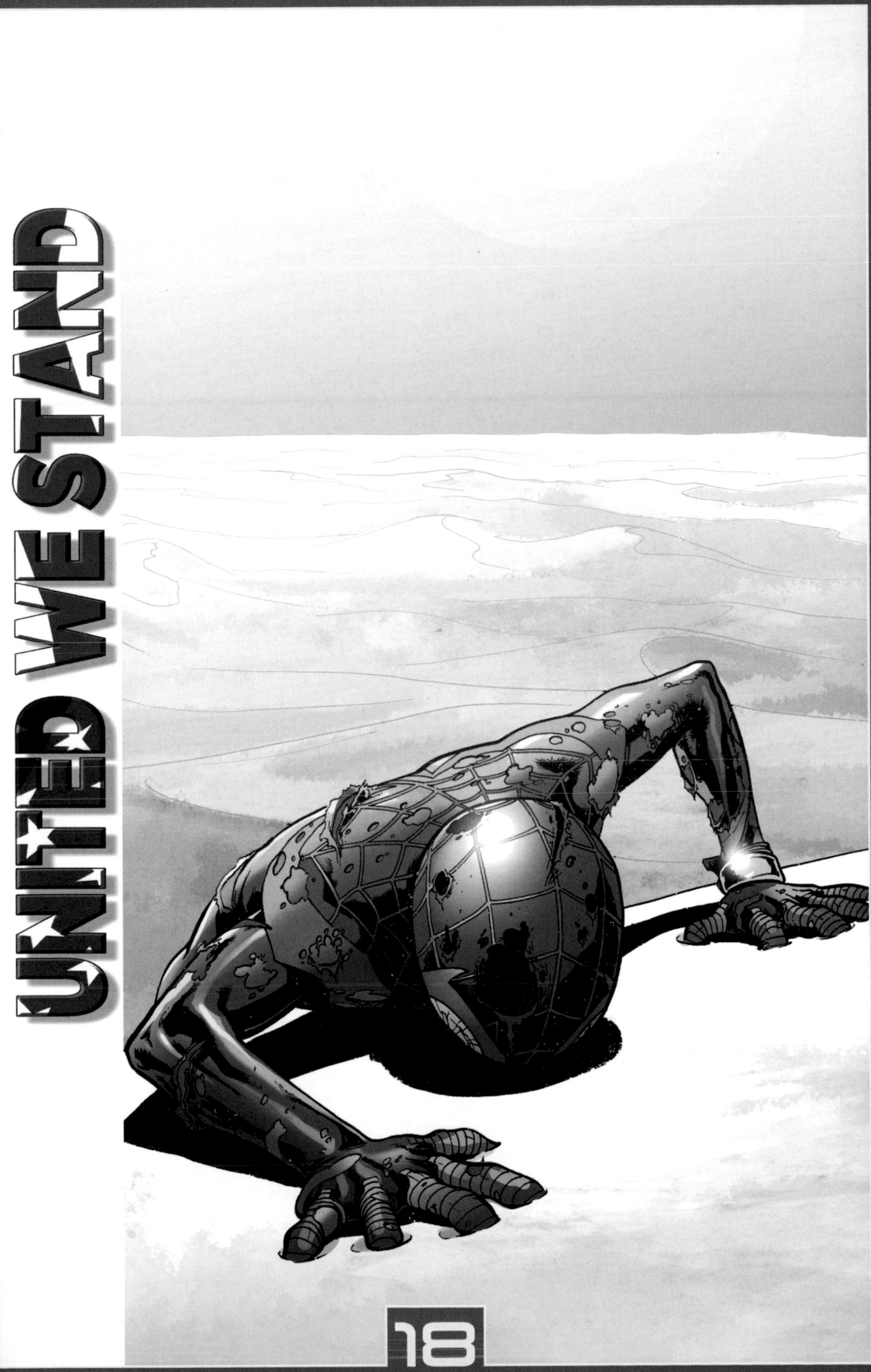
UNITED WE STAND
18

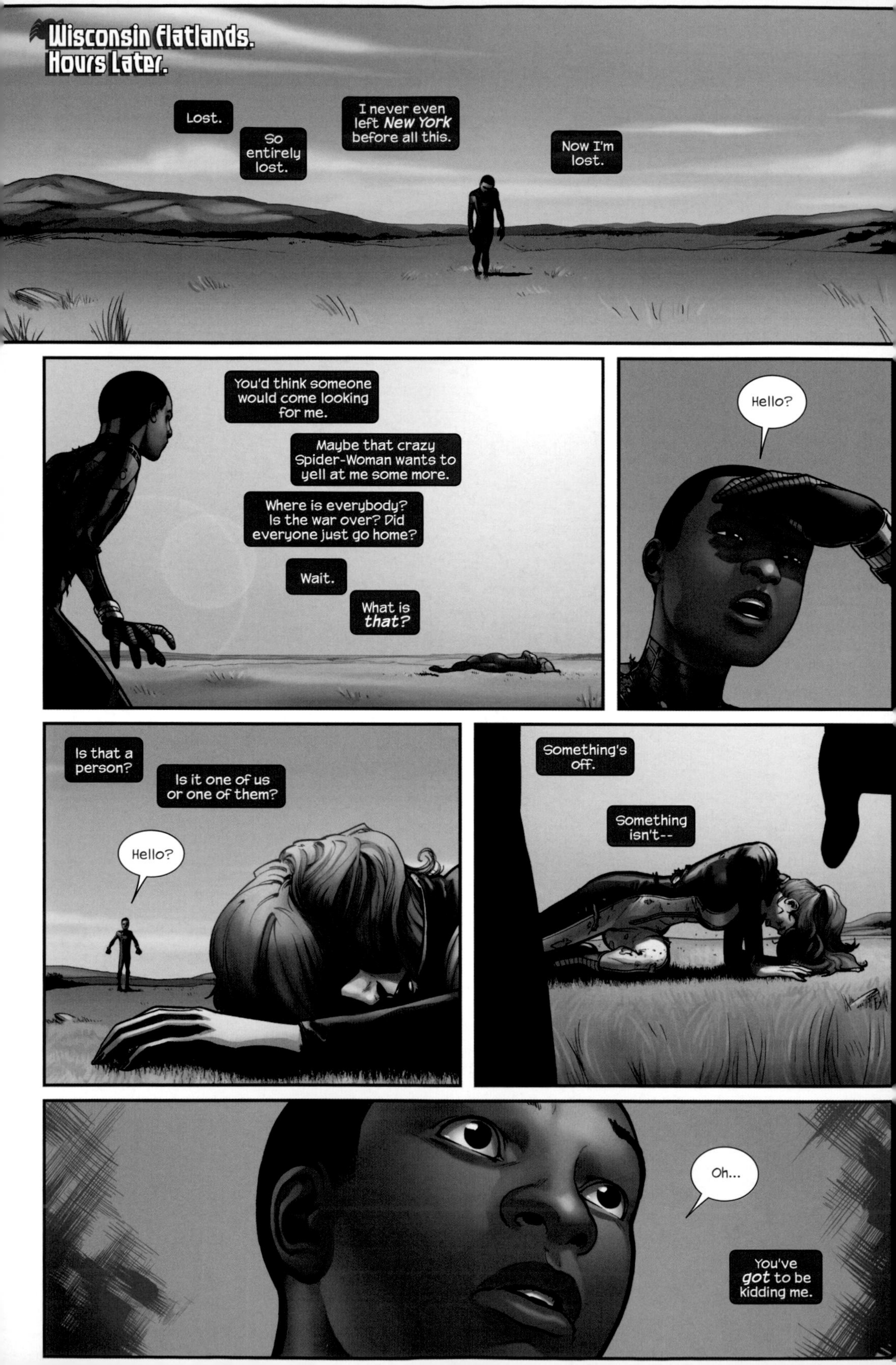
Wisconsin Flatlands. Hours Later.
Lost.
So entirely lost.
I never even left New York before all this.
Now I'm lost.
You'd think someone would come looking for me.
Maybe that crazy Spider-Woman wants to yell at me some more.
Where is everybody? Is the war over? Did everyone just go home?
Wait.
What is that?
Hello?
Is that a person?
Is it one of us or one of them?
Hello?
Something's off.
Something isn't--
Oh...
You've got to be kidding me.

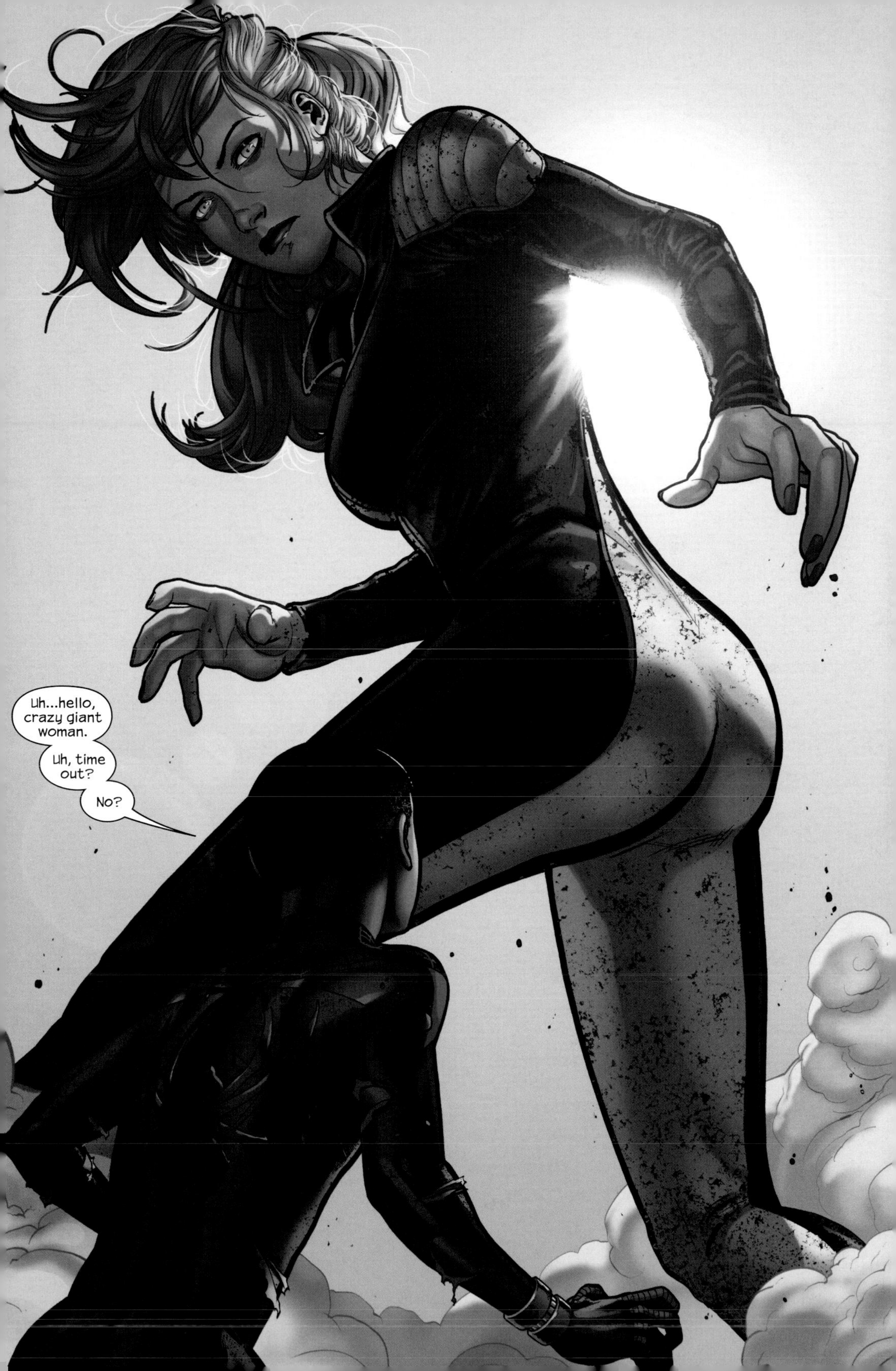
Uh...hello, crazy giant woman.
Uh, time out?
No?

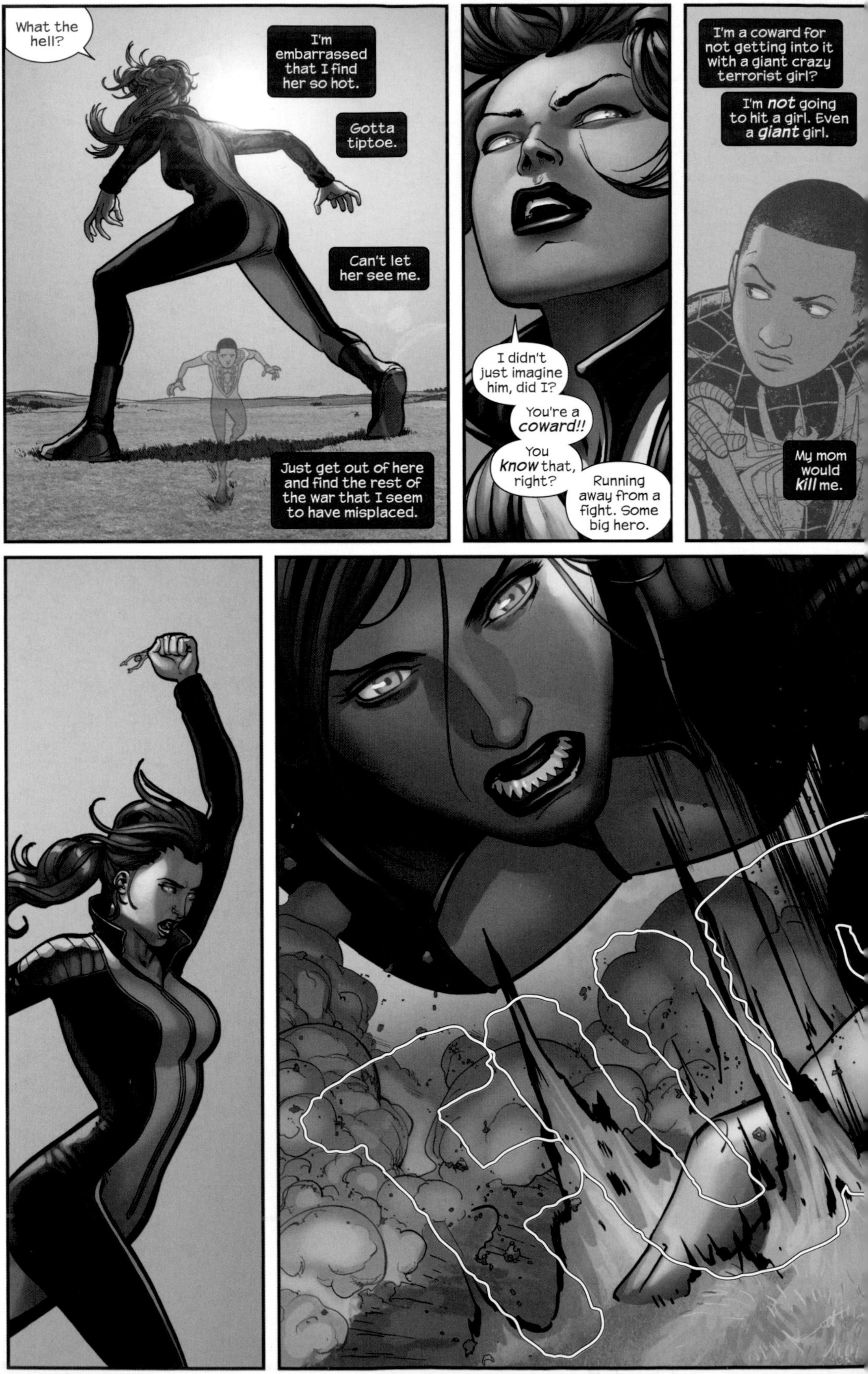
What the hell?
I'm embarrassed that I find her so hot.
Gotta tiptoe.
Can't let her see me.
Just get out of here and find the rest of the war that I seem to have misplaced.
I didn't just imagine him, did I?
You're a coward!!
You know that, right?
Running away from a fight. Some big hero.
I'm a coward for not getting into it with a giant crazy terrorist girl?
I'm not going to hit a girl. Even a giant girl.
My mom would kill me.

Seriously, how did you--?

Gotcha.

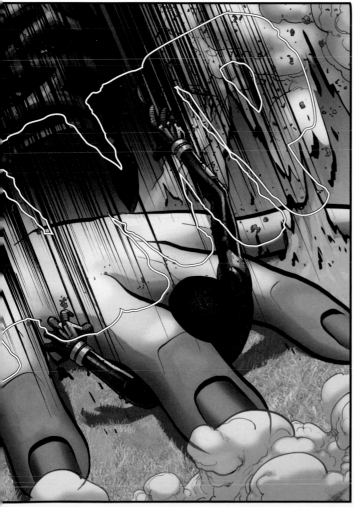

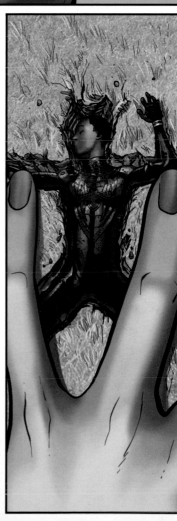

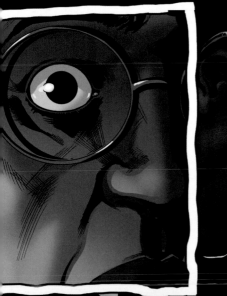

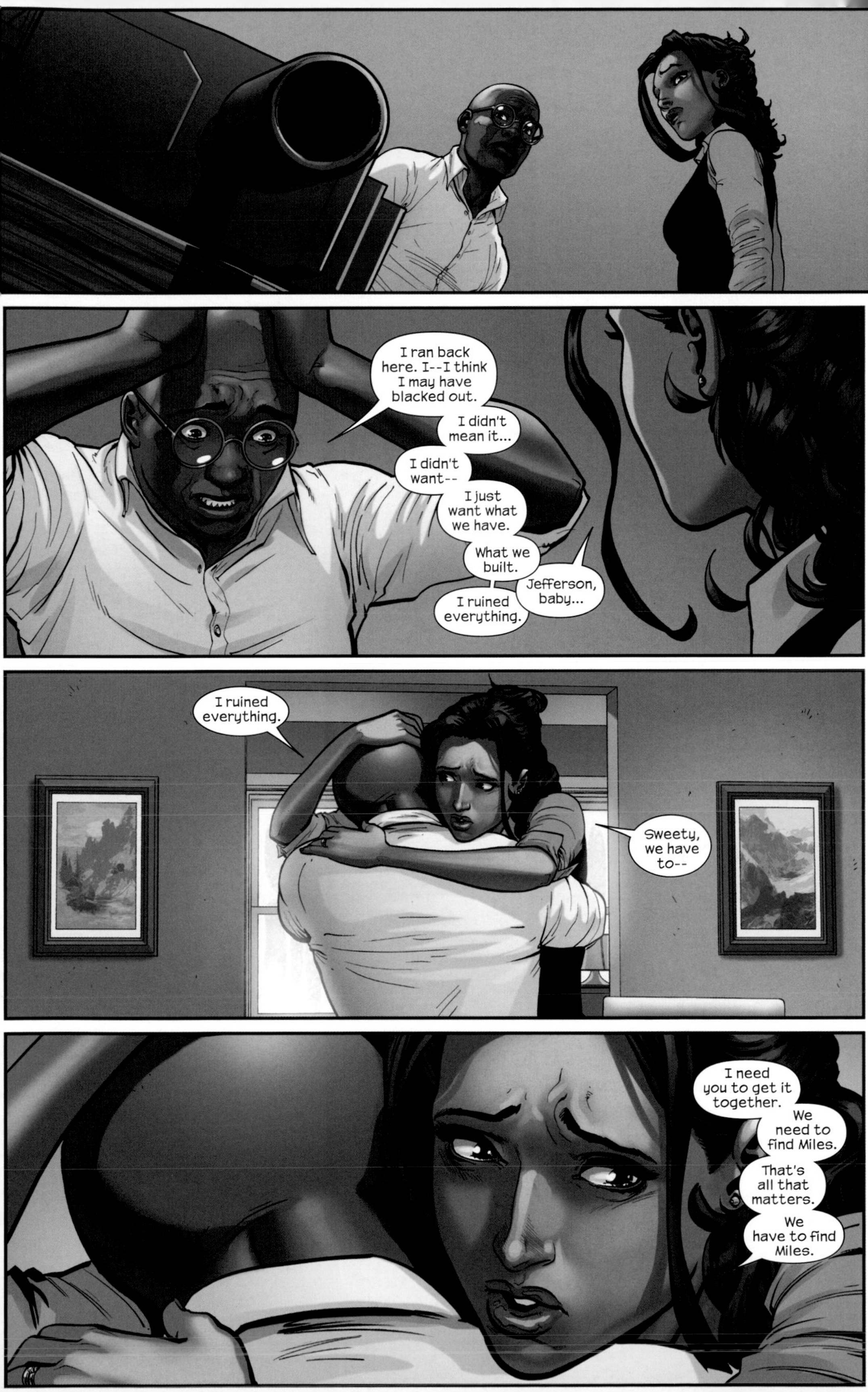
I ran back here. I--I think I may have blacked out.
I didn't mean it...
I didn't want--
I just want what we have.
What we built.
I ruined everything.
Jefferson, baby...
I ruined everything.
Sweety, we have to--
I need you to get it together.
We need to find Miles.
That's all that matters.
We have to find Miles.

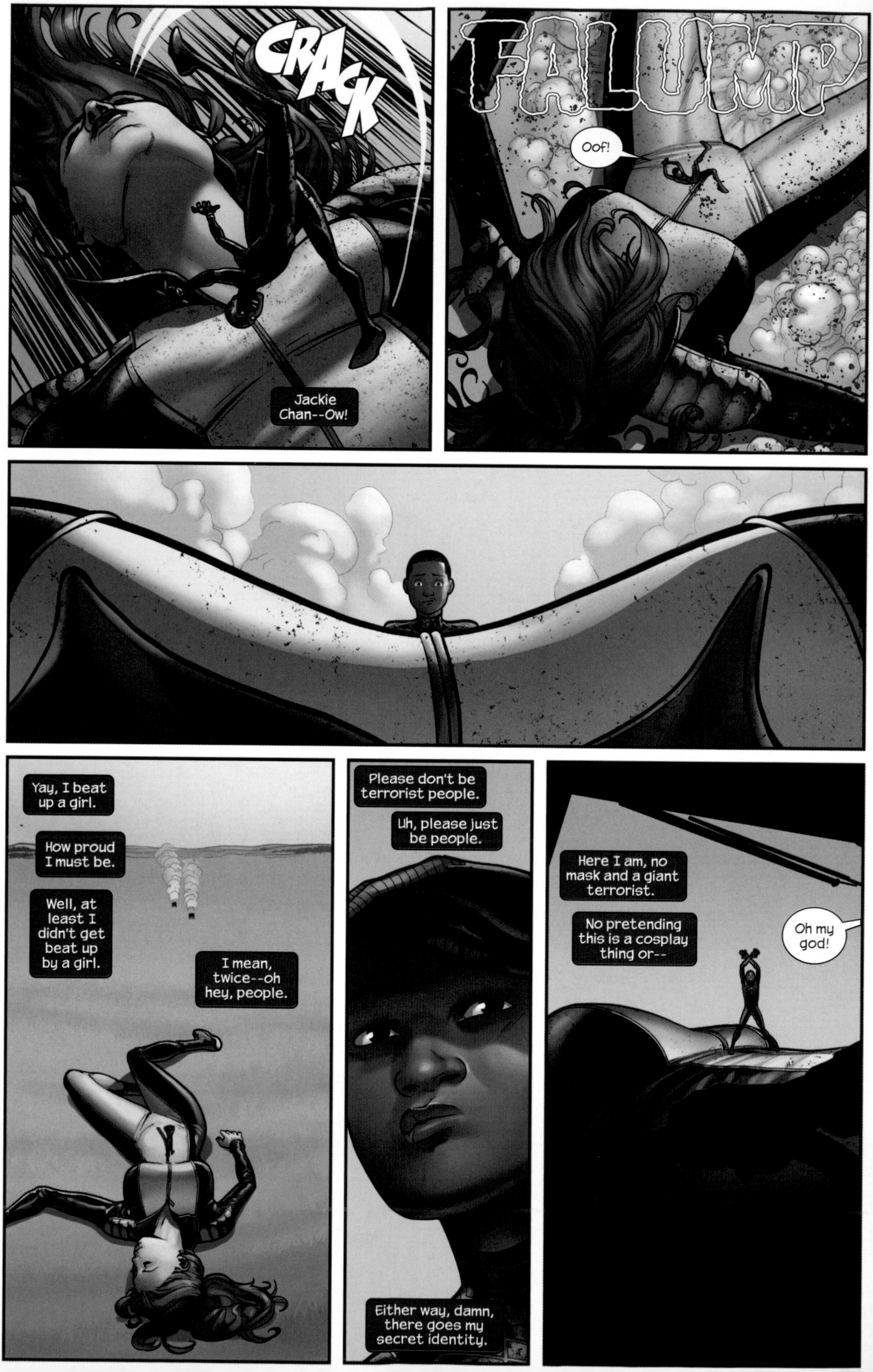
CRACK
Jackie Chan--Ow!
FALUMP
Oof!
Yay, I beat up a girl.
How proud I must be.
Well, at least I didn't get beat up by a girl.
I mean, twice--oh hey, people.
Please don't be terrorist people.
Uh, please just be people.
Either way, damn, there goes my secret identity.
Here I am, no mask and a giant terrorist.
No pretending this is a cosplay thing or--
Oh my god!

Oh my god!

Here comes Spider-Woman to yell at me again.

Uh--

Are you okay?

No.

Nothing broken?

Oh, no.

We intercepted her walkie-talkie communiqué.

Thank God you're okay. What you did today...

I know, I know...please stop yelling at me.

I know I'm too young to be out here.

I know I'm not super hero enough to go to war or be an Ultimate.

I know. You're right.

Just-- help me get home and I'll go home.

Mister President. This is Spider-Woman. I have him.

He's okay. Yes, sir.

The man who saved the President's life is fine.

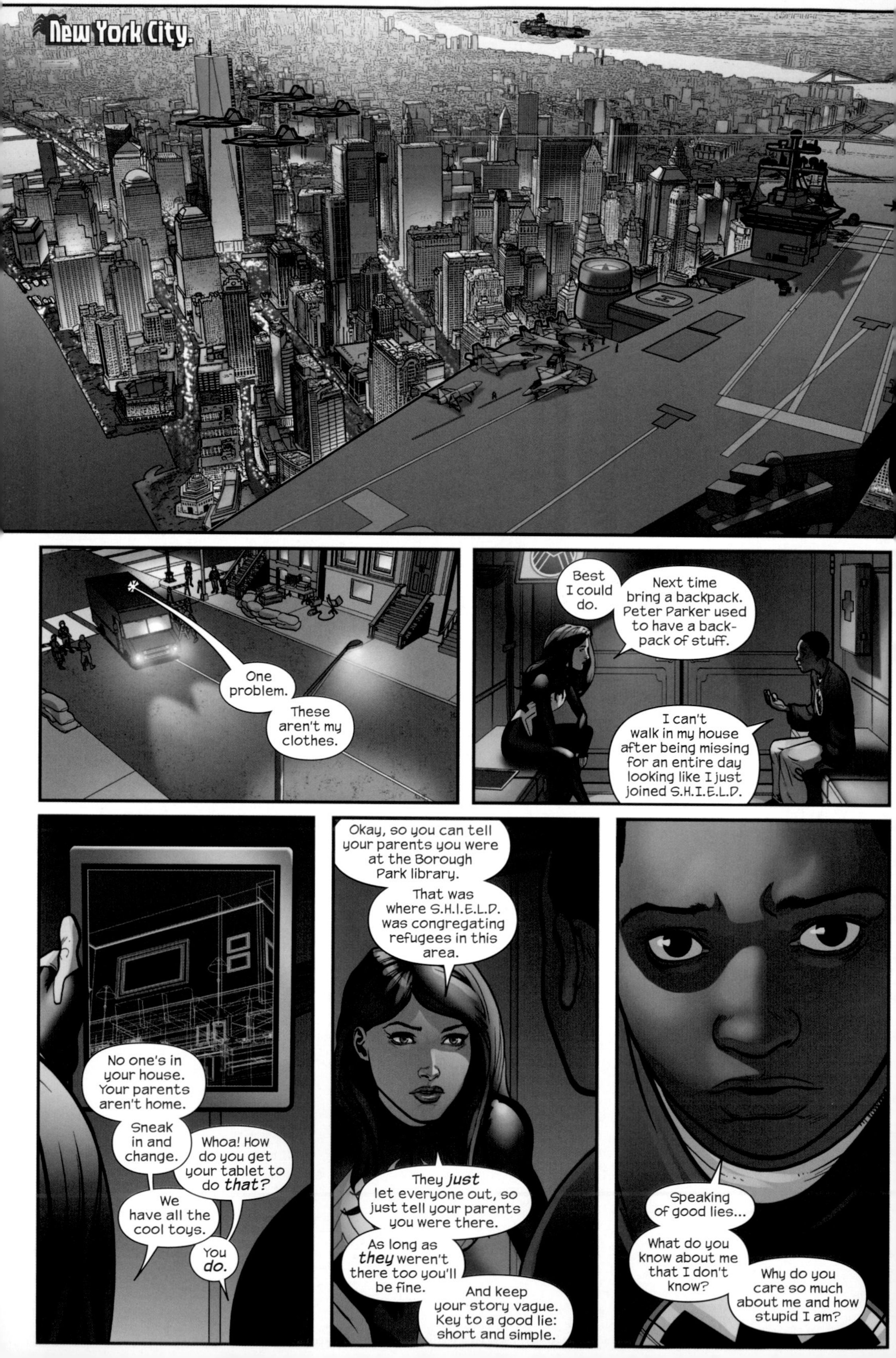
New York City.
One problem.
These aren't my clothes.
Best I could do.
Next time bring a backpack. Peter Parker used to have a back-pack of stuff.
I can't walk in my house after being missing for an entire day looking like I just joined S.H.I.E.L.D.
No one's in your house. Your parents aren't home.
Sneak in and change.
Whoa! How do you get your tablet to do *that?*
We have all the cool toys.
You *do.*
Okay, so you can tell your parents you were at the Borough Park library.
That was where S.H.I.E.L.D. was congregating refugees in this area.
They *just* let everyone out, so just tell your parents you were there.
As long as *they* weren't there too you'll be fine.
And keep your story vague. Key to a good lie: short and simple.
Speaking of good lies...
What do you know about me that I don't know?
Why do you care so much about me and how stupid I am?

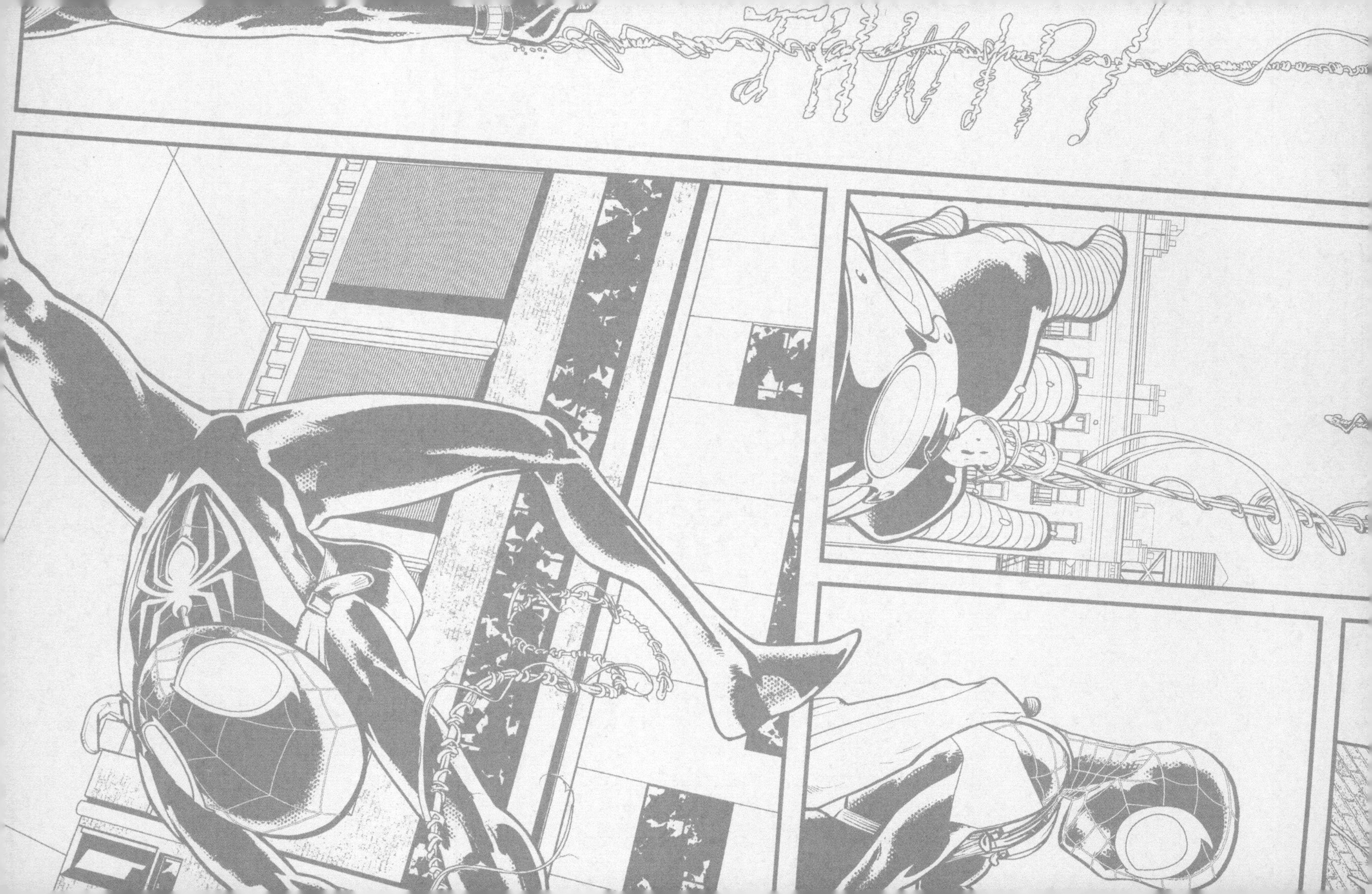
THWIP!

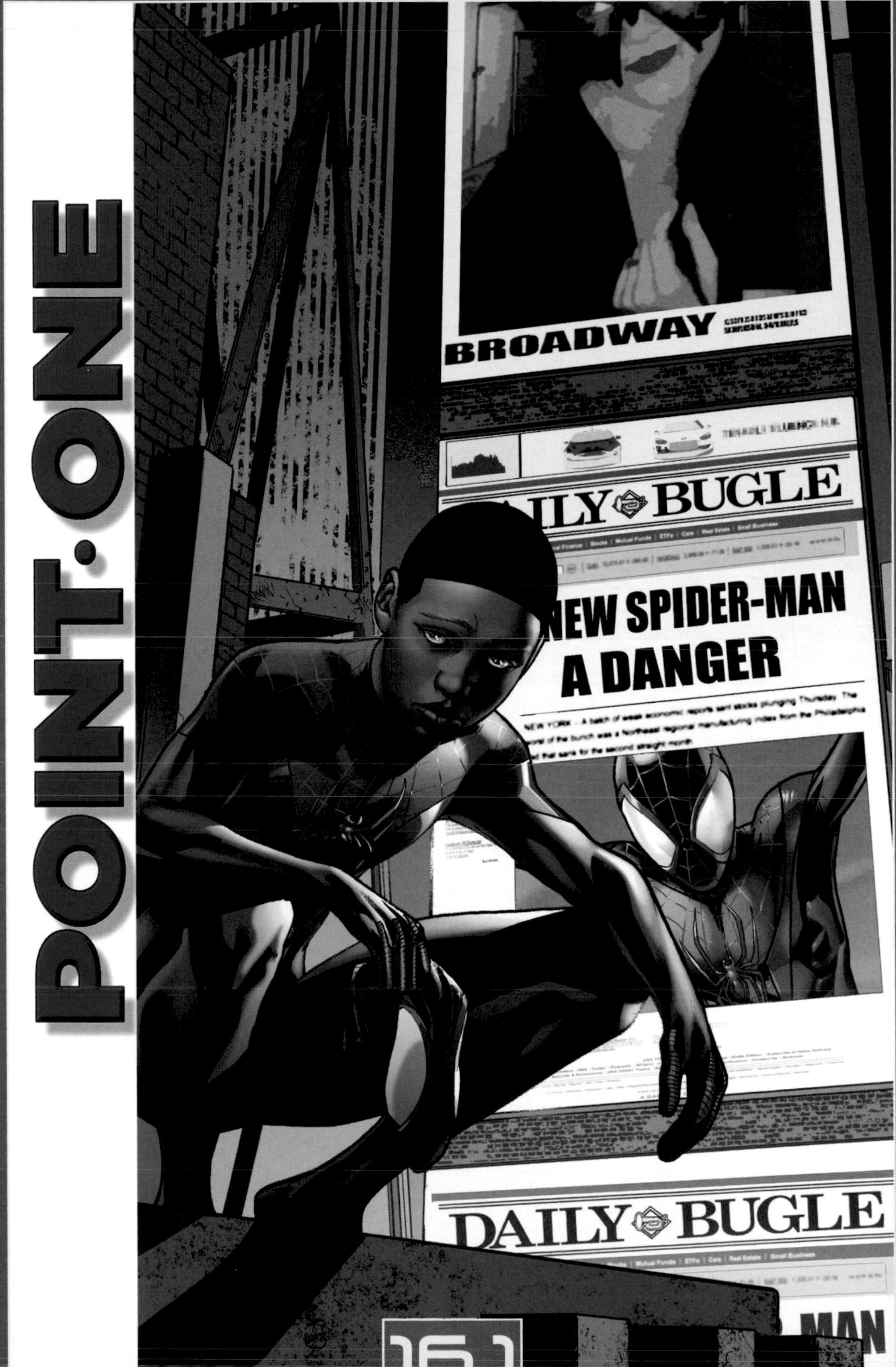
POINT•ONE
BROADWAY
DAILY BUGLE
NEW SPIDER-MAN
A DANGER
DAILY BUGLE
16.1

FLLLBOOM

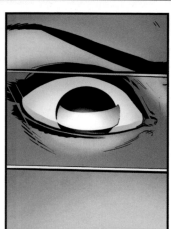

Oh my God!

You are...

just...

...like me.

What? **What** did you say?

They're calling someone. Hold on.

You are...

just...

...like me.

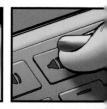

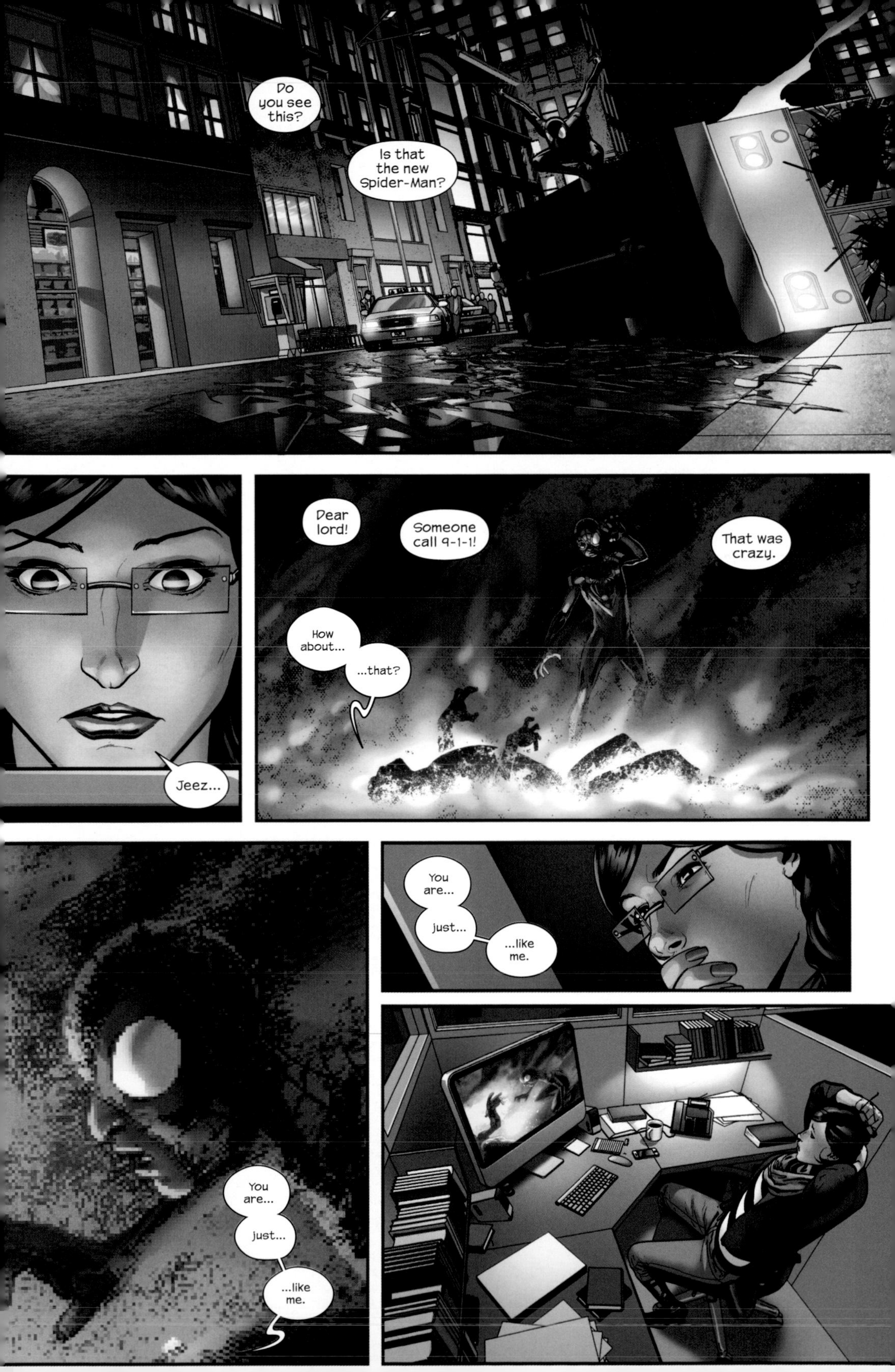
Do you see this?
Is that the new Spider-Man?
Jeez...
Dear lord!
Someone call 9-1-1!
That was crazy.
How about...
...that?
You are...
just...
...like me.
You are...
just...
...like me.

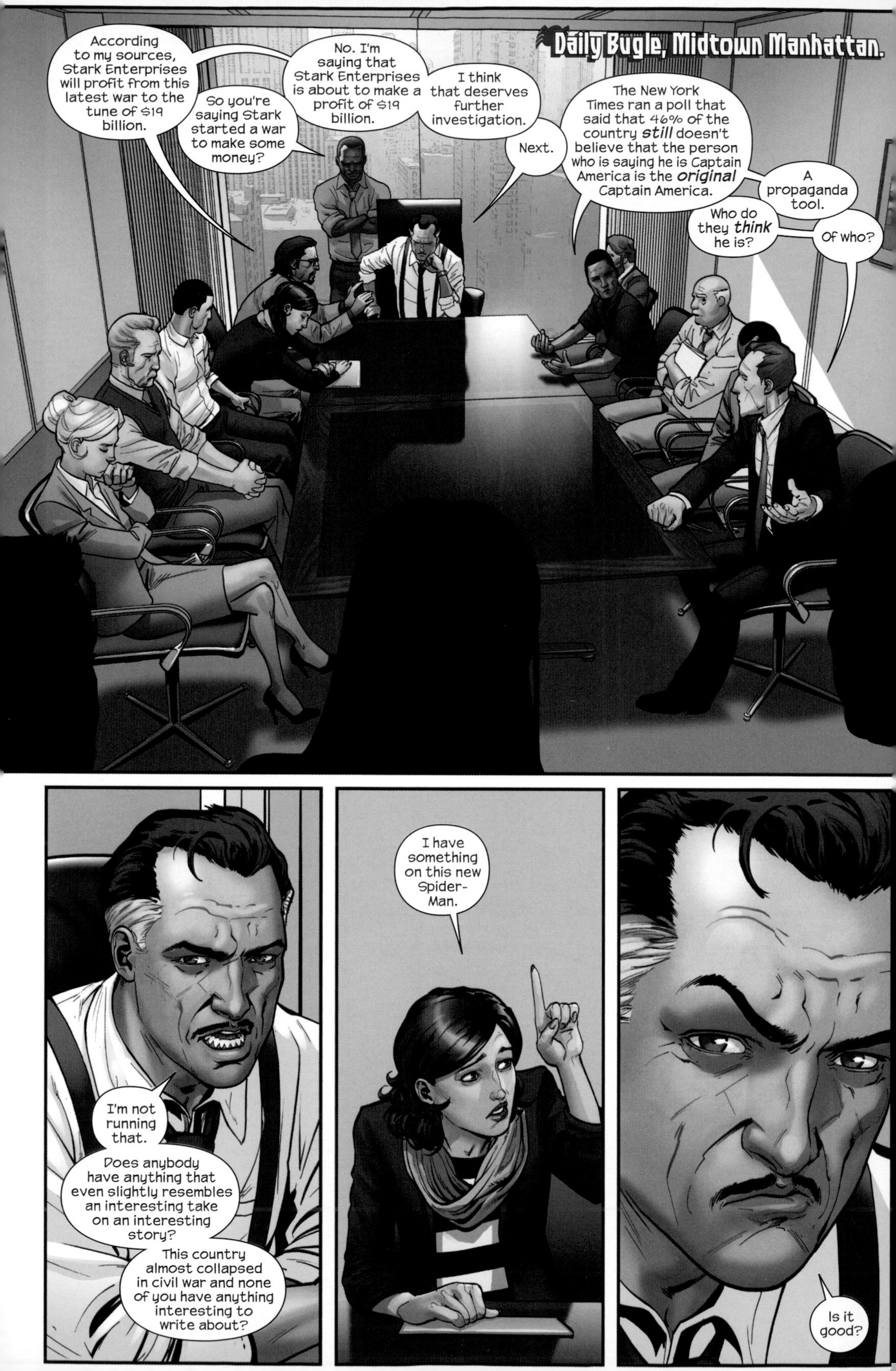
Daily Bugle, Midtown Manhattan.
According to my sources, Stark Enterprises will profit from this latest war to the tune of $19 billion.
So you're saying Stark started a war to make some money?
No. I'm saying that Stark Enterprises is about to make a profit of $19 billion.
I think that deserves further investigation.
Next.
The New York Times ran a poll that said that 46% of the country ***still*** doesn't believe that the person who is saying he is Captain America is the ***original*** Captain America.
A propaganda tool.
Who do they ***think*** he is?
Of who?
I'm not running that.
Does anybody have anything that even slightly resembles an interesting take on an interesting story?
This country almost collapsed in civil war and none of you have anything interesting to write about?
I have something on this new Spider-Man.
Is it good?

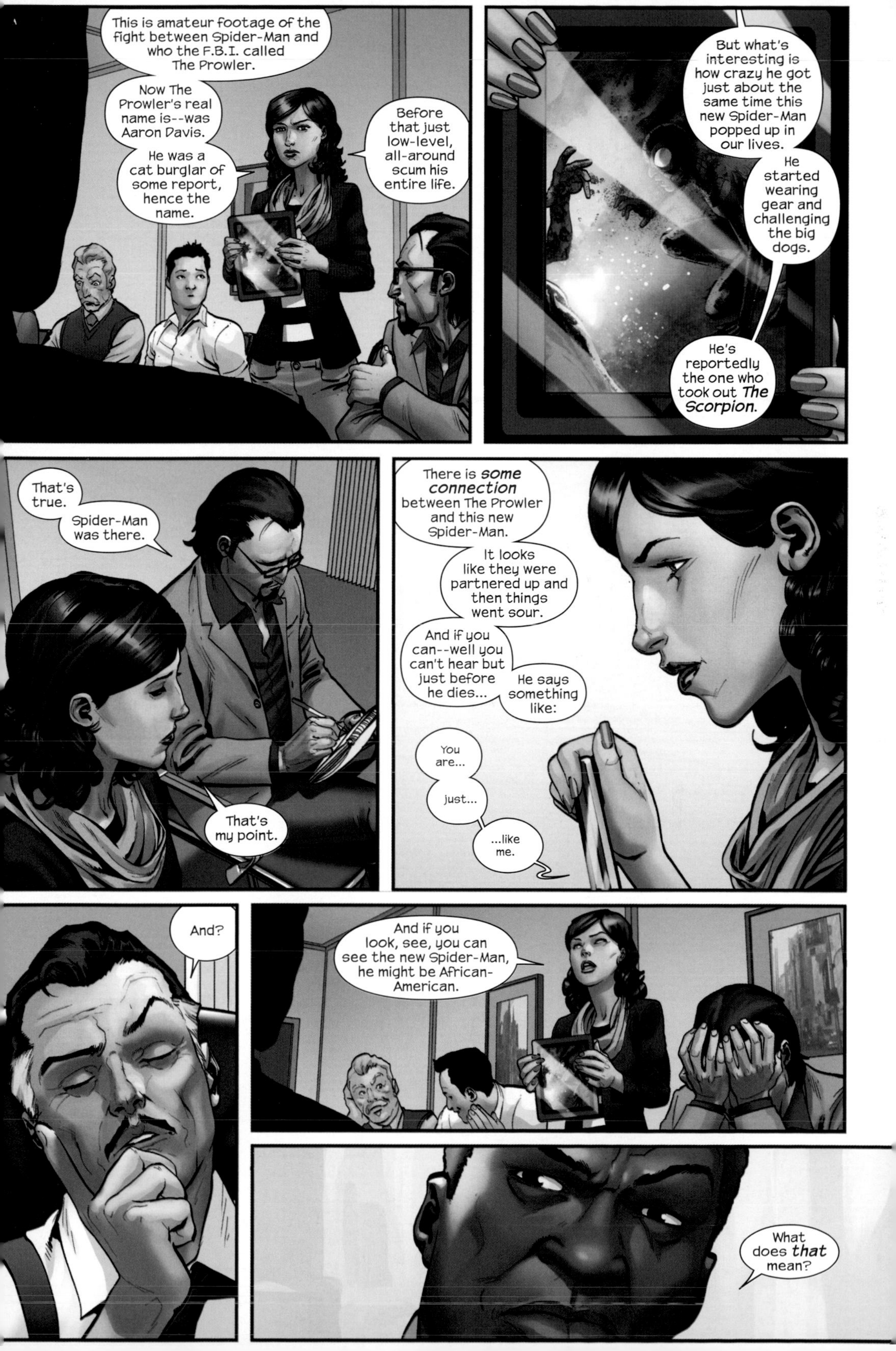
This is amateur footage of the fight between Spider-Man and who the F.B.I. called The Prowler.
Now The Prowler's real name is--was Aaron Davis.
He was a cat burglar of some report, hence the name.
Before that just low-level, all-around scum his entire life.
But what's interesting is how crazy he got just about the same time this new Spider-Man popped up in our lives.
He started wearing gear and challenging the big dogs.
He's reportedly the one who took out *The Scorpion*.
That's true.
Spider-Man was there.
That's my point.
There is *some connection* between The Prowler and this new Spider-Man.
It looks like they were partnered up and then things went sour.
And if you can--well you can't hear but just before he dies...
He says something like:
You are...
just...
...like me.
And?
And if you look, see, you can see the new Spider-Man, he might be African-American.
What does *that* mean?

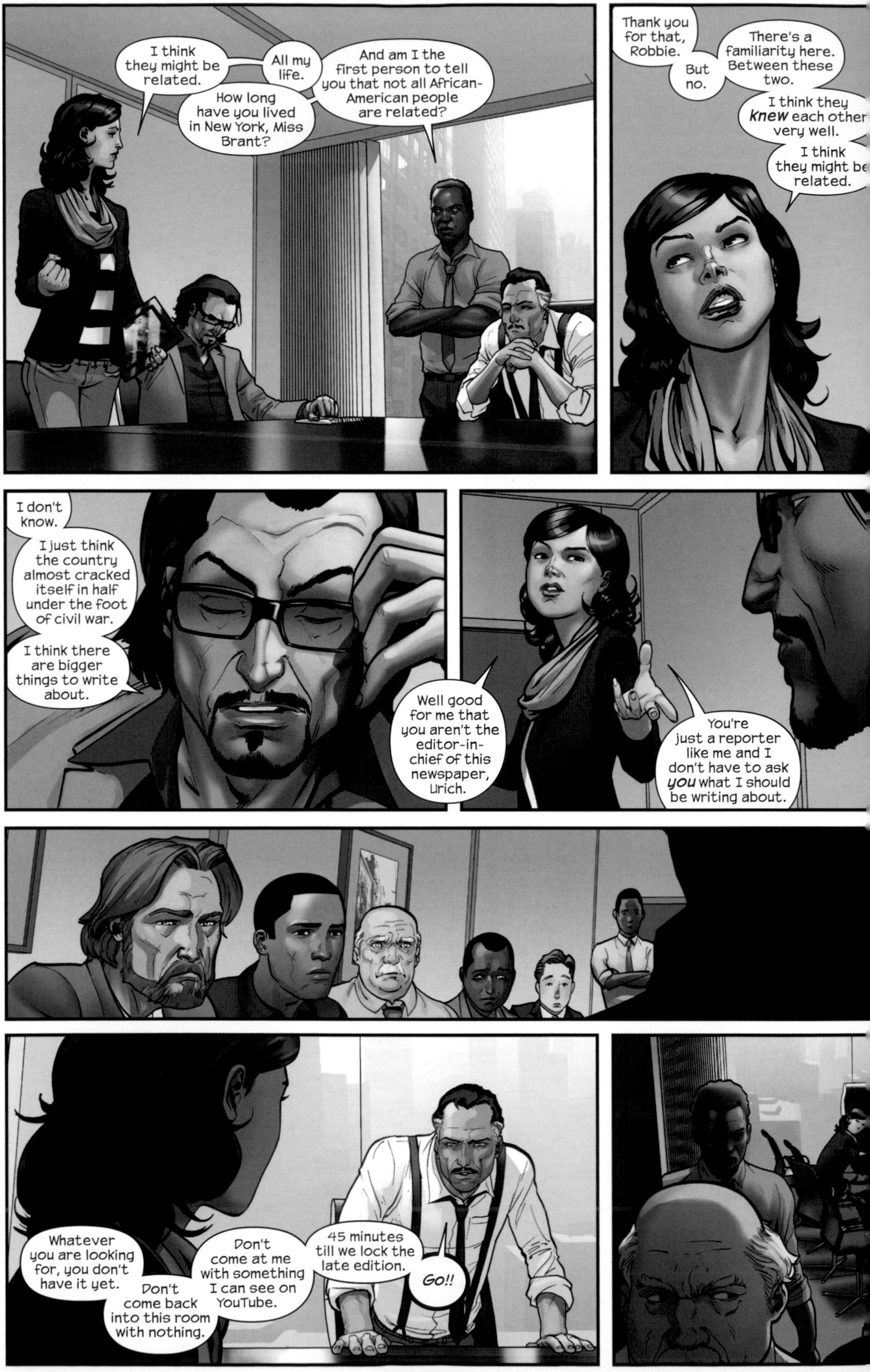

I think they might be related.
How long have you lived in New York, Miss Brant?
All my life.
And am I the first person to tell you that not all African-American people are related?
Thank you for that, Robbie.
But no.
There's a familiarity here. Between these two.
I think they *knew* each other very well.
I think they might be related.
I don't know.
I just think the country almost cracked itself in half under the foot of civil war.
I think there are bigger things to write about.
Well good for me that you aren't the editor-in-chief of this newspaper, Urich.
You're just a reporter like me and I don't have to ask *you* what I should be writing about.
Whatever you are looking for, you don't have it yet.
Don't come back into this room with nothing.
Don't come at me with something I can see on YouTube.
45 minutes till we lock the late edition.
Go!!

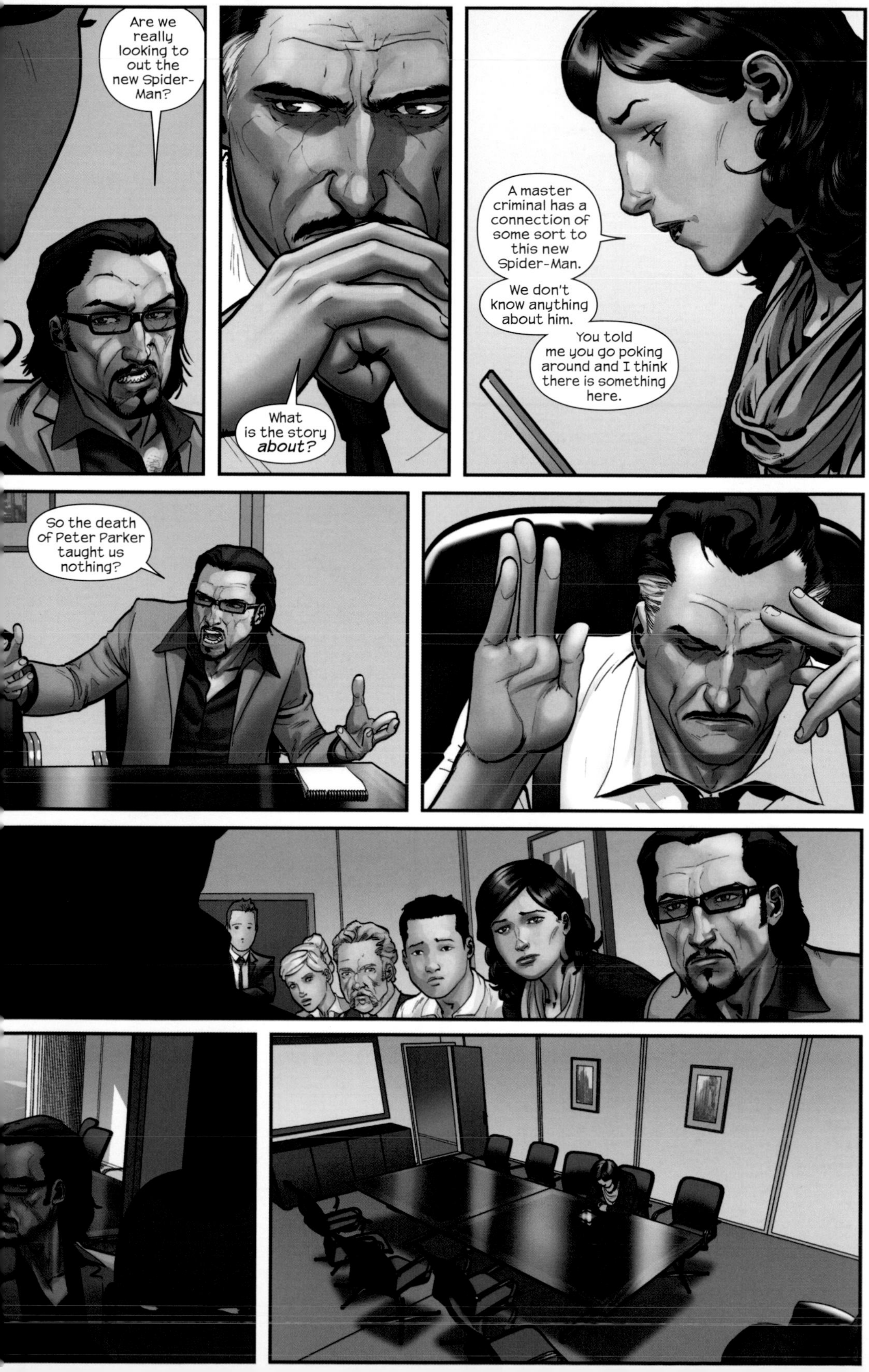
Are we really looking to out the new Spider-Man?
What is the story *about?*
A master criminal has a connection of some sort to this new Spider-Man.
We don't know anything about him.
You told me you go poking around and I think there is something here.
So the death of Peter Parker taught us nothing?

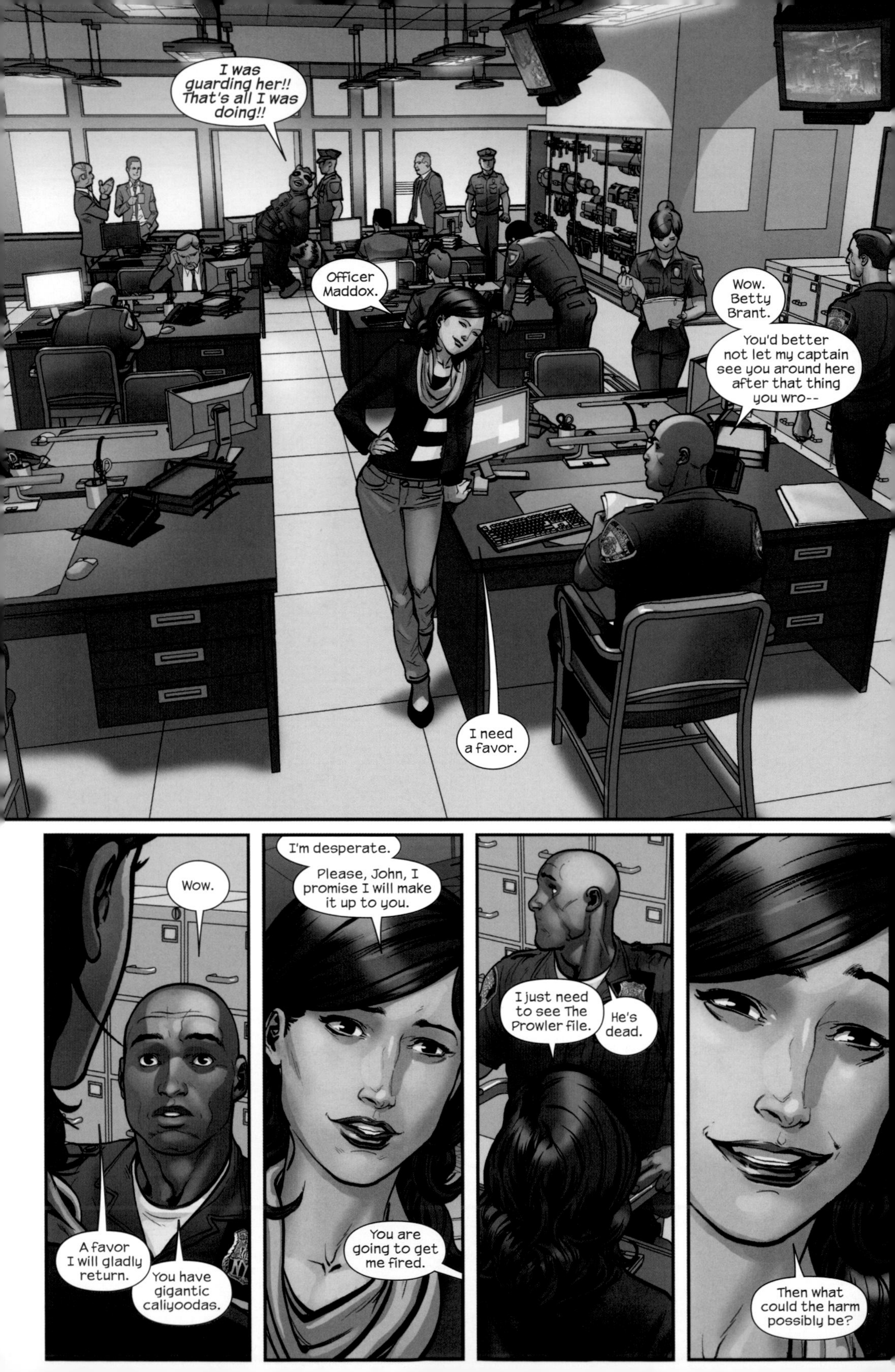
I was guarding her!! That's all I was doing!!
Officer Maddox.
Wow. Betty Brant.
You'd better not let my captain see you around here after that thing you wro--
I need a favor.
Wow.
A favor I will gladly return.
You have gigantic caliyoodas.
I'm desperate.
Please, John, I promise I will make it up to you.
You are going to get me fired.
I just need to see The Prowler file.
He's dead.
Then what could the harm possibly be?

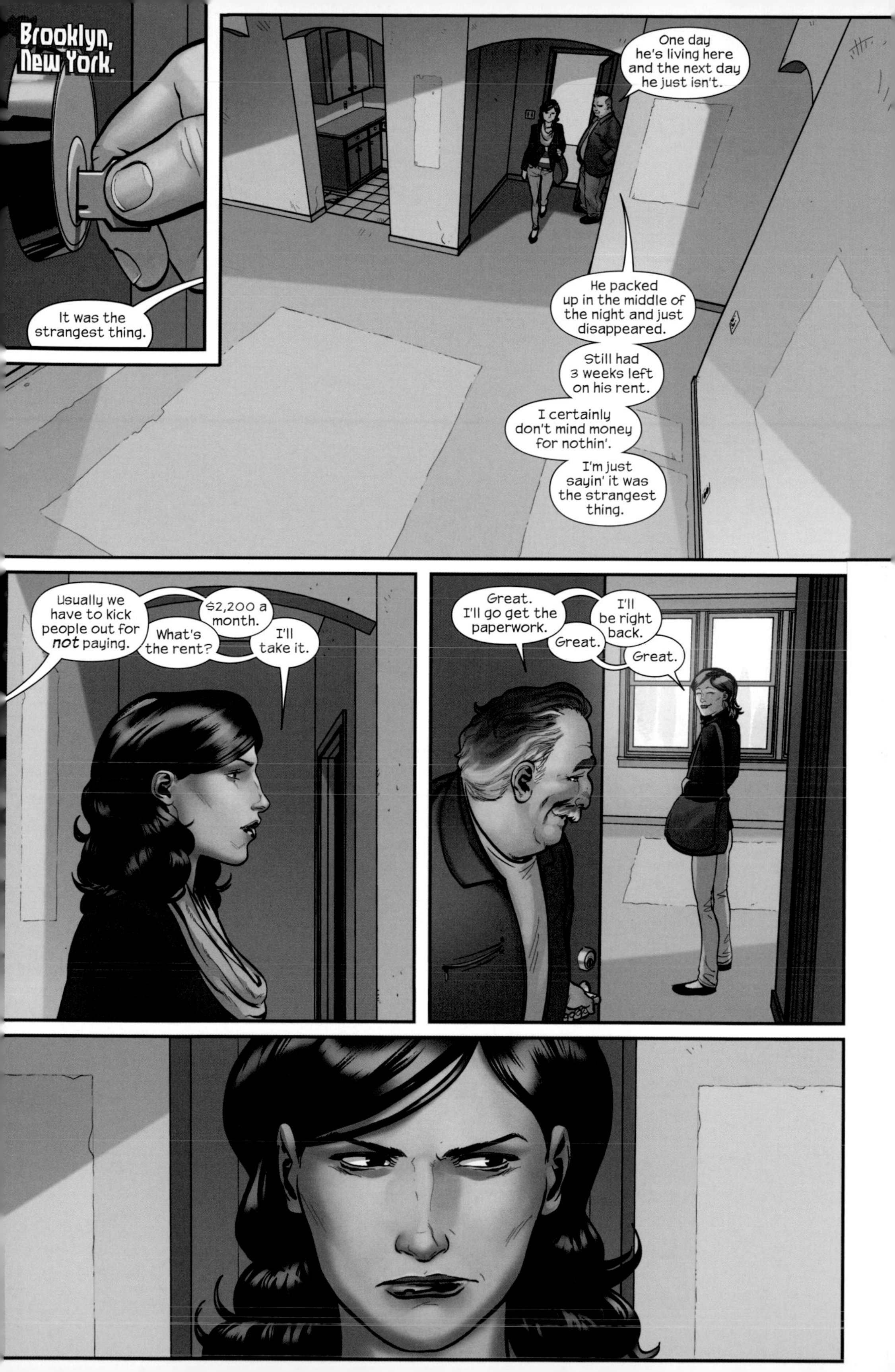
Brooklyn, New York.
It was the strangest thing.
One day he's living here and the next day he just isn't.
He packed up in the middle of the night and just disappeared.
Still had 3 weeks left on his rent.
I certainly don't mind money for nothin'.
I'm just sayin' it was the strangest thing.
Usually we have to kick people out for *not* paying.
What's the rent?
$2,200 a month.
I'll take it.
Great. I'll go get the paperwork.
Great.
I'll be right back.
Great.

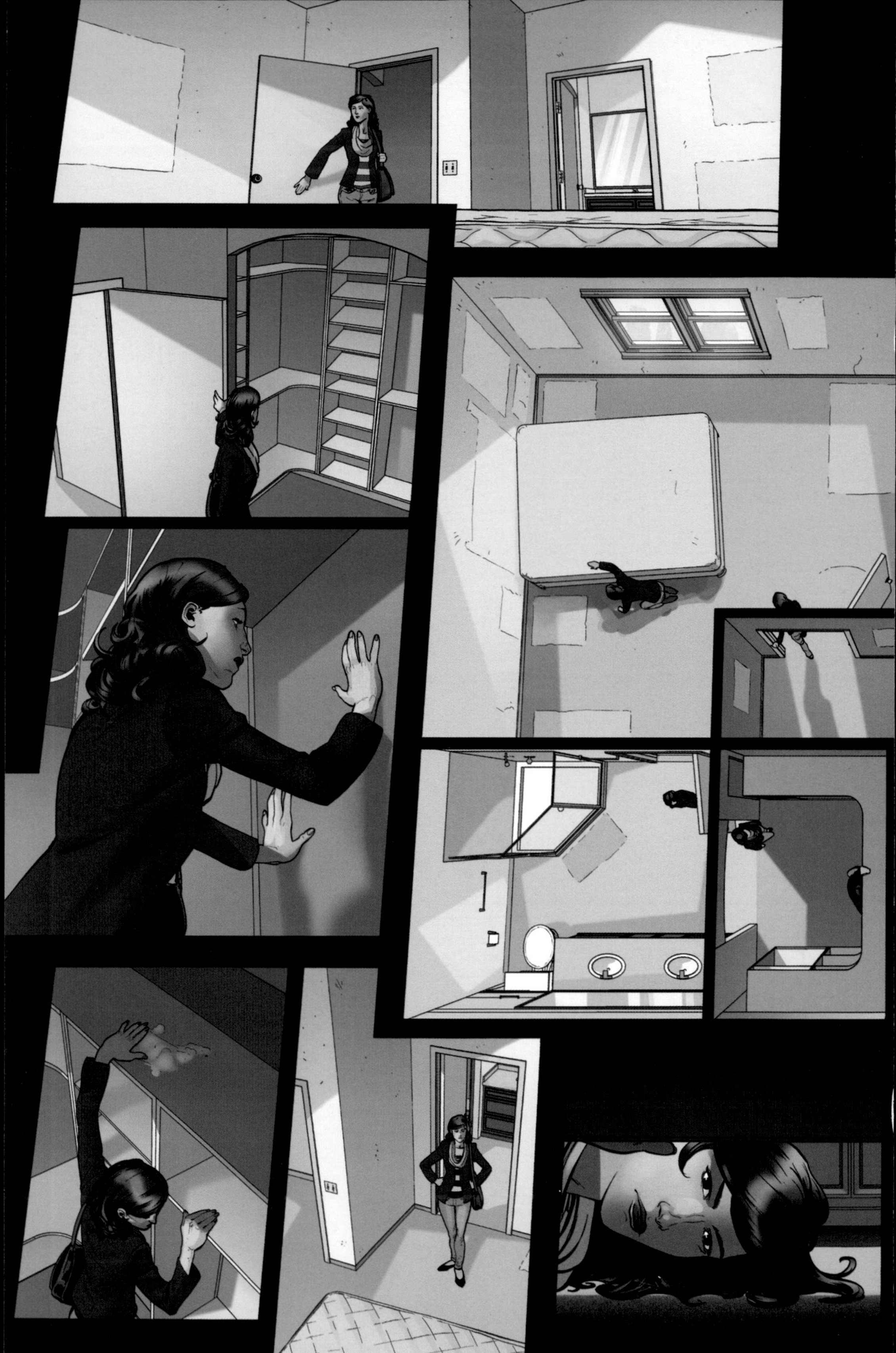

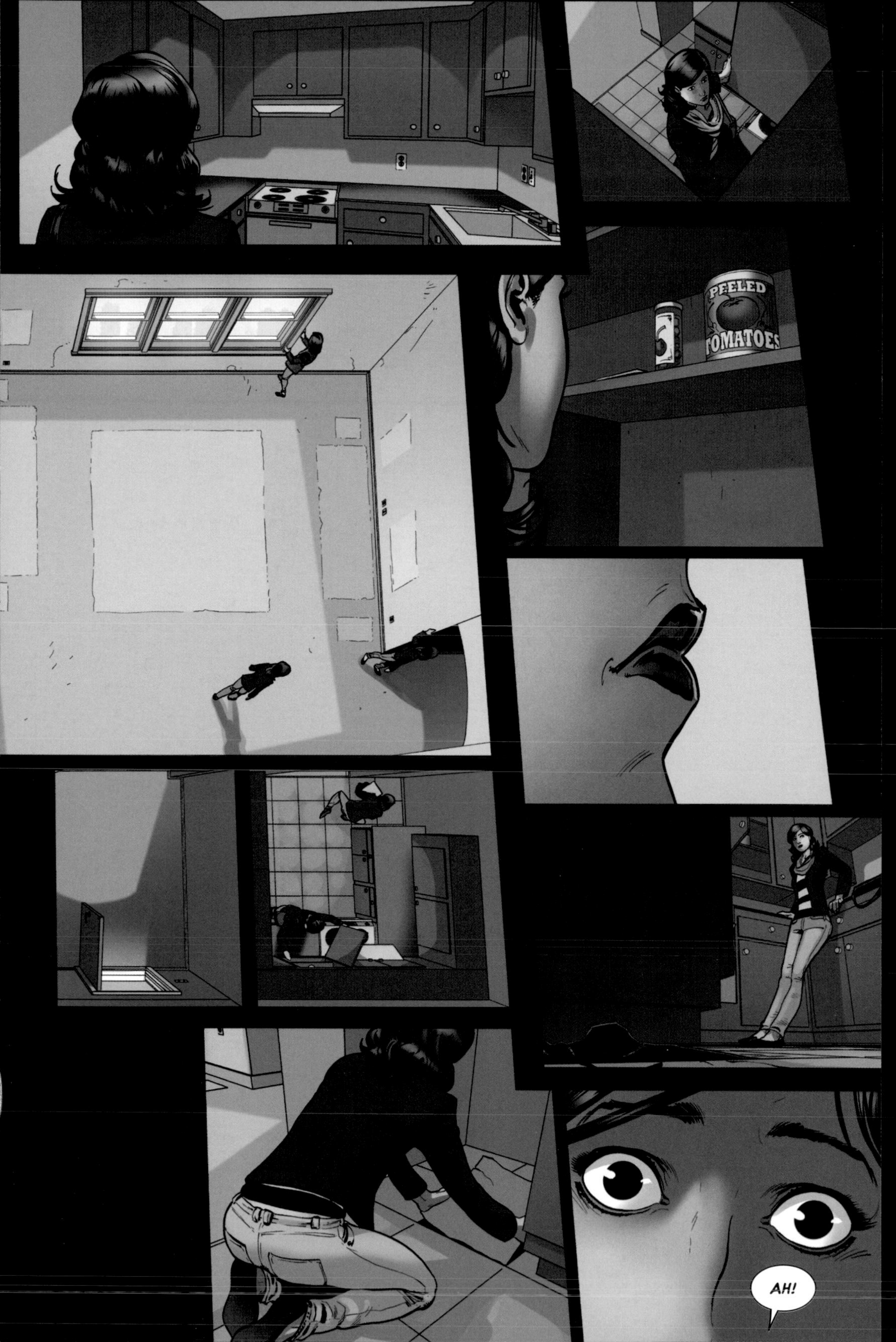
PEELED
TOMATOES
AH!

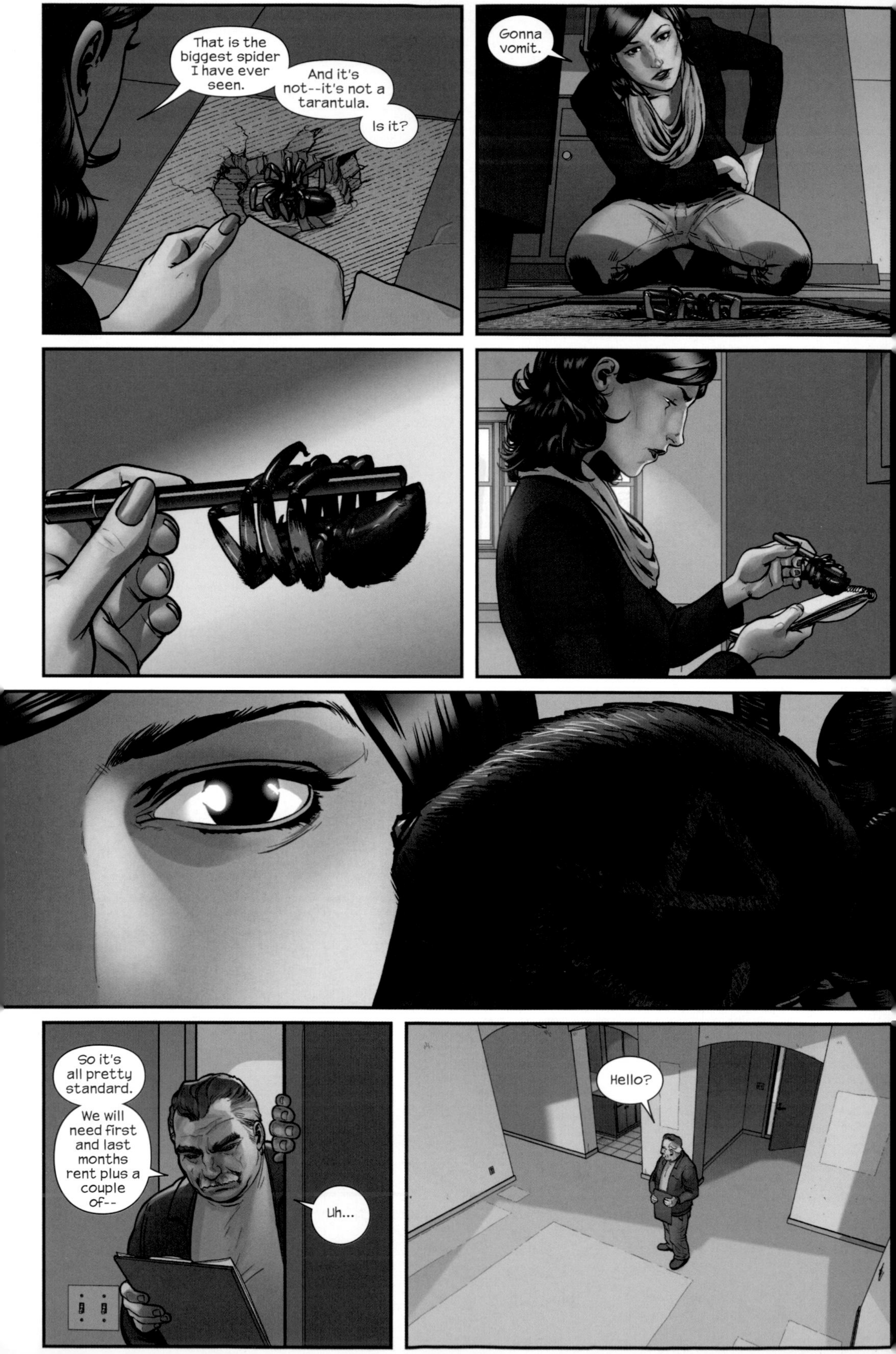
That is the biggest spider I have ever seen.
And it's not--it's not a tarantula.
Is it?
Gonna vomit.
So it's all pretty standard.
We will need first and last months rent plus a couple of--
Uh...
Hello?

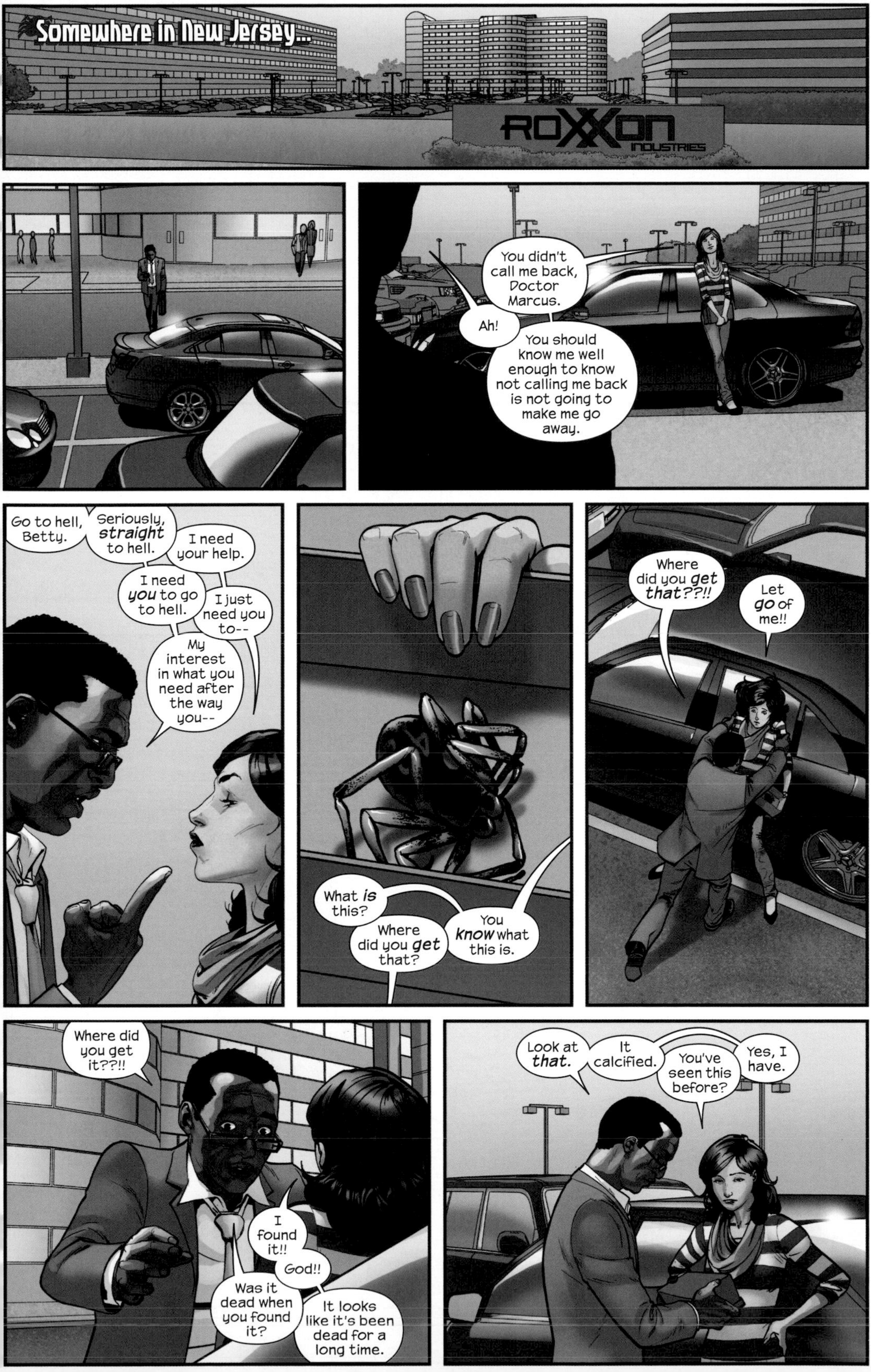
Somewhere in New Jersey...
ROXXON INDUSTRIES
You didn't call me back, Doctor Marcus.
Ah!
You should know me well enough to know not calling me back is not going to make me go away.
Go to hell, Betty.
Seriously, straight to hell.
I need your help.
I need you to go to hell.
I just need you to--
My interest in what you need after the way you--
What is this?
Where did you get that?
You know what this is.
Where did you get that??!!
Let go of me!!
Where did you get it??!!
I found it!!
God!!
Was it dead when you found it?
It looks like it's been dead for a long time.
Look at that.
It calcified.
You've seen this before?
Yes, I have.

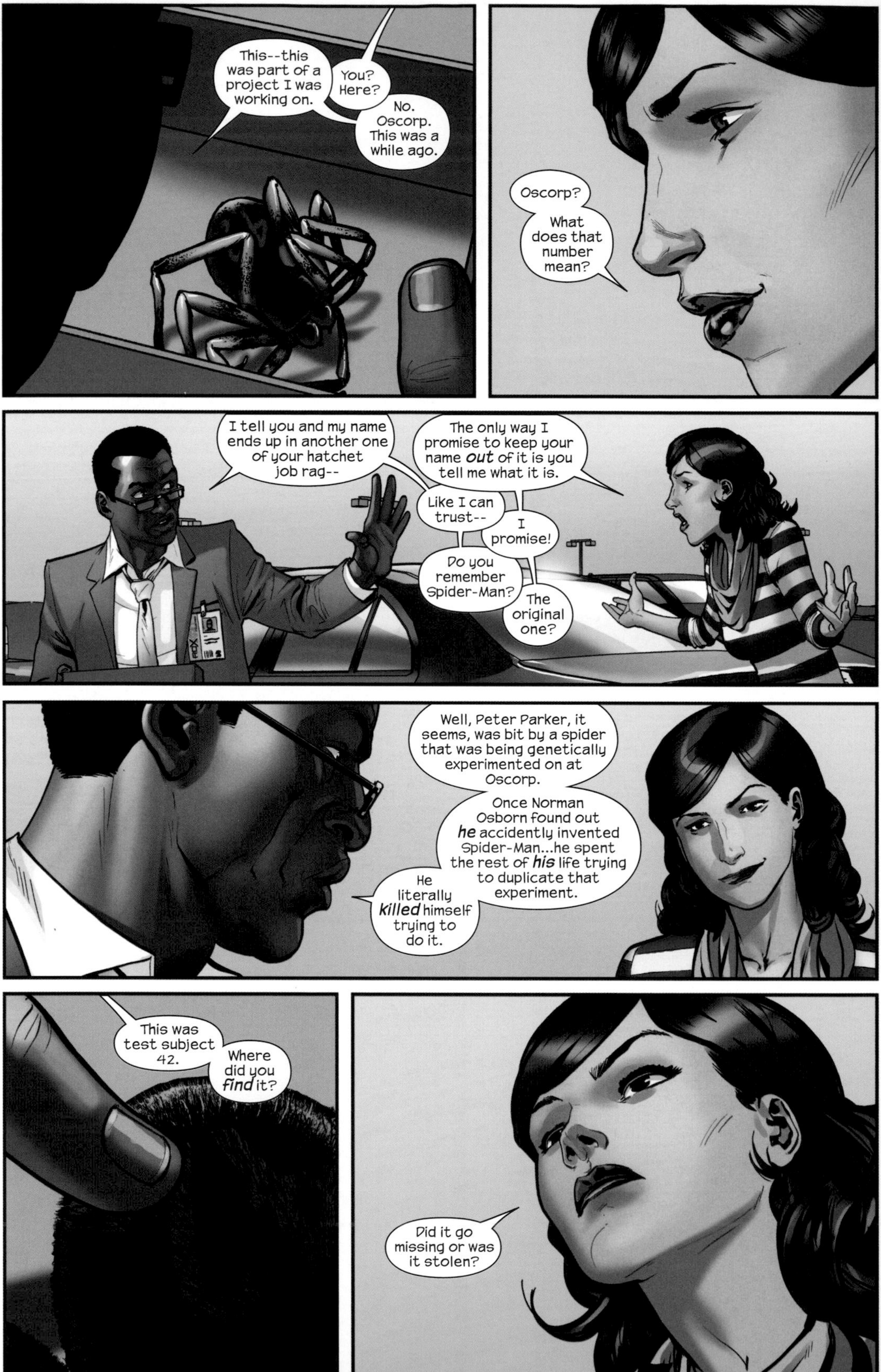
This--this was part of a project I was working on.
You? Here?
No. Oscorp. This was a while ago.
Oscorp?
What does that number mean?
I tell you and my name ends up in another one of your hatchet job rag--
The only way I promise to keep your name *out* of it is you tell me what it is.
Like I can trust--
I promise!
Do you remember Spider-Man?
The original one?
Well, Peter Parker, it seems, was bit by a spider that was being genetically experimented on at Oscorp.
Once Norman Osborn found out *he* accidently invented Spider-Man...he spent the rest of *his* life trying to duplicate that experiment.
He literally *killed* himself trying to do it.
This was test subject 42.
Where did you *find* it?
Did it go missing or was it stolen?

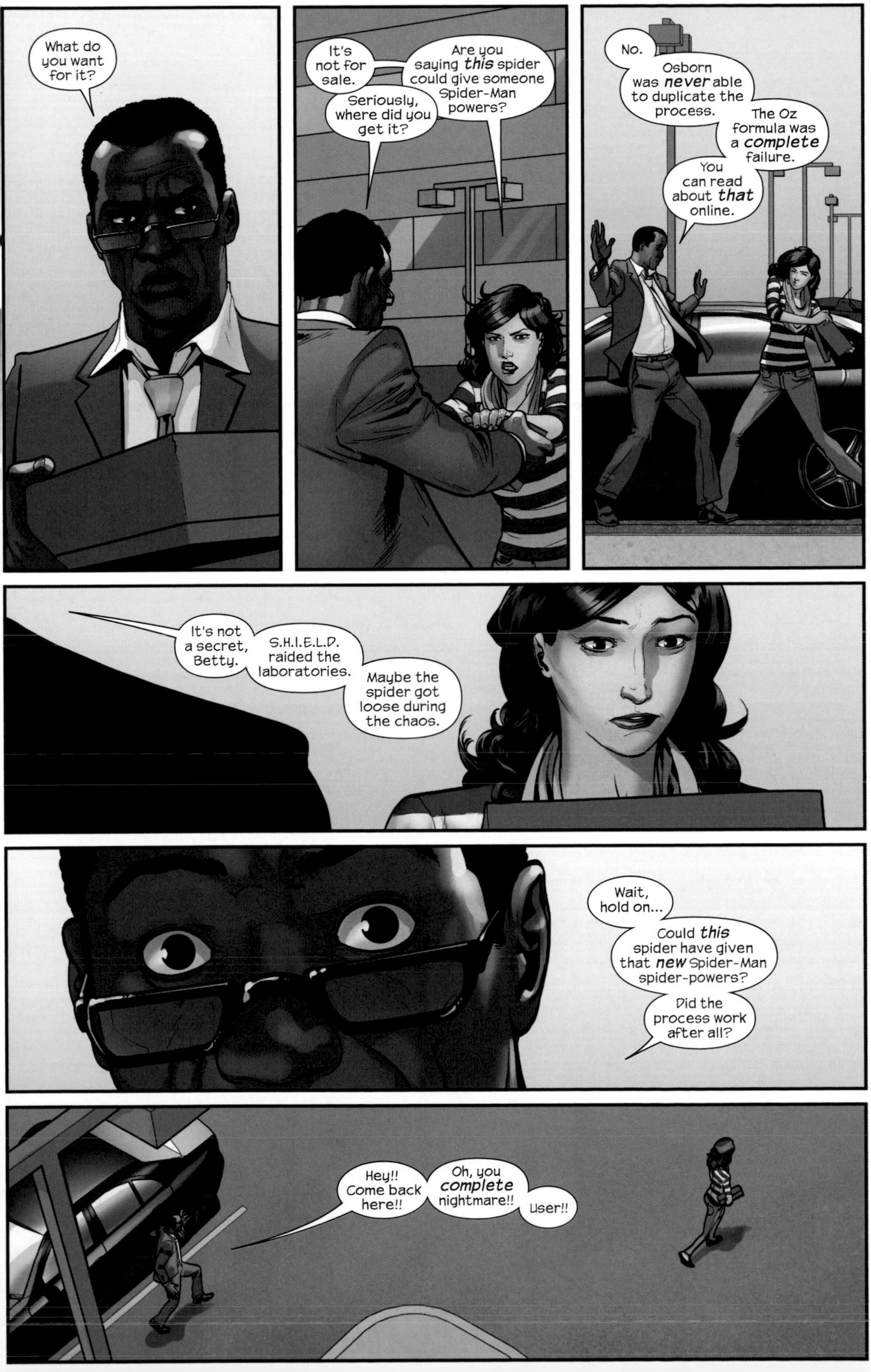
What do you want for it?
It's not for sale.
Are you saying this spider could give someone Spider-Man powers?
Seriously, where did you get it?
No.
Osborn was never able to duplicate the process.
The Oz formula was a complete failure.
You can read about that online.
It's not a secret, Betty.
S.H.I.E.L.D. raided the laboratories.
Maybe the spider got loose during the chaos.
Wait, hold on...
Could this spider have given that new Spider-Man spider-powers?
Did the process work after all?
Hey!! Come back here!!
Oh, you complete nightmare!!
User!!

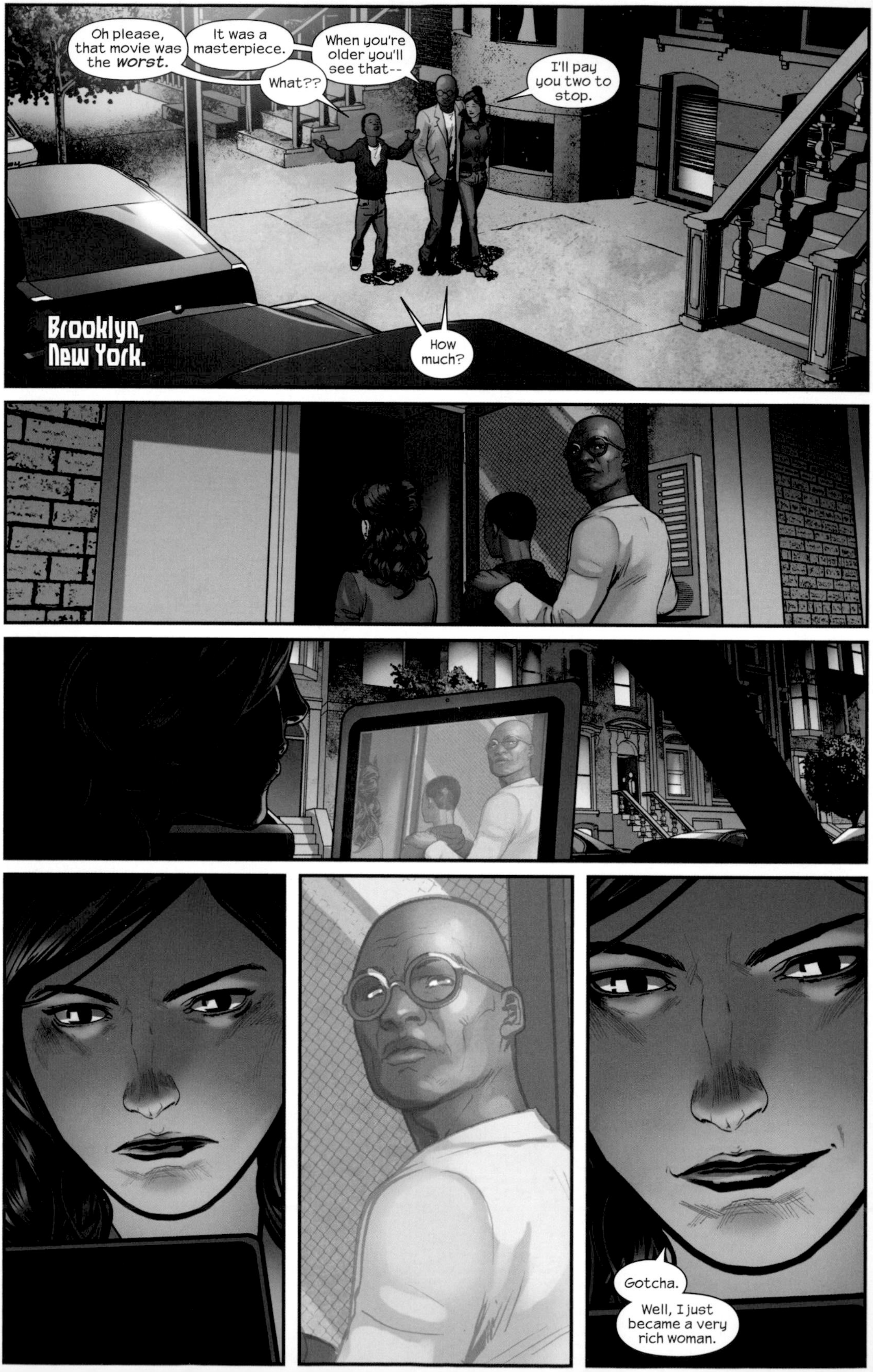

Oh please, that movie was the *worst.*
It was a masterpiece.
When you're older you'll see that--
What??
I'll pay you two to stop.
Brooklyn, New York.
How much?
Gotcha.
Well, I just became a very rich woman.

You don't say.

I know who the new Spider-Man is.

I have physical evidence. I have proof.

It's a great story.

And I want you and I, right now, to work out our financial differences.

We have financial differences?

I don't like how much I make.

I don't like that I'm treated like a lesser reporter because of past indiscretions.

And I would like to rectify all of this in exchange for this world-wide exclusive.

Let me see it.

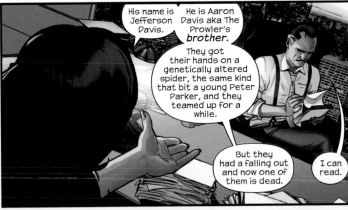

His name is Jefferson Davis.

He is Aaron Davis aka The Prowler's *brother.*

They got their hands on a genetically altered spider, the same kind that bit a young Peter Parker, and they teamed up for a while.

But they had a falling out and now one of them is dead.

I can read.

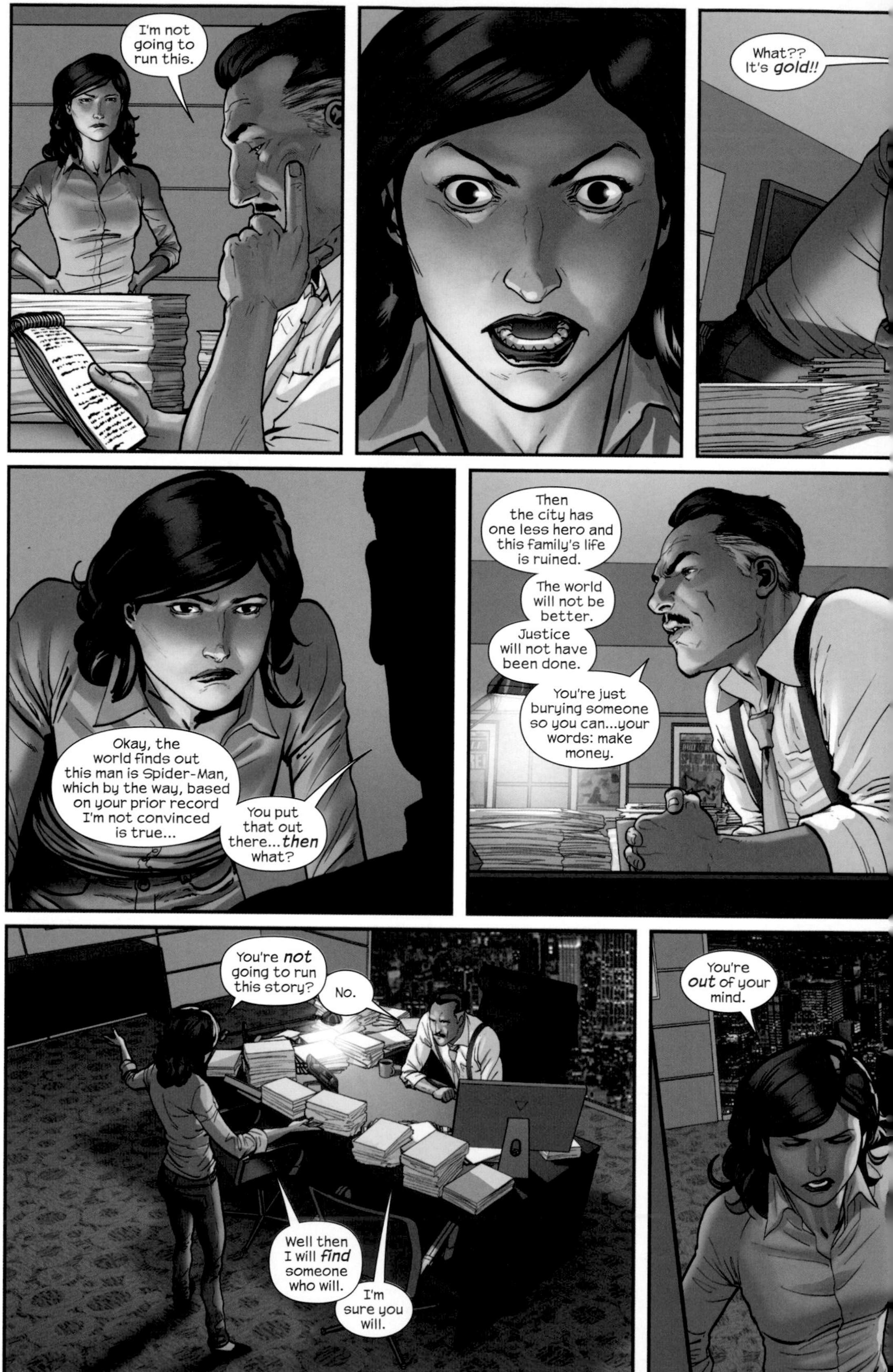
I'm not going to run this.
What?? It's *gold!!*
Then the city has one less hero and this family's life is ruined.
The world will not be better.
Justice will not have been done.
You're just burying someone so you can...your words: make money.
Okay, the world finds out this man is Spider-Man, which by the way, based on your prior record I'm not convinced is true...
You put that out there...*then* what?
You're *not* going to run this story?
No.
Well then I will *find* someone who will.
I'm sure you will.
You're *out* of your mind.

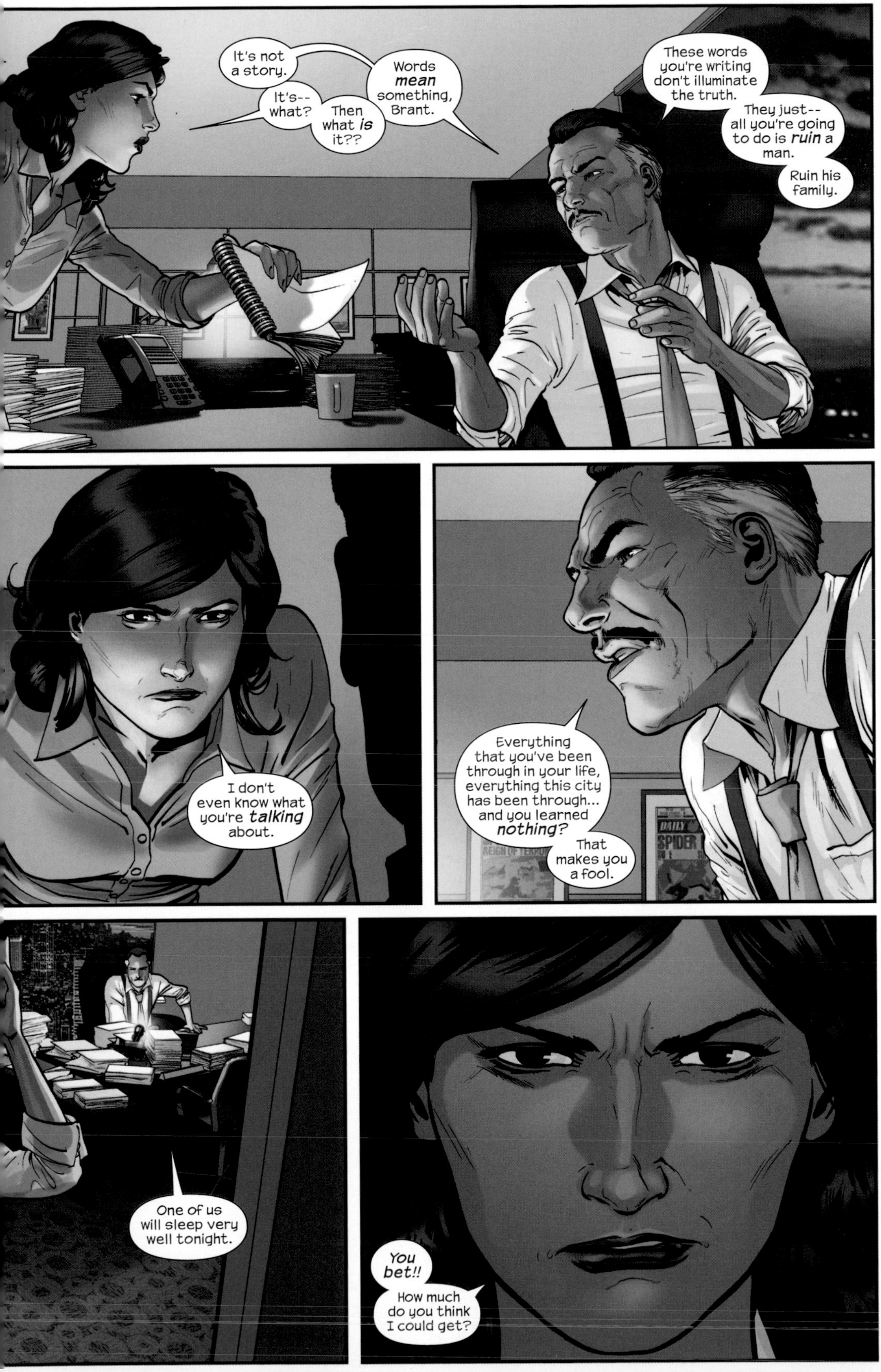

Words mean something, Brant.
It's not a story.
It's--what?
Then what is it??
These words you're writing don't illuminate the truth.
They just--all you're going to do is ruin a man.
Ruin his family.
I don't even know what you're talking about.
Everything that you've been through in your life, everything this city has been through... and you learned nothing?
That makes you a fool.
One of us will sleep very well tonight.
You bet!!
How much do you think I could get?

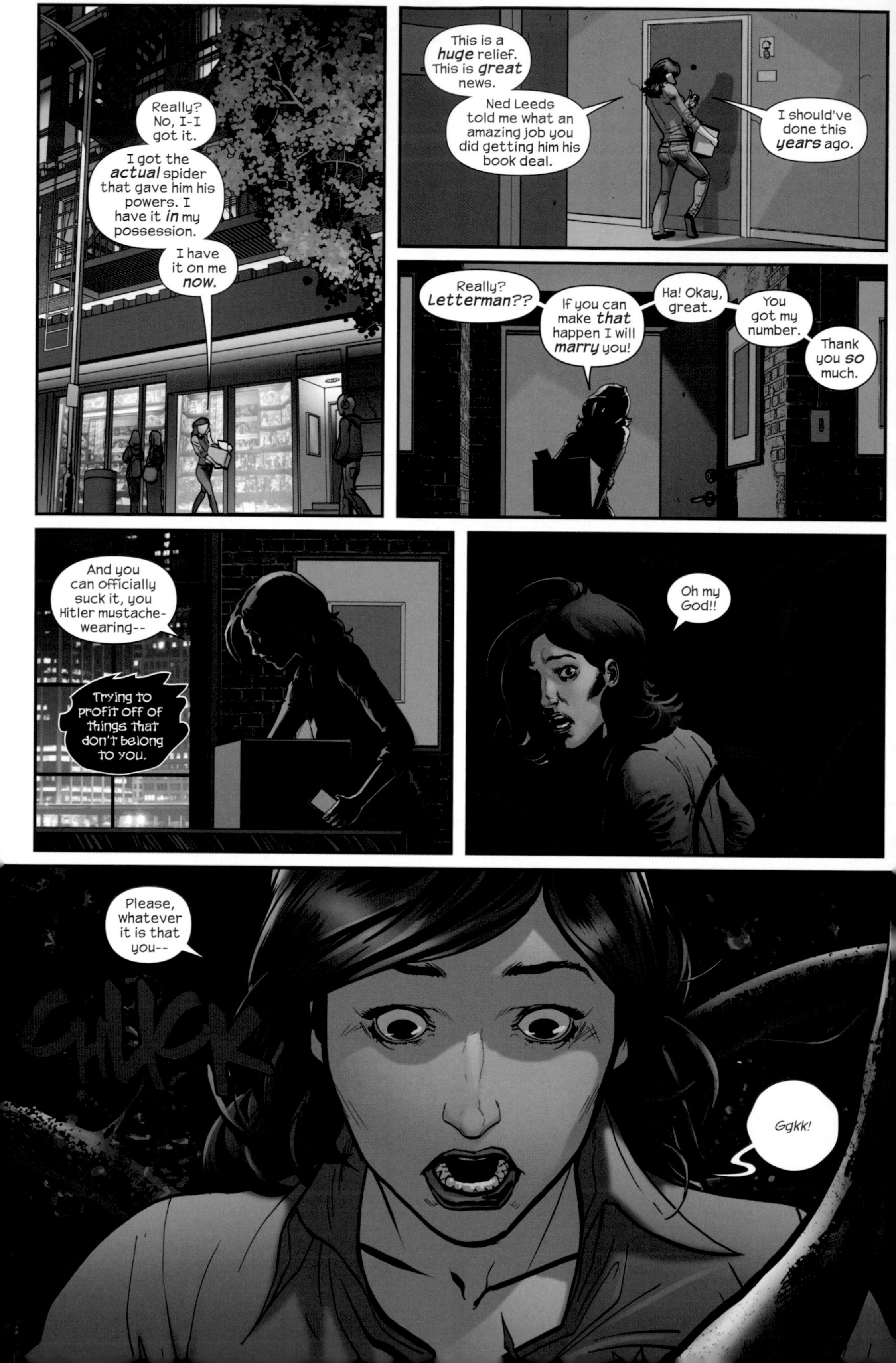
Really? No, I-I got it.
I got the *actual* spider that gave him his powers. I have it *in* my possession.
I have it on me *now.*
This is a *huge* relief. This is *great* news.
Ned Leeds told me what an amazing job you did getting him his book deal.
I should've done this *years* ago.
Really? *Letterman??*
If you can make *that* happen I will *marry* you!
Ha! Okay, great.
You got my number.
Thank you *so* much.
And you can officially suck it, you Hitler mustache-wearing--
Trying to profit off of things that don't belong to you.
Oh my God!!
Please, whatever it is that you--
CHUCK
Ggkk!

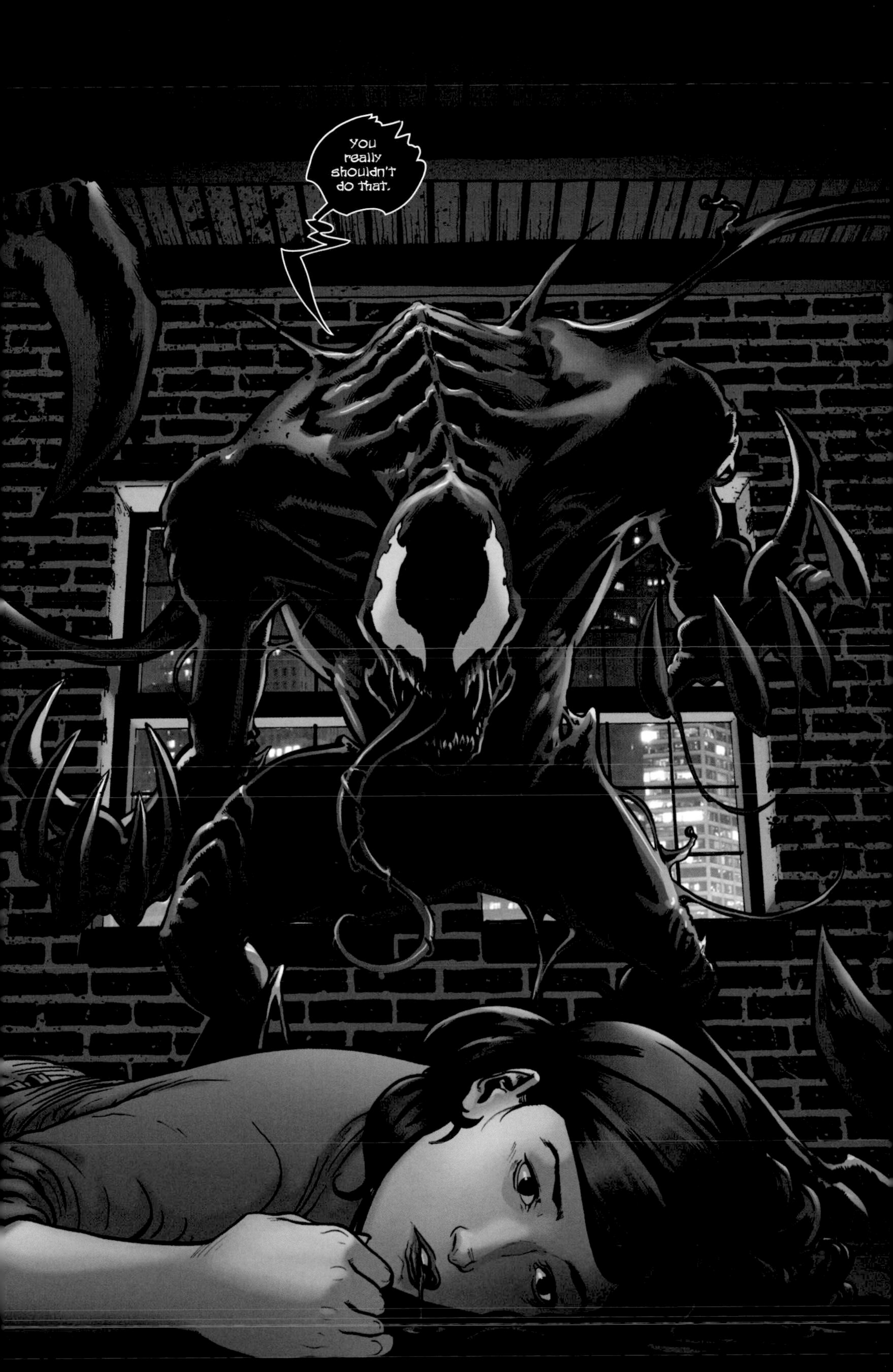
you really shouldn't do that.

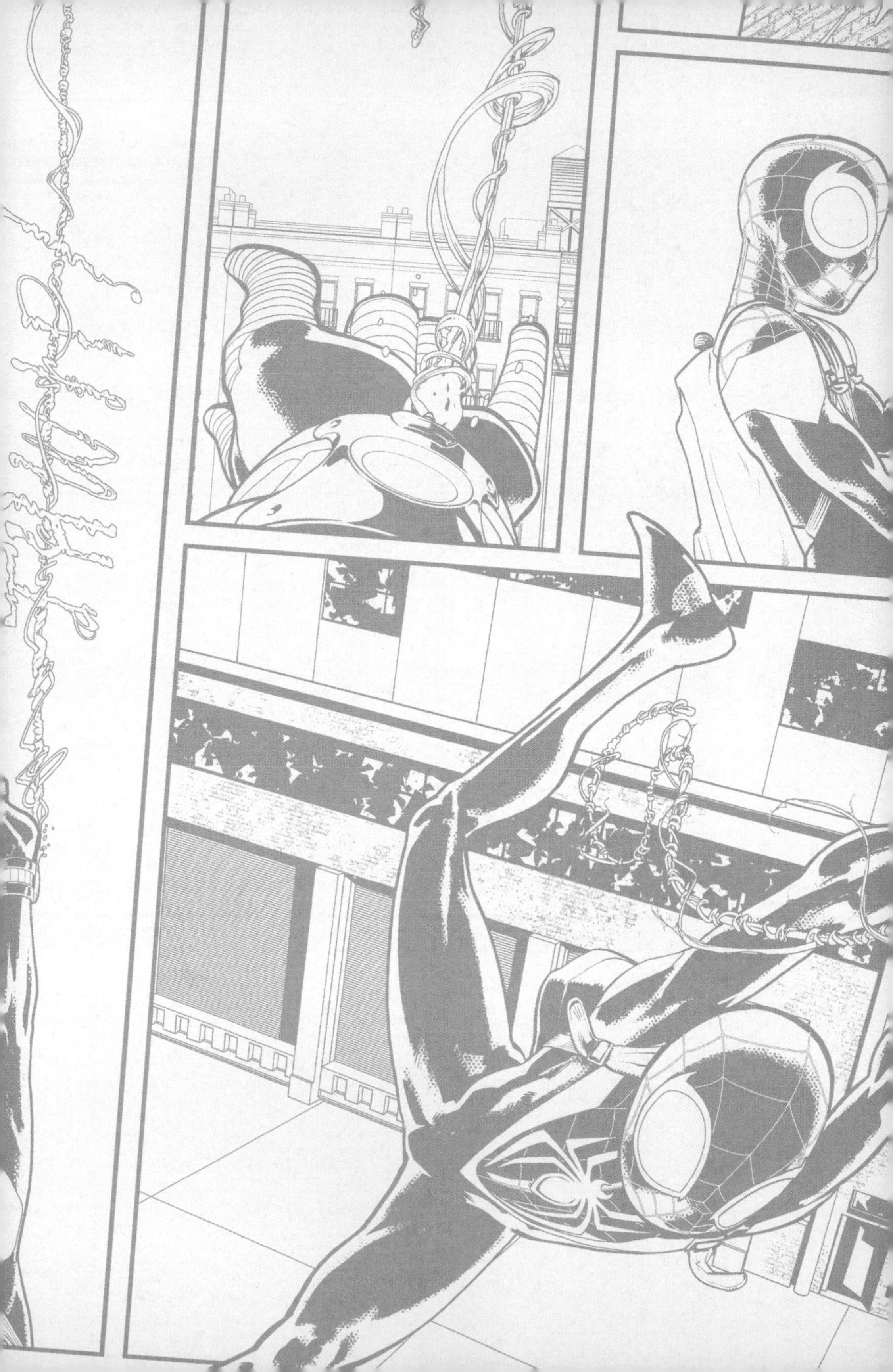

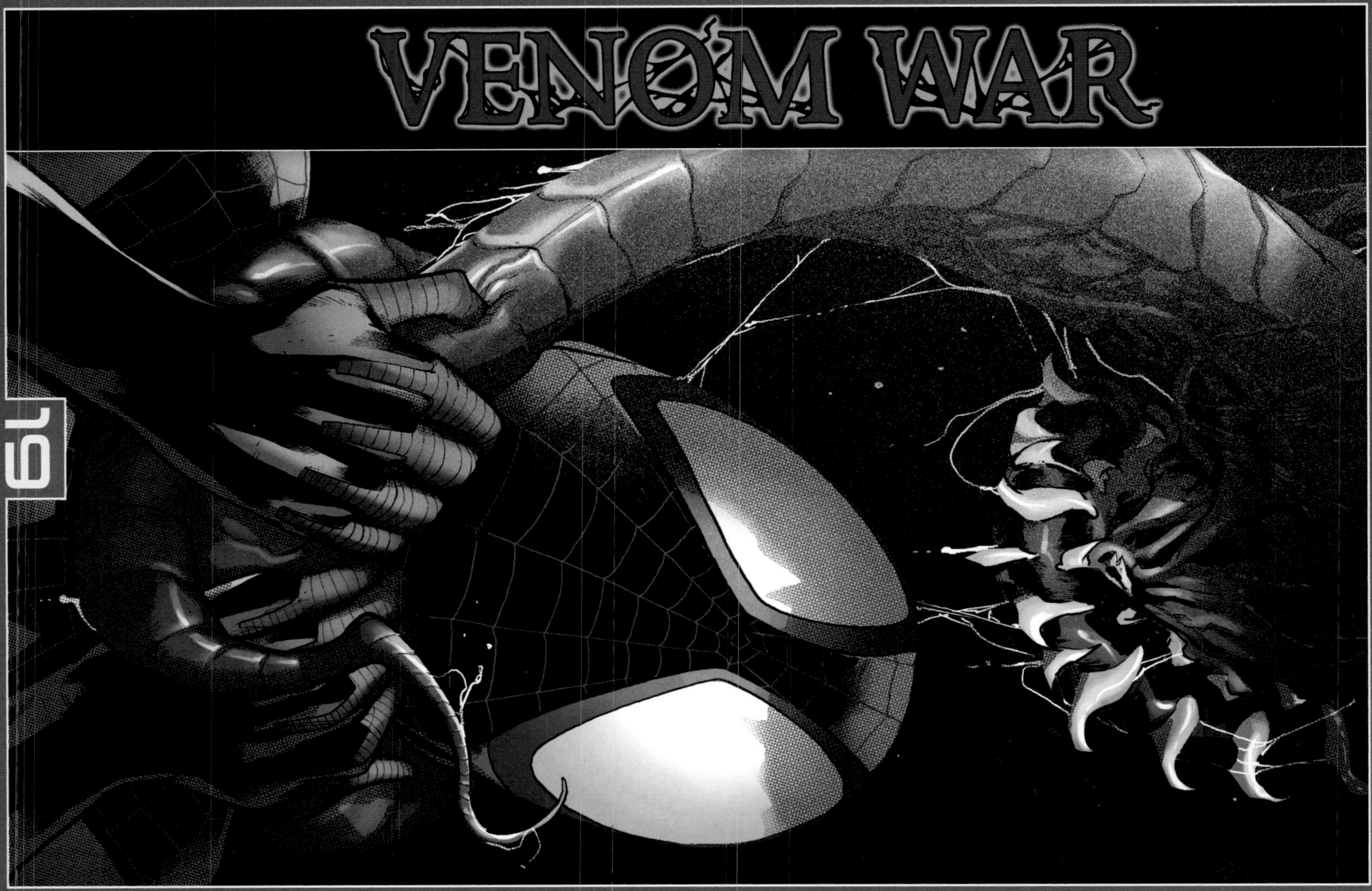
VENOM WAR
19

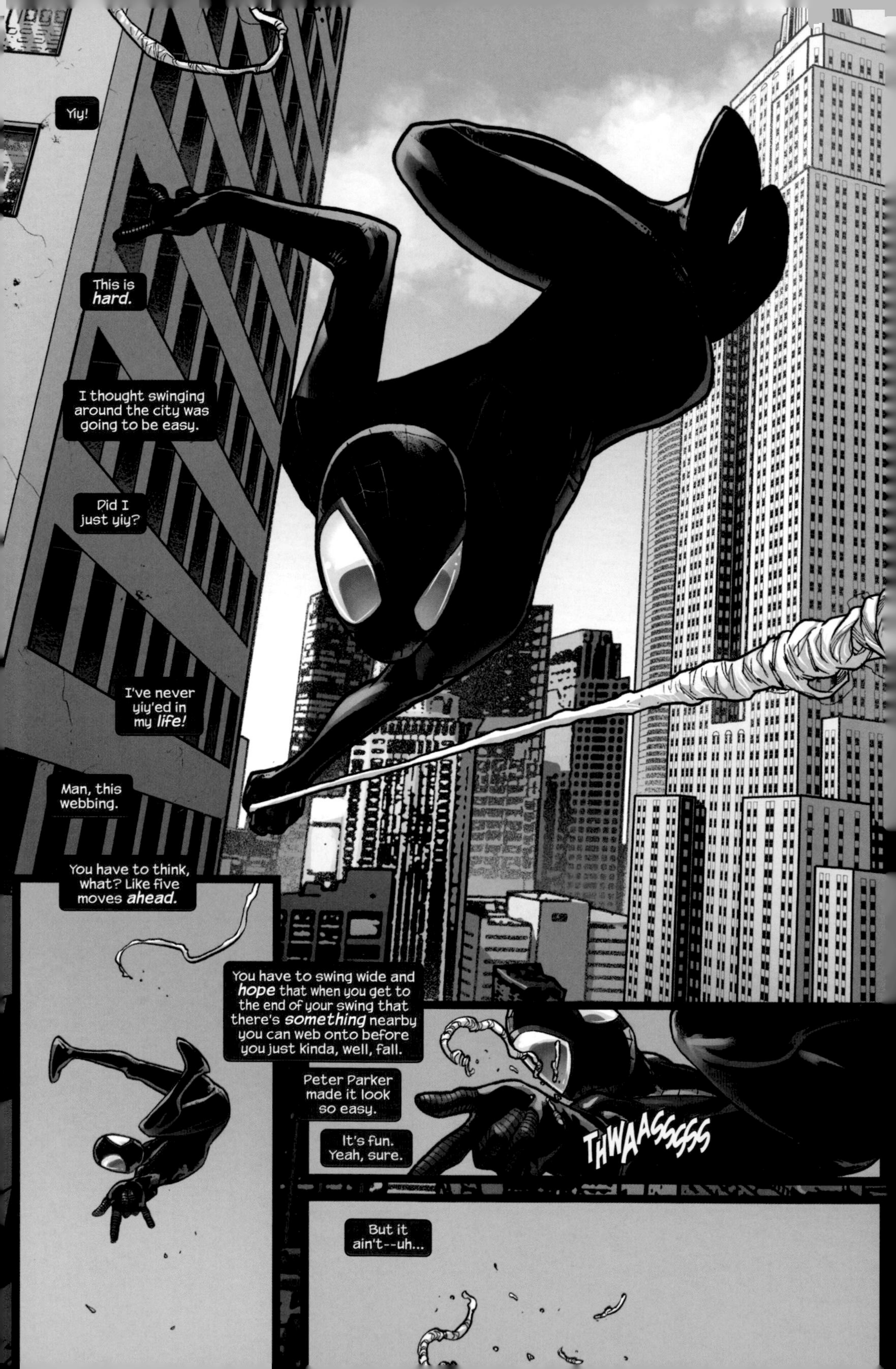
Yiy!
This is hard.
I thought swinging around the city was going to be easy.
Did I just yiy?
I've never yiy'ed in my life!
Man, this webbing.
You have to think, what? Like five moves ahead.
You have to swing wide and hope that when you get to the end of your swing that there's something nearby you can web onto before you just kinda, well, fall.
Peter Parker made it look so easy.
It's fun. Yeah, sure.
THWAASSSSS
But it ain't--uh...

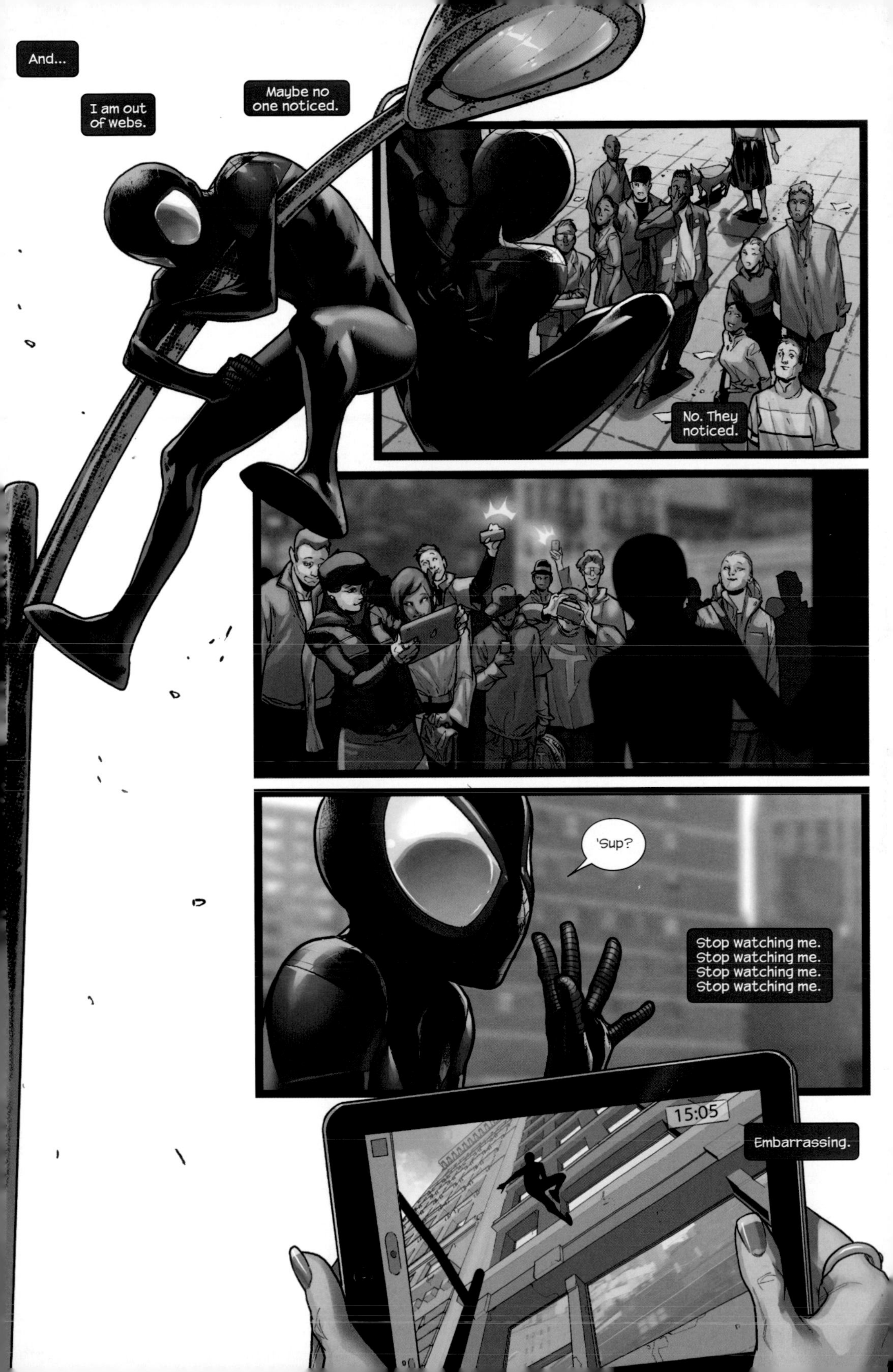
And...
I am out of webs.
Maybe no one noticed.
No. They noticed.
'Sup?
Stop watching me. Stop watching me. Stop watching me. Stop watching me.
15:05
Embarrassing.

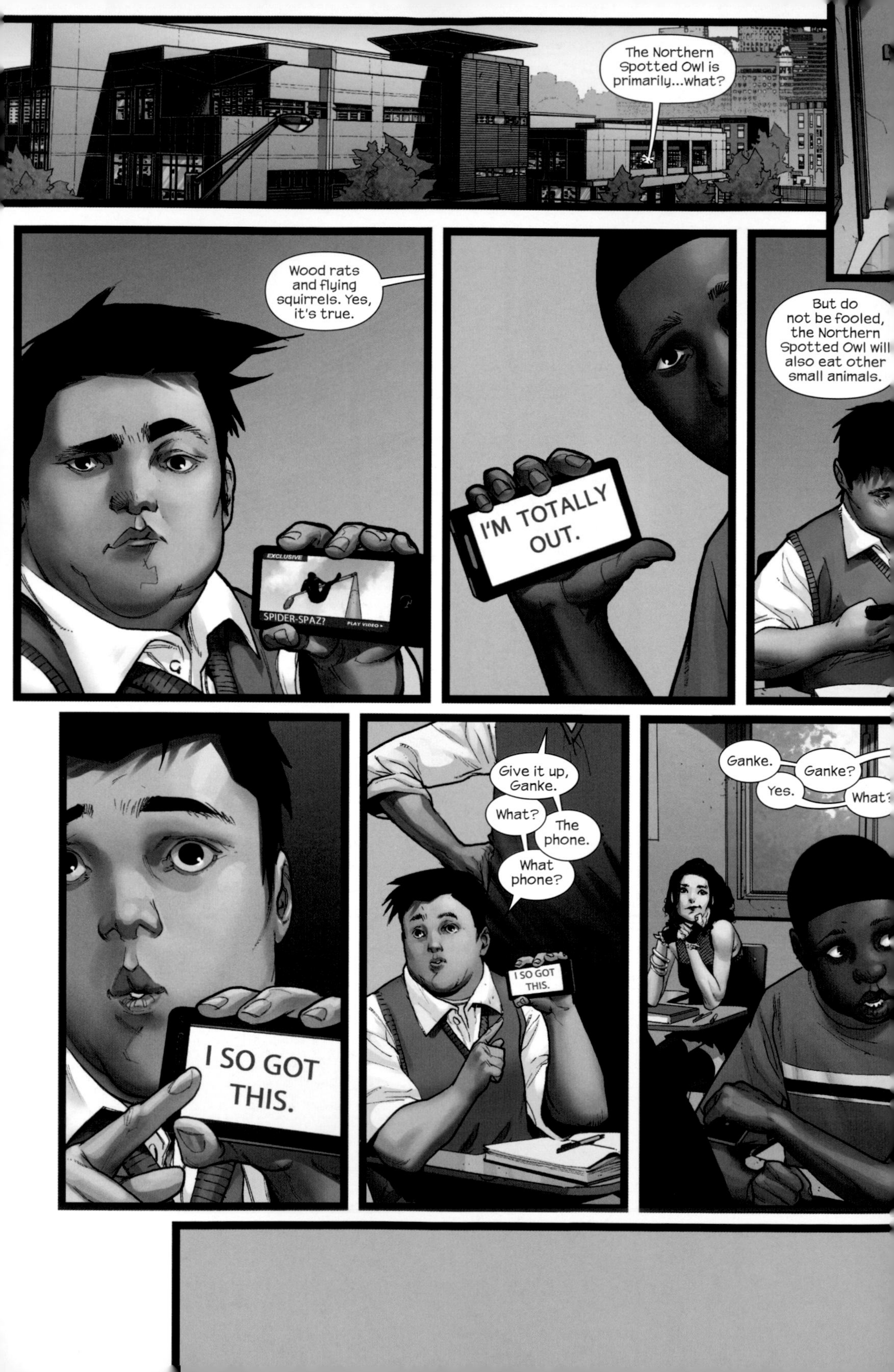

The Northern Spotted Owl is primarily...what?
Wood rats and flying squirrels. Yes, it's true.
EXCLUSIVE
SPIDER-SPAZ?
PLAY VIDEO ▸
I'M TOTALLY OUT.
But do not be fooled, the Northern Spotted Owl will also eat other small animals.
I SO GOT THIS.
Give it up, Ganke.
What?
The phone.
What phone?
I SO GOT THIS.
Ganke.
Ganke?
Yes.
What?

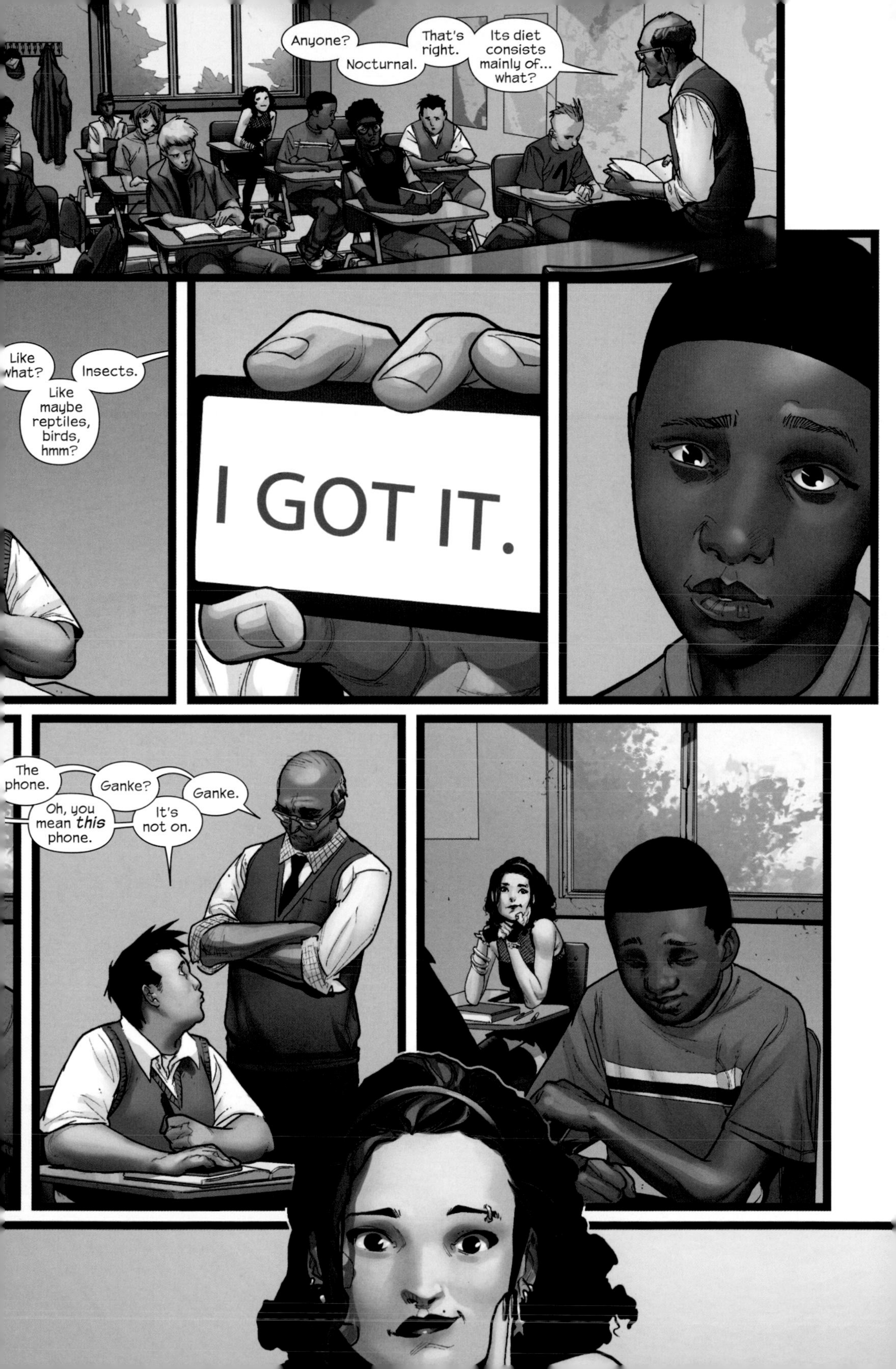

Anyone?
Nocturnal.
That's right.
Its diet consists mainly of... what?
Like what?
Insects.
Like maybe reptiles, birds, hmm?
I GOT IT.
The phone.
Ganke?
Ganke.
Oh, you mean *this* phone.
It's not on.

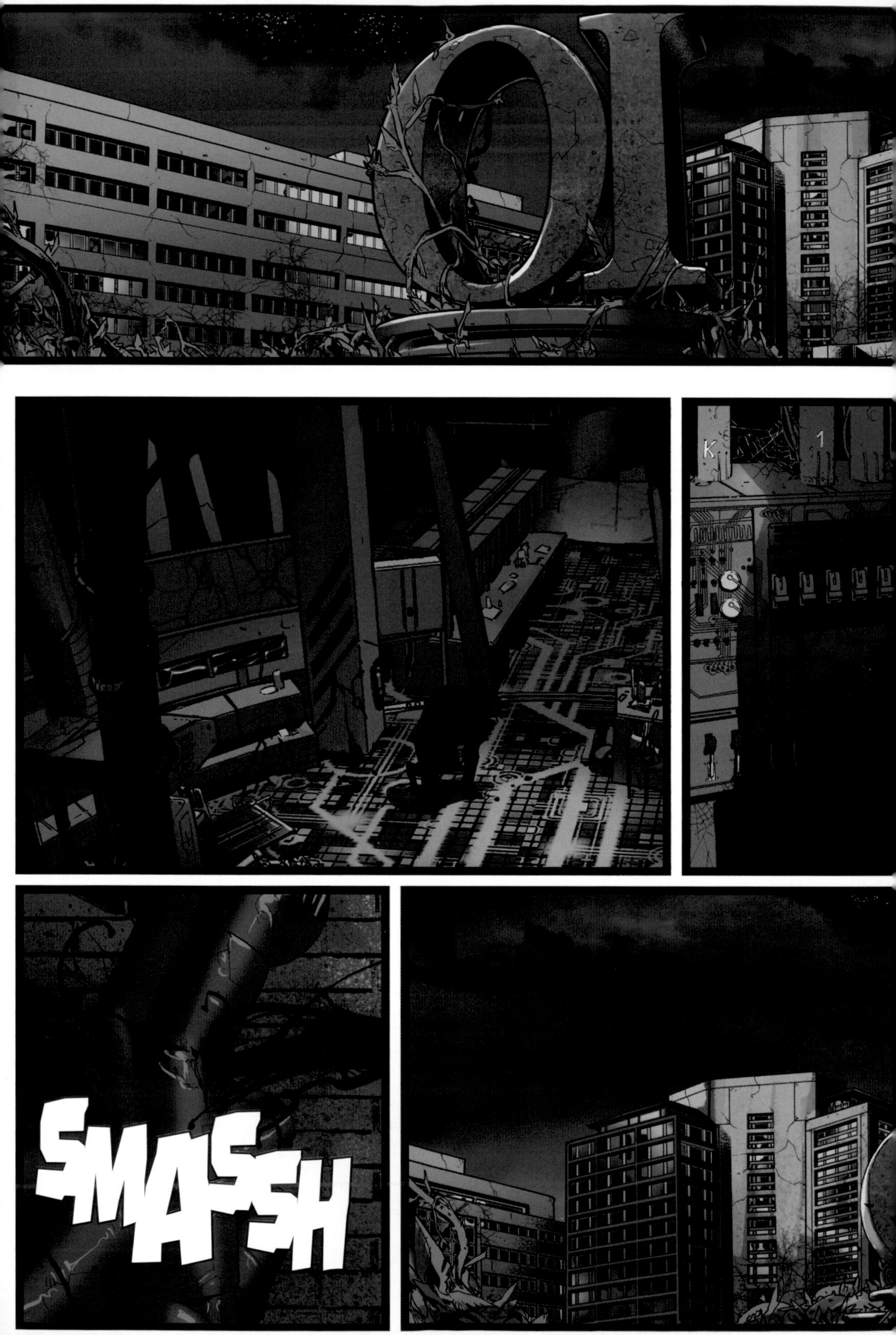
K
1
SMASSH

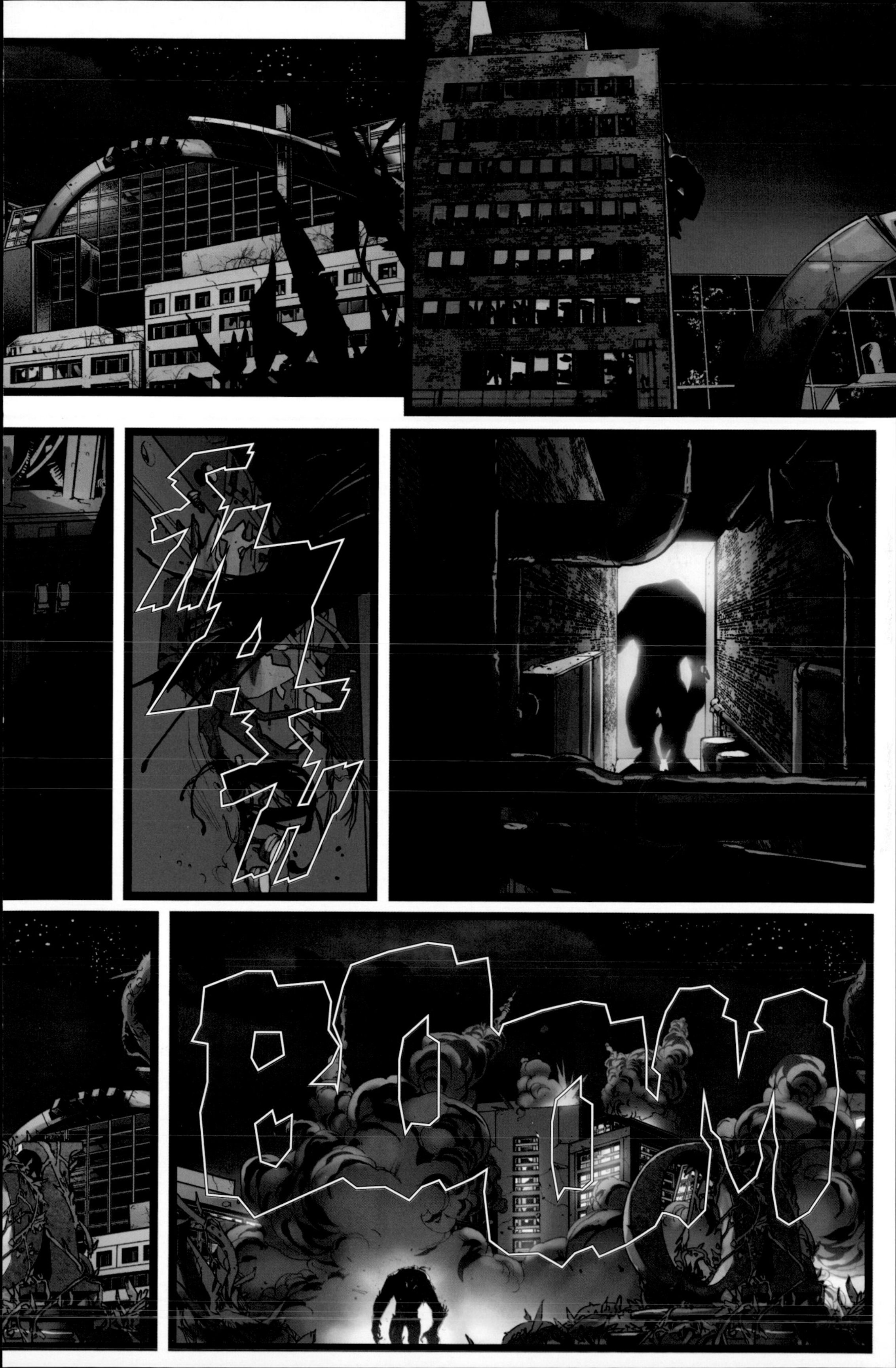
SMASH
BOOM

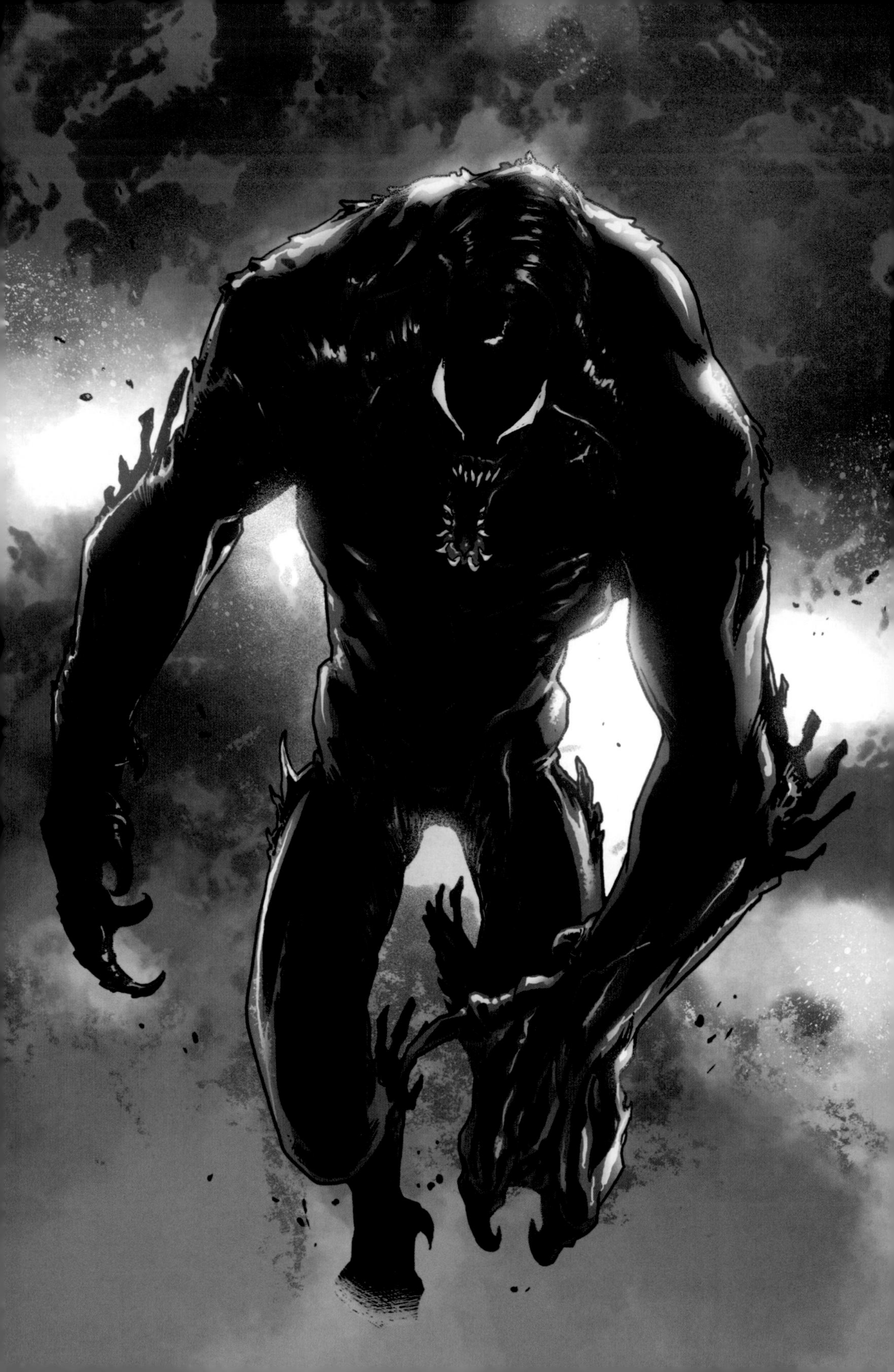

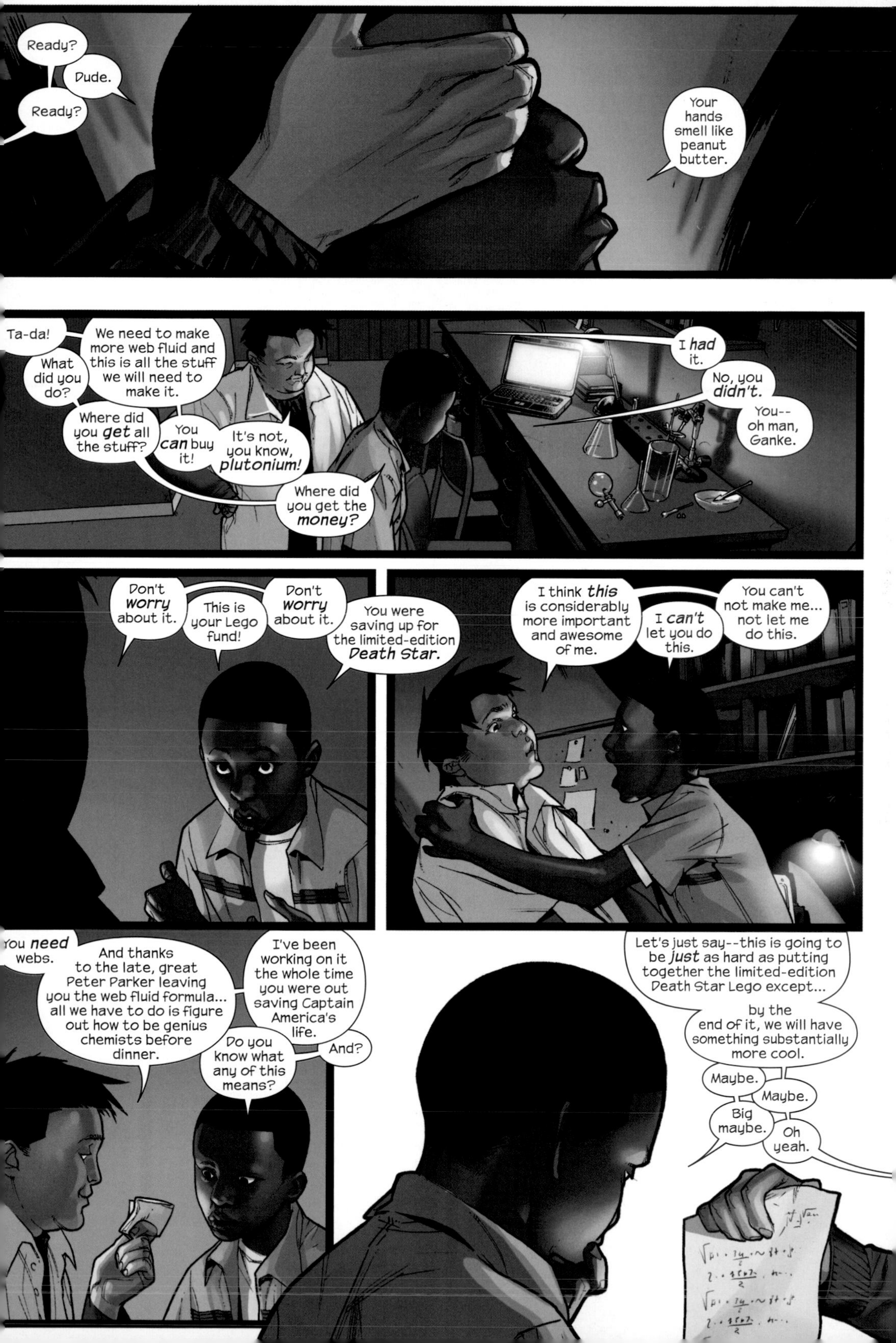

Ready?
Dude.
Ready?
Your hands smell like peanut butter.
Ta-da!
What did you do?
We need to make more web fluid and this is all the stuff we will need to make it.
Where did you *get* all the stuff?
You *can* buy it!
It's not, you know, *plutonium!*
Where did you get the *money?*
I *had* it.
No, you *didn't.*
You-- oh man, Ganke.
Don't *worry* about it.
This is your Lego fund!
Don't *worry* about it.
You were saving up for the limited-edition *Death Star.*
I think *this* is considerably more important and awesome of me.
I *can't* let you do this.
You can't not make me... not let me do this.
You *need* webs.
And thanks to the late, great Peter Parker leaving you the web fluid formula... all we have to do is figure out how to be genius chemists before dinner.
I've been working on it the whole time you were out saving Captain America's life.
Do you know what any of this means?
And?
Let's just say--this is going to be *just* as hard as putting together the limited-edition Death Star Lego except...
by the end of it, we will have something substantially more cool.
Maybe.
Maybe.
Big maybe.
Oh yeah.

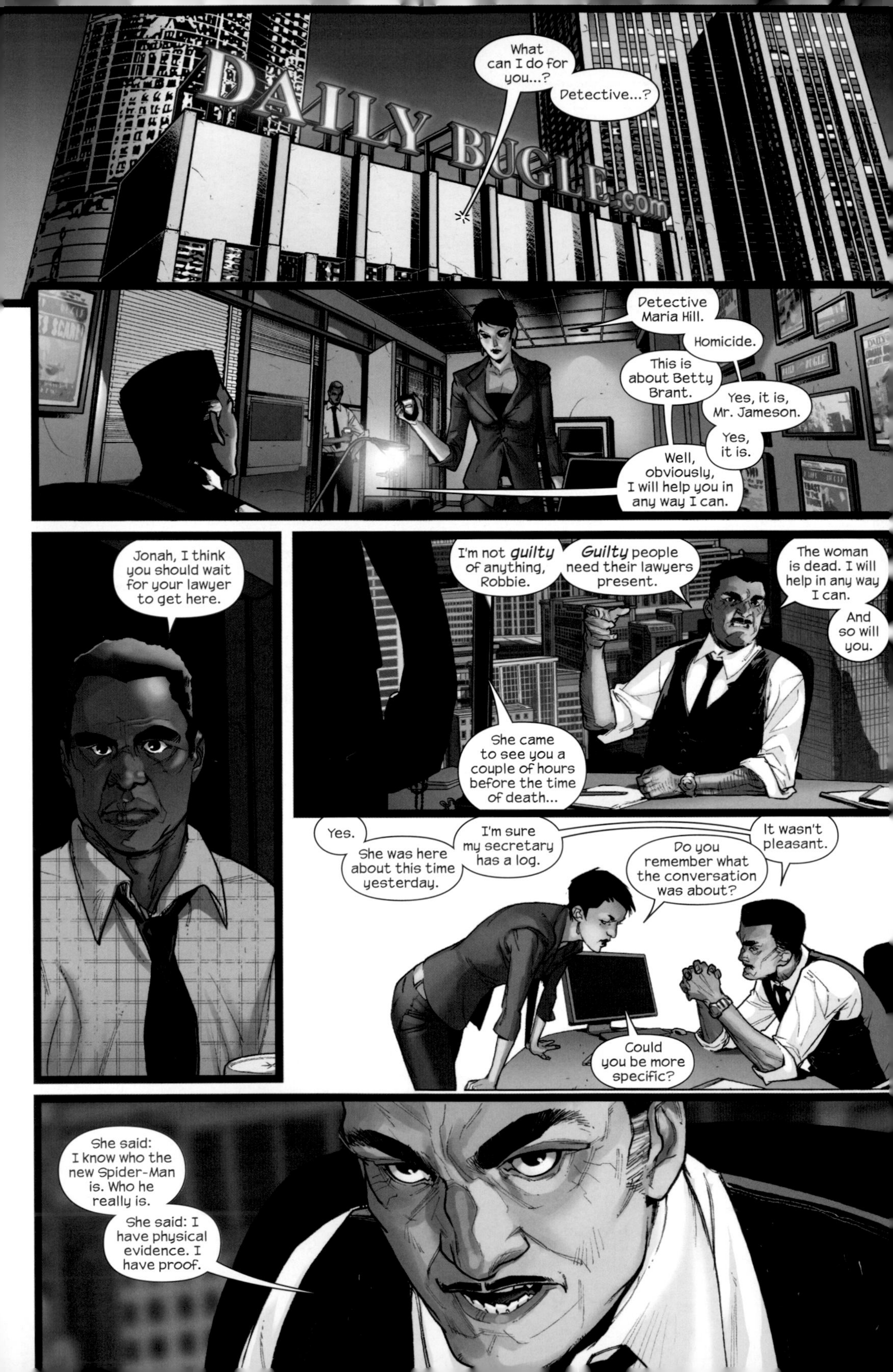

DAILY BUGLE.com
What can I do for you...?
Detective...?
Detective Maria Hill.
Homicide.
This is about Betty Brant.
Yes, it is, Mr. Jameson.
Yes, it is.
Well, obviously, I will help you in any way I can.
Jonah, I think you should wait for your lawyer to get here.
I'm not *guilty* of anything, Robbie.
Guilty people need their lawyers present.
The woman is dead. I will help in any way I can.
And so will you.
She came to see you a couple of hours before the time of death...
Yes.
She was here about this time yesterday.
I'm sure my secretary has a log.
It wasn't pleasant.
Do you remember what the conversation was about?
Could you be more specific?
She said: I know who the new Spider-Man is. Who he really is.
She said: I have physical evidence. I have proof.

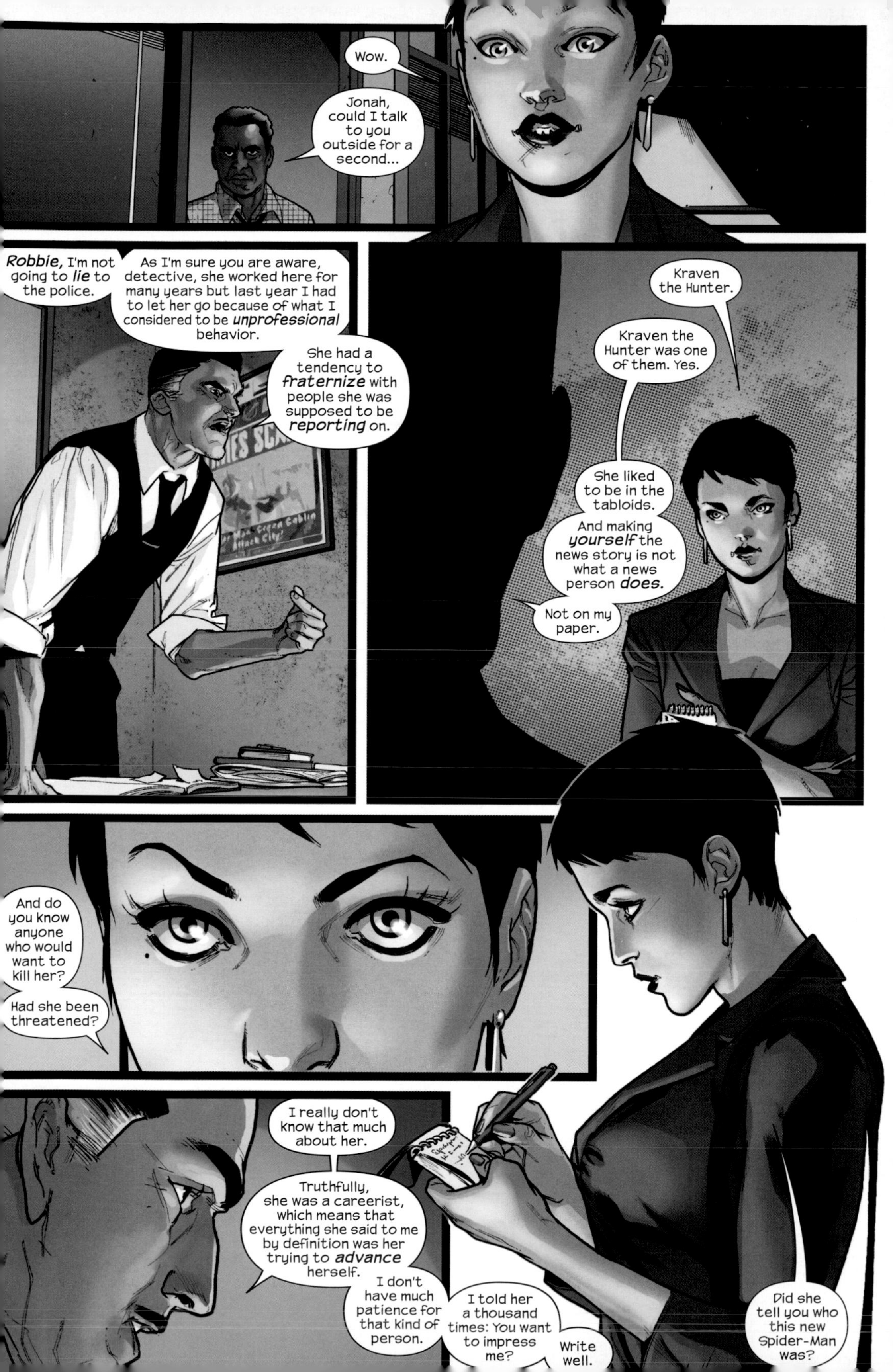

Wow.
Jonah, could I talk to you outside for a second...
Robbie, I'm not going to lie to the police.
As I'm sure you are aware, detective, she worked here for many years but last year I had to let her go because of what I considered to be unprofessional behavior.
She had a tendency to fraternize with people she was supposed to be reporting on.
Kraven the Hunter.
Kraven the Hunter was one of them. Yes.
She liked to be in the tabloids.
And making yourself the news story is not what a news person does.
Not on my paper.
And do you know anyone who would want to kill her?
Had she been threatened?
I really don't know that much about her.
Truthfully, she was a careerist, which means that everything she said to me by definition was her trying to advance herself.
I don't have much patience for that kind of person.
I told her a thousand times: You want to impress me?
Write well.
Did she tell you who this new Spider-Man was?

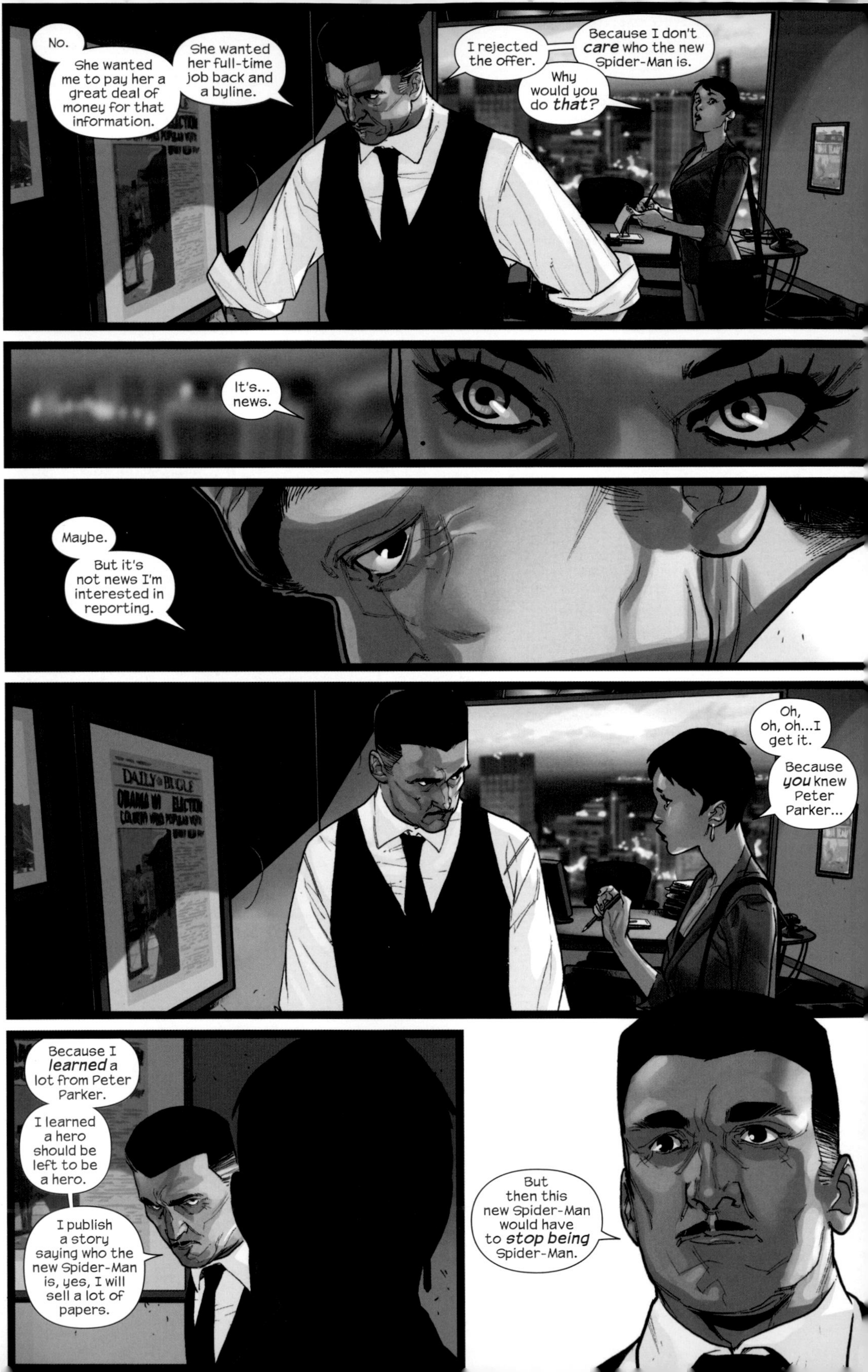
No.
She wanted me to pay her a great deal of money for that information.
She wanted her full-time job back and a byline.
I rejected the offer.
Because I don't *care* who the new Spider-Man is.
Why would you do *that?*
It's... news.
Maybe.
But it's not news I'm interested in reporting.
DAILY BUGLE
Oh, oh, oh...I get it.
Because *you* knew Peter Parker...
Because I *learned* a lot from Peter Parker.
I learned a hero should be left to be a hero.
I publish a story saying who the new Spider-Man is, yes, I will sell a lot of papers.
But then this new Spider-Man would have to *stop being* Spider-Man.

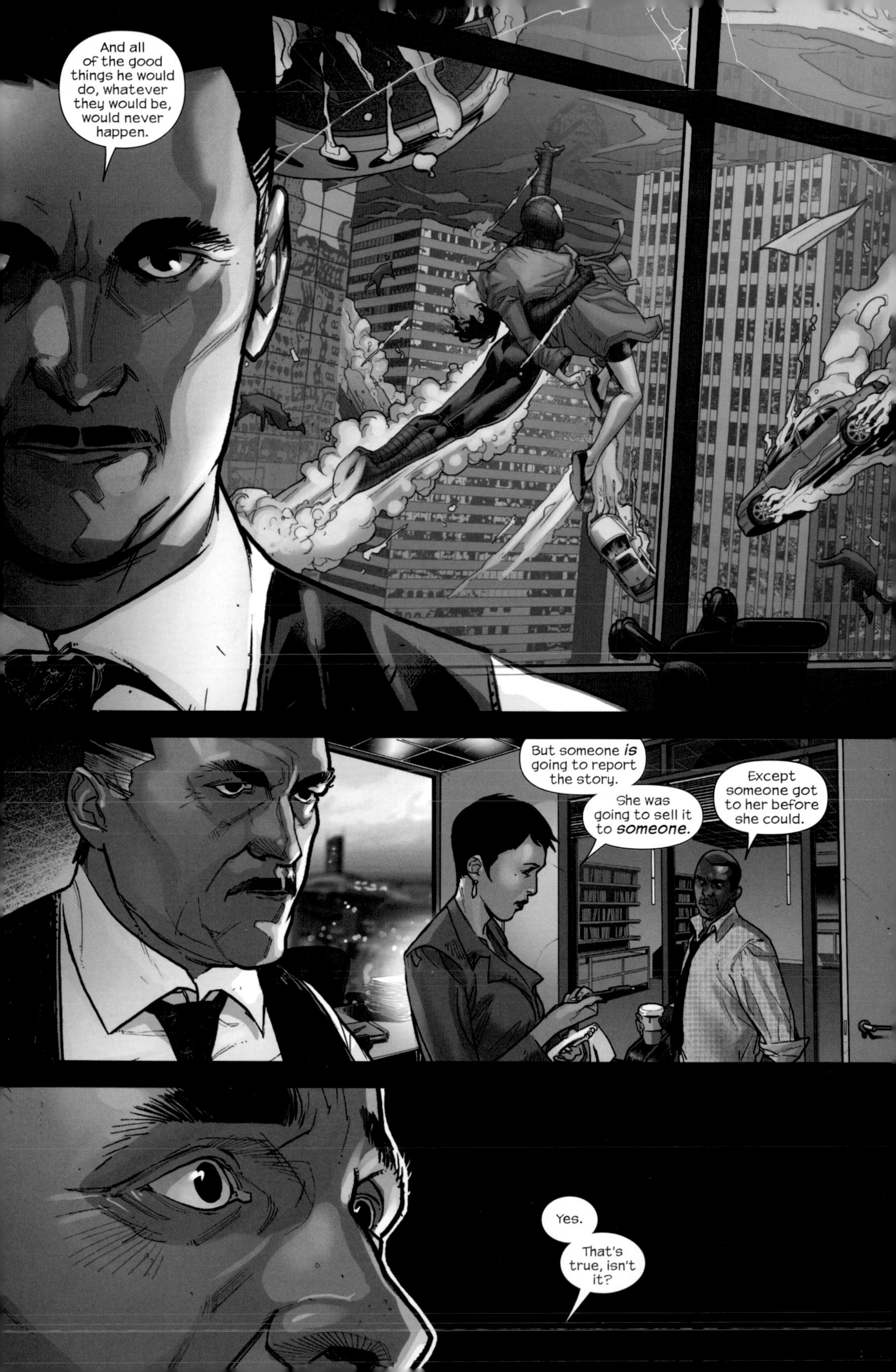
And all of the good things he would do, whatever they would be, would never happen.
But someone *is* going to report the story.
She was going to sell it to *someone.*
Except someone got to her before she could.
Yes.
That's true, isn't it?

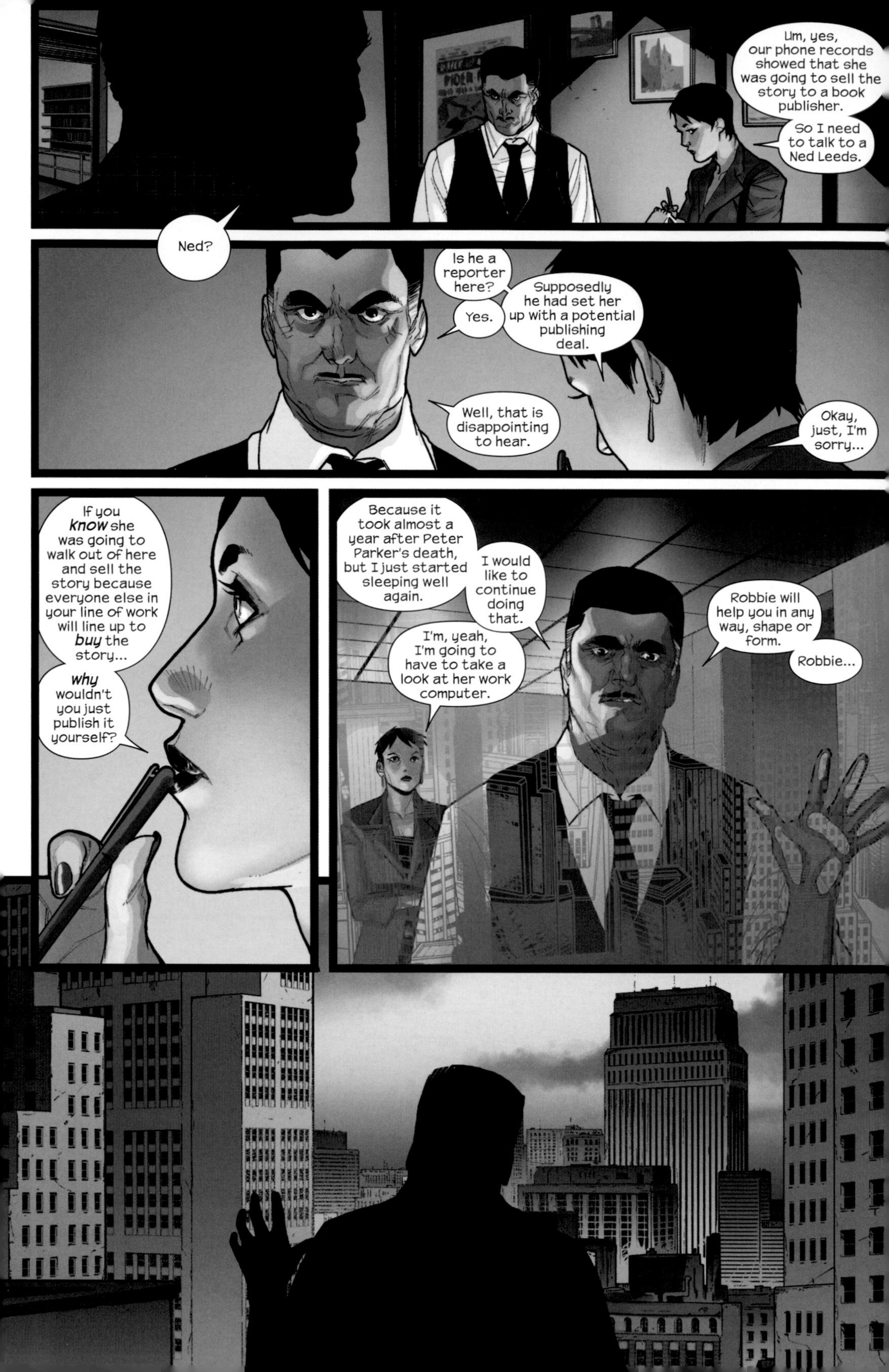

Um, yes, our phone records showed that she was going to sell the story to a book publisher.
So I need to talk to a Ned Leeds.
Ned?
Is he a reporter here?
Yes.
Supposedly he had set her up with a potential publishing deal.
Well, that is disappointing to hear.
Okay, just, I'm sorry...
If you know she was going to walk out of here and sell the story because everyone else in your line of work will line up to buy the story...
why wouldn't you just publish it yourself?
Because it took almost a year after Peter Parker's death, but I just started sleeping well again.
I would like to continue doing that.
I'm, yeah, I'm going to have to take a look at her work computer.
Robbie will help you in any way, shape or form.
Robbie...

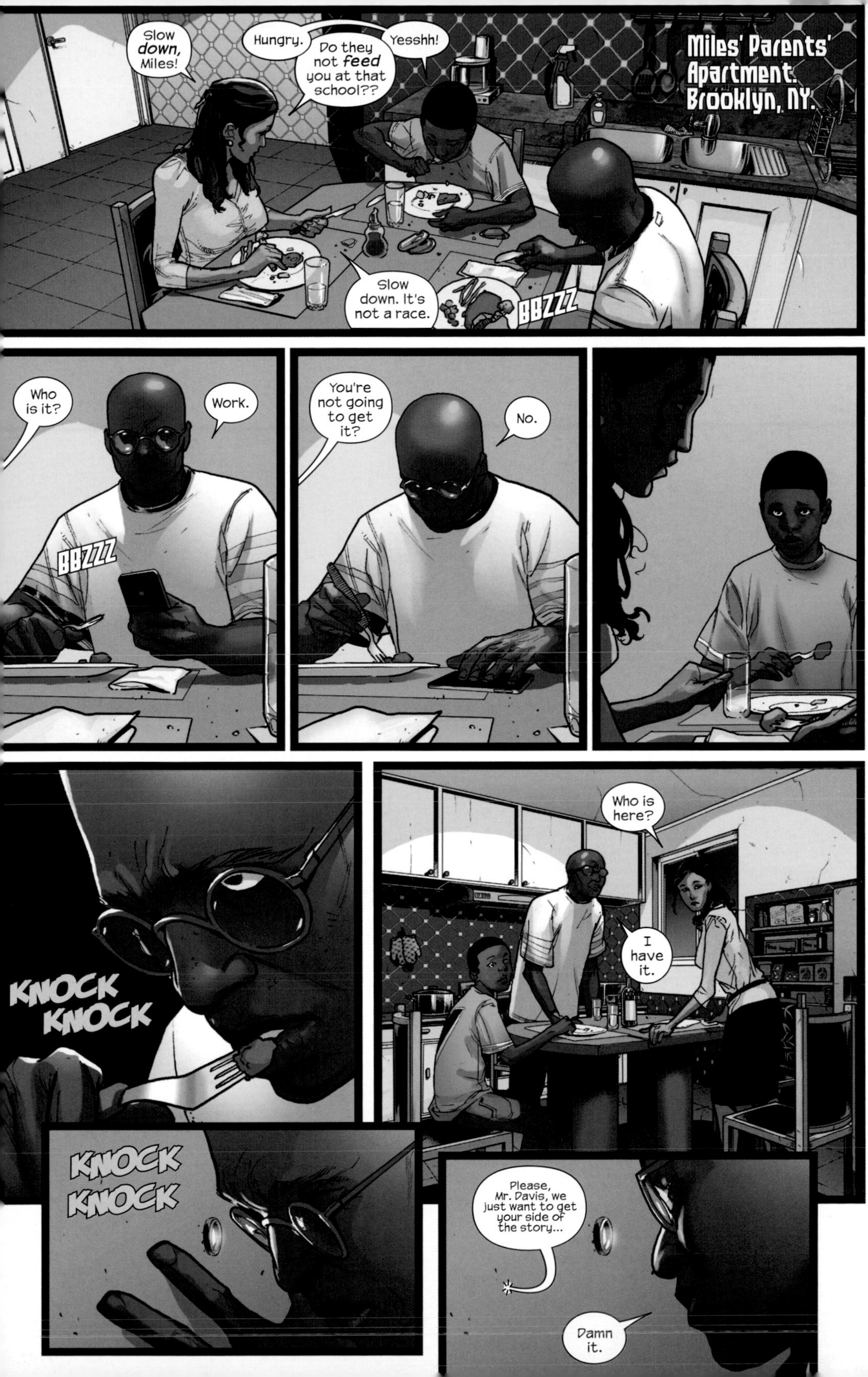
Miles' Parents' Apartment. Brooklyn, NY.
Slow down, Miles!
Hungry.
Yesshh!
Do they not feed you at that school??
Slow down. It's not a race.
BBZZZ
Who is it?
Work.
BBZZZ
You're not going to get it?
No.
KNOCK KNOCK
Who is here?
I have it.
KNOCK KNOCK
Please, Mr. Davis, we just want to get your side of the story...
Damn it.

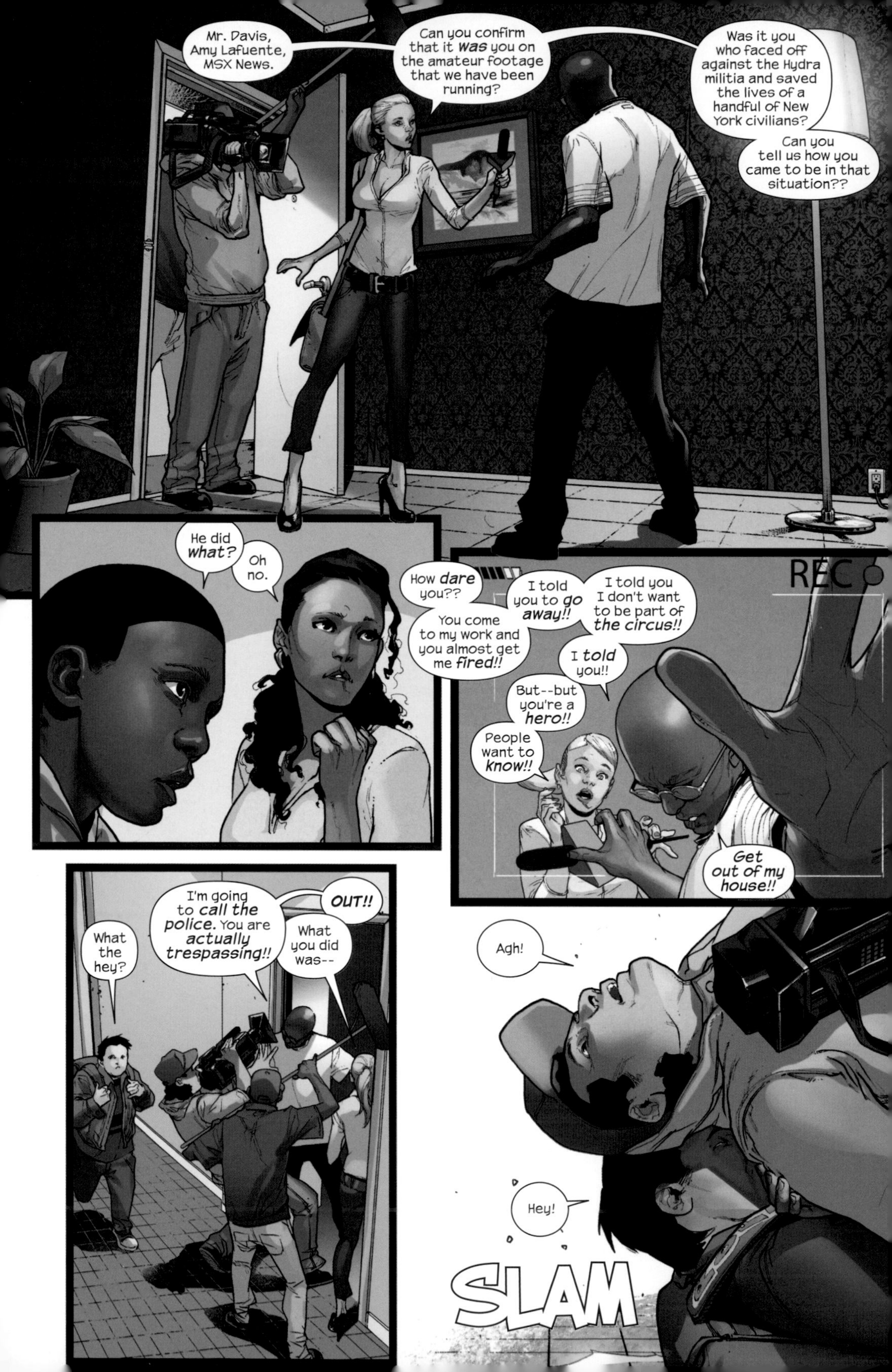
Mr. Davis, Amy Lafuente, MSX News.
Can you confirm that it *was* you on the amateur footage that we have been running?
Was it you who faced off against the Hydra militia and saved the lives of a handful of New York civilians?
Can you tell us how you came to be in that situation??
He did *what?*
Oh no.
REC
How *dare* you??
You come to my work and you almost get me *fired!!*
I told you to *go away!!*
I told you I don't want to be part of *the circus!!*
I *told* you!!
But--but you're a *hero!!*
People want to *know!!*
Get out of my house!!
What the hey?
I'm going to *call the police.* You are *actually trespassing!!*
OUT!!
What you did was--
Agh!
Hey!
SLAM

Ow! My *back!!*

You're on a *kid!*

Yeah, uh, *could you* get off me, please!?

Why didn't you tell me this was *happening?*

24-hour news cycle.

It's a 24-hour news cycle.

It'll go away in 24 hours.

Why won't you *talk* to them and be done with it?

Come on...

Wait, what did you do?

I'm sorry, boy.

Sorry you had to see that.

You fought *HYDRA??!!*

I did too.

We--we have that in common.

Kind of.

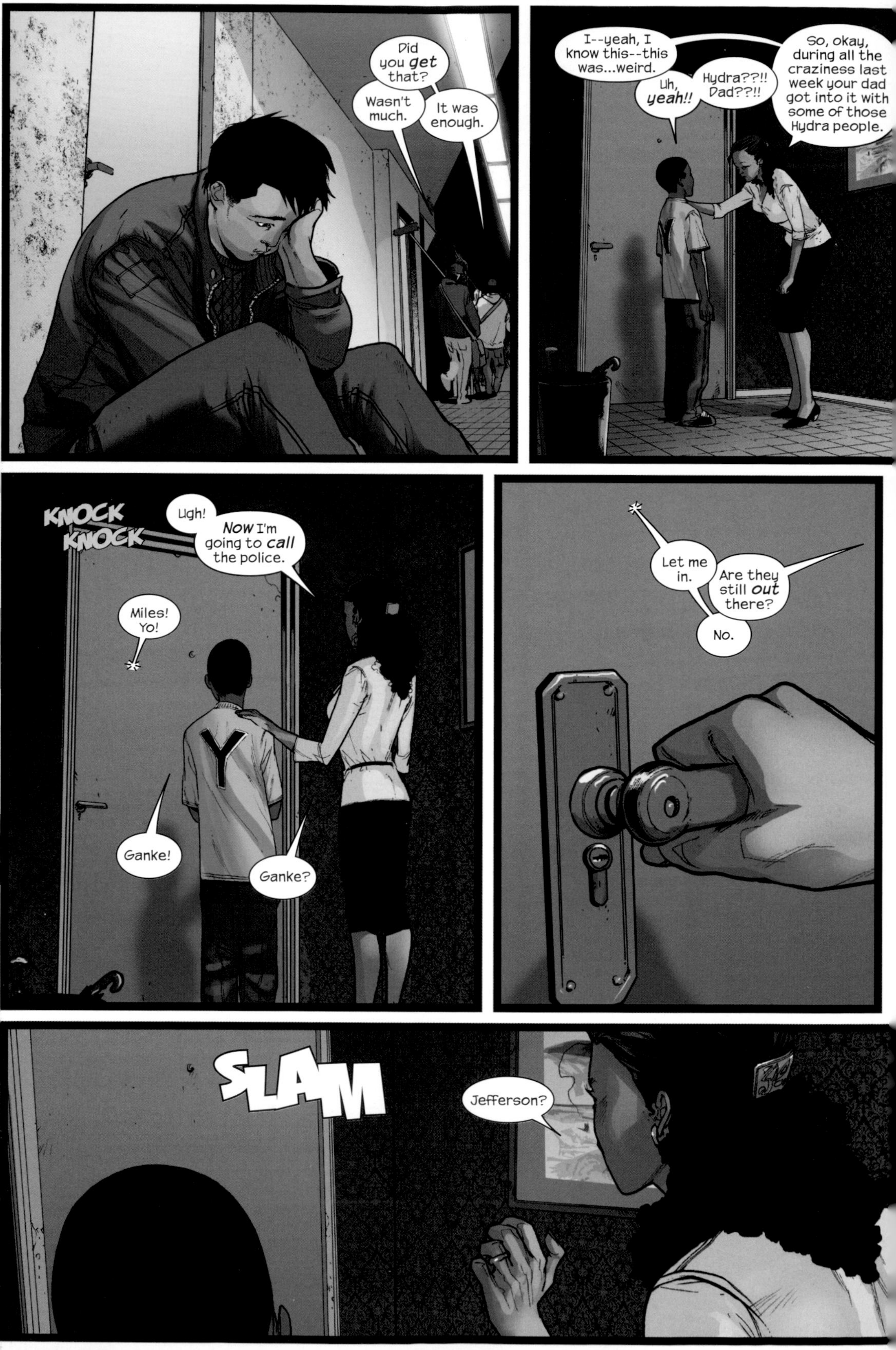
Did you get that?
Wasn't much.
It was enough.
I--yeah, I know this--this was...weird.
So, okay, during all the craziness last week your dad got into it with some of those Hydra people.
Uh, yeah!!
Hydra??!! Dad??!!
KNOCK KNOCK
Ugh!
Now I'm going to call the police.
Miles! Yo!
Ganke!
Ganke?
Let me in.
Are they still out there?
No.
SLAM
Jefferson?

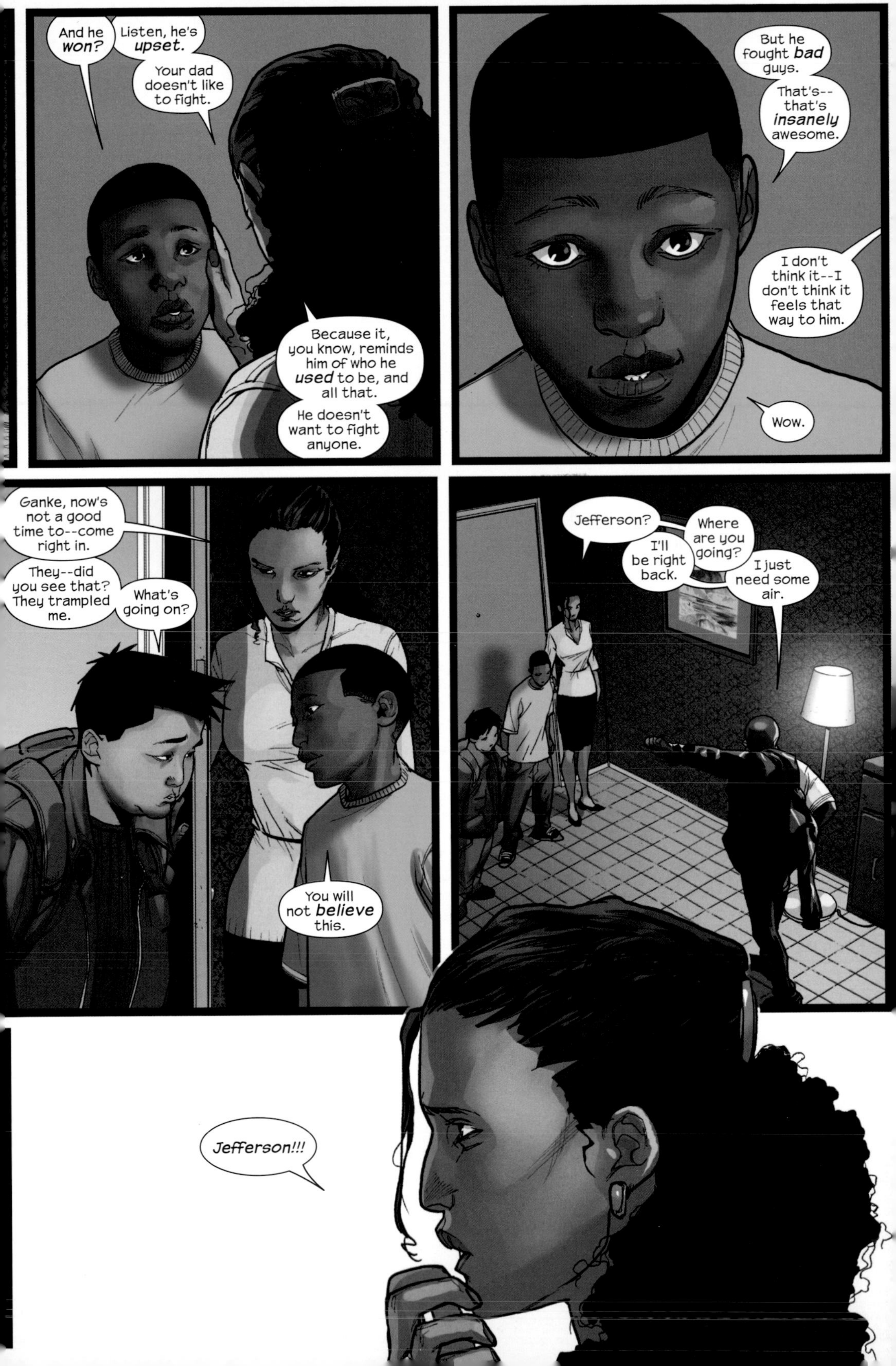
And he *won?*
Listen, he's *upset.*
Your dad doesn't like to fight.
Because it, you know, reminds him of who he *used* to be, and all that.
He doesn't want to fight anyone.
But he fought *bad* guys.
That's-- that's *insanely* awesome.
I don't think it--I don't think it feels that way to him.
Wow.
Ganke, now's not a good time to--come right in.
They--did you see that? They trampled me.
What's going on?
You will not *believe* this.
Jefferson?
Where are you going?
I'll be right back.
I just need some air.
Jefferson!!!

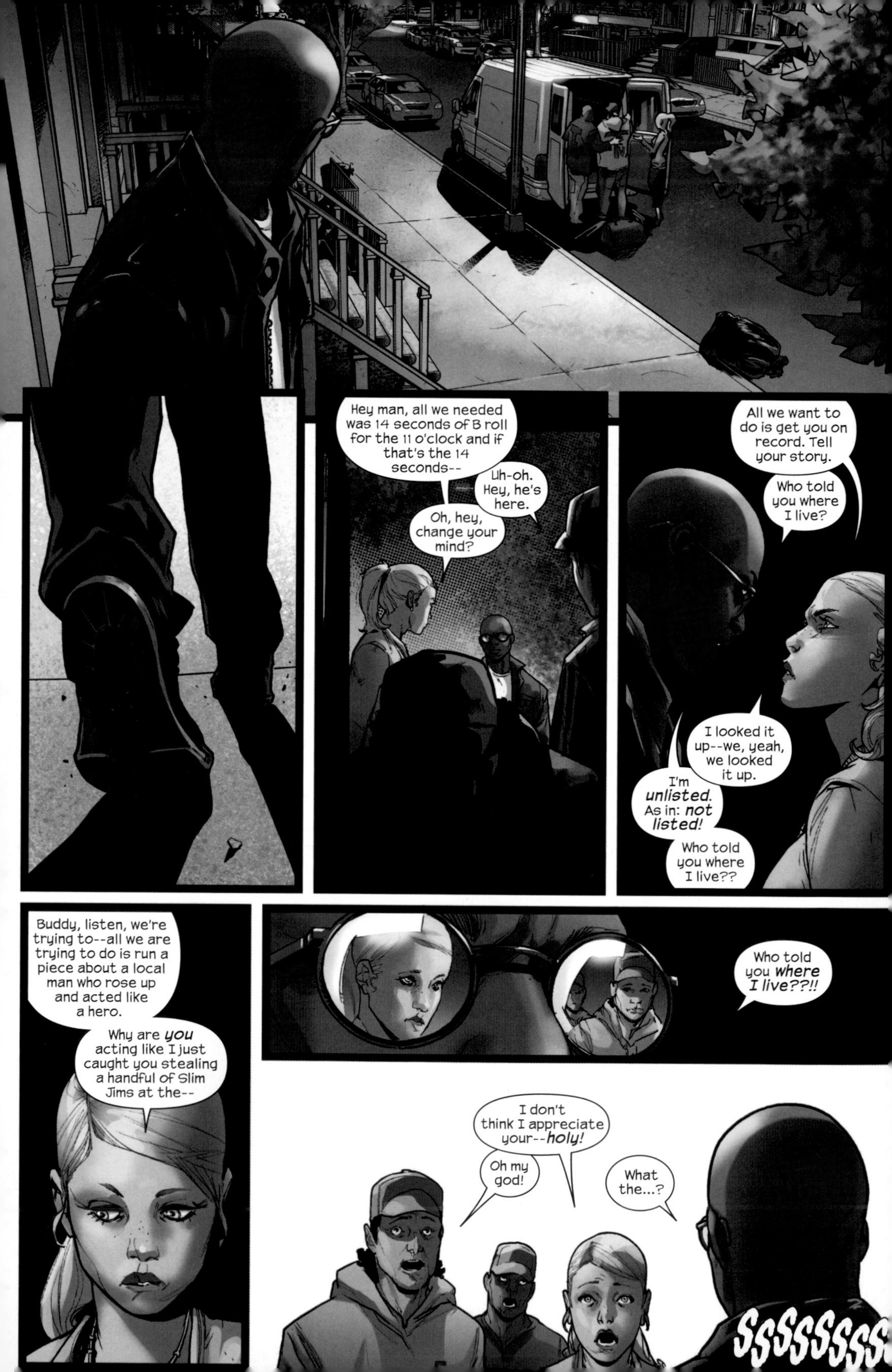

Hey man, all we needed was 14 seconds of B roll for the 11 o'clock and if that's the 14 seconds--
Uh-oh. Hey, he's here.
Oh, hey, change your mind?
All we want to do is get you on record. Tell your story.
Who told you where I live?
I looked it up--we, yeah, we looked it up.
I'm *unlisted*. As in: *not listed!*
Who told you where I live??
Buddy, listen, we're trying to--all we are trying to do is run a piece about a local man who rose up and acted like a hero.
Why are *you* acting like I just caught you stealing a handful of Slim Jims at the--
Who told you *where I live??!!*
I don't think I appreciate your--*holy!*
Oh my god!
What the...?
SSSSSSSS

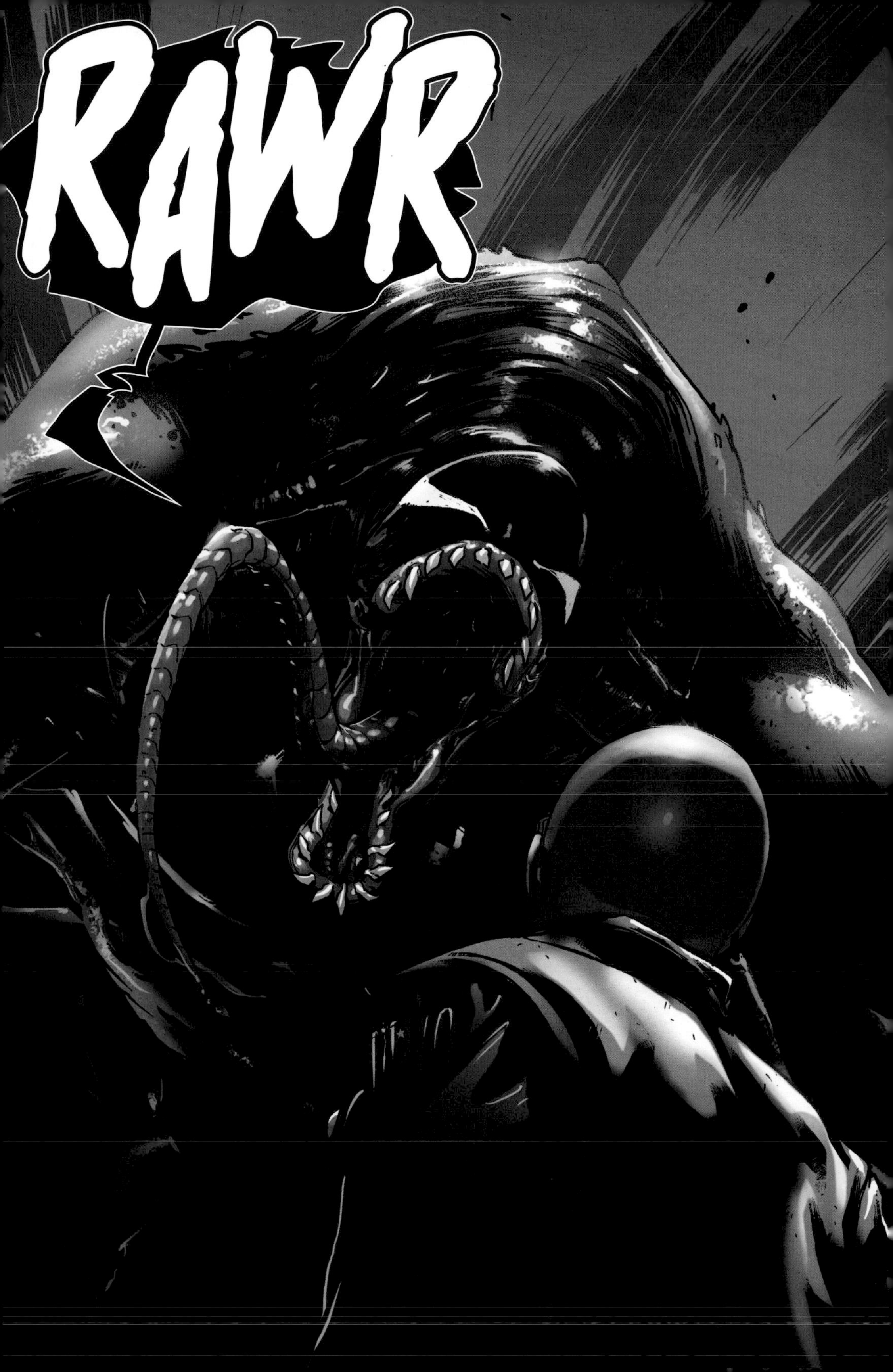
RAWR

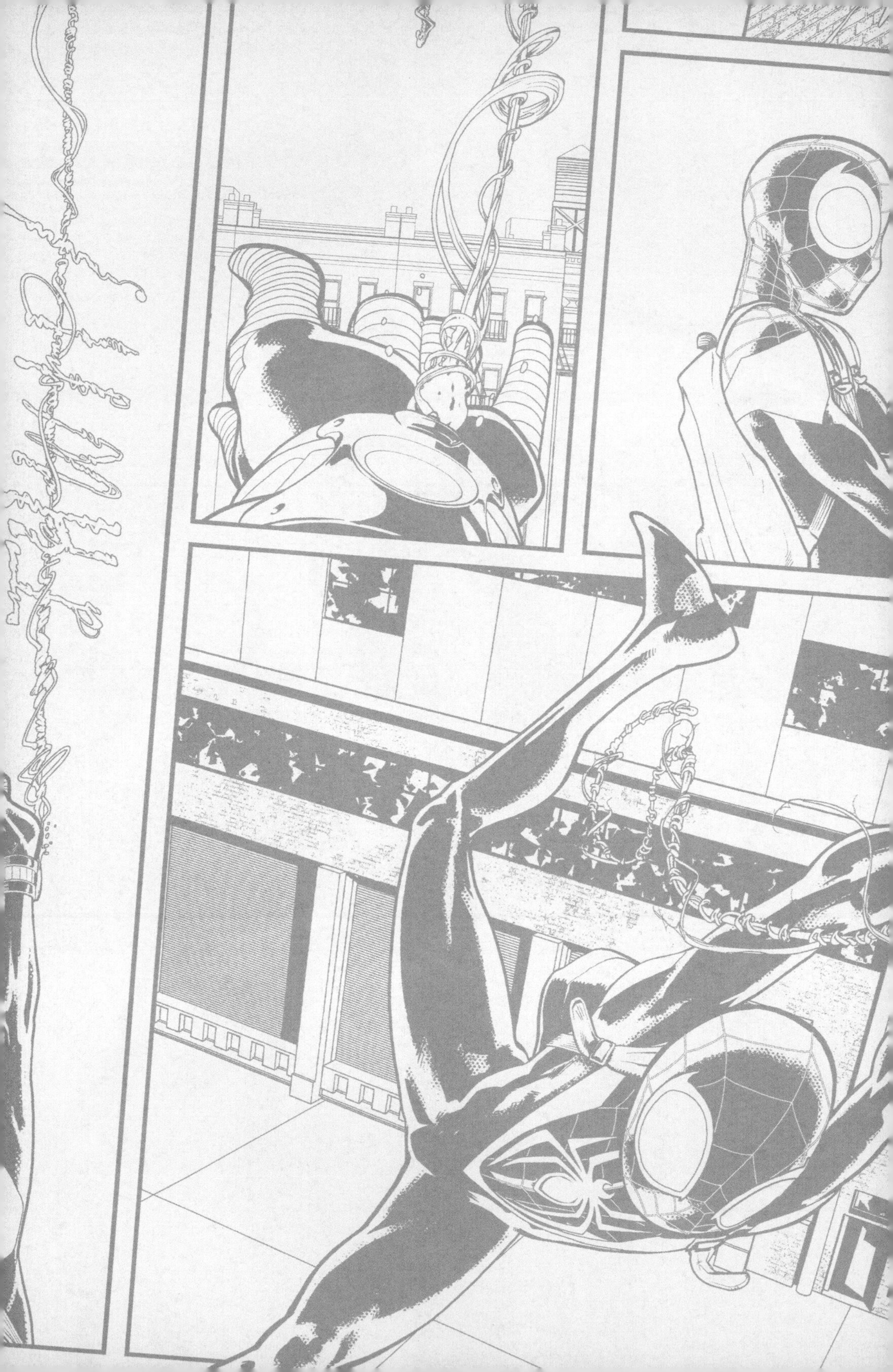

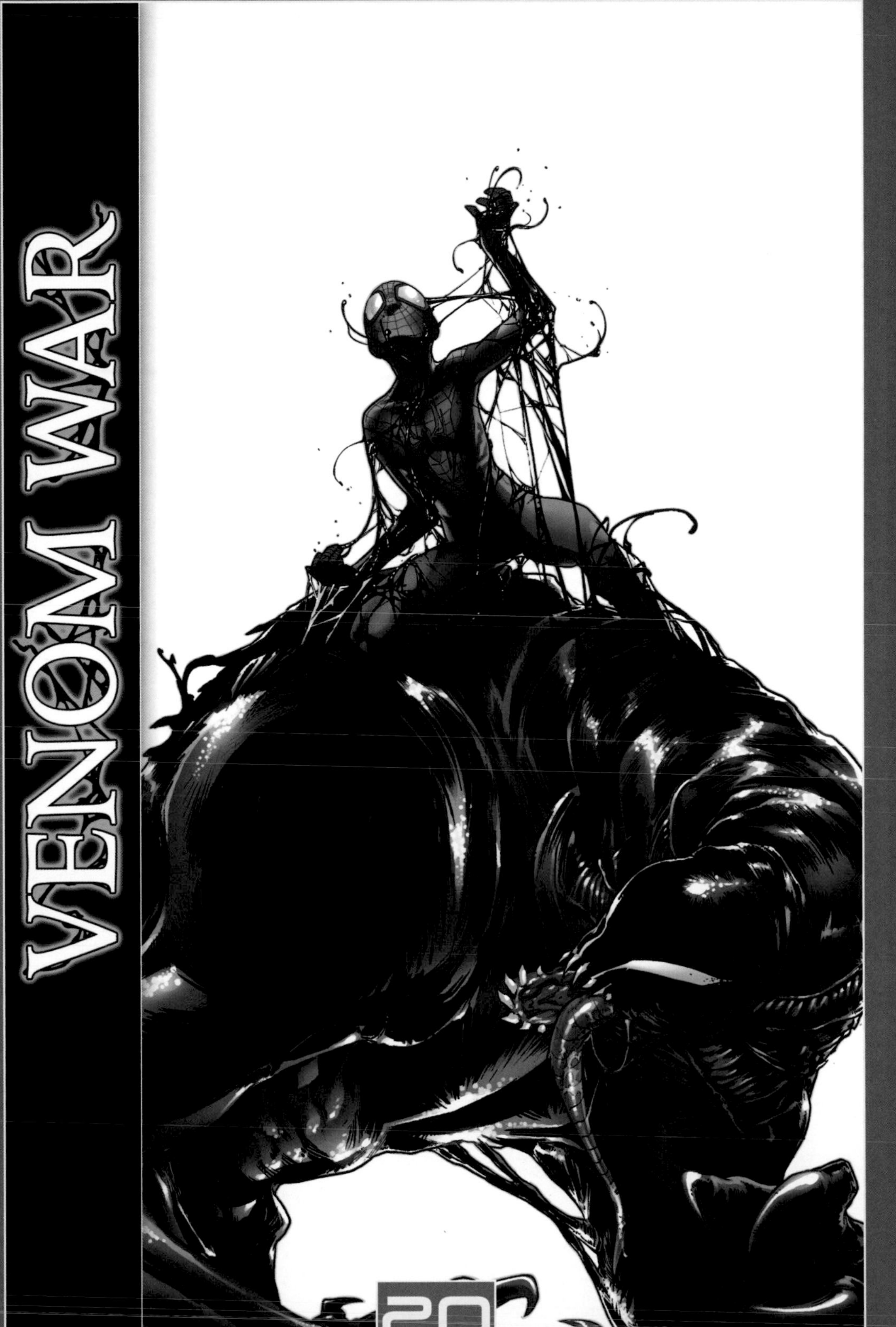
VENOM WAR
20

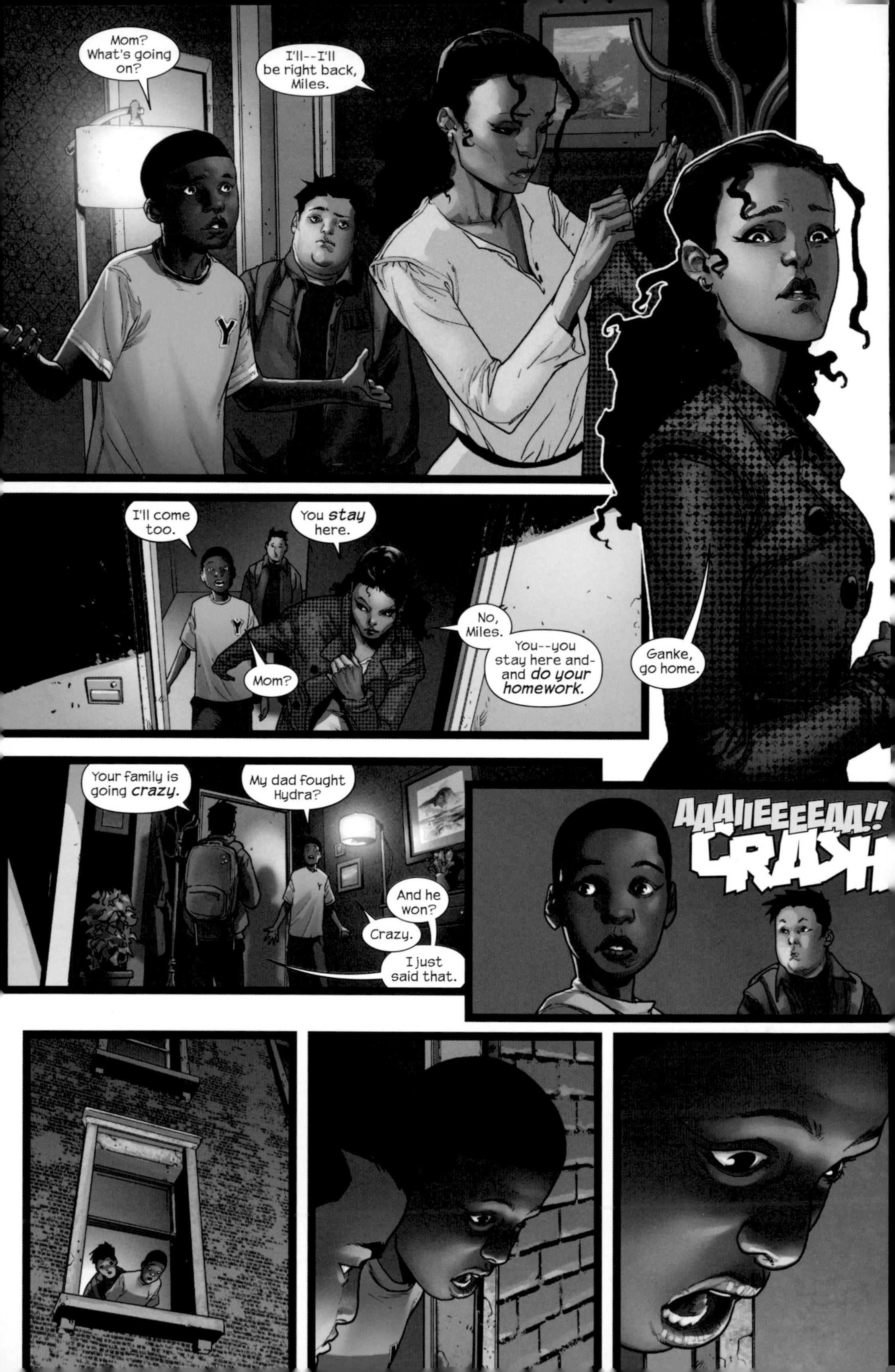

Mom? What's going on?
I'll--I'll be right back, Miles.
Ganke, go home.
I'll come too.
You *stay* here.
Mom?
No, Miles.
You--you stay here and-and *do your homework.*
Your family is going *crazy.*
My dad fought Hydra?
And he won?
Crazy.
I just said that.
AAAIIEEEEAA!!
CRASH

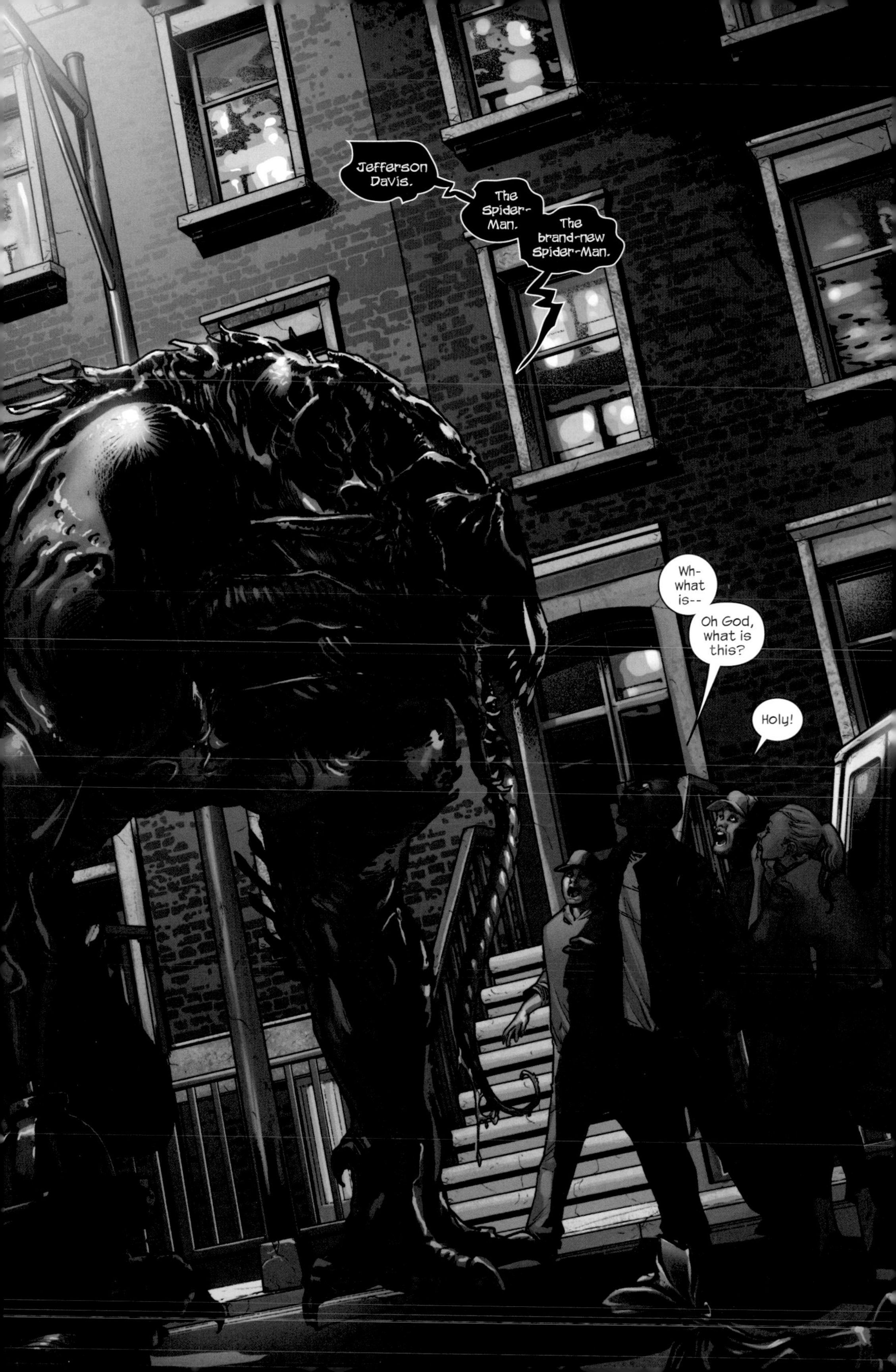

Jefferson Davis.
The Spider-Man.
The brand-new Spider-Man.
Wh-what is--
Oh God, what is this?
Holy!

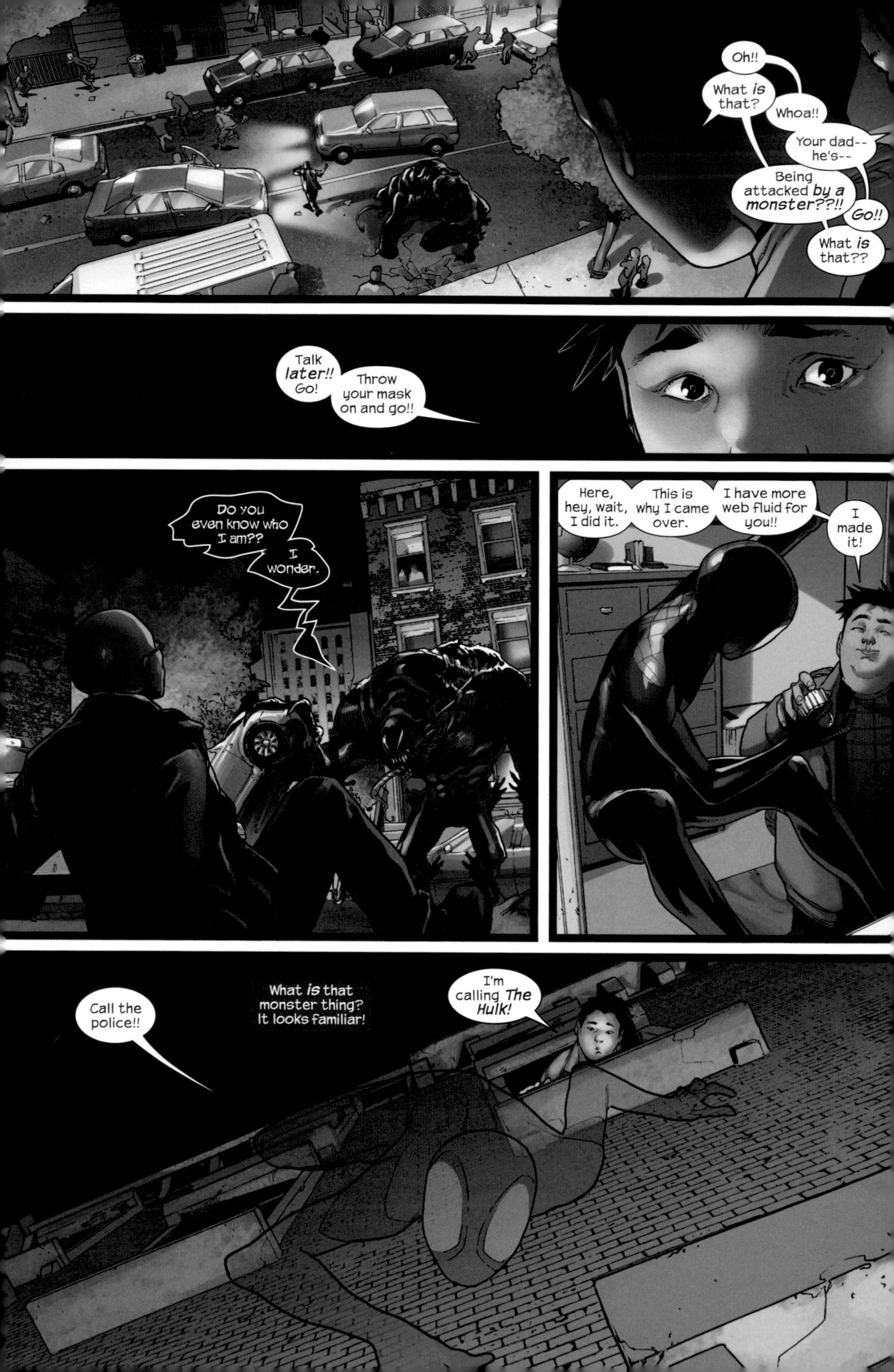
Oh!!
What is that?
Whoa!!
Your dad-- he's--
Being attacked by a monster??!!
Go!!
What is that??
Talk later!! Go!
Throw your mask on and go!!
Do you even know who I am??
I wonder.
Here, hey, wait, I did it.
This is why I came over.
I have more web fluid for you!!
I made it!
Call the police!!
What is that monster thing? It looks familiar!
I'm calling The Hulk!

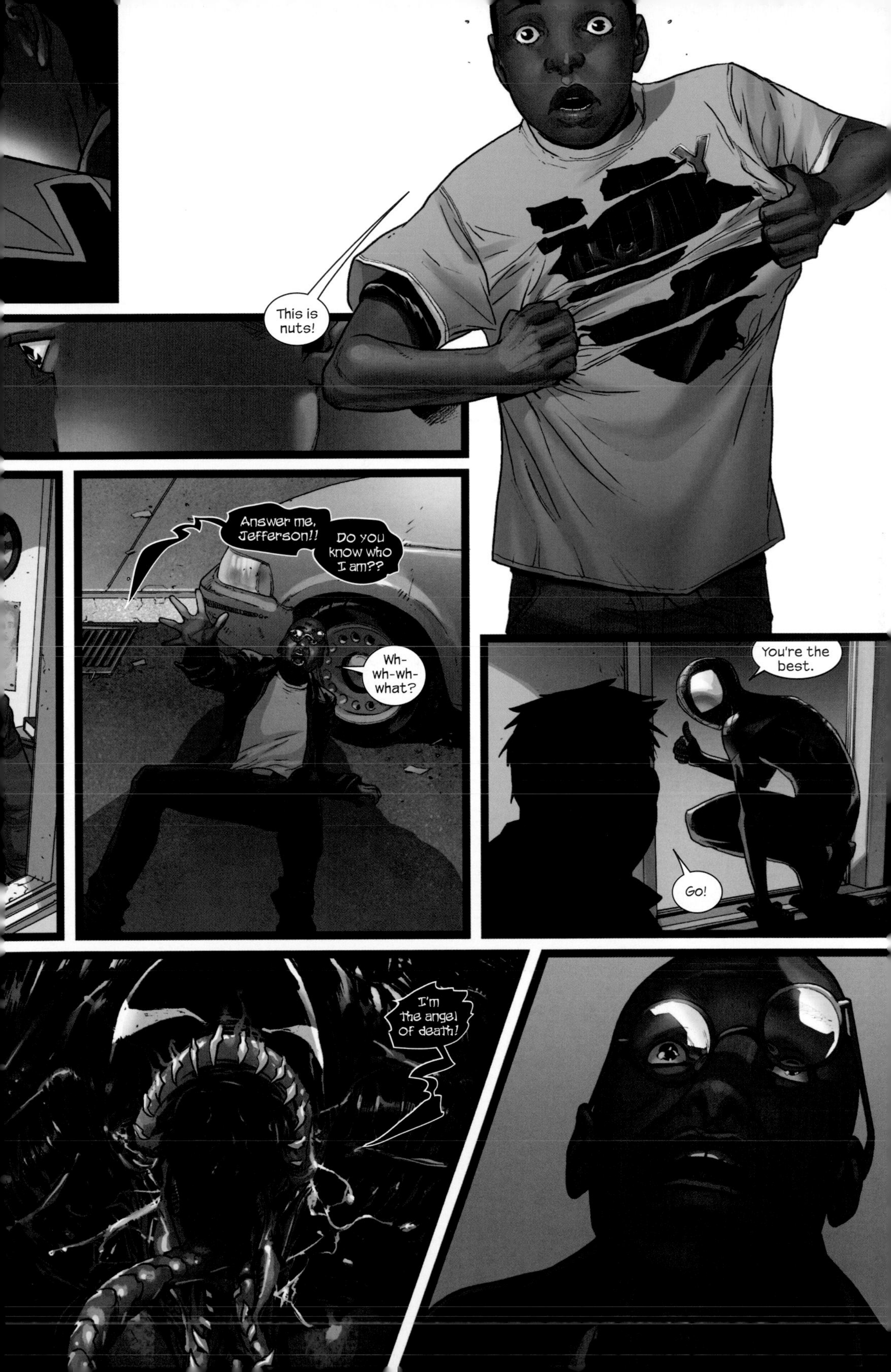
This is nuts!
Answer me, Jefferson!!
Do you know who I am??
Wh-wh-wh-what?
You're the best.
Go!
I'm the angel of death!

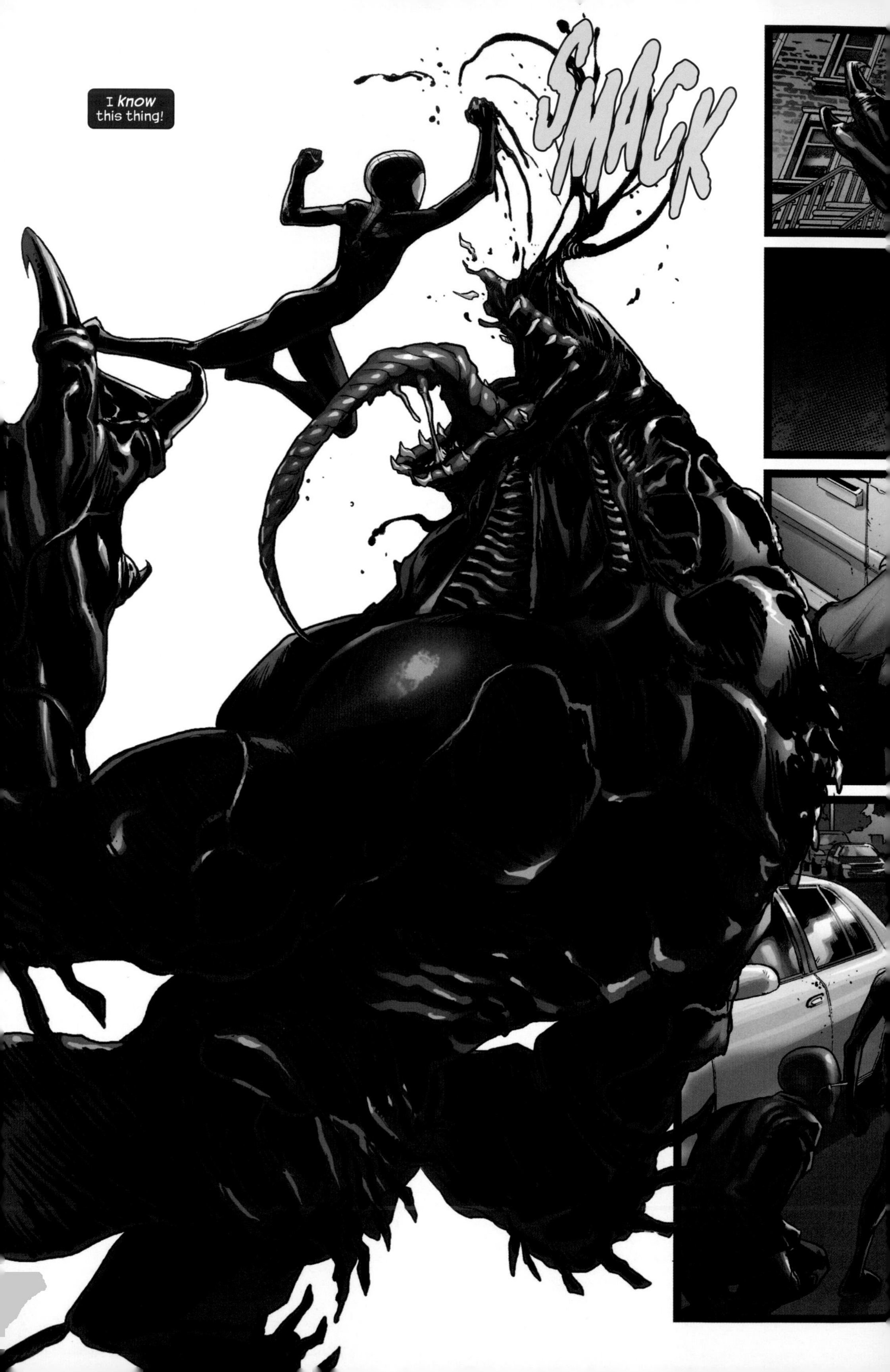
I KNOW this thing!
SMACK

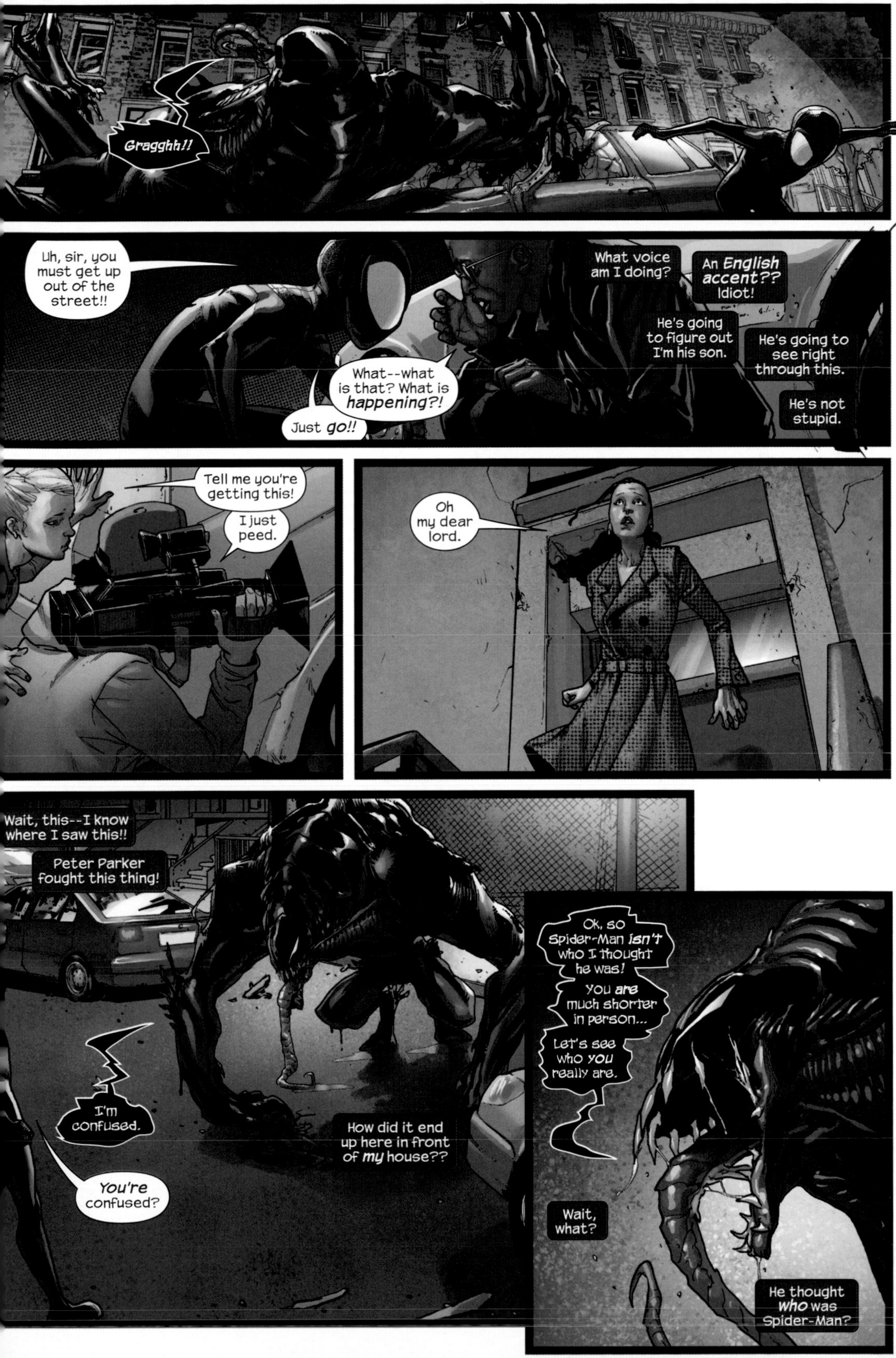

Gragghh!!
Uh, sir, you must get up out of the street!!
What--what is that? What is happening?!
Just go!!
What voice am I doing?
An English accent?? Idiot!
He's going to figure out I'm his son.
He's going to see right through this.
He's not stupid.
Tell me you're getting this!
I just peed.
Oh my dear lord.
Wait, this--I know where I saw this!!
Peter Parker fought this thing!
I'm confused.
You're confused?
How did it end up here in front of my house??
Ok, so Spider-Man isn't who I thought he was!
You are much shorter in person...
Let's see who you really are.
Wait, what?
He thought who was Spider-Man?

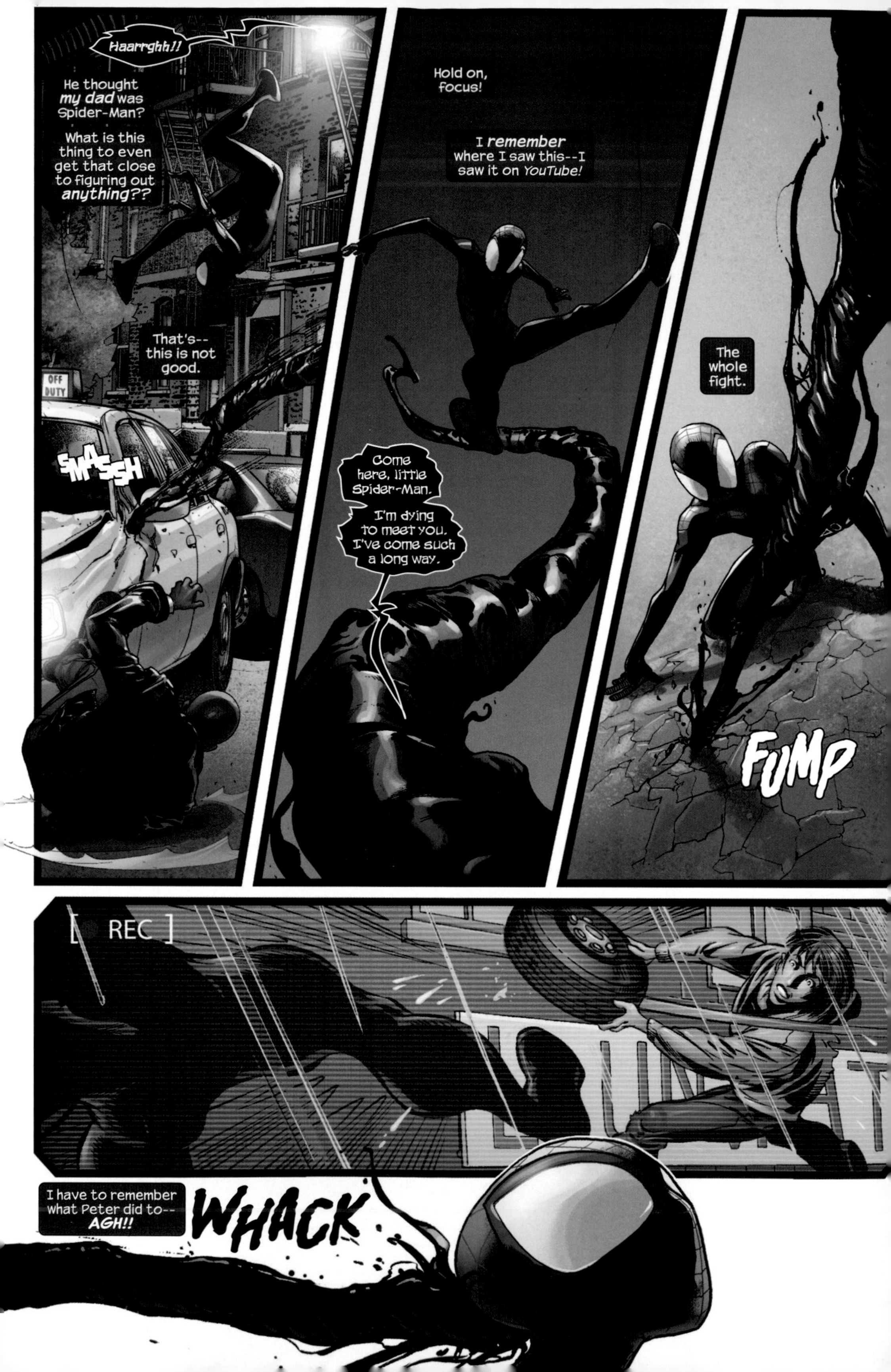
Haarrghh!!
He thought my dad was Spider-Man?
What is this thing to even get that close to figuring out anything??
OFF DUTY
That's-- this is not good.
SMASSH
Hold on, focus!
I remember where I saw this--I saw it on YouTube!
Come here, little Spider-Man.
I'm dying to meet you. I've come such a long way.
The whole fight.
FUMP
REC
I have to remember what Peter did to-- AGH!!
WHACK

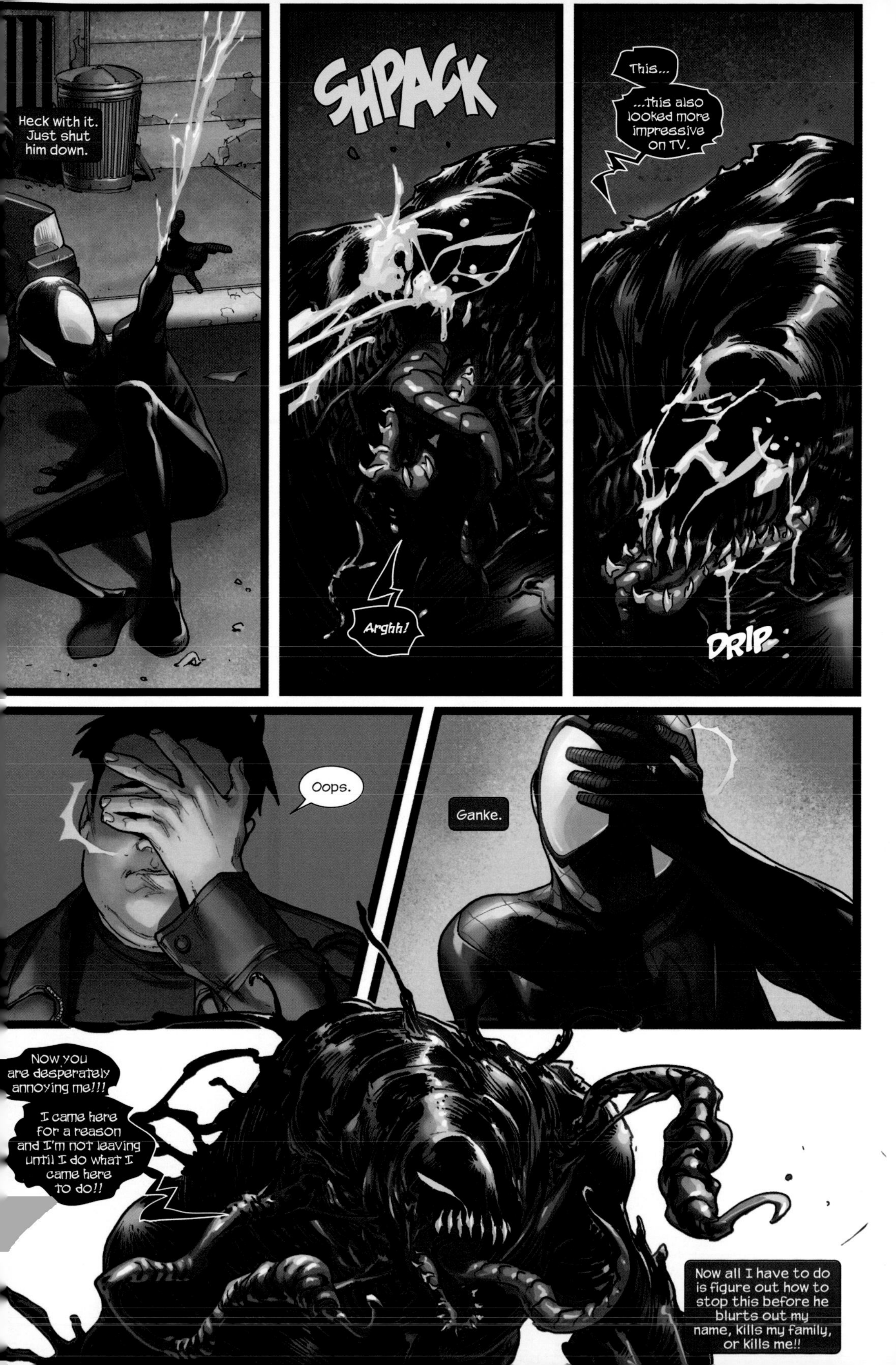
Heck with it. Just shut him down.
SHPACK
Arghh!
This...
...this also looked more impressive on TV.
DRIP
Oops.
Ganke.
Now you are desperately annoying me!!!
I came here for a reason and I'm not leaving until I do what I came here to do!!
Now all I have to do is figure out how to stop this before he blurts out my name, kills my family, or kills me!!

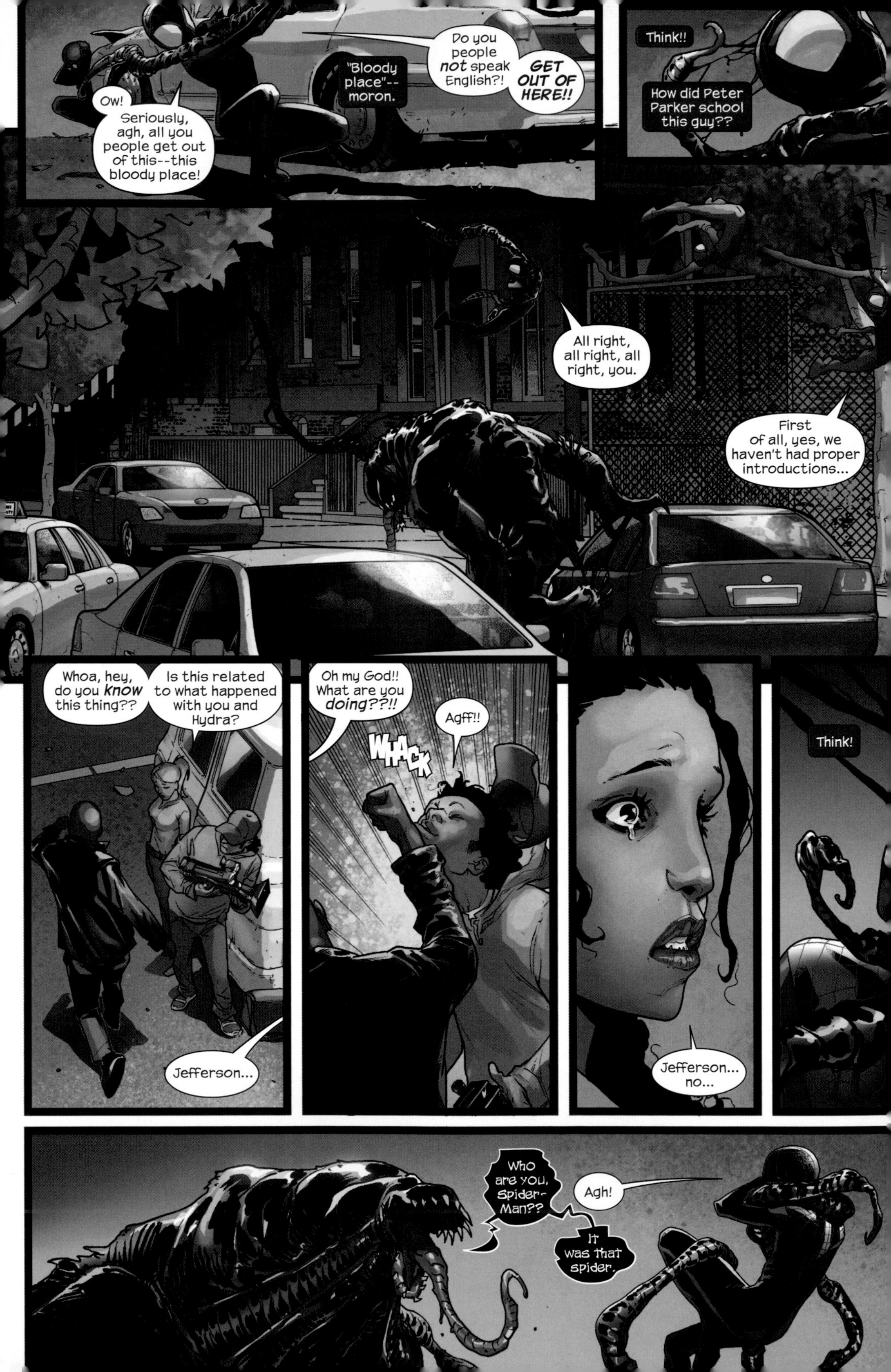
Ow!
Seriously, agh, all you people get out of this--this bloody place!
"Bloody place"-- moron.
Do you people not speak English?!
GET OUT OF HERE!!
Think!!
How did Peter Parker school this guy??
All right, all right, all right, you.
First of all, yes, we haven't had proper introductions...
Whoa, hey, do you KNOW this thing??
Is this related to what happened with you and Hydra?
Jefferson...
Oh my God!! What are you doing??!!
WHACK
Agff!!
Jefferson... no...
Think!
Who are you, Spider-Man??
Agh!
It was that spider.

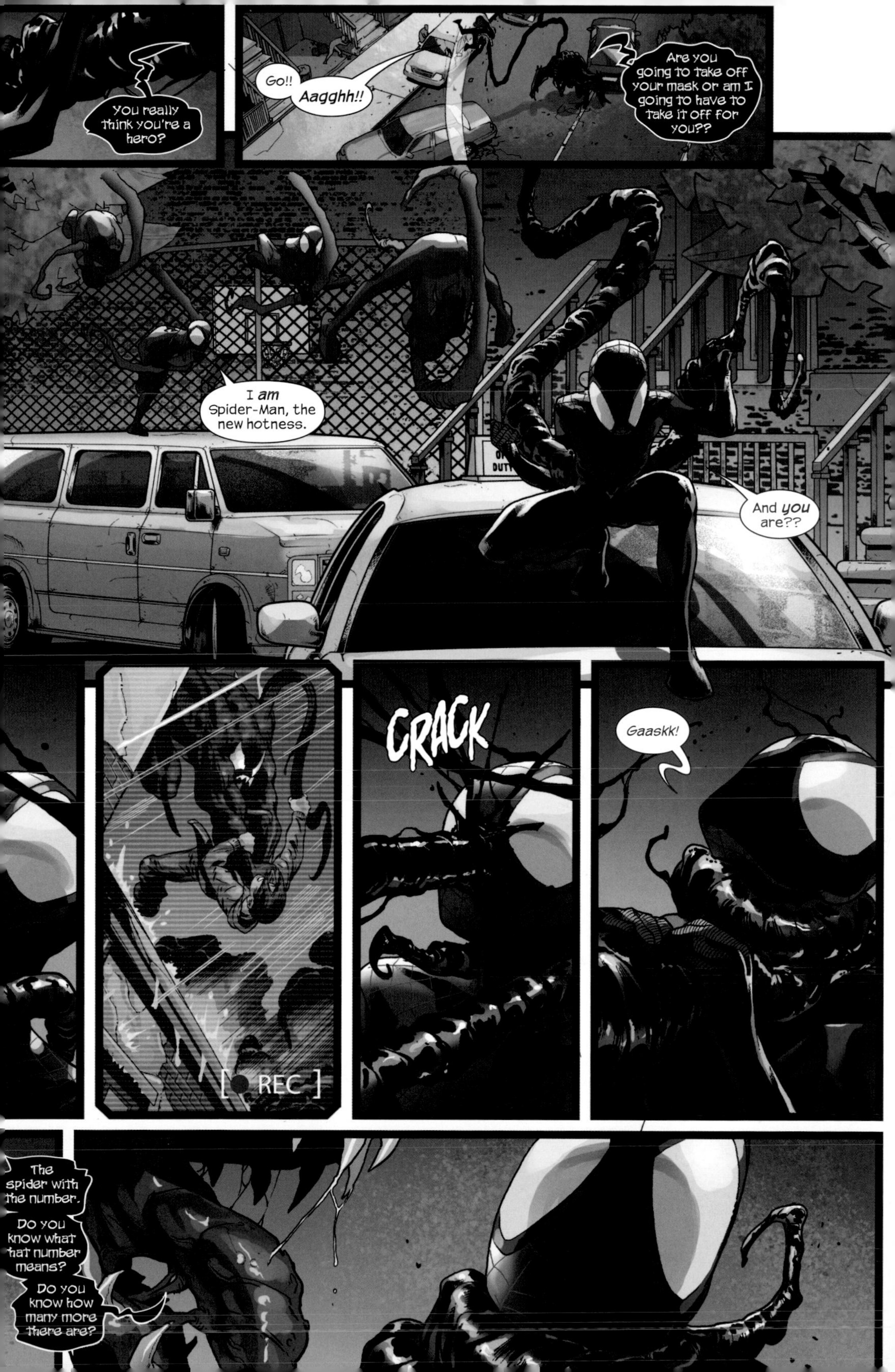

You really think you're a hero?
Go!!
Aagghh!!
Are you going to take off your mask or am I going to have to take it off for you??
I *am* Spider-Man, the new hotness.
And *you* are??
REC
CRACK
Gaaskk!
The spider with the number.
Do you know what that number means?
Do you know how many more there are?

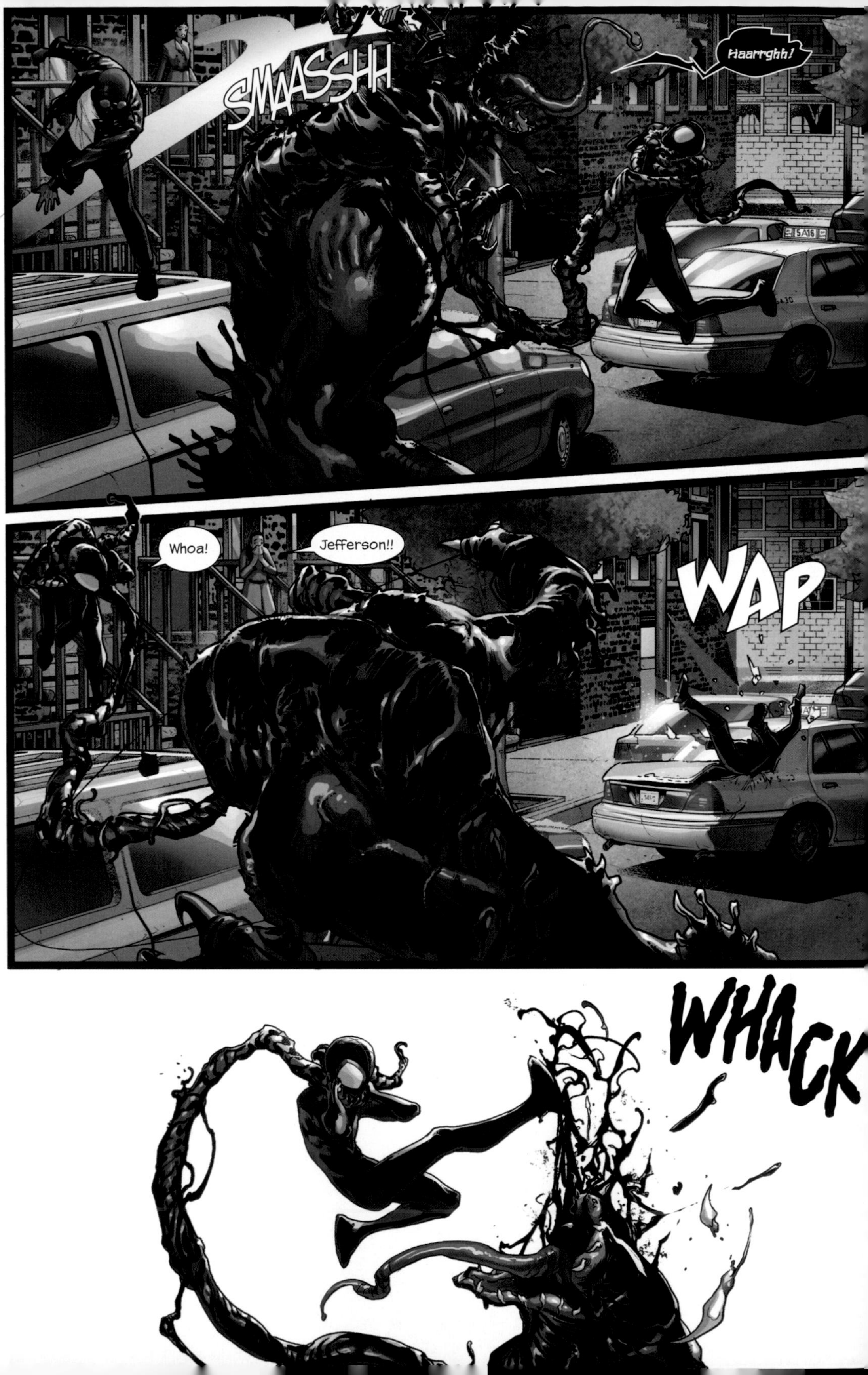

SMAASSHH
Haarrghh!
Whoa!
Jefferson!!
WAP
WHACK

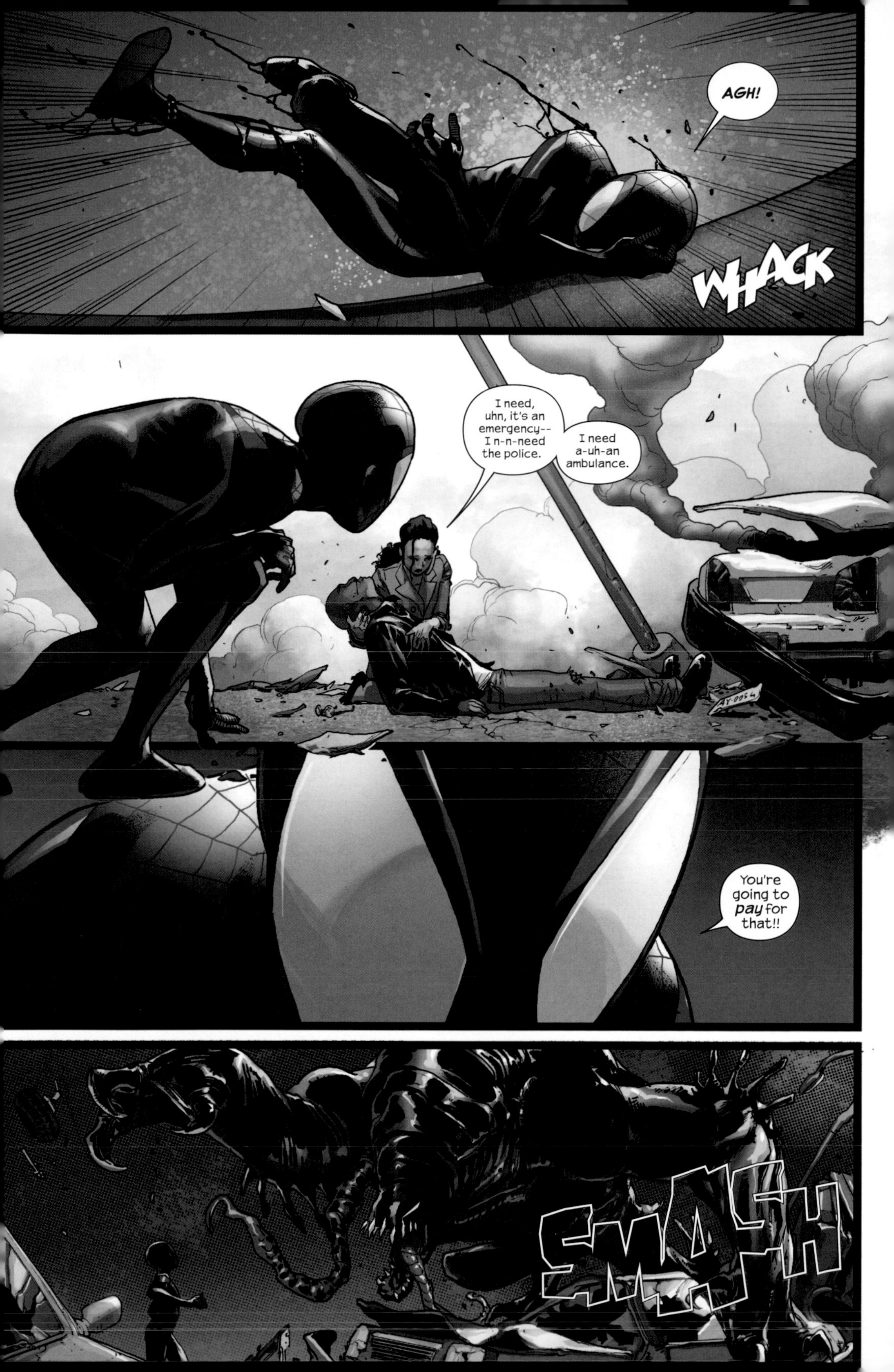
AGH!
WHACK
I need, uhn, it's an emergency-- I n-n-need the police.
I need a-uh-an ambulance.
You're going to *pay* for that!!
SMASH

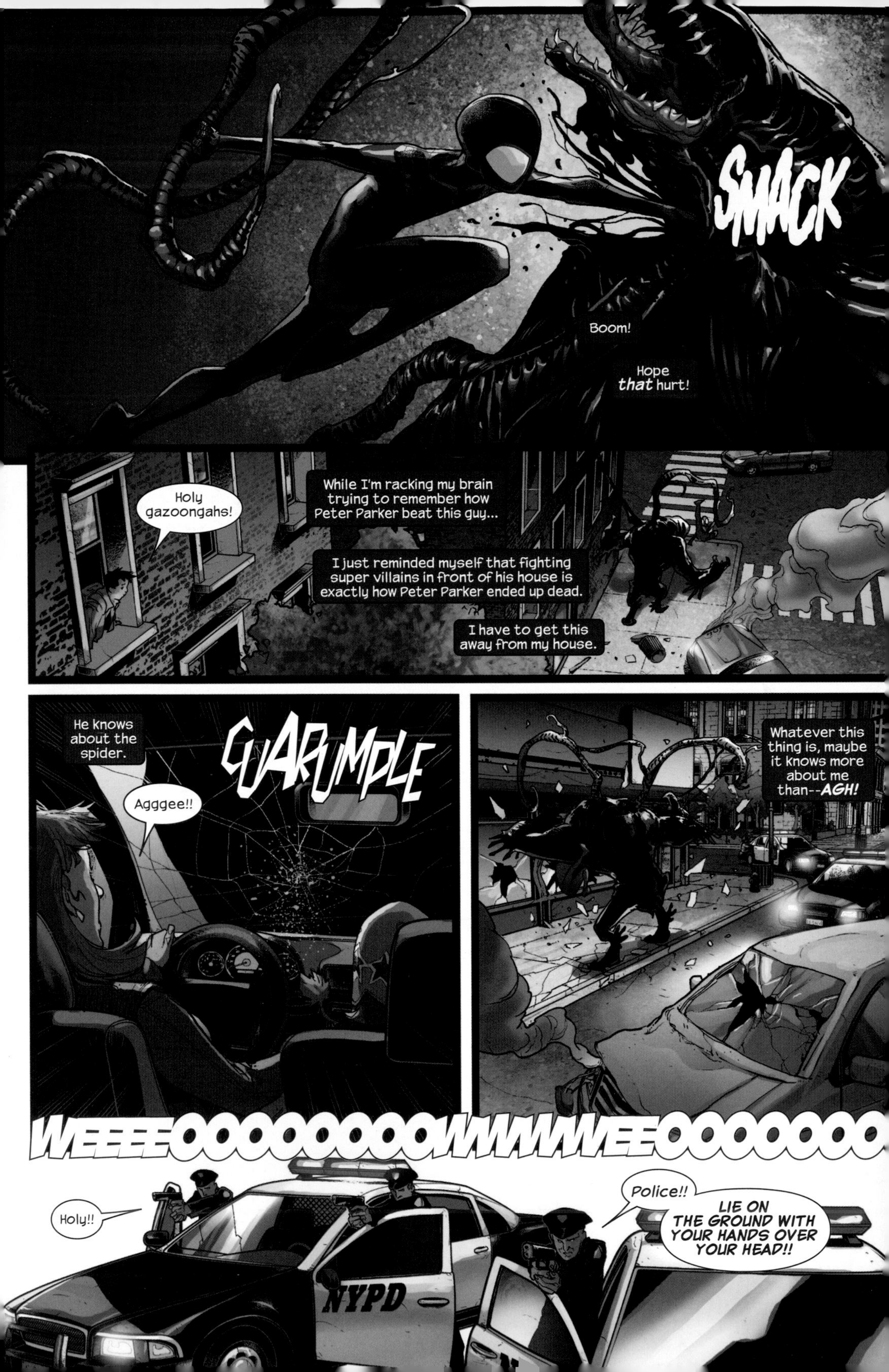
SMACK
Boom!
Hope *that* hurt!
Holy gazoongahs!
While I'm racking my brain trying to remember how Peter Parker beat this guy...
I just reminded myself that fighting super villains in front of his house is exactly how Peter Parker ended up dead.
I have to get this away from my house.
He knows about the spider.
GUARUMPLE
Agggee!!
Whatever this thing is, maybe it knows more about me than--**AGH!**
WEEEEOOOOOOOOOWWWWWEEOOOOOOOO
Holy!!
Police!!
LIE ON THE GROUND WITH YOUR HANDS OVER YOUR HEAD!!
NYPD

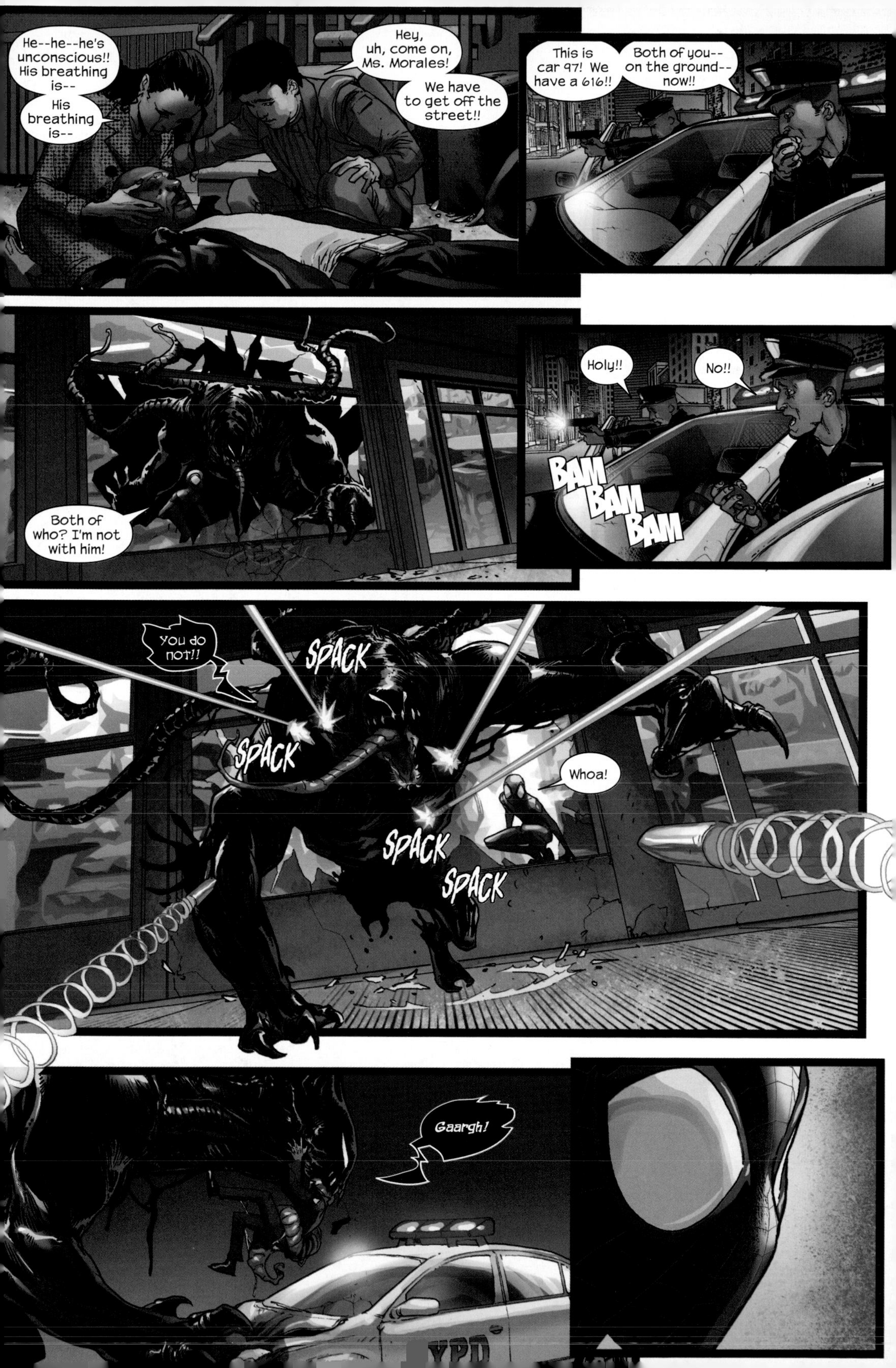
He--he--he's unconscious!! His breathing is--
His breathing is--
Hey, uh, come on, Ms. Morales!
We have to get off the street!!
This is car 97! We have a 616!!
Both of you-- on the ground-- now!!
Both of who? I'm not with him!
Holy!!
No!!
BAM
BAM
BAM
You do not!!
SPACK
SPACK
SPACK
SPACK
Whoa!
Gaargh!

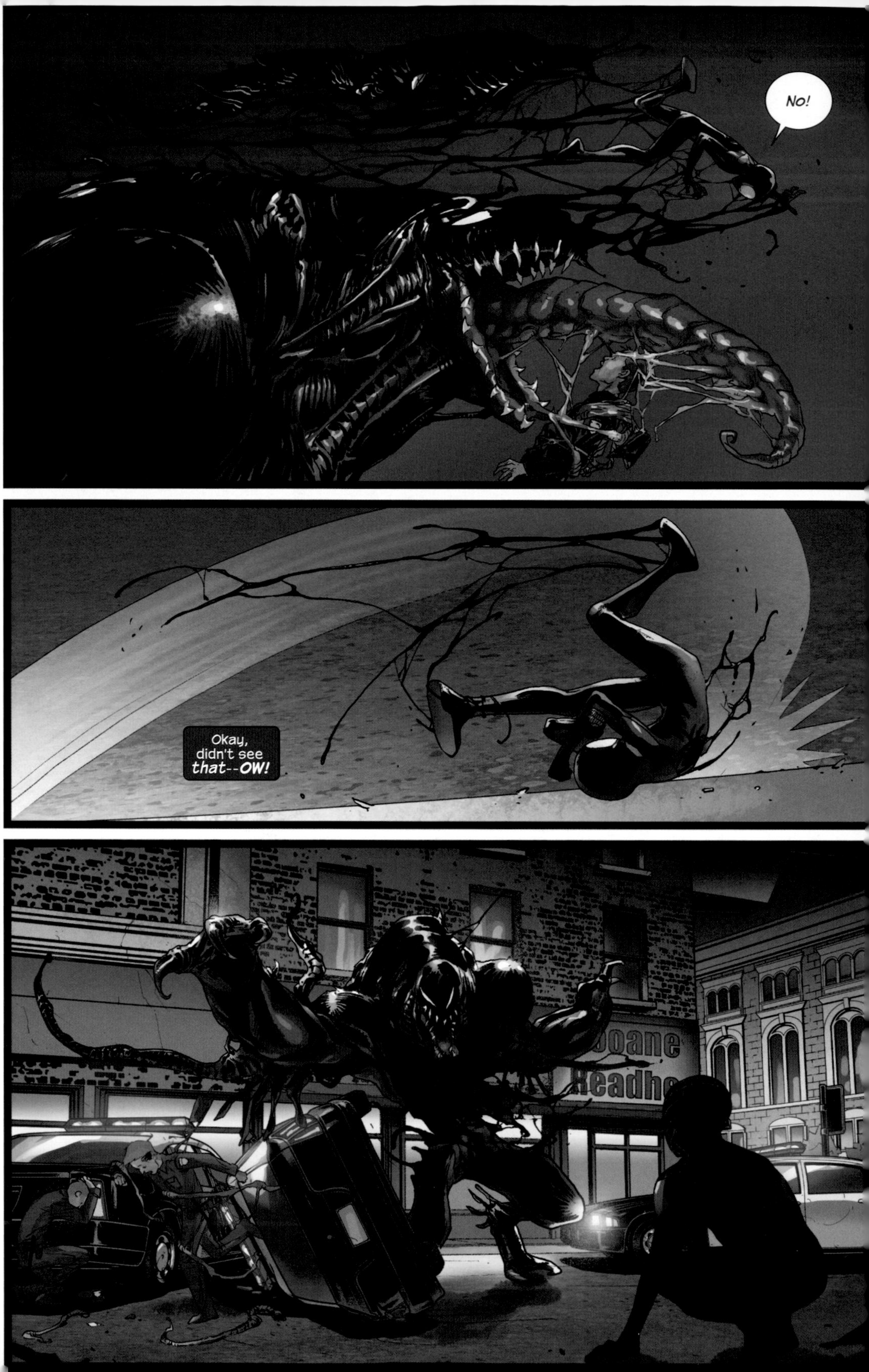
No!
Okay, didn't see *that*--*OW!*

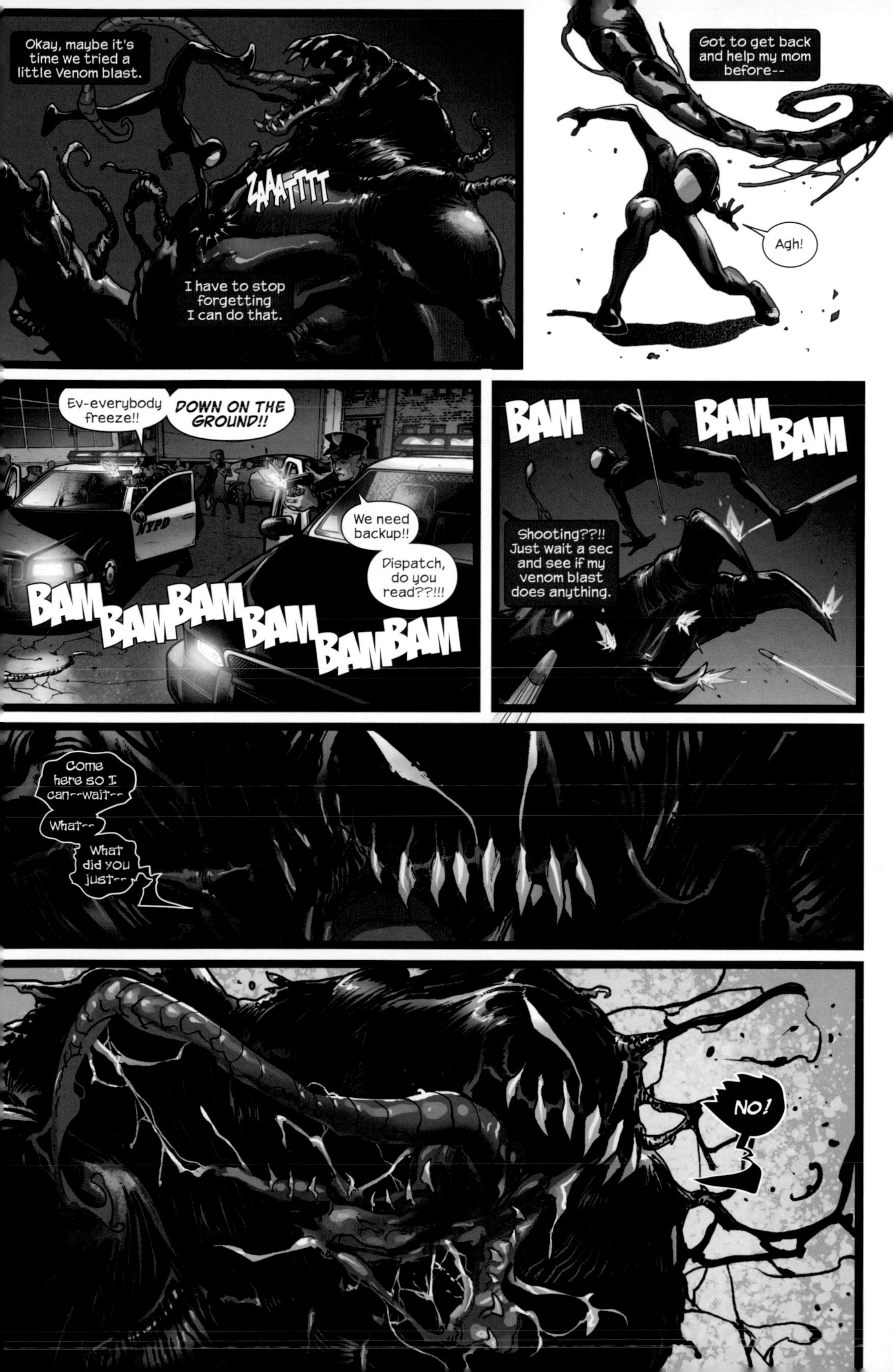
Okay, maybe it's time we tried a little Venom blast.
ZAAATTTT
I have to stop forgetting I can do that.
Got to get back and help my mom before--
Agh!
Ev-everybody freeze!!
DOWN ON THE GROUND!!
We need backup!!
Dispatch, do you read??!!!
BAM BAM BAM BAM BAM BAM
BAM
BAM BAM
Shooting??!! Just wait a sec and see if my venom blast does anything.
Come here so I can--wait--
What--
What did you just--
NO!

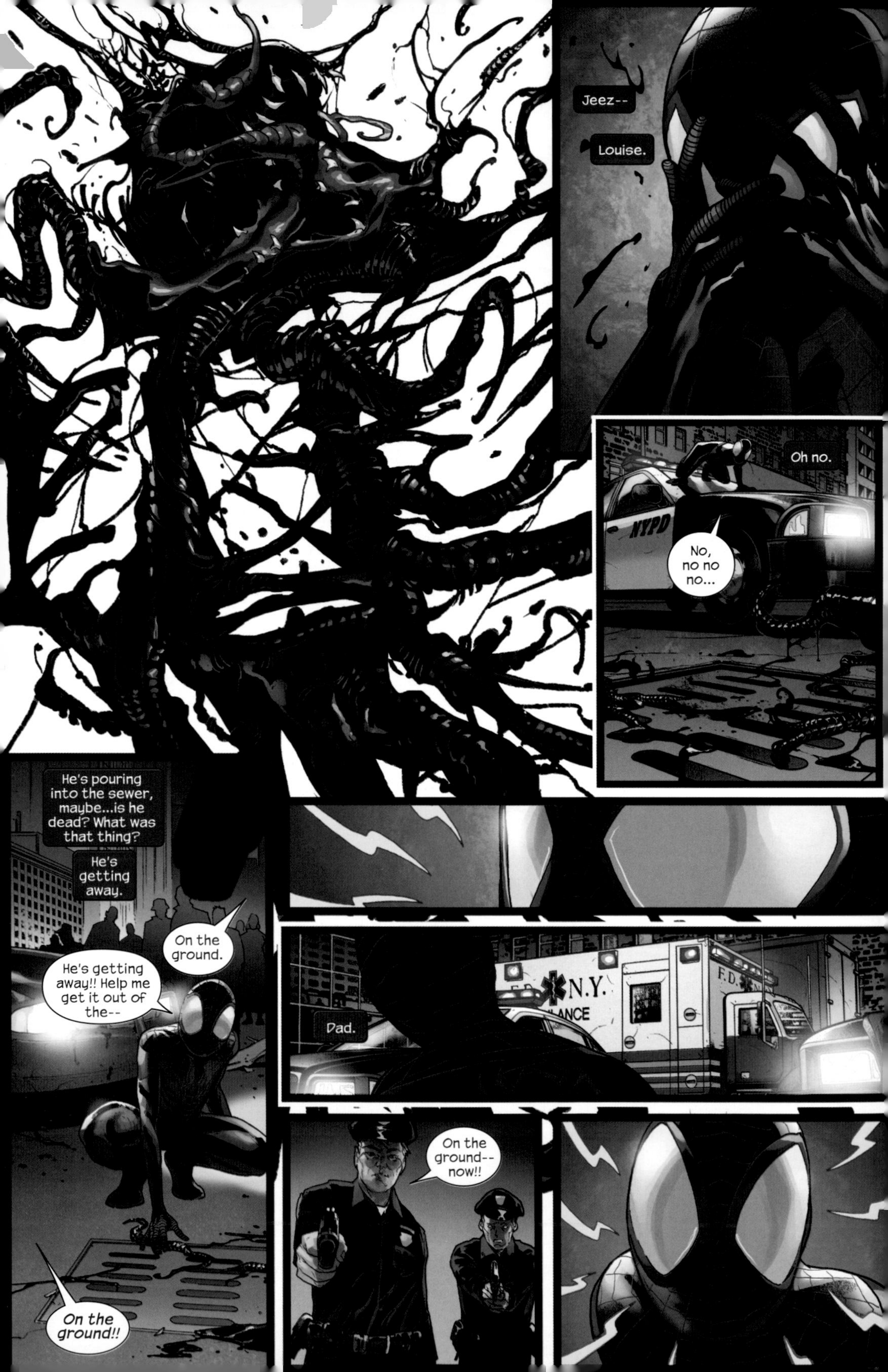
Jeez--
Louise.
Oh no.
No, no no no...
He's pouring into the sewer, maybe...is he dead? What was that thing?
He's getting away.
On the ground.
He's getting away!! Help me get it out of the--
On the ground!!
Dad.
On the ground-- now!!

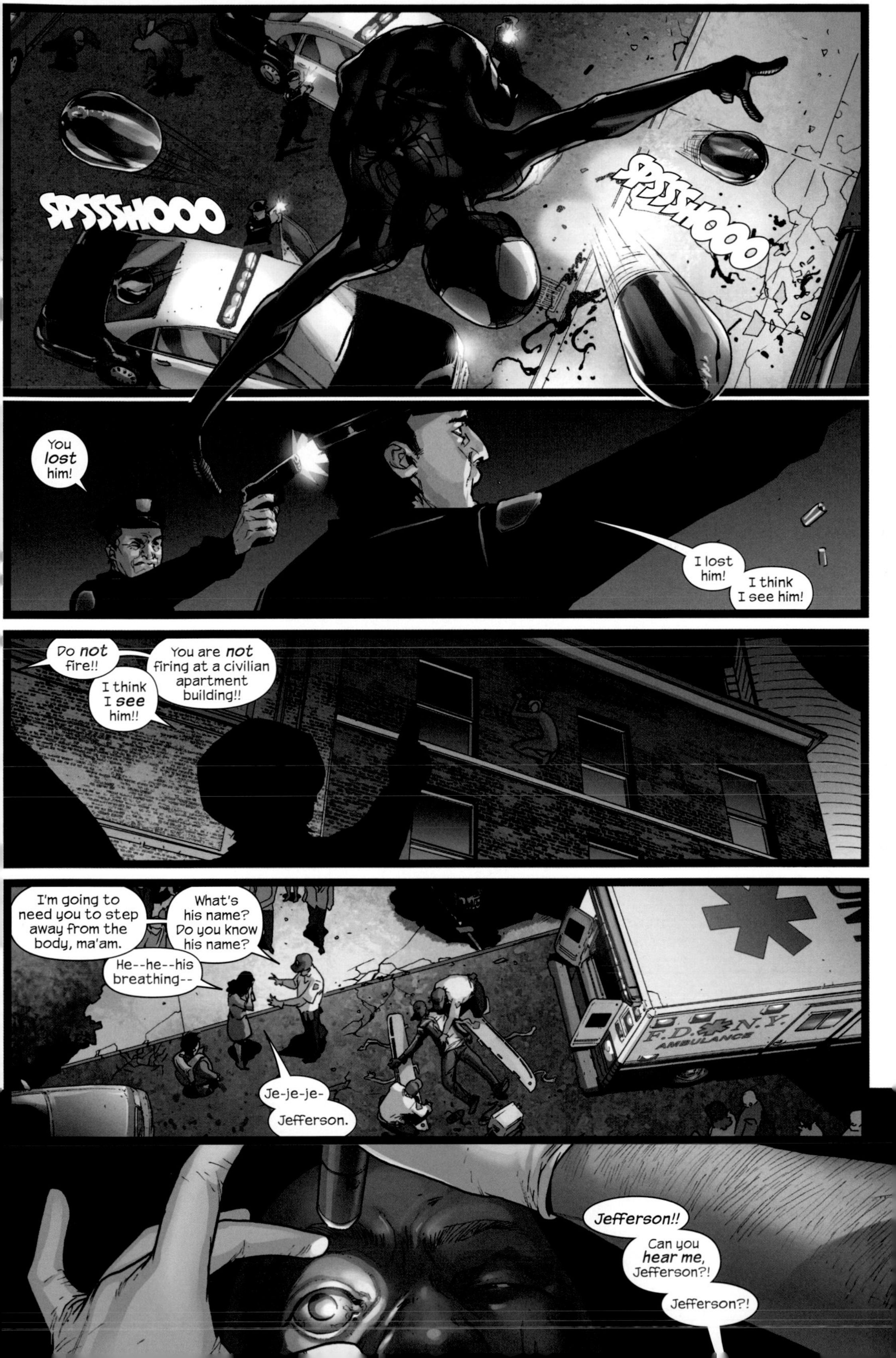
SPSSSHOOO
SPSSSHOOO
You lost him!
I lost him!
I think I see him!
Do not fire!!
You are not firing at a civilian apartment building!!
I think I see him!!
I'm going to need you to step away from the body, ma'am.
What's his name? Do you know his name?
He--he--his breathing--
Je-je-je-
Jefferson.
F.D.N.Y.
AMBULANCE
Jefferson!!
Can you hear me, Jefferson?!
Jefferson?!

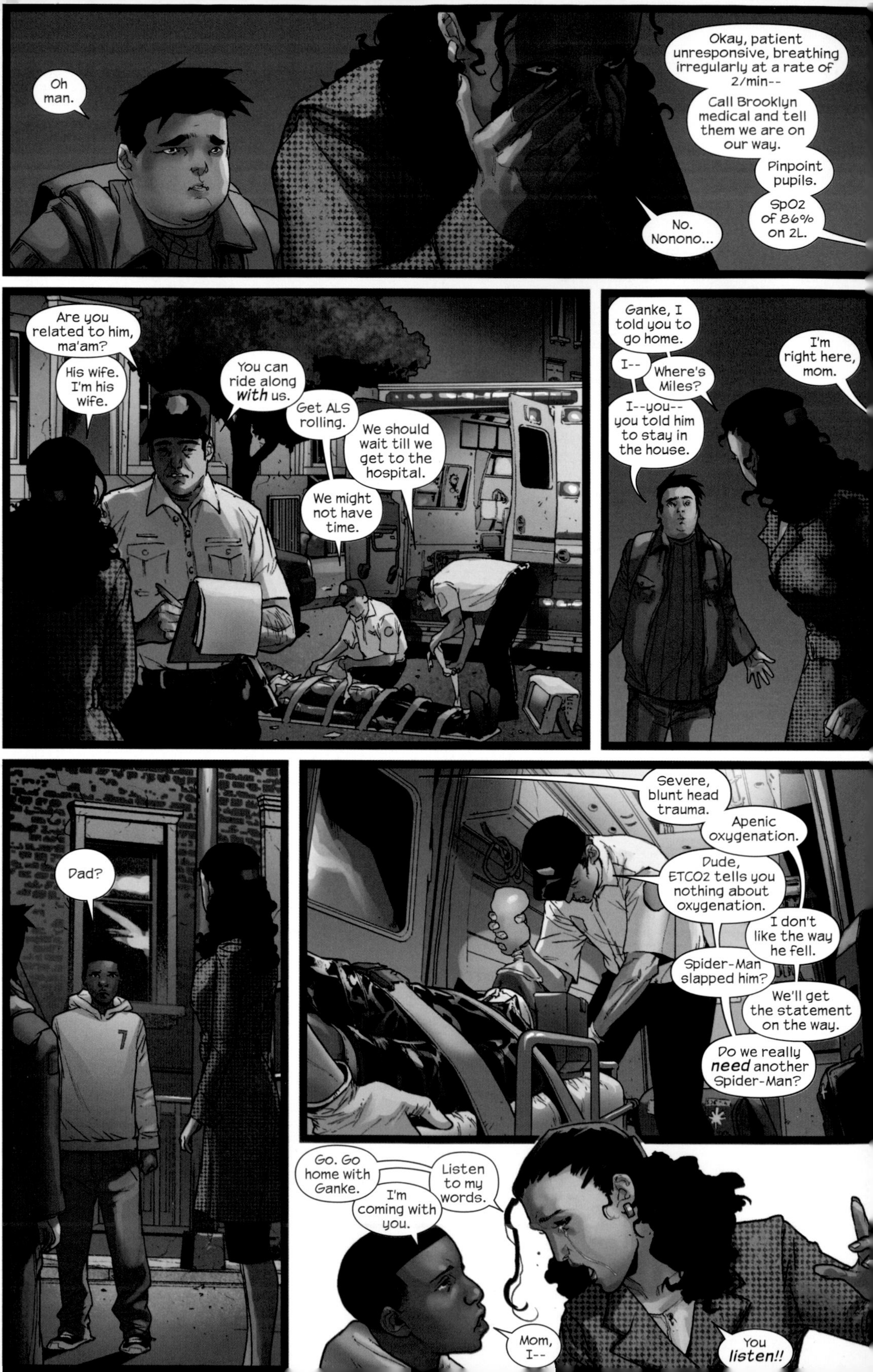

Oh man.
Okay, patient unresponsive, breathing irregularly at a rate of 2/min--
Call Brooklyn medical and tell them we are on our way.
Pinpoint pupils.
SpO2 of 86% on 2L.
No. Nonono...
Are you related to him, ma'am?
His wife. I'm his wife.
You can ride along *with* us.
Get ALS rolling.
We should wait till we get to the hospital.
We might not have time.
Ganke, I told you to go home.
I--
Where's Miles?
I--you-- you told him to stay in the house.
I'm right here, mom.
Dad?
Severe, blunt head trauma.
Apenic oxygenation.
Dude, ETCO2 tells you nothing about oxygenation.
I don't like the way he fell.
Spider-Man slapped him?
We'll get the statement on the way.
Do we really ***need*** another Spider-Man?
Go. Go home with Ganke.
Listen to my words.
I'm coming with you.
Mom, I--
You ***listen!!***

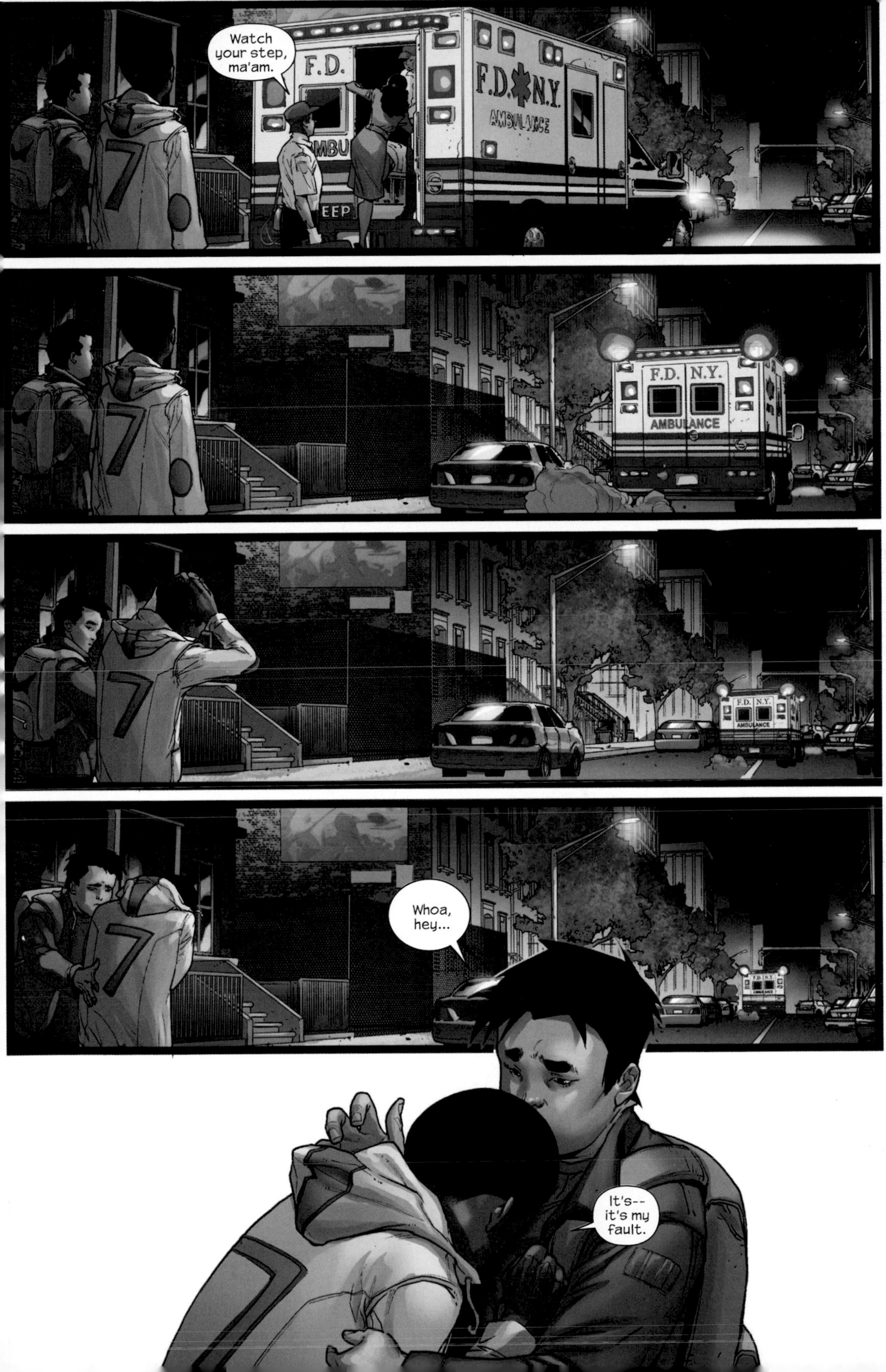
Watch your step, ma'am.
F.D.
F.D. N.Y.
AMBULANCE
F.D. N.Y.
AMBULANCE
Whoa, hey...
It's-- it's my fault.

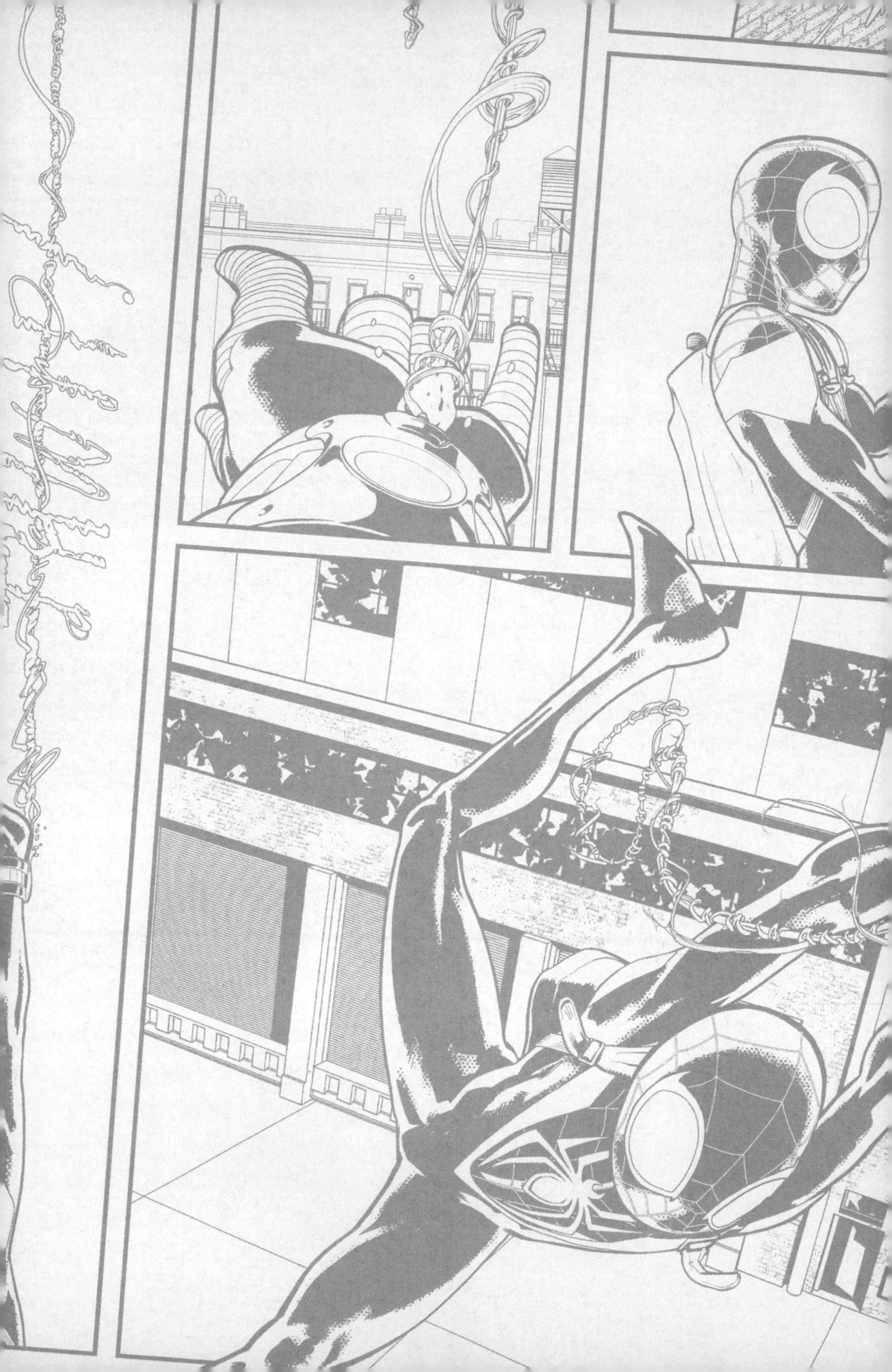

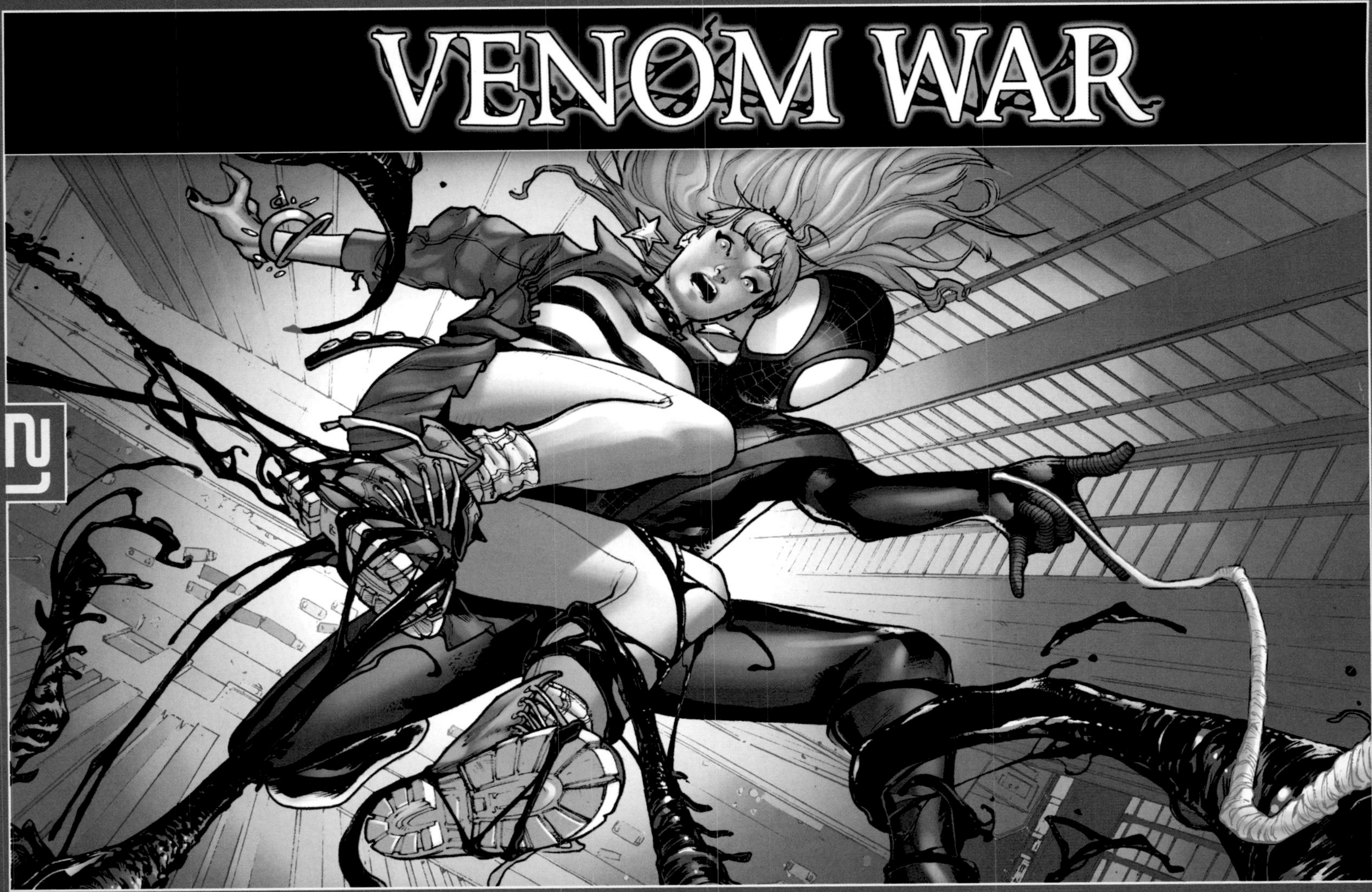
VENOM WAR
21

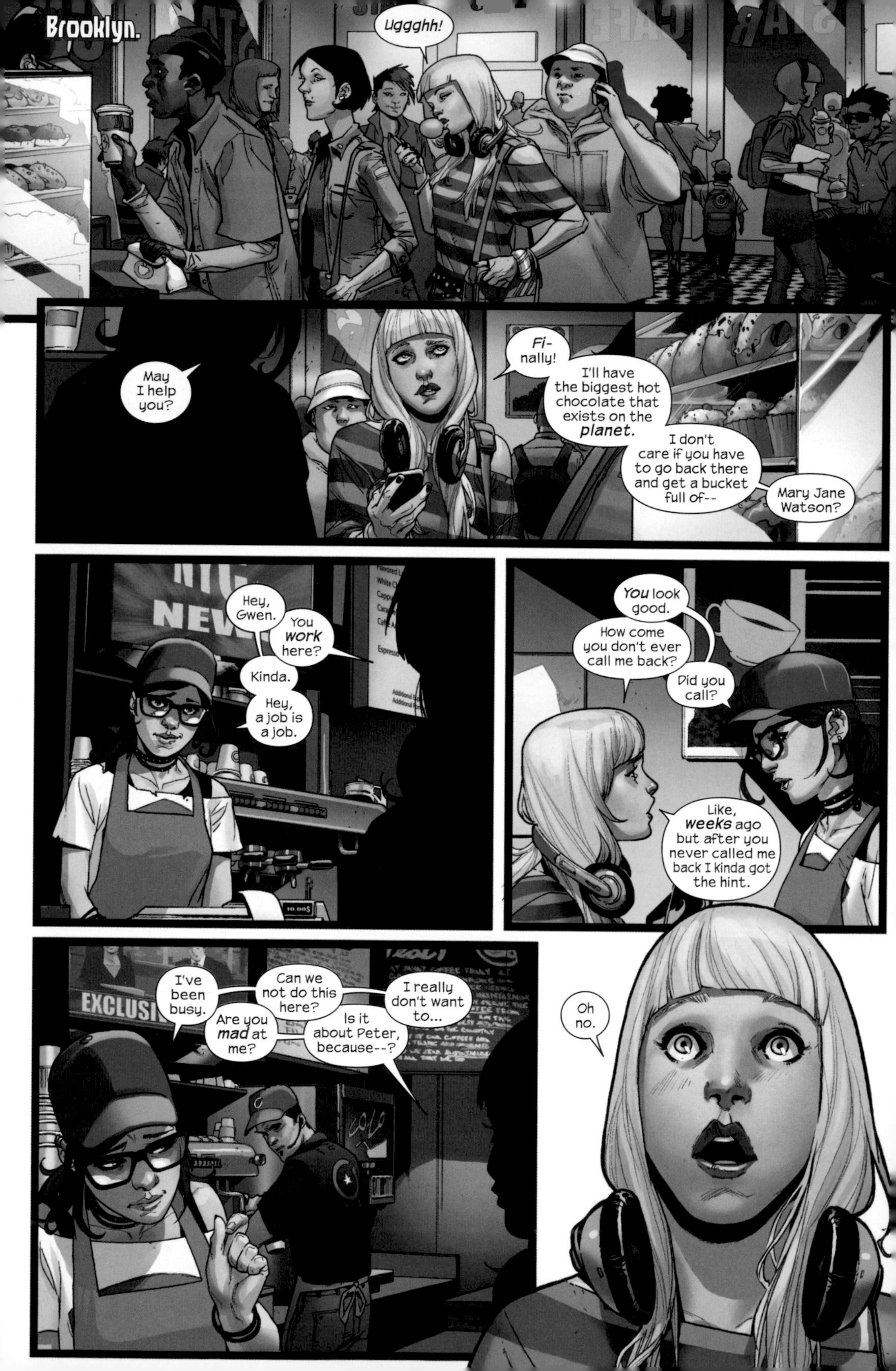
Brooklyn.
Uggghh!
May I help you?
Fi-nally!
I'll have the biggest hot chocolate that exists on the planet.
I don't care if you have to go back there and get a bucket full of--
Mary Jane Watson?
Hey, Gwen.
You work here?
Kinda.
Hey, a job is a job.
You look good.
How come you don't ever call me back?
Did you call?
Like, weeks ago but after you never called me back I kinda got the hint.
I've been busy.
Can we not do this here?
I really don't want to...
Are you mad at me?
Is it about Peter, because--?
Oh no.

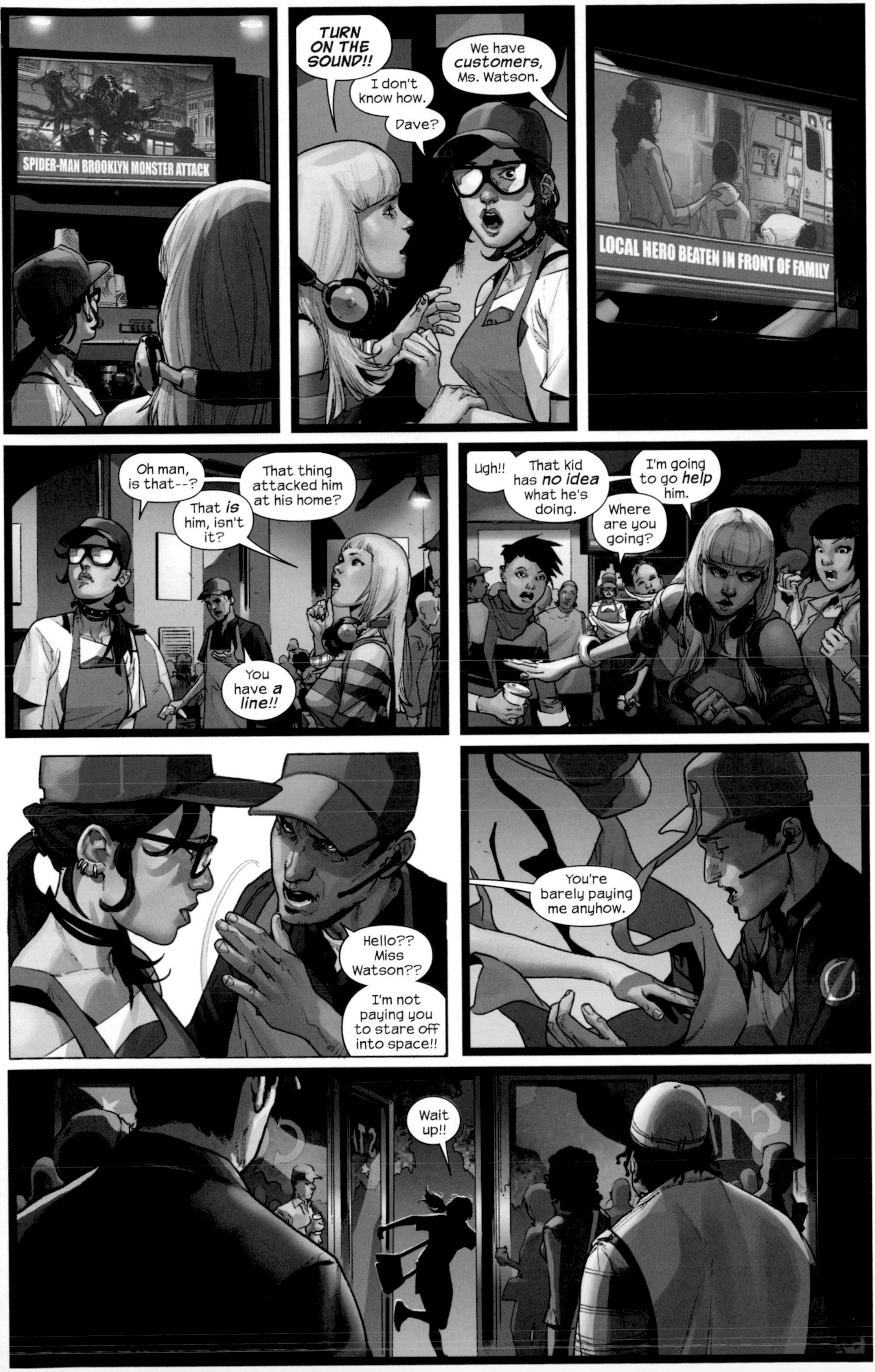

SPIDER-MAN BROOKLYN MONSTER ATTACK
TURN ON THE SOUND!!
I don't know how.
Dave?
We have customers, Ms. Watson.
LOCAL HERO BEATEN IN FRONT OF FAMILY
Oh man, is that--?
That thing attacked him at his home?
That is him, isn't it?
You have a line!!
Ugh!!
That kid has no idea what he's doing.
I'm going to go help him.
Where are you going?
Hello?? Miss Watson??
I'm not paying you to stare off into space!!
You're barely paying me anyhow.
Wait up!!

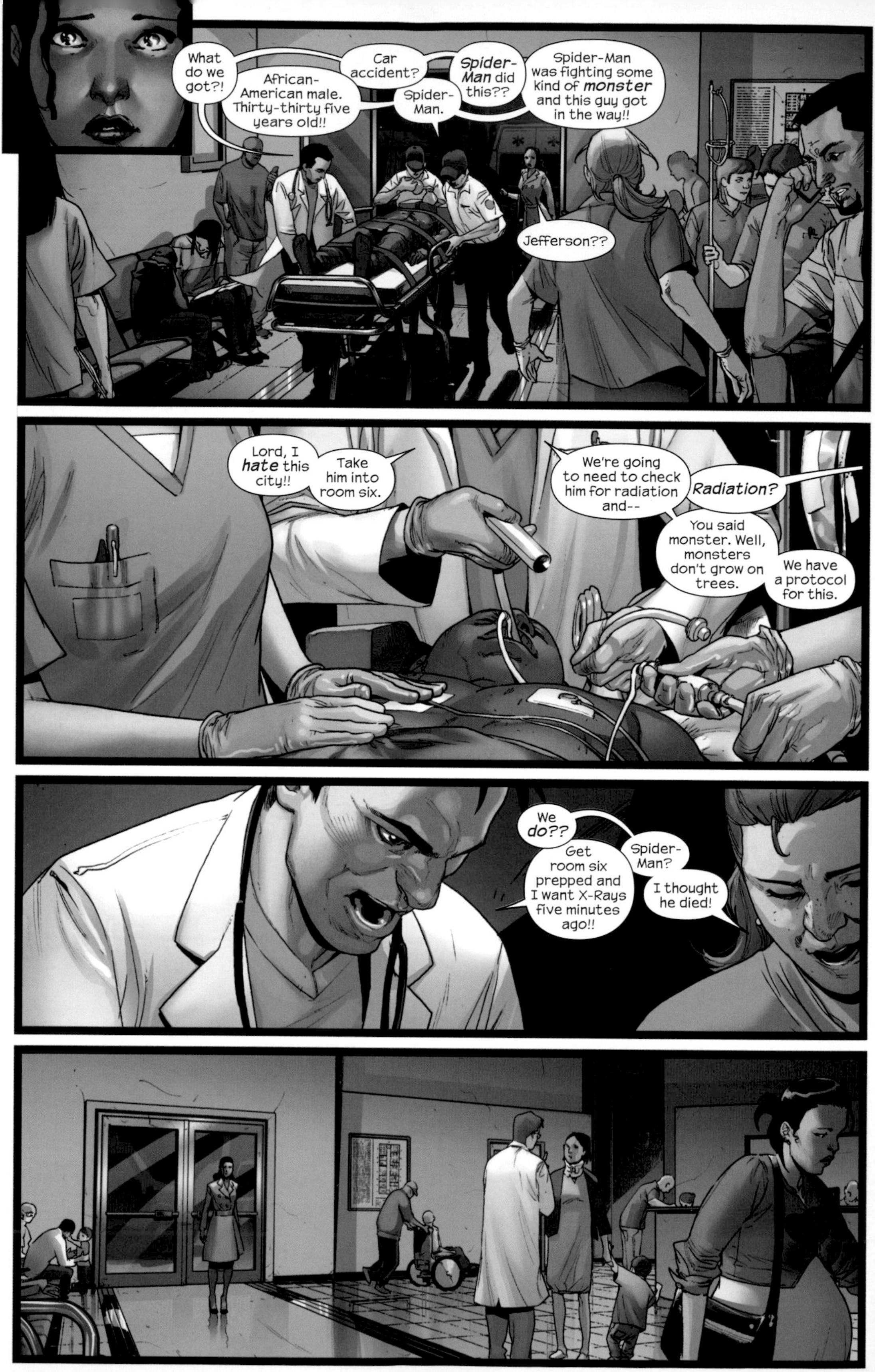
What do we got?!
African-American male. Thirty-thirty five years old!!
Car accident?
Spider-Man.
Spider-Man did this??
Spider-Man was fighting some kind of monster and this guy got in the way!!
Jefferson??
Lord, I hate this city!!
Take him into room six.
We're going to need to check him for radiation and--
Radiation?
You said monster. Well, monsters don't grow on trees.
We have a protocol for this.
We do??
Get room six prepped and I want X-Rays five minutes ago!!
Spider-Man?
I thought he died!

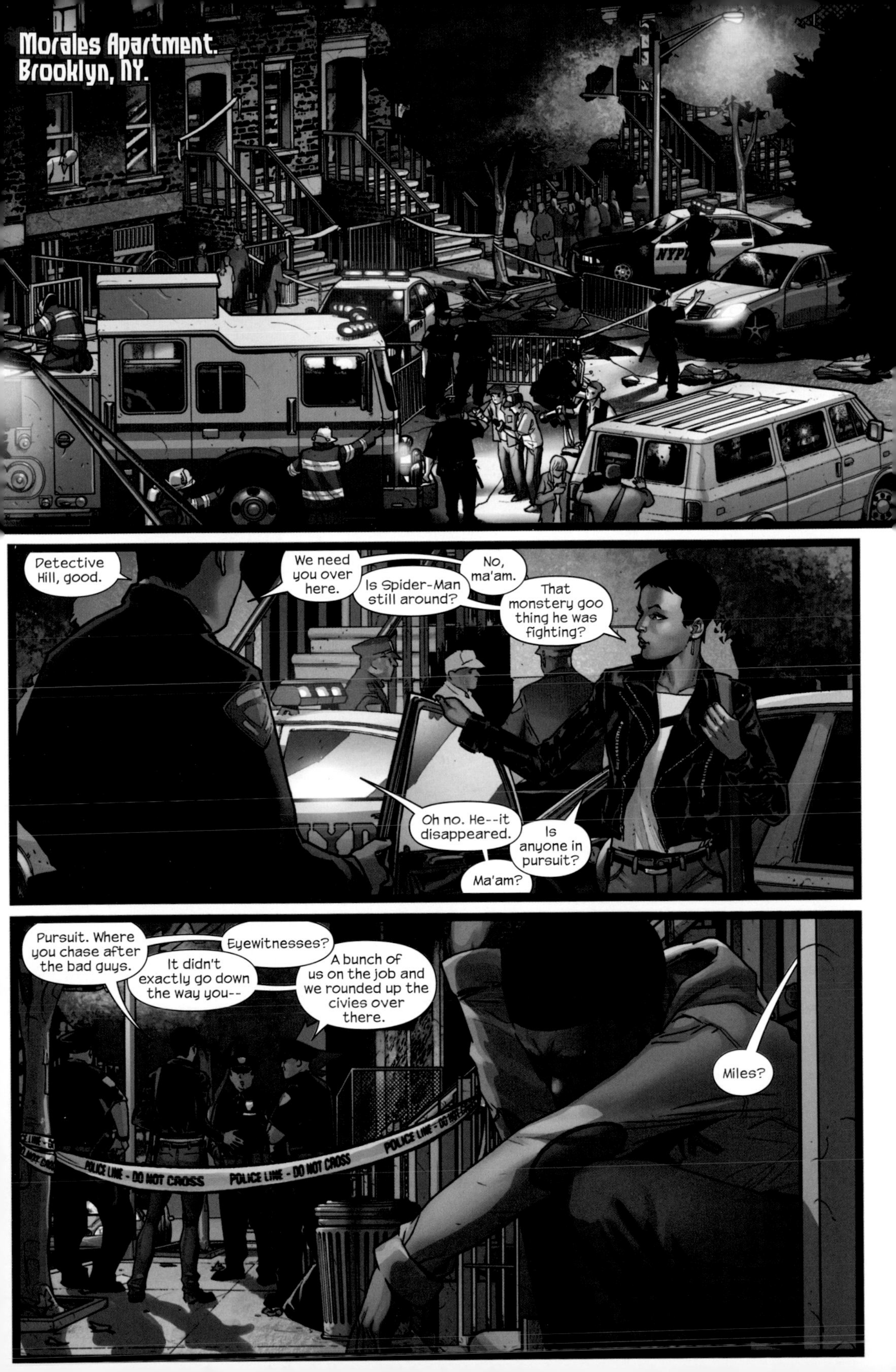
Morales Apartment. Brooklyn, NY.
Detective Hill, good.
We need you over here.
No, ma'am.
Is Spider-Man still around?
That monstery goo thing he was fighting?
Oh no. He--it disappeared.
Is anyone in pursuit?
Ma'am?
Pursuit. Where you chase after the bad guys.
Eyewitnesses?
It didn't exactly go down the way you--
A bunch of us on the job and we rounded up the civies over there.
Miles?
POLICE LINE - DO NOT CROSS
POLICE LINE - DO NOT CROSS
POLICE LINE - DO NOT CROSS

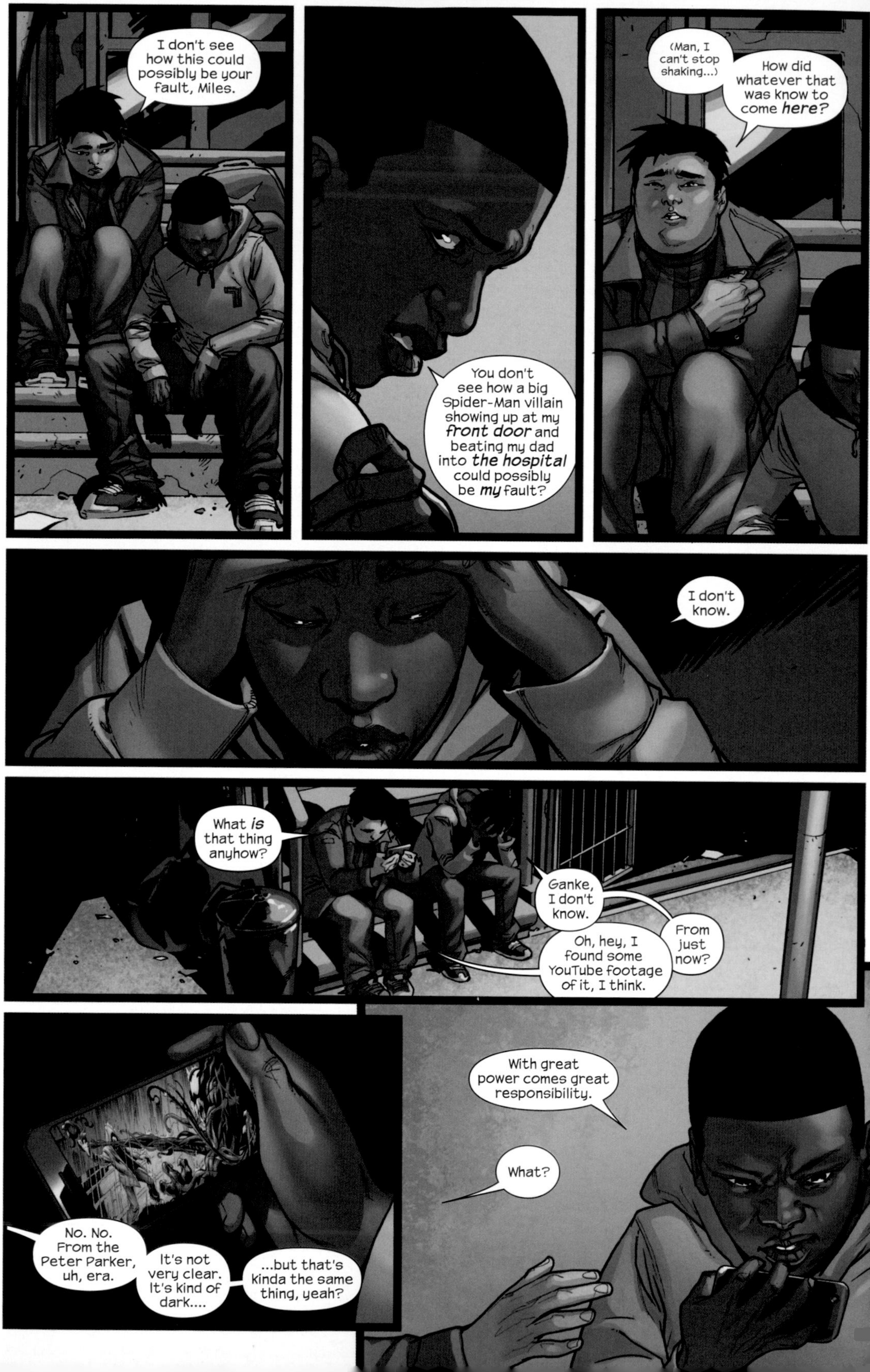
I don't see how this could possibly be your fault, Miles.
You don't see how a big Spider-Man villain showing up at my front door and beating my dad into the hospital could possibly be my fault?
(Man, I can't stop shaking...)
How did whatever that was know to come here?
I don't know.
What is that thing anyhow?
Ganke, I don't know.
Oh, hey, I found some YouTube footage of it, I think.
From just now?
No. No. From the Peter Parker, uh, era.
It's not very clear. It's kind of dark....
...but that's kinda the same thing, yeah?
With great power comes great responsibility.
What?

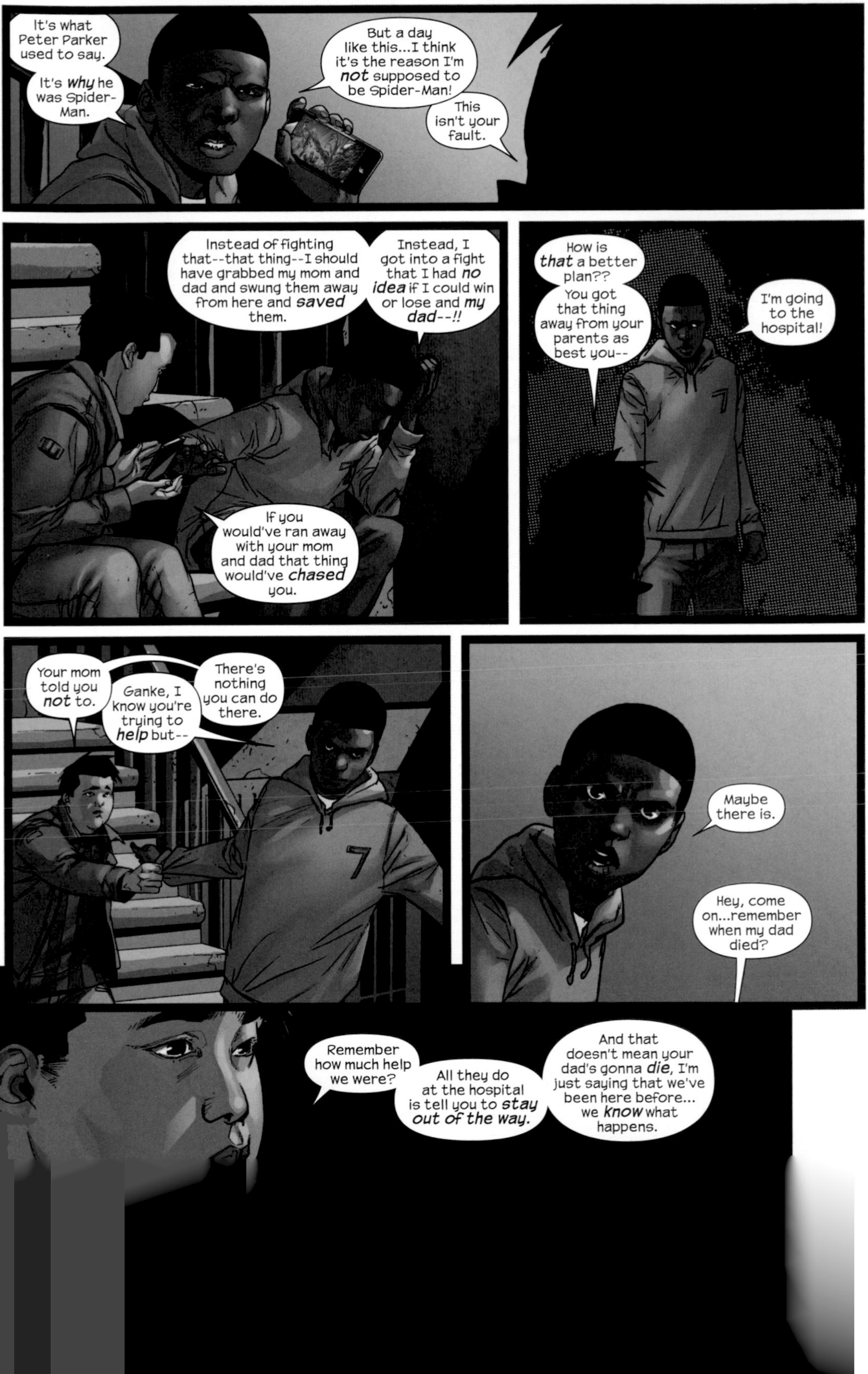
It's what Peter Parker used to say.
It's *why* he was Spider-Man.
But a day like this...I think it's the reason I'm *not* supposed to be Spider-Man!
This isn't your fault.
Instead of fighting that--that thing--I should have grabbed my mom and dad and swung them away from here and *saved* them.
Instead, I got into a fight that I had *no idea* if I could win or lose and *my dad*--!!
If you would've ran away with your mom and dad that thing would've *chased* you.
How is *that* a better plan??
You got that thing away from your parents as best you--
I'm going to the hospital!
Your mom told you *not* to.
Ganke, I know you're trying to *help* but--
There's nothing you can do there.
Maybe there is.
Hey, come on...remember when my dad died?
Remember how much help we were?
All they do at the hospital is tell you to *stay out of the way.*
And that doesn't mean your dad's gonna *die*, I'm just saying that we've been here before... we *know* what happens.

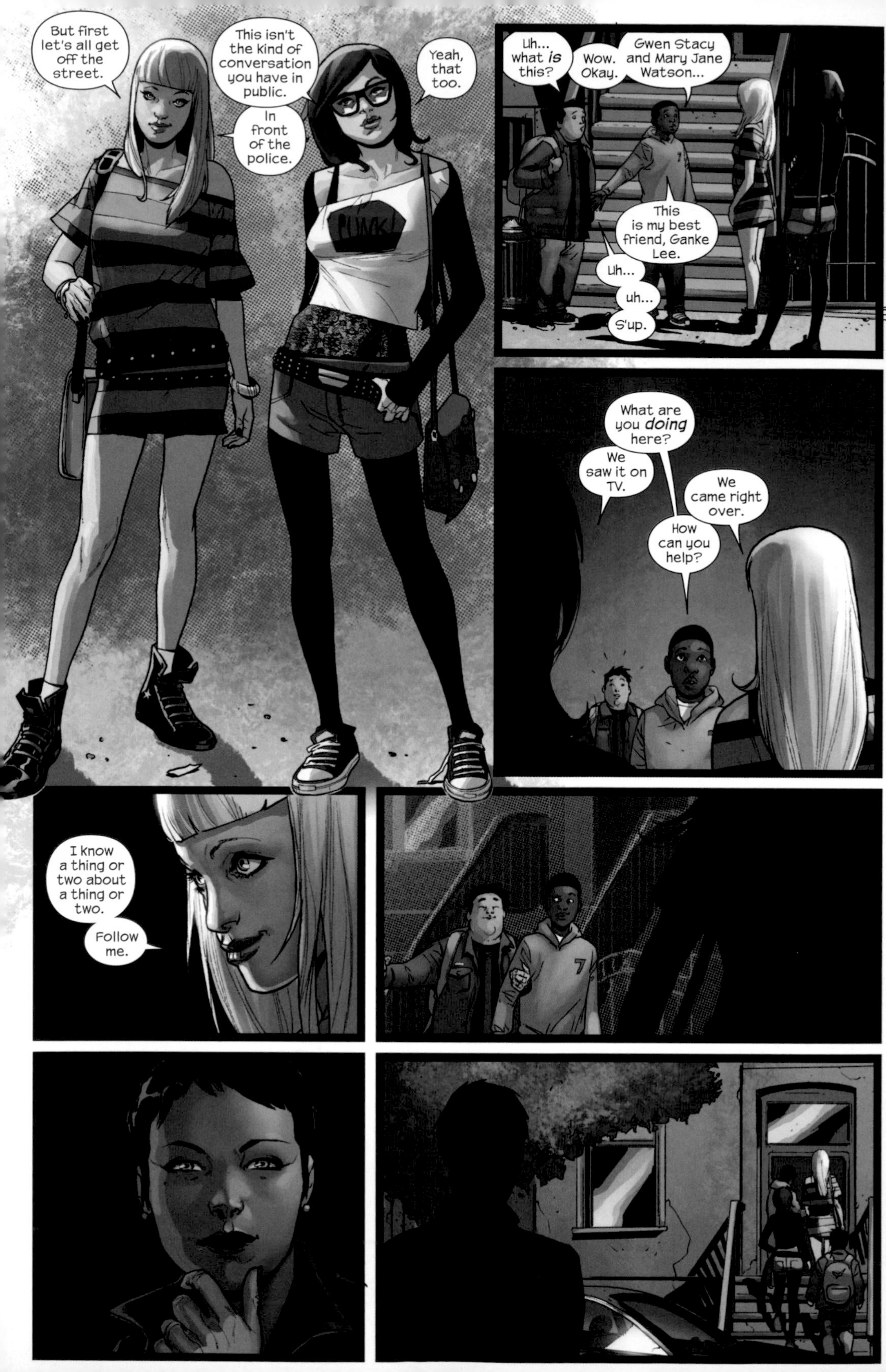

But first let's all get off the street.
This isn't the kind of conversation you have in public.
In front of the police.
Yeah, that too.
Uh... what *is* this?
Wow. Okay.
Gwen Stacy and Mary Jane Watson...
This is my best friend, Ganke Lee.
Uh...
uh...
S'up.
What are you *doing* here?
We saw it on TV.
We came right over.
How can you help?
I know a thing or two about a thing or two.
Follow me.

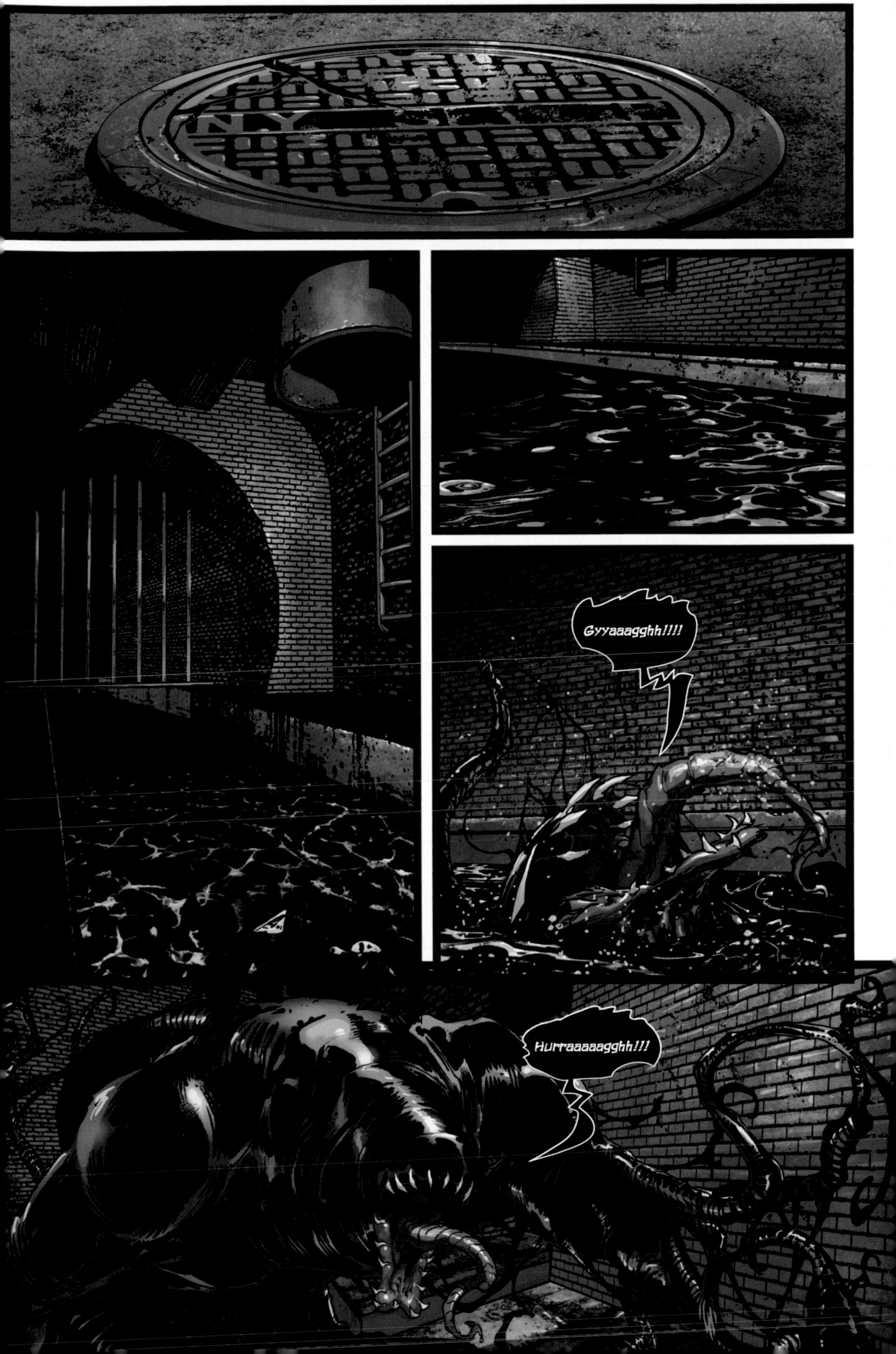
Gyyaaagghh!!!!
Hurraaaaagghh!!!

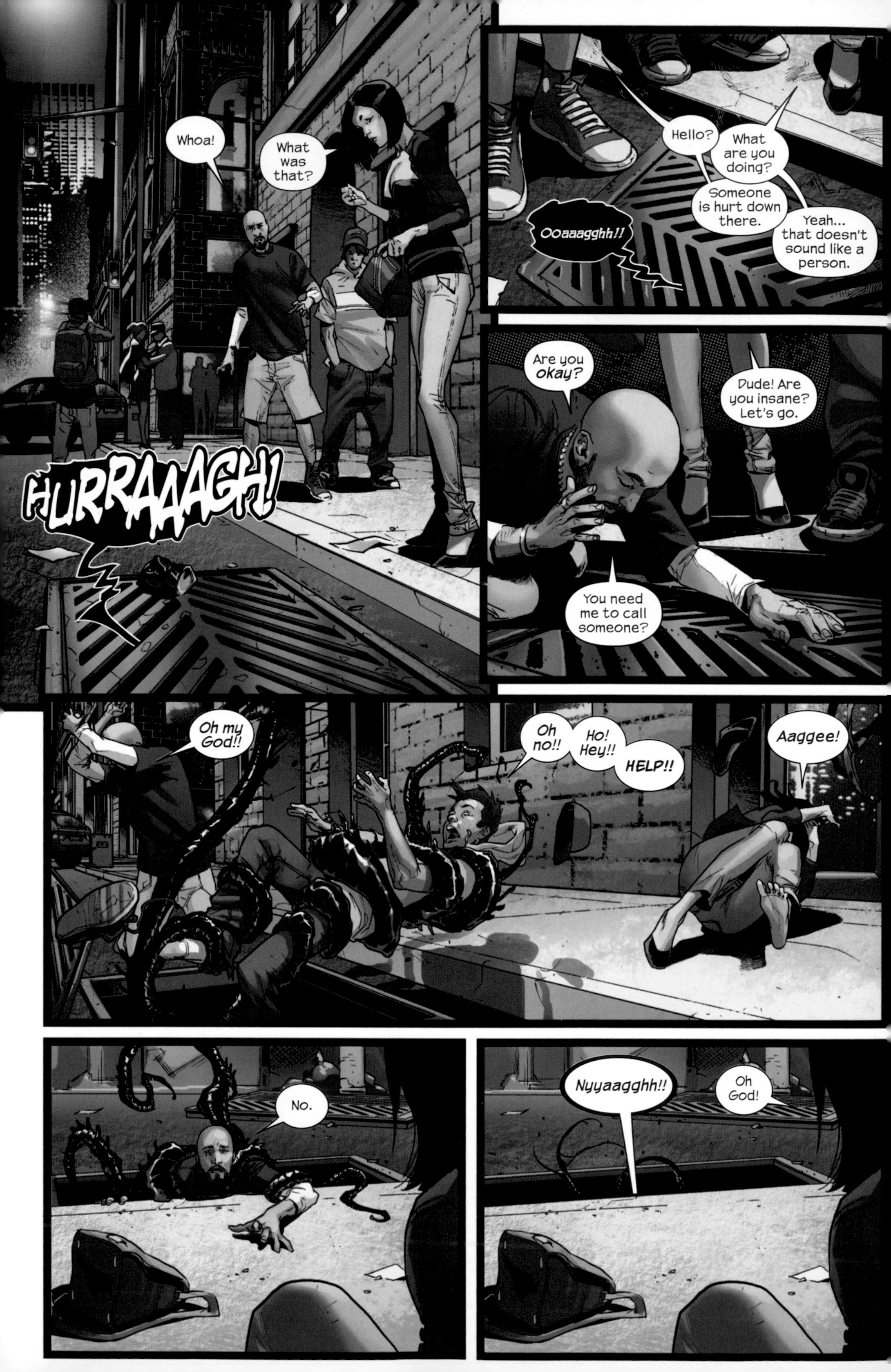
Whoa!
What was that?
HURRAAAGH!
Hello?
What are you doing?
Someone is hurt down there.
Ooaaagghh!!
Yeah... that doesn't sound like a person.
Are you okay?
Dude! Are you insane? Let's go.
You need me to call someone?
Oh my God!!
Oh no!!
Ho! Hey!!
HELP!!
Aaggee!
No.
Nyyaagghh!!
Oh God!

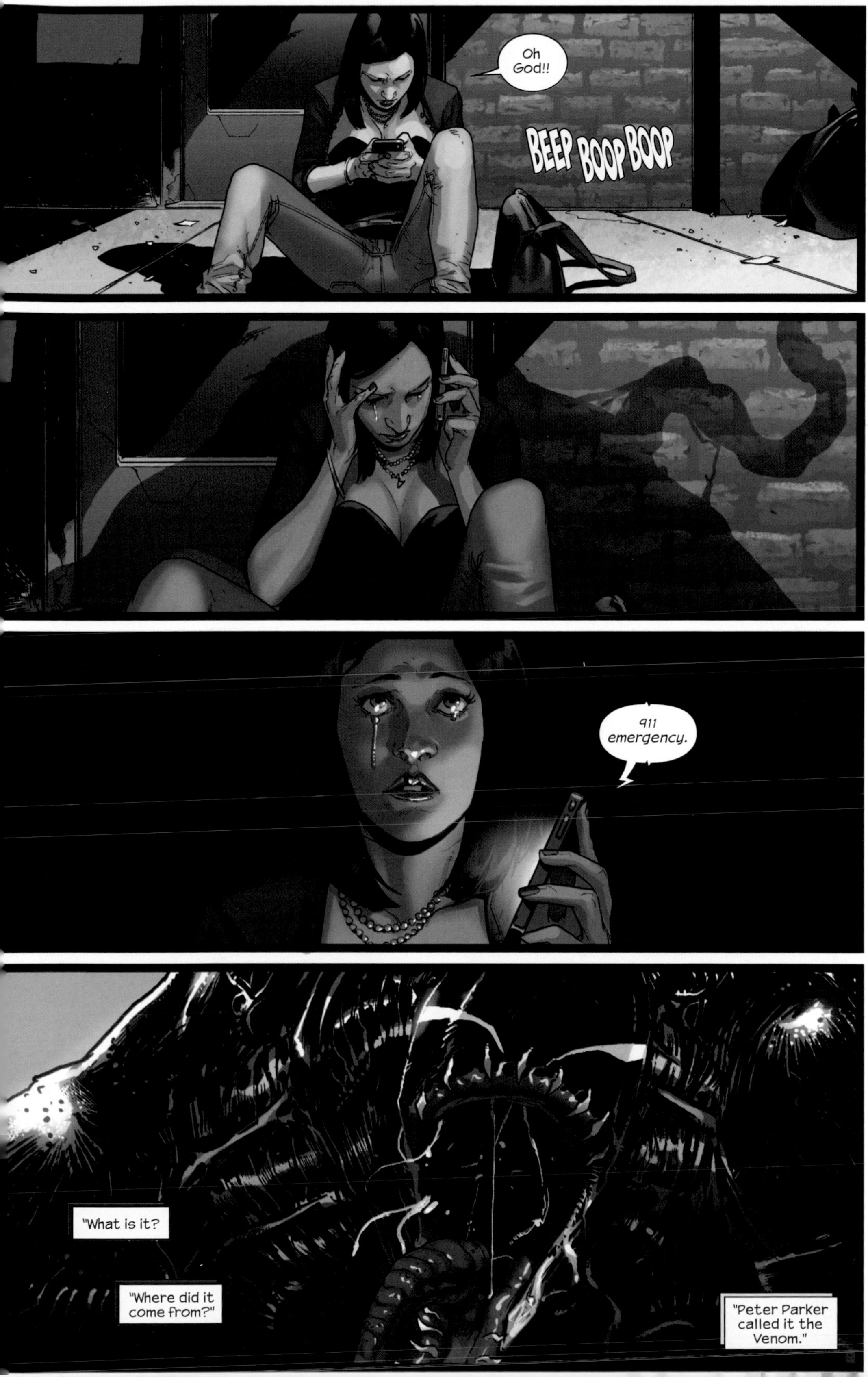
Oh God!!
BEEP BOOP BOOP
911 emergency.
"What is it?
"Where did it come from?"
"Peter Parker called it the Venom."

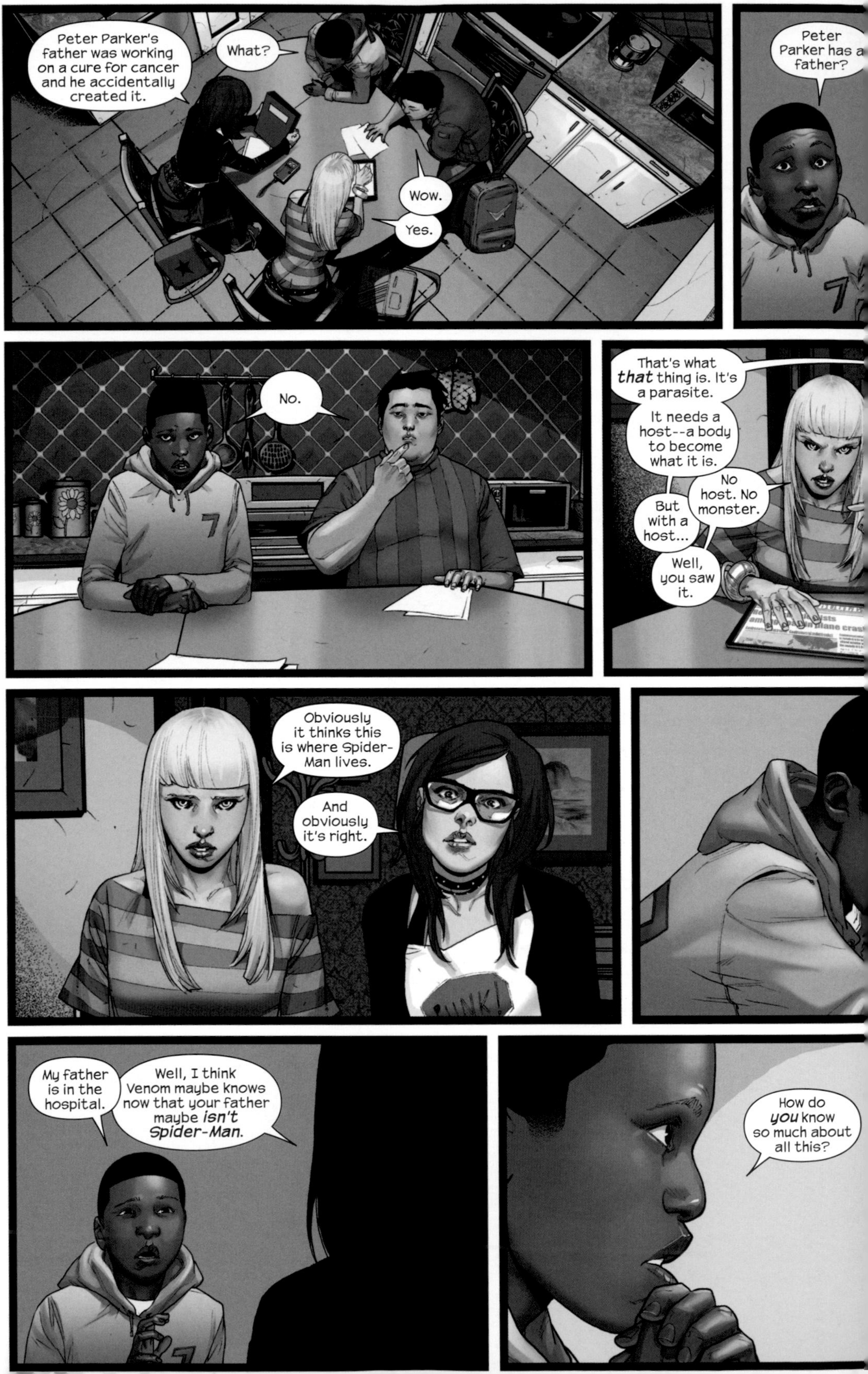
Peter Parker's father was working on a cure for cancer and he accidentally created it.
What?
Wow.
Yes.
Peter Parker has a father?
No.
That's what *that* thing is. It's a parasite.
It needs a host--a body to become what it is.
No host. No monster.
But with a host...
Well, you saw it.
Obviously it thinks this is where Spider-Man lives.
And obviously it's right.
My father is in the hospital.
Well, I think Venom maybe knows now that your father maybe *isn't Spider-Man*.
How do *you* know so much about all this?

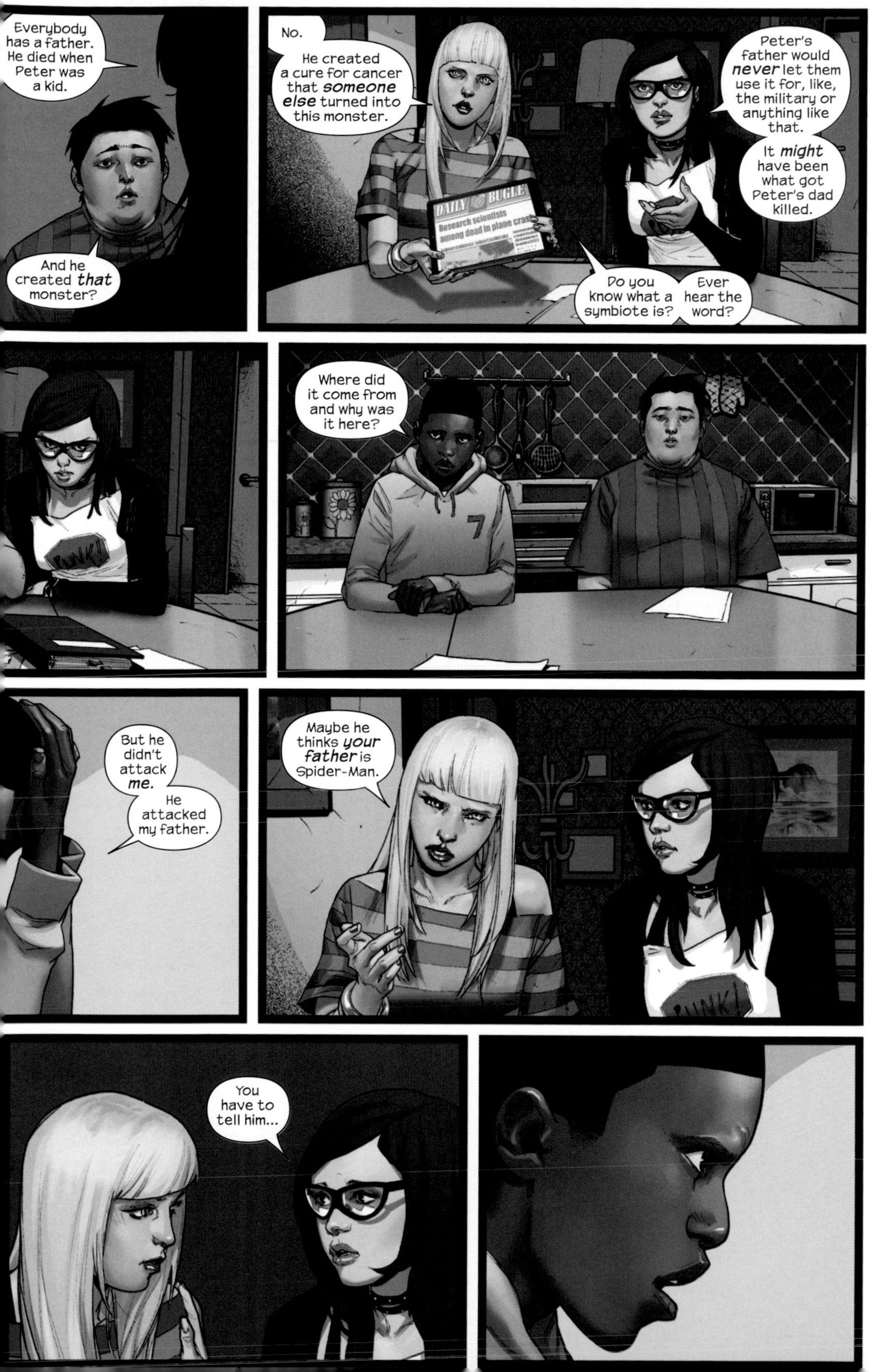

Everybody has a father. He died when Peter was a kid.
And he created *that* monster?
No.
He created a cure for cancer that *someone else* turned into this monster.
DAILY BUGLE
Research scientists among dead in plane cras
Peter's father would *never* let them use it for, like, the military or anything like that.
It *might* have been what got Peter's dad killed.
Do you know what a symbiote is?
Ever hear the word?
Where did it come from and why was it here?
But he didn't attack *me.*
He attacked my father.
Maybe he thinks *your father* is Spider-Man.
You have to tell him...

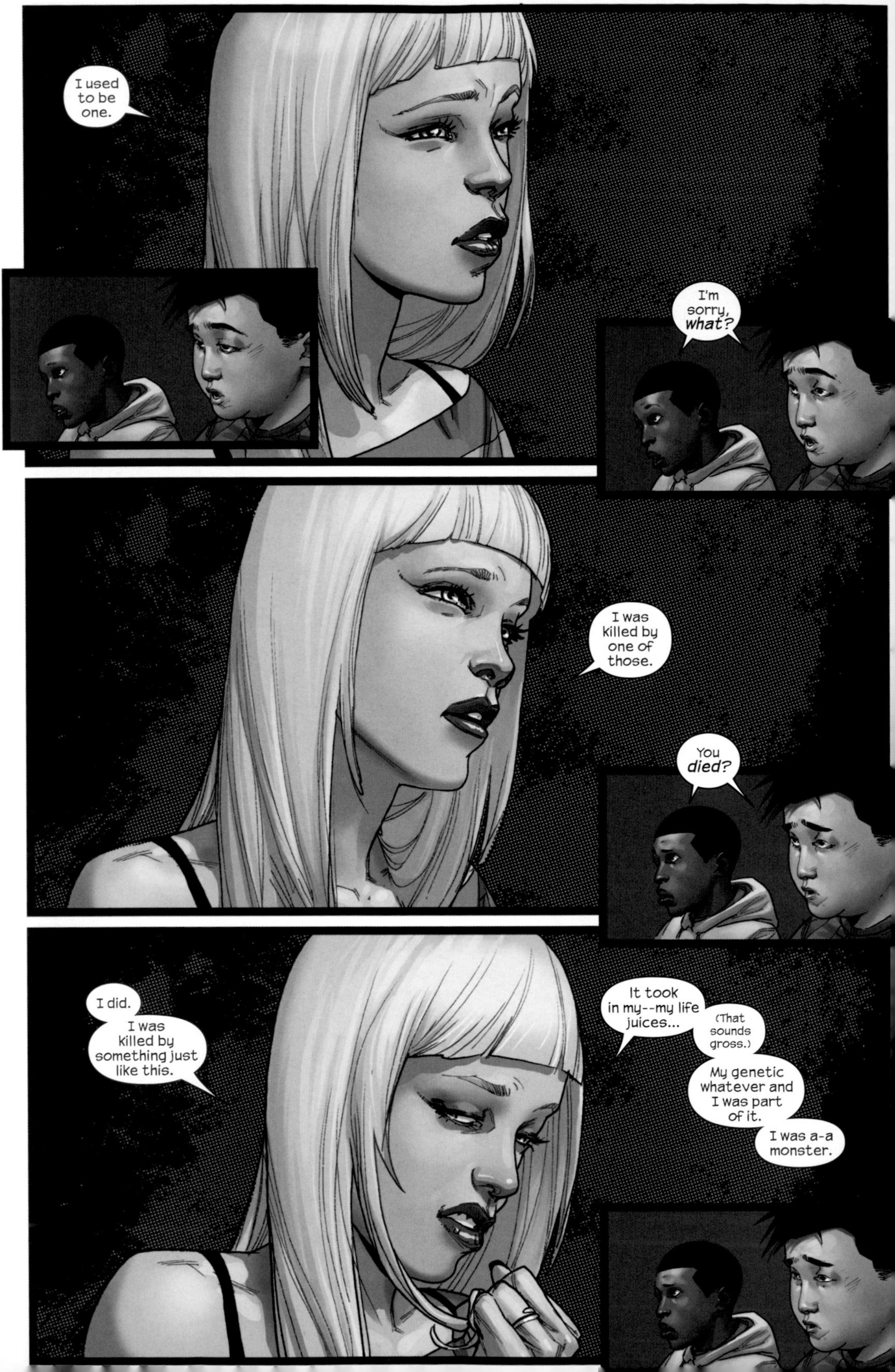
I used to be one.
I'm sorry, what?
I was killed by one of those.
You died?
I did.
I was killed by something just like this.
It took in my--my life juices...
(That sounds gross.)
My genetic whatever and I was part of it.
I was a-a monster.

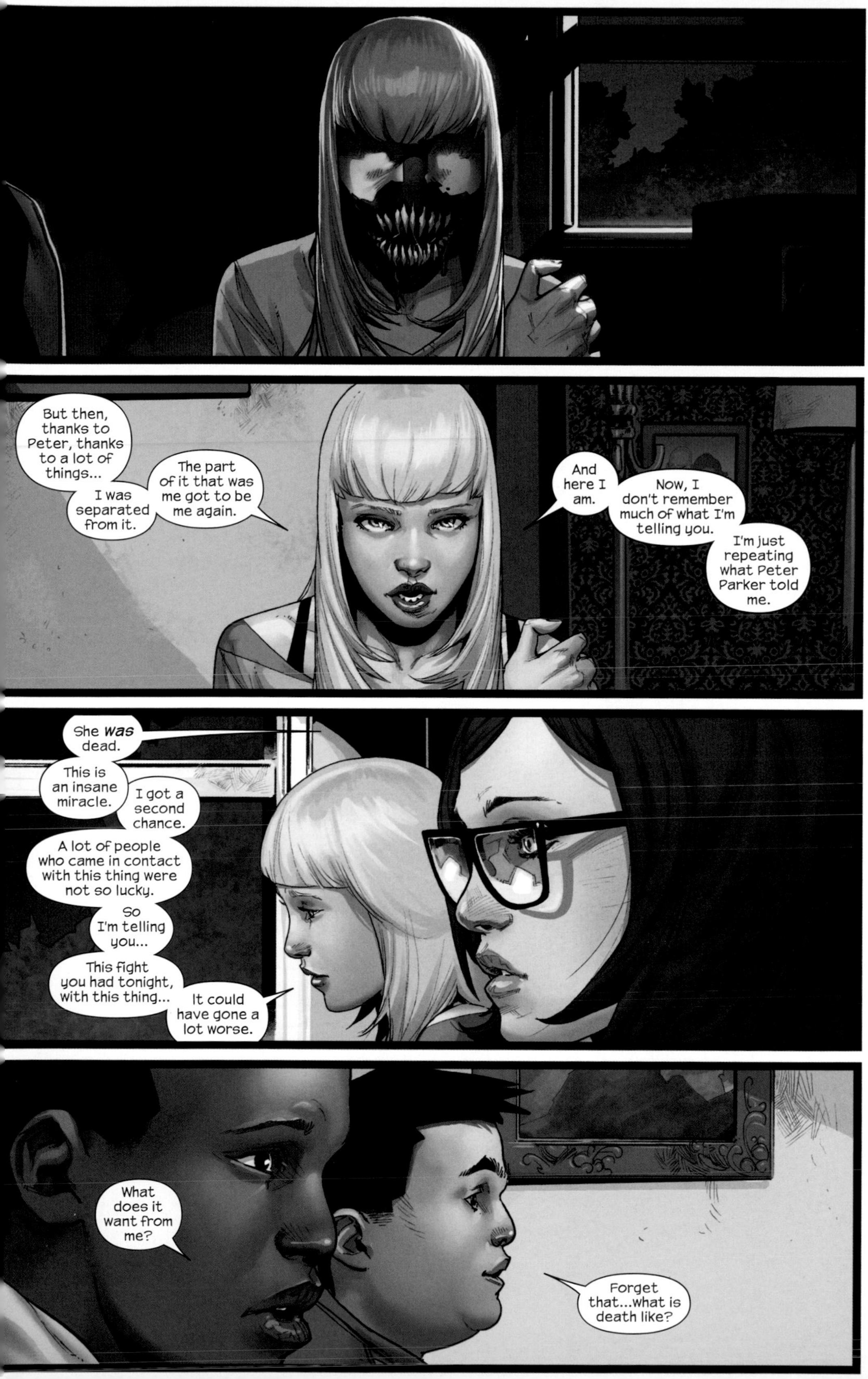

But then, thanks to Peter, thanks to a lot of things...
I was separated from it.
The part of it that was me got to be me again.
And here I am.
Now, I don't remember much of what I'm telling you.
I'm just repeating what Peter Parker told me.
She *was* dead.
This is an insane miracle.
I got a second chance.
A lot of people who came in contact with this thing were not so lucky.
So I'm telling you...
This fight you had tonight, with this thing...
It could have gone a lot worse.
What does it want from me?
Forget that...what is death like?

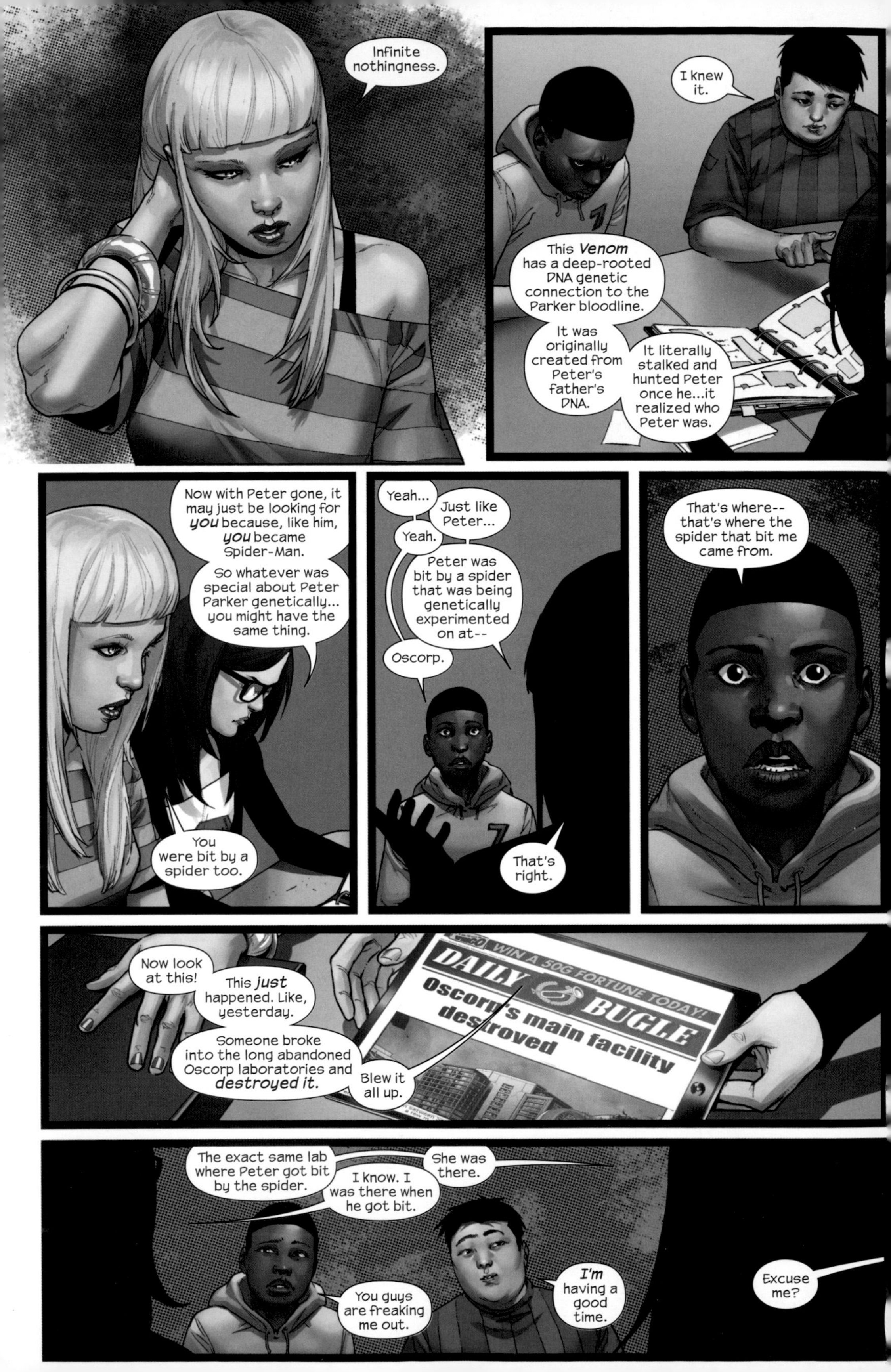
Infinite nothingness.
I knew it.
This *Venom* has a deep-rooted DNA genetic connection to the Parker bloodline.
It was originally created from Peter's father's DNA.
It literally stalked and hunted Peter once he...it realized who Peter was.
Now with Peter gone, it may just be looking for *you* because, like him, *you* became Spider-Man.
So whatever was special about Peter Parker genetically... you might have the same thing.
You were bit by a spider too.
Yeah...
Just like Peter...
Yeah.
Peter was bit by a spider that was being genetically experimented on at--
Oscorp.
That's right.
That's where-- that's where the spider that bit me came from.
Now look at this!
This *just* happened. Like, yesterday.
Someone broke into the long abandoned Oscorp laboratories and *destroyed it.*
Blew it all up.
WIN A 50G FORTUNE TODAY!
DAILY BUGLE
Oscorp's main facility destroyed
The exact same lab where Peter got bit by the spider.
She was there.
I know. I was there when he got bit.
You guys are freaking me out.
I'm having a good time.
Excuse me?

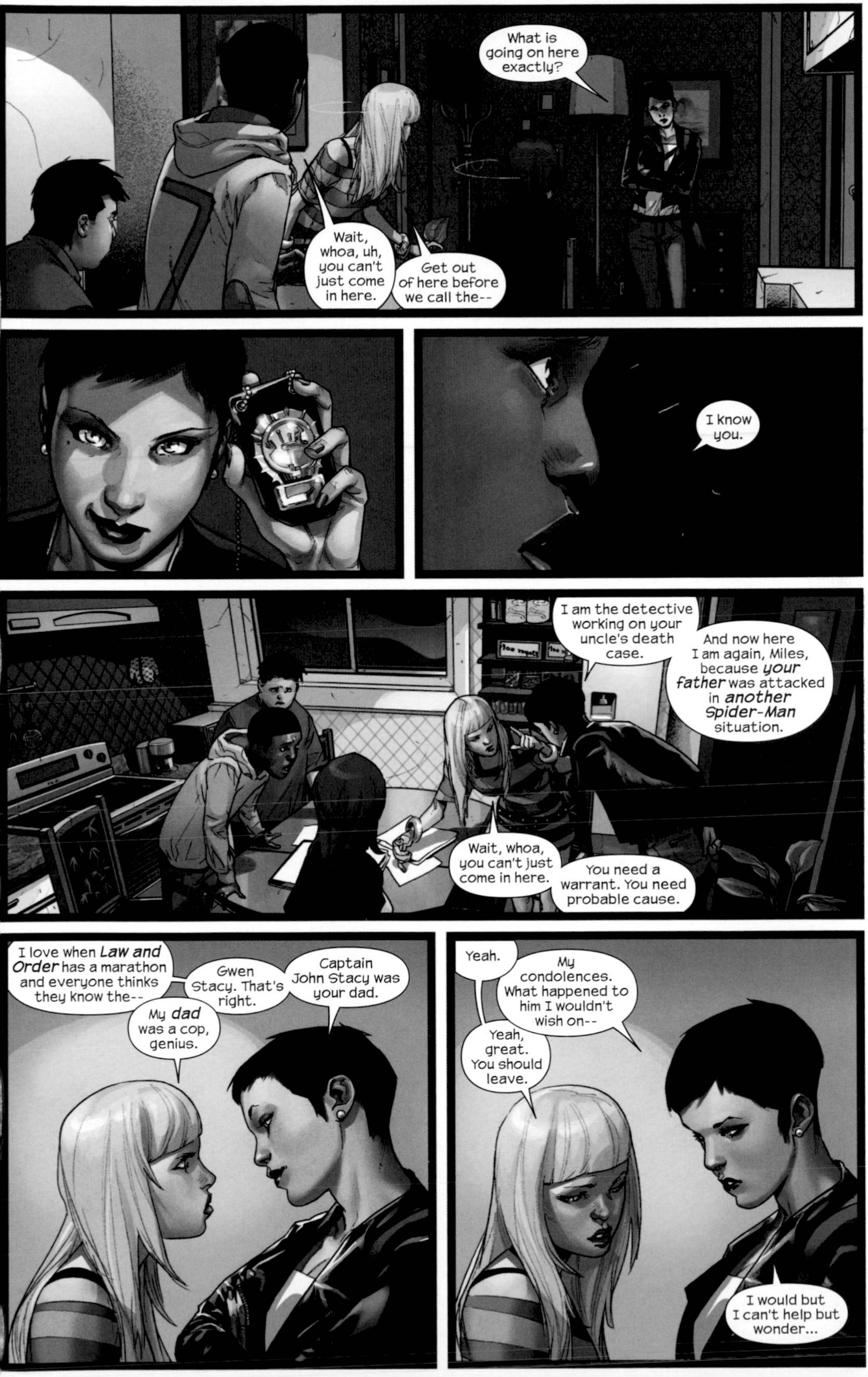
What is going on here exactly?
Wait, whoa, uh, you can't just come in here.
Get out of here before we call the--
I know you.
I am the detective working on your uncle's death case.
And now here I am again, Miles, because your father was attacked in another Spider-Man situation.
Wait, whoa, you can't just come in here.
You need a warrant. You need probable cause.
I love when Law and Order has a marathon and everyone thinks they know the--
Gwen Stacy. That's right.
My dad was a cop, genius.
Captain John Stacy was your dad.
Yeah.
My condolences. What happened to him I wouldn't wish on--
Yeah, great. You should leave.
I would but I can't help but wonder...

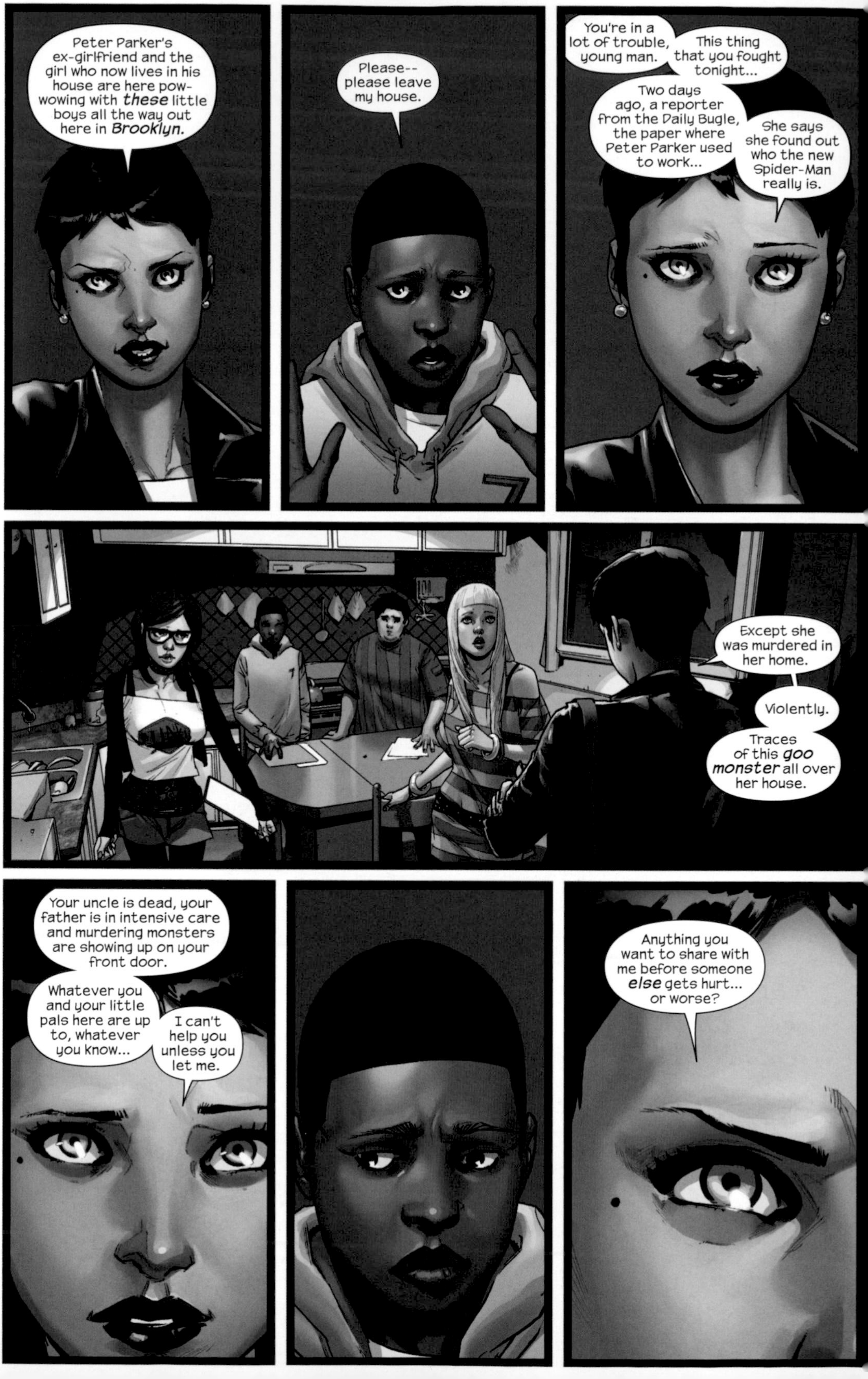

Peter Parker's ex-girlfriend and the girl who now lives in his house are here pow-wowing with *these* little boys all the way out here in *Brooklyn.*
Please-- please leave my house.
You're in a lot of trouble, young man.
This thing that you fought tonight...
Two days ago, a reporter from the Daily Bugle, the paper where Peter Parker used to work...
She says she found out who the new Spider-Man really is.
Except she was murdered in her home.
Violently.
Traces of this *goo monster* all over her house.
Your uncle is dead, your father is in intensive care and murdering monsters are showing up on your front door.
Whatever you and your little pals here are up to, whatever you know...
I can't help you unless you let me.
Anything you want to share with me before someone *else* gets hurt... or worse?

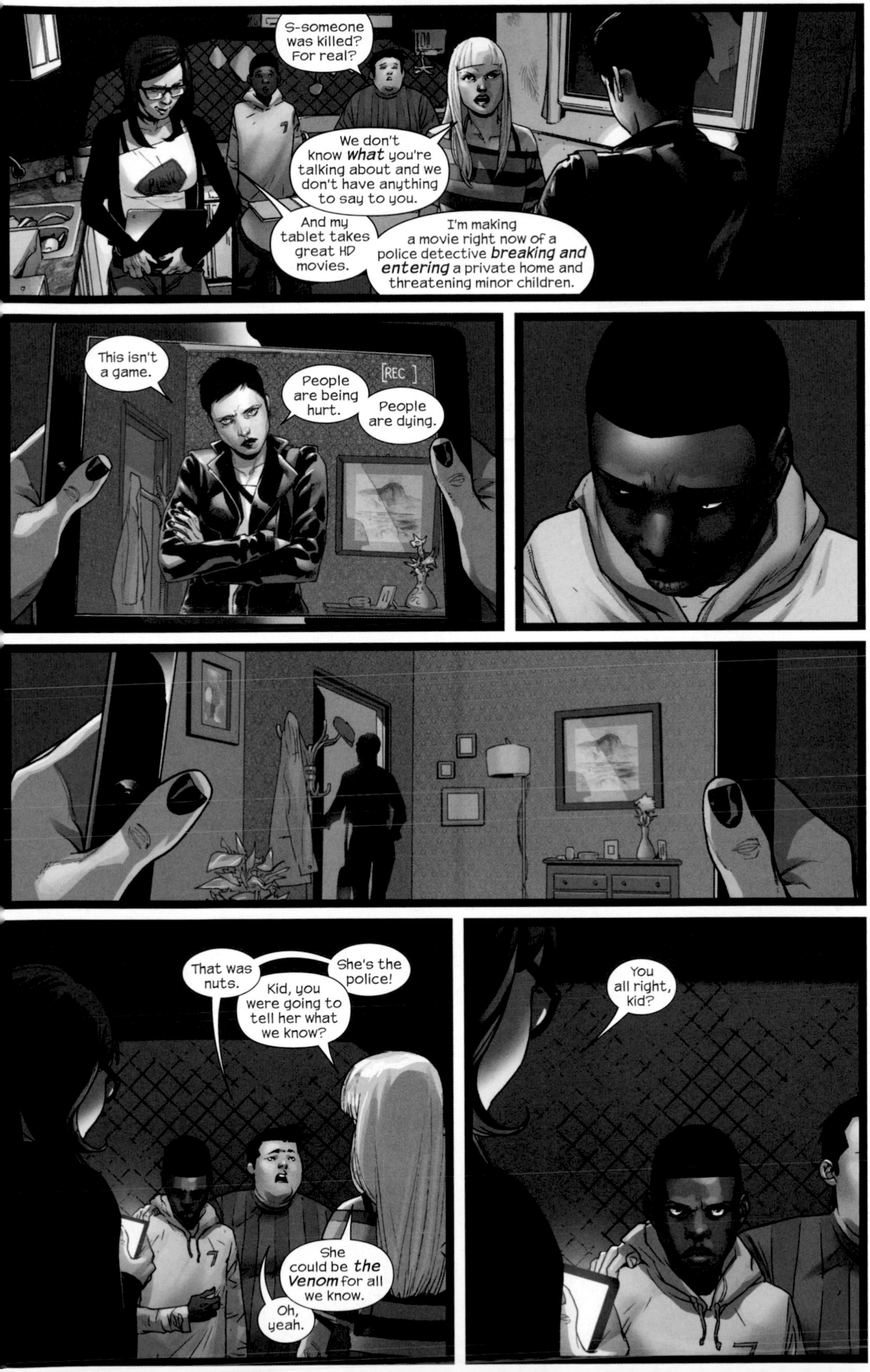
S-someone was killed? For real?
We don't know *what* you're talking about and we don't have anything to say to you.
And my tablet takes great HD movies.
I'm making a movie right now of a police detective *breaking and entering* a private home and threatening minor children.
This isn't a game.
[REC]
People are being hurt.
People are dying.
That was nuts.
She's the police!
Kid, you were going to tell her what we know?
She could be *the Venom* for all we know.
Oh, yeah.
You all right, kid?

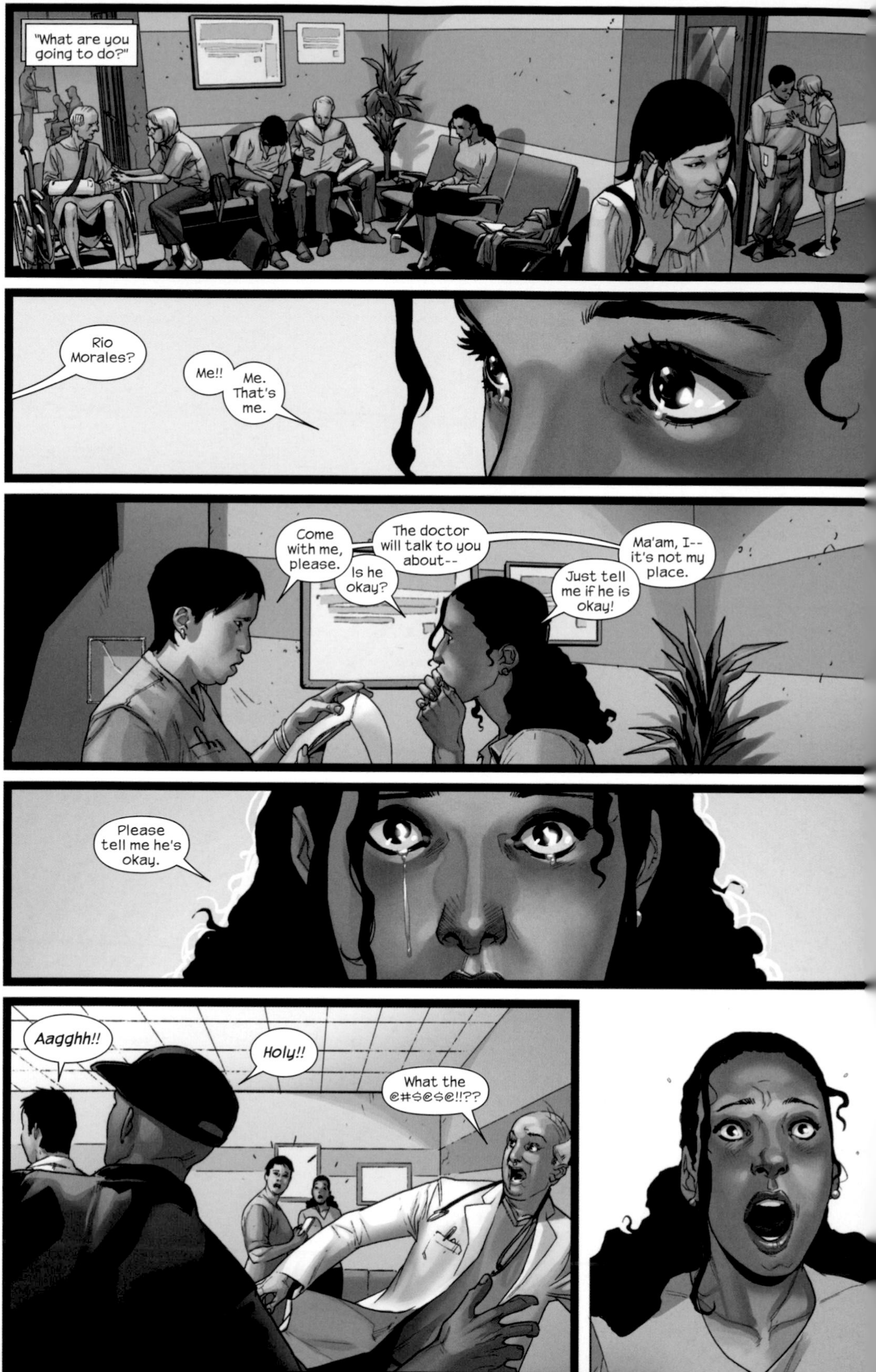
"What are you going to do?"
Rio Morales?
Me!!
Me. That's me.
Come with me, please.
The doctor will talk to you about--
Is he okay?
Ma'am, I-- it's not my place.
Just tell me if he is okay!
Please tell me he's okay.
Aagghh!!
Holy!!
What the @#$@$@!!??

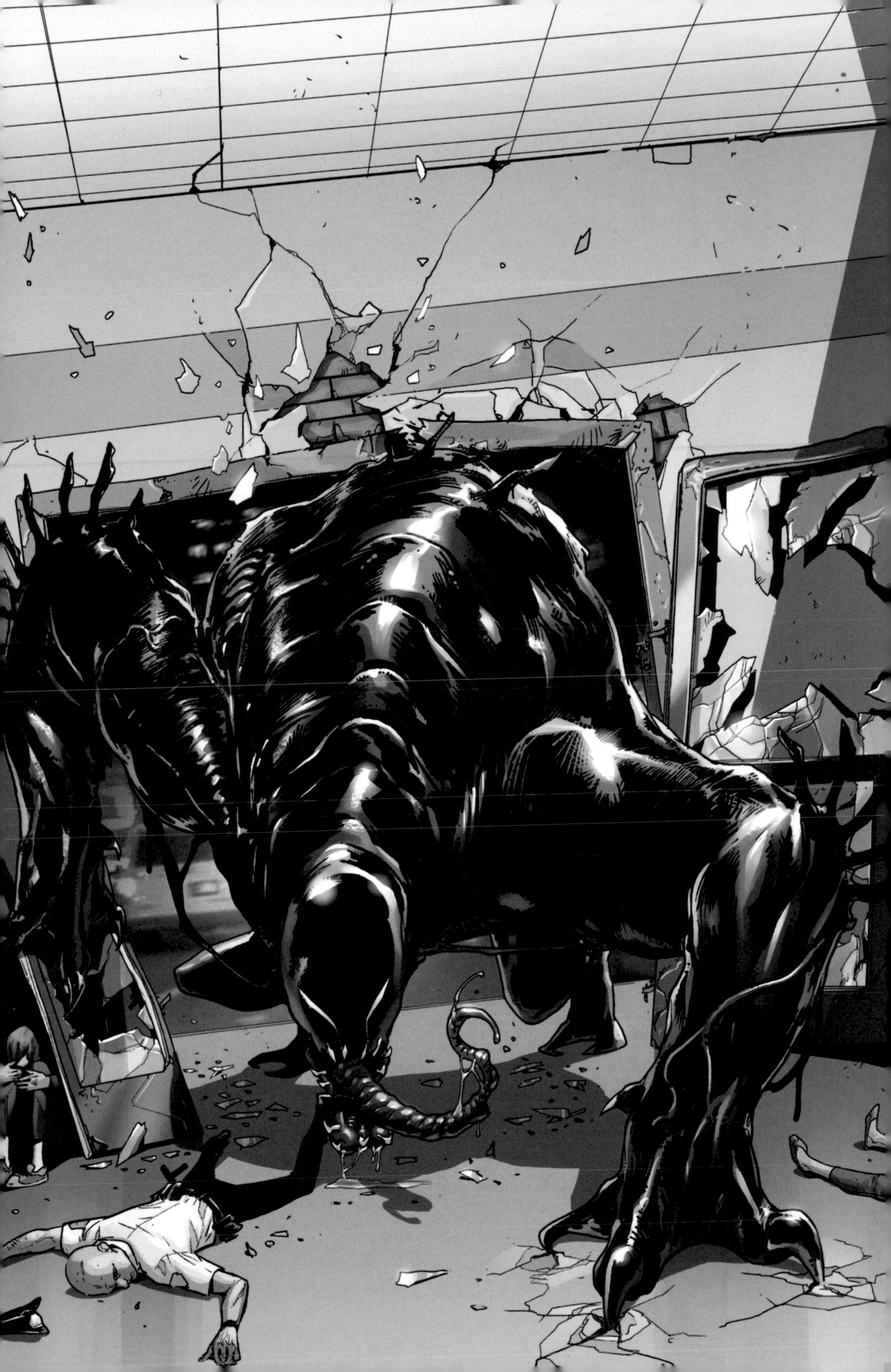

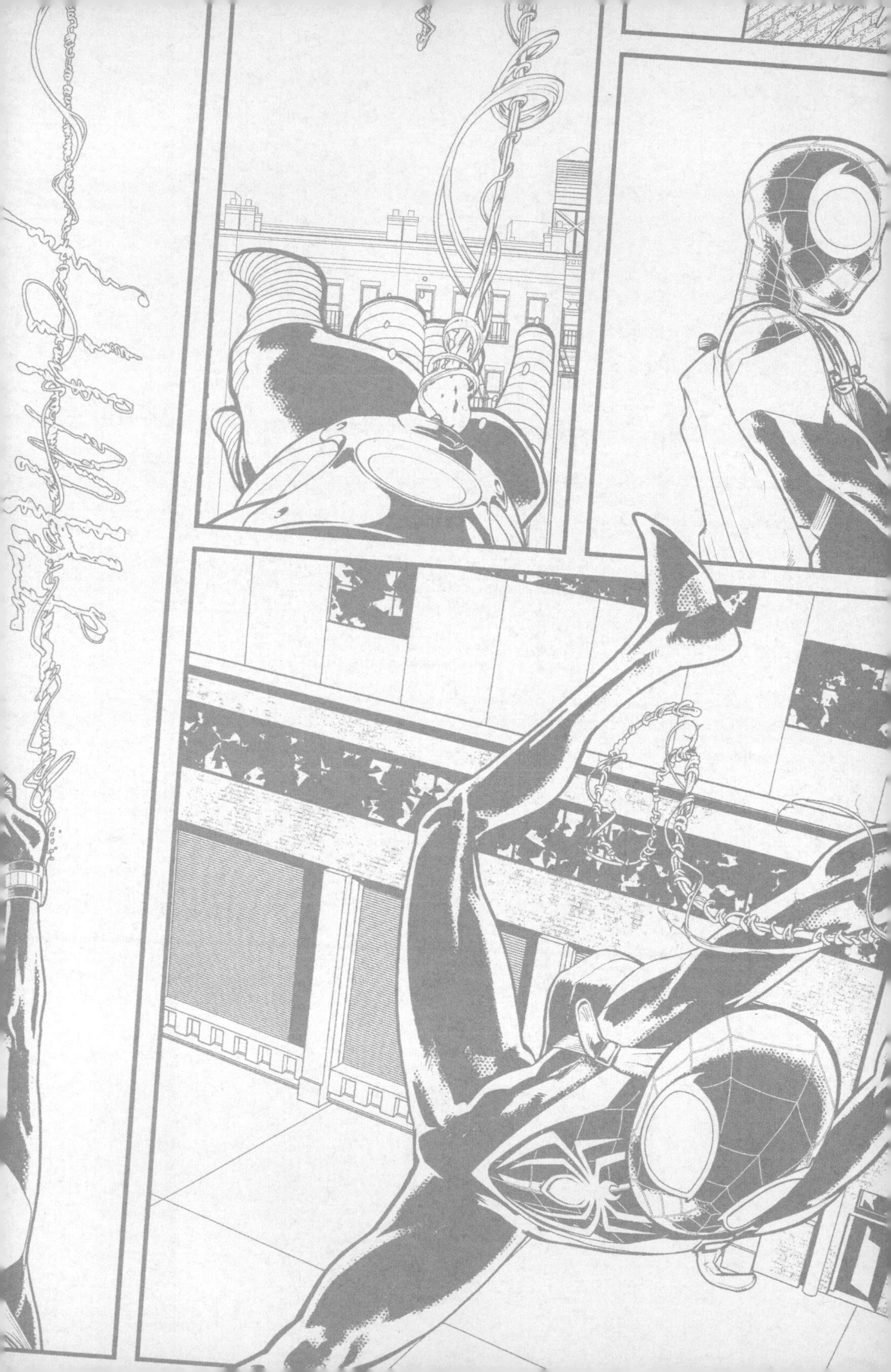

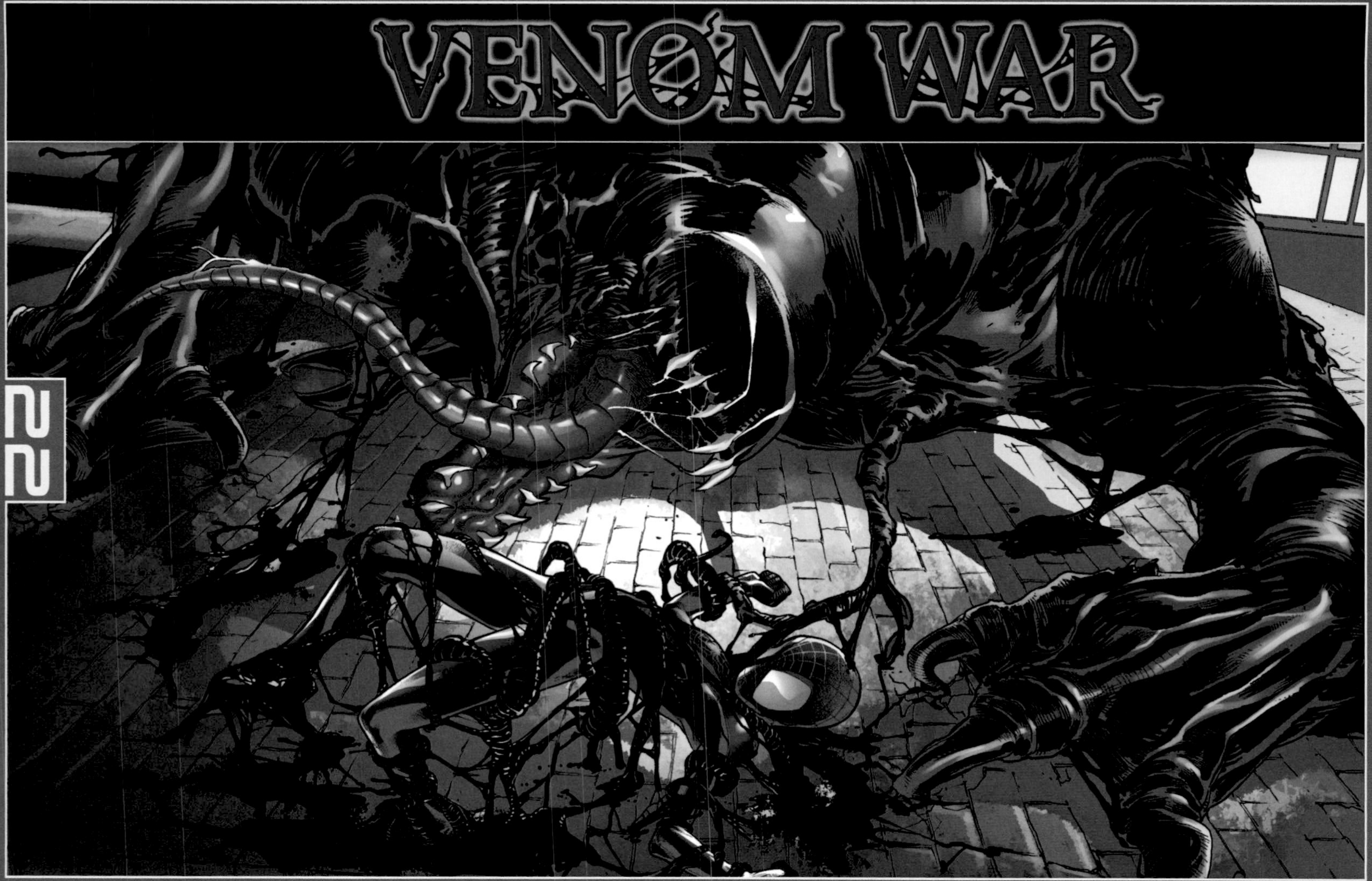
VENOM WAR
22

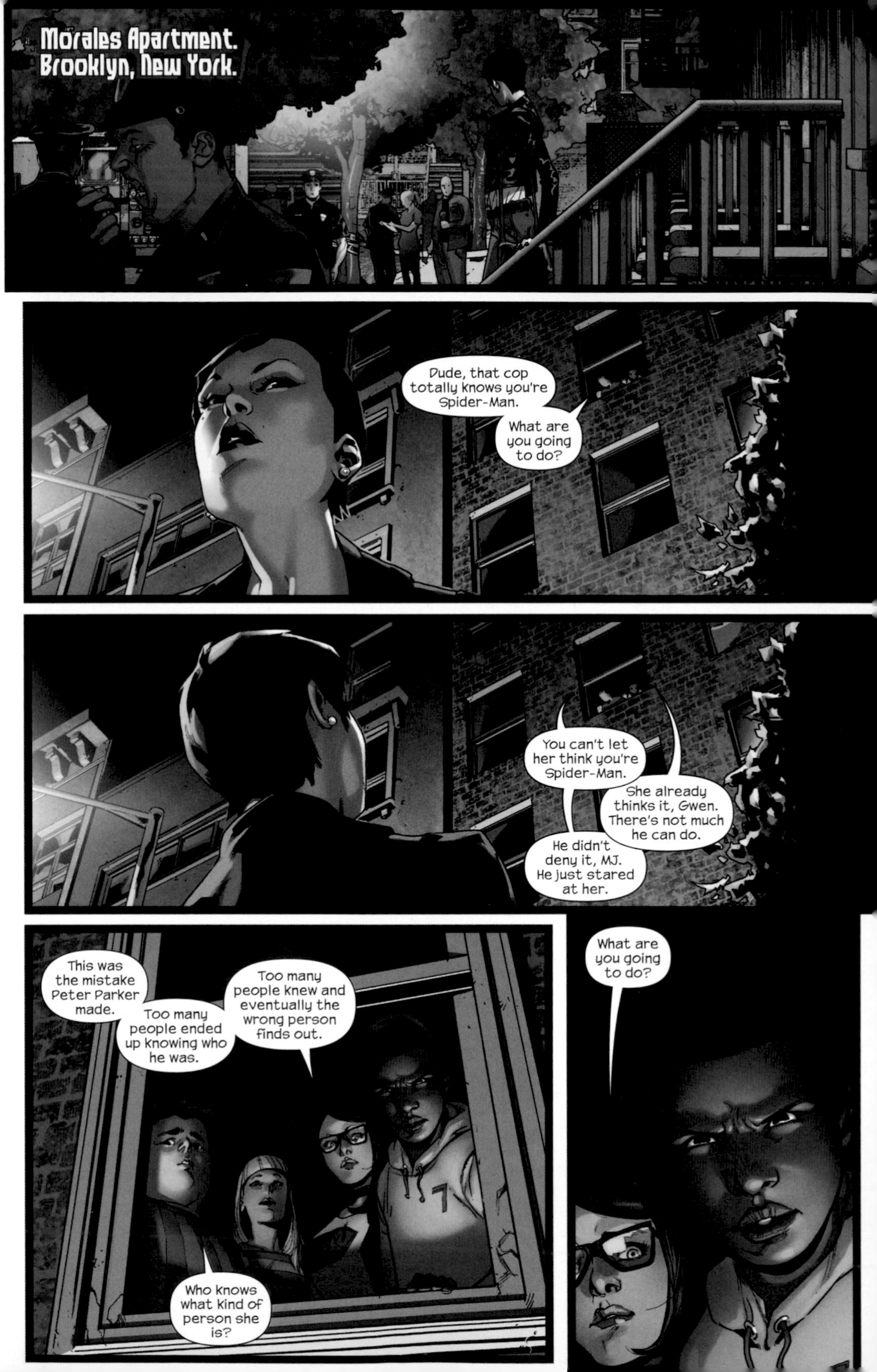

Morales Apartment.
Brooklyn, New York.
Dude, that cop totally knows you're Spider-Man.
What are you going to do?
You can't let her think you're Spider-Man.
She already thinks it, Gwen. There's not much he can do.
He didn't deny it, MJ. He just stared at her.
This was the mistake Peter Parker made.
Too many people ended up knowing who he was.
Too many people knew and eventually the wrong person finds out.
Who knows what kind of person she is?
What are you going to do?

Hey!! You, lady!

Is there something you want to tell me?

You're wrong.

I'm not who you think I am.

Then I'm wrong.

Except I'm not.

There is a monster killing people out on the street!!

And--and--and you walk into my house and accuse me--

You want me to what? To prove it?

I'm a police detective and I used to be an agent of S.H.I.E.L.D.!

How long you think it will take me to frisk you and find your mask?

You--you can't just...

I know you're hurting. I know you're upset.

I know you don't know what's going on here so let me give you some advice--

We gotta 616!!

We have 616!! 616 at Brooklyn General!!

What is it??

That thing-- that thing that was here went there!!

That thing is tearing up the hospital right now!! They called it in!! All units.

Is that-- is that where they took my father?

You'll get there faster than we will.

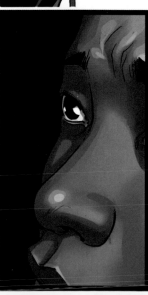

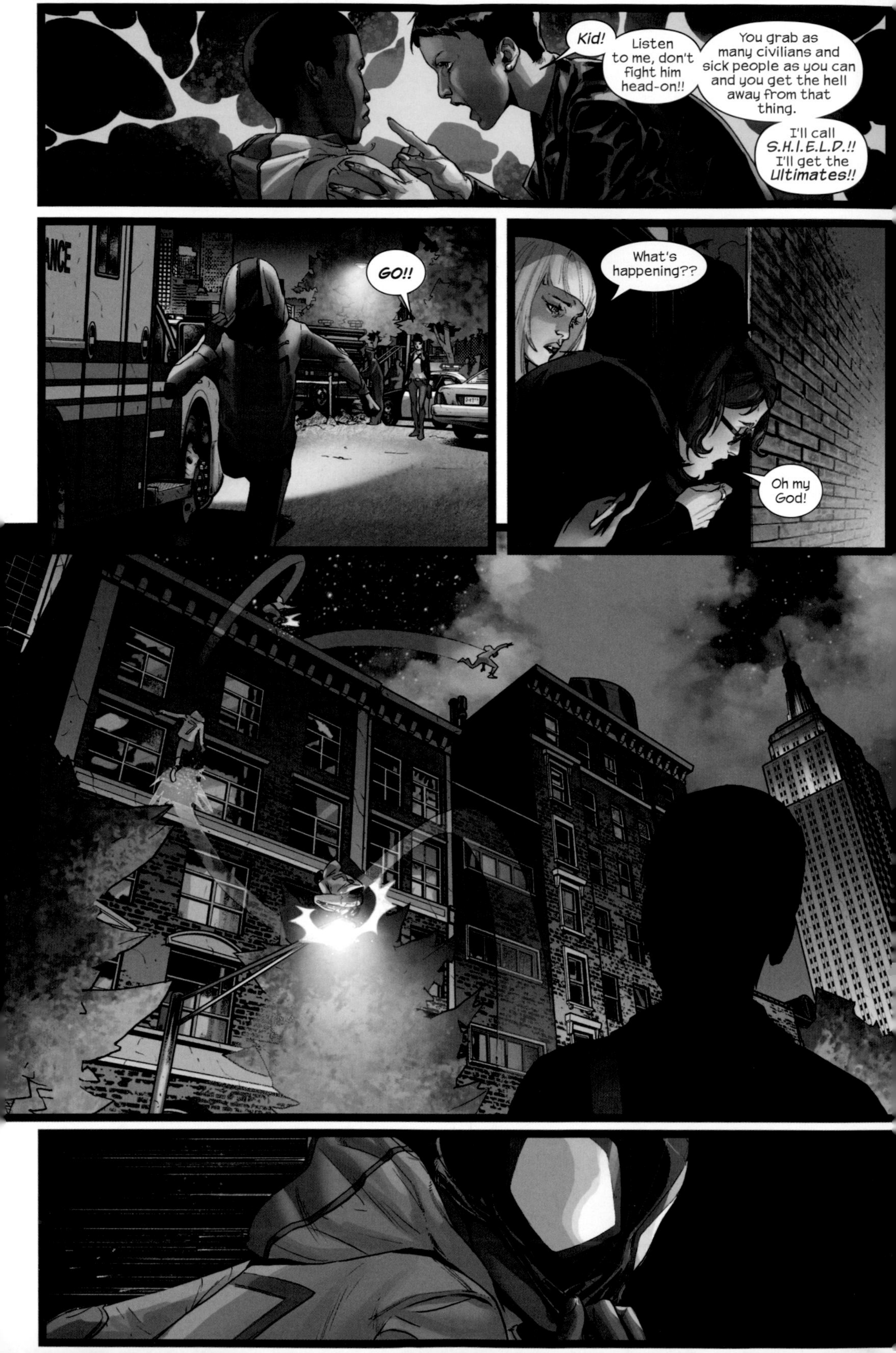
Kid!
Listen to me, don't fight him head-on!!
You grab as many civilians and sick people as you can and you get the hell away from that thing.
I'll call S.H.I.E.L.D.!! I'll get the Ultimates!!
GO!!
What's happening??
Oh my God!

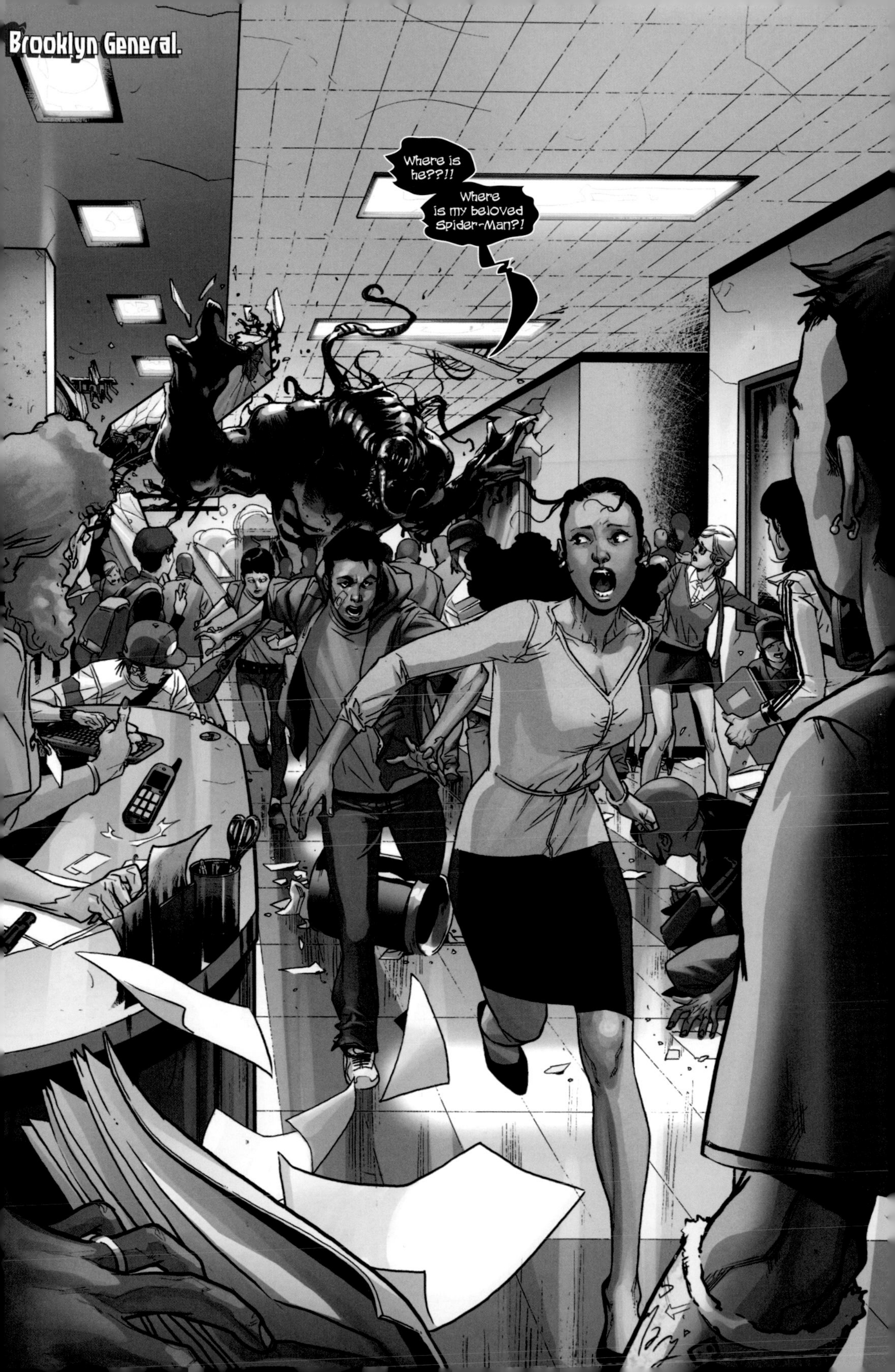
Brooklyn General.
Where is he??!!
Where is my beloved Spider-Man?!

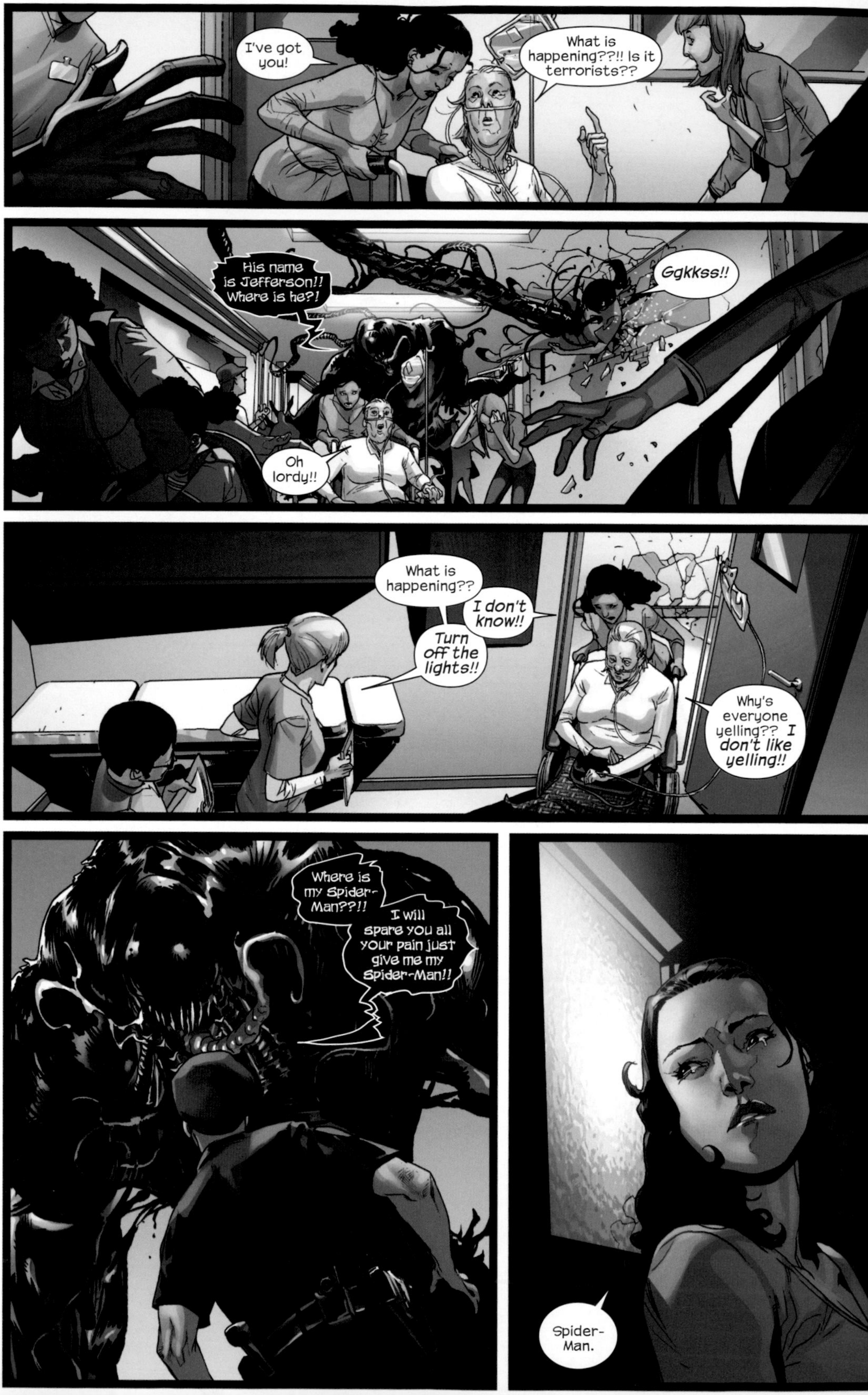
I've got you!
What is happening??!! Is it terrorists??
His name is Jefferson!! Where is he?!
Ggkkss!!
Oh lordy!!
What is happening??
I don't know!!
Turn off the lights!!
Why's everyone yelling?? I don't like yelling!!
Where is my Spider-Man??!!
I will spare you all your pain just give me my Spider-Man!!
Spider-Man.

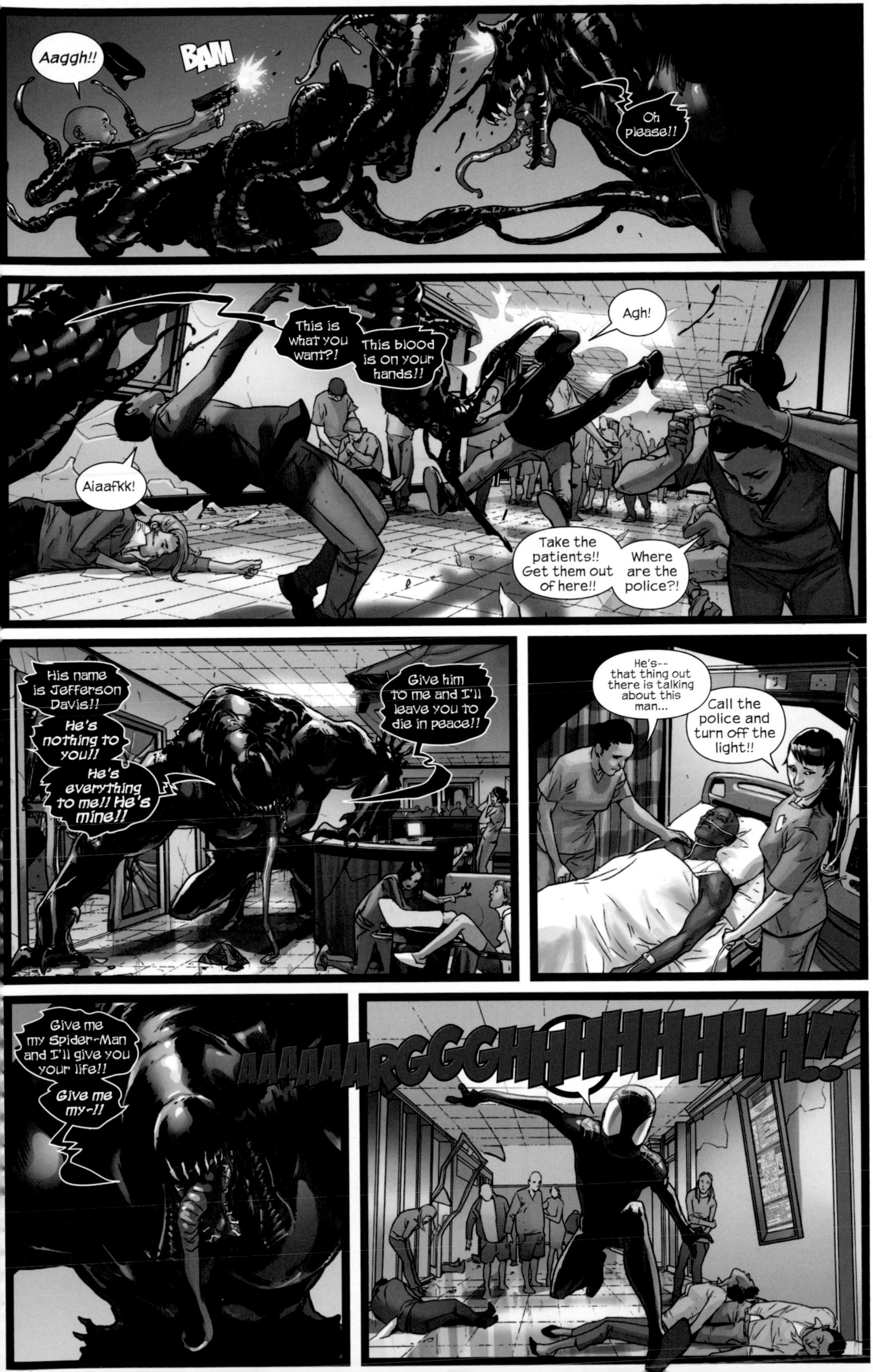
Aaggh!!
BAM
Oh please!!
This is what you want?!
This blood is on your hands!!
Agh!
Aiaafkk!
Take the patients!! Get them out of here!!
Where are the police?!
His name is Jefferson Davis!!
He's nothing to you!!
He's everything to me!! He's mine!!
Give him to me and I'll leave you to die in peace!!
He's-- that thing out there is talking about this man...
Call the police and turn off the light!!
Give me my Spider-Man and I'll give you your life!!
Give me my-!!
AAAAAARGGGHHHHHHHHH!!

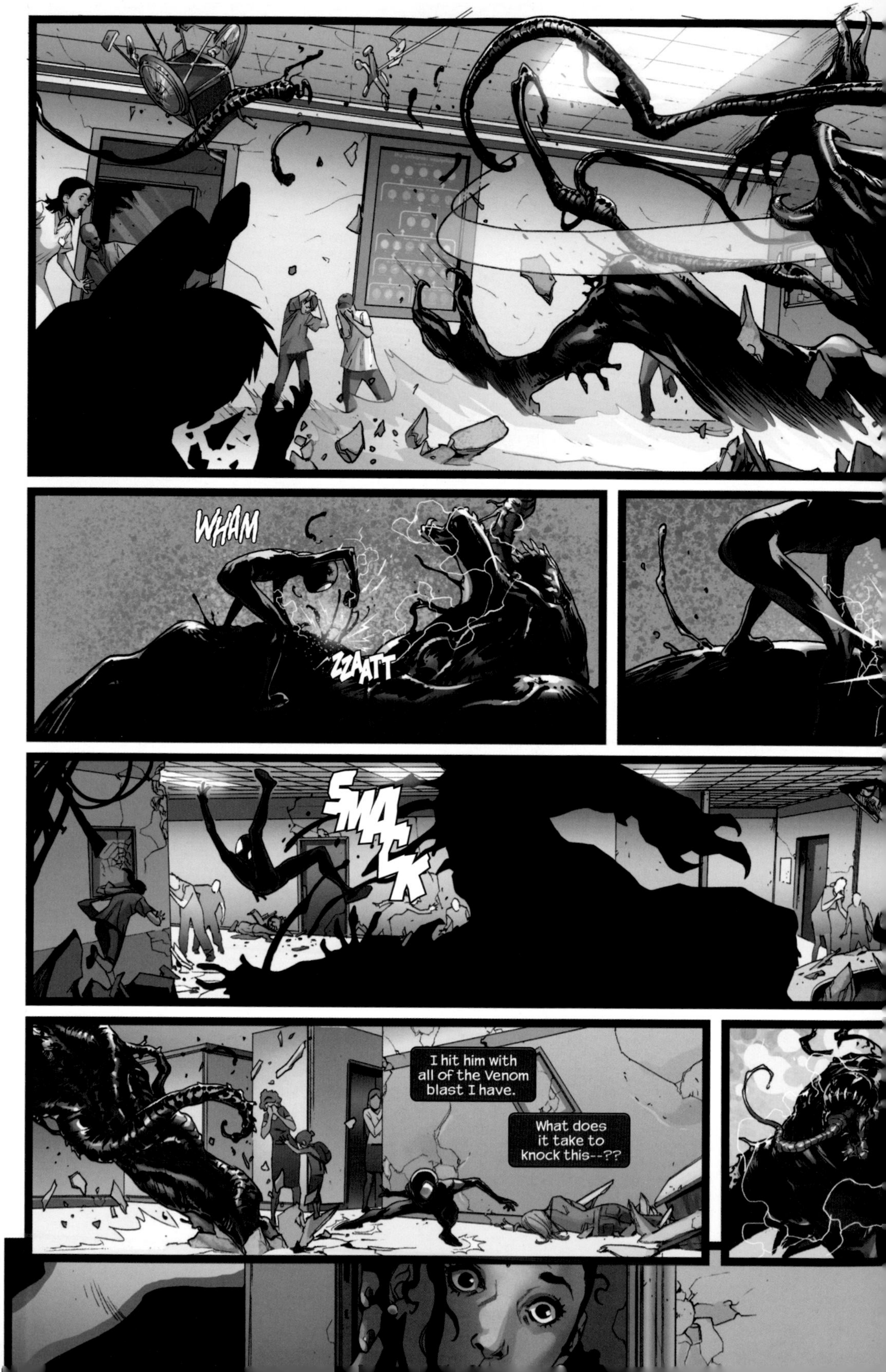
WHAM
ZZAATT
SMACK
I hit him with all of the Venom blast I have.
What does it take to knock this--??

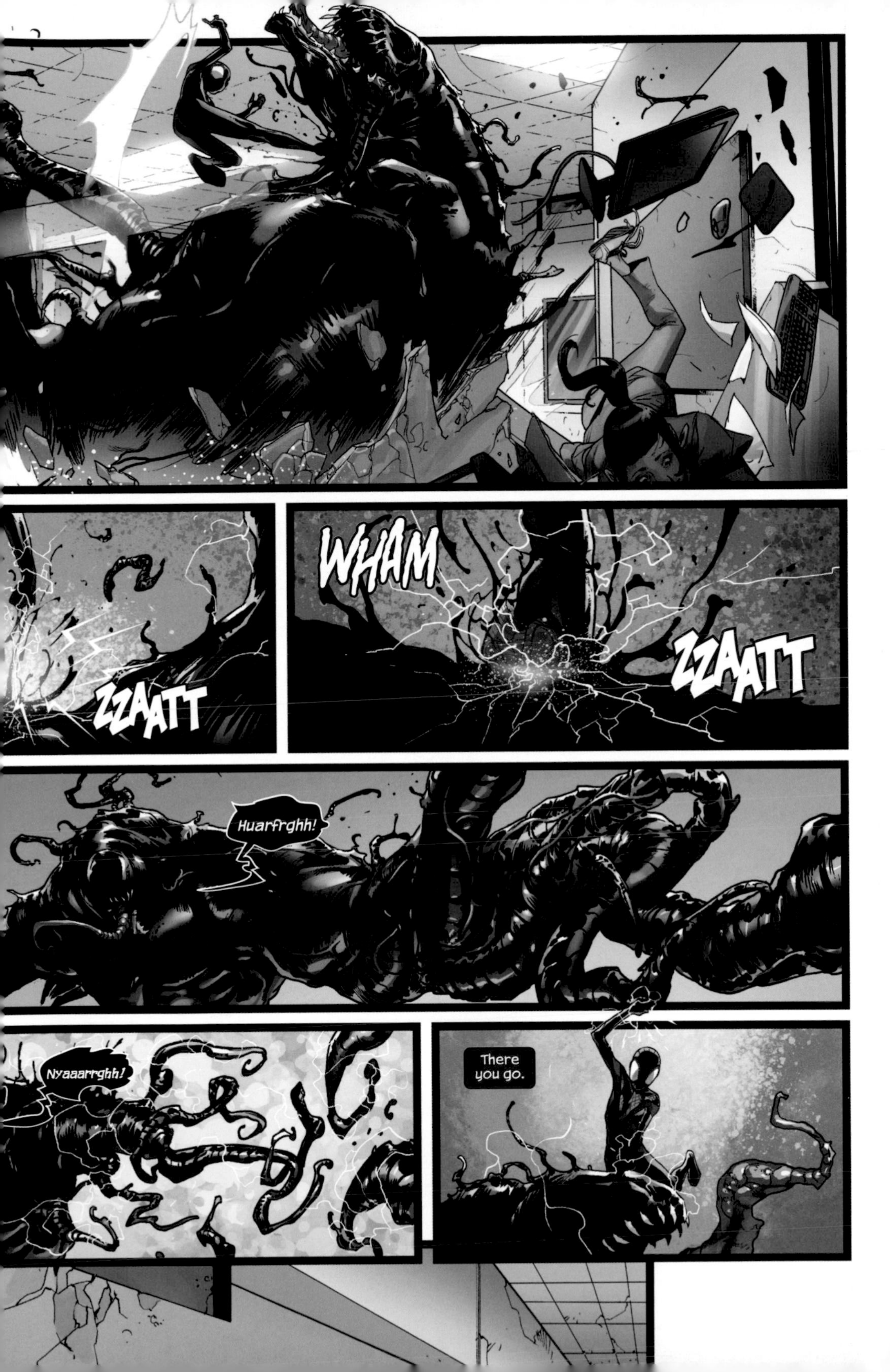
WHAM
ZZAATT
ZZAATT
Huarfrghh!
Nyaaarrghh!
There you go.

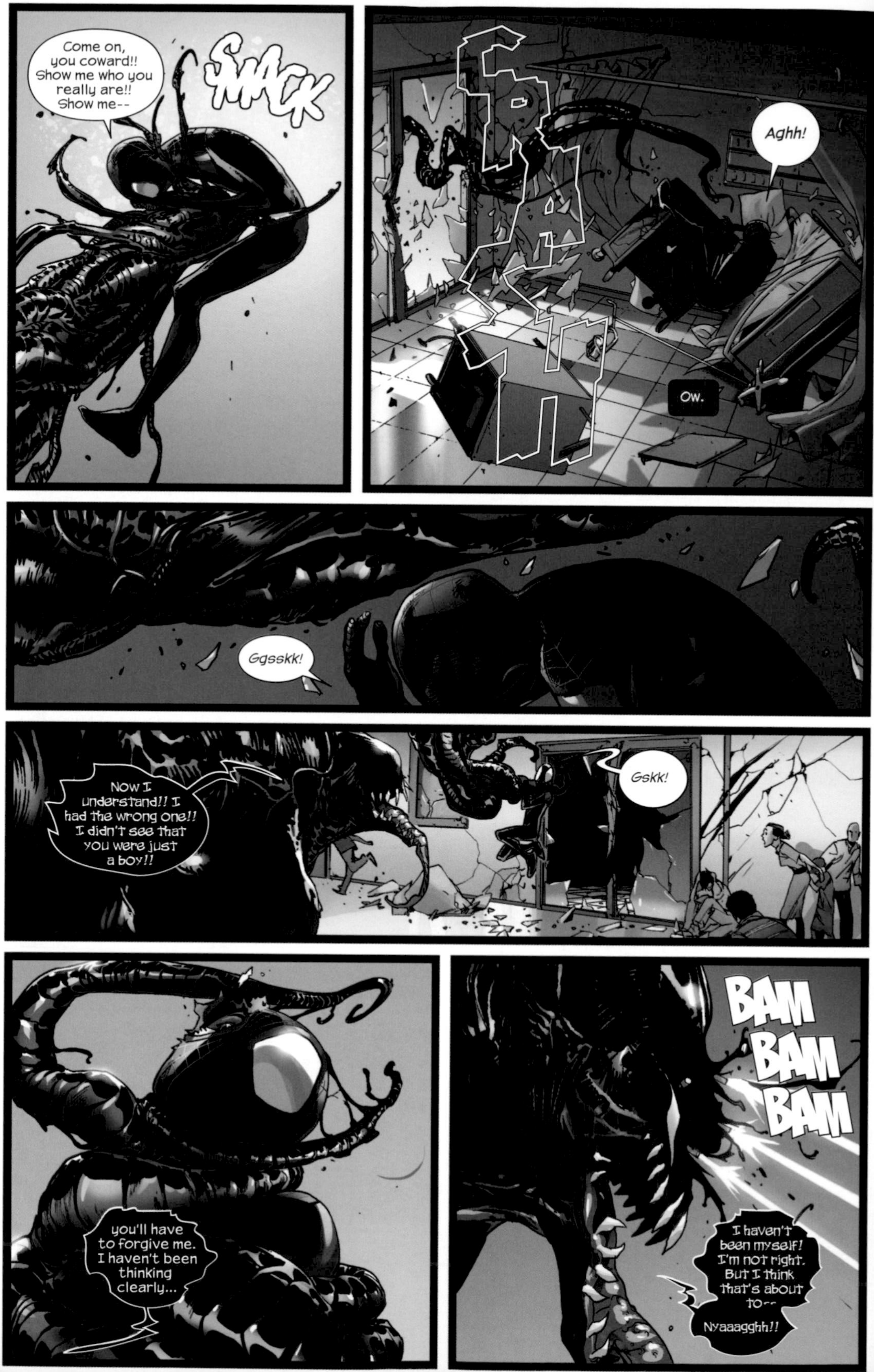
Come on, you coward!! Show me who you really are!! Show me--
SMACK
CRASH
Aghh!
Ow.
Ggsskk!
Now I understand!! I had the wrong one!! I didn't see that you were just a boy!!
Gskk!
you'll have to forgive me. I haven't been thinking clearly...
BAM BAM BAM
I haven't been myself! I'm not right. But I think that's about to--
Nyaaagghh!!

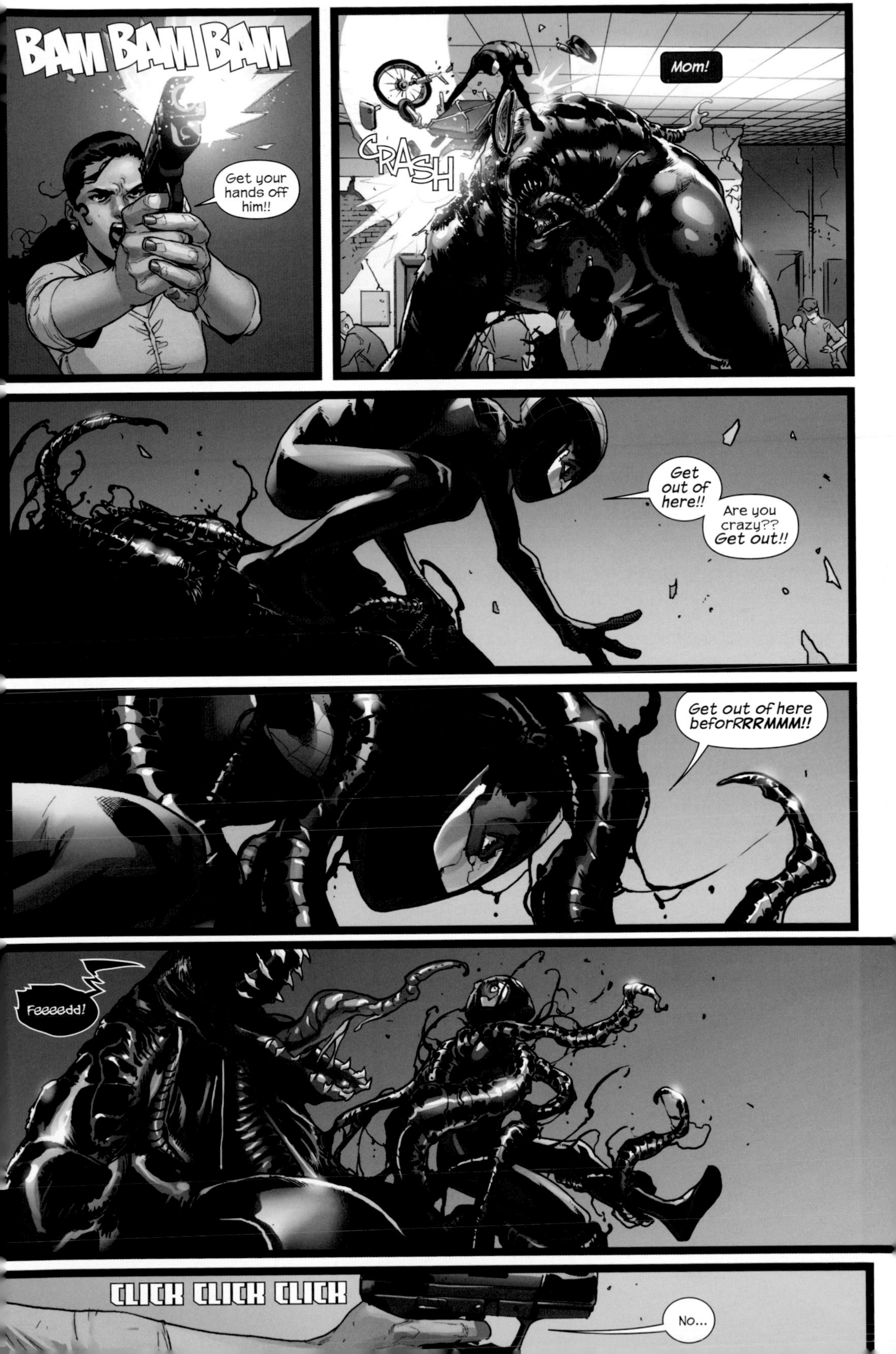
BAM BAM BAM
Get your hands off him!!
CRASH
Mom!
Get out of here!!
Are you crazy?? Get out!!
Get out of here beforRRRMMM!!
Feeeeedd!
CLICK CLICK CLICK
No...

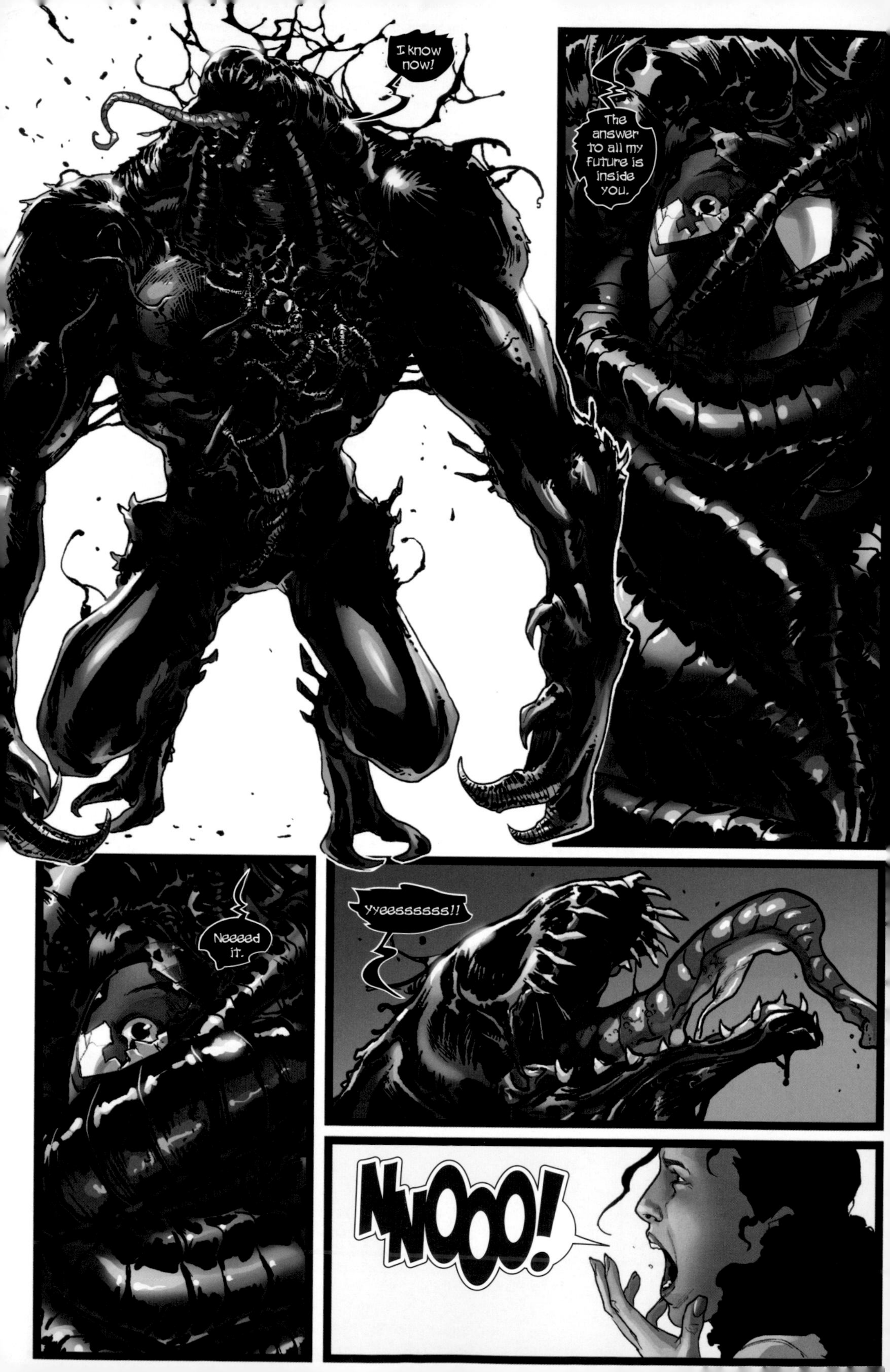
I know now!
The answer to all my future is inside you.
Neeeed it.
Yyeesssssss!!
NNOOO!

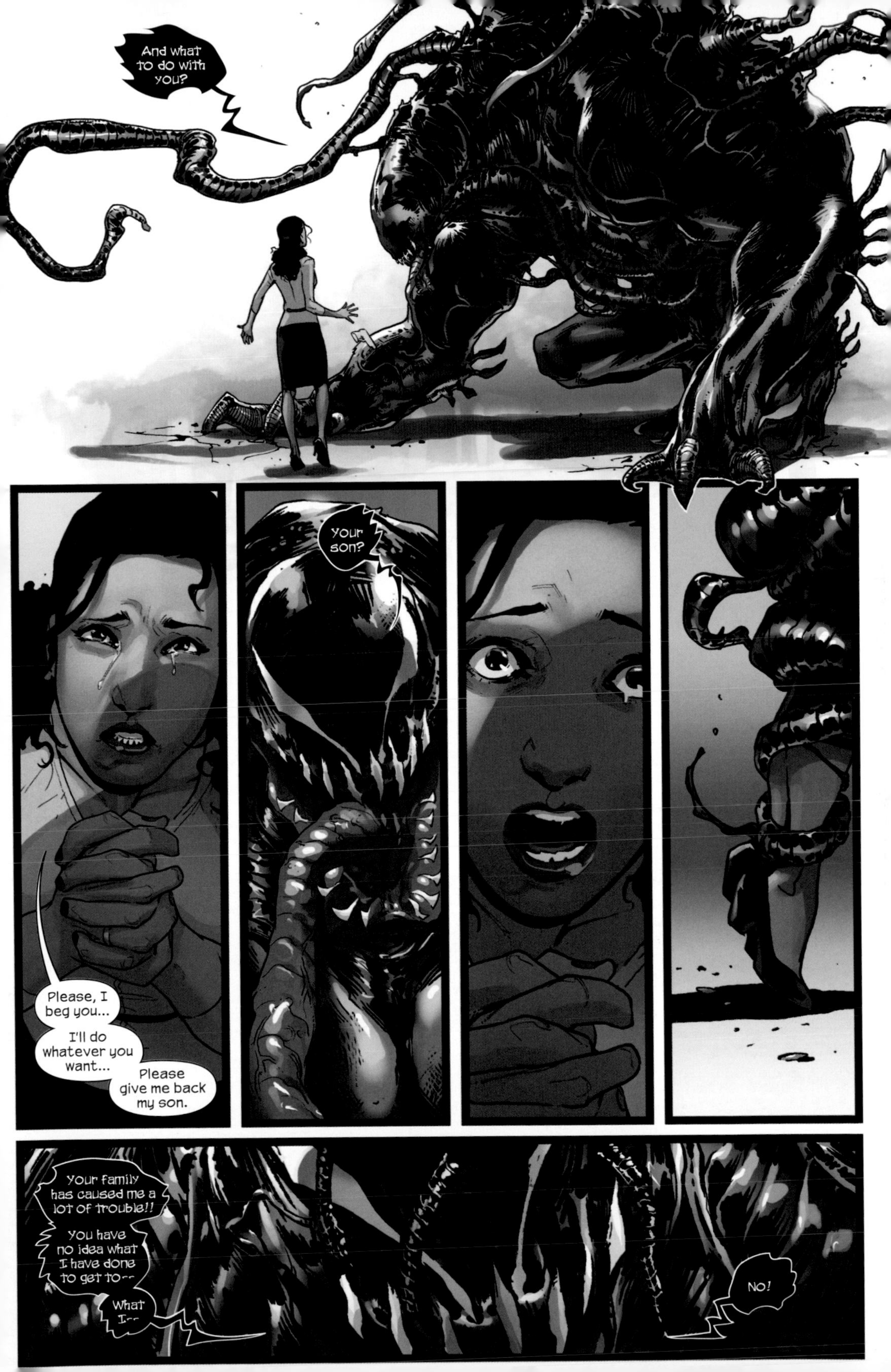
And what to do with you?
Please, I beg you...
I'll do whatever you want...
Please give me back my son.
Your son?
Your family has caused me a lot of trouble!!
You have no idea what I have done to get to--
What I--
No!

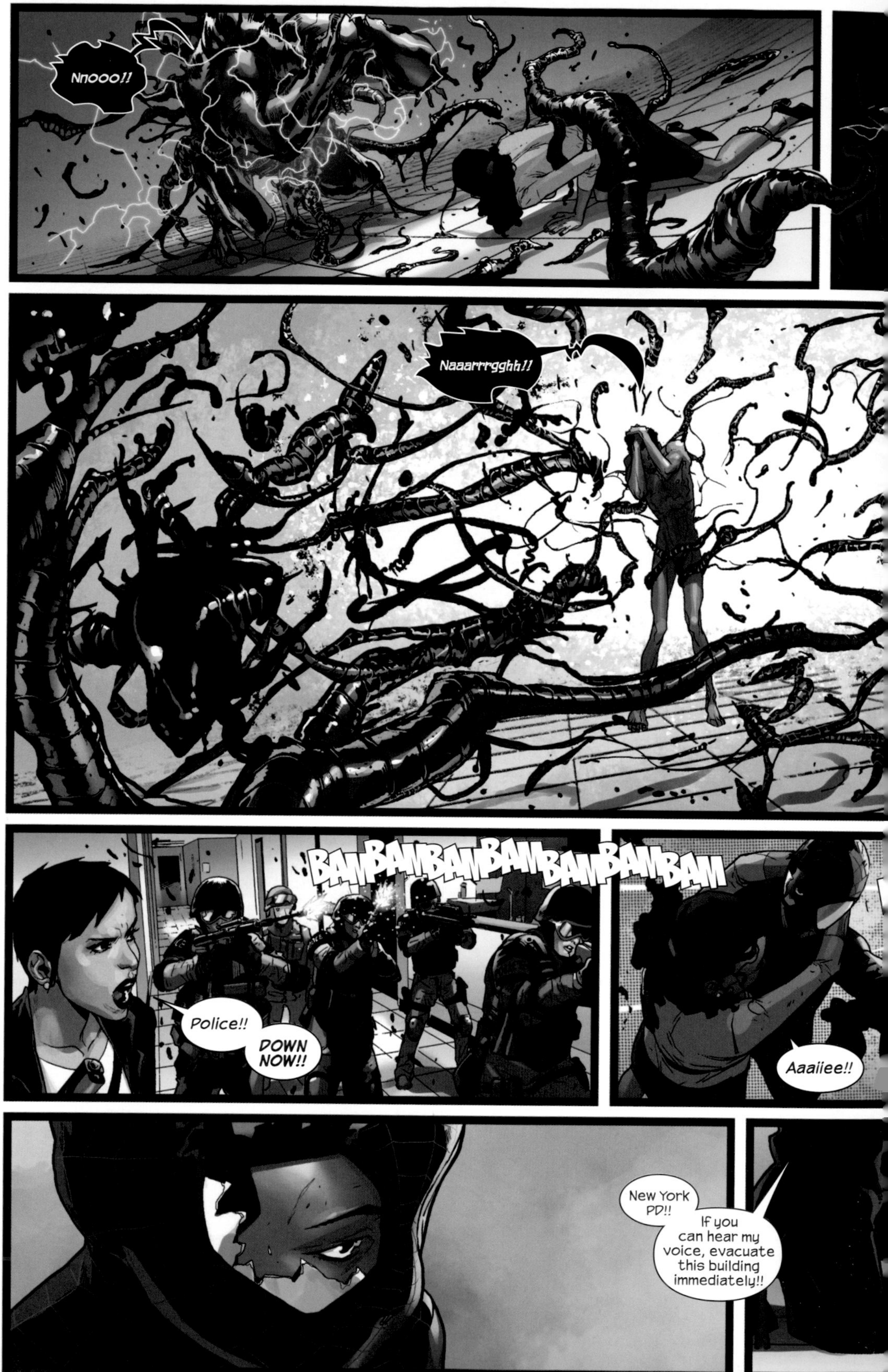
Nnooo!!
Naaarrrgghh!!
BAMBAMBAMBAMBAMBAMBAM
Police!!
DOWN NOW!!
Aaaiiee!!
New York PD!!
If you can hear my voice, evacuate this building immediately!!

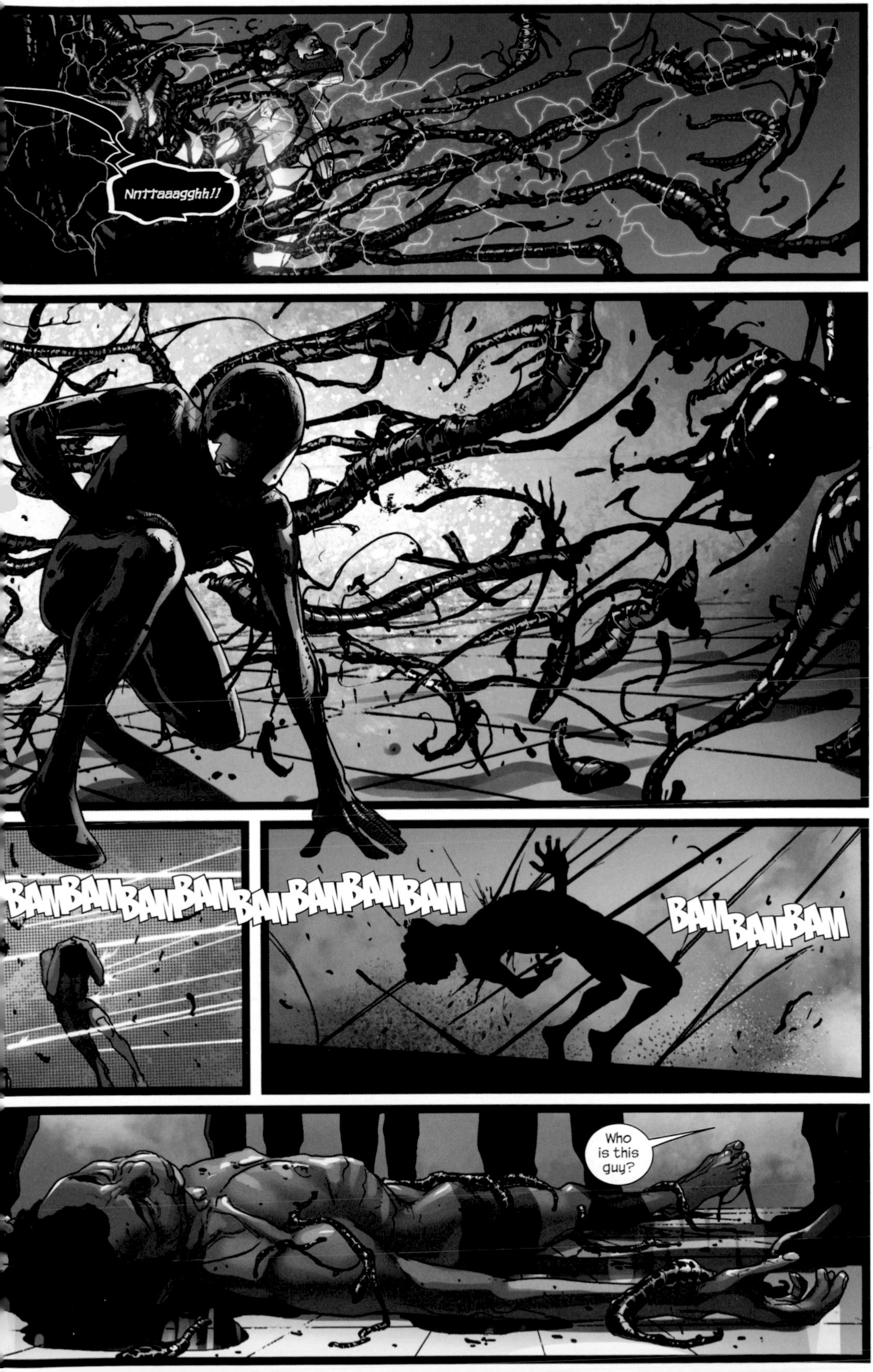

Nnttaaagghh!!
BAMBAMBAMBAMBAMBAMBAMBAM
BAMBAMBAM
Who is this guy?

I have no idea.

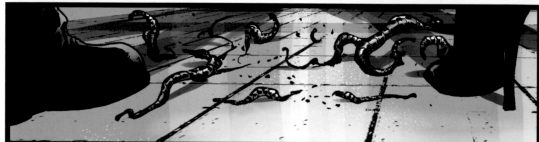

What the--

BAMBAMBAMBAMBAMBAMBAMBAMBAMBAMBAMBAM

SPLAT
SPLAT
SPLAT

Come on, let's get out of--

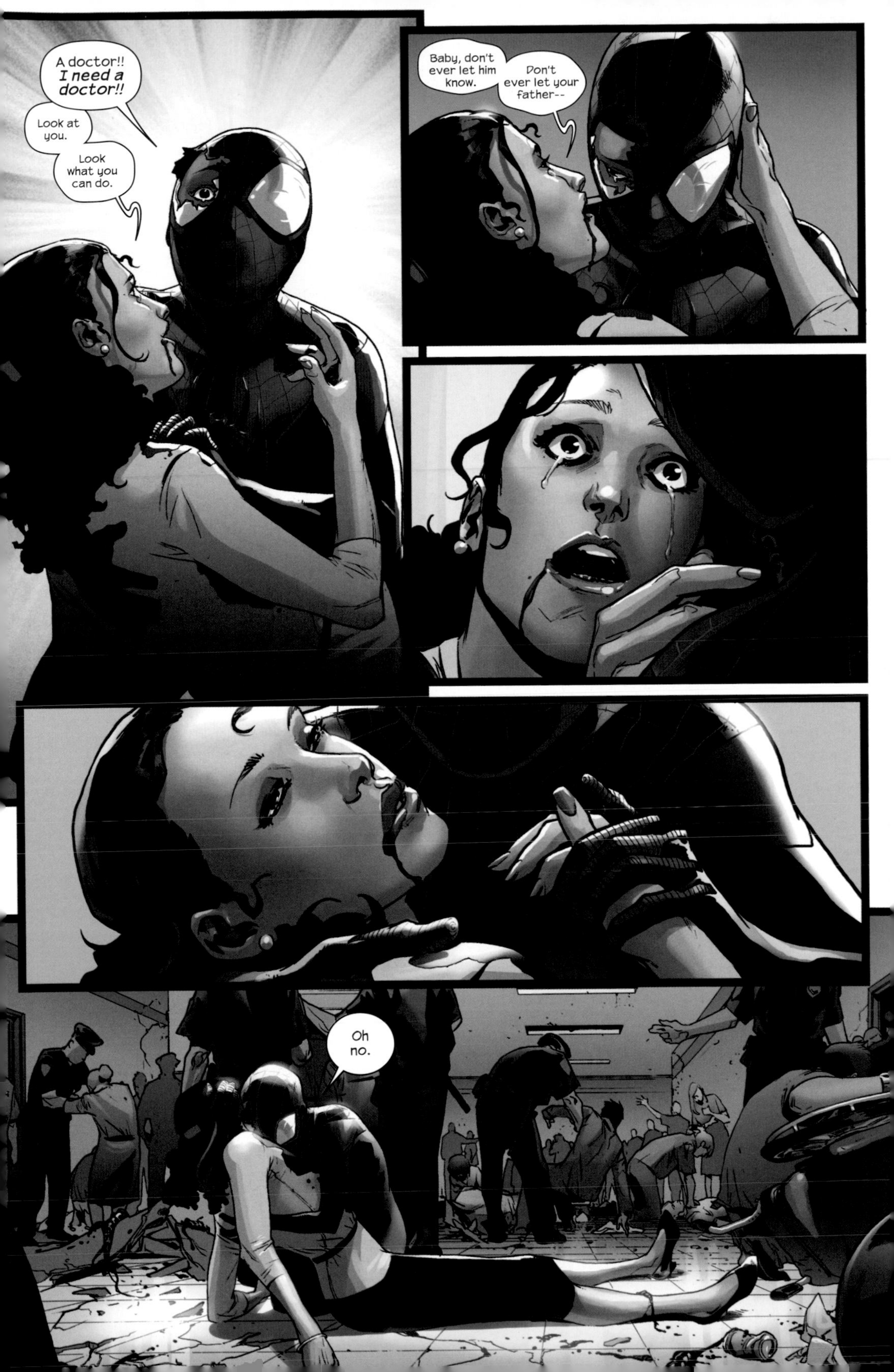
A doctor!! *I need a doctor!!*
Look at you.
Look what you can do.
Baby, don't ever let him know.
Don't ever let your father--
Oh no.

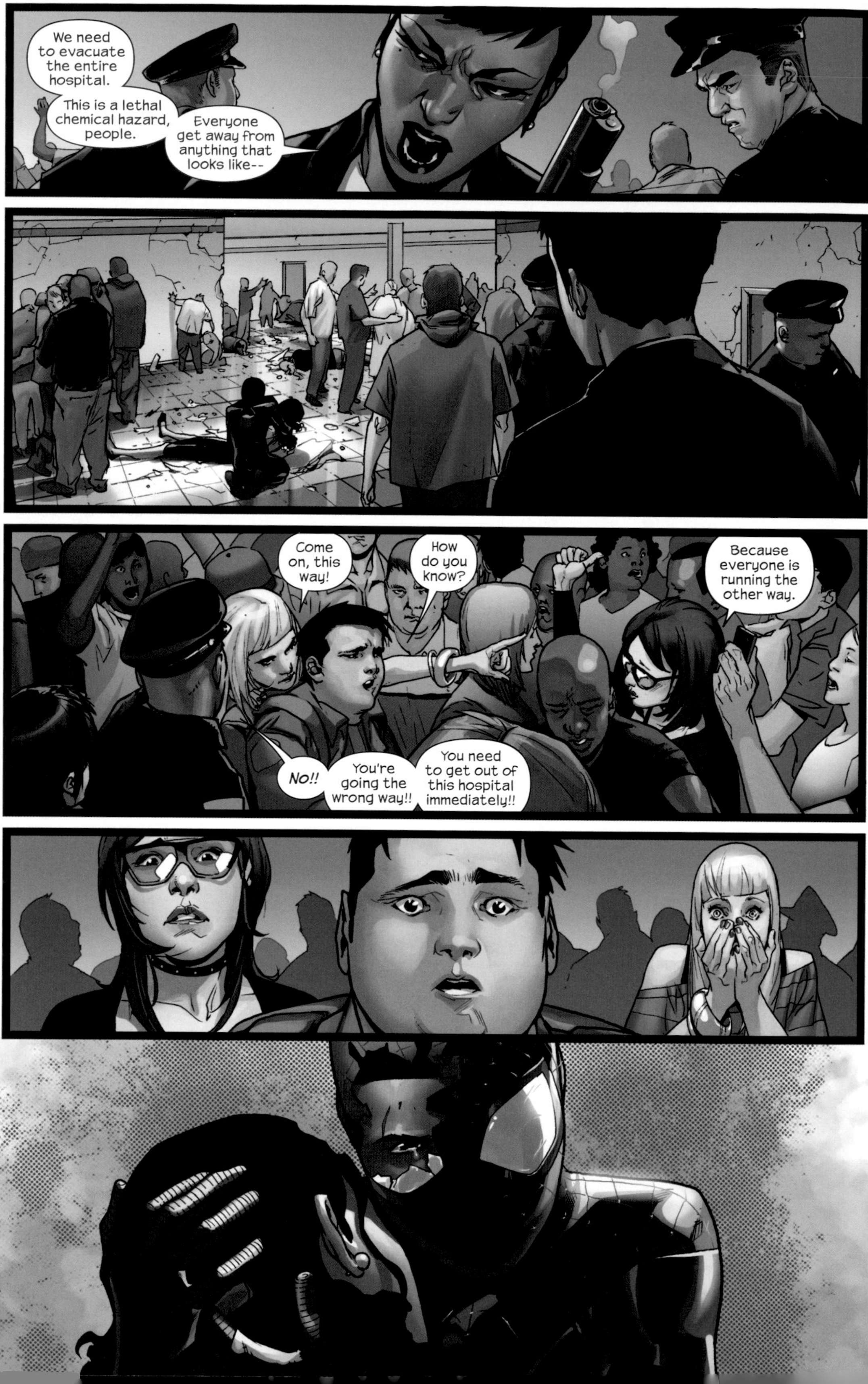
We need to evacuate the entire hospital.
This is a lethal chemical hazard, people.
Everyone get away from anything that looks like--
Come on, this way!
How do you know?
Because everyone is running the other way.
No!!
You're going the wrong way!!
You need to get out of this hospital immediately!!

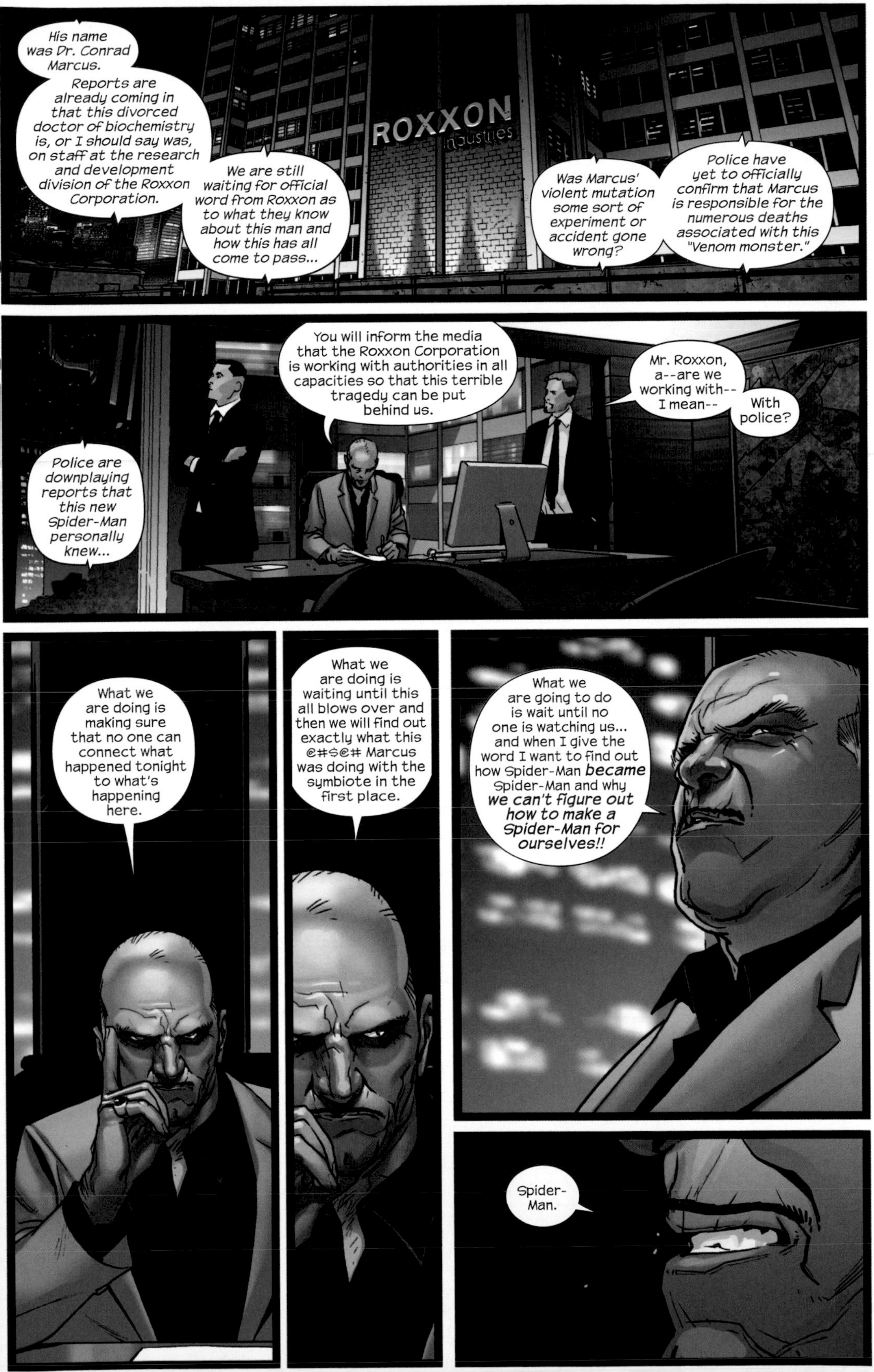
His name was Dr. Conrad Marcus.
Reports are already coming in that this divorced doctor of biochemistry is, or I should say was, on staff at the research and development division of the Roxxon Corporation.
We are still waiting for official word from Roxxon as to what they know about this man and how this has all come to pass...
ROXXON Industries
Was Marcus' violent mutation some sort of experiment or accident gone wrong?
Police have yet to officially confirm that Marcus is responsible for the numerous deaths associated with this "Venom monster."
You will inform the media that the Roxxon Corporation is working with authorities in all capacities so that this terrible tragedy can be put behind us.
Mr. Roxxon, a--are we working with-- I mean--
With police?
Police are downplaying reports that this new Spider-Man personally knew...
What we are doing is making sure that no one can connect what happened tonight to what's happening here.
What we are doing is waiting until this all blows over and then we will find out exactly what this @#$@# Marcus was doing with the symbiote in the first place.
What we are going to do is wait until no one is watching us... and when I give the word I want to find out how Spider-Man *became* Spider-Man and why ***we can't figure out how to make a Spider-Man for ourselves!!***
Spider-Man.

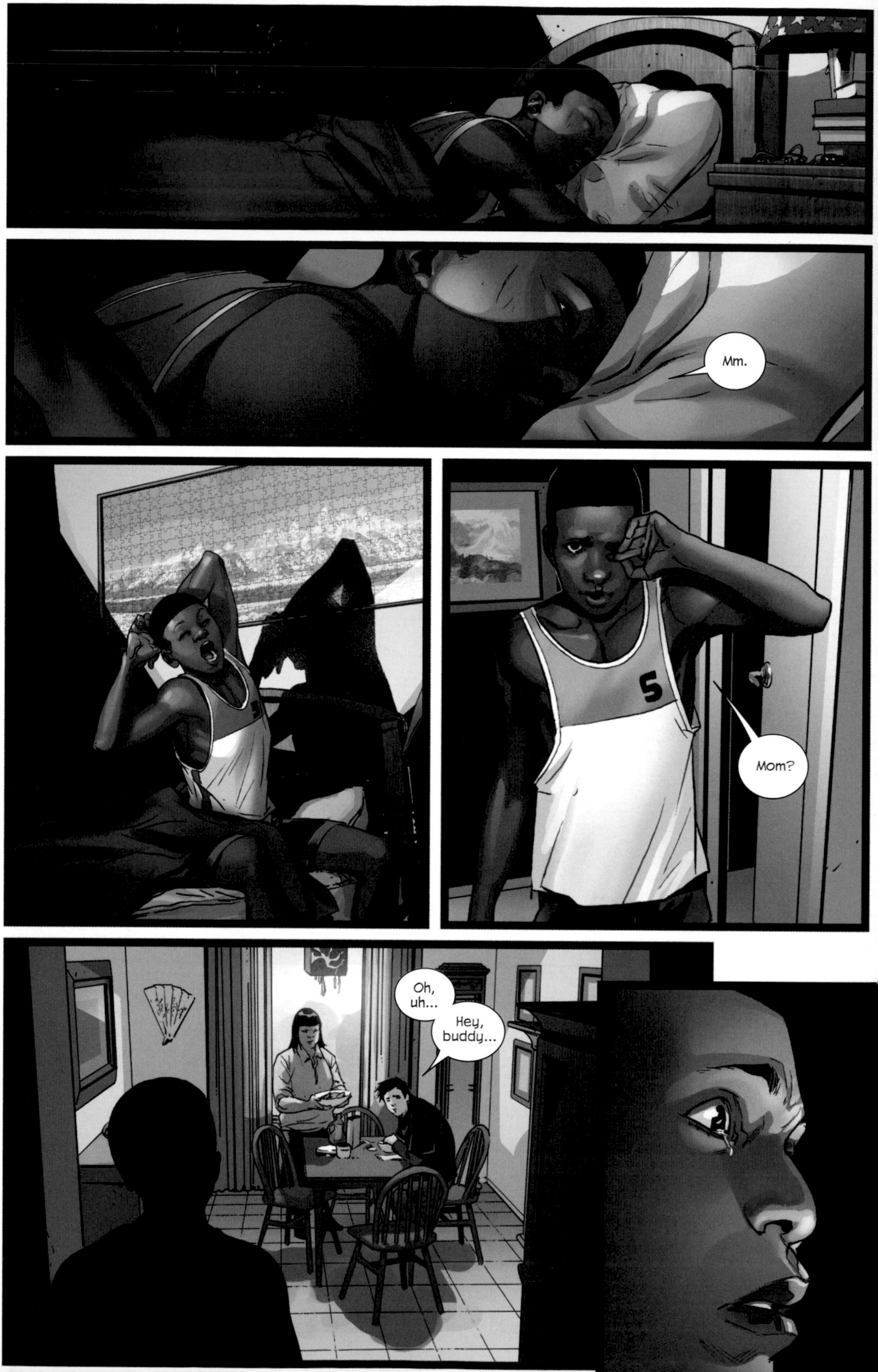
Mm.
Mom?
Oh, uh...
Hey, buddy...

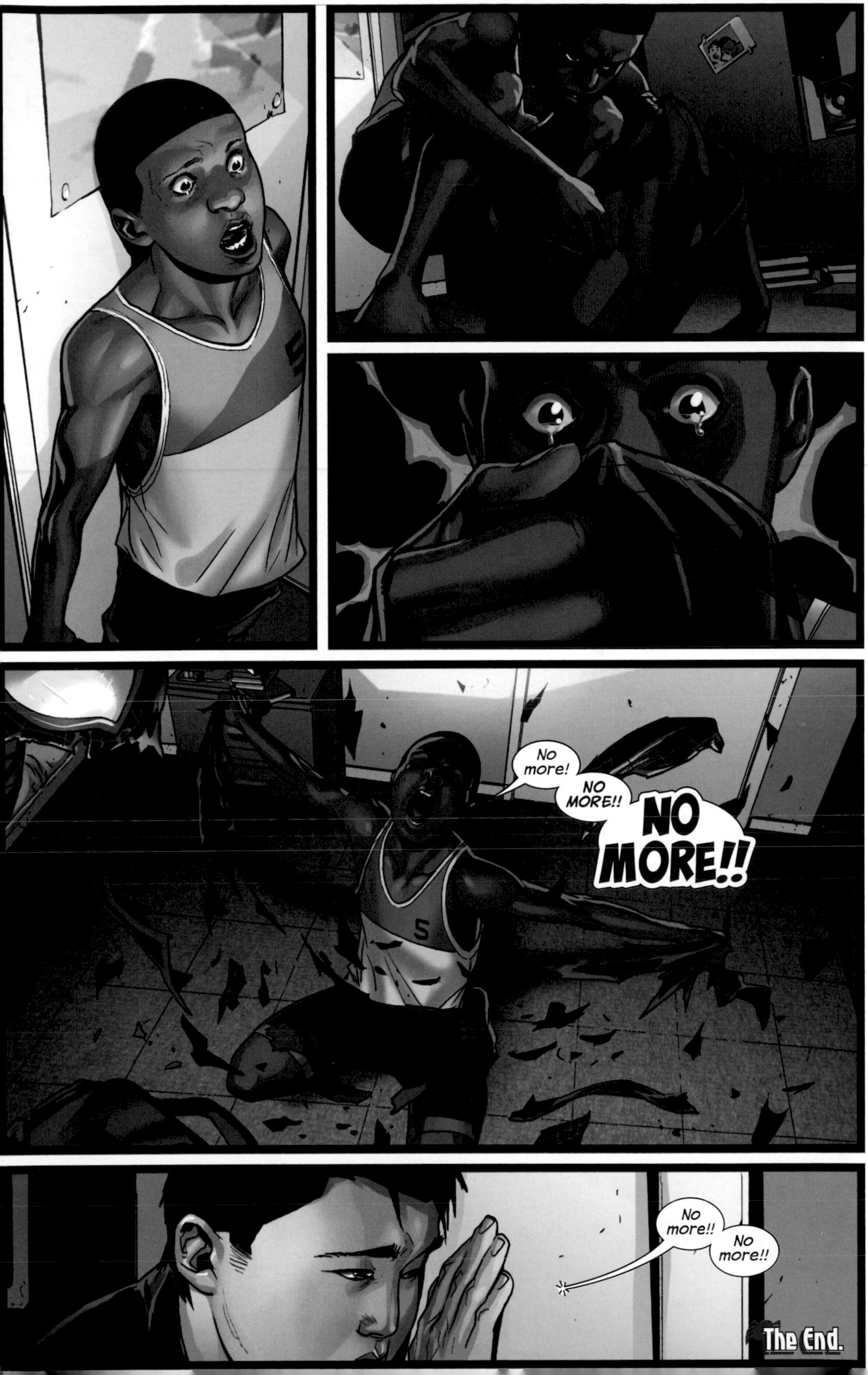
No more!
NO MORE!!
NO MORE!!
No more!!
No more!!
The End.

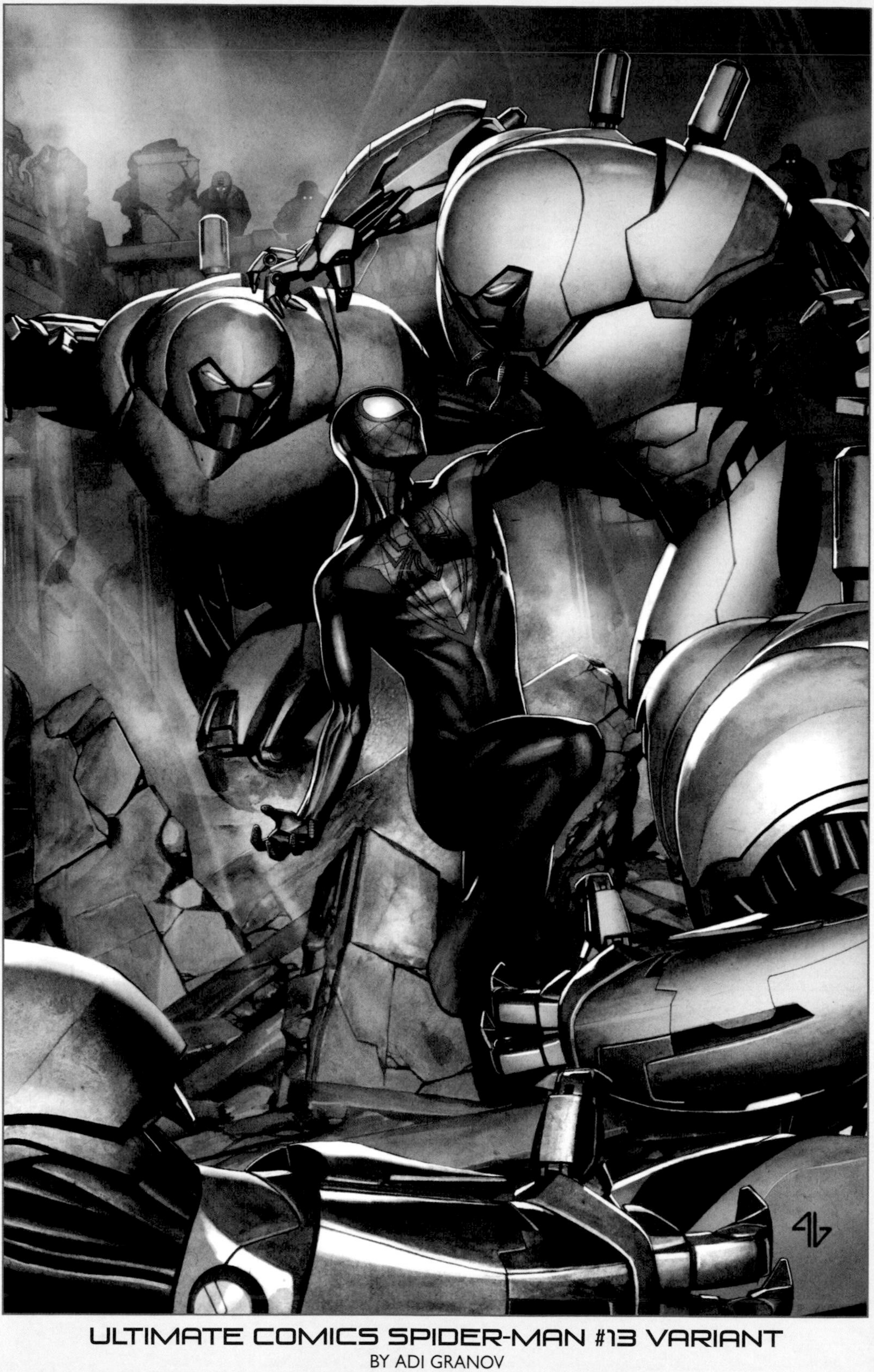

ULTIMATE COMICS SPIDER-MAN #13 VARIANT
BY ADI GRANOV

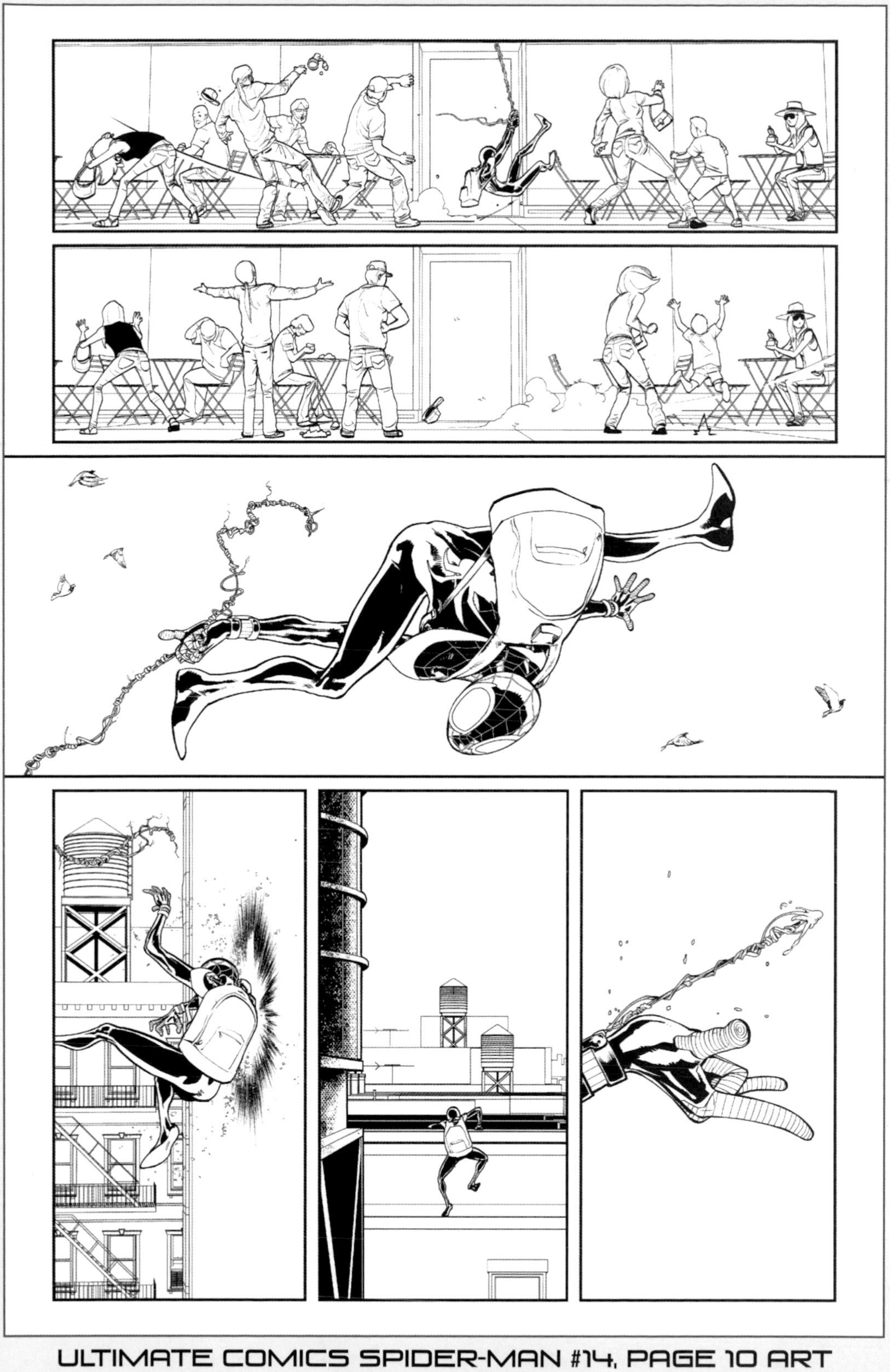

ULTIMATE COMICS SPIDER-MAN #14, PAGE 10 ART
BY DAVID MARQUEZ

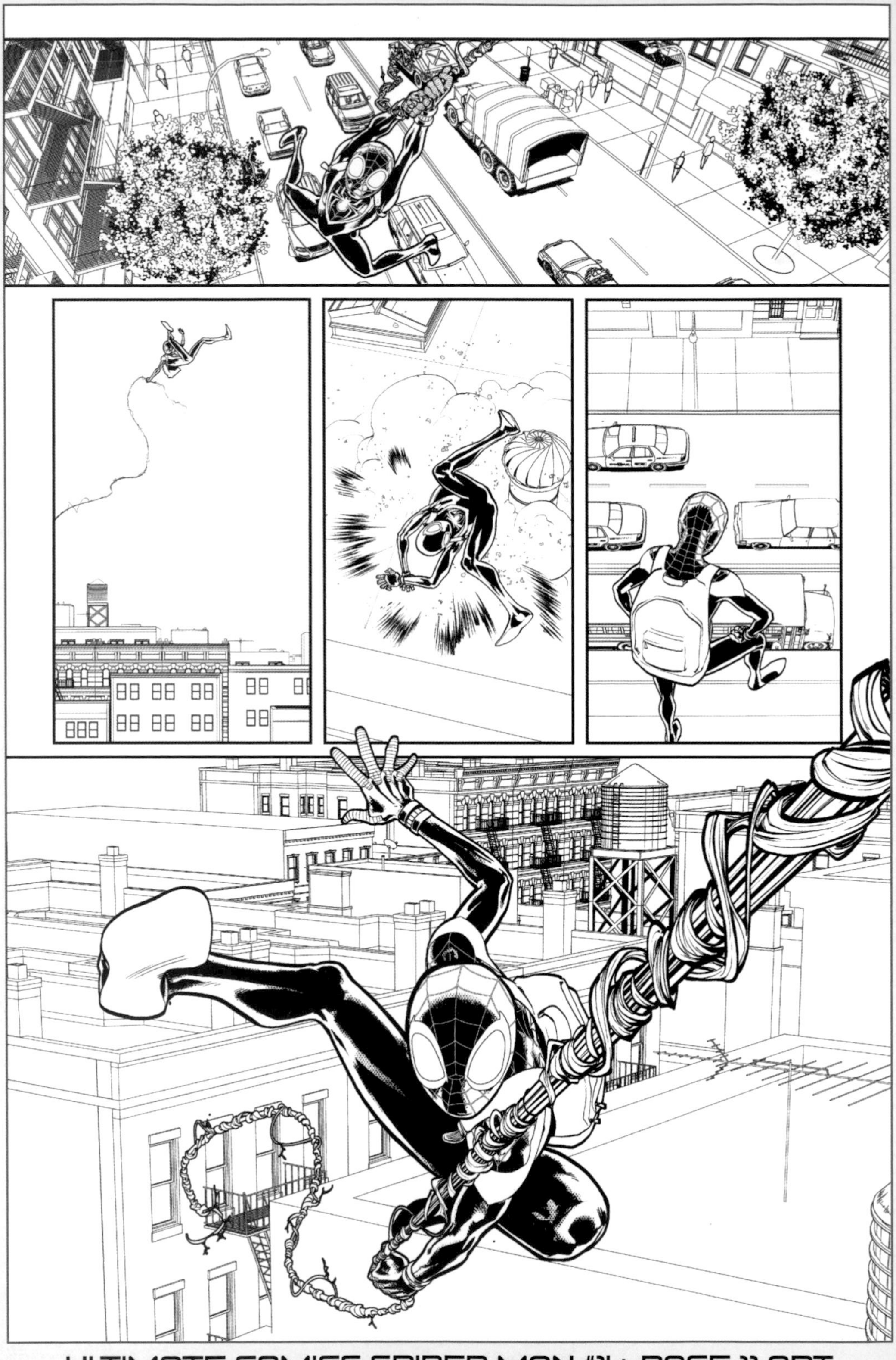

ULTIMATE COMICS SPIDER-MAN #14, PAGE 11 ART
BY DAVID MARQUEZ

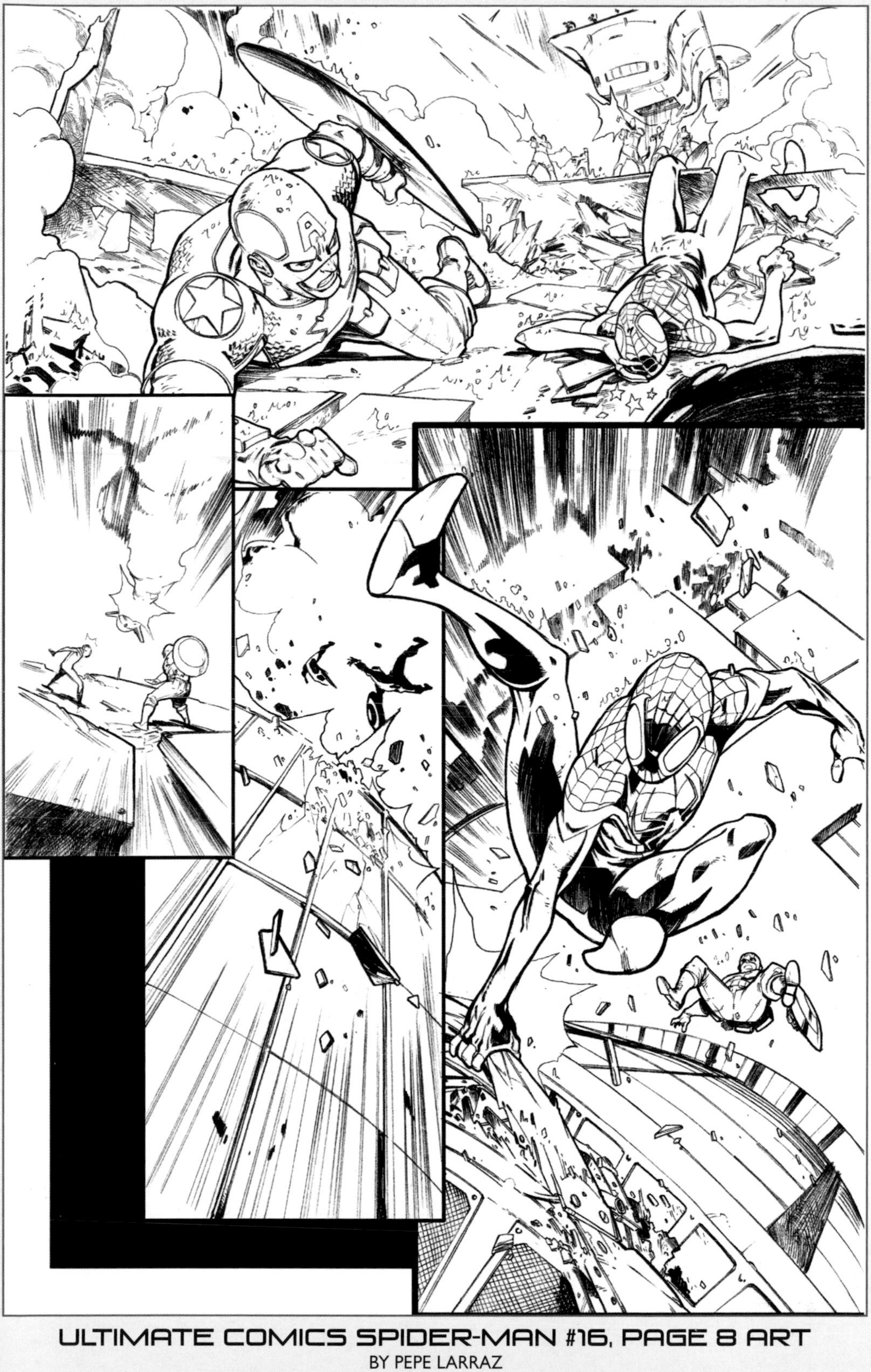

ULTIMATE COMICS SPIDER-MAN #16, PAGE 8 ART
BY PEPE LARRAZ

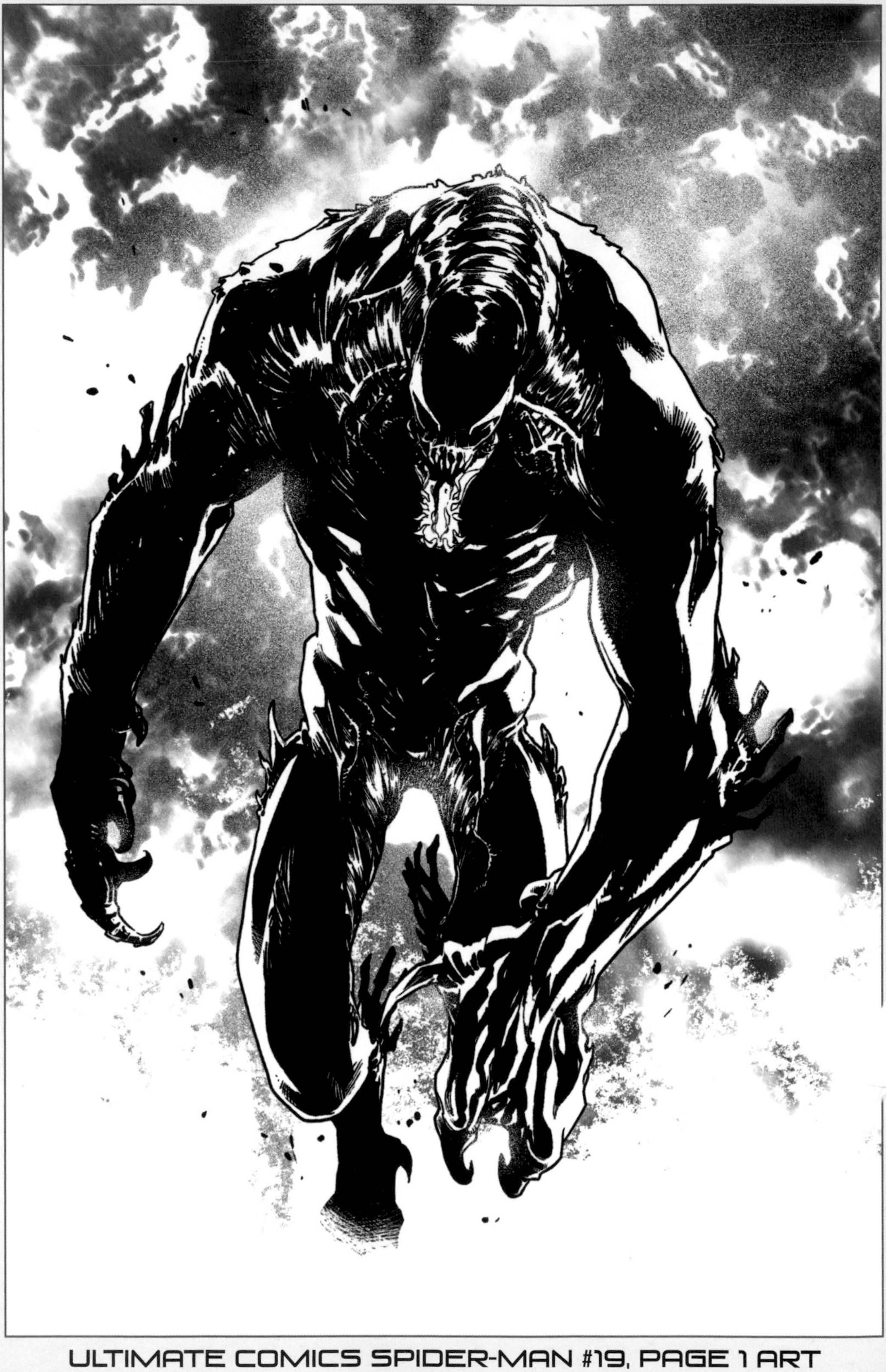

ULTIMATE COMICS SPIDER-MAN #19, PAGE 1 ART
BY SARA PICHELLI